The JULIANTHES

(The Weathered Isles)

•Pireth
Vanguard

of
Corona

◉Pireth
Dancard

Pireth
Tulme
Tinson

Macomber•

The Broken Coast

MIRIANIC

OCEAN

N

THE
DEMON
AWAKENS

BALLANTINE BOOKS
New York

A Del Rey® Book
Published by Ballantine Books

Copyright © 1997 by R. A. Salvatore

Library of Congress Cataloging-in-Publication Data
Salvatore, R. A., 1959–
The demon awakens / R.A. Salvatore
p. cm.
"A Del Rey book."
ISBN 0-345-39149-7
I. Title.
PS3569.A462345D46 1997
813'.54—dc21 96-45628
CIP

Book design by Ruth Kolbert
Endpaper maps by Laura Maestro
Manufactured in the United States of America
First Edition: May 1997
10 9 8 7 6 5 4 3 2 1

❖

*To Owen Lock, for having faith in me
and reminding me to have faith in myself.*

To Veronica Chapman, for her open mind and sharp eye.

To Kuo-yu Liang—energy is infectious.

*And to one other, privately, who found me in a dark place
at a dark time, and lit a candle.*

And, of course, as with everything I do, to Diane and the kids.

CONTENTS

Prelude   *3*

PART ONE
FATE

1   *The Unexpected Kill*   9
2   *True Believer*   20
3   *The Lingering Kiss*   25
4   *The Death of Dundalis*   31
5   *God's Chosen*   41
6   *Carrion Birds*   57
7   *The Blood of Mather*   63
8   *The Preparer*   69
9   *Touel'alfar*   78

PART TWO
PASSAGE

10   *Made of Tougher Stuff*   89
11   *Cat-the-Stray*   99
12   *The* Windrunner   *108*
13   *Running Fast Down a Long, Long Road*   *114*
14   *Jilly*   *122*
15   *Miss Pippin*   *129*
16   *Endwar*   *141*
17   *Black Wings*   *151*
18   *The Test of Faith*   *160*
19   *Truth Be Told*   *179*

20 The Oracle 194
21 Ever Vigilant, Ever Watchful 203
22 The Nightbird 210

PART THREE
CONFLICT

23 The Black Bear 231
24 The Mad Friar 239
25 Brother Justice 243
26 Bradwarden 249
27 The Fat Prophet's Warning 256
28 Siblings 265
29 Of Singular Purpose 274
30 Symphony 286
31 Home Again, Home Again 296
32 Darkness Rising 302
33 The Telling Blow 309
34 Justice 316
35 Escape? 329

PART FOUR
THE RANGER

36 Confrontation 335
37 Catch of the Day 344
38 Mercy Repaid 356
39 The Difference 362
40 Nightbird the Leader 375
41 Tempest 382
42 Reputation 392
43 A Place of Particular Interest 408
44 The Revelations of Spirits 416

PART FIVE
THE BEAST

45 Parting 431
46 The Fiend's Fiend 443
47 One Harmony 449
48 Enemies Ancient 454
49 Hunted 460

50 *Flight*   472
51 *Aida*   478
52 *Through the Maze*   490
53 *Destiny*   498

Epilogue   513

THE DEMON AWAKENS

Prelude

The demon dactyl came awake. It didn't seem such a momentous thing, just a gradual stirring in a deep cave in a far, empty mountain. An unnoticed event, seen by none save the cave worms and those few insomniacs among the bevy of weary bats hanging from the high ceiling.

But the demon spirit had awakened, had come back from its long dormancy into the statuelike form it had left behind after its last visit to the world called Corona. The tangible, corporeal body felt good to the wandering spirit. The dactyl could feel its blood, hot blood, coursing through its wings and mighty legs, could feel the twitching of its mighty muscles. Its eyes flickered open but saw only blackness, for the form, left standing in magical stasis in the deep cave, head bowed and wings wrapped tightly about its torso, had been covered by magma. Most of the fiery stuff of that time long past had bubbled and flowed away from the cavern, but enough had remained to harden about the dactyl's corporeal form. The spirit had come back to Corona encased in obsidian!

The demon spirit fell deep within itself, summoned its powers, both physical and magical. By sheer will and brute strength, the dactyl flexed its wings. A thin crack ran down the center of the obsidian sarcophagus. The dactyl flexed again and the crack widened, and then, with a sudden powerful burst, the beast blew apart the obsidian, stretched its great wings out to the side, clawed tips grasping and rending the air. The dactyl threw back its head and opened wide its mouth, screeching for the sheer joy of the return, for the thoughts of the chaos it would bring again to the quiet human kingdoms of Corona.

Its torso resembled that of a tall, slender man, shaped and lined by corded strands of taut muscle and sporting a pair of tremendous batlike wings, twenty feet across when fully extended and with strength enough to lift a full-grown bull in swift flight. Its head, too, was somewhat human, except more angular, with a narrow jaw and pointed chin. The dactyl's ears were pointed as well, poking up about the demon creature's thin tuft of

3

black hair. Neither did that hair hide the creature's horns, thumb sized and curling in toward each other at the top of the demon's brow.

The texture of its skin was rough and thick, an armored hide, reddish in hue and shiny, as if lit by its own inner glow. Shining, too, were the demon's eyes, pools of liquid black at most times, but shifting to fiery red orbs, living flames, when the demon was agitated, a glow of absolute hatred.

The creature flexed and stretched, extended its wings to their full glory, reached and clawed at the air with its humanlike arms. The demon extended its fingernails, transformed them into hooked claws, and grew its teeth—two pointed canines extending down over its bottom lip. Every part of the demon was a weapon, devastating and deadly. And undeniably powerful though this monster appeared, this demon's real strength lay in its mind and its purpose, the tempter of souls, the twister of hearts, the maker of lies. Theologians of Corona argued over whether the demon dactyl was the source or the result of evil. Did the dactyl bring the weakness, the immorality, to humanity? Was the dactyl the source of the deadly sins, or did it manifest itself and walk the world when those sins had festered to the point of eruption?

For the demonic creature in the cave, such questions hardly mattered. How long had it been? the dactyl wondered. How many decades, even centuries, had passed since its last visit to Corona?

The creature remembered that long-ago time now, savored the thoughts of the streaming blood as army after army had joined in delicious, desperate battle. It cursed aloud the name of Terranen Dinoniel, who had rallied the humans and the elves, chasing the dactyl's armies back to the base of this mountain, Aida. Dinoniel himself had come into this cave after the beast, had skewered the dactyl . . .

The black-winged demon looked down at a darker red tear marring its otherwise smooth hide. With a sickening crackle of bone, the creature's head rotated completely around and bowed, examining the second imperfection of its form, a scarred lump under its lower left shoulder blade. Those two scars were perfectly aligned with the dactyl's heart, and thus, with that one desperate thrust, Dinoniel had defeated the demon's corporeal body. Yet even in its death throes, the dactyl had won the day, using its willpower to bring up the magma from the bowels of Aida. Dinoniel and much of his army had been consumed and destroyed, but the dactyl . . .

The dactyl was eternal. Dinoniel was gone, a distant memory, but the demon spirit had returned and the physical wounds had healed. "What man, what elf, will take Dinoniel's place?" the demon asked aloud in its hollow, resonating voice, always seeming on the edge of a thunderous roar. A cloud of bats shuddered to life at the unexpected noise and flew off down one of the tunnels formed when the lava had flowed from this spot. The dactyl cackled, thinking itself grand to be able to send such creatures—any creatures!—scurrying with a mere sound. And what resolve might the humans and the elves—if the elves were still about, for even in Dinoniel's day they had been on the wane—muster this time?

Its thoughts turned from its enemies to those it would summon as minions. What creatures could the dactyl gather this time to wage its war? The wicked goblins certainly, so full of anger and greed, so delighting in murder and war. The fomorian giants of the mountains, few in number but each with the strength of a dozen men and a hide too thick and tough for a dagger to puncture. And the powries, yes, the powries, the cunning, warlike dwarves of the Julianthes, the Weathered Isles, who hated the humans above all others. Centuries before, powries had dominated the seas in their solid, squat barrelboats, whose hulls were made of tougher stuff than the larger ships of the humans, as the diminutive powries were made of tougher stuff than the larger humans.

A line of drool hung low from the dactyl's mouth as it considered its former and future allies, its army of woe. It would bring them into its fold, tribe by tribe, race by race, growing as the night grows when the sun touches the western horizon. The twilight of Corona was at hand.

The dactyl came awake.

PART ONE

▼

FATE

What song is this, drift through the trees
To lift men broken from their knees?
To untwist hearts from grasping sorrow,
To offer the promise of the morrow?
Hark, what song,
What music sweet?
Warm whispers of the dawn.

Hot blood waft steam in night air cold.
What hopes of treasure, what hunger of gold
Hath brought foul beast from caverns deep
To face the Nightbird, to know endless sleep?
They come for greed.
They come to bleed.
At gentle hands of elven breed.

The shining sword, the horse's run,
The bane of monsters all and one.
To their midst the rider, Nightbird the Ranger,
Flashing Tempest's anger, denying the danger
Cutting and slashing!
Tearing and gashing!
Chasing the nightmares away.

Fast run, you goblins, the Ranger sets his bow,
To let your blood, to stain white snow
Arrow and arrow, the river of red
Fast fall the Evil, to the one is dead.

Hawkwing's fury,
Goblins to bury
In worm's cold domain.

Scatter, goblins, fly and flee!
You'll not outrun Symphony.
Hooves of music rend the gloom
Bearing Nightbird, know your doom!
At Tempest's fall,
So shall you all
To blackness evermore.

Away drifts music, Symphony sweet.
Away goes Nightbird, the forest to greet
In springtime sunshine, of Evil no traces,
Through flowers and lovers, step measured paces
Hark, listen you all
The Nightbird's call
And sleep peaceful lovers, secure.

*—"*THE SONG OF THE NIGHTBIRD*"*

❖ I ❖

The Unexpected Kill

Elbryan Wyndon was up before the dawn. He dressed quickly, fumbling with his clothes in the red light of the hearth's glowing embers. He ran a hand through his touseled straight hair—a light brown shock that bleached pale on its top layers under the summer sun. He retrieved his belt and dagger, which he had reverently placed right near his bed, and Elbryan felt powerful as he ceremoniously strapped the weapon about his waist.

He grabbed the heaviest wrap he could find and rushed out into the dark and chill air, so anxious that he hardly remembered to close the cabin door behind him. The small frontier village of Dundalis was quiet and eerily still about him, sleeping off the well-earned weariness that followed every day's hard labor. Elbryan, too, had worked hard the previous day—harder than normal, for several of the village men and women were out in the deep forest, and the boys and girls, like Elbryan who was nearing his teens, had been asked to keep things aright. That meant gathering wood and tending the fires, repairing the cabins—which always seemed to need repair!—and walking the perimeter of the sheltered vale that held the village, watching for sign of bear, great cat, or the packs of hunting wolves.

Elbryan was the oldest of those children, the leader of the pack, as it were, and he felt important, truly he felt a man. This would be the last time he remained behind when the hunters went off on the season's last and most important expedition. Next spring would bring his thirteenth birthday, the passage from childhood in the hardy land that was the northern wilderness. Next spring, Elbryan would hunt with the adults, the games of his youth left behind.

Indeed he was tired from the previous day's labors, but so full of excitement that sleep had not come to him. The weather had turned toward winter. The men were expected back any day, and Elbryan meant to meet them and lead their procession into the village. Let the younger boys and girls see him then, and afford him the respect he deserved, and let the older men see that the village, under his watchful eye, had fared well in their absence.

He started out of Dundalis, stepping lightly despite his weariness, passing through the darker shadows of the small, one-story cabins.

"Jilly!" The call was not loud but seemed so in the quiet morning air. Elbryan moved up to the corner of the next house, smiling for his cleverness, and peered around.

"It could be today!" protested a young girl, Jilseponie, Elbryan's closest friend.

"You do not know that, Jilly," argued her mother, standing in the open doorway of their cabin. Elbryan tried to muffle his snicker; the girl hated that nickname, Jilly, though nearly everyone in town called her that. She preferred the simple "Jill." But between her and Elbryan, the title was Pony, their secret name, the one Jilseponie liked most of all.

The snicker was soon gone, but the smile remained, all the wider for the sight. Elbryan didn't know why, but he was always happy when he saw Pony, though only a couple of years before, he would have taunted her and the rest of the village girls, chasing them endlessly. One time Elbryan had made the mistake of catching Jilseponie without his male companions nearby, and of tugging too hard on her yellow mane to prove the point of his capture. He never saw the punch coming, never saw anything except how wide the blue sky had suddenly seemed as he lay on his back.

He could laugh at that embarrassment now, privately or even with Pony. He felt as though he could say anything to her, and she wouldn't judge him or make merry of his feelings.

Candlelight spilled out onto the road, softly illuminating the girl. Elbryan liked the image; every day that passed, he found that he enjoyed looking at Pony more and more. She was younger than Elbryan by five months but taller than he, standing about three inches above five feet, while the young man, to his ultimate horror, had not yet reached the coveted five foot mark. Elbryan's father had assured him that Wyndon boys were normally late in sprouting. All jealousy aside, Elbryan found the taller Pony quite a pleasing sight. She stood straight but not stiff, and could outrun and outfight any of the boys in Dundalis, Elbryan included. Still, there was a delicate aura about her, a softness that a younger Elbryan had viewed as weakness, but the older Elbryan viewed as oddly distracting. Her hair, which Jilseponie seemed to be constantly brushing, was golden, silken, and thick enough to lose a hand in; it bounced about her shoulders and back with an alluring wildness. Her eyes, huge eyes, were the richest and clearest blue Elbryan had ever seen, like great sponges soaking in the sights of the wide world and reflecting Jilseponie's every mood. When Pony's eyes showed sadness, Elbryan felt it in his heart; when they soared with sparkling joy, Elbryan's feet moved involuntarily in dance.

Her lips, too, were large and thick. The boys had often taunted Pony about those lips, saying that if she ever stuck them to a window, they would surely hold her fast for all eternity! Elbryan felt no desire to tease when looking at Pony's lips now. He sensed their softness, so very inviting . . .

"I will be back in time for the morning meal," Pony assured her mother.

"The night woods are dangerous," her exasperated mother replied.

"I will be careful!" Pony responded dismissively, before the older woman had even finished the sentence.

Elbryan held his breath, thinking that Pony's mother, often stern, would scold the girl severely. She only sighed, though, and resignedly closed the cabin door.

Pony sighed, too, and shook her head as if to show her ultimate frustration with adults. Then she turned and skipped off, and was startled a moment later when Elbryan jumped out in front of her.

She reflexively cocked a fist, and Elbryan wisely jumped back.

"You are late," he said.

"I am early," Pony insisted, "too early. And I am tired."

Elbryan shrugged and nodded down the road to the north, then led the girl off at a swift pace. Despite her complaints concerning the time, Pony not only paced him but skipped right by him, obviously as excited as he. That excitement turned to sheer joy when they passed out of the town and began their ascent of the ridge. Pony chanced to look back to the south, and she stopped, stunned and smiling, and pointing to the night sky. "The Halo," she said breathlessly.

Elbryan turned to follow her gaze, and he, too, could not suppress a grin.

For stretched across the southern sky, more than halfway to the horizon, was Corona's Halo, the heavenly belt—a subtle tease of colors, red and green and blue and deep purple, a flowing softness, like a living rainbow. The Halo was sometimes visible in the summer sky, but only during the deepest parts of the shorter nights, when children, and even adults, were fast asleep. Elbryan and Jilseponie had seen it on a few occasions, but never so clearly as this, never so vibrant.

Then they heard a distant piping, soft music, perfect melody. It floated through the chill air, barely perceptible.

"The Forest Ghost," Pony whispered, but Elbryan didn't seem to hear. Pony spoke the words again, under her breath. The Forest Ghost was a common legend in the Timberlands. Half horse and half man, he was the keeper of the trees and the friend of the animals, particularly of the wild horses that ran in the dells to the north. For a moment, the thought of such a creature not so far away frightened Pony, but then her fears were washed away by the sheer beauty of the Halo and the fitting melody of the enchanting music. How could anyone, or anything, that could pipe so beautifully pose a danger?

The pair stood on the side of the ridge for a long while, not speaking, not looking at each other, not even realizing that the other was there. Elbryan felt totally alone, yet one with the universe, a small part of majesty, a small but endless flicker in eternity. His mind drifted up from the ridge, from the solid ground, from the sensible experiences of his existence into the unknown, exhilarating joy of spirituality. The name of "Mather" came to him briefly, though he didn't know why. He didn't know anything at that time, it seemed, and yet he knew everything—the secrets of the world, of peace, of eternity—it was all there before him, so simple and true. He felt a song in his heart, though it had no words, felt a warmth in all his body, though he was not at that moment a part of that corporeal form.

The sensation passed—too quickly. Elbryan sighed deeply and turned to Pony. He was about to say something but held the words, seeing that she, too, was immersed in something beyond language. Elbryan felt suddenly closer to the girl, as if they two had shared something very special and very private. How many others could look upon the Halo and understand the beauty of the thing? he wondered. None of the adults of Dundalis, certainly, with their grumbling and grouching, and none of the other children, he decided, who were too caught up in silliness to ponder such thoughts.

No, it was his experience and Pony's—theirs alone. He watched her slowly drift back to the reality about them—the ridge, the night, and her companion. He could almost see her spirit flowing back into that five foot three inch body—a body that was growing more shapely by the day.

Elbryan resisted the sudden and inexplicable urge to run over and kiss Pony.

"What?" she asked, seeing turmoil, even horror, come over his face, despite the darkness.

The boy looked away, angry at himself for allowing such feelings. Pony was a girl, after all, and though Elbryan would openly admit that she was a friend, such deeper feelings were truly horrifying.

"Elbryan?" she asked. "Was it the song, the Forest Ghost?"

"Never heard it," Elbryan retorted, though when he thought about it, he had indeed heard the distant piping melody.

"Then what?" Pony pressed.

"Nothing," he replied gruffly. "Come along. The dawn is not long away." He started up the ridge at a feverish pace then, even scrambling on all fours at times, crunching through the thick carpet of fallen leaves. Pony paused and watched him, confused at first. Gradually a smile found its way back onto her face, her dimples showing the slightest blush of red. She suspected she knew the feelings that Elbryan was fighting, the same feelings she had battled earlier that same year.

Pony had won that battle by accepting, even relishing, those private feelings, the warmth that washed over her whenever she looked upon Elbryan. She hoped Elbryan would wage a gallant war now, with an outcome similar to her own.

She caught up to her friend at the top of the ridge. Behind them, Dundalis sat quiet and dark. All the world seemed still, not a bird calling, not a whisper of wind. They sat together, yet apart, separated by a couple of feet and by the wall of Elbryan's confusion. The boy didn't move, hardly seemed to blink, just sat staring straight ahead at the wide vale before him, though it was too dark for him to even recognize the place.

Pony, though, was more animated. She let her gaze linger on Elbryan until the boy became obviously flustered, then she politely looked away, back to the village—a single candle was burning in one of the houses—and back to the Halo, which was now fast fading in the southern sky. She could still make out the brighter colors, but that special moment of beauty, of innermost reflection, had passed. Now she was again Jilseponie, just Jilseponie, sitting on a ridge with her friend, awaiting the return of her father and the other hunters. And the dawn was approaching. Pony realized that she could make out more of the village, could discern the individual houses, even the individual posts of Bunker Crawyer's corral.

"Today," Elbryan said unexpectedly, his voice turning her about to study him. He was at ease again, the uncomfortable feelings tossed out with the mystery of the night. "They will return this day," he announced with a nod.

Pony grinned warmly, hoping he was right.

They sat in silence as the day grew about them. In the wide vale, the wall of blackness gave way to the individual dark spots that were the evergreens—rows and rows of ancient trees, Corona's oldest soldiers, standing proud, though most were not twice Elbryan's height. The starkness of the scene from this vantage point, in this mounting light, amazed the companions. The ground about the trees caught the morning light and held it fast, for the undergrowth was not dark but was white and thick, a padding of caribou moss. Elbryan loved the stuff—all the children did. Every time he gazed upon the white carpet, he wanted to take off his shoes and pants and run through it barefoot and bare legged, to feel its softness between his toes and brushing against his shins. In many places, the caribou moss was even deeper than his knees!

He wanted to do it, as he had so many times in his earlier years, wanted to cast off his shoes and all his clothes . . .

He remembered his companion, his earlier feelings, and turned away from Pony, blushing fiercely.

"If they come in before the sun gets too high, we'll see them a mile away," Pony remarked. The girl was not looking ahead, though, but at the ridge to the south behind them. Autumn was well advanced, and all the leaves of the deciduous trees, particularly the sugar maples, were bright with colors, shining red and orange and yellow, painting the ridge.

Elbryan was glad that the distracted girl had not noticed his own shade of red. "Coming down that side of the vale," he agreed sharply, catching Pony's attention, and pointing to the wide gentle slope of the vale's northeastern face added, "a mile away!"

Their assessment proved overoptimistic, for the starkness of the scene had confused their sense of distance. They did indeed spot the returning hunters, to their complete joy, but not until the group was moving along the bottom of the bowl-shaped vale, a line of tiny forms far below them.

They watched, chattering wildly, trying to count and to guess who was leading but getting confused as parts of the line wove in and out of the tree shadows.

"A shoulder pole!" Elbryan cried out suddenly, spotting the line that seemed to join two of the men.

"Another!" Pony added happily, and she clapped her hands with glee as more came into view. The hunters would return with carcasses—elk, caribou, or white-tailed deer—slung on shoulder poles, and it seemed to the watching pair as if this hunt had been successful indeed! Their patience fast disintegrated; they leaped out together, running fast down the steeper slope, picking their angle to intercept the returning troop.

From the ridge top, the vale seemed stark and open, but descending into it, Elbryan and Pony quickly remembered just how confusing and intimidating a place it could be. Down among the squat but wide-spreading pines and spruce, vision in all directions was blocked after just a few feet; the companions became separated quickly and spent many minutes just talking themselves back together and then arguing over which direction would lead them to their fathers.

"The sun is in the southeast," Elbryan reminded Pony, squaring his shoulders as he took command of the situation. The sun had not yet come up high enough to peer over the rim of the vale, but they could make out its position easily enough. "The hunters approach from the northeast, so all we have to do is keep the sun just behind our right shoulders."

It seemed logical enough to Pony, so she shrugged and let Elbryan lead and didn't mention to him that if they simply called out loudly, their fathers would likely hear them and guide them in.

Elbryan picked his way determinedly, weaving about the bushy evergreens, not even looking back to make sure Pony was keeping up with him. He moved faster still when he heard the voices of the hunters. His heart pounded when he recognized his father's deep tones, though he couldn't make out what the man was saying.

Pony caught up to him, even passed him over that last expanse, leading the way through the tangle of two wide pines, pushing aside the prickly branches and bursting into a clearing right beside the returning party.

The startled, almost feral, reaction of the hunters froze Elbryan in his tracks and sent Pony ducking for cover. Elbryan hardly heard the sharp scolding his father offered, the boy's eyes basking in the sight, moving from the carcass of a caribou buck, to a deer, to a line of coneys, to . . .

Elbryan and Jilseponie stood perfectly still, stricken. Their fathers, who had come forward to meet the impetuous children, to scold them again for being so far away from Dundalis, let the opportunity pass. The object on the fourth shoulder pole, each man realized, would be enough to get the lesson across.

The sun was up, the day bright, and the village wide awake by the time Elbryan and Pony led the hunting party back into Dundalis. Expressions ran from excitement to awkward fear to blank amazement as the villagers took stock of the kills, especially the last carcass on the shoulder poles, a smallish humanoid form.

"A goblin?" asked one woman, bending low to regard the creature's hideous features: the sloping forehead and the long thin nose, the tiny but perfectly round eyes, now glazed over, sickly yellow. The creature's ears, pointed at the top and with a loose flapping, fat lobe at the bottom, stuck out several inches from its head. The woman shuddered when she considered the mouth, a tangle of greenish-yellow fangs, all crooked but each angled inward. The chin was narrow, but the jowls wide with muscle. It wasn't difficult to imagine the power of the creature's bite or the pain of getting free from those nasty teeth.

"Are they really that color?" asked another woman, and she dared to touch the creature's skin. "Or did it just turn that way after it died?"

"Yellow and green," an old man answered firmly, though he had not been out on the hunt. Elbryan watched the wrinkled and bent elder, Brody Gentle, by name, though the children usually called him "Body Grabber" in mock horror, teasing him and then running away. Old Brody was a snarling type, angry at the world and at his own infirmities, and an easy mark for children, always ready to give chase and never quick enough to make a catch. Elbryan considered the man's true name now, for the first time, and nearly laughed aloud at the contradiction of the surname with Brody's grouchy demeanor.

"Surely is a goblin," Brody continued, obviously enjoying the attention, "big one, too, and they're yellow and green," he answered the second questioning woman, "living and dead, though this one's fast turning gray." He snickered as he finished, a sound of utter contempt that seemed to lend credence to his greater knowledge of the goblin race. Goblins were little seen creatures; many considered them more myth than truth. Even in Dundalis, and in other frontier villages nestled in the Timberlands on the borders of the deep Wilderlands, there had been no confirmed sightings of any goblins for longer than the villagers could remember—with the apparent exception of Brody Gentle.

"You have seen goblins before?" asked Olwan Wyndon, Elbryan's father, and his tone and the fact that he crossed his large arms over his chest as he spoke showed he held many doubts.

Brody Gentle scoffed at him. "Oft have I told the tales!" the old man fumed.

Olwan Wyndon nodded, not wanting to get Brody into one of his legendary fits of outrage. Sitting by the hearth in the village's common house,
Brody had recounted endless tales of his youth, of battling goblins, even
fomorian giants, in the first days of Dundalis, staking out the ground for
proper folk. Most listened politely but turned up their eyes and shook their
heads whenever Brody looked away.

"We had the word of a goblin sighting in Weedy Meadow," offered
another man, referring to another village some twenty miles to the west of
Dundalis.

"A child's word," Olwan Wyndon promptly reminded them all, quieting
nervous whispers before they could gain any momentum.

"Well, we've much work to do, and you've a tale to tell," Pony's mother
intervened. "Better suited for the common house, after a supper of venison
stew."

Olwan nodded and the crowd gradually dispersed, one person taking a
last, long look at the goblin, which was indeed fast turning gray. Elbryan
and Pony lingered long by the corpse, studying it intently. Pony didn't miss
her companion's derisive snort.

"Small as an eight-year-old," the boy explained, waving a dismissive
hand at the goblin. That was something of an exaggeration, but, indeed, the
goblin wasn't much above four feet tall and couldn't have weighed more
than Elbryan's ninety pounds.

"Perhaps it is a child," Pony offered.

"You heard Body Grabber," Elbryan countered. He screwed up his face,
the ridiculous nickname sounding foolish in his ears. "He said it was a big
one." He ended with another snort.

"It looks fierce," Pony insisted, bending low to study the creature more
closely. She didn't miss Elbryan's third snort. "Remember the badger?" she
asked quietly, stealing the boy's bluster. "Not a third the size of the goblin."

Elbryan blanched and looked away. Earlier that year, at the beginning of
summer, some of the younger children had snagged a badger in a noose.
When they came into the village with the news, Elbryan, the oldest of their
group, had taken command, leading the way back to the spot. He
approached the snared creature boldly, only to find that it had chewed right
through the leather bindings. When it came around at him, teeth bared,
Elbryan had, so the legend—and among the children, it was indeed a
legend—said, "run away so fast that he didn't even notice he was running
straight up a tree, not even using his hands to grab a branch."

The rest of the children had fled, as well, but not so far that they could
not witness Elbryan's ultimate humiliation, as the badger, like some vindic-
tive enemy, had waited at the base of Elbryan's tree, keeping the boy up in
the branches for more than an hour.

Stupid badger, Elbryan thought, and stupid Pony for opening that
wound once again. He walked away without another word.

Pony couldn't sustain her smile as she watched him go, wondering if she had pushed him a little too hard.

Every villager was in the common house that night, though most had already heard the tale of the goblin fight by then. The hunting party had come upon a band of six creatures, or actually both groups had come upon each other, stepping out of the thick brush onto an open, rocky riverbank simultaneously, barely twenty paces apart. After a moment of shock, the goblins had thrown their spears, injuring one man. The ensuing fight had been brief and brutal, with many nicks and cuts to both sides and even a couple of bites to the humans, before the goblins, outnumbered two to one, had fled, disappearing into the brush as suddenly as they had appeared. The only serious wound to either side was the hit to the slain goblin—a spear thrust that had punctured the creature's lung. It had tried to flee with its companions but fell short of the brush for lack of breath and died soon after.

Olwan Wyndon told the tale again in full to the gathering, trying hard not to embellish it. "We spent three days looking but found no more sign of the other goblins," he finished.

Immediately a pair of mugs came up into the air from the side of the room. "To Shane McMichael!" the two mug holders bellowed together. "Goblinslayer!"

The cheer went up, and Shane McMichael, a quiet, slender young man just a few years older than Elbryan, reluctantly came forward to stand beside Olwan in front of the blazing hearth. With much prodding, the man was prompted to tell of the fight, of the cunning twist and parry and then straightforward thrust that had come too soon for the goblin to completely dodge.

Elbryan savored every word, envisioning the battle clearly. How he envied Shane!

Afterward, the conversation turned into an exchange of what other people had recently seen, of the report of a goblin sighting in Weedy Meadow, and even a few wild tales from Dundalis folk claiming that they had noticed some huge tracks but just hadn't said anything about it. Elbryan at first listened intently to every word but, gradually taking the cue from his father's posture, came to understand that most of the talk was no more than individual efforts to grab a bit of attention. It surprised Elbryan that adults would act that way, especially considering the gravity of the situation.

Next came a discussion, led by Brody Gentle, of goblinkind in general, from the numerous small goblins to the rare and dangerous disfigured fomorian giants. Brody spoke with an air of expertise, but few in the room hung on his every word. Even young Elbryan soon came to realize that the old man knew little more than anyone else concerning goblins, and Elbryan doubted that Brody had ever seen a fomorian giant. Elbryan looked at Pony, who seemed to be growing quite bored by it all, and motioned to the door.

She was out into the night before he got out of his chair.

"Bluster," Elbryan insisted, joining her. The night was chill, and so the boy moved close to Pony, sharing their warmth.

"But we cannot deny the goblin," Pony replied, motioning to the shed where the creature had been placed. "Your father's tale was real enough."

"I meant Brody—"

"I know what you meant," said Pony, "and I do not believe him either—not completely."

Elbryan's surprise at her qualification of the remark reflected clearly on his face.

"There are goblins," Pony explained. "We know that well enough. So perhaps those who first came to the edge of the Wilderlands to settle Dundalis did have a few fights on their hands."

"Fomorians?" Elbryan asked skeptically.

Pony shrugged, not willing to discount the possibility of giants, not after viewing a dead goblin.

Elbryan conceded the point, though he still thought Brody Gentle more bluster than truth. He couldn't hold that thought, though, or any other negative feelings, when Jilseponie turned to look him directly in the eye, when she, her face only a few inches from his own, locked his olive green eyes with her stare.

Elbryan found his breath hard to come by. Pony was close—too close—and she wasn't backing away!

And she was coming closer, Elbryan realized, her head slowly drifting toward his, her lips, so soft, in line with his! Panic hit him, wrestling hard with a jumble of other emotions that Elbryan did not understand. A part of him wanted to turn away, but another part, a larger and surprising part, would not let him move.

The door to the common house opened with a crash, and both Pony and Elbryan immediately spun away from each other.

The younger children came out in a mob, swarming around the older pair. "What are we going to do?" one of them asked.

Elbryan and Pony exchanged curious looks.

"We must be ready for when the goblins come back," another boy remarked.

"The goblins were never here," Pony interjected.

"But they will be!" claimed the boy. "Kristeena says so."

All eyes turned to Kristeena, a girl of ten who always seemed to be staring at Elbryan. "Goblins always come back for their dead," she explained eagerly.

"How do you know that?" Elbryan asked doubtfully, and his tone seemed to hurt the girl.

She looked down and kicked the dirt with one foot. "My grandmother knows," she answered, her voice suddenly sheepish, and Elbryan felt a fool for making her so uncomfortable. All the gang was quiet, hanging on Elbryan's every word.

Pony nudged him hard. Pony had told him many times that Kristeena was sweet for him, and the older girl, not viewing a ten-year-old as competition, had been charmed by the thought.

"She probably does know," Elbryan said, and Kristeena looked up, suddenly beaming. "And it sounds right." He turned to the shed, and all the younger children flowed about him, following his gaze.

"And if the goblins do come back, we must be ready," Elbryan decided. He looked at Pony and winked, and was surprised when she returned the gesture with a serious frown.

Perhaps this was more than a game.

❖ 2 ❖

True Believer

T wenty-five stood in a line, cloaked in thick brown robes with voluminous sleeves and large hoods that were pulled low to hide their
faces. Quiet and humble, they kept their heads bowed, their
shoulders stooped, and their hands folded before them, though not a digit
showed from beneath the folds of cloth, not a flash of flesh in the whole of
the line.

"Piety, dignity, poverty," the old father abbot, Dalebert Markwart,
intoned in his nasal voice. He stood alone on the balcony above the main
entrance of St.-Mere-Abelle, the most prominent monastery in all the
kingdom of Honce-the-Bear, in the northern temperate zone of Corona.
Intertwined with the rocky cliffs of the southeastern coast, St.-Mere-Abelle
had stood solemn and dark for nearly a millennium, with each generation of
monks adding their toil and craftsmanship to the already huge structure. Its
gray rock walls seemed to grow right from the solid stone, an extension of
the earth's power. Squat towers anchored every turn in the wall; narrow
windows showed that the place was built for somber reflection and defense.
The visible parts of the monastery were impressive; the sea wall alone rose
and melted back into the cliff face for more than a mile. But the bulk of the
place could not be seen from beyond the walls; it was buried under the
ground, in tunnels strong and square, in vast underground chambers—
many smoky from the constant torchlight, others brightened by ways magical. Seven hundred monks lived here and another two hundred servants,
many of them never leaving the place except to go on short visits, usually to
market in the village of St.-Mere-Abelle, some three miles inland.

The new class of twenty-five stood one behind the other. As they were
positioned according to height, Avelyn Desbris, tall and large-boned, was
near the back, with twenty-two before him and only two behind. He could
barely hear the Abbot above the constant groan of the wind, weaving
always through the many rocks. But Avelyn hardly cared. For the majority
of his twenty years, the young man had dreamed of this day, had set his

sights on the Order of St.-Mere-Abelle as surely as any general would focus on his next conquest. Eight years of formal study, eight years of grueling testing, had brought Avelyn to this point, one of twenty-five remaining of the two thousand twelve-year-olds who had begun the process, each desperately vying to gain admittance in this class of God's Year 816.

Avelyn dared to peek out from under his hood at the handful of spectators lining the road before the monastery's front gates. His mother, Annalisa, and father, Jayson, were among that small group, though his mother had taken ill and would not likely make it back to their home in the village of Youmaneff, some three hundred miles from the coast. Avelyn knew with near certainty that this would be the last time he saw her, and likely the last time he'd see his father, as well. Avelyn was the youngest of ten, and his parents had been well into their forties when he was born. His next youngest sibling was seven years his senior, and so he wasn't really close to any of them. By the time Avelyn was old enough to understand the concept of family, half the children had already moved out of the family house.

His life had been good, though, and he had been close to his parents, more so than any of his brothers or sisters had been. The bond had been particularly strong with Annalisa, a humble and spiritual woman, who had encouraged her youngest child to follow the path of God from his earliest recollections.

Avelyn dropped his gaze once more, fearful of discipline should he be caught peeking out from under his hood. Rumors hinted that students of St.-Mere-Abelle had been dismissed for less. He pictured his mother on that day many years before when he had announced that he would enter St.-Mere-Abelle: the tears that had come to her; the smile, gentle, even divine. That image, that confirmation, was burned into Avelyn's thoughts as clearly as if it had been painted and magically illuminated on the inside of his eyelids. How much younger and more vibrant Annalisa had seemed! The last few years had been hard on her, one illness after another. She was determined to see this day, though, and Avelyn understood that with its passing, with his entering St.-Mere-Abelle, the woman would no longer fight against mortality.

It was all right, to Avelyn and to Annalisa. Her goals had been met, her life lived in the spirit of generosity. Avelyn knew he would cry when word reached him of her passing, but he knew, too, that his tears would be selfish—tears for himself and his loss, and not for Annalisa, whom he knew would be in a better place.

A grinding sound, the great gates sliding open, brought the young man from his contemplations.

"Do you willingly enter the service of God?" Father Abbot Dalebert Markwart asked.

The twenty-five responded with a unified "Yes, say I!"

"Show then your desire," the Father Abbot demanded. "Pass ye the Gauntlet of Willing Suffering!"

The line shuffled forward. "My God, our God, one God," they chanted, and they lifted their voices even higher when the first of their ranks entered the gauntlet, stepping between two lines of monks, those who remained of the classes of the previous two years, all armed with heavy wooden paddles.

Avelyn heard the slaps of wood, the unintentional groans, even an occasional cry from the younger students near the front. He fell deeper within himself, chanted with all his strength, and listened to his own words, grabbing at his faith and building with it a wall of denial. So strong was he in meditation that he did not even feel the first few blows, and those that slapped against him afterward seemed a minor thing, a momentary pain, lost in the ultimate sweetness that awaited him. All his life, he had wanted to live in service to God; all his life he had dreamed of this day.

Now was his time, his day. He came through the gauntlet without uttering a single sound beyond the range of his controlled, even-toned chant.

That fact was not lost on Father Abbot Markwart, nor on any of the other monks watching the initiation of God's Year 816. None of the others in Avelyn's line could make such a claim; not one in several years had walked the Gauntlet of Willing Suffering with so minimal complaint.

The huge stone gates of St.-Mere-Abelle slammed shut with a resounding crash that jolted Annalisa Desbris violently. Her husband held her tight then, understanding her pain, both physical and emotional.

Annalisa knew, as Avelyn had known, that she would never see her son in this world again. She had given him over to the service of God, to her ultimate joy, but still, the very real human pain of final parting tugged at her weak heart, stole the strength from her tiny arms and legs.

Jayson supported her, always. He, too, had tears in his eyes, but unlike Annalisa's, which were of joy, Jayson's tears came from a mix of emotions, ranging from simple sadness to anger. He had never spoken openly against Avelyn's decision, but privately the pragmatic man had wondered if his son wasn't merely throwing his life away.

He couldn't say that to frail Annalisa, he knew. A simple word could break her. Jayson only hoped that he could somehow get her home, into her own bed, before she died.

Thoughts of his parents could not hold Avelyn's attention as the group crossed the windblown courtyard and entered the grand entrance hall of St.-Mere-Abelle. Now, the young man did utter an unintended sound, a gasp of disbelief and delight.

The place was not bright, having only a handful of tiny windows set high up on the tall walls. Torches burned at regular intervals, and the massive beams that supported the hall's ceiling seemed to dance in their light. Avelyn had never seen a place so huge, could not comprehend the effort that had been expended to put this hall together. His own village of Youmaneff would fit inside this one hall, with room left over to stable the horses!

The tapestries that lined the place were no less magnificent and intriguing, woven into scenes that held a million details in every square foot—sights within sights, subtle lines and smaller images—that caught Avelyn's eyes and his curiosity and would not let them go. The tapestries covered the walls almost completely, allowing for windows and for racked displays of shining weapons: swords and spears, great axes, long daggers, and a myriad of pole arms with hooked blades and prodding tips that Avelyn did not know. Suits of armor of various designs stood as silent sentinels, every type from the overlapping wooden plates of the ancient Behrenese to the strong metal-plate mail designed for Honce-the-Bear's Allheart Brigade, the personal guards of the King—whoever that might be at the moment. Along one wall stood a gigantic statue, fifteen feet or more, dressed in a heavy leather jack, trimmed in fur and set with spiked metal plates and heavy iron rings. A fomorian, Avelyn realized with a very visible shudder, in the typical battle dress of its warlike race. Beside it, dramatically, were two tiny figures, one just over half Avelyn's height, the other a bit taller, but slender and lithe. The shorter of the pair wore a light leather tunic and arm shields, metal sleeves hooked over the figure's thumbs and running from wrists to elbow. The red beret gave the figure's identity away. It was a powrie mannikin, Avelyn realized. The cruel dwarflike powries were also called "bloody caps" for their gruesome habit of dipping their berets, enchanted pieces made of specially prepared human skin, in their victims' blood until the cap took on—and kept—a shining red hue.

The statue beside the powrie, sporting a pair of nearly translucent wings, had to be a representation of an elf, the mysterious Touel'alfar. Its limbs were slender and long and its armor a silver shining coat of fine interlocking links. Avelyn wanted to go closer to it to study the stern facial features and the incredible craftsmanship of the armor. That thought, and the potential punishment it might bring, reminded the young man of where he was and that many seconds, minutes perhaps, had slipped past him unnoticed. He blushed deeply and lowered his head, taking a quick glance all around. He calmed quickly, though, seeing that all of his classmates were similarly entranced and that the Father Abbot and the other ranking monks seemed not to care.

The initiates were supposed to be overwhelmed, Avelyn suddenly realized, and he looked again around the room, this time more openly, nodding as he began to understand the true nature of the place. The Order of St.-Mere-Abelle was noted not just for its pious and humble priests but also for their long reputation as fierce warriors. The eight years of Avelyn's pretraining had included only minor instruction in the martial arts, but he had suspected that the physical qualifications of the brotherhood, the ability to fight, would become more prominent once inside the monastery.

To Avelyn, it was more of a distraction than anything else. All that the gentle and idealistic young man wanted was to serve God, to foster peace, to heal, and to comfort. To Avelyn Desbris, nothing in all the world, not the treasures of a dragon's hoard, nor the powers of a king, could outweigh that accomplishment.

Now he was on the other side of the great stone gates of St.-Mere-Abelle. Now he had his chance.

So he believed.

❖ 3 ❖

The Lingering Kiss

Things quieted quickly in Dundalis. As the days after the patrol's return stretched out into an uneventful week, and then a second, thoughts of the slain goblin took second place to the very real threat of winter's onset. There was much to be done: the last harvesting, preparing the meat, patching holes in the cottages, and cleaning the chimneys. Every passing day, danger from the goblins seemed more and more remote; every passing day, fewer and fewer men and women went out of the town to walk a patrol.

Elbryan and his friends, some as young as six or seven, saw their chance unfolding. For the adults, the specter of the goblins brought a sobering wariness and then a troublesome distraction. For the younger villagers, whose imaginations were far livelier and whose sense of adventure hadn't yet been tempered by any real loss, thoughts of goblin raids brought excitement, a call to arms, a time for heroes. Elbryan and his friends had offered to walk patrols since the first day of the hunting party's return. Each morning, they approached the village leaders, and each morning, they were politely refused and quickly put to some more mundane task. Even Elbryan, who would be entering the realm of adults that coming spring, had spent almost all the previous week with his head up a dirty chimney.

But the young man held faith and passed his hopes down the line. The adults were tiring of their patrols, he knew, and were growing more and more confident that the goblin incident was a chance thing—a single, unfortunate meeting—and that those creatures which had been chased away would not return to the site of the battle, let alone try to track the humans back to their village, some thirty miles away.

Now, with two calm weeks behind them and no further sightings except for a few wild rumors that were discounted by even the most cautious of Dundalis's folk, Elbryan recognized the lessening of resistance in his father's voice. He was not surprised that morning when Olwan, instead of shaking his head, bent low and sketched out in the dirt a rough map of the area, explaining to his son where he and his friends should be positioned.

Elbryan was surprised, though, and pleasantly so, when Olwan then presented him with the family sword, a short, thick blade of two-foot length. It wasn't an impressive weapon—its blade showed many nicks and more than a little rust—but it was one of the few real swords in the village. "Make certain that every one of your group is well armed," Olwan said seriously. "And make sure that each knows the value, and the danger, of his or her weapon."

Olwan knew what this meant to his son, and if he had smiled or let on in any way that the patrols were no longer really necessary, he would have stolen something from Elbryan, a measure of importance that the young man desperately needed to feel.

"Do you think it is wise to let the children go out with weapons?" Shane McMichael asked Olwan, coming up to the large man soon after Elbryan had run off. "Or to let them go out at all?"

Olwan snorted and shrugged his muscular shoulders. "We cannot spare the men and women," he replied, "and there is the other patrol in the vale, the most likely route for our enemies to take, should they come." Olwan gave another snort, a helpless sound that surprised McMichael, who had always known Olwan as the coolest and most confident head in all the village.

"Besides," Olwan went on, "if the goblins or fomorians get close enough to Dundalis for my son and his friends to see, they will be as well off out in the woods as in the village."

Shane McMichael did not argue the point, though the weight of it grew steadily on his shoulders. Since Honce-the-Bear had been at peace for many years—and goblins and evil giants receding from the thoughts of most people to become little more than fireside tales—Dundalis had not been built for defense. The village was not even walled, as earlier settlements near the Wilderlands had been, and the folk were not well armed. The hunting party of twelve had carried with them more than half the total real weapons of the hundred folk of Dundalis. Olwan was right, Shane McMichael knew, and he shuddered with the thought; if the goblins got close enough for Elbryan and the others to spot them, then all the village would be in danger.

Olwan started away, and McMichael calmed and moved to follow. He really didn't think any goblins would come; none in the village except for pessimistic old Brody Gentle spoke of such darkness.

The patrols began that day, with a score and five youngsters walking the rim of the bowl-shaped vale that held Dundalis. There was one other patrol, a handful of older teenagers, venturing further out, down among the pines and fluffy caribou moss to the northeast. Each of this group nodded respectfully at his younger counterparts as he passed them on the rim; some mentioned that Elbryan's patrols would serve as their vital liaison with the village proper. After that exchange of compliments, even the passing of endless uneventful hours could not dampen the thrill for the youngsters. Elbryan and his friends were not being left out this time, were not being treated as mere children.

As each day slipped past—the weather growing a bit colder, the wind shifting more to the north—the twenty-five in Elbryan's group perfected their patrol routes. Elbryan split them into four teams of five and one of three, which would move from group to group gathering information, while he and Pony served as anchor to them all, holding a position along the highest ridge directly north of Dundalis, overlooking the valley of evergreens and caribou moss. There were several complaints about this arrangement at first, mostly from the older boys who thought that they should serve as Elbryan's second. Some even resorted to teasing Elbryan about his growing relationship with Pony, prompting him to "ride the Pony," and other such crudities.

Elbryan took it all in stride, with the exception of any insults to Pony, which he promptly informed the teasers would bring them serious and painful retaliation. He didn't care about their teasing him though, having at last admitted, to himself and openly, that Pony was his best and most-trusted friend.

"Let the children have their fun," Elbryan, coming into manhood, whispered to Pony as the groups split up.

When he wasn't looking her way, when he had moved off to set up a windbreak of dead wood, Pony regarded him knowingly, a warm smile spreading over her face.

Something else watched the young man from a perch in one of the thicker pines on the ridge. It moved nimbly from branch to branch, crossing over to nearby trees with barely a whisper. It shadowed Elbryan's every move, studying the young leader intently.

To Pony and Elbryan, alert as they were, the creature was invisible and unnoticed. Even if they had looked intently the creature's way, its movements were so fluid and graceful—and always under the cover of pine boughs—that they would have considered the sway of the branches no more than the movement of the wind or a gray squirrel, perhaps.

Another week passed by uneventfully. Work in the village was at full pace, readying for winter. On the ridge and in the vale beyond, the primary enemy became boredom. Elbryan lost half a dozen of his patrol at the beginning of that second week, the youths explaining that their parents needed them about the house and would not let them go out. Elbryan did not miss that every one of those "soldiers" seemed grateful to be relieved of the dull patrols.

Elbryan continued his diligent work, though, reorganizing the routes to cover more ground since he was down to three teams of five, with a couple of messengers.

"We'll lose Shamus tomorrow," Pony said as they sat side by side in a hollow on the high ridge, sheltered from the chill wind by a pair of large pines. The day was late, and gray clouds were rolling in to hide the afternoon sun. "His mother told me this morning this would be his last day out."

Elbryan prodded the ground with the tip of his sword. "His patrol group goes to four, then," he said matter-of-factly.

Pony recognized the frustration in his voice, though he did well to hide it. Elbryan was watching his first command crumbling about him, his soldiers being taken away so that they could help patch roofs or shore up barns. Pony sympathized with the young man, but logically, this was the best scenario they could have hoped for.

"They are being called back home because no enemy has come," she gently reminded him. "Better this than for your patrol to have been truly necessary."

Elbryan looked at her, little luster showing in his normally bright green eyes.

"Or maybe we were necessary," Pony quickly added, trying to salvage some measure of the young man's pride. "How do we know that goblins have not ventured near Dundalis?"

Elbryan cocked his head and ran a hand through his thick layers of straight, light brown hair.

"Perhaps their scouts did come near us," Pony went on. "Perhaps they saw our patrols and realized they would not have an easy time of it against the village."

"We are just children," Elbryan said disgustedly.

Pony shook her head. "And all but the smallest of our group is larger than a goblin," she replied without hesitation, and that truth seemed to lend some credence to her reasoning. "Is not the best army the one so strong that enemies will not dare attack?"

Elbryan didn't answer, but that familiar sparkle lit up his eyes. He turned back to regard the ground in front of him, and the wild design he was cutting with the sword tip.

Pony smiled warmly, feeling that she had done well. It pleased her greatly to help out Elbryan, to guard his emotions. She didn't really believe goblins had come near enough to see the patrols, and neither did Elbryan, but at least this way he could hold out some reason to believe his first real effort at something important by adult standards had not been in vain. The simple fact that they could not be absolutely certain offered Elbryan all the encouragement he needed.

Pony dared to reach out then; the connection was too strong to let the moment pass. She cupped Elbryan's chin in one hand and gently turned him back to face her.

"You have done a wonderful job out here," she said softly.

"Not alone," he started to reply, but she stopped him by putting a finger of her free hand across his lips. Only then did Elbryan realize how close they were, their faces barely two inches apart. He felt warm suddenly, a bit dizzy, a bit frightened.

Pony drifted closer. She kissed him! Full on the lips! Elbryan was terrified and thrilled all at once. He thought he should pull away, spit on the ground, and yell "girl poison!" as was the expected response, as had been his response all the other times Pony, or any of the other girls, had tried to kiss him.

He didn't want to do that; the last notion in his mind was to pull away. He realized then that it had been a long, long time since Pony had tried to kiss him—at least a year. Had she feared his reaction? Had she known he would have spit and yelled out "girl poison," a chant that would have been taken up by every boy in the village?

Or had she known he wasn't ready, until now, to be kissed? That was it, the young man decided as the gentle kiss, their closed mouths barely touching, lingered on and on. Pony knew him so very well, better than he knew himself. Their last few days together, alone for four of every five hours, had brought them even closer.

And now this. Elbryan didn't want it to end. He shifted in his seat, first lifted the short sword, then, realizing that it would be awkward, perhaps even dangerous, dropped it to the ground. He dared to put his arms around Pony's back, dared to pull her closer, feeling the strangely interesting curves and bumps of her body against his own as they came together. He fought a fit of panic—not knowing what he should do, where he should move his hands, or if he should move his hands at all.

All Elbryan knew was that he didn't want the kiss to end, that he wanted something more, though he wasn't really sure what that might be. He wanted to be closer to Pony, physically and emotionally. This was his Pony, his dearest friend, the girl—no, the young woman—whom he had grown to love. He would pass into manhood that spring, Pony into womanhood the following autumn, and soon after, he would ask for Pony's hand . . .

That notion brought fear and Elbryan tried to pull away—and did break the hold long enough to catch his breath. Again, the fears passed, lost in a swirl of warmth as he looked at Pony's shining blue eyes, at her smile, as genuine and joyful as anything Elbryan had ever seen. She hardly had to nudge him to get him to kiss her again, and they settled even more comfortably together.

The kiss shifted, from curiosity to urgency, then back to gentleness. Their clothes ruffled and seemed more of an obstacle than a necessity. Though the air was chill, Elbryan had the feeling he would be warmer without them. His hands did move now, as he lost his fear of touching Pony. He caressed her neck, ran his hand down her side and along the outside of her strong leg. He was shocked as her mouth opened a little bit, as he felt her tongue against his lips, so soft and inviting.

The moment, this most precious moment in all of Elbryan's young life . . .

And then suddenly, it was gone, destroyed by a horrified, and horrifying, scream. The couple jumped apart and to their feet, staring wide-eyed down the long slope to the village, at the swarming forms, at the large plume of smoke—too large to come from any chimney!—rising from one of the houses.

The goblins had come.

Hundreds of miles away, in a windswept, foreboding land called the Barbacan, in a deep cave in a mountain called Aida, the dactyl basked in the sensation of war. The demon creature could feel the screams of those dying in Dundalis, though it had no idea where the battle was being waged. This was an action of a rogue goblin chieftain, perhaps, or one of the many powrie raiding parties, acting on their own initiative, bringing misery to the wretched humans.

The dactyl could not take direct credit, but that mattered little. It had awakened, darkness rising, and already its influence was spreading throughout Corona. Already the goblins, the powries, or one of the other races the demon would claim as minions had felt that awakening and had been given the courage to act.

The creature flexed its great wings and settled back in the throne it had shaped from the obsidian that had formerly served as its tomb. Yes, the dark vibrations were running strong through the stone. The sensation of war, of human agony.

It was good to be awake.

❖ 4 ❖

The Death of Dundalis

Elbryan and Pony were stunned and terrified for many seconds. It was too unreal, too beyond their experience and expectations. Images assaulted them, mingling with imagined scenes even more horrifying, and amid all of it welled utter denial, the hope against obvious reality that this simply could not be happening.

Jilseponie moved first, a single, tiny step, her arm reaching out helplessly. That almost involuntary motion seemed to break her trance and she let out a shriek for her mother and ran full out for home.

Elbryan thought to call out for her, but indecision held his voice and kept him from immediately following. What should he do? What were his responsibilities?

A warrior would know these things!

With great effort, Elbryan tore his gaze from the dreadful spectacle below and glanced all around. He should organize his friends—yes, that was the course, he decided. He would gather together his scouts, perhaps even call in the older scouts from the vale, and charge down into Dundalis in tight formation, anchoring the defense.

But time was against him. He glanced about again, turned to the evergreen and caribou moss valley, and started to call out, thinking to bring in the patrol of older men.

Elbryan fell back behind the twin pines, catching the shout in his throat, gasping for breath. Just over the ridge, facing away from him, he saw the nearly bald head, the pointed ears, the chalky yellow skin of an enemy. With trembling fingers, Elbryan retrieved his short sword, and then he sank even deeper into the hollow, paralyzed with terror.

Pony wasn't armed, having left her club back at the ridge. She didn't care, for she wasn't really running into battle.

The girl was running to find her mother and father, to feel their comforting hugs, to hear her mother telling her that everything would be all right. She wanted to be a little girl again, wrapped tight in her bedsheets, and tighter in Mother's embrace, waking from a nightmare.

This time, though, she was awake. This time, the screams were real.

Pony ran on desperately, blinded by tears. She stumbled to the base of what she thought was a tree, then nearly fainted as it shifted suddenly, as the fomorian giant, huge club in hand, took a long step away from her.

If she had had any breath in her lungs, she would have screamed, and if she had screamed, the giant would have noticed her and squashed her where she stood.

But its focus was the village and not some insignificant little girl, and in a few loping strides it left Pony far behind. She scrambled back to her feet, picked up a couple of rocks of a good size for throwing, and ran on, taking a course that would parallel, but not too closely, the giant. Now, as she entered the area of battle, as she saw the confusion, the fierce fighting, the dead bodies on the road, she was no more a little girl. Now she remembered her training, forced herself to think clearly and concisely. Goblins swarmed everywhere, and Pony spotted at least two other giants, fifteen feet tall and perhaps a thousand pounds of chiseled muscle. Her friends and family could not win! That logical, adult part of Pony—the part that knew that the time of fending off nightmares with bedsheets was long past—told her without doubt that Dundalis could not survive.

"Plan B," she whispered aloud, using the words to steady her thinking. The rules of survival, taught to every child in Wilderlands settlements, declared that the first priority in any catastrophe was to save the village. If that failed, the next task was to save as many individuals as possible. Plan B.

Pony picked her way around the back of the nearest houses, moving in and out of the shadows. She peeked around the corner and stood transfixed.

On the main road of Dundalis, just on the other side of this house, a fierce battle raged. Pony saw Olwan Wyndon first, standing tall in the middle of the human line, calling out commands, forming the group of twenty men and women into a tight circle as enemies came at them from nearly every direction. Pony's first instincts were to try and join that battle group, but she quickly surmised that she would never get in. She clenched her fist hopefully as Olwan Wyndon smashed a goblin's head, dropping the wretch to the dirt.

Then she held her breath as she noticed the man behind Olwan, parrying wildly as two goblins prodded at him with sharp spears.

Her father.

Elbryan held his breath, gasped once, then held it again. He didn't know what to do, then cursed himself silently for what he had already done!

In the hollow of the twin pines, he had lost sight of his enemy—the first, and often fatal, mistake.

Now he had to work hard to deny his terror, had to climb above the emotion and the physical barrier and remember the many lessons his father had given him. A warrior knows his enemy, locates his enemy, and watches its every move. Silently mouthing that litany, Elbryan inched his face toward the edge of the pine. He hesitated momentarily at the very last instant, certain the goblin was just on the other side, weapon poised to smash him as soon as he peeked around.

A warrior knows his enemy . . .

A sudden shift brought the field beyond the pines back into view, and Elbryan nearly collapsed with relief when he saw the goblin had not moved and was still facing away from him, staring into the northern valley. That relief fast transformed into a sinking feeling as Elbryan realized the meaning of this creature's positioning. The patrol in the valley had been spotted, perhaps had even been already engaged, and this goblin had been set as sentry, watching for any other potential human reinforcements while its companions sacked the village.

That thought sparked anger in the young man, enough to overcome his fear. He clenched more tightly his short sword and slowly brought one leg up under him.

Without hesitation, for if he paused, he knew his courage surely would falter, Elbryan slipped out from behind the protection of the tree. Half walking, half crawling, he moved closer to the goblin, quickly covering a third of the distance.

Then he wanted to turn back, to run into the hollow and cover his face. The sounds behind him, from his home, bolstered him, as did the smell of burning wood carried by the wind up to the ridge. With a grimace of determination, Elbyran halved the distance to his foe. No turning back now. He scanned the area, and, as soon as he was confident that this creature was alone, he stood up and rushed out.

Five running strides brought him to the goblin, who didn't hear his approach until the last second. Even as the goblin began to turn, Elbryan's sword came down hard on its head.

The sword bounced out wide. Elbryan was surprised by the force of the impact and that his sword had not cut into the goblin's skull. He thought for one terrible moment he hadn't hit the thing hard enough, that it would turn and skewer him with its crude spear. Desperately, the young man scrambled to the side, trying to ready a defense.

The goblin staggered weirdly, dropped its weapon, and fell to its knees. Its head lolled from side to side. Elbryan saw the bright red gash, the white of split bone, the grayish brain. The goblin stopped moving. Its chin came to rest on its chest, and it held the kneeling pose, quite dead.

Dead.

Elbryan felt his guts churning and labored for his breath. The weight of his first kill descended upon him, bowing his shoulders, nearly driving him to his knees. Again it was the smell of his burning village that cleared his head. He had no time now to ponder, and any sympathetic notions that he might have captured the goblin instead of killing it seemed perfectly ridiculous.

He looked ahead at the evergreen vale and noted to his dismay that a fight was going on down there. Then he looked back at the larger battle for Dundalis.

To where his parents were fighting, to where Pony had run.

"Pony," the desperate young man whispered aloud, and before Elbryan even consciously knew what he was doing, he saw the trees going past him in a blur as he sprinted down the slope toward Dundalis.

Pony made her way around the house, inching toward the battle, wondering how she might get past the ring of goblins to stand beside her father. A cry of agony within the house froze her in place, and she leaned heavily on the frame for support. She took a moment to consider where she was, whose house this was, and she stifled a sob.

"No time for that," she scolded herself, and she focused on the battle raging on the road. Again her shoulders sagged, for though many goblins lay dead or dying on the bloodied ground about the ring of desperate fighters, several humans were down as well. And the goblin ranks, for all the carnage, remained deep, and seemed undiminished.

Above it all stood Olwan, proud and strong and unshakable. He clobbered yet another goblin, bashing in its ugly skull, then raised his arm and called out, trying to rally the others. Pony blinked curiously, for Olwan's arm did not come down, seemed to be going up, up, up. She saw the look of horror and pain that came over the man, then looked higher, past his stretched shoulder, his elbow . . .

The giant's hand covered the tall man's entire forearm. Blocked by the wall of the house, Pony couldn't follow the man's ascent. She wanted to yell out for someone to help doomed Olwan, wanted to scream simply for the sake of screaming.

And then Olwan came flying back into sight, falling in a broken heap on the road right in the midst of the valiant fighters. Their ranks broke apart. They ran every which way, most getting no more than a couple of strides before being buried under a wave of swarming goblins. Pony lost sight of her father immediately, mercifully. She tried to sort out the mob, saw another person—the woman who had taught her to read and write—get pulled down to the ground, saw the goblin spear fast following. And then Pony turned away, stumbling to the back of the house, holding her churning stomach.

There were no lines of defense anymore, no organized pockets of resistance. Everything was confusion, screams and cries of pain. Pony didn't know where to turn, where to run. She saw the image of dead Olwan again, and the last glimpse of her father.

She turned back toward the road, hoping that her dad would come for her, would somehow rush out of the jumble and scoop her away from the danger, would make everything better, as he'd always done.

As if in a grotesque mockery of that hope, a goblin marched around that corner, bearing down on the girl. Pony let out a cry, hurled one of her stones at the creature, and ran off.

Anger held her in place just around the back of the house. She stopped and braced herself, measuring the goblin's footsteps. As it rounded the corner, the girl snapped back her elbow with all her strength, catching the charging creature right under the chin.

Pony spun and jumped on it, flailing wildly with both fists, kicking and kneeing viciously. Stronger than its little body would indicate, the goblin finally pushed her aside and turned its spear.

"Elbryan!"

The call brought the sprinting lad to a skidding halt. He caught the trunk of a young maple and swung about it, turning in the direction of the voice.

Carley dan Aubrey, one of the younger scouts, staggered toward him, his face ashen, both hands clenched firmly to his right side at his waist. Elbryan saw the dark stain near those hands.

"Elbryan!" the nine-year-old boy called again, stumbling forward. Elbryan ran out to meet him, caught him as he fell.

The older boy moved quickly to inspect the wound, forcing Carley's hands away. Elbryan grimaced, and Carley whimpered and nearly vomited, when Elbryan's hand brushed against the broken tip of a spear jutting from Carley's side.

Elbryan pulled back his trembling hand, staring wide-eyed at the bright blood that now covered it. Carley clutched desperately at the wound again, but he could not hope to stem the blood.

Elbryan forced himself to remain steady, to think clearly. He had to get his own shirt off and use it to somehow wrap the wound. And quickly! He tore off his overcoat and pulled open his leather vest, quickly unbuttoning the sleeves of his white shirt. Then he saw the goblin, coming fast, half a spear in its hands. It raised the shaft like a club, bearing down on him.

Elbryan grabbed for his short sword, tried to bring it up in front of him, and fell back as the goblin dove upon him. They came together hard, Elbryan going flat out on his back.

Down they rolled together. Elbryan's sword was up against the creature's side, had cut in a bit, but the angle was wrong, and the goblin's grip surprisingly strong, preventing the boy from driving the weapon home.

Over and over they rolled, tumbling down the slope, punching and thrashing. The ugly goblin face, all twisted teeth and long pointy nose, was barely inches from Elbryan's face, and closer still when the creature began to butt the boy. Elbryan felt his nose crack, felt the warmth of his blood running. He struggled harder, but the goblin would not let him drive his sword home.

Elbryan tugged more fiercely with his other hand instead, increasing the pace of the roll. He caught his ankles on a tree trunk but kicked off, not daring to stop, and the goblin came right over him. Still the creature held on stubbornly, pulling Elbryan over, and they began to roll sidelong again, heads to feet. On the first roll, Elbryan saw his new advantage, and on the second the young man poked the elbow of his sword arm out so it hit the ground and was braced.

When the goblin came over, its own weight forced it down on Elbryan's sword.

The creature went berserk, kicking and thrashing, flopping like a landed fish. Elbryan at first tried to defend himself but when that seemed futile, went on the offensive instead, brutally turning and twisting his blade.

The pair rolled hard into the trunk of another tree, and the goblin abruptly stopped its thrashing. Elbryan, dazed, his breath blasted away, nearly fainted. His thoughts came back in a terrifying rush and he tore free his sword and began hacking wildly, cutting the goblin again and again. He crawled out from under the thing, but kept on attacking it, savagely, primally, his blows wrought of sheer terror. Finally he stopped, realizing it was dead, that it could no longer hurt him. He knelt over it, trying to catch his breath, which would not seem to come to him.

Carley dan Aubrey's whimper brought him back to his senses. He dashed back up the slope, finally getting to the boy.

"Cold," Carley mouthed quietly. Elbryan fell to his knees, reaching for the wound, gingerly touching the spear and wondering if he should pull it free. He looked at the boy, and he held his breath.

But Carley was dead.

Pony ran off, stumbled and fell, then scrambled on all fours—anything to get away. The goblin was behind her; she could imagine it readying its spear, lining up her vulnerable back. She cried out and fell around a corner, flat on her face. Realizing she hadn't been hit by anything, she put her feet back under her and ran on.

Around the back of the house, Thomas Ault, Pony's father, tore his dagger free and let the dead goblin fall to the ground. He looked plaintively at the corner around which his daughter had run, hoping, praying she would somehow escape.

Thomas had done all he could. He felt the sting of the light spears, six of them, in his back, his side, deep in one thigh. He heard the footsteps as the band of pursuing goblins closed the distance to him.

He prayed Pony would get away.

Before Elbryan could start back toward the town, he saw the shadows moving among the trees in the area from which Carley had come. He knew these were not his other friends, knew instinctively the others had fallen. He moved slowly, quietly, away from Carley's body, taking cover behind a larger tree.

Seven goblins came into sight, trotting easily down the slope. They hooted and laughed when they spotted the dead boy, then hooted even louder when they saw their fallen companion, not even pausing as they passed.

Elbryan wanted to jump out at them, to slash them all. Wisdom overruled his rage, though, and he stayed hidden and let them pass. Then he stalked after them, his bloody sword in his bloody hand, hoping one of the creatures would stray from its friends.

The smoke was growing thicker down in the village now. The screams had diminished, but when he crossed an area that offered him a clear view of Dundalis, Elbryan saw the scrambling forms were still thick about the place.

The young man knew it was hopeless, knew that his village was lost, knew all of his friends, his parents, his Pony, were gone.

Elbryan knew it, yet he did not slow his pace and did not alter his course. He was beyond grief, beyond logic, with no tears to cry. He would go down to Dundalis; he would kill every goblin he could catch.

She saw the dead, saw the dying. She didn't know why she hadn't yet been caught, but as she darted from shadow to shadow, from the side of one burning building to the next, she knew that her luck would not hold out for long. All thought of rescuing anyone was gone. All that she wanted now was to get away, far away.

But how? The roads were thick with goblins. Groups of the ugly creatures ran into each house, ransacked the place, and then set it ablaze. They showed no mercy; Pony saw one woman beg for her life, offer herself to the goblins circling about her.

They hacked her down.

The noose was getting tighter, Pony knew. As villagers died, more and more goblins were free to run about. She looked in every direction, trying to find some course out of the town to the trees. But there was no escape, no way to get beyond Dundalis without being seen. And there were other goblins in the woods, coming in a few at a time.

No escape.

Pony squeezed in tight between two buildings and put her head against a wall. She wondered if it would be better to run out into the road and get it over with. "Better that than to wait," she mumbled determinedly, but she found she could not do it, that her most basic instinct for survival would not let her.

Pony took a deep breath. She felt the heat against her hands as this house, too, started to burn. Now where could she run?

The girl cocked her head, suddenly realizing exactly where she was. This was Shane McMichael's house in front of her, Olwan Wyndon's right behind her. Olwan's house, Elbryan's house.

Elbryan's new house!

Pony remembered the building of the place, only two years previously. The whole village had buzzed about the house because Olwan Wyndon was laying a stone foundation.

Pony fell to her knees and began to scrape the ground at the base of Olwan's house. Her fingers bled, she felt the heat growing behind her, but she dug on desperately.

Then her hand broke through into an open area. She reached deeper, perhaps a foot and a half down, and her hand met cold, wet ground. Olwan had used large slabs for the base, and, as Pony suspected, the house hadn't completely settled.

The smoke grew thick about Pony; Olwan's house, too, went up in flames. Still she dug, widening the hole, trying desperately to squeeze under the slab.

The angry young man didn't have long to wait. The goblin band, sentries apparently and not part of the attacking force, did not continue down toward Dundalis but split ranks and filtered left and right into the trees.

Elbryan went left, shadowing a group of three. He heard the continuing screams in Dundalis, more of a pitiful weeping now than any cries of resistance. He saw the houses burning, was close enough to realize that his own house was among them.

That only fueled the young man's outrage. He stalked quietly from tree to tree, and when one of the goblins paused and fell behind the others, he was quickly to the spot.

The kill was swift, a single thrust through the creature's ribs, but not quiet, for the goblin managed to let out a dying cry.

Elbryan tore free his sword and started to run, but too late. He swiped left and right, picking off a pair of thrusting spears as the two other goblins bore down on him, howling and shouting. Their eyes—so full of glee, so uncaring for their fallen comrade—unnerved Elbryan, and he tried hard not to look at them, tried to concentrate on their stabbing spears.

All the while he was backtracking, realizing he had to flee before the other group answered the howling call. The goblin on his left came in hard and straight. Elbryan snapped his sword over and around the spear, angling it past on his right, and he skittered out to the left, up the slope, gaining the higher ground.

All advantage was lost as the young man stumbled, the loose earth slipping out from under his foot. The other goblin ran around the back of its companion and moved higher, coming in at Elbryan from above.

Desperately, he threw himself backward, put a foot under him, and kicked off, flying past the turning spear of the first goblin and rushing to get out of range of the second. He slashed out with his sword as he careened past, gaining hope as he felt it connect with something solid.

Then the world was spinning as Elbryan bounced and rolled. He finally controlled his slide and tried to angle himself so he could stop his roll and come up in a defensive posture. He expected the goblin—perhaps both of the creatures—to be right behind him.

They weren't. The one Elbryan had slashed lay very still on the ground—apparently he had hit it harder than he'd believed. The other was also on the ground, squirming and groaning.

The only explanation Elbryan could think of was that it had charged at him as he had leaped away and had slammed hard against the ground or against a tree trunk. Not one to argue with good fortune, Elbryan scrambled to his feet.

Something tapped him on the shoulder, not hard at first, but then he was flying once more, sidelong this time. He hit the ground in a roll but slammed hard against a tree trunk as he came around. Confused and dazed, Elbryan staggered to his feet.

And all hope flew from him as a fomorian giant, holding a club as large as Elbryan's entire body, casually walked toward him. And Elbryan heard hoots from behind him and knew the other four goblins were on the way.

The young man glanced all around. Nowhere to run, nowhere to hide. He braced himself, used the solid tree as support. When the giant was within one huge stride, Elbryan leaped out, trying to confuse it with sheer savagery. He stabbed and slashed, came in close to the monster's knees and stabbed again, then rolled right between the giant's legs.

But the giant had seen the move dozens of times in its battles with little folk. Elbryan got halfway through before the giant clamped his knees together, holding the youth so securely he could barely draw breath. Elbryan tried to stab the monster again, but the giant squeezed even tighter, and all the young man could do was groan. He managed to turn sideways, and from that perspective could see the giant's club rise up over its head.

A sickening feeling washed over Elbryan. Stubborn to the end, he stabbed again as hard as he could, then closed his eyes.

The air came alive with a strange humming sound. The giant released its grip and Elbryan fell to the ground. He scrambled out, running on for several steps. He heard the continuing whistles and thought for a moment that a swarm of bees had flown up around him. Instinctively he whipped out his hand, and then he cried out for the sudden sting and pulled it back in close.

He turned about, regarding the giant, which was dancing and slapping at the air. Beyond it he could see a pair of the four goblins that were coming in, both of them jerking weirdly and then falling to the ground.

"What?" Elbryan asked in utter confusion. Dots of red, like grotesque chicken pox, covered the giant's face and arms. Looking closer, and then at his own injured hand, Elbryan realized that these were not caused by bees, but were bolts, small arrows, the likes of which he had never seen.

Scores and scores of small arrows, filling the air all about him!

But they hardly seemed to stop the behemoth. The fomorian charged ahead with a tremendous, hideous howl, its cudgel going high. Elbryan, puny and helpless beneath it, held aloft his short sword, though he could not possibly deflect such a mighty blow.

The next volley was concentrated, sixty arrows flying fast for the giant's face and throat, sixty bolts that looked indeed like a swarm of bees. The fomorian staggered once, twice, and then again, as the bolts burrowed in, one on top of the other, a dozen on top of the previous dozen. Finally, the stinging ended, and the fomorian tried to move forward, back toward its prey. But before it could get anywhere near to the young man, the giant went down, choking in its own blood.

Elbryan never saw it; he had fainted dead away.

5

God's Chosen

Brother Avelyn turned hard on the crank, both wood and man groaning with each rotation. When would that bucket finally appear? the young novice wondered.

"Faster," insisted Quintall, Aveyln's work partner and classmate. The class had been divided by birth dates; Avelyn and Quintall had been put together solely because they had been born in the same week, and not for compatibility, either physical or emotional. Indeed, the two seemed obviously mismatched. Quintall was the shortest man in the class of twenty-five, while Avelyn was among the tallest. Both were large boned, but Avelyn was gawky and awkward, whereas Quintall was muscular, a fine athlete.

They were opposites in temperament, as well: Avelyn calm and reverent, always in control, and Quintall a "firework," as Master Siherton, the class overseer, often appropriately referred to him.

"Is it near?" Avelyn asked after a few more unrewarded turns.

"Halfway," Quintall answered coldly, "if that."

Avelyn sighed deeply and put his aching arms into motion.

Quintall offered a disgusted snort; he would have had the bucket up by this time and the pair could have gone off and gotten their midday meal. But it was Avelyn's turn to crank, and the taskmasters were particular about such things. If Quintall tried to sneak in and push that crank, it would likely cost them both their meal.

"He is an impatient one," noted Master Jojonah, a portly man of about fifty, with soft brown eyes and rich brown hair that showed not a speck of gray. Jojonah's skin was tanned and smooth, except for a fan of lines spreading out from each of his eyes—"credibility wrinkles," he called them.

"Firework," explained Master Siherton, tall and angular and thin, though his shoulders were wide, protruding many inches from either side of his skinny neck. Siherton's features befit his rank of class overseer, the disciplinarian of the newest brothers. His face was sharp and hawkish, his eyes small and dark—and smaller still on those many occasions that he squinted ominously at his young students. "Quintall is full of passion," he added with obvious admiration.

Jojonah regarded the man curiously. They were inside the abbey's highest chamber, a long, narrow room with windows overlooking the rough ocean breakers on one side and the abbey courtyard on the other. All twenty-four—one novice had been forced to leave because of illness— brothers of the newest class were out in the courtyard, tending their chores, but the focus of the two masters was Avelyn and Quintall, considered the exceptional novices.

"Avelyn is the best of the class," Jojonah remarked, mostly to gauge Siherton's reaction.

The taller man shrugged noncommittally.

"Some say that he is the best in many years," Jojonah pressed. It was true enough; Avelyn's incredible dedication was fast becoming the talk of St.-Mere-Abelle.

Again, the shrug. "He is without passion," Siherton replied.

"Without human passion because he is closer to God?" Jojonah replied, thinking that he had finally caught Siherton.

"Perhaps because he is already dead," the tall man said dryly, and he turned to glare at his counterpart.

Master Jojonah settled back on his heels but met the penetrating stare firmly. It was no secret that Siherton favored Quintall among this most important class, but the man's overt insult of Avelyn, the choice of every other master—and reportedly of Father Abbot Markwart as well— surprised him.

"We received news this day that his mother died," Siherton said evenly.

Jojonah looked back at the courtyard, to Avelyn at work as always as though nothing was amiss. "You have told him?"

"I did not bother."

"What macabre game do you play?"

Again came that annoying shrug. "Would he care?" Siherton replied. "He would say that she is with God now, and so she is happy; and then he would go on."

"Do you mock his faith?" Jojonah asked rather sharply.

"I despise his inhumanity," replied Siherton. "His mother has died, yet will he care? I think not. Brother Avelyn is so smug within the cocoon of his beliefs that nothing can unbalance him."

"That is the glory of faith," Jojonah said evenly.

"That is a waste of life," Siherton retorted as he leaned out the window. "You, Brother Quintall!" he called.

Both the novices stopped their work and looked up at the window. "Go to your meal," Master Siherton instructed. "And you, Brother Avelyn, do come and join with me at my—at Master Jojonah's chambers." Siherton pulled back into the hall and eyed Jojonah.

"Let us see if our young hero has any heart at all," Siherton remarked coldly, and he stalked off toward the stairwell that would lead him down to the master's quarters.

Jojonah watched him for a long moment, wondering which of them it was, Siherton or Avelyn, who was truly lacking in heart.

"You are using this loss for a most unworthy point," Jojonah insisted when he caught up to Siherton three levels below.

"He must be told," Siherton replied. "Let us not miss the opportunity to measure this man in whom we may soon put so much trust."

Jojonah caught Siherton by the shoulder, stopping him in mid-stride. "Avelyn has spent eight years proving himself worthy," he reminded the taller man. "Unbeknownst to him, he has been under constant scrutiny these last four years. What more would Siherton demand?"

"He must prove that he is a *man*," the hawkish master growled. "He must prove that he can feel. There is more to spirituality than piety, my friend. There is emotion, anger, passion."

"Eight years," Jojonah repeated.

"Perhaps the next class—"

"Too late," Master Jojonah said quietly. "The Preparers must be selected from this class, or from one of the three previous, and not a man among the seventy-five admitted in the last three years has shown the promise of Avelyn Desbris." Jojonah paused and spent a long while studying the other man. Siherton knew the truth of Jojonah's words, and seemed now caught within that truth, helpless in the face of reality. His arguments against Avelyn would be duly noted, but they rang hollow in light of the choices before the abbey. And even with any credible arguments, Siherton's posture, bordering on anger, on outrage, seemed so out of place.

"Why, my dear Siherton," Jojonah said a moment later, figuring it out, "you are jealous!"

Master Siherton growled and turned away, heading for the door to Jojonah's private room.

"Our misfortune to be born between the showers," Jojonah said, sincerely sympathetic to Siherton's frustration. "But we have our duty. Brother Avelyn is the best of the lot."

The words stung Siherton profoundly. He stopped at the door, bowed his head, and closed his eyes, conjuring images of the young Avelyn. Always working or praying; there were no other recollections of Avelyn to be found. Strength, or weakness? Siherton wondered, and he wondered, too, about the potential danger of having one so devout getting involved with the precious stones. There were pragmatic matters concerning the magic which might not sit well in a man so deep in faith, in a man so obviously convinced that he understood the desires of God.

"Father Abbot Markwart is quite pleased with the young man," Jojonah remarked.

True enough, Siherton had to admit, and he understood that he would not win any debate he might wage against the selection of Avelyn as one of the Preparers. The position of the second Preparer remained wide open, though, and so the tall master decided then and there that he would use his energy to put forth a student better to his liking. Someone like Quintall, a young man full of fire and full of life. And, because of that passion, because of worldly lusts, a man who could be controlled.

He was not surprised; his lip didn't quiver.

"Pray tell me, Master Siherton, was it peaceful?" he heard himself ask.

Master Jojonah was glad to hear the sympathetic question. Avelyn's lack of initial response to the news that his mother had died had lent credence to Siherton's complaints. "The messenger said that she died in her sleep," Jojonah interrupted.

Master Siherton eyed his peer sternly, considering the lie, for the messenger, a young boy, had only delivered news of the death and had offered no details surrounding it. Master Jojonah hadn't even conversed with the messenger. In a rare display of sympathy, with Jojonah glaring at him out of the corner of his brown eye, Siherton let it go.

Avelyn nodded, accepting the news.

"You will want to leave at once," Siherton offered, "to join your father at your mother's gravesite."

Avelyn stared him incredulously.

"Or you may choose to stay," Jojonah put in immediately, seeing the lure. If Avelyn left St.-Mere-Abelle for any reason, he would have to wait until the following year to enter. His reentry would be guaranteed, but his position as a Preparer—though he had no idea that he would be offered such a position or even that there was such a thing—would be lost.

"My mother is already buried, I assume," Avelyn responded to Siherton, "and my father has surely left her grave to return home. Given the short time since their departure from St.-Mere-Abelle, he has yet a long road before him."

Master Siherton squinted ominously and leaned close over Avelyn, glaring openly. "Your mother has died, boy," he said slowly, accentuating each syllable. "Do you care?"

The words hit young Avelyn hard. Did he care? He wanted to punch out at the tall master for even insinuating otherwise. He wanted to fly into a rage, tear the room—and anyone who tried to stop him—apart!

But that would be a disservice to Annalisa, Avelyn knew, an insult to the memory of the gentle woman. Avelyn's mother had lived in the light of God. Avelyn had to believe that, else all of her life—and all of his own life—would be no more than a lie. The reward for such a life, for such a good heart, was a better existence in a better place. Annalisa was with God now.

That thought bolstered the young man. He straightened his shoulders and looked squarely at the imposing Master Siherton.

"My mother knew that she would not make it home," he said quietly, aiming his words at Jojonah. "We all knew it. She lived on, in sickness, only to see me enter the Order of St.-Mere-Abelle. It was her glory that I join the Abellican Church, and I would be stealing that glory if I left now." He sucked in his breath, bolstering his declaration.

"The Order of St.-Mere-Abelle, God's Year 816," Brother Avelyn said without the slightest quiver in his voice. "That is my place. That is the vision that allowed Annalisa Desbris to pass on peacefully from this world."

Master Jojonah nodded, seeing the calm and logical reasoning, and at once impressed with, and frightened of, the depth of this young man's faith. It was obvious that Avelyn had loved his mother dearly, and yet, there was a sincerity in his demeanor. In that, Jojonah could clearly see Siherton's point. Either Avelyn had a direct line to God or the young man simply had no idea of what it was to be human.

"May I go?" Avelyn asked.

The question caught Jojonah off guard, and as he considered it, he came to realize that Avelyn's stoicism was, perhaps, not so deeply rooted. "You will be excused from your duties this day," the master stated.

"No," Avelyn replied without hesitation. He bowed his head as soon as he realized that he had just spoken against a master's command, an offense that could lead to exile from the abbey. "Please allow me to continue my duties."

Jojonah looked to Siherton, who was shaking his head disgustedly. Without a word, the tall master stalked from the room.

Jojonah suspected that young Brother Avelyn should be careful in the coming weeks. Master Siherton would see to his dismissal if given any real cause. The gentle master hesitated for a long while, making sure that Siherton would be far away by the time that Avelyn left the room.

"As you wish, Brother Avelyn," Jojonah subsequently agreed. "Be away, then. You have a few minutes left for your midday meal."

Avelyn bowed deeply and exited the room.

Jojonah folded his hands on his desk and spent a long while staring at the closed door. What was it about Avelyn that really bothered Siherton? he wondered. Was it, as Siherton insisted, the young man's apparent inhumanity? Or was it something more profound? Was Avelyn, perhaps, a higher standard, a shadowy mirror, held up before all the monks of St.-Mere-Abelle, a testament of true faith that seemed so rare in these times, even in the holy abbey?

That thought shook Jojonah as he looked around at his decorated chamber, at the beautiful tapestry he had commissioned from the gallery of Porvon dan Guardinio, among the most respected artists in all the world. He considered the gold leaf highlighting the carved hardwood of the room's support beams, the rich rug from some exotic land, the cushiony chairs, the many baubles and trinkets on his vast bookshelf, every one of them worth more gold than a common laborer would make in a year.

Piety, dignity, poverty, that was the pledge offered upon entering the Order of St.-Mere-Abelle. That was the standard. Jojonah glanced around the room again, reminding himself that most of the other masters, even some of the tenth-year immaculates, had chambers more richly adorned.

Piety, dignity, poverty.

But pragmatism, too, should be part of that pledge, so said Father Abbot Markwart, and so had declared the abbey's previous leaders, dating back more than two centuries. In Honce-the-Bear, wealth equalled power, and without power, how could the Order hope to influence the lives of the common folk? Wasn't God better served by strength than by weakness?

So went the widely accepted argument that allowed for relaxing some aspects of the holy pledge.

Still, Master Jojonah could see why a student such as Avelyn Desbris would so unnerve Master Siherton.

That night, Avelyn retired to his room, thoroughly exhausted, both emotionally and physically. He had spent all his waking hours at demanding work, volunteering for the most difficult parts of each task. He had lost count of the buckets he had cranked up from the well—somewhere near fifty—and had gone right from that heavy work to removing loose stones near to the northern end of the abbey's top wall, pulling them free and piling them neatly for the masons who would follow the next day.

Only the call to vespers, the ceremony heralding eventide, had interrupted Avelyn's frantic pace. He went quietly to the service, then skipped his evening meal altogether and went right to his chamber, a five-foot-square cubicle with a single stool, which doubled as a table for Avelyn's candle, and a cot—little more than a flat board and a blanket—that folded down from one wall.

The work was ended now, and the ache settled in. Despite his weariness, Avelyn Desbris could hardly sleep. Images of his mother flooded his thoughts; he wondered if he might see a vision of her now, a visitation of her spirit before it went to its place in heaven. Would Annalisa come to say good-bye to her youngest child, or had she already said her farewells to Avelyn in the courtyard outside of St.-Mere-Abelle?

Avelyn rolled off the cot and fumbled with his flint and steel, finally getting the candle lit. He glanced around in the shadowy light, as if expecting Annalisa to be standing in a corner waiting for him.

She wasn't, to Avelyn's ultimate disappointment.

The young man settled on the edge of his cot, head bowed, hands resting on his sore thighs. He felt the first tears leaking from his eyes and tried to deny them. To cry would be a weakness, Avelyn reasoned, a lack of faith. If what he believed, what he truly held in his heart, could not sustain him in a time of death, then of what value was it? The Abellican Church, the ancient scriptures, promised heaven to those deserving, and who could be more deserving than gentle and generous Annalisa Desbris?

A tear rolled down Avelyn's cheek, then another. He dropped his head lower, brought his hands up to cover his eyes, his wet eyes.

A sob lifted Avelyn's bowed shoulders. He tried to deny it, tried to fight back. He recited the Prayer of the Dead, the Prayer of the Faithful, the Prayer of Eternal Promise, all in a row, forcing his voice to hold steady.

Still the tears came; every so often his even tone was broken by a sniffle or a sob.

He went through the recitals again, and again. He prayed with all his heart, wrapping the words around images of his mother, often intoning her name between lines of verse. He was on the floor then, but did not know how he had gotten there. On the floor and curled up like a baby, wanting his mother, praying for his mother.

Finally, after more than an hour, Avelyn composed himself and sat back on the cot, taking several deep breaths to fight away the last of the sobs. He thought long and hard then, considering his grief, searching his soul for the weakness that had come into his faith.

Soon enough, he had his answer, and Avelyn was glad. He was not crying, he realized, for Annalisa, for he did indeed hold faith that she had passed on to a deserved better existence. He was crying for himself, for his brothers and sisters, for his father, for all who knew Annalisa Desbris and would not be graced by her presence in this life again.

Avelyn could accept that. His faith was intact and solid, and so he was not desecrating the memory of his mother. He moved to blow out the candle, then changed his mind and settled back on the cot. Still his eyes searched the corners of the shadowy room for his mother's spirit.

Perhaps he would find her in his dreams.

Two men walked quietly away from Brother Avelyn's closed door. "Are you satisfied?" Master Jojonah asked Master Siherton when they were far away.

Indeed Siherton had been pleased to hear Avelyn crying, to know that the too-dedicated young man was possessed of human emotions, but the sound of Avelyn's sobs had not changed the stern master's general attitude toward Avelyn. He gave a slight nod to Jojonah and started away.

"I have been given the blessings of Father Abbot Markwart to show young Brother Avelyn the stones," Jojonah called after him.

Siherton stopped dead in his tracks, fought down the angry protest that rose in his throat, and then nodded again, only slightly, and continued on his way.

It was settled then. Brother Avelyn Desbris would be one of the Preparers.

Avelyn tried to keep his head bowed, his eyes to the floor, as befitted his lowly station, but he couldn't help notice some of the splendors that surrounded him as he followed Master Jojonah through the winding corridors of the Abbot's Maze, the most private and revered place in all of St.-Mere-Abelle, and one that a first-year novice would certainly not expect to visit.

Jojonah's explanation for the tour had been weak, some remark about an area that needed cleaning. After only a few weeks in the abbey, Avelyn knew enough about the routine to understand that students much older and more experienced than he were the normal choice for any tasks, however menial, in the Abbot's Maze. He also knew that nothing special was going on, that many of the older students would have been available to Master Jojonah.

His questions were kept private though, for it was not his place to ask anything of the masters. Only to obey, and so he was, walking as quietly as he could beside the plump man, keeping his head bowed but still stealing an occasional glance at the splendor: the gold leaf bordering every side door, the wondrous and intricate carvings on every beam of wood, the mosaic tile patterns on the floors, the tapestries, so rich in detail that Avelyn figured he could spend hours and hours lingering over but one of them. Master Jojonah talked constantly, though he said nothing of interest—slight remarks about the weather, a storm that had hit twenty years before, the passing of his favorite baker in the town of St.-Mere-Abelle, a surprisingly off-color remark about the man's "lusty" wife. None of it diverted Avelyn's attention from the wonders of the place, though he did listen somewhat, fearing to miss any questions directed his way.

They stopped before a heavy door—and what a door! Avelyn could not help but lift his eyes at the sight of the thing, at the layers and layers of painted carvings, scenes of battles, of Saint Abelle being burned at the stake, of the healing hands of Mother Bastibule. Scenes of angels conquering demons, of the mighty demon dactyl screaming in agony as its own lava poured over it, consuming it. Scenes of the Halo, the heavenly gift, enwrapping all the others, an oval because of the angle at which it was portrayed. It started, if such a complete thing could be said to start, at the bottom left corner of the door, and led the observer's eye upward across the portal to the top right. And on the way, as Avelyn's eyes scanned, it seemed to him as if the history of the world, of the faith, unfolded to him, the images packed so that one led to another easily, with enough distinction so that each made an impact, however brief, like the flowing of time.

He wanted to kneel and pray; he wanted to ask who the artist—or artists, for certainly no one man could have created all of this—might be, but realized before the words left his mouth that any name would be inconsequential, for certainly the carvers and illuminators who had done this had done so at the explicit intervention of God. He alone, who called all the men and women of the world His children, might have done this.

"You know of the Ring Stones?" Master Jojonah asked abruptly, and the words sounded sharp and out of place to Avelyn. He nearly jumped, and turned with a start, surprised that a master would be so foolish as to speak in the presence of such beauty.

Then the impact of the question hit him fully.

"You know?" Jojonah asked again.

Avelyn swallowed hard, trying to discern his best response. Of course he knew of the Ring Stones, the heavenly gifts to St.-Mere-Abelle, the source of all the magic in the world. Avelyn didn't know much, though, just the common rumors about how the stones would fall from the heavens into the hands of waiting monks, to be blessed by the Father Abbot that their special powers be realized.

"We are the Keepers of the Stones," Master Jojonah said after a moment, Avelyn still making no move to respond.

The young monk nodded slightly.

"It is our most holy duty," Jojonah said, moving to the door and lifting the heavy latch that held it. Avelyn blinked; amid the wonders of the door, he hadn't even noticed the huge latch!

"The stones are the proof of our faith," Jojonah remarked, pushing wide the door.

Avelyn stood as if turned to stone. "The proof of our faith," he whispered under his breath, hardly believing that a master of St.-Mere-Abelle had uttered those borderline blasphemous words. Faith needed no proof—indeed the very value of faith was loyalty to beliefs without proof!

Of course Avelyn would not protest aloud, and even his silent musings were washed away as the heavy door opened silently, on balanced and oiled hinges, to reveal the greatest splendor of all.

The room inside was well lit, though Avelyn saw no torches and didn't smell the usual odor of burning wood. They were far below ground in one of the abbey's interior chambers, so there could be no window. But there was indeed light inside that room, such a light as to make Avelyn think of a cloudless midsummer day. It filled every corner, every crack in every stone, and reflected brilliantly off the glass covers of the many cases set about the room, and off their contents, as well, hundreds and hundreds of polished stones.

The Ring Stones!

Jojonah moved into the room, Avelyn practically stumbling behind him. The young monk made no pretense of keeping his gaze low now, looking left and right as they passed each case, marveling at the gems, the reds and blues, amber-colored stones and violet crystals. One case of a dozen or so smooth stones, a dark gray in hue but somehow seeming even blacker than night, caught Avelyn's attention and made him shudder, though he did not know why. In another case he saw clear stones—he recognized them as diamonds—and he paused again, and noted that Jojonah, too, had paused, allowing him to linger.

Avelyn studied the way the light worked off the many facets of the diamonds, of how it seemed to delve within the stone itself, swirling down to crystalline depths. Then he realized the truth.

"The diamonds are the source of the light," he said, and he bit his lip immediately when he realized that he had spoken out of turn.

"Well done," Master Jojonah congratulated, and Avelyn relaxed somewhat. "What do you know of the Ring Stones?"

"They are the source of all the magic in the world," Avelyn recited.

Jojonah nodded but said, "Not exactly true."

Avelyn stared at him hard.

"The Ring Stones are the source of all goodly magic," Master Jojonah explained.

"God-given magic," Avelyn dared to put in.

Jojonah hesitated—a pause not consciously caught by Avelyn, but one that he would recall in years to come—then nodded. "But there are, too, the Earth Stones, the source of evil magic, the power of the dactyls," said Jojonah. "They are not numerous, by God's grace, and can only be used by those demons—who, by God's grace, are even less numerous!" He ended with a chuckle, but Avelyn was hard-pressed to see any humor in a discussion of the demon dactyls.

Jojonah cleared his throat uncomfortably. "And there is magic in the Touel'alfar, as well," he said. "In their melodious singing, so it is said, and in the metal their gardens 'grow' from the soil."

"Grow?" Avelyn asked.

Master Jojonah shrugged; it was not important. "Tell me of the Ring Stones," he prompted. "Who gathers them?"

"The brothers of St.-Mere-Abelle," Avelyn answered immediately.

"From where?"

"They fall from the sky, from the Halo, into the waiting hands of—"

Jojonah's chuckle stopped him short. "They fall with a speed greater than that of an arrow in flight," the master explained. "And they are hot, my novice friend, so hot as to burn the flesh and the bone beneath it!" Jojonah chuckled again as he described to Avelyn an image of a young monk standing in a field, as holed as the cheese of Alpinador, an incredulous look on his face, a group of glowing rocks on the ground behind him.

Avelyn bit hard on his lip. He realized that Jojonah wasn't mocking him, but could not understand why he was being told these things.

"Where do we get them?" Jojonah asked suddenly.

Avelyn started to say, "The Halo," but stopped short, realizing that that ground had already been covered. His expression blank, he merely shrugged.

"Pimaninicuit," Jojonah said.

Avelyn's expression did not change.

"An island," the master explained. "Pimaninicuit. That is the only place where the sacred stones may be collected."

Avelyn had never heard such a thing.

"If you ever utter that name to any who do not know it, without the express permission—no, the express instruction—of the presiding father abbot of St.-Mere-Abelle, all of the powers of the abbey will be put into focus to bring about your execution."

Avelyn knew why he had never heard the name before.

"When do we get them?" Jojonah asked, changing the subject so abruptly that he had Avelyn thoroughly flustered. Again the young monk could only shrug helplessly, wanting to know but afraid to know. There was something most sacred, yet particularly unmysterious, and thus unholy, in all of this, a tingling of ecstasy combined with a slightly foul taste that Avelyn Desbris could not ignore.

"The stones do not come to ground often," Jojonah explained, sounding more like a scholar than a priest. "They do not fall frequently, but they do fall regularly." He led the way to the left-hand wall of the large chamber, and as they neared, Avelyn could see that the murals carved there were, in fact, charts, astronomical charts. Avelyn, who had often spent hours at a time gazing at the wondrous night sky, recognized some of the points. He noted the four-starred girdle of Progos-Behemoth the Warrior, the most prominent constellation in the northern sky, and the arcing stars that marked the handle of the Farmer's Bucket, the one he had to walk away from his parent's back door in order to see, for it always lingered right above their roof. Corona, with its Halo, was certainly evident, and prominent, being the center of it all, as Corona was the center of the universe.

Looking closer, Avelyn noted grooves in the wall. At first he thought them the borders of the known spheres, for he had heard theories of the universe as a series of overlapping, interlocking heavenly spheres, the invisible bubbles that held the layers of stars in place. When he realized that most of the grooves were near Corona, connecting the sun and the moon, and the five planets, he came to understand the truth. Those grooves were of a practical and not aesthetic nature, serving the mechanics of the chart so that the heavenly bodies could be kept in motion. Avelyn carefully noted the position of Sheila, the moon, and stared at it long enough to realize that it was indeed moving, ever so slightly, along its path about Corona.

"Six generations," Master Jojonah explained, after he had given Avelyn several quiet minutes in which to study the fabulous chart. "Or nearly," he added when Avelyn turned to him. "A hundred and seventy-three years will pass between each of the offerings."

"Offerings?"

"The stone showers," Jojonah explained. "Consider yourself blessed, my novice friend, for you live in a time of the showers."

Avelyn breathed hard and stared again at the chart, as if expecting little lines of falling stones to appear between the Halo and Corona.

"Have you ever witnessed one of the stones at work?" Jojonah asked suddenly, drawing Avelyn from his contemplations. The young man stared at him wide-eyed with hope and eagerness, his hands clenching and opening at his sides.

Jojonah pointed to a case near to the middle of the room, and motioned for Avelyn to approach it. As soon as his back was turned to the master, Avelyn heard a click from the wall and suspected that Jojonah had thrown some sort of lever, probably hidden within the tapestry of the star charts, to unlock the case. The master soon joined him at the case and slowly slid back the glass top.

There were several various stones within, all smooth and polished. Jojonah's hand reached for one of two of the shiny gray stones. "The soul stones," he explained. "Hematite, by name." He held the stone tightly in his right hand, then reached back in with his left and took out a different gem, mostly clear, but with a slight shading of yellow-green. "Chrysoberyl," he said. "A stone of protection, in this clear form. Always a wise choice when dealing with the dark hematite!"

Avelyn didn't really understand, but he was too overwhelmed by all of this to think of interrupting with a question.

Jojonah dropped the chrysoberyl into the pocket of his thick robe and moved far from Avelyn, facing the younger man directly. "Count to ten," he instructed, "that I might have time to cast the enchantment. Then place your hands behind your back and raise your fingers, however many you choose, in a slow and clear sequence of seven distinct numbers. Take care to remember your sequence!"

The master closed his eyes and began to softly chant. Avelyn hesitated for a moment, trying to digest the newest information. He collected himself quickly and did as instructed, alternating the number of raised fingers behind his back. Through it all, Master Jojonah continued his soft chant, his eyes never fluttering, all of his body seeming locked in place.

A moment later, the master opened his eyes. "Seven, three, six, five, five, two, and eight," Jojonah said, seeming quite pleased with himself.

"You heard what was within my mind!" Avelyn gasped.

"No," Jojonah quickly corrected. "I left my physical body and ventured behind you. I merely watched as you raised your fingers."

Avelyn started to respond but held the thought private, though his labored breath and incredulous expression revealed volumes.

"Not so hard a task!" Master Jojonah said suddenly, exploding with delight. "The hematite is a powerful tool, among the most powerful stones of all. Using it to walk out of body barely touches at the edge of its true magic. Anyone trained in the stones could do it. Why even you . . ." Jojonah's voice trailed off, a tease that anxious Avelyn could not ignore.

"Brother Avelyn," the master said in all seriousness a moment later, "would you care to try?"

Before he could even begin to consider the offer, Avelyn nodded so forcefully that he was sure he must have looked incredibly simple. His feet, too, were moving before his conscious thought could stop them, as if he were being drawn to the stone.

Jojonah nearly laughed aloud at the spectacle, and held forth the hematite. Avelyn reached for it, but the master pulled it back.

"It is a powerful stone," the master said somberly, "one that could put you somewhere you do not belong. Take care in your travels, my young friend, for you may soon be lost!"

Avelyn retracted his hand a few inches, wondering if he was being a bit foolish here. The temptation was too strong, though, and he reached out again, and this time, Jojonah let him take the hematite.

Its feel was impossibly smooth, almost liquid. It was heavier than Avelyn had expected, quite solid and dense. He ran his fingers over it repeatedly, felt something deeper within it, a place of mystery, of magic. He looked to Jojonah and saw that the master was clutching the chrysoberyl close to his heart.

"It will prevent our spirits from crossing," Jojonah explained. "That would not be a wise choice."

Avelyn nodded and backed off a few steps. Jojonah put his free hand behind his back. "All in your due time," he said softly. "I will know when you are in the hold of the magic, and then I will begin."

Avelyn hardly heard him. Already the young monk was falling into the depths of the stone. To his rubbing fingers, the hematite felt truly liquid then, and inviting. Avelyn stared at it for a long while, then closed his eyes, but saw it still. It was expanding before him, engulfing his hands, then his arms. Then he was falling, falling.

He resisted, and the hematite receded dramatically, almost forcing him from the trance. But Avelyn caught his fears in time and started the journey once more.

His hands were gone, then his arms. Then all was gray, then black.

Avelyn stepped out of his body. He looked back and saw himself standing there, holding the stone. He turned back to Jojonah, saw most distinctly the chrysoberyl, fiercely glowing and encasing all of the master in a thin white bubble, a ward that Avelyn knew his spirit could not pass.

He started toward Jojonah, giving the man a wide berth. He felt incredibly light, felt as if by will alone he could rise from the ground and fly.

Behind the master, Avelyn watched the sequence of fingers: one, three, two, one, five.

"Go higher," he heard Master Jojonah prompt.

Avelyn was surprised that he could even hear the voice in this state. He understood the command and willed himself off the ground, drifting effortlessly toward the ceiling.

"There is no physical barrier that can stop you," Jojonah remarked. "No barriers at all. Have you seen the roof? There is something on the roof that you should know."

Despite the thrill, Avelyn flinched as he drifted through the room's ceiling. He marveled at the loose structure of the wood, at the density of the higher room's tile floor.

There were several monks, men a few years Avelyn's senior, in the chamber above. Avelyn felt himself grinning, felt his physical form in the lower room grinning, as he passed, the men totally oblivious of him.

Then the grin was gone. Something tugged hard at the young monk, some dark temptation that he should enter one of these men, that he could push out the host spirit and possess the body!

He was beyond them before that dangerous notion fully registered, drifting higher, through the next ceiling into an empty room, then through that ceiling and the next and the next and the next, this last one much thicker. Then he was outside, though he felt none of the physical sensations, the warmth of the sun or the chill of the ocean breeze. He saw that he was rising above one of the highest spots of St.-Mere-Abelle, coming right out of the roof. Still he went higher, and Avelyn feared that he would never stop the ascent, that he would drift through the clouds, out to the Halo, the stars. Perhaps he would shine in the heavens above, a fifth light on the girdle of Progos-Behemoth!

He dismissed that ridiculous notion and turned his spirit about, looking at the roof of the abbey. From up here, St.-Mere-Abelle appeared as a thick and stretched snake, winding its way along the top of the sea cliff. Avelyn saw a commotion in the courtyard, far to the side, as a group of young monks labored at the well and with the abbey's horses and mules.

"Come back," bade a distant voice, Master Jojonah's voice, reaching Avelyn through his physical form. The disconnection was not complete, the young monk realized, and he shuddered to think of what a complete break from his own physical form might mean.

Shocked back to his senses, Avelyn turned his attention to the high roof directly below him. He had seen this roof before, from one of the higher points of the abbey, but looking on it from this vantage point revealed a most clever design, an image that could not be seen from a lower angle. Carved into the roof were four arms, two sets, hands lifted high, palms open and holding stones.

The journey back was quicker, until Avelyn got into the room directly above the Ring Stone chamber. This time the temptation of the other bodies pulled at him even harder. He felt himself being drawn in. He pictured the hematite as another living being, commanding him, whispering promises of power into his spiritual ear.

Avelyn felt something touch his hand—not his spiritual hand, but the physical one, the one clutching the stone. He sensed the chrysoberyl again, that magical barrier, and then his spirit was pulled to the floor, through the floor, careening back to his waiting body.

Avelyn nearly jumped when he opened his physical eyes again, seeing Master Jojonah so very close.

"One, three, two, one, five," the young monk said abruptly, trying to satisfy whatever curiosity held the older man.

Jojonah waved his hand and shook his head, uninterested. "What did you see?" he asked.

Avelyn noted that Jojonah held both stones again, though he didn't remember giving the hematite back to the man.

"What did you see?" Jojonah pressed, moving even closer.

"Arms," Avelyn blurted. "Two sets, palms open . . ." Before he could finish, Jojonah fell away, gasping, laughing, crying all at once. Avelyn had never seen such a display, couldn't begin to decipher it.

"How?" Avelyn asked with enough force to bring Jojonah back to his senses. "The stones," Avelyn clarified when he had the man's attention. "How could this be?"

Jojonah launched into a rushed explanation, more the regurgitation of a prepared speech than anything spontaneous. He talked of the humours of the body joining together with the alien humours of the stones to create the seemingly magical reaction. He even compared what had happened to Avelyn with the tablets giving to a monk with a stomachache to induce a belch or a fart.

As he listened, Avelyn felt the mystery melting around him. For the first time since they had entered the room, there was no reverence in Master Jojonah's voice, just the dry lecturing tone of an instructor. Avelyn didn't buy into it, any of it. He could not explain what had just happened to him, but he knew instinctively that this talk of "alien humours" belittled the experience. There was indeed a mystery here that no tumble of fancy words could lay bare; there was something here of a higher order. Master Jojonah had called the stone showers "offerings," and to Avelyn, that description seemed exactly wrong. "Graces" was a more appropriate term, the young monk decided there and then. He glanced around the room again, from stone to stone, his reverence of these gifts from God tenfold what it had been when first he had entered the chamber.

"You should be among those select few who make the journey," Master Jojonah declared, and the weight of the statement drew Avelyn back to him.

"To Pimaninicuit," Jojonah explained, his grin widening as Avelyn's brown eyes widened. "You are young and strong and full of God's voice."

Tears collected in Avelyn's eyes and began to stream down his face at the mere thought that he might be among the chosen few to get so very close to the greatest gift of God.

Jojonah dismissed him then and he left the room as if in a trance, overwhelmed indeed.

When he was gone, Master Jojonah replaced the stones, closed the case, then went to the wall and moved the hidden switch to lock it fast. All the while, the master considered the weight of what he had witnessed. A first-year novice should not have been able to activate the magic of the stone, despite what he had told Avelyn about hematite. Even if a novice had managed to fall into the magic, the control should have been above him, a quick and random out of body experience, culminating with a gasping, disbelieving, thoroughly overwhelmed young man.

For Avelyn to control the magic enough to get behind Jojonah's back and see the finger sequence was incredible. For the young man to use the stones and drift out of the room, out of the abbey, and see the design on the roof was truly amazing. Jojonah would not have believed it possible. The master paused and lamented his own weakness. He had been in St.-Mere-Abelle for more than three decades, and had only been able to use the hematite that way for the last three years!

Jojonah pushed his own self-pity away and smiled about Avelyn. The young monk was a good choice, a God-given choice indeed, to go to Pimaninicuit.

Carrion Birds

S he came back to consciousness never expecting to see the wide sky again. She opened her blue eyes even as she moved her hands in frantic waves, trying to rid the small hole of the thick odor of charred wood.

A slanting ray cut in through the smoke, a single shaft of light that beckoned the girl back to the land of the living. She followed it as if in a dream, gingerly reaching up to touch the piece of lumber that had fallen to partially block the hole.

The wood was warm. Jilseponie understood then that she had been unconscious for a long time. She found she could put her arm against the beam firmly as long as she kept her sleeve between tender flesh and the wood.

The girl pushed hard, but the beam would not give. Stubborn as ever, summoning her rage to bolster her muscles, Pony set her legs under her as firmly as she could and pushed again, with all her might, groaning with the strain.

The sound of her own voice stopped her cold. What if the goblins were still out there? She settled back and sat very still, listening intently, not even daring to breathe.

She heard the cawing of the birds—carrion birds, she knew. But nothing else came to her—not the whimper of a survivor, not the whining, grating voice of a goblin, not the guttural grunts of the fomorian giants.

Just the birds, feeding on the bodies of her fallen friends.

That horrid thought set Pony into violent motion. She set her legs again and pushed with every ounce of strength she had, groaning but too angry to consider the implications of her noise should the goblins still be around.

The beam lifted an inch and shifted to the side, but Pony could not maintain its weight and it came down heavily, with a decidedly final thud. Pony knew that she could not move it again from this new angle, and so she didn't even try. Now she squirmed and squeezed. She got her arm through, then her head and one shoulder, and held there for a moment, trying to catch her breath, so relieved to have her face, at least, out in the open sunlight once again.

That relief lasted only until the girl glanced around. This was Dundalis—she knew that logically—but it was no place Pony had ever seen before. All that remained of Elbryan's house was a few beams and the stone foundation; all that remained of Dundalis was a few beams and a few stones.

And bodies. Pony only saw a couple from this angle, a goblin and an older woman, but the stench of death hung as thickly in the air as the smoke from the fires. A substantial voice within Pony's head told her to crawl back into the hole, to curl up and cry, perhaps even to die, for death—be it heaven, be it empty blackness—had to be preferable to this.

She spent a long while halfway in and halfway out, teetering on the edge of hysteria, of hopelessness. She made up her mind simply to crawl back in, but something, some inner resolve the young woman did not yet understand, would not let her.

Again came the wriggling, the tearing of clothes and scraping of skin, the frantic pull and twist that, at last, freed her from the hole. And then came the next long pause, lying on the ground on her back, her thoughts swirling down a multitude of paths, every one of which seemed to lead to no place but despair.

With great effort, Pony pulled herself up from the ground and walked from between the piles of rubble that had been the houses of Olwan Wyndon and Shane McMichael. The main road remained, crushed stones and packed dirt carefully edged for drainage, and that alone confirmed to Pony that she was indeed in Dundalis, in the remains of what had been her home. Not a single structure stood. Not a single person or even a horse remained alive. Nor were there any living goblins or giants, Pony realized with small relief. Only the vultures, dozens and dozens, some circling overhead, most on the ground feasting, tearing at skin that had been warm to Pony's touch just the day before, pecking at eyes that had locked with her own, shared gaze and shared thought.

Pony turned with a start, visualizing the fight on the road, the last she had seen of her father. There were the bodies; she saw Olwan, crumpled and broken in the same spot where she had seen him fall. And then she could look no more, fearing that she would find Thomas Ault, her father dear, among the dead. Of course he was dead, Pony told herself, and so was her mother, and so was Elbryan, and so was everyone.

The girl, feeling so helpless and so little, nearly fell to the ground, but again that stubborn instinct kept her upright. She noted the great numbers of dead goblins, even a couple of giants. One group in particular, a pile of many monstrous corpses together in the road, posed a curious riddle. They had fallen as if they had formed a defensive ring, yet there were no human bodies near them. Just the goblins and a lone giant, slumped together, soaked in blood from the many small wounds on each corpse. Pony thought she should go closer to investigate, but she hadn't the stomach.

She stood and stared, and a numbness came over her, stealing her emotions. The riddle was lost, for Pony was too exhausted to pause and ponder it, to pause and think of anything—too defeated and bedraggled to do anything except stagger out of the village, moving south along the road, then turning west at the first fork, moving toward the dying sun.

Subconscious instinct alone guided her. Weedy Meadow was the closest village, but Pony really didn't think that the place would be any different. Surely all the world had fallen to ruin; surely all the people were dead, were being pecked and torn by vultures.

Sometime later, as dusk descended, Pony's senses warned her that she was not alone. To the right, she saw a slight shiver of one small bush. It could have been a ground squirrel, the girl reasoned, but she knew in her heart that it was not.

To the left came a titter, a tiny voice whispering softly.

Pony kept moving straight ahead. She cursed herself for not having had the wisdom to collect a weapon before leaving Dundalis. It wouldn't matter, she quickly reminded herself, and perhaps this way, defenseless, the end would come more quickly.

So she went on, stubbornly, looking straight ahead, ignoring any signals that she might not be alone, that goblins might be behind every tree, watching her, laughing at her, taking good measure of her, perhaps even arguing among themselves over which one would be given the pleasure of the kill—and the pleasures that might come before the kill.

That thought nearly dropped Pony to the ground, reminded her of Elbryan, of the moments before the disaster, of the kiss . . .

Then she cried. She walked straight ahead, kept her shoulders squared.

But she could not deny the tears, and the guilt and the pain.

She slept fitfully at the base of a tree, in open view right beside the road, shivering from the cold, from the nightmares that she feared would haunt her forever.

Those dreams were mercifully gone when she awoke, and no images could she conjure of the village, of her family and her friends. All that the girl knew was that she was out on the road somehow, somewhere.

She knew that she was in pain, physical and emotional, but the reason for the latter escaped her conscious memory.

She didn't even know her own name.

The giant was there, facedown in the blood and dirt, in the same place Elbryan had last seen it, just a few feet from where he had fainted. At that horrible moment, the monster had been lifting its club to squash Elbryan; now it was dead.

And so were a dozen other goblins, scattered all about the area.

Elbryan sat up and rubbed his face, noting the cut and dried blood on one of his hands. His thoughts careened suddenly back to Pony and the kiss at the twin pines atop the ridge. Then they came full force back to the present, through those minutes of horror—the goblins in the woods; poor Carley; the smoke from Dundalis; Jilseponie running, running for the town, screaming every step. It had all been so unreal, had all happened much too quickly. In the span of a few unbelievable minutes, Elbryan's entire world had been thrown down.

The young man knew all that, as he sat in the dirt, staring curiously at the somehow dead giant. He knew nothing would ever be as it had been.

He struggled to his feet and approached the fomorian tentatively, though he realized from the amount of blood and from the absolute stillness of the creature that it was certainly dead. He moved to the head and knelt, studying the many wounds.

Puncture wounds, as from arrows, only much smaller. Elbryan recalled the humming sound; he conjured an image of buzzing bees. He found the nerve to inspect more closely, even to put his thumb on the edge of one prominent wound and push the skin back.

"No bolt," he remarked aloud, trying to make sense of it all. Again he thought of bees—giant bees, perhaps, that stung and stung and flew away. He sat back again and began a quick count, then shook his head helplessly when he realized the giant had at least twenty such wounds on its exposed face alone and no doubt countless others all over its fifteen-foot frame.

The young man simply had no answers now. He had thought himself dead, and yet he was not. He had thought Dundalis doomed . . .

Elbryan scrambled to his feet, did a quick check of the dead goblins in the area. He was somewhat surprised, and a bit humbled, to find that even the two he had struggled against, even the one he had thought slain by his own sword, also showed many mysterious puncture wounds.

"Bees, bees, bees," Elbryan chanted, a litany of hope, as he dashed from the area, down the slope toward Dundalis. The words, the hopes, fell away in a stifled gasp as soon as the village, the charred rubble that had been the village, came into view.

He knew that they were dead, all dead. Even from this distance, fifty yards from the northernmost point of the village, Elbryan felt in his heart that no one could have survived such a disaster. His face ashen, his heart pounding—but offering no energy to arms that hung slack at his side or to legs that seemed suddenly as if they each weighed a hundred pounds—the young man, feeling very much a little lost boy, walked home.

He recognized every body that had not been caught by flames—the parents of his friends; the younger men, just a few years older than he; and the younger boys and girls who had been taken from patrol by their parents. On the charred threshold of one ruin, he saw a tiny corpse, a blackened ball. Carralee Ault, Pony's cousin, Elbryan realized, for she was the only baby in town. Carralee's mother lay facedown in the road, just a few feet from the threshold where lay the baby. She had been trying to get back to Carralee, Elbryan understood, and they had cut her down as she had watched the house, her house, burn down about her baby.

Elbryan forced himself to stay away from such vivid empathy, realizing that he could easily lose himself in utter despair. The task became all the harder as he approached one large group of slain goblins and giants on the road, as he walked past the area of heaviest fighting, as he walked past the body of Olwan, his father.

Elbryan could see his father had died bravely, and understanding his father's stern and forceful way, he was not surprised. Olwan had died fighting.

But that mattered not at all to Elbryan.

The boy staggered on toward the ruin of his own house. He snorted, a crying chuckle, as he saw that the foundation, of which his father was so proud, was intact, though the walls and ceiling had collapsed. Elbryan picked his way into the still-smoldering ruin. One of the back corners had somehow escaped the flames, and when the roof had fallen in, it had angled down, leaving a clear space.

He pushed aside a timber—gingerly, when he heard the remaining roof groan in protest—and went down to his knees, peering in. He could make out two forms, lying against the very back corner.

"Please, please," Elbryan whispered, picking a careful path to that spot.

The goblin, the closest form, was dead, its head bashed. Unreasonable hope pushing him on, Elbryan scrambled over the thing to the next body, sitting in the very corner.

It was his mother, dead as well—of smoke, Elbryan soon realized, for she had not a wound on her. In her hand she clutched her heavy wooden spoon. Often had she waved that thing at the children, Elbryan and his friends, when they were bothering her, threatening to warm their bottoms.

She had never used it, Elbryan only then remembered. Not until this day, he silently added, looking at the slain goblin.

All the images of her in life—waving that spoon, shaking her head at her impetuous son, teasing Olwan, and sharing a wink with Jilseponie as if they knew a secret about Elbryan—came flooding back to the boy in an overwhelming jumble. He moved in further and sat beside his mother, shifting her stiffening form that he might hug her one final time.

And he cried. He cried for his mother and father, for his friends and their parents, for all of Dundalis. He cried for Pony, not knowing that if he had rushed into town as soon as he had awakened, he would have spotted the battered girl stumbling down the south road.

And Elbryan cried for himself, his future bleak and uncertain.

He was in that corner of his house, that tiny link to what had been, cradling his mother, when the sun went down, and there he remained all through the cold night.

❖ 7 ❖

The Blood of Mather

"The blood of Mather!" scoffed Tuntun, an elf maiden so slight of build that she could easily hide behind a third-year sapling. Tuntun's normally melodic voice turned squeaky whenever she got excited, and several of the others cringed and some even put their hands over their sensitive, pointed ears. Tuntun pretended not to notice. She batted her huge blue eyes and her translucent wings, and crossed her slender arms imperiously over her tiny, pointy breasts.

"Mather's nephew," replied Belli'mar Juraviel, never taking his gaze from Elbryan as the boy moved about the ruins of his house. Juraviel didn't have to look Tuntun's way to know her pose, for the obstinate elf struck it often.

"His father fought well," remarked a third of the gathering. "Were it not for the fomorian—"

"Mather would have slain the fomorian," Tuntun interrupted.

"Mather wielded Tempest," Juraviel said grimly. "The boy's father had nothing more than a simple club."

"Mather would have choked the fomorian with his bare—"

"Enough, Tuntun!" demanded Juraviel; even in a shout, the elf's voice rang like the clear chime of a bell. It didn't bother Juraviel, or any of the others, how loud their conversation had become, for though Elbryan was barely fifteen yards away from them, they had erected a sound shield, and no human ear could have discerned anything more than a few chirps, squeaks, and whistles, sounds easily enough explained away by the natural creatures in the area. "Lady Dasslerond has declared this one a fitting choice," Juraviel finished, calming himself. "It is not your place to argue."

Tuntun knew she could not win this debate, so she held fast her defiant pose and began tapping her foot on the ground, all the while staring at young Elbryan—and not liking what she saw. Tuntun had little fondness for the big, bumbling humans. Even Mather, a man she had trained and had known for more than four decades, had more often than not driven her away with his pretentious purpose and stoicism. Now, looking at Elbryan, this sniveling youngster, Tuntun could barely stand the thought of seven years of training!

Why did the world need rangers, anyway?

Belli'mar Juraviel suppressed a chuckle, for he liked seeing Tuntun flustered. He knew the maiden would make his life miserable if he embarrassed her now, though, so he leaped up high, his little wings beating hard, lifting him a dozen feet from the ground; he came to rest on a low branch, a better vantage point for watching the movements of this boy who would replace Mather.

Mercifully, Elbryan's grief had brought with it exhaustion, and the boy had found some sleep. He remained in the house, cradling his mother, gently stroking her hair even after the first waves of slumber had come over him. He awoke with the dawn—and with resolve.

He came out of the house, eyes still moist with tears, his mother's body in his arms. Now Elbryan steeled himself against the scene of devastation. He found strength in duty, and that duty lay in burying the dead. He put his sword in his belt, found a spade, and began to dig. He buried his parents first, side by side, though the task of filling the grave, of putting cold dirt on the bodies of those whom he had most loved, nearly destroyed him.

He found Thomas Ault and several other men next, and only then did the already weary youngster realize the scope of his task. Dundalis had been home to more than a hundred folk; how long would it take to bury them all? And what of those youngsters who had been slaughtered on the hill? And of the other patrol, who had battled in the wide pine valley among the caribou moss?

"One day," Elbryan decided, and even his own voice sounded strange to him in this surreal situation. He would spend just this one day gathering the bodies, collecting them for a mass grave. That would have to suffice.

But then what? Elbryan wondered. What might he do after the task was completed? Where might he go? He thought of Weedy Meadow, a day of hard marching. He thought of pursuing the goblins, if he could find any tracks. Elbryan shook that away immediately, knowing the rage within him, the hunger for revenge, could cloud his judgment, could consume him. His next task was clear to him, for the moment at least, and though it pained him immeasurably to think of success, he knew he had to find the body of Jilseponie Ault, his dear Pony.

And so he searched, pulling corpses from the ruins of houses, collecting the fallen and laying the bodies side by side on the field that had been Bunker Crawyer's corral. Half the day slipped by, but Elbryan had no thoughts of food. His search for Jilseponie grew more agitated as the hours slipped by. Soon he was bypassing the closest bodies, leaving them where they lay, focusing his search, though he realized that in his desperation, he was, perhaps, being inefficient and he had little time to waste. Such a scene of carnage would no doubt bring other scavengers—great cats and bears, perhaps—and Elbryan couldn't be sure that the goblins wouldn't return. So he ran on, hauling bodies, peeking under rubble, kicking aside piles of dead goblins to see who might be underneath. He tried to keep a mental note of his macabre collection, tried to match it against the people of Dundalis by sorting their names house by house.

The task overwhelmed him; he couldn't be sure, couldn't even be certain of the identity of so many of the charred bodies. One of them must have been Pony.

By mid-afternoon, Elbryan knew he was defeated, knew he could not hope to properly bury all the corpses. He had two score lined up in the field, and so he decided to bury them alone. The rest . . .

Elbryan sighed helplessly. He took the spade, went to the field, and began to dig. He transferred the grief, rising again within him, into rage, and went at the earth as if it, and not the goblins, had assaulted Dundalis, had stolen from him everything in the world that was familiar and comforting. Everything, everyone that he loved.

His muscles complained, but he didn't know it; his stomach groaned from lack of food, but he didn't hear it.

Even Tuntun was impressed by his stamina.

Elbryan lay down to sleep at the base of the ridge that night, outside Dundalis. "Pony," he said aloud, needing to hear a voice, any voice, even his own.

The elves quietly encircling him paused and cocked curious ears. Tuntun thought the boy might be calling to his mount, but Juraviel, who had been more attentive to the boy and his relationships, knew the truth.

"Please don't be dead," Elbryan said to the quiet wind. He closed his eyes, wet again with tears for his mother and father, for all his friends and all his community. "I can survive this," Elbryan said determinedly, "but only with you." He lay back on the ground and crossed his forearms over his face. "I need you, Pony. I need you."

"A very needy young boy," Tuntun remarked.

"Some sympathy," Juraviel scolded.

A short distance away, Elbryan sat bolt upright, confused.

Juraviel glared at Tuntun, for the female's sour attitude had forced the words out before any sound screen could be cast up.

Elbryan drew out his short sword, glancing warily into the shadows. "Come out and face me!" he commanded, and there was no fear in his voice.

Tuntun nodded. "Oo, so brave," she said sarcastically.

Juraviel responded with a nod of his own, but his admiration was sincere.

The young man, so suddenly no more a boy, had passed through grief and through fear. He was indeed brave—it was no act—and would willingly face whatever enemy he found without fear of his own death.

After a few moments, Elbryan's nerves began to wear thin. He moved to the nearest tree, stalked about it, then darted to the next. The elves, of course, had little trouble keeping ahead of him, silent and out of sight. After a few minutes, the young man began to relax, but, exhausted though he was, he realized he should not remain so vulnerable here out in the open. He couldn't think of any defensible spots nearby, but perhaps he could strengthen this one. He went to work quietly, methodically, using the lace of his shirt, his belt, anything he could find to secure saplings into snares.

The elves watched every move, some with respect, some with a hugely superior attitude. Elbryan's traps couldn't catch a squirrel; certainly any elf could run into one, untie it before it ever went off, then reset it as he scampered out the other side!

"Blood of Mather!" Tuntun remarked more than once.

Juraviel, Elbryan's chief sponsor with Lady Dasslerond, took it lightly. He remembered Mather at the start of the legendary ranger's career, a bumbling boy no more adept and probably not even as resourceful as this Elbryan.

Within the hour, Elbryan had done all he could—and that was not much. He found a tall pine with low-hanging branches and slipped underneath them into the natural tent. Only the keenest of eyes could have picked him out within that blocking canopy, but of course, his field of vision likewise was severely limited. He put his back to the tree trunk, put his sword across his lap. Nagged by a distinct feeling that he was not alone and believing that he would be safe if he could just make it to the dawn, he tried hard to stay awake. But weariness overtook him, caught him where he sat, and brought his eyelids low.

The elves gradually closed in.

Something brought Elbryan awake. Music? A soft singing he could not quite discern? He had no idea how long he had slept. Was morning close? Or had he slumbered right through the next day?

He forced himself to his knees and crawled to the edge of the over-hanging canopy, carefully pushing aside one of the branches.

The moon, Sheila, was up, but not yet directly overhead. Elbryan tried to calculate the duration of his rest, knew it had been no more than a couple of hours. He paused and listened hard, certain there was something out there beyond his vision.

A soft melody vibrated in his ear, somewhere just below his consciousness. Quiet and sweet were the notes, but that did little to comfort Elbryan.

It went on and on, sometimes seeming to rise, as if his enemies were about to rush out at him from the shadows but then it diminished to near nothingness once again. Elbryan clutched the sword hilt so hard his knuckles whitened. It wasn't Pony out there, he knew; it wasn't anything human. And to the young man who had somehow survived a goblin raid, such a conclusion meant it could only be one thing.

He should have stayed hidden. Rationally, Elbryan knew his best defense lay in concealment, the best he could hope for against returning goblins was to keep as far away from them as possible. But thoughts of his slain family and friends, of Pony, spurred him on. Despite very real fears, Elbryan wanted revenge.

"I told you he was brave," Juraviel whispered to Tuntun as Elbryan slipped out from under the pine boughs.

"Stupid," Tuntun corrected without hesitation.

Again Juraviel let the insult to Elbryan pass. Tuntun had thought Mather stupid, as well—at first. Juraviel motioned to his companions and started away.

The teasing fairy song, remaining at the very edge of his consciousness, led Elbryan on for many minutes. Then abruptly it was no more, and for Elbryan, the sudden silence was like waking up from a dream. He found he was standing in the middle of a nearly circular clearing, a small meadow ringed by tall trees. The moon was above the easternmost boughs, casting slanted rays upon him, and he realized how foolish he had been—and how vulnerable he now was. Ducking low, he started for the edge of the clearing but stopped almost immediately and stood up straight, eyes wide, mouth hanging open.

He spun in a complete circle, watching as they stepped into the clearing's perimeter, dozens of creatures of a type he did not know. They were no taller than he and couldn't have weighed close to his ninety pounds. They were slight of build, delicate, and beautiful, with angled features, pointed ears, and skin that seemed almost translucent in the soft light.

"Elves?" Elbryan whispered, the thought coming from somewhere far back in his memories, the stuff of legends so remote the flustered young man had no idea what to make of these creatures.

The elves joined hands and began to walk in a circle about him, and only then did Elbryan realize they were indeed singing. The syllables came clear to him, though they joined into words he could not understand, distant melodic sounds he somehow recognized as part of the earth itself. Soothing sounds, and that made defiant Elbryan panic even more. He glanced all around, tried to focus on individual creatures that he might discern their leader.

Their tempo increased. Sometimes they held hands, and other times they let go long enough for every other elf to turn a graceful pirouette. Elbryan couldn't focus; every time he sorted out an individual, some movement at the edge of his vision, or some higher note in the chorus, distracted him. And by the time he looked back to the original spot, the individual elf had blended away, for surely they all looked alike.

The dance intensified, the pace, the spins. Now whenever the elves broke apart for their pirouettes, those not spinning lifted off the ground as if by magic—for Elbryan could not see their delicate wings in the moonlight—floating and fluttering to land back in place.

Too many images assailed poor Elbryan. He tried to push them away, closed his eyes, and several times took up his sword and started a charge, meaning to break through the ring and run off into the forest. Every attempt proved futile, for though he started straight, the young man inevitably turned with the flow of the dancers, going around in a circle until the multitude of images and the sweet melody distracted him and defeated him.

He realized then he had dropped his sword and thought it might be a good idea to pick it up. But the song . . .

The song! There was something about it that would not let him go. He felt it, a tender vibration all along his frame, more than he heard it. It caressed him and beckoned him. It brought images of a younger world, a cleaner and more vibrant world. It told him these creatures were not of the evil goblin race; these were friends to be trusted.

Elbryan, so full of grief and rage, fought that last notion fiercely and so remained standing much longer than usual for a mere human. Gradually, though, his resolve drained away and so did his strength. He accepted the invitation of the soft earth.

He was lying down; that was the last thought that came to him.

"Blood of Mather," muttered Tuntun as the elvish caravan started off, Elbryan moving with their line on a floating bed woven of silken strands, feathers, and music.

"You keep saying that," replied Juravel. As he spoke, the elf fingered a green stone, serpentine, feeling its subtle vibrations. Normally such trivial magic would prove useless against one as wise as Tuntun, who had seen the birth and death of several centuries, but the female was clearly distracted by her distaste for this night's work.

"I *shall* keep saying it!" Tuntun insisted, but her bluster was lost in the *whoosh* of a sapling. The agile elf managed to slip her foot out of Elbryan's belt snare and come dropping back to the ground, though even with her wings fluttering hard, she hit rather unceremoniously.

Her glare at Juravel was almost threatening as laughter erupted about her. She knew, as did all the gathering, that there was no possible way she could have stumbled into such a coarse trap had not a bit of magic been worked.

It wasn't hard for Tuntun to guess who had worked it.

❖ 8 ❖

The Preparer

T he schedule was grueling, designed to find weakness and break those who were not fit for the daily rigors of the Order of St.-Mere-Abelle. For the four chosen Preparers candidates, Avelyn and Quintall, Thagraine and Pellimar—two students from the class of God's Year 815—life was even more difficult. In addition to their daily duties as first- and second-year students at the abbey, they were given the extra chores of preparation for their journey to Pimaninicuit.

After vespers, their classmates knelt to pray for one hour, spent an hour with their letters, then retired early to meditate and sleep, to reinvigorate their bodies for the tasks of the next day.

But after vespers, the four Preparers began a four-hour regimen, each with an appointed master. They studied the Halo, the charts that determined the astronomical data which would indicate the time of the showers. They learned of seamanship, of how to navigate by the stars of the night sky—and of how those stars would change when the ship carrying the monks crossed certain latitudes. They learned how to tie ropes in a variety of ways, knots necessary for the many uses aboard a sailing vessel. They learned sea etiquette, the rules of the wide waters, and they learned, most of all, the properties of the various stones and of how they must prepare the stones immediately after the shower.

For Avelyn, the night lessons were the promise of his greatest aspirations. He was with Master Jojonah most nights, and Avelyn lived up to his reputation as the finest student to enter St.-Mere-Abelle in many decades. After only two weeks, his predictions of astronomical shifts were perfect, and within the first month, he could recite all the known magical stones, from adamite to turquoise, their reputed properties, and the greatest known magical effects which had been brought about by each.

Master Jojonah watched the young brother with mounting pride, and Avelyn recognized that the older man considered him a protégé. There was security in that, Avelyn came to realize, but also responsibility. Some of the other masters, Siherton in particular, watched him closely, very closely, seeking an excuse to berate him. It seemed to Avelyn as if he had fallen into the middle of a running rivalry between the two older men.

That bothered the young monk profoundly. To see such human frailty in the masters of St.-Mere-Abelle touched the very core of Avelyn's faith. These were men of God, the men closest to God, and such petty actions on their part diminished the very meaning of the Abellican Church. All that should have mattered was the retrieval of the stones. Toward his fellow Preparers, young men he would compete against for the coveted two positions of those who would actually step onto the island of Pimaninicuit, Avelyn felt no rivalry. He exalted in their successes as much as in his own. If they proved the better, he believed, then that was obviously God's will. The proven better two must go to the island; all that mattered was the success of the journey, the retrieval of God's highest gift to humanity.

It quickly became apparent to the watching masters that Avelyn Desbris would be one of the two. During the long hours put in at night, not one of the other three came close to him; they were still mired in charting the stars when Avelyn had moved on to the specific humours that caused the "magical" reaction, having already passed through the recognition of the stones by touch as well as sight and the recognition of their potential intensity by their brightness, shape, and hue. After only five weeks of a four-year training program, the first position of Preparer was nearly secured. If Avelyn did not take ill, the competition to go onto the island of Pimaninicuit had been narrowed to three monks fighting for one slot.

The daytime training was not as easy or as inspiring for Avelyn. He found the many prayer rituals boring, even trite, in light of the revelations he was finding every night. The candle ceremonies, the water bucket lines, the stone carriers bringing material to the newest sections of the abbey, the gift of the class of God's Year 816, simply did not measure up against the mysteries of the God-given stones. Worst of all, and most intense of all, was the physical training. From sunrise to noon each day, with only an hour break—half for a meal and half for a prayer—the students assembled in a courtyard for a lesson in the martial arts or ran barefoot along the rough walls of the abbey or swam in the frigid waters of All Saints Bay. For months they learned to fall and roll; they hardened their bodies by slapping, slapping, slapping one another until their skin grew less sensitive. They walked through attack and defense routines, slowly, endlessly, building in their sore muscles memories of the moves. For the first year, they would study barehanded techniques, punching and grappling. After that, the monks would move on to weapon mastery. And through it all, bare-handed and with weapons, they would square off against each other, pounding on each other relentlessly. Physical perfection was the goal; it was said that a monk of St.-Mere-Abelle could outfight any man alive, and the masters seemed determined to keep that reputation intact.

Avelyn was not the worst of his class, but he was certainly not near the best: Quintall. The short, stocky man went at the martial training as eagerly as Avelyn went at the nighttime studies. As the year progressed, as Avelyn further separated himself from the other three candidate Preparers, he came to dread his daytime matches against any of them, particularly Quintall. There was supposed to be no anger toward an opponent, only respect and mutual learning, but Quintall growled whenever the masters paired him against Avelyn.

Avelyn understood the man's motives. Quintall was carrying over the nighttime rivalry. He could not beat Avelyn at the Ring Stone studies, but he gained a measure of superiority during the day. In most of the maneuvers, the monks were supposed to pull their punches, but Quintall often blasted the breath from Avelyn; there was no striking above the shoulders allowed, but more than once, Quintall knifed a "serpent hand" across Avelyn's throat, dropping him to his knees, gasping for breath.

"Is this how you plan to get to the island?" Avelyn quietly asked after one such mishap. The slips had become too common; Avelyn honestly believed Quintall meant to eliminate the competition.

The look the stocky man gave him in reply did little to allay the monk's mounting suspicions. Quintall's grin was certainly as far from Godlike as anything Avelyn had ever seen, and the fact that their training with weapons, where wounds could easily become more severe, was not far away, brought goose bumps to the scholarly young man.

What bothered Avelyn even more was that if he could recognize what was going on here, then so could the masters, who watched every move of every student so closely. The Order of St.-Mere-Abelle took its physical training seriously; perhaps Avelyn was expected to defend himself against such tactics. Perhaps this training was not so far removed from the nighttime training, which Avelyn considered more important. If he couldn't survive in the courtyard of the abbey, after all, what chance did he have on the high and wild seas?

He watched Quintall walk away from him, his stride so confident, even cocky. Avelyn folded his hands and bowed his head, closed his eyes and began to plot his defense for the next time he and Quintall were paired.

All the troubles of the day were lost each night when Avelyn went to his true work, usually under the tutelage of Master Jojonah. Sometimes that work entailed exhaustive study, reading text after text and reciting procedures so many times in rapid succession that Avelyn would often continue reciting them after he had gone to sleep. Other nights Avelyn and Master Jojonah would simply spend on the roof, huddled against a chill ocean breeze with no fire between them. They would sit and stare at the stars. An occasional question might pass between them, but otherwise their vigil would be as silent as it was dark. Master Jojonah's instructions were vague at best, but Avelyn came to understand them in his heart. He was to watch the night sky, to learn every twinkle of light, to become so familiar with the visible stars that he would not only know their given names but also might create pet names of his own for them.

Avelyn loved those nights. He felt so close to God, to his dead mother, to all humanity, living and dead. He felt a part of the larger and higher truths, a oneness with the universe.

But the quiet awe of stargazing placed a distant second on Avelyn's preferred list of duties. His real zest and heart came shining through on those nights he and Master Jojonah worked with the stones. There were nearly fifty different types at the abbey, each with its own particular properties, and each individual stone with its own particular intensity. Some stones had multiple uses—hematite, for example, could be used for simple out-of-body experiences, for possession of another's body, for domination of another's spirit, and also to heal another's physical wounds.

Avelyn knew all the uses of all the stones, and gradually he was coming to sensitize his fingers to the magical humours within any stone he touched. Handed two similar stones, Avelyn could quickly discern which was the stronger.

Jojonah nodded on each occasion as if expecting that of any student, but in truth the master was again amazed by the young man's prowess. There were in the abbey no more than four other monks, three of them masters and one Father Abbot Markwart himself, who could so distinguish magical intensity, and that fact had been the determining factor in Dalebert Markwart's ascension to the highest rank, for his chief rival could not determine magical intensity in individual stones.

And here before Jojonah's astonished eyes was a young novice, a man of only twenty winters, performing feats that would tax the Father Abbot of St.-Mere-Abelle to the very limits of his powers!

"The night is cloudy," Avelyn dared to note, one dreary and cold November evening as he followed Master Jojonah up the winding staircase of a tower, toward the perch where they would normally sit and study the stars.

Master Jojonah kept quiet and continued on his way, and Avelyn knew better than to press the point.

Avelyn was even more surprised, when he came to the tower top, to find Master Siherton and the Father Abbot waiting for them. Siherton held a small diamond, and from it came enough light for Avelyn to discern the man's features clearly. The young man bowed low and kept his gaze on the floor stones even when he straightened, focusing his attention on the joints among the rocks, each black line seeming so distinct in the harsh diamond light. He had been in St.-Mere-Abelle for several months and had only gazed upon Father Abbot Markwart a handful of times, usually at vespers, when the older leader would sometimes come forth and oversee the celebration.

The three older men moved to the edge of the tower and talked among themselves. Avelyn tried hard not to eavesdrop, but he did catch snatches of the conversation, mostly Siherton complaining vigorously that this was against strict procedure. "This is neither a requirement nor a sensible test for any first-year student," the tall and hawkish master argued.

"Not a test, but a show," Jojonah argued, unintentionally lifting his voice.

"A show-off, more likely," sneered Siherton. "The place has already been secured," he went on. "Why must you press on with it?"

Jojonah stamped his foot and pointed an accusing finger at Siherton; Avelyn was quick to look away from that uncomfortable sight. How it bothered him to see masters bickering! Particularly when he realized that they were arguing over him!

Now Avelyn began to recite his evening prayers so that he might hear no more. He did catch one reference by Master Jojonah to the morning routine, something about its being too dangerous.

Finally, Father Abbot Markwart halted the conversation with an upraised hand. He led the two masters back to Avelyn and bade the young man to look up at him. "It is unusual," he said calmly. "And know you, Masters Siherton and Jojonah, that it is neither a test nor a show and irrelevant to the decisions to be made concerning Pimaninicuit. Suffice it to say that it is for my pleasure, for my curiosity."

He focused on Avelyn then, his face serene, comforting. "I have heard much about you, my son," he said quietly. "Your progress has been monumental in Master Jojonah's estimation."

Avelyn was too awestruck to beam.

"You have used the stones?"

It took a long moment for Avelyn even to register the question. He nodded dumbly.

"You have walked high with hematite, so says Master Jojonah," Abbot Markwart went on. "And you have lit the hearths of many rooms with the small celestite crystals."

Avelyn nodded again. "The greatest was the hematite," he managed to say.

The Father Abbot smiled gently. "Satisfy my curiosity," he bade Avelyn. He held out his left hand and opened it to show Avelyn three stones: malachite, ringed with various shades of green; shining, polished amber; and a silvery piece of chrysotile, the largest of the three resembling a sheet of straight bars, long and narrow lying side by side.

"Do you know them?" Markwart asked.

Avelyn sorted them out in his mind. He did indeed know the magical properties of these three, though those properties seemed oddly disparate for Father Abbot Markwart to be presenting them together. He nodded.

Markwart handed him the stones. "Do you feel their intensity?" he asked, looking hard into Avelyn's eyes. He needed to know the truth, Avelyn realized. Markwart needed to be absolutely certain.

Avelyn fell into the stones, closed his eyes, and passed the items one at a time into his free hand that he might weigh their magical strength. He opened his eyes a moment later, staring hard at the Father Abbot, and nodded again.

"Why must we use such a combination?" Master Jojonah dared to interrupt.

Father Abbot Markwart, his eyes glowing fiercely in the diamond light, waved a hand to silence the master. Nonetheless, Jojonah began to protest again, but Markwart cut him short.

"I warned you of the conditions!" the old Father Abbot growled.

Avelyn swallowed hard; he had never imagined such ferocity coming from the gentle man, the most Godly man in all the world.

"I'll not allow the ruby to be used anywhere near St.-Mere-Abelle." Father Abbot Markwart went on. "I'll not take such a chance for the sake of your student's pride." He turned back to Avelyn and smiled again, but there was little gentle or comforting in that hungry grin. "If Brother Avelyn cannot utilize the simple stones I have given to him, then he has no right even to hold this one." He ended by bringing forth his other hand, turning it over, and opening it to reveal the most beautiful, perfect jewel that Avelyn had ever seen.

"Corundum," the Father Abbot explained. "A ruby. Before I give this to you, understand that what I ask of you is dangerous indeed."

Avelyn nodded and reached out for the jewel, too stunned to fully appreciate the gravity in the old man's voice. Markwart handed it over.

"The puzzle is before you," the Father Abbot explained. "There are no ships in. Sort it out." With that, he walked to the far edge of the tower and motioned for the two masters to join him.

Avelyn studied them intently. Father Abbot Markwart appeared wickedly intense, the gleam in his eyes seeming almost maniacal, and certainly frightening. Master Siherton wouldn't even look his way, and Avelyn could sense that the man desired his failure. Master Jojonah was the most intense, but in a kinder way. Avelyn could smell the man's fear—fear for Avelyn's safety—and only then did the young monk appreciate the weight of this performance and the danger.

"Sort it out," the Father Abbot said again urgently.

Avelyn bowed his head and considered the stones. The ruby was thrumming in his hand, its magic intense and straining for release. Avelyn knew what he could do with that jewel, and when he stopped to consider the implications for the other monks if he used the ruby first, the puzzle seemed not so difficult. Father Abbot Markwart had pointedly mentioned that there were no ships in; Avelyn knew where he was supposed to go. Malachite, amber, serpentine, ruby, in that order.

Avelyn paused and considered the sequence and the implications. He would have to have not one but two other stones already in use when he called forth the powers of the ruby. He had once used two stones together—a hematite and a chrysoberyl, that he might walk out of body with no urge to take possession of any form he passed. But three?

Avelyn took a deep breath, consciously keeping his eyes from the eager gazes of the onlookers.

Malachite first, he told himself, and he walked to the outer edge of the tower, overlooking the sea, black and thunderous a hundred yards below. Avelyn clutched the malachite firmly, felt its magic tingling and coursing through his hand, then his arm, and into all his body. And then he felt lighter, strangely so, almost as light as he did when spirit-walking with hematite. He went over the tower's edge with hardly a hesitation, his body beginning a gentle, controlled fall.

Avelyn tried not to think of the reality of his position as the tower walls slipped past his descending form. The cliff wall below the tower was less smooth and far from sheer, and the young monk had to constantly push himself away, angling down and out from the abbey.

As he neared the pounding surf, Avelyn shifted the amber into the hand holding the malachite and brought forth its powers as well.

He touched down easily atop the surf, berating himself for not simply walking his body horizontally across the cliff to land atop the wharf instead. No sense in worrying about that now, he decided; so he kept the malachite functioning until he caught his balance, then, with a deep breath, let it go.

Only the amber was functioning now, and it kept him above the water. With another deep and steadying breath, his confidence in the stone growing, Avelyn walked out across the dark waters, his feet barely making the slightest depression on the rolling surface.

He looked back over his shoulder several times as he moved out from the abbey. He had to get far enough away so that using the ruby would not pose any risk to the structure, and even farther than that, considering the angle of the tall tower, if he wanted the two masters and the Father Abbot truly to witness the demonstration.

Now Avelyn called upon the serpentine, a stone he had never before put to any real test. He knew its reputed properties, of course, but he had never attempted to use them. Master Jojonah had done so once in Avelyn's presence, when he had retrieved a jewel from a hot hearth, and the young monk had to focus on that now to take faith that the serpentine would protect him.

All too soon, the moment was upon him. He was far out from shore, standing firm on the rolling waves, the serpentine shield strong about him. Avelyn put the ruby in his hand.

"He might have slipped under the waters," Siherton said dryly. "A great and difficult task we will have in retrieving the stones."

Father Abbot Markwart chuckled, but Master Jojonah didn't appreciate the levity. "Brother Avelyn is worth more to us than all the stones in St.-Mere-Abelle combined," he asserted, drawing incredulous looks from both his companions.

"I think, perhaps, that you have become too close to this novice," the Father Abbot warned.

Before the old man could go on, though, his breath was stolen away as a tremendous fireball erupted out at sea, rings of searing flames spreading out wide from a central point that the three knew to be Avelyn.

"Pray that the serpentine shield was in full!" Markwart gasped, thoroughly stunned by the intensity and size of the blast. The ruby was strong, but this was ridiculous!

"I told you!" Master Jojonah said over and over. "I told you!"

Even Siherton had little in the way of rebuttal. He watched, as impressed as his companions, as the fireball widened and churned, as the ocean hissed in protest so loudly that the three could hear it clearly, as the top waters turned to steam and rose in a thick fog. Brother Avelyn was strong indeed!

And probably dead, Siherton realized, though he was too shaken to make the point at that moment. If Avelyn had concentrated so much of his energy into the ruby, then likely he had let the serpentine shield slip. Then likely he was now a charred thing, drifting to the bottom of the harbor.

The three waited a long time, Jojonah growing ever more concerned, but Markwart resignedly saying, "A pity," many times, and Siherton seeming on the verge of a chuckle.

Then came a sound not so far below them, a deep breath as one might take after great exertion. They rushed to the edge and peered over, Siherton holding the diamond low, focusing its light downward to reveal a haggard-looking but very much alive Brother Avelyn, the malachite clenched tightly in one hand, his other hand working at the wall, pulling his nearly weightless body upward. Avelyn's brown robes were tattered and dripping; he had the stench of burned hair about him.

He got near the tower's lip and Jojonah pulled him over.

"Some of the flames got through," a shivering Avelyn explained, bowing his head in shame, holding his arms wide to display the damage to his robe. "I had to let go of the amber's power briefly and dunk myself."

Only then did Jojonah realize how blue Avelyn's lips appeared. He looked sharply at Siherton, and when the master didn't respond, Jojonah snatched the diamond from him. The light went out for just a moment, then returned, brighter than ever. And warmer. Jojonah held the diamond close to Avelyn, and the young monk felt its warmth flowing into his aching, frozen form.

"I am sorry," Avelyn said to Father Abbot Markwart through chattering teeth. "I have failed." He held his hand out limply, returning the four stones.

Father Abbot Markwart burst out into the most heartfelt laughter Avelyn had ever heard. The cackling old man pocketed the four stones, then clenched his empty fist, and from a ring on his finger, set with a tiny diamond, he brought forth a light of his own. He motioned for Siherton to follow and started for the stairs.

Master Jojonah waited until the pair had gone, then lifted Avelyn's head so the young brother could look directly into his soft brown eyes. "You will be one of the chosen pair who go onto the island of Pimaninicuit," he said with all confidence.

He led Avelyn down from the tower then, to the warmth of the lower levels. Avelyn undressed and wrapped a blanket about himself, then sat alone with his thoughts in front of a blazing fire. Though the trial of the four stones, the high wall, and the cold sea had exhausted him, he did not sleep that night.

Touel'alfar

It was warm; Elbryan felt that first, felt a soft, moist sensation gently touching all his skin. Gradually his consciousness came floating back to him, as if from a far distant place. He spent a long while lying very still, bathing in the comforting sensation, the warmth, holding that clear consciousness away. For the boy who had just witnessed such carnage and loss, the semiconscious state was preferable.

It wasn't until a memory of Dundalis, of his dead parents, slipped through his defenses, shocking away the quiet and the calm, that he opened his olive green eyes.

He was on a mossy bank, a gentle slope that put his head comfortably above his feet. A warm fog hung thick about him, caressing his body and dulling his senses. Visibility was but a few feet and Elbryan, shuffling up to his elbows, soon realized that sound traveled little farther than that, caught up and deadened in the tangible mist. He was in a forest, he understood— he was ankle deep in fallen leaves. Elbryan's instincts—something about the air, perhaps, the aroma—told him this was not the slope leading out of Dundalis up to the ridgeline, the slope where he had met the . . .

The what? Elbryan wondered, having no explanation of who or what those delicate winged creatures might be.

Despite the bruises from his fights with the goblins, the minor wounds, and the discomfort of the night spent in the corner of his ruined house, the young man felt no pain, no soreness in his limbs. He sat up straight, then rolled to put his legs under him. Gradually he came up in a crouch, studying the area intently, trying to get some bearings on where he might be.

The forest was an old one, judging from the gnarled and twisted trunks of those nearby trees he could discern through the mist. The sun seemed a gray blur above him, a lighter spot in the sky. "West," Elbryan decided after studying it for a moment, his instincts, his internal directional sense, sorting things out. The boy believed the sun to be in the west, halfway from noon to sunset.

He didn't have much time before the night settled around him. He stood up, but stayed low, feeling vulnerable despite the thick mist. His reasoning told him to get out of that fog so that he might survey the area, but his physical senses did not want him to leave the soothing mist.

He overruled the physical and started up the slope, thinking to get above the gray blanket. He moved quickly, stumbling often and cursing himself silently for every stick-snapping sound. He climbed within the fog for only a few minutes and came out of it so suddenly he nearly stumbled again from the shock. At the same moment that the air grew clear about him, strong winds buffeted him—not gusts but a continual blow. Elbryan looked down the slope curiously, just the few feet to the unmoving mist. It appeared to him as if the mist was somehow blocking, or at least escaping, the winds, but how could that be?

Elbryan's eyes widened with yet another unexplainable mystery as he continued to survey the ascent before him, going up, up, up from his position, dwarfing him, making him feel totally insignificant and tiny. He knew that he was nowhere near Dundalis; this mountain was nothing like the gentle, tree-covered hills of his homeland. He was on the western face of but one mountain in a great, towering range, looking down at a mist-shrouded vale, oval-shaped and nestled between the many overlooking peaks. Not so far above him, Elbryan could see the snow on this mountain and on all the others, a whitecapping that the young man suspected might be perpetual.

He shook his head helplessly. Where in Corona was he? And how had he come to this place?

The young man's eyes opened even wider then, and he glanced all around frantically. "Am I dead?" he asked the wind.

No answer, no hint, just the murmur, an endless string of mysterious whispers.

"Father?" Elbryan cried, and he scrambled three steps to the right, as though that might make some difference. "Pony?"

No answer.

His heart was racing, blood pumping furiously. Soon he was gasping for breath in utter panic. He started to run, first left, then up, then, when that course proved too difficult, back to the right, all the while calling out for his father or mother or for anyone.

"You are not dead," came a sweet, melodic voice from behind.

Elbryan paused for a long while, catching his breath, composing himself. Somehow he knew the speaker was not human, that no human voice could chime so sweetly, so perfectly.

Slowly, concentrating on his breathing more than anything else, Elbryan turned.

There stood one of the creatures he had seen in the glade, a bit shorter than he and probably no more than three-quarters his weight. Its limbs were incredibly slender, but they weren't bumpy and bony like Jilseponie's had been when she was much younger. This creature's limbs didn't look skinny, any more than did the supple branches of a bending willow. Nor did this creature, so tiny, seem weak. Far from it; there was a sureness, a fluid solidity to the creature that warned Elbryan this tiny foe would be more difficult than any of the goblins he had battled, perhaps more difficult even than the giant.

"Come back down where it is warmer," the creature bade Elbryan, "into the mists where the wind does not blow."

Elbryan looked back at the vale—and realized for the first time that no treetops were poking through the gray canopy, as if all the trees had stopped at exactly that level. Elbryan had the distinct feeling the mist and the treetops were somehow connected.

"Come," said the creature. "You are not dead and are not in danger. The danger has passed."

Elbryan winced at the reference to the tragedy of Dundalis. The way the words were spoken, however—plainly and without any apparent deception—allowed Elbryan to relax somewhat. Instead of sizing up the diminutive creature as a potential enemy now, he regarded it in a different light. He noticed for the first time how delicate and beautiful this one seemed, with angular features perfectly sculpted and hair so golden that even Pony's thick, lustrous mane could sparkle no brighter. It was as if the being shone of its own accord, an inner light making the flowing hair glow and shimmer. The creature's eyes were no less spectacular, two golden stars, they seemed, bright with childish innocence, yet deep with wisdom.

The creature started down the slope but stopped at the very edge of the fog, realizing the young man was making no move to follow.

"Who are you?" came the obvious question.

The creature smiled disarmingly. "I am Belli'mar Juraviel," it answered honestly and motioned again toward the mist, even took another step down, so that its shins disappeared into the grayness.

"What are you?" Elbryan said with more confidence. He suspected the creature would confirm it was an elf, but he realized even such an honest and expected answer would give him little information, for he really didn't know what an elf was.

The creatures stopped again and turned back to regard him. "Do you know so little?"

Elbryan glared at Juraviel, in no mood for cryptic talk.

"The world is a lost place, I fear," Juraviel went on. "To think we have been forgotten in a mere century."

Elbryan's scowl melted away in curiosity.

"You really do not know?"

"Know what?" Elbryan snapped back defiantly.

"Of anything beyond your own race," Juraviel clarified.

"I know of goblins and of fomorian giants!" Elbryan insisted, his voice and his ire rising.

Juraviel had a response for that, a remark concerning the relative unpreparedness of Dundalis in the face of such knowledge. If this boy knew of the evil races, then why was his village so utterly ill equipped to deal with a simple raiding party? The elf politely kept the question to himself, though, understanding the wounds were too raw in this young one. "And do I fit into your knowledge of such creatures? Am I goblin or fomorian?" Juraviel asked calmly, that melodic voice alone destroying any possible comparisons to the croaking and growling monsters.

Elbryan chewed on his lip for a moment, trying to find an appropriate response. Finally, he shook his head.

"Come," Juraviel bade him, the diminutive fellow turning again toward the mist.

"You haven't answered my question."

When Juraviel turned back this time, his expression was more stern. "There is no answer that can be conveyed with simple words," he explained. "I could tell you a name, and you might have heard the name before, but that will give you little of the truth and more of the myth."

Elbryan cocked his head, obviously lost.

"Your prejudices twined with the name will conflict with your perceptions," Juraviel went on. "You asked me my own name, and that I willingly gave, for the words 'Belli'mar Juraviel' bring no preconceptions with them. You asked what I am, and that I cannot tell you. That is something Elbryan Wyndon of Dundalis must learn for himself."

Before the startled young man could even ask how Belli'mar Juraviel might have come by his name, the creature turned and strode into the mist, disappearing from sight. Elbryan rocked back on his heels, fumbling with his thoughts. Then he realized that he was alone again, and utterly lost. His choices were simple, and there seemed none better than following this creature, whatever it might be.

Elbryan sprinted down the slope, back into the grayness, and found a smiling Juraviel waiting for him just a few feet beyond the mist's edge. At first, Elbryan wondered why he hadn't seen the figure from outside the mist, then he realized that he could not see the trees from out there, either, though they were tall and thick about him now, just five steps in.

Too many questions, the young man decided, and he didn't even want to know the answers at that moment, his curiosity overwhelmed.

Juraviel walked down the slope at an easy pace, Elbryan right behind him. Not so far down, they moved beneath the misty canopy, and the forested valley came clear to Elbryan. Again he was amazed. He felt warm and serene, despite all that had happened, despite his very real fears. He didn't feel lost anymore and if he was dead—and he was again beginning to believe that to be the case—then death was not so bad!

For the forest, this place, was more beautiful than anything young Elbryan had ever seen. The undergrowth was lush and thick but seemed to part before them as they made their way along smooth trails that always seemed as if they would end just a few feet in front of the pair but went on, apparently in any direction that Belli'mar Juraviel chose. The creature wasn't following a trail, Elbryan believed, but was making one, walking as easily and openly through the underbrush as a man might wade through a shallow pond. As soon as he recovered from that spectacle, Elbryan was overwhelmed again, this time by the myriad vivid colors and delicate aromas, by the chirping of countless birds, the winsome song of an unseen brook, the bleating of some distant creature. The whole place was a song; Elbryan's every sense was on its edge, and he felt more alive than he had ever felt before.

His mind fought against that perception. He forced himself to remember Dundalis, to replay the horror, that he might find a fighting edge. He thought of escape, though he knew not where he might run, or even why he would wish to. He looked at the low branches of a nearby tree and visualized a weapon he could fashion from one of them, though a weapon, any weapon, would surely seem out of place here. His stubbornness held for many minutes, a testament to the young man's strong willpower. But even the memories of the recent tragedy could not hold firmly to Elbryan as he walked for the first time through the forest that was home to the elves, to Belli'mar Juraviel's folk. Dark thoughts could not be sustained in the place where Juraviel's people danced and played.

"Can you at least tell me where I am?" a flustered Elbryan asked some minutes later, Juraviel going along as if in a trance, ignoring the young man completely.

After a dozen more skipping steps, the creature paused and turned. "On your maps, if it is on your maps, this place is named simply the Valley of Mists."

Elbryan shrugged; the name meant nothing to him, though he was glad to learn that it might be on some map, at least. If that was true, then he probably was not dead.

"Truly, it is Andur'Blough Inninness, the Forest of Cloud, though few of your people would recognize that name, and those who did would not likely admit it."

"Do you always talk in riddles?"

"Do you always ask foolish questions?"

"What is foolish about wanting to know where I am?" Elbryan asked angrily.

"And so I have told you," a calm Juraviel replied. "Does that change anything? Do you feel comforted now, to know that you are in a place that you do not know?"

Elbryan growled softly and brought both his hands up to ruffle his light brown hair.

"But then," the elf went on in condescending tones, "humans must name everything, must map it and place it in some tidy little package and category, that they believe they have found some measure of control over what cannot be controlled. A false sense of godliness, I suppose."

"Godliness?"

"Arrogance," Juraviel clarified. "My young human!" he said suddenly, excitedly, clapping his delicate hands together in mock glee. "You are in Andur'Blough Inninness!"

Elbryan screwed up his face and shrugged.

"Exactly my point," Juraviel said dryly, and started on his way.

Elbryan sighed and followed.

Half an hour passed uneventfully, Elbryan walking and looking about, constantly awed by the beauty and the richness of Andur'Blough Inninness. Mostly, though, the boy's gaze drifted back to the curious creature leading him.

"Do those work?" he asked on impulse, blurting out his thoughts before he even realized he was speaking.

Juraviel stopped short and turned to regard the obviously embarrassed Elbryan, standing perfectly still on the trail and pointing forward at Juraviel.

Juraviel's smile calmed Elbryan considerably. "A logical question," the creature remarked, understanding Elbryan's curiosity, and then he added, with exaggerated relief, "at last."

Elbryan's expression soured.

"But why would you wish to know?" the ever-elusive Juraviel answered. "To gain advantage in a battle, perhaps?" He quickly added, "Not that you and I shall ever battle, of course," as soon as he noticed Elbryan's muscles go tense.

That declaration relaxed the young man, and so, of course, Juraviel put in, "Except during . . ." and then paused and let the teasing thought hang empty in the air.

Thoroughly flustered, feeling very out of place both physically and emotionally, Elbryan took a deep breath and removed himself from his anxiety—as simply as that. He merely let his fears and dark thoughts fall somewhere behind him, concentrating only on the present. It might have been resignation, a simple conclusion that he could do nothing about anything anyway, but to Juraviel, the obvious change that came over the boy was promising. Certainly an emotional detachment would prove healthier for this young human who had been through so much and who had so many more trying experiences ahead of him.

With a widening smile, Juraviel started his wings fluttering, bent his knees, and leaped into the air, a half jump, half flight to the lowest branch of a nearby maple.

"They work," Juraviel announced, "for short hops and to break a fall. But, no, we cannot fly as do the birds." He came back to the ground, his face suddenly serious as he contemplated his own words. "A pity."

Elbryan nodded, in full agreement. How wonderful it would be to fly! He imagined the wind, the green treetop canopy speeding below him . . .

"Your time here will not be unpleasant unless you make it so," Juraviel announced immediately and grimly before the grin could even begin to spread across young Elbryan's face.

Elbryan stared at the creature curiously, caught off guard by the sudden change of demeanor.

"Know that there are those among my people who do not believe you belong," Juraviel went on, his voice stern. "There are those who do not see in you the likeness of Mather."

"I know of no person by the name of Mather," Elbryan replied with all the courage he could muster. Again came that feeling of detachment, summoned consciously, an attitude that he had nothing to lose, had already lost all there was.

Juraviel shrugged, a flitting little movement of his slender shoulders. "You shall," he promised. "Hear me now clearly, young one. You are not a prisoner, yet you are not free. As long as you remain in Andur'Blough Inninness, your conduct must be controlled, as your training shall be guided."

"Training?" Elbryan started to ask, but Juraviel didn't pause long enough to hear him.

"Stray from the rules at your own peril. Ask not for a second chance when the harsh justice of the Touel'alfar falls upon you."

The threat was open and clear. Elbryan, with that typical Wyndon pride, squared his shoulders and tightened his jaw, a movement that Juraviel seemed to take no note of whatsoever. The name Juraviel had given his people, Touel'alfar, had a distinctly familiar ring, and Elbryan was certain he had heard it in conjunction with tales of the elves.

"You may rest now," Juraviel finished. "I will show to you your duties with the rising of the sun."

"And rest well," he finished, his voice grim and somber, "for your duties are many and will weary you indeed!"

Elbryan wanted to shout out that he would do as he pleased, when he pleased. He wanted to proclaim his independence loudly and openly, but before he got the first stuttered word out of his mouth, Juraviel hopped into a short flight once more. The delicate creature stepped lightly onto a branch and jumped again immediately, disappearing into the thick brush so completely and easily that Elbryan blinked and rubbed his eyes.

He stood there, in the valley of Andur'Blough Inninness, doubting what he had seen, doubting all that had happened. He wanted his mother and his father. He wanted Pony, that they might have another chance to warn the village before the goblin darkness descended. He wanted . . .

He wanted too much, all at once. He sat down right in the dirt at his feet and fought hard against his emotions, for he did not want to cry.

From Juraviel's perspective, the first meeting had gone quite well. He knew there would be many doubts raised about Elbryan, particularly by Tuntun, and he knew how difficult Tuntun could be! But after speaking with the boy, Juraviel was even more convinced that this was indeed the true bloodline of Mather, and an appropriate ranger-in-training. Elbryan had that same impish quality about him as Mather, a love and luster of life, lurking just below the surface. The boy could control it, could find that necessary place of detachment . . . and yet, Elbryan could not resist the question about the wings. He had to know, and then, when he did know, he couldn't help but imagine the wonder of soaring through the air. Just by the expression on Elbryan's face, Juraviel had read the boy's every wonder-filled thought and had relished each of them as much as had Elbryan.

It was good that the boy could think such things at this darkest time in his life, was good that he could press on logically, stoically. Tuntun was wrong, Juraviel knew without any doubt at all; this one had character.

Elbryan wanted to eat, or fall asleep, even looked for a place, a moss bed, perhaps, where he might lie down. That notion was lost along with so many others, fleeting thoughts banging into a wall of images. Andur'Blough Inninness, with all its sounds and colors, all its vivid images, called to him, teased him. Juraviel had said nothing about his remaining where he was, so Elbryan got up, brushed himself off, and started walking again among the trees.

He spent the remainder of the afternoon caught up in the sights and smells. He found a stream filled with yellow fish that he did not know, and watched them for more than an hour. He spotted a deer, its long white tail bobbing, but as soon as he tried to get closer, it caught wind of him and leaped away, disappearing as completely as Belli'mar Juraviel had into the shadows.

For all the sights of that wondrous afternoon, for all the relief of existing simply in the present and not in the most terrible past or the uncertain future, Elbryan was even more greatly overwhelmed as dusk descended.

The hole opened in the middle of the fog that covered the elven valley, showing the deep blue sky. Slowly that hole widened, all sides drawing away evenly, perfectly, and Elbryan, watching in sheer amazement, knew that something supernatural, some magic, guided the mist. Soon the sky was clear above him, the first stars twinkling into view.

Elbryan ran about in search of an open meadow, wanting to see this spectacle more clearly. He found a hillock, bare of trees, and scrambled up its side, stumbling more than once, for his eyes remained fixed on the sky.

The fog had receded now to the edges of the vale, and there it hung, blurring the dark shadows of the towering mountains, blurring the boundary between earth and sky. Elbryan had stopped at the top of the hillock, but he felt as if he were still going up, still ascending to those brilliant, twinkling dots. There was a music that swelled about him, he suddenly realized, a beautiful harmony, and it, too, seemed to draw him higher to walk among the stars, to dwell in their light and mystery. Questions too profound flitted about his consciousness.

He knew not how many minutes, perhaps even hours, had passed when he at last came from that trance. The night was dark about him; his neck ached from holding the position for so long.

Though he was back on earth, spiritually, the music remained, soft and wonderful, emanating from every shadow, from every tree, from the ground itself.

No horrible memories could come to him while he was listening to that elvish song, no fears could gain hold. Slowly, determinedly, Elbryan moved down the hillock, looking back often to the sky. Then he forced himself to stare at the darkest spot he could find, that his eyes could adjust more completely.

He paused and very carefully turned a circuit, listening intently, trying to focus on the sound. His direction chosen, he started off, determined to find the singer.

Many times that night, Elbryan believed that he was close. Many times, he rushed around a bend in the trail or jumped out from behind a tree, expecting to catch an elf at song, and once he thought he glimpsed the light of a distant torch.

The song was strong, though not loud, with many voices joining in, but Elbryan never caught a glimpse of any of the singers, saw no elf nor any other creature the rest of that night.

Juraviel found him at dawn, curled in a hollow at the base of a wide oak.

It was time to begin.

PART TWO

▼

PASSAGE

Often I sit and stare at the stars, wondering, wandering. They are to me the shining symbol of all the unanswered questions of human existence, of our place in this vast sky, of our purpose, of death itself. They are sparkles of unanswerable wonder, and, too, the beacons of hope.

The night sky is what I liked most about my years in Andur'Blough Inninness. At dusk, when the fog rolled back to the forest edge, it shrouded the known world, blocked the stark mountain shadows in soft and subtle mystery, and the stars came out shining clearer than anywhere else in all the world. That magical mist drew me up—my spirit and even my physical body, it seemed—into the heavens, above the tangible world, that I might walk among the stars and bathe in the lights of mystery, in the secrets of the universe unveiled.

In that elven forest, under that elven sky, I knew freedom. I knew the purest contemplation, the release of physical boundaries, the brotherhood with all the universe. Under that sky that posed to me so many questions, I dismissed mortality, for I had become one with something that was eternal. I had ascended from this temporary existence, from a place of constant change to a place of eternity.

An elf may live for a handful of centuries, a human for a handful of decades, but for both that is but the start of an eternal journey—or perhaps a continuation of a journey that had begun long before this present conscious incarnation. For the spirit continues, as the stars continue. Under that sky, I learned this to be true.

Under that sky, I talked to God.

—ELBRYAN WYNDON

CHAPTER

❖ 10 ❖

Made of Tougher Stuff

Elbryan rolled his breeches up over his knees—not that the worn and ragged pants would stay that way for long!—and touched the dark water with his toe.

Cold. It was always cold; the boy didn't know why he even bothered testing it each morning before plunging in.

From somewhere in the thick brush behind him, he heard a call, "Be quick about it!" The words were not spoken in the common tongue of Honce-the-Bear but in the singsong, melodious language of the elves, a language Elbryan was already beginning to comprehend.

Elbryan glared over his shoulder in the general direction of the voice, though he knew he would not see one of the Touel'alfar. He had been in Andur'Blough Inninness for three months, had watched winter settle over the land just outside the elven valley and in a few places within the enchanted vale. Elbryan didn't know exactly where Andur'Blough Inninness was located, but he suspected they were somewhere in the northern latitudes of Corona, beyond the Wilderlands border of Honce-the-Bear. By his reckoning, the winter solstice had passed, and he knew Dundalis, or what was left of the village, was likely under several feet of snow. He remembered well the hardships, and the excitement, of Dundalis in the winter, the gusting wind throwing icy particles against the side of the cabin, the piles of blowing snow, sometimes so deep that he and his father had to break through a drift just to get outside!

It wasn't like that in Andur'Blough Inninness. Some magic, probably the same enchantment that brought the daily blanket of fog, kept the winter season much warmer and more gentle. The northern end of the valley was carpeted by snow, but only a few inches, and the small pond up there was frozen solid—Elbryan had once seen a handful of elves dancing and playing on the ice. But many of the hardier plants had kept their summer hue, many flowers still bloomed, and this reedy bog, the one place in all the valley that Elbryan had truly come to hate, had not frozen. The water was chilly, but not more so than it had been on the first day Elbryan had been told to go in, back when the season was still autumn.

The boy took a deep breath and plunged one foot in, held the pose for a moment until the numbness took away the sting, then dipped in his second foot. He picked up his basket, cursed when one pant leg slipped down into the water, then waded out through the reeds. The cold mud squishing through his toes felt good, at least.

"Be quick about it!" came the predictable call again from the brush, and it was repeated several times, sometimes in elven and sometimes in the common human tongue, by different voices in different places. The elves were taunting him, the boy knew. They were always taunting, always complaining, always pointing out his all too numerous shortcomings.

To his credit, Elbryan had pretty much learned to ignore them.

Parting one patch of reeds, the boy found his first stone of the day, bobbing low in the water. He scooped it out and dropped it into his basket, then moved along to a group of nearly a dozen bobbing stones. He recognized which ones were too high in the water, and plunged them under, trying to saturate the spongelike rocks a bit more before taking them out. When he squeezed them, extracting the now-flavored liquid, the elves would inevitably complain about how little he had collected.

It was yet another part of this unchanging daily ritual.

Soon the basket was full, so Elbryan hauled it back to the bank and collected another one. Thus it went for the bulk of the morning, for the bulk of every morning: the boy moving carefully about the chilly bog, collecting ten baskets of milk-stones.

That was the easy part of Elbryan's day, for then he had to haul the heavy baskets, one at a time, nearly half a mile to the collecting trough. He had to be fast, for he could lose precious time at this point and then would have to suffer almost continual insult from the unseen elves. "Five miles laden, five miles empty," was the way Belli'mar Juraviel had described this part of his work. Ironically, the laden section of each trip seemed the easiest to Elbryan, for the elves often set traps for him on the journey back to the bog. These weren't particularly nasty traps, designed more to embarrass than to injure. A trip line here, a disguised patch of slick mud on a corner there. The worst part of falling victim to one of the snares was hearing the laughter as he tried to extract himself from whatever had hold of him, be it a thorny bush or some of those silken elven strands, which, Elbryan found out soon enough, could be made as sticky and clingy as a spiderweb.

He got his reward for his morning's toils when he returned to the bog to collect the tenth loaded basket. There, every day, he would eat his midday meal—though at first, it was usually halfway through the afternoon before Elbryan got a chance to taste it. The elves would set out a grand table, steaming stew and venison, sometimes roasted game fowl, and piping hot tea that warmed the boy from his head to his cold toes. Always it was a hot meal they set, and Elbryan soon understood why. The elves would put the food out at exactly the same time every day, but if he was not fast enough, *"tolque ne'pesil siq'el palouviel,"* or, "the steam would be off the stew," as one particularly nasty elf, a deceivingly delicate maiden named Tuntun, had often chided him.

So Elbryan ran, stumbling with his ninth basket, knowing that any stone he dropped into the dirt would be useless for that day. Carefully placing the basket at last at the trough, the boy then sprinted full out the half mile back to the bog. He ate a cold lunch every day at first, but gradually, as the terrain became more familiar and his legs became stronger, as he grew to recognize and thus avoid many of the devilish elven traps, he graduated to warm food.

This day, Elbryan resolved, that tea would burn his tongue!

He put the ninth basket down by the trough right on schedule, took one deep breath, clearing his thoughts and remembering the last layout of the elvish obstacle course. For only the third time in all these weeks, the lunch had not yet been set out when Elbryan had collected the ninth basket. On those first two occasions, the hopeful lad had fallen victim to ever more cunning elvish traps. "Not this time," he said quietly, determinedly, and he started his sprint.

He spotted mud at one sharp bend; without slowing, Elbryan leaped atop a stone at the elbow of the trail and skipped off it, landing beyond the slick area. With the aid of a slanting sunbeam poking down through a break in the leafy boughs, he then spotted a series of nearly translucent trip lines, of height ranging from ankle to knee, blocking one long straight section of the trail. Elbryan considered veering off the trail, crashing through the brush, then slowed, thinking he should just walk past this obvious trap.

"Not today," Elbryan growled, and he put his head down and ran on, full speed. He found his visual focus quickly, locking his eyes upon a point just one step ahead, and high-stepped his way through the region, getting his feet up over every single trip line.

Laughter trailed him as he sped away, and Elbryan sensed that there was some measure of admiration in it.

Within a couple of minutes, his goal—the bog, the basket, the meal— was in sight, down the last stretch of path. Here, high stones lined both sides of the trail, making passage off the path nearly impossible unless Elbryan took a circuitous route quite deep into the underbrush.

He slowed to a near walk, opting for caution and understanding that an extra few seconds would make no difference in the quality of his meal.

They had dug a pit—how could they have done that so quickly?—and had cleverly covered it with a layer of dirt and fallen leaves, supported by a trellis of woven sticks. Despite the addition of the pit, the path appeared almost exactly the same as it had on all of his previous returns.

Almost exactly.

Elbryan crouched and tamped down his feet, thinking to take a few run-ning strides and then leap the trap. He stopped before he had really begun, though, catching the sound of a soft titter on the breeze.

A smile widened on the boy's face. He wagged his finger at the under-brush. "Well done," he congratulated, then he moved to the edge of the apparent pit and pulled aside the phony trellis.

The real pit, he discovered was several feet beyond the apparent pit. He would have leaped clear of the phony, only to drop heavily into the real one.

Now it was Elbryan's turn to laugh, as he discerned the dimensions of the true trap, then easily leaped it, leaving the last few feet of the path, the last expanse to the food, open to him.

"Not this time!" he yelled loudly, and there was no return laughter from the brush, no sound at all. *"Ne leque towithel!"* he repeated in elvish.

Elbryan slowly passed the last tree, home free, so he thought.

Something zipped by him, just under his chin. He heard a thud at the side and turned to see one of those tiny elvish arrows half buried in a tree. A second bolt whistled behind him, turning him with a start, and only when Elbryan noticed the silvery filament trailing this arrow did he understand what was happening.

There came a third and a fourth, all dangerously close.

"Not fair!" the boy yelled, trying to move—and discovering that the sticky strands were already grabbing at him. He looked at the brush help-lessly, at the steaming stew, just a few strides away.

More arrows whistled past, each trailing a strand, each tightening the web about Elbryan, holding him from his meal.

"Not fair!" he yelled repeatedly, tearing at the strands. He managed to pull a few down—a couple of arrows came out of the tree, other strands pulled free of the arrow fletchings—but that helped only a little, as the now-loose strands clung to the boy's clothing, entangling him even more.

Another arrow came by and slashed across Elbryan's forearm as he struggled. His protest came out as a snarl, words stolen by the stinging pain, and he stopped his thrashing and clutched at his arm.

"Cowards!" he yelled in total frustration. "Goblinkin! Only a coward would shoot from the boughs. Only a coward of goblin heritage would attack someone who has no weapons with which to strike back!"

The next arrow razored painfully across the back of his neck, drawing a line of bright blood.

"Enough!" came a stern voice from the brush, a voice that Elbryan rec-ognized—and was certainly glad to hear.

Protests, laughter, taunts all came back in reply from many different places.

"Enough, Tuntun!" Belli'mar Juraviel demanded again, and the elf came forth from the brush, moving to young Elbryan. Tuntun, bow in hand, came out from across the way and moved quickly to follow on Juraviel's heels.

"Calm, my friend," Juraviel prompted poor Elbryan, the boy thrashing about and only entangling himself even more. "The strands will not let go until Tuntun commands them." Juraviel turned and glared at the female then, and she sighed resignedly and muttered something under her breath.

Almost immediately, the strands began to fall from Elbryan, except for those still tight in the line from the tree to the brush where Tuntun had tied them off, and those which the young man had inadvertently twisted and turned about his limbs. Finally, with Juraviel's help, Elbryan got free, and he immediately stormed up to Tuntun, his green eyes flaring dangerously.

The elf looked up at him calmly, smiling, perfectly relaxed.

"I earned that meal!" the boy stormed.

"So go and eat it," Tuntun replied, and snickers came at Elbryan from every bush. "You needn't worry that it will burn your tongue."

"Elbryan," Juraviel warned when he saw the boy ball his fist at his side. Tuntun held up a hand to her elvish companion, silently bidding Juraviel to let her take care of this situation. Juraviel knew what was coming, and though he did not like it, for he thought it too soon in the boy's training, he did on some levels agree that the lesson might be necessary.

"You want so badly to strike me." Tuntun tittered.

Elbryan fumed but couldn't, in good conscience, punch this diminutive creature, half his weight, if that, and a girl besides!

Tuntun's bow came up, faster than Elbryan could follow, and the elf let fly an arrow, down the path. It struck the bowl of stew, overturning it and making a mess of the meal. "You'll get nothing more this day," Tuntun said sternly.

The knuckles on both of Elbryan's hands were white by this point, and the muscles along his jaw strained taut. He started to turn away, thinking that he had to hold his control, had to let all the insults pass, but before he got halfway around, Tuntun slapped her bow across the back of his head.

Elbryan let fly a wide-arcing left hook as he spun back toward the elf. He missed miserably, Tuntun ducking low under the predictable blow, and kicking him twice in rapid succession, once on the inside of each knee.

Elbryan stumbled and squared himself; Tuntun tossed her bow aside, held up both her empty hands, and motioned for Elbryan to come on.

The boy paused. The forest was silent, totally silent, about him, and Juraviel made not a move nor any indication of how Elbryan should proceed.

It was his choice to make, he realized, and so he crouched low, hands out wide, feeling his balance on the balls of his feet. He waited, and waited some more, until Tuntun relaxed, and then he sprang like a hunting cat.

He caught the air, nothing more, and didn't even realize that the elf was not in front of him until he heard wings fluttering behind him and felt a series of sharp punches on the back of his head.

He wheeled, but Tuntun turned with him, staying behind him and punching out a veritable drum roll on his upper back. Furious, Elbryan finally launched himself sideways, putting some ground between him and his elusive opponent.

"Blood of Mather!" Tuntun said sarcastically. "He fights as any lumbering human might!"

Juraviel wanted to respond that Mather had fought the exact same way in the first years of his training, but he let it pass. Let Tuntun have her fun this day, the elf decided; that would make his victory all the sweeter when Elbryan finally proved himself.

On cue, Elbryan came back in, measuring his steps this time, not taking his eyes off the dancing elf. Tuntun was on the ground again, swaying slowly, hands waving before her.

Elbryan saw an opening and let fly a combination—left jab, step, and right cross. He meant to retract the left, which missed, that he could roll his shoulders and put some weight behind the right. He meant to do a lot of things, to follow the combination with a shoulder tackle or another quick one-two if the opportunity presented itself. He found, however, that as soon as his left arm extended, his fist flying so tantalizing near Tuntun's swaying head, that his moment of control had passed.

Tuntun turned in accord with the punch, her head fading back across to Elbryan's right, her right hand catching the boy's wrist and pushing outward, her left hand coming back in and catching the outside of his elbow, driving in.

As Elbryan's arm locked, and before he could even step in and begin the cross, Tuntun turned her right wrist over and down.

Elbryan had no choice but to follow, scampering out to the left a step before tumbling hard to the ground, crashing into one nearby bush. To his credit, he didn't fight the roll or even try to break his fall. He went right over and came back out low, scrambling for Tuntun's legs.

The elf straightened and stiffened, and leaned forward over the lunging boy's head and shoulders.

Tuntun's strength surprised Elbryan, for he could not break the elf's position, and then he was surprised even more as Tuntun locked her hands together and brought them down hard onto the tender area just below Elbryan's right shoulder blade.

The boy felt the strength leave that side of his body. He staggered down again, was barely even conscious that his hold on the elf was broken. He noted the elf's spring, heard the wings fluttering. He went up fast to his knees, realizing that he was vulnerable. He heard a snicker, then felt the explosion as Tuntun, half turning and landing easily on one foot right between the boy's ankles, let fly a kick with the other, up between Elbryan's thighs to catch him right in the groin.

The boy went down hard, clutching and groaning, feeling suddenly weak and nauseous.

"Tuntun!" he heard Juraviel protest, and it seemed to him as if the elf's voice had come from far away.

"He fights like a human," Tuntun answered indignantly.

"He *is* a human!" Juraviel reminded.

"All the more reason to kick him hard." The laughter from the forest was painful to Elbryan, at least as much as his wounded groin. He remained on the ground for a very long time, eyes closed, curled in a fetal position.

Finally, he opened his eyes and rolled to find Juraviel alone standing near him. The elf offered a hand, but Elbryan stubbornly refused, struggling shakily to his feet.

"Suffer the barbs, my young friend," Juraviel offered. "They are not without merit."

"Lick a bloody cap," Elbryan cursed, a common insult among humans, but one referring to powries. Elbryan hardly knew what a "bloody cap" was, and so the meaning of his own curse was lost on him.

It wasn't lost on Juraviel, though, for the elf had battled the fierce, evil powries many times over the centuries. Recognizing the boy's ultimate distress and embarrassment, Juraviel generously let the insult pass.

Elbryan walked a crooked path to the food and stubbornly salvaged what he could. That done, he hoisted the last basket and started back the half mile to the trough.

Juraviel followed silently, some distance behind. He wanted to make the most of Tuntun's painful lesson, but he wasn't sure that Elbryan was in any frame of mind to learn.

Titters came at Elbryan from the shadows several times as he walked. He ignored them, didn't even hear them, lost in his self-pity, consumed by frustrated rage. He felt so alone and isolated, felt as if he would have been better off had these vile elves not come and rescued him from the fomorian.

Back at the trough, Elbryan began his more difficult work. He took up one of the saturated stones and squeezed it with all his strength over the trough. When the porous thing was light once more, the flavored bog water extracted, Elbryan tossed it near the basket and took up the next. All too soon, before he had even finished with the first basket, his forearms ached from the effort.

Juraviel walked past Elbryan to the trough and dipped his cupped hands in. He stared at the water for a moment, eyeing its hue, then sniffed its delicate bouquet. The combination of bog water and milk-stones, as the elves called them, produced some of the sweetest juices in all of Corona. From this raw product, the elves would make their intoxicating wine, *Questel ni'touel* to the elves, but known to the wide world simply as "boggle." The swamplike connotation of the name was usually completely lost on the humans, who thought the term a mere reference to their state of mind after but a few sips of the potent liquid. Not that many humans had ever tasted the elixir, for the elves did not deal openly in the juice. Their contacts in the wide human world were discrete and few, but the elves did enough trading so that they could bring desired items, curiosity pieces mostly, and a sampling of songs of the few human bards who could bring them pleasure, into their valley.

"A good take today," Juraviel commented, hoping to draw the boy from his sour mood.

Elbryan grunted and did not reply. He took up another stone, held it high over the trough and squeezed with all his might, hoping to splash the juices enough to wet Juraviel.

The elf was too quick and wary for that.

Juraviel nodded at the surprising effect, though, taking note of the boy's gain in strength after just a few short weeks. He thought to leave Elbryan then, but decided to try one last time to calm the boy, to put a positive meaning on the embarrassing and painful lesson. "It is good that you have such spirit," Juraviel said, "and better still that you keep it under such control."

"Not so tight a rein," Elbryan replied, growling with each word. To accentuate his point, Elbryan lifted the next stone, and, instead of holding it over the trough, hurled it into the brush nearby, an act of defiance and of finality. Even if he went and retrieved it, the liquid within the stone had been tainted and was no good.

Juraviel stared solemnly at the spot where the stone had bounced for a long moment. He tried to view things through Elbryan's eyes, tried to sympathize with the frustration, tried to remember the terrible tragedy the youngster had suffered just this past season.

It was no good. For whatever had happened, today and in the days and weeks before, this stubborn behavior could only lead to disaster. Juraviel turned on Elbryan swiftly and suddenly, wings lifting the elf into a short hop. One hand grabbed the back of Elbryan's hair, the other cupped under the boy's chin, and though Elbryan, at least as strong as the elf, got his arms up to defend, when Juraviel turned his arms, turned Elbryan's head, the boy had no chance to resist. Juraviel took full advantage, put Elbryan off balance and kept on twisting, angling the boy over the trough. Quite a bit of juice might be ruined, but Juraviel figured the loss was worth it.

He put Elbryan's head under the liquid, brought him up, sputtering, then dunked him again. The third time, he held the boy under for what seemed like minutes, and when he brought Elbryan up and subsequently let him go, the stunned boy fell to the ground, gasping desperately.

"I am your friend," Belli'mar Juraviel said sternly. "But let us both understand the situation from the proper perspective. You are *n'Touel'alfar*, not of the People. You have been brought into Andur'Blough Inninness to be trained in the way of the rangers. This is fact; it has begun and there can be no turning back. If you fail in this, if you do not prove yourself worthy of elven friendship, you cannot be let out into the world with the knowledge you have attained of our home and of our ways."

Even as Elbryan started to protest, horrified at the thought of becoming a prisoner, Juraviel finished grimly, "Nor can you stay."

Elbryan's thoughts shifted to the illogic of it all. He couldn't leave, and he couldn't stay. How could that be?

The boy's jaw drooped as he realized the only remaining possibility, as he considered that Tuntun would carry out his execution, if Juraviel would not, without hesitation.

Humbled, he said not a word, but went right back to his work, as Juraviel left him.

That night, Elbryan sat upon the bare hillock that he claimed as his own, under the starry canopy, alone with his thoughts. Images, memories of the time of his past life, a few weeks that sometimes seemed as a few minutes and other times a few centuries, careened about the edges of his consciousness. He tried to concentrate on the present, on the simple beauty of the starry sky, or on the future, the questions of infinity, of eternity. Inevitably, though, that led Elbryan to thoughts of mortality and thus to the recent fate of his family and friends.

Piled in the emotional jumble were Elbryan's mixed feelings concerning the elves. He did not understand these creatures, so gay and full of almost childish spirit at one moment, so deadly and stern at the next. Even Juraviel! Elbryan had thought the elf his friend, and perhaps Juraviel was, in his own inhuman way, but the ferocity and ease with which Juraviel had put the boy under the trough water was amazing and frightening. Elbryan had always thought himself a bit of a warrior. He had killed goblins, after all, though his body was far from maturity. Yet measured against the speed and agility of the elves, the fluidity of their movements, substituting perfect balance for lack of weight and strength, Elbryan truly felt a novice. Juraviel, lighter and smaller, had put him down with astounding ease, a simple movement for which Elbryan had no counter.

So now here he was, in a land enchanting and terrifying, sharing the forest with these creatures that he could not understand and could not defeat. Sitting on that hillock that night, Elbryan felt as if he were alone in the universe, as if everything around him—the world and the elves, the goblins that had attacked Dundalis and the folk he had known in the village—were but a dream, *his* dream. Elbryan realized the arrogance of that notion, an almost sinful pride, but he was so much out of control, so insignificant, so vulnerable, that he suffered the barbs of his conscience for the sake of his sensibilities.

On that hillock, under that sky, Elbryan dared to play God, and that emotional game allowed him to sleep finally in peace and to wake with the determination to go on, with the gritty confidence that today, this day, he would eat hot stew for lunch. He collected his baskets and ran for the bog.

And when he slipped back beside the tenth and last basket, he saw steam still rising from his tea.

It was difficult, exhausting work, repeated every day, endlessly. But it was not without its benefits. As the weeks became months, and they became a year, and then two, Elbryan was hardly recognizable as the short gangly boy that Jilseponie had once beat up. His legs grew strong and agile from carrying loads and dodging traps. His chest and shoulders grew broad and thick, and his arms, particularly his forearms, bulged with iron-hard muscles.

By the tender age of sixteen, Elbryan Wyndon was stronger than Olwan had been.

And Olwan had been the strongest man in Dundalis.

❖ 11 ❖

Cat-the-Stray

"Corner table, Cat," called Graevis Chilichunk, the barkeep and proprietor of Fellowship Way, reputedly the finest inn in all the great city of Palmaris. Fellowship Way, or the Way, as it was commonly called, was not a large establishment, boasting only a dozen small, private rooms and a single common bedroom in the upstairs guest quarters, and a tavern that could hold no more than a hundred, and that with most folks standing. But Graevis, a fat, balding man, perpetually smiling, full of laughter and cheer and with the warmest of hearts, had made the place the best of the cheapest, so to speak. The noble visitors to Palmaris mostly stayed at the more haughty establishments, those near or within the duke's castle, but for those who knew, for the lesser merchants and the frequent wanderers, there was no better place in the world than Fellowship Way. In the Way, a single piece of silver would get you a hot meal, and a mere smile, whether you were a paying customer or not, would coax from Graevis or from most of the other usual patrons or workers a marvelous tale. In the Way, the hearth was always blazing, the beds were always soft, and the song was always loud.

The young woman sighed deeply, paused a moment, then consciously worked hard to erase the perpetual frown from her face as she made her way to the three men calling her from the corner table. She was aware of their eyes upon her as she approached; always the men looked at her that way. She was in her mid-teens, but had the shapely body of a woman five years older. She was not tall, just four inches above five feet, but that only made her golden hair appear even thicker and longer. She brushed at it and shook it as she crossed the room, for with her sweat and the grease from the meal she had just helped prepare, it clung uncomfortably to her neck.

"Ah, the pretty lady!" one of the men cooed. "Be a good girl for me," he added, winking lewdly.

The young woman—Cat-the-Stray, she was called by the folk of the Way—tried unsuccessfully to hide her scowl. She caught herself quickly, though, and covered it with a smirk she thought must have appeared, at least a little, as a smile. Not that the seated drunk was even looking at her face; his eyes never seemed to angle quite that high.

Another deep breath steadied her. She thought of Graevis, dear Graevis, the man who had rescued her from a past she could not remember, the man who had taken in a broken little girl and, with his warm smile and warm heart, helped her to heal, at least enough so that she had become functional once again. Out of the corner of her eye, she noticed the movements, a dance they seemed, of Pettibwa Chilichunk, Graevis' boisterous wife. When she had first come to know the woman, Cat had thought her simple. Pettibwa was forever laughing, dancing with her tray from one table to the next. She got pinched at every stop, hugged by every patron who left at night, but she never seemed to care. Indeed, Pettibwa loved every moment of it. If she had a free hand when a man pinched her on her ample buttocks, she would pinch him right back; often she would grab a man along the path of her table-to-table dance and sweep him with her across the room. And it was all done in such good fun that neither Graevis nor any suitor of her unsuspecting dance partner ever seemed to care.

It took grim Cat a long while to learn the truth of Pettibwa. The woman was not simple, far from it. Pettibwa just had an unrivaled love of life and of other people.

Cat loved her—as much as she had loved her own mother, she believed, for though she could not remember her own mother, she couldn't imagine loving anyone more. Sometimes that thought only made the young woman even sadder than usual.

She took the order from the three—no surprise here, just three more mugs of the cheapest ale—then turned to the bar. She stopped short when the winker gave her rump a solid slap, and she stood there, suffering their laughter. She wanted to turn and lay him out flat on the floor, and anyone who had witnessed Cat's temper knew that she could have done it easily enough, but her eyes met the gaze of Graevis, soaking in his smile. By all his motions—bobbing head, sparkling brown eyes—he was silently telling her to let it pass.

Not that Graevis wouldn't protect her. He had taken her in, heart and soul, and loved her at least as much as he loved his own son, the surly Grady. No man would ever take advantage of Cat while Graevis drew breath—and Pettibwa, too, for that matter—but in the Way, a slap on the rump was not to be made into a big deal, especially not considering the everyday actions of the boisterous proprietress.

The young woman didn't look back as she made her way across the crowded floor to get the drinks.

"Take it as a compliment, me deary," Pettibwa remarked in her "commoner accent," as she strolled to the bar beside her adopted daughter.

"I shall have to wash my dress in the morning," Cat-the-Stray replied, her speech not as stilted as the older woman's, though it hinted at her four years with the Chilichunks.

"Bah, ye're always so serious!" Pettibwa replied, pinching the young woman's cheek. "Sure'n ye've come to know the feelings ye stir in menfolk."

The young woman blushed and looked away.

"No, ye're not a pretty one, now are ye?" Pettibwa cooed with smiling sarcasm, stroking Cat's hair. "If only ye'd smile, me girl, then all the world'd be smiling back at ye."

The young woman closed her eyes and felt the gentle, unthreatening stroke on her hair. Had her mother done it that way? She sensed that her hair had been much shorter then, back when she was young and all the world seemed a great adventure, back when the devils were just fireside stories to make your skin tingle or imagined demons upon whom children could wage war.

The moment ended all too soon, Cat-the-Stray tuning back to the bustle of the lively room about her. She offered a meek smile and a nod to Pettibwa, who returned them with a wink. The older woman collected her tray and rushed away, blending into the continuing party just a step from the bar.

"If he's to bother ye, ye just be letting me know about it," Graevis said to her as he put the three ales in front of her. "Ye're not to play with him if ye're not wanting to."

Cat-the-Stray nodded and smiled weakly again. She knew that Graevis spoke truthfully; she, and not the patrons, was in control in here. But she knew, too, the atmosphere of the Way, and the last thing in the world the young woman wanted was to make things difficult for Graevis and Pettibwa, her saviors.

She took up her tray and weaved across the room, getting back to the corner table with hardly a drop spilled. Master Wink-and-Slap twisted his face at her again and gave a breathless burst of laughter, his throat no doubt numb from the drink. "Might that we be getting together when the hearth's burning low," he stated more than asked. "I've a gold piece to be rid of."

Again that hoarse laughter, this time accompanied by the other two.

Cat ignored it and methodically placed the mugs on the table.

"Two gold, then, and ye best be worth it," the dirty man offered, and when Cat continued to ignore him, he roughly grabbed her by the arm.

Her other hand came across, hooked his thumb, and bent it back over his wrist so quickly that the man, senses blurred by drink, hardly understood what was happening. Suddenly he was off balance, and then he was sitting on the floor, the pretty barmaid gliding out of reach. His friends howled with glee.

Cat suffered his insults, but couldn't dismiss the realization that Pettibwa would have handled it differently, better. Pettibwa would have proclaimed that two gold was an insult to a woman of her talents, and might have gone on to insist that she would never bed a man, no matter the money, who did not understand the meaning of the word "bath."

Pettibwa would have extracted herself delicately, subtly, turning the joke back on the rude man, making him the fool but with such cunning that he probably wouldn't even realize it until she was across the room.

Now, the man continued sputtering. Cat caught the word "whore," and then she was not surprised to see Graevis, several of the other regulars in tow, crossing the room, their faces suddenly grim.

Cat suffered the inevitable apology, the insincere man only offering it at the end of his twisted arm. The young woman pointedly turned away then, not wanting to watch as Graevis none too gently threw the drunk out into the street, and then pushed his two wretched friends out behind him.

Perhaps worst of all for the young woman were the host of other eager young men ready to defend her honor, offering everything from a thrashing of the man to his very life. One in particular, handsomely dressed and well groomed, with light brown eyes that sparkled with intelligence and a calm demeanor that hinted at good breeding, nodded the young woman's way and smiled slightly, an invitation for Cat to name him as her champion. She eyed the young man for a long moment—the way he sat, the way he moved—and she had no doubt that he was well trained in the use of the slender sword that hung comfortably at his hip. On a single word from her, he would thrash all three of the drunks to within an inch of their lives.

Cat knew it, and knew that many others would have defended her as well. That should have come as a compliment, but Cat-the-Stray hated being the center of attention, hated the patronizing, the would-be heroes, who, with the sole exception of Graevis, wanted exactly the same thing as the bounced drunk. Their course was more gentlemanly, less straight-forward, but their goal through honor, Cat knew, was precisely the same as the drunk had attempted through offered gold.

She worked for another hour, and when her smile did not return, Graevis graciously bade her to take an early night. Cat resisted, fearing that her leaving would only put more work on Pettibwa's shoulders, but the older woman pooh-poohed that notion and almost forced Cat through the side door, into the family's private chambers. Cat looked back apprecia-tively, and over Pettibwa's large round shoulder, she saw again the hand-some well-dressed young man, watching her go, lifting his glass of wine in apparent toast to her.

She scurried away, suddenly uncomfortable.

All the bustle of the common room disappeared as soon as the heavy door was closed, leaving the young woman in happy solitude—almost, for a moment later, she noticed that Grady Chilichunk was in the house, moving about his little room.

Cat sighed again; the last thing she wanted now was to spend any time near Grady. He was a handsome man of thirty years, nearly twice Cat's age, with sharp brown eyes. Physically, by all accounts, he was the image of his father in Graevis' younger days, but by Cat's estimation, Grady could not have been more different than Graevis in temperament. Since her first days in the house, Grady had made the young woman uncomfortable. Not in a lewd way, like the drunk in the bar, or even in a teasing way, like the handsome young man. In four years, Grady had never once looked at the flowering young woman lustfully. To Cat-the-Stray, his adopted sister, he was always polite, too polite. Stiff even, and as the young woman had grown wiser to the ways of the world, she came to understand that Grady saw her as a threat to what he considered his rightful inheritance.

It wasn't that Grady honestly cared for Fellowship Way. He was hardly ever in the place. He liked the money the establishment brought in, though, and the young woman already understood that if Graevis and Pettibwa left Fellowship Way to her, even partially, Grady would not be pleased.

"What are you doing in here?" he asked, coming from his room. His proper speech rang in sharp contrast to the street dialect of his parents. Grady saw himself as above that lowly station, Cat understood. He fancied himself an important man, and frequented the more expensive establishments near the duke's castle, and had even been in the castle on many occasions. It struck Cat that he must know the well-dressed gentleman in the bar; perhaps the man had even come to the Way on Grady's invitation.

"Have you no work?" he snapped at her.

Cat-the-Stray bit her lip, not liking his condescending tone. "I've done more this one night than you have in the last two seasons," she replied.

Grady glared at her. "Some were made to work in life," he began evenly, "others to live and enjoy."

Cat decided that it wasn't worth arguing. She shook her head, tossed her apron to the back of a nearby chair, gathered up her cloak, and headed out into the Palmaris night.

A chill breeze was blowing off the gulf, moaning as it wound its way past the many two- and three-story houses of the great city. Palmaris was second in size in all the Kingdom of Honce-the-Bear only to Ursal, the throne seat, further upriver, though neither were reputedly as populous as the great, crowded cities of the southern kingdom of Behren. To Cat-the-Stray, who had grown up on the edge of the Wilderlands, in a village where ten people together was considered a crowd, the place had, at first, been overwhelming. Even now, after nearly four years in Palmaris, when she knew every street, where to go, where to avoid, and when the dark image of the great Masur Delaval and the smell of brine and the wind filled with crisp wetness had become very familiar to her, she could not consider the place her home. Even now, surrounded by the love of the Chilichunks, the place was not home, could never replace the fleeting image of a cabin that she held so dear.

She loved Graevis and Pettibwa, even Grady, but they were not, could not be, her parents, and Grady would never take the place of a true friend she sensed that she had once known.

Cat-the-Stray winced as the thoughts careened back in time. She had blocked away so much, could only remember fleeting images, a certain look, a kiss that she wasn't even sure had really happened. And the name, all the names, were gone from her mind—that was the worst thing of all! She could not remember her friend's name, could not remember her own name!

"Cat-the-Stray," she whispered distastefully into the cold night air, watching the mist of her breath float away, and wishing the title would go with it. It had been given to her affectionately, she knew, and with all sympathy for her pitiful predicament, and so she had not argued.

The young woman made her way around the back of the inn, down a dark alley that inspired no fear, and up a gutter, to the one section of Fellowship Way's roof that was not slanted. The lights of Palmaris spread wide before her, the lights of the night sky wide above her. This was her secret place, her place of contemplation. She came up here as often as her duties allowed to be alone with her memories, to try to piece together who she was and where she had come from.

She remembered wandering into a village, dirty and wounded, covered in soot and blood. She remembered the tender manner in which she had been brought in, followed by relentless questions that she could not answer. Then came the long journey, tagging along with a merchant caravan that had swapped crafted items to the people of the small frontier village in exchange for pelts and great trees that would be used as masts for the sailing ships built in Palmaris. Graevis Chilichunk had been on that caravan, coming north to the Wilderlands to pick up some very special wine, boggle by name. He had taken to the poor lost girl—he was the one who had given the girl the name of Cat-the-Stray—and the villagers had been more than willing to part with the orphan and with many of their own weaker folk, since they were in fear of a raid similar to the one that had sacked the neighboring settlement, Cat's settlement.

Cat rested back against a sooty chimney, the warm bricks taking a bit of the bite from the night chill.

Why couldn't she remember the name of her village or of the one where Graevis had found her? On several occasions, she had started to ask Pettibwa and Graevis about it, but every time she had stopped short, some part of her fearing to remember. Neither of her adopted parents pressed her to remember; Cat had overheard them talking one night, making a pact that they would let the girl heal in her own time. "Perhaps she will never remember," Pettibwa had said. "Perhaps that would be better."

"And she's got her new name now," Graevis agreed. "Though if I'd've thought it would stick, I'd've chosen differently!"

And they laughed, and it was not in any way an insult to the girl, just their joy at being able to help one so in need.

Cat loved them with all her heart. Now, though, she was beginning to think it was time for her to figure out who she was and where she had come from. She looked up at the sky. Some streaks of clouds had moved in, giving a different perspective to those stars still visible. It was often possible to look at familiar things in a different way, Cat realized. She let the night canopy absorb her, used it to filter back through the painful barriers. She had seen this sky all her life and used that commonality to recall another place.

She remembered running up a forested slope, looking back to her village, nestled in a sheltered vale, and then turning her gaze above it, to the southern sky, to the faint colors of the Halo.

"The Halo," Cat-the-Stray muttered, and she realized that she had not seen the phenomenon since she had come to Palmaris. Her face screwed up with concern. Did such a thing as the Halo even exist, or was her memory a mere fantasy?

If it did exist, then her memory was correct, then she had found yet another image of her lost life.

She considered going back into the Way and inquiring about this Halo right then, but her concentration was broken by a sharp, metallic sound.

Somebody was climbing up the gutter.

Cat did not get overalarmed—until she saw a familiar dirty face come over the edge of the roof.

"Ah, me lovely," said the drunk from the bar. "So ye come up here to meet with me."

"Be on your way," Cat warned, but the man rolled up over the edge of the roof and started to rise.

"Oh, I'll be having me way," he said, and then Cat heard yet another man coming up the gutter, and realized she was in trouble. They had followed her, all three, and she knew well enough what they meant to do to her.

Quick as her namesake, the young woman leaped across and put her knee heavily into the drunk's chest, knocking him flat to the roof. She slapped away his grabbing hands, then slugged him twice in the face.

Then she was up, meeting the second intruder with a foot in his face as his head came above the roof edge. His head snapped back; he started to say something in protest, and Cat kicked him again, right in the jaw.

With a groan, he fell away into the blackness, dropping heavily atop the last of the three, then both of them going down hard to the cobblestones. Two kicks and two down, but it had taken too long. Even as Cat started to turn back for the first, the drunk's arms came about her and locked about her chest, squeezing her tight.

She felt his hot breath on her neck, smelled the stench of the cheap ale. "There, there, me pretty one," he whispered. "If ye're not to fight me, ye'll like it all the more."

He nibbled her earlobe, or tried to, but she snapped her head back hard into his face, stunning him.

The one memory that Cat-the-Stray held completely from her past was not an image or a name, but a feeling, a deep frustrated rage. She let that memory out now, on the roof of Fellowship Way in Palmaris. She let all the tears and all the unanswered screams come out, channeled them into a level of violence that the drunk could not have foreseen.

Her hands raked at his arms; she stuck one arm between her torso and the drunk's arm, and let her legs fall out from under her, twisting and squirming.

"Might be more the fun if ye fight!" the drunk squealed, but he wasn't paying attention and had let the young woman get her face close to his clenched hands.

Cat-the-Stray clamped her teeth over one of his knuckles and bit him hard.

"Ah, ye whore!" he yelled, and lifted his other hand to pound her.

But he had broken his grip, and Cat turned and ducked, accepting the blow across the back of her shoulders, not even feeling it through the turmoil of her emotions. She came around and up and right back in, clawing at his face, raking for his eyes. He pulled her hands out wide, and she used the opening to head-butt him again.

She tore her hands free and grabbed him by the hair. He punched her hard on the side of the head, but she only loosed a feral scream, and tugged down hard with both her hands, while she jumped and curled one leg. She heard the crack of bone as her knee connected with his face. He shot back up straight, then fell over backward, but Cat was not done with him.

She came in hard, screaming all the while, driving her knee into his throat.

"Enough!" he whined, gagged. "I'll let ye be."

That wasn't the point; Cat would not let him be. She hit him a score of heavy blows; she kicked him, she bit him, she clawed him. Finally, battered and bleeding from a dozen wounds, he managed to get to his feet and he ran headlong to the ledge and dove right over it.

Following across the roof, Cat noticed that there was a light below in the alley. She came to the edge, expecting one of the man's companions to be coming up the gutter, and hoping that to be the case.

She stopped, taken fully by surprise. The drunk lay very still, groaning softly, blood running from his many wounds and from the side of his broken head. The man she had kicked from the gutter was down as well, sitting against the building wall across the alley, one hand supporting him, the other clutching his shin. The leg had splintered in the fall; Cat could see the jagged edge of a bone poking through the skin.

The third drunk was up, hands high above his head and facing the wall directly below Cat, a sword's pointed tip tight against the middle of his back.

"I heard a scream," said the handsome man from the Way, the one with the sparkling light brown eyes, the one with the purest white smile. "I took my leave soon after you departed," he explained, "figuring there was nothing left in the place worth watching."

Cat felt the blood rushing to her face.

"Some hero I prove to be," the man said, bringing his sword back in a salute to the young woman. "By my eyes, it seems as if I saved these three!"

Cat-the-Stray had no idea what to respond to the gallant man. Her rage bubbled away, and she turned from the alley, walking back into the solitude of the darkened rooftop.

After a few uncomfortable minutes, the man called up to her, but before she could answer, she heard a commotion as several others, Graevis among them, came rushing into the alley.

Cat-the-Stray didn't want to face them. She was embarrassed, she was ashamed, and she just wanted to be left alone. That was not possible, she realized, nor could she slip down the other side of the building without having half of Palmaris searching frantically for her. She took a deep breath and moved to the gutter, then down, meeting the eyes of no one, falling into the bosom of Pettibwa as soon as she spotted the woman, and whispering for Pettibwa to please take her to her room.

❖ 12 ❖

The Windrunner

The hours were endless, up before the dawn and not to bed again until the midnight hour had passed. Brothers Avelyn, Quintall, Pellimar, and Thagraine learned to survive, even thrive, on no more than four hours of sleep. They were taught the deepest forms of meditation, where a twenty-minute break afforded them all the recuperation they needed to press on with their training for several more hours. They studied with their respective classmates throughout the day, learning their religious duties and expectations, the day-to-day functions of the abbey, and the fighting techniques. After vespers, the training shifted to lessons concerning the sacred stones—the collection process, the preparation ceremony immediately after collection, and the various magical properties of each type of stone. In addition, all four were taught the ways of the sea, spending many hours on a small boat rocking in the waves on the rough, frigid waters of All Saints Bay.

Avelyn could not keep up with his three companions in the matters of fighting or seamanship; and in the religious training, the young brother grew more and more frustrated. It seemed that as every ceremony became ingrained within him, it lost a bit of its mystery, and thus, its holiness. Were the fifteen Holy Orders of God, the rules of righteousness, truly God inspired, or were they merely rules of keeping order within a civilized society? Such questions would have broken Avelyn were it not for the training after the sun had set. For in the Ring Stones, the young man found his ideals satisfied. The mysteries of stone magic could not be explained away by human desires of control and order. To Avelyn, these stones were truly the gift of God, the magic of the heavens, the promise of eternal life and glory.

So he suffered the brutal hours of the day, the fighting in which Quintall almost always bested him. By the beginning of the third year, the level of jealousy among the four began to rise noticeably. Avelyn and Thagraine had been formally named as the Preparers, the two monks who would leave the chartered ship and go onto the island of Pimaninicuit to collect and prepare the stones, while Quintall and Pellimar would remain aboard, going onto the island only should one of the chosen pair falter. Sea journeys were not considered safe in God's Year 821, the year of the stone showers, and replacements might become necessary.

Quintall was easily the best of the four in matters of martial arts. The man was impossibly strong, his stocky frame and low center of gravity giving him the leverage he needed to punish Avelyn endlessly. On more than one occasion, the lanky Avelyn was convinced that Quintall meant to kill him. What better way to get to Pimaninicuit?

The thought was more than a little unsettling to gentle Avelyn Desbris, and he thought it ironic that Quintall's anger was no more than proof that he, and not the stocky, ferocious man, was the better choice for Pimaninicuit. Avelyn knew in his heart that if the situation were reversed, if Quintall and not he had been chosen to go to the island, he would support the man with all his heart, taking his comfort in the fact that he was allowed to go on the journey and holding faith that the masters, and not he, were better judges of the students. Besides, at night, and especially on those occasions when the chosen students actually handled the stones, Brother Avelyn easily proved that he was the proper choice. By the fourth year, none, not even the masters, could bring forth the stone magic more completely, more effortlessly, than Avelyn. Even skeptical Master Siherton, whatever reservations he continued to hold about Avelyn as a fellow human being, had to admit that the man was the obvious choice, the God-given choice, for Pimaninicuit. Siherton maintained his tight bond with Quintall and lobbied for the younger man to be included—as Thagraine's replacement and not Avelyn's. By the third year, Master Siherton also became invaluable as a mediator between the two rivals from the class of God's Year 816, coaxing Quintall into easing up on his jealousy of Avelyn.

The first three months of God's Year 821 were full of excitement and anticipation throughout St.-Mere-Abelle. Nearly every day—when the weather was calm enough for the younger monks to go out into the courtyard—the students would glance repeatedly at the dark waters of All Saints Bay, shaking their heads whenever an iceberg floated by but always remarking that it would not be long. As Bafway, the third month, whose end marked the spring equinox, neared, the whispers became a contest to see who might first spot the square sails of the chartered ship.

Bafway proved to be a long, uneventful month. The spring equinox passed, and every time the weather seemed to be improving, another cold front would sweep down from Alpinador, chopping the waters of All Saints Bay into frothing, threatening whitecaps.

As the fourth month, Toumanay, slipped past, the quiet whispers became open discussions, with even the older brothers—even some of the masters—joining in, the older and more experienced holy men admitting that this was indeed a blessed time and a ship was indeed on its way to St.-Mere-Abelle. The only secret remained the subsequent destination of that ship, for only the masters and the four chosen monks knew the magical name Pimaninicuit.

Brother Avelyn's thoughts were full of that island and of the long voyage ahead of him. He hardly considered the dangers, though he knew from his studies that on several occasions, the monks who had set out for Pimaninicuit had never returned, taken by storms or powries or by the great serpents of the Mirianic Ocean. Even on successful voyages to Pimaninicuit, more often than not, one or more of the four monks did not return, for disease was a very real fact of life aboard ship. What Avelyn focused on, therefore, was the destination, the isle itself. From the texts he had studied, he conjured images of lush gardens and exotic flowers, pictured himself standing in a garden with multicolored stones raining down around him, divine music playing in the air. He would run barefoot through the stones, would roll in them, would bask in his God.

Avelyn knew the absurdity of his fantasy, of course. When the showers arrived, he and his fellow Preparer would be hidden underground, sheltered from the pelting meteors. Even after the showers ceased, the pair would have to wait some time before handling the heated stones, and then the work would be too furious and desperate to pause and contemplate God.

But for all the harsh reality, for all the possibilities that he would not survive, Avelyn watched the watery horizon for hint of those square sails most intently of all. To his thinking, this was the pinnacle of his existence, the greatest joy that a monk of St.-Mere-Abelle might know, the closest, before death, that he could ever get to his God.

Toumanay was less than half finished when the two-masted caravel appeared, gliding swiftly through the choppy waters to the sheltered harbor before St.-Mere-Abelle. Avelyn spent the entirety of the morning in silent prayer, as instructed, and was shaking so badly when he was at last summoned to Father Abbot Markwart's chambers that Master Jojonah had to lend him a supporting arm. The other three chosen were already in the spacious office when Avelyn and Jojonah arrived. All of the masters of St.-Mere-Abelle were there, along with the Father Abbot and two men Avelyn did not know, one tall and slender, the other shorter, much older, and so skinny that Avelyn wondered if he had eaten in a month. Avelyn quickly discerned that the taller man was obviously the captain of the chartered vessel. He stood with an air of superiority, posture perfect, hand on gilded rapier. He had a garish scar running from ear to chin that seemed to Avelyn somehow gallant, and, unlike his scruffy companion, he was clean shaven except for a neatly trimmed mustache, rolling out from the sides of his mouth and curling up. His eyes were dark brown, so dark that the pupil was hardly distinguishable from the iris; his hair was long and black and curly, and under one arm he had tucked a great hat, with an upturned brim and a feather on one side. The rest of his dress, though weathered, was rich, particularly a golden brocade and jewel-studded baldric. That garment held Avelyn's attention acutely, for he sensed that at least one of those jewels, a small ruby, was more than ornamental.

Avelyn tried not to stare, confused as to why this man, who was not of the Order of St.-Mere-Abelle, was in possession of a sacred stone—and right in front of Father Abbot Markwart! Surely the Father Abbot and the masters recognized the jewel for what it was.

Avelyn calmed quickly; surely they did recognize the jewel, and apparently, it did not bother them. Perhaps, the younger brother reasoned, the stone had been given as payment for the ship, or perhaps it had only been loaned, a helpful tool for the perilous voyage. Avelyn shook it all away.

The older man caught Avelyn's attention only because of his constant squinting, his bulbous eyes darting about nervously from man to man, head bobbing and trembling on his turkey neck. His clothing seemed nearly as old as he, worn out so badly in many places that Avelyn could see the darkly tanned skin beneath. He was dirty and gray, his hair cropped short and badly trimmed, and his beard untended. Avelyn had once heard the term "salty dog" in reference to seamen, and he thought that appropriate indeed for this one.

"Brother Quintall, Brother Pellimar, Brother Thagraine, and Brother Avelyn," the Father Abbot said, indicating each monk, and each, in turn, bowing to their guests. "I give you Captain Adjonas of the good ship *Windrunner*, and his first hand, Bunkus Smealy." The proud captain made no motion, but Bunkus bowed to each in turn so violently that he nearly toppled, and would have, had it not been for his proximity to Father Abbot Markwart's huge desk.

"Captain Adjonas knows your course," Markwart finished, "and you may trust that his is the finest ship on the Mirianic."

"The tide will be favorable an hour after the dawn," Adjonas said in a clear and strong voice—a voice befitting a man of his station, Avelyn thought. "If we miss the tide, we will lose an entire day." The stern man steeled his gaze upon each of the four monks, letting them know right up front that the ship was his domain. "That would not be a wise thing to do. We shall be running against the weather at least until we have turned south of All Saints Bay. Each day we spend this far north brings the very real chance of complete ruin."

The four young monks exchanged glances; Avelyn was sympathetic to the captain's wishes and actually took some comfort in the man's commanding, if cold, demeanor. He saw that his three companions apparently didn't share his feelings, for Quintall openly scowled as if he were offended by a mere ship's captain speaking so forcefully to him.

Father Abbot Markwart, also sensing the sudden tension, cleared his throat loudly. "You are dismissed," he said to the four, "to an early meal and to your rooms. You are excused from all your duties this day, and all the ceremonies. Make your peace with God and prepare yourselves for the task before you."

They left the office then, unescorted, and Quintall began openly complaining even as the door shut behind them.

"Captain Adjonas will be in for a long journey indeed if he thinks that he commands," the stocky man said, to the nodding replies of both Thagraine and Pellimar.

"It is his ship," Avelyn said simply.

"A ship bought," Quintall replied immediately and brusquely. "Adjonas commands his crew to execute the task they were paid to do, but he does not command us. Understand that now. On the *Windrunner*, you and Thagraine answer only to Pellimar, and Pellimar answers only to me."

Avelyn had no response to that. The pecking order for the voyage had indeed been determined in just that manner. While Thagraine and Avelyn, as Preparers, were paramount to the mission, Quintall and Pellimar had been given higher positions on the voyage to and from Pimaninicuit. Avelyn could accept that. If things got rough out on the seas, as expected, Quintall, the most physically impressive of the four, would be best prepared to handle any situation.

Avelyn left the group then, heading for his room as the Father Abbot had ordered. He was some distance down the corridor and still he heard complaining near the Abbot's door. He suspected that Quintall and the others kept up their complaining for some time, long after he was kneeling beside his simple cot, falling deep into important prayer.

The morning ceremony was the grandest event that Avelyn had seen in his four and a half years at St.-Mere-Abelle. More than eight hundred monks, every member of the Order, including four score who were not living at the abbey any longer but were serving as missionaries all along All Saints Bay, lined the docks, lifting their voices in common song. The bells of the abbey pealed repeatedly, drawing curious onlookers from the nearby village of St.-Mere-Abelle. The ceremony began before dawn, intensified as the sun glistened on the horizon across the waters, then went on and on, one prayer after another, each song louder than the previous.

The four crewmen of the *Windrunner*'s boat, which was bouncing noisily against the wooden dock, sat through it all with smirking faces, thoroughly amused and certainly not impressed. As the day brightened, Avelyn could see the rest of the thirty-man crew lining the deck of the caravel, the ship resting at anchor some fifty yards out in the harbor.

The sailors cared nothing for this all-important mission, Avelyn realized, beyond their payment of gold—and whatever other trinkets Father Abbot Markwart had included in the bargain. Avelyn considered again the sacred stone woven into Captain Adjonas's baldric, and the thought disturbed him more than a little. If the man, like his crew, was so obviously nonreligious, then he should not possess such a gem, not for any reason.

This was just the first hint, Avelyn understood, and he began to suspect that the long voyage—they were expected to be away for near to eight months—would be trying in more ways than physical.

First hand Bunkus Smealy interrupted the ceremony an hour or so after the dawn, calling out in a crusty voice, "Time for going!"

Father Abbot Markwart, closest to the craft, looked at the man, then turned back to the suddenly quiet gathering. He motioned to Siherton, and the hawkish master led the four chosen brothers to the edge of the dock. "Go with God's graces," he said to each as he stepped into the rolling craft. Avelyn nearly fell over the side, and banged his leg hard against the edge of the dock. He caught the look that crossed between Quintall and Siherton. Quintall seemed disgusted, but Siherton was unbending, silently imparting to the aggravated Quintall that his duties were paramount to his personal feelings.

Avelyn watched that stare, and the return look Quintall offered to the master, and he understood that, while Quintall hated him and was jealous of him, the man would indeed protect him at all costs on the journey to and from the island.

Or at least, *to* the island.

Songs followed them out across the harbor, and Quintall led them up the netting to the deck of the *Windrunner*, where Captain Adjonas, face as stern as ever, waited.

"With your permission, sir," Quintall said evenly, as he had been instructed. Adjonas gave a curt nod, and Quintall paced by him, the other three monks in tow.

Avelyn remained at the taffrail—an ornate railing about waist high that encircled the stern deck—for some time, watching the walls of St.-Mere-Abelle diminish, as the drifting voices raised in joyous song faded. Soon the rugged hills of the coast were but a gray blur and the *Windrunner*, whose mainmast had appeared so tall and impressive in the sheltered harbor, seemed a tiny thing indeed, dwarfed by the overwhelming power of the vast Mirianic.

❖ 13 ❖

Running Fast Down a Long, Long Road

E lbryan froze as he heard the crusty snow crunch under his feet. His breath came slow and steady, and he let that sensation spread throughout his tense body, easing muscles, finding a solid harmony, a more perfect balance. He could see the deer's shoulder over the next rise. Its head had not come up; it had not heard the slight noise.

That slight noise had sounded so clearly to Elbryan!

The young man paused then to consider the extent of his progress. Only the previous autumn, his fourth in Andur'Blough Inninness, he had not been able to get within fifty feet of such a wary creature. Only the previous autumn, he would not even have noticed his last slight misstep. The elves had worked him hard, very hard. He continued his daily gathering of the milk-stones, though now he ate a hot meal every time, easily avoiding even the most cunning of the elvish traps. No longer was the rest of the day his own, though, for the elves had filled his afternoons and early evenings with lessons on the ways of beast and plant. He had learned to identify the various plants and their properties, often medicinal. Elbryan had learned to walk nearly silently—though he still thought himself clumsy when measured against the graceful elves! He had learned truly to understand and recognize the perspective of those animals watching him, that he might better blend into the forest background. He had learned to observe the world through the senses of each animal, understood now each creature's fears and needs. To a squirrel and a rabbit, he could become perfectly unthreatening, coaxing the beast to feed right from his hand. And to a deer, perhaps the most skittish creature of all . . .

He was barely a half dozen steps away, unnoticed, on open ground.

His focus went back to the task at hand, to the six most difficult steps of all. He considered the air around him, the slight breeze in his face. Winter was still present in this part of Andur'Blough Inninness, but its grip was fast loosening. The deer was having little trouble finding grass through the spotty layer of snow, and its treasurelike find had it, perhaps, a little less alert than usual.

Elbryan couldn't suppress his widening smile. Eagerness welled within him, the very real hope that this time he would touch that animal. He took another step, then another.

Too quickly, with too little time to find his center of balance.

The deer's head came up, ears twitching, scanning; Elbryan's smile vanished. He went forward with all speed, scrambling over the low ridge. He dove and reached, desperate to slap the creature, though he knew perfectly well that this kind of closing rush was not what Juraviel and Tuntun wanted from him.

Would his victory prove tainted?

The point was moot, anyway, for Elbryan never got close to touching the elusive deer. A single great leap sent the beast flying away, disappearing so quickly into the twigs and branches of the forest lining the small meadow that it was lost to Elbryan's sight before he ever recovered from his lunging roll.

The young man shifted to a sitting position and sagged on the wet ground. Juraviel came to him at once, the elf grinning and nodding. *"Elu touise!"* Juraviel exclaimed and patted the young man on the back. "So very close!"

"I lost control," Elbryan said despondently. "At the last, and most crucial moment, my eagerness overcame my movement."

"Ah, but you miss the point," the elf replied. "You *kept* control for all this time, closing perfectly."

"I did not touch the deer!"

"But you have approached the goal," Juraviel cried. "You have just begun, my young friend. "Think not of the failure but of the triumph. Never have you gotten this close; but you shall again, and when you do, you will know better and will temper your eagerness."

Elbryan looked at the elf long and hard, glad for the words. Put in that manner, this was indeed a day of celebration. He hadn't touched the deer, that was true, but his progress beyond his last few fumbling attempts was marked.

Just as the young man's smile began to widen, Tuntun came out of the brush, walking back from the spot where the deer had disappeared. She moved right in front of Elbryan and put her tiny hand up to his face.

He smelled the scent of deer on her fingers.

"Blood of Mather." Tuntun snorted sarcastically as she moved away, the all too familiar phrase that Elbryan had grown tired of years before. He looked back at Juraviel for support and found that the elf was working hard to hide his grin.

Elbryan sighed deeply. He tried to keep a perspective on his gains. Could any of the men of Dundalis, could his own father, have ever gotten that close to a deer? Still, Elbryan wasn't among those folk anymore, and in measuring his progress in all areas but physical strength against the elves of Andur'Blough Inninness, he felt a novice indeed. It was hard for the young man to appreciate all he had learned when he considered all he had left to learn.

Juraviel offered him a hand, and Elbryan took it, though in truth the elf could do little to help the large man rise. There was very little boyishness left in Elbryan's frame. He stood three inches over six feet, tall and muscular, and his two hundred and twenty lean, strong pounds put him at more than three times the weight of the average elf. Not that Juraviel and the others weren't strong; it constantly amazed Elbryan how much power an elf packed into its tiny frame, power he felt all too often in the sting of a practice sword's strike during his sparring sessions!

Together, with Tuntun nearby but comfortably—for herself *and* for Elbryan—out of sight, the pair enjoyed the fine day as they made their way to the southern end of the enchanted valley, the area of Andur'Blough Inninness where winter had never found a hold. They chatted easily, Juraviel doing most of the talking, explaining this plant and that, talking of ways to bind a wound, then shifting the subject back to where Elbryan had performed well and where he had failed in his quest to slap the deer. Such were Juraviel's methods, his enchanting and engrossing conversation techniques, that Elbryan hardly realized this to be perhaps the most important part of his training, these daily chats, anecdotal and enjoyable.

They walked down confusing trails, often branching, seeming to go in circles, seeming as if they merely ended until that apparent end was reached. Elbryan still could not navigate this area, but he was gaining some understanding. Juraviel let him lead often and corrected him whenever he went wrong—which was not often any longer—and soon the pair came into the low dell called Caer'alfar: Elvenhome. It was a place of thick grass and lines of trees, with houses built in the boughs above the ground. It was a place of flowers and song, where the forest was not so thick and the sky could be seen from many vantage points. This was the very center of the mist that blanketed Andur'Blough Inninness during the light of day, and yet Caer'alfar was rarely covered, a small hole remaining in the gray canopy, unnoticeable from anywhere but this low meadow, that the elves might enjoy the sun as well as the stars.

Dozens of elves were about this day, some sparring with practice weapons, others dancing. Some rested back against the trees or lay comfortably in the soft grass, drinking their sweet *Questel ni'touel* wine. Here and there debates sprang up concerning the value of the spirits and what they should bring in trade, for the spring caravan would soon depart, a group of elves going to their secret contacts in the frontier villages.

All in all, the peaceful scene struck a chord in Elbryan about how out of place he was, and yet, he somehow felt as if he belonged. He had been coming into Caer'alfar regularly since the turn of the year, and now the elves hardly gave him a thought as he walked in. No longer was he an outcast—he even joined in their nightly party of song and dance—and yet, he was so obviously different. For Elbryan, his entire existence seemed as it had been on those occasions many years back in Dundalis when his father and mother invited friends to the house. Sometimes Elbryan would be allowed to stay up late, sometimes he would even be allowed to join in their dice games for a bit before retiring. How grown up he had felt! And yet, he was not really a part of that game, of that group. His parents and their adult friends had accepted him with smiles that he now realized were somewhat condescending.

So it was with the elves. He could never truly be one of them.

He and Juraviel continued their conversation until Tuntun walked by, eyeing Elbryan derisively and tapping her smooth cheek and chin. Elbryan understood—so did Juraviel—and the elf motioned for the young man to go to his place. Above all else, the elves were meticulous about grooming. Elbryan was expected to bathe daily, to keep his clothing clean, and since his beard was splotchy and uneven, not yet that of a man, to keep his face clean shaven. That was the one task which always seemed to elude the young man—until Tuntun inevitably pointed it out—although, with the impossibly fine-edged elven knife, shaving was neither painful nor troublesome.

Elbryan moved grudgingly to his lodging, a low, wide house on the bottom boughs of a thick-limbed elm. He collected his bowl, towel, and knife, but before he began, remembered that he had not yet asked Juraviel when they would again stalk a deer, something the eager young man greatly wanted to know.

He slipped down from the tree house and moved about Caer'alfar, spotting Juraviel talking with another elf across the way. Elbryan smiled sneakily and went into a crouch. Perhaps the only creature more difficult to surprise than the wary deer was the forest elf! Using all his skills, the young man picked his way through the trees, scampering across the opening, finding cover wherever he could. The other elves took little notice, hardly caring for his games, and Juraviel and his companion remained apparently oblivious.

Elbryan put his back to a tree barely a dozen feet from the pair and considered his next move.

"Within six strides," Juraviel was saying in the elven tongue. "Perhaps five. And the deer did not notice."

"Well done!" the other congratulated.

Elbryan nearly fainted away. He recognized the voice, melodic and higher pitched than Juraviel's, as that of Lady Dasslerond, the High Lady of Caer'alfar and of all Andur'Blough Inninness.

And she was speaking of him! Elbryan held steady his breath, paying close attention, for though he could understand the melodic language, many individual words might elude him if he was not careful. With Lady Dasslerond speaking of him, the young man didn't want to miss a thing.

"In the fighting, too," she went on, "he is losing much of the clumsiness that comes with his human heritage, and what a combination of power and grace he shall be when one of his stature learns to wield the sword as an elf!"

Elbryan peeked around the tree to see Juraviel nodding his agreement. He forgot all about his game of surprising the pair then, and used his stealth ability to extract himself from the area, return to his tree house—which was closer to the ground than the sky—to shave and to prepare himself for his next sparring session, one he suddenly intended to win.

Early that evening, Elbryan walked onto the low meadow, ringed by tall, thick pines and capped by the starry canopy. He carried only a long smooth pole, his weapon. The elf was already there, and Elbryan breathed a sigh of relief when he noted that it was not Tuntun waiting for him.

He could never catch Tuntun off her guard; she relished the sparring matches, acting as if they were her personal forum for punishing the young man. After his first few encounters with the surly elf, Elbryan had wondered what it was that so prompted her desire to punish. Soon enough the young man had realized that it was for no particular act but merely because he was not elvish.

His opponent this night was Tallareyish Issinshine, an older and calmer member of the elvish band. He was a quiet sort and rarely talked with Elbryan, though, according to Juraviel, Tallareyish had the finest singing voice in all of Andur'Blough Inninness. Elbryan had sparred with him only once, very early in his training, and had been put down rather easily.

"Not this time," the young man muttered under his breath as he walked determinedly to the center of the meadow. He moved to a spot five feet from the sprite and bowed low, as did Tallareyish, in respect.

Elbryan presented his long pole horizontally in front of him; the elf responded by crossing his two smaller poles, replicas of slender elvish swords, in the air before him.

"Fight well," Tallareyish said, the proper beginning.

"And you," Elbryan answered, and on he came, full of fury and determination. His skills had improved, so he had heard Juraviel say, and now he meant to show how much.

He started with a cunning feint, boring in, mock spear leading, as if he meant to overrun the diminutive elf, and then pulling to an abrupt stop and swishing his weapon hard to the side. He had to guess, of course, which way agile Tallareyish would spin, and even though he guessed correctly that the elf would go to his right, his swipe was batted aside, not once but three times, before it ever got close to hitting the mark.

Tallareyish came right back in, wooden swords dancing and weaving, cutting figure eights and then darting straight ahead suddenly, viciously. Elbryan could not watch them and try to react. He had to anticipate, and so he did, flipping his spear over one hand counterclockwise and then back again, then again clockwise, then back the other way. He hardly saw the elf's attacks, but he took comfort in the clicking sounds as the twirling pole picked off each one.

"Well done!" Tallareyish commented, pressing the attack with every word.

Elbryan's green eyes sparkled with pride. He kept his focus, though, and knew that he had to get off the defensive posture. He had spent many hours with Juraviel playing the game the elves called *pellell*, resembling something close to a three-tiered chess match, and he had learned well the value of taking the initiative. At this point, Tallareyish was playing white, pressing the attack, but Elbryan meant to reverse that.

Over went his spinning pole, clockwise to his right, then it went over again, and then a third time, Elbryan sliding his foot further to the right with each spin. Tallareyish turned in pursuit and came forward, one step, left foot. Elbryan tensed.

Another step, right foot.

Elbryan caught his long pole in both hands to stop its spin. He threw it out diagonally to his left, then let go with his left hand, planted the pole against his right hip with his elbow, and swept it back across in front of him, forcing Tallareyish to fall a step to the side, forcing the elf's wooden weapon away.

The eager young man rushed through the opening, shuffling a few steps past Tallareyish's right flank, then cut a swift pivot, grabbing his pole down low with both hands and sweeping it back.

It swished through the air, hitting nothing, and Elbryan's eyes widened in shock as he came to realize that Tallareyish had followed his move perfectly, had run out right behind him. Elbryan was not surprised, therefore, when the elf's poles smacked him, but not so hard, on the rump and the back of the knee. His leg nearly buckled, but he managed to swing about, his pole still flying in a desperate, wide arc.

Tallareyish ducked low under it and double-poked his weapons, stabbing at the young man's belly twice, though neither connected. The elf came forward suddenly, furiously, as Elbryan halted the flow of his pole and snapped it back to the ready, a beautiful recover.

And one that might have worked against a human or a goblin. Tallareyish, though, was diving low before the pole ever got back in front of Elbryan. The elf went into a headlong roll, right between the young man's widespread legs, came up to his feet behind the yelling and turning Elbryan, and reversed his momentum, stabbing both his poles back over his shoulders.

Elbryan was already into his responding turn but not far enough, and the elf's blades poked him hard in the kidneys. Waves of pain buckled the young man's legs. He continued to swing, but he was down on one knee then, and his blurred vision didn't even register that Tallareyish had moved again.

The next hit, a heavy slash, caught the young man across the shoulder blades and laid him out facedown on the wet grass.

Elbryan lay still for a long, long while, his eyes closed, his thoughts whirling. He had come in so full of hope, and had gone down so very hard.

"Well done," he heard above him—Juraviel's voice. The young man rolled over and opened his eyes; he was surprised to find that Tallareyish was no longer there, that Juraviel was apparently speaking to him, was, for some reason that Elbryan could not understand, congratulating him.

"Do you often salute corpses?" Elbryan asked sarcastically, each word strained from the pain.

Juraviel only laughed.

"I heard you," Elbryan said accusingly.

The elf stopped his grinning and painted a serious expression, understanding the sudden gravity and frustration in the young man's tone.

"You and Lady Dasslerond," Elbryan clarified. "You said that I had come far in fighting as well."

Juraviel's expression hardly changed, as if he didn't understand the point Elbryan was trying to make.

"You said that!" the frustrated young man accused.

"Indeed," replied Juraviel.

"But here I am." Elbryan spat, pulling himself to his knees and tossing aside his pole—a useless piece of wood, by his current estimation. He flinched as he straightened and grabbed at his kidney.

"Here you are," Juraviel agreed, "fighting better than any, Tuntun included, would have believed possible."

"Here I am," Elbryan corrected grimly, "spitting grass."

Juraviel laughed aloud, something the young man obviously did not appreciate. "Two in three," the elf remarked.

Elbryan shook his head, not understanding.

"Tallareyish's maneuver," Juraviel explained. "The roll through your legs. Two in three attempts, it will work; the third equals complete disaster."

Elbryan quieted and considered the thought. He didn't like his odds in that prospect—only one in three—but the mere fact that he had forced Tallareyish into so desperate a routine—and any routine that held a reasonable chance of utter failure was indeed desperate—surprised him.

"And of the two that work, only half will gain a solid strike," Juraviel went on. "Even worse, you have now seen the 'shadow dive,' as we call it, and you will never, ever be taken by it again."

"Tallareyish was worried," Elbryan said quietly.

"Tallareyish was nearly beaten," Juraviel agreed. "You executed the plant of your staff on hip perfectly, and your step timing was without error. Even in running behind you was Tallareyish forced off his balance; that is why his passing strikes were of little consequence. Your turn, and subsequent blows, would have forced a close-quarters parry, at the very least, and no elf desires that with one of your size and strength."

"So he dove ahead," Elbryan concluded.

"He was stumbling anyway," Juraviel explained. "And only that stumble allowed your mighty swipe to go over his head." The elf gave a chuckle. "Had it connected, I fear that Tallareyish would still be lying facedown on the field!"

Elbryan managed a smile. To think that he had almost won! To think that he had put one of the agile elves off his balance!

"When first we began the sparring, any elf in Caer'alfar could defeat you easily, with hardly any effort," Juraviel said. "We drew lots each night to find your opponent, for none, other than Tuntun, wanted to waste time in battling you."

Elbryan chuckled, not surprised that predictable Tuntun enjoyed issuing the beatings.

"Now your opponents are selected carefully, as we bring to you different fighting styles, ones that we believe will offer you the greatest challenge. You have come far."

"I have far to go."

Juraviel would not argue the point. "You heard my conversation," he replied. "Our Lady was not exaggerating when she spoke of your potential, my young friend. With your great strength, and the elven sword dancing style, you will be the match of any man, of any elf, of any goblin, of any fomorian. You have been with us only four years and a season. You have time."

That last sentence brought a strange feeling over Elbryan. He was indeed grateful for the kind and optimistic words, and felt better, much better, about his loss to Tallareyish. But now something else tugged at him and put him on edge. What might come next for him? Elbryan had come to think of his life with the elves as a permanent arrangement, had figured that he would live in Andur'Blough Inninness for the rest of his mortal days. The notion of going out from the enchanted valley, perhaps of walking with his own kind again, scared him.

But also intrigued him.

Suddenly the world seemed much wider.

❖ 14 ❖

Jilly

C at-the-Stray was more than a little surprised, and embarrassed, when her would-be rescuer ventured into the Way the following week. To his credit, the gentleman did not approach her directly, nor did he leer at her or make any remarks whatsoever that made the young woman feel uncomfortable.

For her part, Cat kept her distance, offering a shy smile once or twice but mostly looking the other way. A part of her was very glad that the handsome man had returned, but another part of her, a very large part, was more than a little uncomfortable with the whole situation. She was closer to seventeen than sixteen now, by all appearances no more a girl, and surely the thought of the handsome man imparted intriguing, warm thoughts.

The man left early, tipping his floppy beret to Cat as he exited, his light brown eyes sparkling gaily, and the young woman was both relieved and upset that this second meeting had ended so abruptly. She shrugged it away, though, and went about her work, giving the stranger not another thought.

He came into the Way again the following week.

Again, he was more than polite, the perfect gentleman, not pressuring Cat to even so much as offer a greeting to him. He watched her more closely this time, though, and whenever she looked back, his eyes widened with intensity.

His intentions were becoming quite clear.

That night, alone in her room, Cat-the-Stray found it more difficult to dismiss her thoughts of the man. She wondered what life might be like for her in the years to come, away from Pettibwa and Graevis perhaps. She dared to fantasize about a life without work in Fellowship Way, about a life in a home of her own, with children of her own. That notion inevitably led her back to images of her own childhood, of her mother . . .

Cat-the-Stray shook her head violently, as if trying to launch the disturbing half memories right out of her ear. Suddenly the fantasy became a horrid thing that had no relevance to her present life. Her place was in the Way, with Graevis and Pettibwa. This was her home and, though she did not yet realize it, this place was also her shield against memories too terrible for her to face.

But the handsome gentleman came back again the night after the next, and then again the next week, and, predictably, the whispers started that his heart had been stolen by a certain barmaid. Cat-the-Stray tried to ignore the whispers and the sidelong glances, but even Pettibwa, cheery cheeked and grinning slyly, caught Cat's gaze and nodded her head in the man's direction more than once.

"Will ye wait the man at the table near to the window for me?" the conniving woman asked often, always with some excuse close at hand.

Cat-the-Stray could hardly refuse, but she went to the man with a cold demeanor indeed, asking what he fancied and pointedly clarifying that she was referring to food or drink only. Again to his credit, the gentleman did not press the young woman, but ordered some wine only.

He was in the tavern the next week, as well, and this time, Pettibwa, seeming a bit frustrated with the young woman, was more straightforward about insisting that the man was Cat's to serve. Even more disheartening to the frightened young woman, Pettibwa left the Way a short while later, only to return with Grady.

"Gone on about long enough by me own thinking," Cat heard the woman say to her son, to which Grady laughed and eyed Cat directly. He moved from his mother immediately and took Cat by the hand, pulling her along toward the man who had become such a regular in the tavern.

Cat resisted, tugging back, until she noted that half the patrons were watching and smiling, obviously understanding what was going on.

Cat pulled her hand from Grady's grasp. "Lead on, then," she muttered grimly, as if he was some powrie captain walking her to the plank of his barrelboat.

The gentleman smiled in recognition of Grady when he noticed the approach.

"My greetings to you, Master Bildeborough," Grady said, sweeping a low bow.

"And mine to you, Master Chilichunk," Bildeborough replied, though he didn't bother to get up from his seat and likewise bow.

"I believe that you are acquainted with my . . ." Grady fished for the right word, and Cat, blushing fiercely, wanted to smack him on the back of the head.

"My sister," Grady finished. "By adoption, of course."

"Of course," Bildeborough agreed. "She is much too beautiful to be a blood sister of yours!"

Grady's lips seemed to disappear, but in truth, there was indeed little family resemblance between him and Cat-the-Stray. The young woman was undeniably beautiful, even in her plain barmaid's dress. Her hair was long and golden, her eyes a startlingly clear and rich shade of blue, and her skin silken smooth and slightly tanned. Everything about her seemed to fit perfectly—her nose, eyes, and mouth in perfect proportion, her legs and arms long and slender but certainly not skinny. Her gait enhanced that perception as well, for she walked with ease and fluidity, always balanced.

"Cat-the-Stray is her name," Grady said, eyeing the young woman somewhat contemptuously. "Or at least, that is the name Graevis, my father, gave to her when she was taken in."

"Orphaned?" Bildeborough asked, seeming genuinely sympathetic.

Cat nodded, and her expression told the gentleman to let it go, which, of course, he did.

"And Cat," continued Grady, "I give to you Master Connor Bildeborough of Chasewind Manor. Master Bildeborough's father is the brother of Baron Bildeborough, who presides over the outlands of County Palmaris, third only to the duke, and of course, they both to the King himself."

Cat realized that she should have appeared more impressed, but in truth, little about society had ever meant anything to her. She smiled at the man, at least—and from Cat-the-Stray, that was something!—and he returned the grin.

"I do thank you for the introduction," Connor said to Grady, his tone begging the man to take his leave. Grady was more than willing to comply, practically shoving Cat right onto the man's lap as he moved behind her. Grady then gave a curt bow and rushed away, back to a wide-smiling Pettibwa.

Cat backed away, glanced over her shoulder, and straightened her dress. She knew that her face was bright red, and felt the perfect fool, but Connor Bildeborough was no novice to the ways of courting.

"For all these weeks, I have come back to the Way hoping that you would once again find yourself in danger," he said, taking Cat completely off her guard.

"Such a wonderful wish," the young woman replied sarcastically.

"Well, I merely wanted to prove to you that I would be willing to rescue you," said Connor.

Cat did well to keep the grimace from her face. Her pride didn't appreciate that condescending notion—she was never one to think she needed anyone's protection—but again she managed to check the defensive reflex, consciously reminding herself that this man truly meant no harm.

"Is not that the way it is supposed to happen?" Connor asked lightly, pouring half his wine into an empty glass on the table, then handing Cat the original glass, from which he had not yet sipped. "The young damsel, caught by fiends, rescued by the gallant hero?"

Cat couldn't quite decipher his tone, but she was quite certain that he was not mocking her.

"Rubbish," Connor went on. "Perhaps I came here hoping that I would get into a bit of a stew, so to speak, that you might rescue me."

"And why would I want to be doing that?"

Cat could hardly believe she had spoken the words, but her horror vanished when Connor laughed heartily. "Why, indeed?" he said. "After all, I was a bit late in getting to the three who came after you, and as I said on that night, I believe that I did more to help their cause than your own!"

"Are you mocking me?"

"I am admiring you, young lady," Connor replied without hesitation.

"Am I to swoon, then?" Cat asked, growing bolder and more sarcastic. "Should I run from the Way and hunt up some willing rogues, that your pride be assuaged?"

Again came the heartfelt laugh, and this time, despite herself, Cat found herself laughing with Connor.

"You are the spirited one," Connor remarked. "A bit of the wild pony in you, not to doubt!"

Cat's laugh was buried in confusion as soon as she registered the analogy. Something about the comparison, something she could not grasp, tugged hard at her, begging for release.

"My apologies," Connor said a few moment's later. "I meant no disrespect."

That wasn't it at all, Cat silently replied, but to Connor, she said nothing.

"By my heart, my remark referred not at all to your virtue, which I would not question," Connor went on sincerely.

Cat nodded to him and managed a smile. "I have my work . . ." she started to say.

"Might we walk when you are done?" Connor asked boldly. "I have waited these weeks—more than a month it has been—just to be told your name. Might we walk?"

Cat didn't know what to reply. "I must ask Pettibwa," she explained, only to buy herself some time.

"I will assure her of my honor," Connor asserted and started to rise.

Cat caught him by the shoulder—her strength seemed to surprise him—and held him back. "No need," she assured him. "No need."

She smiled at him again, pushed the wineglass, from which she had not sipped, back in front of him, and took her leave.

"Oh, by me eyes, he's a handsome one!" Pettibwa beamed when she caught up to Cat in the small kitchen behind the bar area a short while later. The older woman clapped her pudgy hands before her, her toothy smile nearly taking in her ears. She clapped her hands again, then wrapped Cat in a bone-crushing hug.

"I had not noticed," Cat replied coolly, not returning the hug and trying hard to keep her expression blank as Pettibwa jumped back to arms' length.

"Hadn't ye, now?"

"You embarrassed me."

"Meself?" Pettibwa said innocently. "Ah, but, me girl, ye'd never find one sweet for ye if I left ye to yer own doings. Why, ye act like no man's a good man!" The woman gave a bawdy wink. "So tell me now that ye're not feeling a bit warm in yer belly, and a bit o' the tingling, when ye look upon Master Bildeborough."

Cat blushed fiercely, all the confirmation Pettibwa needed.

"No reason for embarrassment," the woman said. "It's all so natural." She hooked one finger in the cleavage of Cat's dress, pulled the dress lower, and shook her hand about, so that the young woman's breasts jiggled. "And what are ye thinkin' these are for?" Pettibwa asked.

Cat's look was one of pure horror.

"For catchin' men and feeding babies," the woman said with a wink. "And ye can't get the latter without the former!"

"Pettibwa!"

"Oh, go on then!" Pettibwa shot back. "I know ye think he's handsome, and who wouldn't? And well mannered and up to his waist in the gold, too. Nephew of the Baron himself! Why, even me Grady's speaking highly o' the man, and ye be knowing, by Grady's words, that the man's speaking highly o' Cat-the-Stray. Sure there's a sparkle in his eye when he's looking on ye, and his pants are gettin' a bit too ti—"

"Pettibwa!"

The older woman laughed riotously, and Cat took the welcomed break in the conversation to consider her words. Grady was all for this, so said Pettibwa, but Cat knew that had little to do with the demeanor of her would-be suitor. If she was set up with a nobleman, the gain for Grady would be twofold. First, he'd have the prestige of being related to the nobility, a sure invitation to any important social event, and most of all, with Cat's needs attended to by outside money, she could have no claim on the lucrative Fellowship Way.

So Grady's enthusiasm for this alliance held little weight with Cat, but Pettibwa's exuberance was a bit harder to dismiss. Through all the bawdy talk, Cat could see that her adopted mother was indeed thrilled at the prospect of Cat being courted, especially by one as influential and handsome as Master Connor Bildeborough of Chasewind Manor.

So what did Cat think? That was the real question, the only one that truly mattered, but the young woman couldn't look at things that way, not now, not with Pettibwa beaming more brightly than ever.

"He asked me to walk with him when I am done with my work," Cat admitted.

"Oh, do!" Pettibwa said. "And if he means to kiss ye, then let him," she said, tapping Cat on the cheek.

"But these," Pettibwa went on, hooking her finger again and giving Cat's breasts another jiggle, "these'll wait a bit."

Cat blushed again and looked away, pointedly did not look down. Her breasts had developed late, just past her sixteenth birthday, and, though by any standards they only added to her beautiful, feminine form, she had never been comfortable with them. They represented another side of the girl, a womanly side, sensual, sexual—a part that Cat's free and girlish spirit was not yet ready to admit. Graevis used to wrestle with her, had helped her to mature her fighting skills, but once those breasts had swelled, the man stayed away. It was as if they were a boundary between Cat and her beloved adopted father, a signal that she was not his little girl any longer.

In truth, Cat had never been his "little girl." That had been reserved for another man, in some place far away, a place that Cat could not remember.

She wasn't ready to grow up yet, not all the way.

And yet she couldn't ignore the advances of handsome Connor Bildeborough, not at the price of breaking Pettibwa's heart.

She went for the walk, and truly had a lovely time, for she found that Connor was as easy to talk to as he was to look at. He let her lead the conversation, down any avenue of her choosing, and was careful not to question her too personally on any points. She told him only that she was not really the daughter of the Chilichunks, but had been adopted in a faraway village called, according to Graevis, Weedy Meadow. "Have you ever heard a name so foolish?" she said, embarrassed. She went on to explain that she didn't know where she had been before that, didn't know of her family or her real name.

Connor left her at the door of the private quarters behind Fellowship Way. He didn't even try to kiss her, not on the face anyway, only took her hand in his own and put it gently to his lips.

"I will come back," he promised, "but only if you so desire."

Before she could even consider the question or the implications, Cat found herself mesmerized by the way his lashes closed upon those beautiful brown eyes. He was tall—he had to be close to six feet—and slender, but his body was hard with well-honed muscles. Strange emotions swirled in Cat as he lightly touched her arm, vaguely familiar feelings but ones she had not felt in several years.

"May I, Cat?" he asked.

"No," she replied, and his expression became crestfallen. "Not Cat," she explained quickly, and then, with a most curious expression, she said, "Jilly."

"Jilly?"

"Or Jill," the young woman replied, seeming sincerely confused. "Jill. Jill, not Cat. They used to call me Jilly."

Her excitement mounted with each word, and so did Connor's. "Your name!" he exclaimed. "You've remembered it!"

"Not Cat, never Cat," Jill said firmly. "It is Jilly, Jill. I am sure of it!"

He kissed her, right on the lips, but he backed off at once as if in apology, as if to let her know that it was unintentional, a consequence of his sudden joy.

Jill let it go without a word.

"You must go and tell Pettibwa," Connor bade her, "though surely I hate to part with you now." He tipped his chin toward the door behind the young woman.

Jill nodded and moved to leave, but Connor caught her by the shoulder and turned her about to face him.

"May I return to Fellowship Way?" he asked in all seriousness.

Jill thought of some smart remark about the tavern being a public place, but she held her tongue and merely nodded, offering a warm smile. There followed a tense moment—Jill, and probably Connor, not sure if he would try to kiss her again.

He didn't; he just grabbed her hand in both of his, squeezed it warmly, then turned and walked away.

Jill wasn't sure if she was glad of that or not.

Pettibwa accepted the news with the purest joy—Jill was afraid that the woman would be hurt when she cast off the name Graevis had given to her. Far from it, though, the woman bubbled with joyful tears. "Not fittin' to be calling ye Cat when ye're no more a girl," she said, wrapping Jill in a hug, falling over her so heavily that the strong young woman could hardly hold them both upright.

Jill went to bed that night full of warm feelings, some pleasant, others too intense, too uncomfortable for her to understand. Her thoughts careened back and forth between the realization of her true name and her experience with Connor. So much had happened in a single night! So many emotions and memories had come rushing to the surface. Now she knew her name: Jill—though she knew that she was more often called Jilly.

And that feeling when Connor was close to her! How could she sweat so much on such a cool night?

That feeling, too, seemed something out of her past, something wonderful and terrifying all at once.

She couldn't place it, and didn't try. She knew her name now, and suspected that alone would begin to bring other memories back to her. And so it was with a true jumble of emotions, a purely teenage churning confusion, fear and warmth, happiness and the verge of terror, that the young woman, no longer Cat-the-Stray, drifted off to a sleep of the sweetest dreams and the starkest nightmares.

CHAPTER

❖ 15 ❖

Miss Pippin

T hey were out beyond sight of land all too quickly, rolling on great swells and an aroma so thick that Avelyn felt as if he could float atop it. They were busy every minute, checking and rechecking lines, adjusting the rigging, for the *Windrunner* hadn't been out to deep sea in several years and Captain Adjonas was clearly nervous. Old Bunkus Smealy seemed to take extra pleasure in ordering the monks on any particularly dangerous task.

But the old sea dog couldn't fathom the level of physical training these four men had endured. He ordered Thagraine and Quintall up the yard of the mainmast, and so up they went, faster than any crewman on the *Windrunner*. Smealy sent them far out on the yard, and they went easily, hanging under, hand over hand, adjusting the rigging and then sliding down the ropes to stand on the deck right beside the first hand.

"Well, next for ye—" Smealy began, but Quintall cut him short.

"Take care, Master Smealy," the monk said calmly. "We are as part of the crew, and as such, will work—" He paused, his stare boring into the man. They were about the same height, but Quintall carried an extra fifty pounds, every one of them hardened muscle. "—as the crew works," Quintall finished ominously. "If you entertain thoughts of working the brothers of St.-Mere-Abelle beyond what you demand of the regular crew, then accompany those thoughts with visions of swimming."

Smealy squinted perhaps a dozen times in the next few seconds and lifted a hand to scratch hard at his gray hair—to kill a few lice, Avelyn figured. The twitchy little man looked across the open deck, past the staring eyes of the crewmen, to the tall, regal figure of Captain Adjonas.

Quintall suspected that he and his fellow brothers might be fighting very soon, but so be it. He had to set the ground rules right away or this would be a long and perilous journey indeed. This was Adjonas' ship, that Quintall did not dispute, but the abbey had paid well for this transport and the brothers had not been put aboard as slaves.

To the relief of the monks—though Quintall felt a bit of disappointment—Adjonas tipped his great feathered hat to the monk and nodded slightly, a clear sign of respect.

Quintall glowered at Smealy, the old sea dog trembling with frustration. Smealy glanced at each of the four monks, spat something unintelligible, then stormed away, taking out his rage on the nearest crewmen.

"You took a chance," Pellimar remarked.

Quintall nodded. "Would you have us treated as cattle?" he asked. "We would all be dead before we ever reached Pimaninicuit." He grunted and started away.

"Not all, perhaps," Thagraine remarked, stopping Quintall short.

Avelyn and Pellimar held their breath at the bold words. The monks still carried some jealousy, Avelyn—and obviously Thagraine—realized, concerning which pair would go onto Pimaninicuit.

Quintall turned slowly. Two long strides brought him right up to Thagraine. "You might have fallen from the mast," he said bluntly, his tone making the statement sound like a threat. "And then I would journey to the island."

"But I did not fall."

"And I did not push you," Quintall stated. "You have been given your duty, and I mine. I will get you to Pimaninicuit." He glanced Avelyn's way. "Both of you, and if Captain Adjonas or Bunker Smealy—or any others aboard the *Windrunner*—conspire differently, they will answer to Quintall."

"And to Pellimar," the fourth monk added.

"And to Thagraine," the man said, smiling.

"And to Avelyn," Avelyn was compelled to add. The bond was immediate and secure, the four monks putting aside their personal squabbles in light of potentially more dangerous enemies. Avelyn, who had worked so closely with Quintall for more than four years, found that he believed the man wholly. He looked at Thagraine, who by fate had become his most trusted ally, and he smiled when he noted that the man and Pellimar, who had been together a year longer than had Avelyn and Quintall, had clasped wrists firmly, staring eye to eye.

It was indeed a good start.

No land came in sight for three days, the *Windrunner* making a direct run to the southeastern point of the Gulf of Corona, the northern tip of the region known as the Mantis Arm. They saw a light after dusk on that third day, far to the south but obviously high above the waterline.

"Pireth Tulme," Captain Adjonas explained to his guests. "The Coastpoint Guards."

"Whatever it may be," Pellimar put in, "it is good to see a sign of land again."

"You will be seeing it often over the next two weeks," Adjonas replied. "We will run the length of the Mantis Arm near to the shore, then to deeper water in a straight run to Freeport and Entel."

"And then?" Pellimar's voice was full of anticipation.

"And then we have just begun," Quintall put in firmly. The stocky man knew their course better than his three companions, as part of his private training with Master Siherton. The dangers of such a voyage were many, but perhaps most prominent among them was the danger to the mind. Pellimar seemed too eager, as if he expected Pimaninicuit to be quite close to Entel, but in truth, the *Windrunner* would likely spend the better part of four months getting to the island, and that was assuming favorable winds. Even if they arrived at Pimaninicuit early, they would only spend their days encircling the island, awaiting the day of the stone showers.

"Then we turn more directly south," Captain Adjonas added.

"In sight of land?" Pellimar asked.

Adjonas scoffed at the absurd notion. "The only land to be seen would be the coast of Behren."

"We are not at war with Behren," Pellimar promptly put in.

"But the southern kingdom has little control over its raiders," Adjonas explained. "To be in sight of land would mean to be in sight of pirates." He snorted and walked away, but paused, looked back, and motioned to them.

The four began to follow.

"Only you," Adjonas said, pointing to Quintall.

The stocky man followed the captain into his private quarters, leaving his three curious companions out on the deck with the cold, wet wind and the distant light of Pireth Tulme.

Quintall returned to them much later that evening, belowdecks in the closet-sized compartment they now called their home. There was something weird about his smile, Avelyn noted, something misplaced.

Quintall took Thagraine's arm and led him out of the cubby, then the stocky man returned alone.

"Where?" Pellimar asked.

"You will learn soon enough," Quintall replied. "I think two is enough for one night." He moved to his bunk as Pellimar and Avelyn exchanged unknowing shrugs. Their curiosity only heightened as Quintall chuckled repeatedly, until he fell away into a sound slumber.

Thagraine was likewise chuckling the next day on the deck. Avelyn wasn't sure the man had ever rejoined them the previous night, and indeed he looked haggard but certainly not displeased. The stoic Avelyn dismissed it, all of it. Apparently Quintall and Thagraine's secret posed no threat, so whatever it might be really didn't matter. For now Avelyn had his duties, and his goal was growing closer with each gliding league.

Pellimar, though, was not so patient. He prodded Quintall repeatedly, and when he got nowhere with the stocky man, he went to his older friend. Finally, after the bright sun had nearly reached its zenith, Quintall and Thagraine exchanged nods.

"The ceremony of necessity," Quintall explained with a grin—a rather lewd grin, Avelyn thought.

"A fine one," Thagraine put in. "Not so long in the trade, I'd guess."

Avelyn narrowed his eyes, trying vainly to decipher the cryptic talk.

"Not here," Pellimar breathed hopefully, having apparently figured it all out. Avelyn looked at him for some clue.

"Only for Captain Adjonas," Quintall explained, "and for the four of us, who have earned the captain's respect."

"Not so long a trip then!" Pellimar cried. "Direct me!"

"Ah, but you have rigging to tie," Thagraine teased.

"And I'll work all the better after the—"

"Ceremony of necessity," Thagraine and Quintall said together, laughing. Quintall nodded his approval and Thagraine led the eager Pellimar away.

"What are you talking about?" Avelyn demanded.

"Poor dear Avelyn," chided Quintall. "Sheltered in your mother's arms, you have never learned of such treasures."

Quintall would say no more about it, leaving Avelyn chewing his lip in frustration for the rest of the afternoon. Avelyn stubbornly decided that he would ask no more, that he would overcome his curiosity, treating it as a weakness.

That discipline lasted only until the four took their supper, a bowl of lumpy, lukewarm porridge in the tight quarters of their small room, when Quintall talked of taking "first watch."

"We set no watch," Avelyn protested. "That is the job for the common crew." The monk certainly wanted no part of a night watch on the decks, for a soaking rain had started, and even the smelly, damp cabin was better than walking the slick decks, or even worse, climbing the masts.

"I am second," Thagraine said quickly, to Pellimar's dismay.

"Fear not," Quintall said to Pellimar, "for I am sure that Thagraine's watch will not last long." That brought a laugh from both men, obviously at Thagraine's expense.

Avelyn shoved his plate forward forcefully, angered now at being left out of their little secret. It wasn't until Quintall had left, though, that he finally got the clue he needed.

"She's a fine one," Pellimar remarked, quite offhandedly. Thagraine's face as he glanced Avelyn's way showed that he was disappointed; that alone clued Avelyn in to the fact that Pellimar had slipped.

"She?" Avelyn asked.

"The ship's whore," Thagraine admitted, scowling at Pellimar. "I am thinking that your watch, Brother Pellimar, just became the fourth."

"Third," Pellimar insisted. "If Avelyn desires a ride this night, he can wait until I've finished!"

Brother Avelyn sat back, thoroughly overwhelmed. The ship's whore? The ceremony of necessity? His hands grew clammy—more out of sheer fear than anticipation. He had never expected such a thing, could not comprehend that his companions, on the most important journey of their lives should they live a century, would surrender to such base urges.

"Surely you are not offended," Thagraine scoffed at him. "Ah, but it is simple embarrassment, then. Why, my dear Pellimar, I do believe that our companion here has never ridden a woman."

Ridden a woman? The coarse image burned in Avelyn's mind. To hear his fellow monks speaking of something as sacred as love in such crude terms did surprise and offend him.

He said nothing, though, fearful of making a fool of himself. Avelyn understood that he could lose more than a little respect from the other three, and that any mistakes could cost him dearly as the weeks aboard the *Windrunner* dragged on.

"You go after Thagraine," he said to Pellimar, trying to keep his voice as steady as possible. "I will wait for another time." He turned to lie on his cot then, noting the judging look Thagraine was sending his way. There would be a measure in this of his manhood, Avelyn realized, a test he could not fail. To completely lose the respect of Thagraine, or any of the others, could jeopardize it all. There were replacements for Pimaninicuit, after all, and Quintall, so strong and virile, Quintall, no doubt practiced in the arts of lovemaking, Quintall, who would likely visit this woman daily at the very least, was next in line for the island.

But the thought of actually going to see the woman terrified Avelyn. Thagraine's perception of his sexual past was indeed accurate. All his adult life had been devoted to his studies; there had been no time for such diversions. He tried to push it all from his mind and find solace in sleep, but he got another shock when Thagraine and Pellimar began speaking in quite familiar terms of a certain maidservant and two of the cook's helpers back at the abbey.

"More practiced than any of them," Thagraine assured Pellimar, speaking of the ship's woman.

"Yes, but the young one," Pellimar argued, his voice almost wistful. "Bien deLouisa was her name, was it not?"

Avelyn's stomach churned; he knew the woman, hardly more than a girl. She worked in the kitchen at St.-Mere-Abelle, a beautiful young lady with long black hair and dark, mysterious eyes.

And now these two fellow brothers were comparing her lovemaking techniques!

Avelyn found he could hardly breathe. Had he been so blind as that? He had never even suspected that anything so sordid could go on at St.-Mere-Abelle.

He didn't sleep well at all that night.

The weather was rough over the next few days—mercifully so, in Avelyn's estimation, because he and his companions were kept very busy, attending rigging, a dangerous yet thrilling exercise in the gusting winds, and crawling in the dark belowdecks, checking for leaks in the hull. At one point, they even took up buckets as part of a bailing line.

The grueling schedule, though, allowed Avelyn the opportunity to put off his more personal problems. He knew what would be expected of him—the other three viewed sexuality as a test of manhood—and, on one level, at least, he was indeed intrigued. More than that, however, Avelyn was simply terrified. He had never known a woman in that way, and didn't know how he would react. Every time he passed that cabin door, a small stateroom just behind the quarters of Captain Adjonas, he trembled.

His sleep every night was fitful, tossing and turning even more than did the *Windrunner* on the rough swells. All his dreams melded into that singular, mounting fear. He began to envision monsters behind that door, a horrid caricature of a woman, of his mother even, leering at him as he entered, eager to destroy his finer feelings, to steal his very soul. But even those nightmares were not quite that simple, for Avelyn's other instincts, more base than any he had ever allowed himself to feel, often made him attack that female demon as fiercely as she attacked him, wrestling and kicking, biting in furious, uncontrollable passion. He awoke always in a cold sweat, and one time found himself in an even more uncomfortable position.

It had to happen: the weather cleared. The *Windrunner* glided easily over calmer seas, the southern reaches of the Mantis Arm's coast a gray blur to the west. The four monks were on deck when Bunkus Smealy informed them that they would have no formal duties that day, that they might go about their business. "I know ye've a bit of prayin' to catch up on," the old sea dog said, mostly to Quintall, with a lewd wink. "Say a prayer for me, if ye'd be so kind."

"One for every man on the ship," Thagraine piped in, bringing on a cackling fit of laughter in Smealy. The old man ambled away on bowed legs.

"I could indeed use a round of morning exercise," Thagraine added jubilantly when they were alone once more. He rubbed his hands together and started aft.

Quintall caught him by the shoulder. "Avelyn," the stocky man said. Thagraine turned to regard him. "We have all tasted the sweetness of Miss Pippin," Quintall explained, "except for our brother Avelyn."

Three sets of eyes bore down on the young monk, who felt small indeed. "Go," the nervous young monk bade Thagraine, before he hardly considered his options. "I am weary from the days of storm."

"Hold!" Quintall said forcefully, stopping Thagraine before he had taken a single step. To Avelyn, he asked, "Are you to join with the barrel-bumpers, then?"

Avelyn's eyebrows rose with curiosity. He had heard the term before, and he knew Quintall and the others used it for the common seamen, but he had no idea what it meant. Now, putting it so obviously in sexual terms only confused poor Avelyn even more.

"Yes," Quintall remarked quietly, "that might be more to your liking." Thagraine and Pellimar chuckled; Avelyn noted that they tried to stifle the laughs and were thus somewhat sympathetic to him, at least.

"I know not of what you speak, Brother Quintall," he replied bluntly, firming his jaw. "Perhaps you would tell me what a 'barrelbumper' might be."

That brought a loud snort from Pellimar. Thagraine nudged him hard.

Avelyn scrunched his face with distaste and disbelief. To see other members of his order acting so . . . *juvenile* was the only word he could think of to describe it, pained him greatly.

"Do you see that barrel," Quintall happily explained, pointing across the open deck to a single keg set far forward.

Avelyn nodded gravely, not liking where this was going.

"It has a small hole in one side," Quintall went on, "for those who cannot use the woman."

Avelyn took a deep breath, trying to calm his mounting anger.

"Of course, you'll have to pay on your appointed night," Quintall finished.

"The night you are *in* the barrel!" Thagraine howled, and all three broke into laughter.

Avelyn saw nothing at all humorous in the ridiculous joke, nor did the few crewmen close enough at hand to hear the insults. For Avelyn, this was a most sacred mission, the most important duty of the Abellican Church, and to profane it so by indulging in a shipboard orgy, was surely blasphemous.

"The woman was sanctioned by Father Abbot Markwart," Quintall said suddenly, sternly, as if he had read Avelyn's thoughts—not so difficult a feat, given the man's sour expression. "In his wisdom, he knows the trying times of a shipboard voyage and would have us reach Pimaninicuit healthy of mind and body."

"And what of soul?" Avelyn asked, but Quintall snorted at the notion.

"The choice is yours," Quintall finished.

Avelyn didn't think so, not at all. He had been called onto the table, so to speak. His actions now carried serious consequences concerning his future dealings with his three companions. If he didn't have their respect, he couldn't expect their loyalty, and given the level of jealousy that had been creeping about the four since they had become the chosen Preparers. . .

Avelyn took a bold step, cutting between Quintall and Thagraine. The stocky man willingly fell back, a smirk on his dark face—darker now for the week of beard—but Thagraine put his arm out to hold Avelyn back.

"After me," the monk said firmly.

Too angry for debate, Avelyn hooked his arm under, then up and over Thagraine's and gave a sharp tug to put the monk off balance. Avelyn then let go and dropped into a leg sweep that left Thagraine lying flat on the deck. Not wanting to continue the struggle, Avelyn was up and walking fast before the felled monk could respond.

Quintall's laughter followed him.

Captain Adjonas came out of his room as Avelyn neared. He looked at the flustered young monk, then across the deck at the other three. His grin was telling when he looked back at Avelyn, and he merely tipped his great feathered hat and continued on his way.

Avelyn didn't look back. He stalked up to the stateroom and lifted his hand to knock, then thought that perfectly ridiculous and simply walked in.

He caught her by surprise, wearing only a dirty nightshirt. She jumped when he briskly entered, pulling the covers from her bed up before her.

She wasn't what he expected—and was certainly not the monster of his dreams. She was younger than he, probably just a year or so past twenty, with long black hair and blue eyes that had long ago lost their sparkle. Her face seemed tiny, framed by the voluminous hair, but cute, if not beautiful, and her frame, too, was small and thin. Avelyn suspected that to be from lack of food not from any desire to be fashionable.

She looked at Avelyn curiously, her fear fast fading. "One o' the monks, then?" she asked in a throaty voice. "He said there'd be four, but I thought I'd seen all . . ." She paused and shook her head, apparently confused.

Avelyn swallowed hard; she was so oblivious of her partners that she didn't even know how many of them had visited her.

"Are ye?"

"What?"

"A monk?"

Avelyn nodded.

"Well, good enough then," she said, and she tossed the blanket onto the bed, then reached for the hem of her short shirt, pulling it up.

"No!" Avelyn said, near panic. He noted bruises on her legs, his eyes drawn down despite his good intentions. And the dirtiness of the woman assaulted him. Not that he was any cleaner; it amazed Avelyn how difficult it was to stay washed in the middle of so much water.

"Not yet," Avelyn quickly clarified, seeing the woman's stunned expression. "I mean . . . what is your name?"

"Me name?" she replied, and then she thought about it and chuckled and shrugged. "Yer friend calls me Miss Pippin."

"Your real name," Avelyn insisted.

The woman looked at him long and hard, obviously confused and surprised but also seeming a bit intrigued. "All right then," she said at length. "Call me Dansally. Dansally Comerwick."

"I am Avelyn Desbris," the monk responded.

"Well, are ye ready then, Avelyn Desbris?" Dansally asked, pulling up the hem a bit more and striking a teasing pose.

Avelyn considered the sight from two widely disparate viewpoints. Part of him wanted to take her up on the offer, to rush right over and crush her under him; but another part, the part that had spent more than half of Avelyn's life in fervent effort to elevate him and all of mankind somehow above this level—above following base, animalistic urges without thought, without reason—could not accept it.

"No," he said again, walking near her and gently moving her hand away so that the nightshirt slipped back down over her legs.

"What would ye have me do?" the confused woman asked.

"Talk," Avelyn answered calmly, under control.

"Talk? And what would ye have me say?" she asked, a mischievous, lewd sparkle coming to her blue eyes.

"Tell me where you are from," Avelyn bade her. "Tell me of your life before this."

If he had slapped her, she would not have looked more wounded. "How dare ye?" she asked.

Avelyn couldn't hide a smile. She seemed insulted, as if he had gotten too personal with her, and yet she was offering willingly what should have been the most personal thing of all! He held up his hands and backed off a step.

"Please sit, Dansally Comerwick," he bade, motioning at the bed. "I mean you no harm."

"I am here for a reason," she said dryly, but she did sit on the edge of the bed.

"To give us comfort," Avelyn said, nodding. "And my comfort will come in the form of conversation. I would like to know you."

"To save me, then?" Dansally asked sarcastically. "To tell me where I wandered from the righteous path and guide me back to it?"

"I would never presume to judge you," Avelyn said sincerely. "But indeed I would like to understand this, which I apparently cannot comprehend."

"Have ye never felt a bit funny then?" she asked, again with that teasing sparkle. "A bit itchy?"

"I am a man," Avelyn assured her in all confidence. "But I am not certain that my definition of the term and that of my companions is nearly the same."

Dansally, not a stupid woman, settled back and digested the words. She had spent the four days of the storm alone—except for the regular visits of Quintall, who never seemed to get enough of her. In truth, though, Dansally had felt alone for so very long—for all the voyage to and from St.-Mere-Abelle and for years before that.

It took more than a bit of coaxing, but at last Avelyn got the woman to answer his questions, to speak with him as she might a friend. He spent the better part of two hours with her, sitting and talking.

"I should go back to my duties now," Avelyn said at last. He patted her hand and rose, heading for the door.

"Are ye sure ye'll not stay just a bit longer?" Dansally asked. Avelyn looked back to see her stretched languidly on the bed, blue eyes sparkling.

"No," he answered quietly, with respect. He paused a moment, considering the wider picture. "But I would ask a favor."

"Don't ye worry," Dansally replied with a wink before he could begin to ask. "Yer friends'll look on ye with respect, don't ye doubt!"

Avelyn returned her smile warmly. He found that he believed her, and he walked back out into the sunlight truly relieved, but not in the way that the others, particularly Quintall, could ever have guessed.

Avelyn visited Dansally at least as often as all the others, sitting and talking, laughing, and one night even with Dansally crying on his shoulder. She had lost a baby, so she told him, stillborn, and her outraged husband had thrown her out into the street.

As soon as the story came pouring out, Dansally pulled away from Avelyn and sat staring hard at the man. She couldn't believe she had so opened up to him. It made her more than a bit uncomfortable, for Avelyn, with his clothes on, had reached her in ways that the others never could, had touched a very private part of her indeed.

"He was a dog," Avelyn said, "and no better. And a fool, Dansally Comerwick, for no man could ask for a better companion."

"There goes Brother Avelyn Desbris," Dansally said with a huge sigh. "Savin' me again."

"I would guess that you need less saving than most," Avelyn replied. His words, the sincerity of his tone, struck her dumb. She dropped her gaze to the floor and the tears came again.

Avelyn went to her and hugged her.

The *Windrunner* made great time, cutting southwest from the southern reaches of the Mantis Arm in a direct run to Freeport. Adjonas swung her out wide at first, explaining that it would not do to be too close to treacherous Falidean Bay, where the water could rise forty feet in twenty minutes and the undertow of the tremendous flood tide could pull a sailing ship against gale winds and smash it to bits on the rocks.

They put into Freeport only briefly, with but a handful of sailors going ashore in the boat. The *Windrunner* caught the next tide away from the unlawful and dangerous place, and they were soon into Entel harbor.

Entel was the third largest city in Corona, behind Ursal, the throne seat, and Palmaris. The wharves were long enough in water deep enough for the

Windrunner to dock, and Adjonas gave leave for all hands to go ashore, in two shifts.

On Quintall's orders, the four monks ventured out together to see the city. Pellimar suggested that they pay a visit to the local abbey. Thagraine and Avelyn nodded, but pragmatic Quintall overruled that choice, fearing that any discussion of what might have brought four brothers of St.-Mere-Abelle so far south could lead to some uncomfortable questions. The secrets of Pimaninicuit were the domain of St.-Mere-Abelle only; according to Master Siherton, even the other abbeys of the Abellican Church knew little concerning the source of the magic stones.

Avelyn remembered the speech Master Jojonah had given him when first they had talked about the island, the stern warning that to utter even its name to any without sanction of Father Abbot Markwart was punishable by death, and he agreed with Quintall's logic.

So they spent the day walking and marveling at the sights of the great city, at the thick rows of exotic flowers in the tree-lined green that centered the place, at the shining white buildings, at the frantic bazaar, the largest open market that any of them had seen, reputably the largest open market in all Honce-the-Bear. Even the vivid, bright colors of the clothing of Entel's inhabitants struck the four as unusual. The city, it was said, was more akin to those of exotic Behren than to any in Honce-the-Bear, and Avelyn, after half a day of one astounding sight after another, decided that he would indeed enjoy a visit to Behren.

"Another time, perhaps," he whispered, looking over his shoulder as he made his way back aboard the *Windrunner*, the sun dipping over the city.

Resupplied, the *Windrunner* put out the next day, sails full of wind with a favorable tide, sailing fast to the south.

Avelyn got his wish sooner than expected, for, without explanation, Captain Adjonas put his ship into the next harbor in line, Jacintha, just a score of miles to the south, but across the mountain range that divided the kingdoms.

The three nervous monks looked to Quintall for answers, but he had none, caught as completely off his guard as the others. He went at once to the captain, demanding an explanation.

"None know the southern waters better than the sailors of Behren," Adjonas explained. "What winds we should catch, what troubles we might face. I have friends here, valuable friends."

"Take care that your questions do not lead your contacts to the way to Pimaninicuit," Quintall whispered ominously.

Adjonas straightened, the blood rushing to his face, making that garish scar seem all the more imposing. But Quintall did not back down an inch. "I will accompany you to your . . . friends."

"Then change out of your telling robes, Brother Quintall," Adjonas replied. "I'll not guarantee your safety."

"Nor I yours."

The pair, along with Bunkus Smealy, went out late that afternoon, leaving the nervous gazes of three monks and thirty crewmen at the rail. Pellimar relieved his tensions with a visit to the woman—to Avelyn's satisfaction, his companions still didn't know her real name—but Avelyn and Thagraine remained at the rail, watching the sunset and then the lights of the structures that lined the harbor.

Finally came the welcome sound of oars and the boat, all three safely aboard. "We are out in the morning, at first light," Adjonas said sharply to Smealy and to the nearby crew when the three gained the deck.

Thagraine and Avelyn exchanged grave looks, given the man's uncharacteristic tone and the severe look on Quintall's face.

"The waters are not clear, by any reports," Quintall explained to his brothers.

"Pirates?" asked Thagraine.

"Yes, that and powries."

Avelyn sighed and moved back to gaze at the unfamiliar landscape, layers of lights lifting up to the darkness of the great range known as the Belt-and-Buckle. He felt so far from home, and now, with the vast open Mirianic looming before him and the talk of fierce powries, he began to understand that he had much further yet to go.

He, too, visited Dansally that night. Brother Avelyn needed a friend.

❖ 16 ❖

Endwar

lbryan's fifth summer in Andur'Blough Inninness was among the very best times in all his young life. He was no more a boy but a young and strong man, with all traces of his youth gone except for a mischievous streak Tuntun feared he would never be rid of. He continued his ritual with the milk-stones, running out eagerly each morning, attacking the task with pride, for he could see the difference the continual exercise had made on his tall, graceful form. His legs were long and covered with muscle, and his arms had grown huge, each muscle clearly defined. When Elbryan bent his fist forward and flexed, he couldn't put his other hand— and his hands were not small by human standards!—halfway around the bulging forearm.

But even with all that mass, there was nothing awkward about the young man. He danced with the elves, he fought with the elves, he skipped along the winding trails of Andur'Blough Inninness. His light brown hair had grown long, to his shoulders, but he kept it clean and neatly trimmed, pushed back from his face, which he still kept clean shaven.

He was welcomed in every elven ritual now—in every dance, in every celebration, in every hunt—but still, perhaps more than ever, Elbryan felt alone. It wasn't that he craved human companionship; he continued to fear that thought greatly. It was simply Elbryan's realization of how different he was from these creatures, and not just in stature. They had taught him to view the world as an elf might, with utter freedom and often more veiled in imagination than reality. Elbryan found that he could not possibly maintain such a stance. His sense of order was simply too strong, his sense of right and wrong too keenly developed. He expressed that sentiment to Juraviel one quiet afternoon, he and the elf out on a long walk, talking of the plants and animals.

Juraviel stopped in his tracks and stared at the young man. "Could you expect differently?" he asked simply.

It wasn't the wording but the way Juraviel spoke that offered Elbryan comfort. For the first time, he realized that perhaps the elves were not expecting him to be as one of them.

"We are showing you a different way to view the world about you," Juraviel explained, "one that will aid you in your journeys and trials. We are giving you tools that will put you above your kin."

"Why?" Elbryan asked simply. "Why was I chosen for these gifts?"

"Blood of Mather," Juraviel replied, a phrase the young man had heard all too often, usually derisively, from Tuntun. "Mather was your uncle, your father's oldest brother."

As he spoke, Elbryan found his mind drifting back to a specific place and moment, a time nearly five years previous, when he had stood on the ridge outside of Dundalis, Pony beside him, looking up at the glowing Halo. Though his mind conjured that image, that feeling, and placed him squarely within that space and time, he remained alert to Juraviel's every word.

"He died very young, so it was believed by your father and the others of the Wyndon family."

"I remember—" Elbryan stopped short. He didn't know what he remembered. He had a feeling that his father had mentioned a lost older brother, Mather perhaps, and it must have been so, because Elbryan now knew he had heard that name before he had ever met with the Touel'alfar.

"The boy Mather was nearly killed," Juraviel went on. "We found him in the woods, mauled by a bear, and brought him to Caer'alfar. It took him some time to heal, but he was strong, as is the way of your heritage. Afterward, we could have let him return to his family, but many months had passed and the Wyndons, by all the reports of our scouts, had moved along."

The elf paused, as if wondering how he should proceed. "In centuries past," he began solemnly, "our peoples were not so secluded. Elves and humans lived near each other, often trading stories and goods and sometimes living together in a single community. There were even marriages, two that I know written of, between elf and human, though few offspring ever came from such unions."

"What drove our peoples apart?" Elbryan asked, for he thought that the world, particularly concerning his race, was a more tragic place for the change.

Juraviel chuckled. "You have been in Andur'Blough Inninness for five years," he replied. "Have you noticed the absence of anything?"

Elbryan crinkled his brow. What could possibly be missing from so enchanted a place as this?

"Children," Juraviel prompted at length. "Children," he repeated, his voice low. "We are not like humans. I might live a millennium—I am nearly halfway to that point already—and sire no more than one, or perhaps two, children."

Juraviel paused again, and it seemed to Elbryan as if a cloud passed over the elf's angular features. "Three centuries ago, the dactyl awakened," he said.

"Dactyl?" Elbryan asked.

"Demon," Juraviel clarified. He turned away from Elbryan, walked to the edge of a small clearing, and lifted his head to the heavens and his voice in song.

"When the eyes of sentries turn inward,
When the hearts of men covet,
When love is lost to lust.
When the ways of merchants turn cheating,
When the legs of women bow,
When gain is ill not just.
Then look ye men to darkness.
Then see the smoke-filled sky.
Then feel the rumble 'neath your feet
And know 'tis time to die.
So turn your swords away from kin
Your hatred far from kind,
And see the charge of goblin and dwarf
To which lust has left you blind.
Thus find your hearts and enemies true
And all ill ways forsake
And know the time for righteousness!
The dactyl has come awake!"

Many images flitted through Elbryan's imagination as Juraviel sang: scenes of war and terror, scenes so very much like Dundalis on that awful day when the goblins came. By the time Juraviel finished, the young man's cheeks were wet with tears, and Juraviel's were as well, Elbryan noted when the elf turned back to him.

"Dactyl is the name we give to it," Juraviel said softly, "though truthfully the awakening of the demon is more an event of the whole world than of a specific being. It is our own folly—that of human and in times long past, of elf—that allows the dark creature to walk the earth."

"And when the demon awakens, then there is war," Elbryan reasoned from the song. "Like the battle that claimed my family."

Juraviel shrugged and shook his head. "Often there are such battles when humans and goblins live near each other," he explained. "On the wide seas, sailing ships often meet the low boats of powries, with predictable results."

Elbryan nodded; he had heard of the fierce powries and their reputation for destroying human ships.

"It was three centuries ago when the dactyl last awakened," Juraviel said. "At that time, I and my people traded openly with humans. We were many more. Many more, though not as many as the humans. *Co'awille*, 'Endwar,' we call that horrible time, for four of every five elves were killed." He sighed resignedly. "And since we do not procreate prolifically . . ."

"You had to run away," Elbryan reasoned. "For the very survival of your race, you had to seclude yourself from the other races."

Juraviel nodded and seemed pleased by the perceptive reasoning. "And so we came to Andur'Blough Inninness," he said, "and to other such places of mystery. Aided by the holy humans and their precious gifts, the magical stones, we made these places our own, secluded and veiled from the eyes of the wider world. Know that the dactyl was defeated in that time long past after great cost, but gone, too, was our time in this world. And so we live on, here and there, under blankets of cloud, under cover of darkness. Our numbers are small; we cannot afford to be known, even to the humans whom we consider our friends."

"Some of you do," Elbryan remarked, thinking of Tuntun.

"Even Tuntun," Juraviel replied with a laugh. But his smile did not last. "She is jealous of what you have."

"I?"

"Freedom," Juraviel went on. "The world is open to you, but not to Tuntun. She does not hate you."

"I will believe that right up until the next time we spar," Elbryan replied, drawing a laugh from his elven friend.

"She fights hard," Juraviel admitted. "And on you, she is particularly strict. Is that not proof that she is your friend?"

Elbryan stuck a blade of grass between his teeth and considered the viewpoint.

"Tuntun knows that your life may be difficult," Juraviel finished. "She desires you to be properly prepared."

"For what?"

"Ah, that is the question," Juraviel answered, his finger pointing into the air, his eyebrows arched. "Though we have forsaken the ways and places of the humans, we have not forsaken your race. It is we, the elves of Caer'alfar, who train those known as rangers, the protectors, usually of people who have no idea they need protecting."

Elbryan shook his head; he had never heard of rangers, except for occasional references by the elves.

"Mather was a ranger," said Juraviel, "one of the finest. For near to forty years he kept a line a hundred miles long secure from goblins and fomorian giants alike. His list of victories is far too long to be recited here, if we had a week to spare."

Elbryan felt a strange sense of family pride. He remembered again that morning on the ridge, viewing the Halo, hearing the name of Mather distinctly within his mind.

"And so you shall be," Juraviel finished. "Elbryan the Ranger."

The elf nodded, then walked away. Elbryan understood that his lesson was at its end and understood, too, that this lesson might have been the most important of all during his time in Andur'Blough Inninness.

"There, do you feel it?"

Belli'mar Juraviel held his hand up, begging silence, then shifted his sensitive bare feet about on the stone face. A moment later, feeling the subtle vibrations running clearly into him through his toes, he gave a grim nod.

"Many miles north and west," Tallareyish remarked, looking that way as if he expected some vast horde of darkness to be charging down toward Andur'Blough Inninness.

"Lady Dasslerond has been told?" Juraviel asked.

"Of course," an elf by the name of Viellain, one of the oldest in Caer'alfar, answered. "And scouts have gone out. There are reports of a trench, a great upheaval, not twenty miles beyond our valley."

Juraviel looked to the north, to the wild lands beyond his elven home and far beyond the settlements of any humans. "Do you know this place?" he asked of Viellain.

"It should not be so hard to find," Tallareyish answered quickly, as eager as Juraviel to glimpse the evidence. The pair looked at Viellain, their expressions revealing much.

"The scouts will pass by the trench, if there is indeed such a marker, then continue far to the north," the old elf explained. "Thus they shall not return to Caer'alfar for many days."

"But Lady Dasslerond should be informed," Tallareyish reasoned, guessing that Viellain, usually a stickler for rules, was coming around to their way of thinking.

"We can reach this place and return before the sun has set tomorrow," Juraviel said, "if we can find it."

"The birds will know," Viellain assured him. "Always, the birds know."

The glade was strangely quiet this night, with no elves in the area—or at least none showing themselves, for Elbryan had been around the Touel'alfar long enough to realize that a host of sprites could be within a dozen paces and even he, now so attuned to the forest, would not suspect it unless they chose to make their presence known.

Still, he was fairly certain that he was alone this night, except for his opponent, standing in the shadows across the way.

The young man held his breath when the elf came out into the moonlight. Tuntun.

Elbryan clutched his staff and set his heels. He had not battled Tuntun in many weeks; he was determined now to give the upstart elf a bit of a surprise.

"I shall not stop beating you until you cry out my name," Tuntun taunted, moving to the center and twirling her longer pole, the size of an elven sword, in a circle, while her second weapon, a stick fashioned as a dirk, worked in tighter circles over her fingers. Around and around the weapons went, reminding Elbryan of her uncanny dexterity. Tuntun could roll four coins at a time on each of her hands; she could juggle a dozen daggers, or even flaming brands, effortlessly.

But that quickness and precision would not be enough, Elbryan told himself. Not this time.

He stalked in, his staff horizontal before him, right hand palm up, left palm down. Normally, the combatants would speak the rules before a match, but with these two there was little need for such ceremony. After all these years, Tuntun and Elbryan understood each other perfectly; between these two, there were no rules.

Elbryan went into a crouch, and Tuntun wasted no time in going on the attack, sending her sword straight ahead. Elbryan let go of his staff with his left hand, turned his right hand over, then back. The overhand parry deflected the stabbing blade, but the second attempt, the undersweeping slap designed to send the elf's sword flying up high, was far too slow to catch up to Tuntun's retracting movement.

Elbryan caught the staff again with his left hand, holding steady, his defenses set.

But then he surprised Tuntun. Fighting logic said that he, with the heavier weapon and more lumbering moves, should have allowed Tuntun the initial attacks, playing black on the chessboard. Any offensive mistake would leave Elbryan dangerously vulnerable to the elf's darting blades.

But on the young man came anyway, pressing furiously. He started with an overhand, underhand parry sweep again, but instead of catching the staff with his left hand as it came swishing back to horizontal, he turned his right hand over once more. Halfway through the next sweep, Elbryan's powerful forearm flexed tight, catching the pole in mid-swing, and he brought its low end snapping in against his side, catching it under his right arm, then lowering and thrusting its tip like a spear.

Tuntun, almost expecting the attack from this man who so hated her, was not caught by surprise. She backed through the first swishes, then ducked under the thrust, crossing sword and dagger in an X above her head to keep the pole harmlessly high. She expected then to find an opening for a counter but had to stay defensive as she realized the young man wasn't yet through with his surprisingly adept routine.

Elbryan brought the pole right back in, before Tuntun's crossed blades could shift it to either side. Then he sent it straight out a second time, cutting short the thrust as the elf predictably ducked. He brought the leading end of the pole up and back over his head, launching the pole into an immediate spin, catching it again in his left hand after it went once around, then stepping forward forcefully. Now firmly held in both hands, his staff made a second twirl, then came arching diagonally toward the ground, toward Tuntun.

The elf squealed and threw her sword out to the side, blade vertical, its tip nearly touching the ground. The staff smacked it with all the young man's considerable weight and strength behind it, and Tuntun went flying backward, skipping and hopping, even flapping her gossamer wings, to absorb the tremendous shock.

Elbryan smiled grimly and came on, twirling and swinging, poking, stabbing, thrusting—anything to keep the elf moving backward and off her balance.

His success was partly gained by surprise. Soon the cunning elf had a new and more respectful measure of him, and her parries—and the distance she kept between herself and her opponent—became more appropriate.

And so they fought, evenly matched, for a long while, poles sometimes slapping together so rapidly that it occurred to Elbryan that, if they had some kindling, they might light a fire from friction alone! Each scored minor hits, each felt minor stings, but neither seemed to gain the advantage as the minutes continued to slip by.

Inevitably the hits, particularly on Elbryan, became more substantial as weariness caused some sloppy defensive posturing. Tuntun was tiring, too, Elbryan knew, and if he could land but one solid blow, the fight might be at its end.

Elbryan slashed across in front of him and felt his staff smacked once, twice, perhaps a half dozen times before he even completed the pass. One solid blow, indeed, he thought, but landing that hit would prove no easy task!

That point came clearer a split second later, as the last of Tuntun's sword parries hit hard enough to force his staff out just wide enough for the elf to dart straight ahead and sting the fingers of Elbryan's trailing hand with her dirk.

He needed something new, something Tuntun had not seen from him and could not expect. Something daring, even desperate, like the shadow dive Tallareyish had used to defeat him. Tuntun was growing more confident, he realized. She felt she had his measure.

She was ripe for the plucking.

A series of swipes, stabs, and forward strides put Elbryan in the desired position. He shifted back on his heels, reading the elf's next attack perfectly and easily sliding too far away for the small sword to reach.

Then he came ahead in a rush, hands apart and holding firm, swiping the staff across left to right in front of him, up high so that Tuntun could not stop it and had to duck it.

She did, perfectly, but Elbryan kept his staff moving, letting go with his left hand and using his right merely to keep the staff's turn intact and balanced. He caught the weapon mid-pole, again in his left hand, an overhand grasp as it came around his back and swiped it across in the same direction, this time with only the one hand and using his hip, the back half of the staff still behind it, for leverage.

Again Tuntun—though surprised the second swing had come the same way and not on the predictable backhand—managed to dodge, this time rolling around the tip of the pole, turning a complete spin back to her right.

But Elbryan wasn't more than half done. As his staff came sweeping around to horizontal in front of him, he caught it in his right hand, quickly flipped his left hand under the weapon, then stepped ahead and to the left in swift pursuit and launched the third swipe, again left to right, by pulling his right hand in while thrusting his left out.

Tuntun's only avenue of escape was straight down to the ground, and so she took it unceremoniously.

Elbryan did not check the flying momentum, continuing his own spin and letting the staff fly out to its full extension, catching it down low in both hands, as he might have held a club in his younger days when at play smacking rocks far into the air.

Around he went, all the way around, though he knew that it was dangerous to turn his back for even a split second on one as swift as Tuntun. He yelled out as he came back to face her, dropping to one knee, swiping low with all his strength.

The staff swished harmlessly through the air. Tuntun was gone!

The man's mind whirled through the possibilities, all jumbled with the horror that he had erred, that he was about to get clobbered. He realized immediately that Tuntun could not have stepped left or right without his noticing and certainly couldn't have gone low under the cut with him dropping to one knee.

That left only one possibility, an escape borne on translucent wings.

As his swing crossed before him, Elbryan turned his left shoulder down and fell into a roll that left him on his back in the grass. He pulled with all his great strength, tearing out the staff's momentum, halting its flow and turning it perpendicular to the ground.

Down came Tuntun, her wing-fluttering hop exhausted, her sword pointed below her, leading. She had meant to pounce right upon stupid Elbryan's back, driving her wooden practice sword into the back of his neck. How her blue eyes widened when she saw the pole's tip come up to meet her descent!

She batted futilely with her sword, then, that failing, tried to stab down at Elbryan. Her breath came out in a rush as she plopped down hard, the staff's butt end secure against the ground, its tip stabbing hard into her chest between her lowest ribs.

She held there for a long moment, up high on the eight-foot pole, her sword nowhere near supine Elbryan. She dropped the sword—unintentionally, Elbryan knew, for it fell harmlessly to the side—so the young man graciously pulled the pole out straight so Tuntun wouldn't fall off balance to either side. She landed on her feet, skittered back away from the weapon, but soon fell, gasping desperately for breath.

Elbryan, his weapon dropped, was at her side in a moment. He thought himself foolish as he neared the unpredictable Tuntun, expecting that she would find the strength to drive her dirk into his face, thus claiming a draw.

But Tuntun had no such strength. She couldn't even talk, and her dirk, like her sword before it, slipped uselessly from her weakened hand. Elbryan knelt beside her, his arm about her shoulders, comforting her.

"Tuntun," he repeated over and over, for he feared she was hurt, that she might die out here in the practice glade with no one near her except this man she so despised.

But finally she was breathing somewhat steadily again. She looked up at Elbryan, sincere admiration in her eyes. "Fairly won," she congratulated. "I thought . . . you had over . . . stepped . . . your ability, but your recovery . . . was truly remarkable."

Tuntun nodded and rose unsteadily, then walked from the glade, leaving Elbryan kneeling in the grass.

He hardly knew how to react. After so many long months, he had scored his first win.

The row of trees, short and wide apples, ran almost perfectly straight, then jumped back a dozen feet, up a ridge twice an elf's height, and continued on straight again from there. The upheaval was recent, that much was perfectly clear, for the soil on the torn side of the ridge was loose and deep brown, pocked here and there by a root, but with no fresh, aboveground growth. Something had reached into the middle of this line of apple trees and simply pulled back a third of the row.

"This is one of Brother Allarbarnet's groves," remarked Tallareyish. The other two nodded their agreement, for Allarbarnet, a wandering monk of St. Precious Abbey of Palmaris, was not unknown to them or to any reasoning creature of Corona. He had wandered the lands—the Wilderlands and not the civilized regions of his birth—more than a century before, planting lines of apple seeds in hope that his fruit would encourage the people of the kingdom of Honce-the-Bear to explore the wider world. Brother Allarbarnet—the canonization process for the man had already begun, and the abbots expected that he would be sainted within the decade—had not lived to see his dream realized; indeed, it had not yet been realized, but many of his groves had grown and flourished. Unknown to the humans, Brother Allarbarnet had been named an elf-friend, and had often been aided by the elves or by the rangers the elves had trained. So these three knew of the man and his work, knew of his groves, and knew that they were always planted in straight lines.

What, then, had so altered this one?

There could be only one answer, for no living creature, not even one of the great dragons of the north, could so tear this amount of ground in such an even, tidy manner.

"Earthquake," Juraviel muttered, but even given his grim demeanor, his melodic voice could sound only a bit ominous.

"From that direction," Tallareyish agreed, pointing to the north in the direction, they all knew, of the wastelands of old, a torn and battered mountainous region known as the Barbacan.

"Not so unusual an event," Viellain reminded the pair. "Quakes happen in all times."

Juraviel understood his fellow's reasoning and knew the elf was speaking those words for his sake mostly. For Juraviel's anxiety was clearly etched on his fine features—how could it have been otherwise when he had been speaking to his protégé Elbryan about this very subject not a week's time past?

Viellain was right, Juraviel knew logically. Earthquakes and thunderstorms, swirling tornadoes, even exploding volcanoes, were more often than not natural events. Perhaps it was coincidence.

Perhaps, but Juraviel knew, too, that such events might accompany a larger and darker phenomenon, that earthquakes that could tear the earth as here, that goblin raids upon villages, like the one that had orphaned Elbryan not five years before, might signal something evil indeed.

He looked to the north again, peering hard just above the horizon. If the day had been clearer, his keen eyes might have spotted something, some flicker, some confirmation. For now, the elf could only worry.

Had the dactyl awakened?

❖ 17 ❖

Black Wings

They took it slowly, very slowly, with eager Connor coming to understand Jilly's needs and hesitation. He sensed the way she tensed every time he moved near her, every time his face was within a few inches of hers, his lips and hers seeming to pull together as if magnetic.

But Jill inevitably turned away, her face flushed with frustration as deep as that which Connor felt. On those first few occasions, Connor took the rejection personally, as a slight, despite Jill's proclamations otherwise. He couldn't help but feel that she did not find him attractive, that she somehow revolted her. No novice in the ways of love, the nephew of Palmaris' baron was surprised and pained but also intrigued. Jilly was a challenge he had not before faced and one he was determined to overcome.

Gradually, as he came to see the light in Jill's eyes every time he entered the Way—a more and more common occurrence—the proud young man began to understand and accept that her problem was within the mysteries of her past and not with him. That realization didn't lessen the challenge, though, and Connor found he wanted Jill more desperately than he had ever wanted any woman. To Connor Bildeborough, Jill became perhaps the ultimate challenge of his young life. So he would be patient, would spend his nights walking with Jill and talking. His other needs could be taken care of in the many brothels that openly offered their wares in the city, but of course he didn't need to tell Jill, his Jilly, about that.

For Jill's part, her night always got better when Connor entered the Way. She found herself thinking about him constantly, even dreaming about him. She took him to her private place, the roof down the alley, and together they sat for hours watching the stars, talking comfortably. It was up there that she finally allowed Connor to kiss her—actually kissing him back—though she kept it brief and pulled away as soon as those dark wings of some past event she did not understand began to flap up around her. In kissing him—in kissing anyone, she supposed—Jill was sent back to a moment of pain, an event in her past too painful for her to remember.

But she suffered that pain, and let Connor kiss her, every once in a while.

It was up on that rooftop, under a sky that was streaked by clouds and stars, that Connor first mentioned the prospect of marriage.

Jill found it hard to breathe. She couldn't look at the man but kept her eyes locked on the stars, as if seeking refuge high above. Did she love Connor? Did she know what love was?

She knew it made her happy to be with Connor but also that it terrified her. She couldn't deny the longings, how parts of her body seemed to grow very warm, how she felt as if she were on the verge of trembling whenever she looked upon him. But neither could Jill deny the fear of getting too close—to Connor or to any man. The sweetness was there, but somehow just out of Jill's reach.

Her first instinct told her to refuse the proposal. How good a wife might she be, after all, when she wasn't even sure who she really was? And how long would Connor remain with her when even a kiss was a strained thing, something she had to force past this great black block that she did not understand?

But what of Pettibwa and Graevis? Jill had to consider. What of her duty to the couple who had taken her in and given her a home? How much better their lives would be to know that she was well wed! Perhaps her ascension into local nobility would even raise their own station in life, and Jill would treasure that above all else.

Jill finally found the nerve to look back at Connor, to stare into those marvelous brown eyes, sparkling more now in this starry light than she had ever seen.

"You know that I love you," he said to her, "only you. All these weeks, nay months, I've sat beside you, wanting to make love to you, wanting to wake beside you. Ah, my Jilly, do say you love me. If you do not, then I shall walk into the Masur Delaval and let the cold waters take me, for never again will this body know warmth."

The words sounded so beautiful to the young woman, except for his reference to her as "Jilly," which she really didn't like much, which made her feel like a little girl. She believed him with all her heart, and she had come to love him, so she thought. What else could it be called, after all, considering that her smile came so easily whenever he was in sight?

"Will you wed with me?" he asked softly, so softly that Jill really didn't hear the words but felt them as if they were transferred to her by his gentle touch as he ran the tip of his finger from the side of her nose and down her cheek.

She nodded and he kissed her, and she let him hold her close, their lips together for a long while, and all that time, while Connor was making soft, satisfied noises, Jill was beating back black wings, was furiously fighting to divorce her mind from the current situation, was remembering beer orders from her work in the Way, was thinking of the man she had seen get run down by a rushing cart the week before—anything so that the moment would not send her careening back across the lost years to something, some horrible event, that she could not face.

The reaction of Pettibwa and Graevis to the news of the marriage was not hard to predict. The bartender nodded, smiling, and gave his precious Cat—he still called her that—a generous and warm hug. Pettibwa was distinctly more animated, hopping up and down, breasts and belly bouncing wildly, and clapping her hands together, her cheeks fast streaking with an outburst of tears. All that Graevis and Pettibwa had ever wanted for the girl was for her to be happy: as unselfish a love as anyone could ever know. And now that seemed so certain. To wed nobility! Jill would never want for anything, so they believed. She would dress in the finest gowns and attend the highest social events in Palmaris, even in Ursal!

Their reaction confirmed to Jill that she had made the right choice. Whatever her personal problems, the sight of Graevis and Pettibwa so animated and so sincerely happy warmed her heart. With all that they had done for her, how could she have ever chosen otherwise?

The wedding was planned—by Connor's family, of course, since they had the wealth to do it right—for late summer, and with all of the preparations ahead of them, Connor and Jill actually saw less of each other over the next few months than before the proposal.

"Finished already?" Grady called as he descended the wide, sweeping staircase of House Battlebrow, the most renowned brothel in all of Palmaris.

Connor, sitting back on one of the plush chairs in the lobby, turned an absent gaze his companion's way.

"What, only one this night?" Grady chided. "To be sure then, there are at least two disappointed ladies in the house!"

"Enough, Grady," Connor replied, his commanding tone leaving little doubt as to which was the dominant one in this relationship. Grady's standing was nowhere near Connor's, and the only reason the baron's nephew suffered the almost constant companionship of the upstart commoner was for the sake of his adopted sister.

Grady knew too much about Connor's nighttime pursuits for the nobleman to discard him, and though Grady had never even hinted at blackmail, Connor understood him well enough to fear him.

"What is wrong, my friend?" Grady asked, tying his belt and sliding into the chair beside Connor. "Your cheer has been left behind, I fear. Might the bonds of approaching matrimony be tightening?"

"Hardly," Connor replied. "Would that the day were the morrow! How long I have waited!"

Grady spent a long moment digesting those words, trying to find any hidden meanings.

"And do not doubt my love for your sister," Connor went on. "She is surely the most beautiful, the most tantalizing and teasing . . ." He let it go with a profound sigh.

Grady put his hands in front of his mouth to hide his grin. "So it seems that she is driving you mad," he offered. "Her charms have put you into the arms of three women a night for, lo, these five months!"

Connor glared at him, hardly appreciating the sarcasm. "And if you tell her a single word of it, I shall stick my sword into your belly and wriggle it about," he warned, and there was little doubt he meant every grim word.

But Grady understood he had the upper hand and he would not back away. "You do so like sticking and wriggling," he teased.

"As any true man must!" Connor insisted. "Am I to let Jilly drive me to madness? But that does not mean I love her any less. Understand that. So fine a wife."

"Have you bedded her?"

Connor's expression forced Grady to lean the other way, fearing the man would slap him. "An honest question," Grady protested, "and not one aimed in protection of my sister's honor. Know that I would bed her myself, except for the consequences I would face from my parents."

"And from me." Connor's words sounded as a low growl.

"No longer do I desire such a thing, of course," Grady wisely conceded. Even hinting that he still had amorous desires for Jill to Connor would be akin to reaching under a crowning eagle to pull away its meal. "She is for you, and only you. A swooning girl, if ever I saw one. No man but Connor Bildeborough could bed her now, but by force."

"And what of Connor Bildeborough?" Grady bravely pressed. "Has Jill surrendered?"

"No," the frustrated nobleman admitted. "But the time is near."

"End of midsummer, I should say," Grady agreed, "or will you wait that long?"

"I give her until the wedding night," Connor replied. "She is fearful—virgins always are—but of course, my rights on that night are absolute. She will offer it, or I shall take it!"

Grady wisely bit back a remark questioning the virginity of his adopted sister. It really didn't matter; all that mattered was what Connor believed.

And indeed Connor believed! Grady could see that in his every fidget, in his almost animal-like intensity. Why, even the practiced whores of House Battlebrow were losing their charms for him!

"Dear Jilly," Grady mumbled under his breath as Connor rose furiously from the chair and stormed across to the exit. "You teasing little wench. Putting your maidenhead on a barbed hook and jiggling it before the baron's nephew." Grady silently applauded his conniving little sister, though his perception of her actions almost scared him; he had never thought her capable of such a beautifully treacherous play. "Ah, good enough for both of them, I say," Grady remarked more loudly, addressing a pair of ladies sitting on the bottom step of the wide stairway as he walked past in pursuit of Connor. The women cocked their heads curiously. "I'll be rid of you, dear sister," he went on, speaking to himself once more, "and let Connor Bildeborough learn in his own time that you were not worth the waiting!"

Another prostitute entered from the street just before Grady went out. He cupped her chin in his hand, drawing a smile from her. "The little teasing wench," he said, moving near the woman, who was one of his favorites. "Poor Connor will learn soon enough that she hasn't your charms nor your talents."

He kissed her, then rushed out behind Connor. The night was young but getting on, and Connor would soon enough have to get to the Way to meet Jill. But perhaps he'd have time for a few drinks and a dice game before.

It was a ceremony that had all of Palmaris talking; the women swooning, the men standing tall, feigning importance, wishing they were in the carriage in Connor Bildeborough's place as it made its winding way through the streets. Any reservations that the nobleman's family had held toward the peasant orphan girl had been washed away when they met Jill, truly beautiful both inside and out. Now, seeing her adorned in a white gown of satin and lace, her long, thick blond mane pinned up on one side and hanging loose on the other, she seemed made for royalty. There were even whispers that the young woman was indeed of royal blood, and a host of rumors as to her past made their way through the crowds.

It was all nonsense, all pretension, but in Honce-the-Bear in God's Year 821, that was the way things were done.

For Jill, her face was a mask of paint and false smiles. She looked a princess but felt like a little lost girl. On the one hand, she couldn't deny the pleasure of dressing so beautifully, of knowing she was the center of attention. On the other hand, being the center of attention truly terrified her. It was bad enough that the carriage would roll through every part of the large city, bad enough that more than five hundred people would be in attendance at the church when she and Connor were wed, but the thought of what would come later, after the grand ball . . .

"I have waited long enough," Connor had said to her that morning, following the words with a kiss on the cheek. "Tonight."

And then he had left Jill with the thought. She hadn't even been able to kiss him yet without those black wings of that awful past flapping up around her, but she knew what he expected—one of his house servants had described it to her in great detail.

She had smiled at Connor before he left, trying to be comforting. She dreaded the night to come.

The ceremony went off perfectly—solemn yet joyous, ladies crying, men standing tall and handsome. After the carriage ride, the newlyweds came to a hall filled with music and drink, with ladies and gentlemen spinning about, twirling and laughing. It was loud and rushing, exhilarating. Jill rarely drank more than a single glass of wine, but this night, Connor kept foisting glasses upon her, and she kept taking them. He was trying to loosen up her inhibitions, and she was, too.

Or maybe she was just trying to blur the terror.

She found herself in the arms of dozens of men whom she did not know, gentlemen all, by blood if not by deed. More than one whispered something lewd in her ear, more than one tried to get a hand somewhere it should not be. Even a bit drunk, Jill was agile, and she got through the dancing with her purity intact.

The ball ended far too soon, at Connor's insistence, which brought more than a few randy comments.

Jill suffered them as she had suffered everything else, quietly and privately, looking at Graevis and Pettibwa as they stood beside the Bildeboroughs. This was for them, Jill constantly reminded herself, and in truth, she had never seen them, particularly Pettibwa, looking so happy.

When the guests were excused, Connor took Jill across the town to the mansion of his uncle, the Baron Bildeborough. They entered quietly through a side door of the west wing, proceeding to the guest quarters, which were empty, save a pair of handmaidens Baron Bildeborough had put at Connor's bidding. The two young women—younger than Jill even, though she had just passed eighteen—took Jill to the private chamber, a room that made her feel tiny indeed! The ceiling was high, the walls covered in grand tapestries, and both the bed and the hearth were of heroic proportions. For Jill, who had spent her life so simply, it seemed somehow obscene; a dozen people could sleep comfortably on that bed, and she needed a stepping stool to even get onto it!

She said nothing as the handmaidens helped her to get out of her great gown, making suggestions all the while as to how she should proceed, of this trick or that trick they had heard about. "A lady must be well practiced in the ways of lovemaking for royalty," one of them remarked.

"Is there a girl in Palmaris that Connor Bildeborough could not bed?" the other added.

Jill thought she would throw up.

When the tittering pair finally left, Jill was sitting on the edge of the great cushiony bed, wearing only a simple silk nightgown that was too low cut, both front and back, and didn't go nearly far enough down her legs. The night was chill for late August and the room drafty, but the handmaidens had lit a small fire in the hearth. Jill was just moving for it when the door swung open and Connor, dressed in the black pants and white shirt he had worn for the wedding and ball but without his boots, without his jacket, and without his belt, entered.

She started for the hearth; he cut her off and wrapped his arms about her.

"My Jilly," he whispered, the word lost as his lips brushed against her neck.

Connor backed off almost immediately, his face crinkled in confusion. He could feel her tension, she knew, and that notion alone allowed her to relax a bit. Connor knew her so very well; he could sense her fear. He would be gentle with her, she believed, would give her all the time she needed. He loved her, after all!

Even as that thought cascaded down through Jill's body, easing the muscles, Connor grabbed her and pulled her to him roughly, crushing his lips against hers. She hadn't even time to consider the rush of passion, so surprised was she. She didn't fight back, not at first, just stood there perfectly still.

She tasted his lips, felt his tongue brushing through.

In her mind, she heard a scream, agonized. The scream of a dying child, of her mother, of her village.

"No!" Jill growled, pushing him back.

She stood before him, panting.

"No?"

Jill could not find the breath to answer, to explain. She just stood there, shaking her head.

"No?" Connor yelled again, and he slapped her across the face.

Jill felt her knees buckle and she would have gone down, except Connor was on her again, squeezing her tight, kissing her all about the face and neck. "You cannot deny me," he said.

Jill squirmed and twisted, not wanting to hurt him, even sympathetic to him, but simply unable to comply with his needs. Finally she worked her arm up under his and broke the hold enough so that she could move back a step.

"I am your husband," Connor said evenly. "By law. I will do as I please with you."

"I beg of you," Jill said, her voice barely a whisper.

Connor threw up his arms and spun away from her. "You have kept me waiting all these months!" he roared. "I have dreamed about you, about this night. Nothing else in all the world matters but this night!" He spun back to face her, now several steps away.

Jill felt as if she must be the most horrible person in the world. She wanted to give in to Connor, to give him what he deserved for his patience. But those wings, those black wings, that distant scream!

Connor's demeanor changed again, suddenly. "No more," he declared, his voice low, even threatening. Jill watched helplessly as he tore open his shirt, leaving it back on his shoulders, then squirmed out of his pants.

She had never seen a nude man before, and certainly not like this! But whatever feelings the sight of Connor's body—and he was indeed a beautiful man—might have inspired were washed away by the fear, by the black wings, by feelings that Jill could not understand.

Even worse, there was no love, no tenderness in his face as he stalked back to her, just heated desire, an almost angry passion. "Look at me!" he demanded, grabbing Jill by the shoulders and turning her roughly, forcing her to face him directly. "I am your husband. I will do as I please, when I please!" As if to accentuate his point, he reached over with one hand and tore down the side of Jill's nightgown, pulling it low enough to reveal one of her breasts. The sight of it, round and firm and creamy white, seemed to calm him for a moment.

"You approve of my appearance," he concluded.

Jill looked down. Her nipple stood hard, but it was not for love, not for excitement, just fear and a cold sensation that coursed through her entire body. Connor brought his hand to it and pinched it hard.

Jill winced and pulled away. "I beg of you," she whispered again.

Her hesitance incited his rage once more. Connor grabbed her and pulled her down, and before she could move to protest, he was on top of her, his knee between her legs, forcing them apart.

"No!" she begged, and she could feel him prodding at her, tearing at her nightgown to get the material out of his way.

His passion seemed to mount, driving him on, forcing him closer, rougher.

Jill gasped for air that would not come. She heard the flapping wings, the screams, the dying. She pulled and turned, looking away as his hungry mouth descended, but he only pursued, pinning one of her arms, putting all of his weight atop her.

The screams, distant, agonized. Her mother dying!

Jill scraped her forearm on the sharp edge of the stone hearth. She looked up to see she was trapped by the raised hearth, no room to squirm, her head close to the stone. And Connor would not relent, prodding and pushing.

Her mind was lost to the swirl of the past—to the screams, to the sights, the smells of torn bodies swelling, growing thick with decay. She was there again, in that most horrible place, with no escape, with the death and the fire.

The fire.

She saw the ember fall from a log, orange glowing like the eye of some hideous night creature. She closed her hand on it and felt no pain, was beyond pain.

And then she turned and stuck it into the face of her attacker, into the face of this thing that was atop her, this thing that had killed her mother, had murdered all of her village. It howled and fell away, and Jill rolled out from under it and scrambled to the bed.

Her surroundings confused her. She saw the man—it was a man, it was Connor!—rise to his feet, clutch at his face, and run screaming out of the room.

Waves of pain assaulted her suddenly; she threw the ember back into the fireplace.

What had she done?

She fell upon the bed, crying, clutching her burned hand in the other and pressing both of them under her, against her breasts. Her sobs did not relent for many minutes, for half an hour perhaps, for all of an hour. She did not stop, did not look up when she heard the door open, when she heard the sound of footsteps—more than one set—approaching.

She did not stop crying when she was grabbed roughly and turned about, her arms pinned out wide to the sides, her legs hooked under the knees and similarly pulled out wide.

The handmaidens had her securely, and Connor, the burns on his face mercifully not so bad, approached, wearing only his shirt, and with that garment open wide.

"You are my wife," he said grimly.

Jill had no more fight left in her. She looked up pleadingly at the two women that held her, but both seemed impassive, even somehow pleased by it all, by the sight of her, and of Connor—seemed pleased by her help-lessness and their part in it.

She looked back as Connor climbed up onto the bed, moving right atop her.

She shook her head. "I beg," she whispered.

Connor thrust against her, but she felt no stabbing point.

Connor lifted his head up from her, and he seemed to her truly hurt and saddened. He spun away in frustration, shifting off the bed right back to his feet.

"I cannot," he admitted, looking back sharply, his eyes reflecting a simmering rage. "Take her out of here and lock her in a room," he demanded of the handmaidens, who immediately and none too gently moved to comply. "We shall let the magistrate, Abbot Dobrinion, determine her fate in the morning. Take her!

"And then return to me," Connor added, speaking to the handmaidens, but aiming the words at Jill's heart. "Both of you."

❖ 18 ❖

The Test of Faith

H our after endless hour, day after endless day, the *Windrunner* glided lazily across the sparkling glassy surface of the South Mirianic. The sun became the enemy; the air grew uncomfortably hot. All the time.

Avelyn thought his very skin would slip off his body, a great rag, and fall rumpled to the deck. He burned and blistered, then browned, darker and darker, taking on the leathery appearance of those seasoned sailors around him. He tried to keep clean shaven, as did his monk companions, but there was no blade fine enough, and soon all three had scraggly beards.

The worst of it was the boredom. All they could see in any direction was the flat bluish-gray line of the horizon. Moments of excitement—a whale spout, the flight of a dolphin beside the prow, a run of bluefish churning white the water—came all too rarely and lasted barely seconds, to be inevitably replaced by the emptiness of the open sea. All romantic notions Avelyn had held concerning sea voyages were long gone, washed away by the slow, creaking, rolling reality.

He visited Dansally often, and for hours at a time. She was forbidden to come out of her cabin and preferred it that way, both she and the captain fearing what might happen if the common sailors, men who had been away from women for great lengths of time, caught her sweet scent. Thus she kept her cabin door securely locked.

Avelyn also noted that his three monk companions, apparently tiring of Dansally, visited her far less often. He was glad of that, though he wasn't certain why. Dansally didn't seem to mind at all the duties of her profession, and Avelyn had come to accept her work as a part of who she was. As he had said to her on his initial visit, it was not his place to judge her.

He believed that with all his heart, and yet he couldn't deny he was glad to see that the others, including Captain Adjonas, were spending less time with her. He came to know aspects of Dansally that his companions would never think to look for—her witty sense of humor, tenderness, and her regrettable resignation for her station in life. Avelyn came to hear her dreams and ambitions, uttered rarely and never to anyone else, and he, alone among all the men the woman had known, tried to encourage those dreams, to give the woman some respect for herself. The issue of physical intimacy did not come up between them during those weeks, for both of them had found a more special intimacy, far more satisfying.

And so the days went, the sun, the stars, the endless swells and sparkles. The one relief for the monks and crewmen alike came on cloudless nights, for the colors of the Halo were much clearer here than in the northern zones. Soft blues and purples, vivid oranges and sometimes a deep crimson lined the night sky, lifting hearts and spirits.

Even prosaic and gruff Quintall appreciated the beauty, saw the Halo as a sign of God, and took faith whenever those colors appeared.

"Starboard ho!" came the cry one bright morning the second week out of Jacintha.

Quintall peered at the horizon, hopeful, though he knew from his discussions with Adjonas that they were not near to halfway to Pimaninicuit, and any other land they might sight would only tell them that they were far off course.

"Whale to starboard!" the lookout cried a moment later. "Must be a dead one, 'cause he's not moving."

Farther back along the deck, Avelyn was close enough to hear Captain Adjonas mutter, "Damnation."

"Is it bad fortune to spot a dead whale?" the innocent monk asked.

"No whale," Adjonas answered grimly. "No whale." He headed forward, Avelyn in his wake, and Bunkus Smealy, Pellimar, and Thagraine falling in line. Quintall was already at the rail, pointing far out and down.

Adjonas took up his spyglass and peered in the direction. He shook his head almost immediately and handed the instrument to Quintall—a move that Bunkus Smealy apparently did not like.

"No whale," Adjonas said again. "Powrie."

"Powrie?" Avelyn said, confused. Powries were skinny dwarfs, barely four feet in height.

"Powrie vessel," Adjonas explained. "Barrelboats, they're called."

"That is a boat out there?" Pellimar asked in amazement.

Quintall nodded, bringing down the glass. "And keeping fair time with us," he added.

"They've no sail," argued Pellimar, as if logic alone should dismiss the possibility that this was a powrie craft.

"Powries need no sail," Adjonas answered. "They pedal, turning a shaft to a great fan aft of the ship."

"Pedal?" Pellimar scoffed, thinking the notion ridiculous in so vast a sea, where distance was measured in hundreds of miles.

Adjonas' voice was grim and unrelenting. "Powries do not tire."

Avelyn had heard as much. Powries were not often seen, except in times of war when they were dealt with all too often. Their battle prowess was the stuff of legend, of terrifying fireside tales. Though diminutive in stature, they were said to be stronger than an average man and with incredible stamina. They could suffer brutal hits with club or sword and keep on fighting, and they could wage battle for hours at a stretch, even after a forced march of many miles.

"So far out," Quintall remarked. "Surely there's no land within ten days' sail."

"Who can know the minds of Powries," Adjonas replied. "They have been quite active of late, so my friends in Jacintha informed me. They slip into the shipping routes and take their fill, then move back to deep water, following the blues or the cod or other favored fish. A hardy and stoic type, do not doubt; powries have been said to be out on the open water for a year and a half at a stretch."

"But what would they do with their booty?" Avelyn reasoned innocently, drawing looks from the other five. "If they waylay ships, what goods do they extract and where, then, do they drop off their newfound cargo?"

Adjonas and Bunkus Smealy exchanged grim glances, telling the four monks that they simply did not understand this enemy.

"They take lives," Adjonas answered calmly. "They waylay ships simply to kill. They attack only to pillage enough stores to get them to the next ship and for the simple thrill of the hunt and torture."

Avelyn blanched, so did Thagraine and Pellimar, but Quintall only let out a low growl and turned his gaze back in the direction of the distant powrie ship.

"But for us to pass so close to one of them," Pellimar offered nervously. "What dumb luck is that? We'd not even have seen the craft if we were but a hundred more yards to port."

"But they would have seen us," Adjonas replied. "Our sails break the horizon for miles, and powries have magic of their own, do not doubt. It is said that they have friends that swim under the sea, returning to them with whispers of passing ships. This is not dumb luck, my good brother Pellimar."

"What could they know of us?" Quintall demanded, not turning back to face the others.

"Only that we are a lone ship far from home," Adjonas was quick to answer.

"Of our mission?" Quintall pressed.

"Nothing," Adjonas assured him. "It is doubtful that any aboard the powrie craft would even recognize your abbey robes."

Quintall nodded. "Then run away from them," he instructed.

Avelyn and the others held their breath as they watched Captain

Adjonas' face tighten. Avelyn feared that Quintall, in issuing such a clear order, might have overstepped his bounds this time.

"Hard to port!" Adjonas screamed out, then he calmed and turned to his first hand. "Fill our sails, Mister Smealy," he instructed. "I've no desire to do battle with powries."

Smealy ran off. Adjonas let his dagger-throwing gaze linger on Quintall's back for a long while, then calmly turned and, with a quick nod to the other three monks, walked away.

Avelyn moved to the rail and shaded his eyes with his hand, peering hard into the vast gray-blue expanse. He thought he caught sight of the barrel-boat but couldn't be sure—it might have been no more than the shadow of a wave.

The *Windrunner* veered hard to port, sails filling and pushing the square-rigged caravel on with tremendous speed. But the powries tailed her; the lookout called down repeatedly, his tone growing thick with frustration and fear, that the barrelboat was keeping pace, was even beginning to close a bit.

Now at the taffrail the four monks and Captain Adjonas watched the powries' progress. Avelyn could see the craft clearly now; no longer did he confuse the strange barrelboat with any wave shadows.

Adjonas looked up at his sails, then at his crew, tacking frantically to keep them as full of wind as possible.

"An amazing design," Quintall remarked of the closing craft. "Why is it that we humans have not copied it?"

"There is a human barrelboat in Freeport," Adjonas replied, "and several were constructed in Ursal for use on the river. But men are not powries. The quarters within such a boat are tight—far tighter than even your small cabin on the *Windrunner*. And men have not the powrie endurance. The dwarves can pedal all day, while most men tire within the hour—or after a couple of hours, at most."

Quintall nodded, his respect for the stoic, tireless enemy redoubled. "If the powries will not tire, then we cannot simply keep up the run," he remarked.

"I will set bowmen firing flaming arrows upon the vessel when it closes a bit more," Adjonas answered, his tone far from hopeful. "But most of the craft is underwater, with little above to aim at, and none of that critical. Hopefully we will be able to keep our pace swift enough so that the powries' initial ram causes little damage. Then we will fight them—what choice do we have?—as they try to board us."

Quintall was shaking his head before Adjonas even finished. "We cannot allow them to ram," he argued. "Any damage would slow us, at the least, and that we cannot afford. We have less than a week of extra time—and that if our calculations to our destination are correct and the winds hold."

"I see few options," Adjonas remarked.

The other three monks were looking grimly at the distant barrelboat or at each other, shaking their heads, but Quintall had turned his thoughts in a different direction, digesting all the information that Adjonas had given him of the enemy.

"Tell me," he said at length, "how swift will a barrelboat run if its great fan becomes entangled?"

Adjonas looked at him curiously.

"We have extra netting," Quintall added.

"The fan is not so exposed," Adjonas said. "Even if we placed the netting perfectly in the barrelboat's path, it would not likely snag on anything except the catch hooks protecting the fan."

"Suppose that we did not simply place the net but rather took it to its destination?" Quintall asked slyly, drawing a confused look from all but Thagraine, who had caught on and was more than eager.

"That would be foolhardy," Adjonas began, but he stopped as the hatch of the barrelboat flipped open and a red-capped head popped into sight. Up came a skinny arm, holding a funnel-shaped tube.

"Humans!" the powrie shouted through the funnel. "Yach, trader, give her up! You cannot outrun us, yach you cannot, nor can you hope to give a fight. Give her up, I say, and some of you might be spared."

Adjonas looked all around at his now-stationary crew. He saw the expressions there, the sudden faint hope in the powrie's promise.

Bunkus Smealy spoke for many of them by Adjonas' estimation. "Might that we should harken to his words, Captain," the first hand said. "If we offer them no fight—"

Adjonas pushed him aside and walked in from the rail so that all on deck could see him. "They shall kill us, every one!" he shouted. "These are powries, bloody caps, looking to wet their berets in human blood. They'll not let a ship sail from them, nor do they have room for prisoners! If we stop, or even slow, they'll only ram us all the harder."

Even as Adjonas spoke, a flaming quarrel arched over the taffrail of the *Windrunner*, slashing into the rear sail. Three crewmen ran to the small fire immediately, minimizing the damage.

"Yach, how long can you keep up the run, trader?" the powrie howled, and then he disappeared, closing the hatch behind him.

"Who are your best swimmers?" Quintall asked, moving up to the captain. Adjonas looked at him curiously.

"The *Windrunner* is a ship of cold northern waters," he replied. "As a habit, we do not swim."

Quintall nodded grimly and turned to his three brothers. He hated risking them all but realized the success of the mission hinged on their actions right now. Before he ever finished his motion, Avelyn, Pellimar, and Thagraine dropped their robes to the deck and began stretching their muscles and swinging their arms.

"We are swimmers," Quintall explained. "Even in the cold northern waters. Fetch me a net."

Adjonas motioned to Bunkus Smealy; this was Quintall's operation now, and the *Windrunner* captain, with no other apparent options, was more than willing to give the sturdy monk his chance.

The four were at the port rail out of sight of the barrelboat soon after. Quintall tossed the net into the water, and Thagraine went in right behind it, taking hold.

Adjonas grabbed Quintall by the shoulder. He pulled a stone from his baldric, a small red ruby, and handed it over. "Only if you see a need," he explained. "That stone is more valuable than all my ship."

Quintall looked it over curiously. He could feel the magic within it, a faint pulsing of energy. He nodded to Adjonas, then unexpectedly handed the stone to Avelyn. "Not a man alive knows the power of the stones better," he said to his companion. "Use it well if we find the need."

Avelyn took it and fingered it for a few moments, feeling the energy clearly, understanding the purpose of the stone as surely as if it had spoken to him. He moved to put it in his loincloth but didn't feel secure with that, so he popped it into his mouth instead, rolling it behind his teeth.

Then they went in, swimming fast to join Thagraine, who was still bobbing with the net, many yards behind the swift-running *Windrunner*.

They split into two groups, with Thagraine and Quintall holding the net between them while swimming out to the side, trying to find an angle to the closing barrelboat, and Pellimar and Avelyn putting themselves right in line with the craft, keeping low in the water in case that hatch should open again or in case the powries had some other method of looking out.

Adjonas watched nervously from the taffrail. He knew things about powries and about the sea that the four monks apparently did not. If the barrelboat got by the net holders, for example, they would never catch up and Adjonas couldn't turn about for them. They would be stranded in open water, and thus, surely doomed. Even more dangerous, powries were said to have waterborne friends, often ones with a distinctive dorsal fin.

The captain nodded, confident that even if brave Quintall knew all of this, he still would have gone into the South Mirianic with the net.

"Swim hard!" Quintall gurgled to his companion, moving fast to close the remaining distance. The barrelboat was moving much more swiftly than it appeared, for it cut no prow wake, as did the *Windrunner*. Thagraine worked as furiously as he could, flailing arms and legs, but he would not have gotten to the mark had not Quintall, the other end of the netting hooked about his broad shoulders, tugged him along.

Exhausted, the two men dove under for the last expanse, swimming so the craft would pass right over them. Fortunately, the water was crystal clear.

Up ahead, Avelyn and Pellimar waited anxiously. They would have to get aboard the barrelboat, whatever the outcome of Quintall's attempt. If the net failed, then these two would have to find some way to stop the powries. Avelyn rolled his tongue over the ruby. The stone wouldn't be nearly strong enough, he realized, to take out the wet barrelboat's sturdy hull.

The barrelboat closed—fifty yards, forty, twenty—cutting the water smoothly.

Then it jerked suddenly and its straight run shifted to the diagonal. Avelyn and Pellimar swam with all speed. Pellimar reached the drifting boat first, pulling himself cautiously up its slick, rounded side. He shuffled for the hatch and got there just after it opened.

The first powrie out was truly stunned. The fan had snagged on some seaweed or on something the caravel had dropped, so the dwarves thought, and it was not so uncommon an occurrence. But to see a human standing on the deck!

The sight was no less amazing to Pellimar, who had never seen a powrie up close. The dwarf stood just over four feet, with gangly arms and legs that seemed too skinny to support its barrel-like torso.

The dwarf's expression did not change, its pale, wrinkled face staring openmouthed as Pellimar hit it with a solid right cross.

The monk stared at his wounded hand, and at his opponent, so much more solid than it appeared! The hard-headed powrie shook its head vigorously, lips flapping.

Pellimar hit it again, a series of three quick left jabs, then brought his right leg up hard, snapping out his foot to connect right under the powrie's jaw. The dwarf's head snapped back, and it fell to the deck and rolled over the side of the barrelboat.

But another was in its place, this one not surprised. Pellimar, quick as a cat, hit it, too, with three solid punches—a left, right, left combination—but the monk's impetus was lost when his right hand, still pained from the first hit, connected that second time.

Avelyn, rushing in behind his brother, saw Pellimar jerk suddenly and then fall to the side, a bright red line across his chest. There before Avelyn stood the powrie, its short sword dripping Pellimar's blood. The dwarf squealed in rage, seeing its victim falling off the side, seeing a chance to heighten the color of its already bright crimson beret tumbling into the Mirianic. That moment of distraction gave Avelyn his chance.

He could have bent low and barreled into the dwarf, but he sensed its solidity and saw another powrie coming through the hatch behind it. Putting his personal safety aside, Avelyn had to consider the greater good.

He ran forward and slid down to the deck, scrambling fast and taking the ruby from his mouth. He rubbed it in his hand, calling forth its magic, finding its center of energy and bringing that to a volatile level.

The powrie came across with a backhand slash, but Avelyn managed to duck beneath it. He reached between the powrie's legs and tossed the stone upward, toward the hatch. Then, guided purely by his survival instinct, Avelyn curled his legs under him and came up fast.

The ruby, shining with power, arced lazily over the open hatch. The next powrie coming out saw its sparkle and, mesmerized, reached for it. The dwarf caught the gem securely, but surrendered his hold on the ladder. Thus, when Avelyn and the other powrie came up suddenly, rising over the stone holder, the surprised dwarf fell back down into the barrelboat, glowing ruby in hand.

Avelyn clung to the powrie's sword arm for all his life. He had one hand below him and managed to push the hatch back as they descended, Avelyn rolling right over the hatchway, the deceivingly agile powrie hopping to its feet atop the now-closed portal. The dwarf lifted its sword, grinning evilly, and let out a wail that shook Avelyn to the marrow of his bones as he lay prone not far away.

But then the dwarf was flying, the hatch spinning through the air behind it, and a stream of thick black smoke poured from the open hole.

The jolt sent Avelyn tumbling, and he didn't fight the motion. The blast had not likely killed half the powries—the barrelboat was nearly as large as the *Windrunner*!—and they would be up on deck soon enough.

And Avelyn had no desire to face another.

Quintall and Thagraine came up breathless after setting the net in place. By the time Quintall got near the barrelboat a powrie was in the water, and Brother Pellimar was tumbling close behind.

With their heavy bodies and spindly limbs, powries were not strong swimmers, and Quintall easily overtook the dazed creature, pushing it under the water and gaining a seat atop its shoulders. The powrie struggled desperately, but the powerful man locked his legs tight and fought to keep his balance.

The dwarf would not find the surface ever again.

Once in the water, Avelyn found Quintall treading high not so far away, half his body clear of the sea. The sight surprised Avelyn at first—until he noted the "seat" his companion had found. Thagraine, some distance to the side, had Pellimar under one arm, swimming as hard as he could for the turning caravel.

As soon as his grim business was finished, Quintall, easily the strongest swimmer, relieved Thagraine of his burden and nearly kept up with his two companions, despite the added weight of an unconscious Pellimar.

Adjonas watched it all anxiously, moving along the rail as his ship executed a turn. The barrelboat was disabled temporarily, but the fight was hardly over. The captain ordered archers into place and told them to take whatever shots presented themselves if the powries came out through that smoke, which was already diminishing.

Then he watched, because there was nothing else he could do. The *Windrunner* came right about, bearing down on the four monks, and on the barrelboat. There were indeed powries on her deck now, some with heavy crossbows, taking potshots at the swimming monks.

Even worse for the monks, Adjonas knew, was the trail of blood the wounded Pellimar was leaving in the water.

Thagraine was first to the *Windrunner*, grabbing frantically at a line thrown from the deck. He had barely taken hold, Avelyn twenty yards away, and Quintall and Pellimar that distance again, when the lookout gave a not-unexpected cry.

"Dorsal fin!" he shouted. "Shark, white shark!"

"Get them up quickly!" Adjonas howled, moving to the rope to lend a hand. "More ropes into the water!"

One thrown rope splashed right near Avelyn, but understanding the frantic lookout and the newest danger, he refused it, turning about for Quintall and Pellimar.

"Brother Avelyn!" Thagraine shouted from his perch on the *Windrunner*'s rail. "You and I are the Preparers! They are expendable!"

The words assaulted Avelyn with the force of a cold slap. Expendable? These were monks of St.-Mere-Abelle! These were human beings!

With a growl, Avelyn pushed on, finally reaching the tiring Quintall. To Avelyn's surprise, Pellimar bobbed in the water behind the stocky man.

Avelyn asked no questions, nor did Quintall, who was swimming hard for the rope. Avelyn finally reached Pellimar and hooked his arm around the bobbing man's shoulder.

A crossbow quarrel skipped across the water right beside Avelyn's face as he turned. He saw it, then—a dorsal fin sticking fully two feet out of the water—and though he had never seen or heard of sharks before, he could well imagine the horrors that lay beneath the telltale fin.

The shark closed, as did the *Windrunner*. A dozen men—Quintall, Thagraine, and Adjonas among them—had the rope in hand and were pulling it taut even as Avelyn desperately grabbed its other end.

He couldn't lift himself even a bit, had all that he could handle and more in simply keeping his grasp on the rope and on limp Pellimar.

But they got him up to the rail, Quintall grabbing Pellimar and hauling the man onto the deck, Avelyn dangling dangerously low. He heard the screams of the crewmen and looked down, one foot still in the water, as the great dark shape, fully twenty-five feet in length, glided under the *Windrunner*, under Avelyn.

A split second later, the terrified monk was standing on the deck.

"Big one," Adjonas remarked, noting the shark.

Bunkus Smealy turned his greasy grin on Avelyn, holding one hand up, his thumb and index finger about five inches apart. "With teeth this long," he said cruelly.

There were a dozen powries on the deck of the barrelboat, Adjonas noted, but none would go into the water with the great shark so close and so obviously agitated. Powries and sharks worked in concert, so it was said, but apparently there were limits to such friendship.

A wicked grin widened on the captain's face; he decided to test that unlikely truce.

"Give them a bump," he told Bunkus Smealy, and the first hand shrieked with glee and ran to the wheel.

It wasn't a full ram—no sensible captain would pit his ship against the strong hull of a powrie barrelboat—but enough of a nudge certainly to send all but one of the powries on deck rolling into the water. The *Windrunner*'s archers opened up hard as the ship crossed beside the powrie craft, leaving three more dwarves dead in the water.

A second, smaller dorsal fin joined the first in its tightening ring.

How the dwarves scrambled!

"Get us away," Adjonas called to his crew. The sharks would feed on the dead, and the frantic actions of those still alive combined with the widening blood spill would likely bring more in, he knew. No powrie would dare go into the water to try and untangle the netted fan with frenzied sharks so close.

Even worse for the powries, though neither Adjonas nor any other aboard the *Windrunner* could have foreseen it, the drifting barrelboat appeared remarkably like a wounded whale to the crazed sharks.

The barrelboat, rolling from the contact with the *Windrunner*, with water rushing in the open hatchway, soon disappeared under the waves.

The excitement on the *Windrunner* did not dissipate until the powries were left far behind. The monks had been the heroes of the fight, but Avelyn heard crewmen muttering "foolhardy" as often as "brave." The sailors were a tough bunch, proud and cynical, and if he or Quintall or any of the others expected a congratulatory pat on the back, they were disappointed.

Avelyn and Thagraine took the severely wounded Pellimar into Dansally's quarters, and found the woman was versed in more skills than the sensual. Soon after, the man was resting as comfortably as possible, and Avelyn left the room.

He found Quintall standing with Adjonas, the captain, looking weary, leaning against the mainmast.

"Powries," he was muttering when Avelyn walked up. "More bloody caps than ever on the Mirianic, north and south. They have multiplied on their isles, the Julianthes, it would seem, bursting from their shores. Their attacks will only increase in number and in purpose."

Quintall shrugged away the grim words. "How fares Pellimar?" he asked Avelyn.

Avelyn sighed helplessly. "He may live," he replied, "or he may not."

Quintall nodded, then suddenly exploded into action, his roundhouse punch catching Avelyn square on the jaw, dropping the man in a heap to the deck. "How dare you?" Quintall yelled.

Sailors looked up from every corner of the deck; Adjonas eyed the stocky man with disbelief.

Avelyn pulled himself up, wary of another blow, thoroughly confused by Quintall's actions.

"You are the chosen Preparer," Quintall scolded. "Yet you risked your life to save Pellimar."

"We all risked our lives by going out," Avelyn argued.

"We had no choice in the matter," Quintall retorted, so angry that his spittle sprayed forth with every word. "But when the danger to the *Windrunner* was ended, when the powries were stopped and the way was clear, you went back into the dangerous waters."

"Pellimar would have been eaten!"

"A pity, but not important!"

Avelyn swallowed his next retort, knowing that it would be a useless argument. He had never imagined such a level of fanaticism, even from stern Quintall. "I could not leave him, and you."

Quintall spat on the deck at Avelyn's feet. "I asked you not for help, and would have refused it if offered. The way to our destination was cleared, the threat to the *Windrunner* ended. You should have gone aboard and stayed aboard. What a waste Pellimar's life, and my own, would have been had Avelyn, too, died in the water!"

Avelyn had no response. The argument was indisputable. He pulled himself up, nodding in agreement, though in his heart he knew if the situation arose again he would again go back to the pair.

"We do not know that the way to Pimaninicuit is now clear," Adjonas whispered, protecting the sacred name.

"Pellimar is no good to us in any case," Quintall was fast to respond. "Even if he lives, he'll not likely crawl out of bed for many days."

Avelyn studied the stocky man intently. The mission was all important— Avelyn agreed and he would sacrifice his own life for the good of the voyage. But to ask him to let another die?

Avelyn shook his head, though fortunately Quintall and Adjonas missed the movement. No, the young monk decided, that he could not, would not, do.

"Remember," Quintall said to him gravely.

"I will go to Pellimar," Avelyn replied, taking comfort in the subtle vow the words implied, one that Quintall could not comprehend. "Dansally tends his wounds."

"Who?" Quintall asked as Avelyn walked away.

Avelyn smiled, not surprised.

Pellimar's condition did not much improve as the days slipped past. The weather remained hot and clear, and no more barrelboats came into view.

Perhaps it was the boredom, the heat, or the tasteless provisions, but the crew grew increasingly uneasy, even hostile. More than once, Avelyn heard Bunkus Smealy and Adjonas in a shouting match, and every time the monk walked the open deck now, he felt burning gazes of hatred on his back. The crew were blaming the monks for their discomfort, for this whole journey. Quintall had warned Avelyn and Thagraine of this, as Adjonas had warned Quintall. The *Windrunner* was usually a coast hugger. Journeys into the wide, vast ocean were extremely rare, and rumors told of a madness that often grabbed at a crew. Ships had been found, so the stories went, intact and seaworthy, but with not a crewman aboard. Some said it was the work of ghosts, or evil monsters of the deeper waters, but most rational, experienced sailors attributed it to fear and suspicion, to the long days of emptiness and the undeniable feeling that the sea would never end, that the ship would sail and sail until there was no more to eat and no more to drink.

It got so bad by the sixth week out of Jacintha that Adjonas, to Avelyn's utter dismay, opened privileges of Dansally to other members of the crew. It had to be done in a calm fashion, so the captain ordered, and every time Avelyn saw another of the filthy sailors going to Dansally's door, his heart sank a bit lower, and he chewed a bit more of his skin from his lip.

Dansally took it in stride, accepting her lot in life, but her expanded duties left her little time for her talks with Avelyn, something the monk, and now the woman, dearly needed.

Even the extra privileges did little to improve the mood of the increasingly surly crew. The situation came to a frightening head one especially hot humid morning. Quintall spent the better part of an hour in a sometimes heated discussion with Captain Adjonas. Finally, Adjonas seemed to nod his assent, and then he called Bunkus Smealy to his side.

More yelling ensued, mostly by Quintall, and when Smealy at last tried to counter, the stocky monk snapped his hand under Smealy's chin and lifted the man from the deck by the throat.

Avelyn and Thagraine rushed to Quintall's side, Thagraine pointing out that all the crew was watching with more than passing interest.

"It proves my point, Captain Adjonas," Quintall remarked, giving

Smealy a little shake. "He is the leader of the unrest, a man to be thrown over as food for the sharks."

Adjonas calmly put his hand over Quintall's arm, easing it and his first hand down. Smealy pulled away, coughing and, predictably, turned to the crew for help.

"Utter one word of encouragement to them," Quintall threatened, "and all my attacks, and those of my companions, will be directed at you. Both your arms and both your legs will be broken and useless when you hit the water, Bunkus Smealy. How long could you stay afloat, waiting for the *Windrunner* to turn about and find you?"

The greasy man blanched. "We're too far out," he said to his captain, his plea sounding as a whine. "Too far!"

"The island—" Adjonas started to say.

Smealy stopped him with a snarl. "There ain't no island!" he yelled, and the murmurs of the crewmen, seeming closer now than a moment before, were in agreement.

Adjonas turned a worried glance at Quintall. They had another month of sailing, at the least, and the captain honestly wondered if his crew would show that much patience. They had been carefully picked, most had sailed with Adjonas for nearly a decade, but weeks on end out of sight of land were unnerving.

"Three months!" the captain yelled suddenly. "Before ever we started from Jacintha, I told you that we would find three months of travel before our destination was reached. Yet, we've not yet marked the end of our second month out of St.-Mere-Abelle. Are you cowards, then? Are you not men of your honor?"

That backed them off, though they continued grumbling.

"Know by my word," Quintall said to Smealy as the first hand, too, retreated, "that I hold you personally responsible for the actions of the crew."

Smealy never blinked and didn't dare look away from the dangerous monk until he was halfway across the deck.

"It will only worsen if Pimaninicuit is not easily found," Adjonas quietly warned the three.

Quintall fixed him with an icy stare.

"We are on course, and on time," Adjonas assured him, feeling the need to calm the man, "according to the maps I was given."

"They are accurate to the league," Quintall growled in response.

Indeed they were, for four and a half uneasy weeks later, the lookout cried out, "Land to forward!"

All the crew rushed to the forward rails, and soon enough the gray haze became more substantial, became the undeniable outline of an island, conical in shape. Gray became green as they closed, lush vegetation thick on the slopes.

"By my estimation we have nearly a week to spare," Adjonas remarked to the four monks—for Pellimar, though still very weak, was up on the deck again. "Should we go ashore and scout—"

"No!" Quintall snapped to everyone's amazement. The captain's recommendation seemed perfectly logical.

"None but the Preparers may go ashore," Quintall explained. "Any others who touch the shores of Pimaninicuit will find their lives forfeit."

It was a strange decree, one that caught Avelyn so much by surprise that he hardly noticed Quintall had openly proclaimed the name of the island.

The words caught Captain Adjonas off his guard as well, an unexpected proclamation and one that was hardly welcomed by Adjonas. His crew had been aboard ship for so long, with only the short break in Entel. To keep them out now, with land so close and inviting—land likely covered with fruit trees and other luxuries they had not known on the open sea—was foolhardy indeed.

But Quintall would not relent. "Circle the island close once that we might discern where best to put the Preparers ashore, then sail out to deeper water out of sight of the island," he instructed the captain. "Then sail back in five days."

Adjonas knew he was at a critical point here. He didn't agree with Quintall, not at all, but now with Pimaninicuit in sight, he had, by agreement with the Father Abbot, to let the monk take command. This was the purpose of the voyage, after all, and Father Abbot Markwart had made no secret of Adjonas' place in all this. On the open seas, he was the captain; at Pimaninicuit, he would do as told, or all payment, and the sum was considerable, would be forfeit.

And worse.

So they circled, spotting one promising lagoon, and then sailed out to deeper waters for the longest five days of the trip, particularly for Avelyn and Thagraine.

Avelyn spent all the last day in prayer and meditation, mentally preparing himself for the task ahead. He wanted to go to Dansally and tell her of his fears, of his inadequacy for such a task, but he resisted the urge. This was his battle alone.

Finally, he and Thagraine, carrying their supplies, slipped down the rope off the side of the *Windrunner* into the boat, Pimaninicuit looming large before them.

"We need be far out when the showers begin," Quintall explained to them, "for the stones have been known to cause great damage. When it is ended, we will sail back here."

A cry from the stern stole the conversation, and the monks and Adjonas turned as one to see one of the crew, a boy of no more than seventeen who had been especially sea-crazed, dive off the ship into the water, then begin swimming hard for the shore.

"Mister Smealy!" Adjonas roared, turning a stern eye on all the crew. "Archers to the rail!"

"Let him go," Quintall said, surprising Adjonas. Quintall realized that shooting the desperate man in front of the crew would likely cause a mutiny. "Let him go!" Quintall yelled louder. "But since he has chosen the island, he will find his work doubled." He bent low and whispered something to Thagraine then, and Avelyn doubted that it had anything to do with putting the fleeing man to work.

Avelyn and Thagraine rowed away from the *Windrunner* moments later and the ship raised sail immediately, fleeing for the safety of the deeper waters far from Pimaninicuit. On board Quintall launched right away into lies about the dangers to the foolish seaman, about how the monks, and the monks alone, were trained to withstand the fury of the showers. "He will not likely live to return to the *Windrunner*," Quintall explained, trying to prepare the volatile crew for the blow that would surely come.

Thagraine was out and running as soon as the small boat brushed its bottom on the black sands of the island beach. They had passed the mutineer on the water, far to the side, and Thagraine had made a mental note of his direction and speed.

Avelyn called out to his companion, but Thagraine only ordered him to secure the boat, and did not look back.

Avelyn felt a sinking feeling in the pit of his stomach. He hauled the boat to a sheltered point in the lagoon and tipped it low, filling it with water and securing it on the shallow bottom.

Thagraine returned to him soon after.

Avelyn winced, seeing the man alone. He knew what instructions Quintall had offered.

"There is much to eat," Thagraine said happily, trembling with excitement. "And we must seek out a cave."

Avelyn said nothing, just followed quietly, praying for the young sailor's soul.

The next two days, mostly spent huddled in a small cave on the side of the single mountain, overlooking the beach and the wide water, were perfectly unbearable. Thagraine was most ill at ease, pacing, stalking, and muttering to himself.

Avelyn understood the man's distress and knew that Thagraine's agitation could cost them both much when the showers came. "You killed him," the younger monk remarked quietly, taking care so that his statement did not sound as an accusation.

Thagraine stopped his pacing. "Any who step on Pimaninicuit forfeit their lives," he replied, straining hard to keep his tone even.

Avelyn didn't believe a word of it; in his mind, Thagraine had acted as a tool for the murderous Quintall.

"How will they know when we are finished?" Thagraine asked suddenly, wildly. "How will they even know when the showers occur if they sail so far from the island?"

Avelyn eyed him carefully. He had hoped to draw the man into a discussion of his action against the sailor, to ease the man's mind, at least for now, that they might concentrate on their most-important mission. But his words hardly seemed to calm Thagraine; quite the opposite, the man, obviously racked with guilt, paced all the more furiously, slapping his hands together repeatedly.

The showers, by their calculations, were now overdue. Still the pair huddled near the edge of the cave, looking for some sign.

"Is it even true?" Thagraine protested every few minutes. "Is there a man alive who can bear witness to such a thing?"

"The old tomes do not lie," Avelyn said faithfully.

"How do you know?" Thagraine exploded. "Where are the stones, then? Where is the precious day?" He stopped, gasping for breath. "Seven generations," he shouted, "and we are to get here within the week of the showers? What folly is this? Why, if the abbey's calculations are off by only a month, or a year perhaps . . . are we to stay huddled in a hole all that time?"

"Calm, Thagraine," Avelyn murmured. "Hold fast your faith in Father Abbot Markwart and in God."

"To the pit of Hell with Father Abbot Markwart!" the other monk howled. "God?" He spat contemptuously. "What does God know when he calls for the death of a frightened boy?"

So that was it, Avelyn realized: guilt, pure and simple. Avelyn moved to take Thagraine's hand, to try and offer comfort, but the older monk shoved him away and scrambled out the narrow mouth of the cave, running off into the brush.

"Do not!" Avelyn cried, and he paused only a moment before following. He lost sight of Thagraine immediately, the monk disappearing into the thick underbrush but headed, predictably, for the open beach. Avelyn moved to follow, but as soon as he got out of sight of the cave, something, some inner voice, called to him to stop. He looked back in the direction of the cave, then out over the hillside to the water. He noted that the sky had turned a funny color, a purplish, rosy hue the likes of which Avelyn had only seen at sunrise or sunset, and then only on the appropriate horizon. Yet the sun, in this region of long days, was still hours from the western rim and should have been shining bright and yellow in the cloudless sky.

"Damnation," Avelyn sputtered, and he scrambled with all speed back to the shelter of the cave. Inside, from that higher perch, he spotted Thagraine, running wildly along the beach, and he saw, too, a gentle rustling on the water far out from the shore.

Avelyn closed his eyes and prayed.

* * *

"Where are you, damned God?" Thagraine cried, stumbling along the black sands of Pimaninicuit. "What cost do you exact from your faithful? What lies do you tell?"

He stopped then, suddenly, hearing the splashing.

He grabbed at his arm a moment later, felt a line of blood there, and noticed a small stone, a smoky crystal, lying on the black sand before him.

Thagraine's eyes widened as surely as if God himself had answered his questions. He looked back and turned and ran with all speed for the cave, crying for Avelyn every step.

Avelyn couldn't bear to watch, nor could he bear to look away. Fiery rocks streaked down before the cave entrance, slicing holes in the wide leaves of trees and bushes. The rocky hail was light for some time, gradually increasing to the point where it punished the very ground of Pimaninicuit.

And through the deluge, Avelyn heard his name. He peered out, stunned, as a torn and battered Thagraine came into view beyond the thinned foliage, the man bleeding in so many places that he seemed one great wound. He stumbled forward pitifully, holding out his arms toward the cave.

Avelyn set his feet under him. He knew that it was foolhardy for him to go out, but how could he not? He could make it, he told himself grimly. He could get to Thagraine and shelter the man back to the cave. He tried not to think of the choice that would then befall him, of tending to either Thagraine or to the sacred stones, for his period of opportunity for sealing the enchantment of the stones was narrow indeed.

But Avelyn would have to worry about that when the time came. Thagraine was barely twenty strides away, stumbling forward, when Avelyn started out.

He saw it at once, a dark blot high above, and he knew, somehow he knew, its deadly path.

Thagraine spotted him then, a hopeful, pitiful, smile widening on his bloody face.

The stone streaked down like an aimed arrow, smashing into the back of Thagraine's head, laying him out flat on the ground.

Avelyn fell back into the cave, into his prayers.

The storm intensified over the next hour, wind and rocky rain pounding the island, battering the ground above Avelyn's hole so forcefully that the monk feared it would collapse upon him.

But then, as abruptly as it began, it ended, and the skies cleared quickly to deep blue.

Avelyn came out, frightened but determined. He went right to Thagraine, a torn and bloody pulp. Avelyn meant to turn him over, but he could not find his breath when he looked at the fatal wound, a gaping hole smashed right through Thagraine's skull, brain matter splattered all about.

The object of Thagraine's death, a huge purple amethyst, held Avelyn's attention. Gently, reverently, Avelyn reached into the back of his dead companion's head and pulled forth the stone. He could feel the power thrumming within it, the likes of which he had never before imagined. Surely this was greater than any stone at St.-Mere-Abelle! And the size of it! Avelyn's hands were large indeed, yet even with his fingers fully extended he could not touch all edges of the stone.

He went to work, put all thoughts of Thagraine and of the boy Thagraine had killed far out of his mind, and went with furor to the task he had trained to do for all these years. He prepared the amethyst first, coating it with special oils, giving it some of his own energy through intense prayer and handling.

Then he went on, letting his instincts guide him to which stones were the most full of heavenly energy. Many showed no magical power at all, and Avelyn soon realized that these were the remnants of previous showers, brought up to the surface by the battering of the storm. He selected an egg-sized hematite next, and then a ruby, small but flawless to his trained eye.

On and on he went. Only those stones he selected and treated would hold their power; the others would become the waste of Pimaninicuit, buried by the black sands and the resurgent foliage over the next seven generations.

Late that night, the monk fell, thoroughly exhausted, upon the beach bordering the lagoon. He did not wake up until long after the dawn, his precious cargo intact in his pack. Only then did Avelyn take the time to note that dramatic change that had come over Pimaninicuit. No longer did the island seem so plush and inviting. Where trees and thick brush had grown was now only battered pulp and blasted stone.

It took great effort for the monk to get the sunken boat raised and floating, but he somehow managed. He thought that he should fill it with fruits or some other delicacy, but in looking around at the near-total devastation, Avelyn realized that opportunity was lost. On another note, Avelyn could not help but laugh at the absurd, useless treasure that lay strewn all about him. In an hour's time, he could collect enough precious—though nonmagical—gemstones to finance the building of a palace finer than that in Ursal. In a day, he could have more wealth than any man in all Honce-the-Bear, in all the world, perhaps, including the fabulously rich tribal chieftains of Behren. But his orders concerning Pimaninicuit had been explicit and unyielding: only those stones treated to retain their magic could be brought from the island. Any other gems taken would be considered an insult to God himself. The gift of the showers was given to two monks only, and whatever they might prepare, they might take. Not a ruby, not a smoky quartz, more.

Thus, Avelyn simply sat staring outward, too overwhelmed even to eat, and waited for the *Windrunner*.

The sails came into sight late the next day. Like a robot, beyond feeling, Brother Avelyn got into the boat and pushed away. Only then did he think that perhaps he should retrieve the body of Thagraine, but he decided against that course.

What better fate and final resting place for an Abellican monk?

❖ 19 ❖

Truth Be Told

He hardly noted the passing of the days, the weeks, so enthralled was he with the horde of God-given treasures. While Adjonas tended to the crew and their course, the three remaining monks—even Pellimar, whose condition had steadily improved—worked with the stones. The powrie slash had not been without consequence to Pellimar, though, tearing the muscles about the monk's left shoulder. His arm hung practically useless, with no sign that it would ever improve.

They encountered no powries on the voyage back from Pimaninicuit, and Avelyn wasn't concerned in any case. He above all others sensed the throbbing powers of some of the gemstones. If a barrelboat showed itself, Avelyn was confident he could use any one of a dozen different stones to destroy it utterly.

Most intriguing of all was the giant purple amethyst, with so many different crystal shafts. Its bottom was nearly flat, and placed on the floor it resembled some strange purple bush, with stems of various heights rising at many angles. Avelyn could not discern the purpose of the magic, except to note that there was a tremendous amount of energy stored within those crystals.

Some of the stones, such as the hematite, were placed in a small tumbler and rolled for hours on end, smoothing them to a perfect finish. Others had to be treated with oils for many days, that their magic be locked permanently within them. All three monks knew the process, and knew each stone, except for that amethyst.

They couldn't tumble it—it was too large for the container—and they hardly knew where to begin with their oils. Avelyn made it his personal work, and he treated the giant crystal with prayers, not physical salves. He felt as if he was giving a bit of himself to the stone each time, but that was acceptable, as if it were some communion with his God.

The talk among the monks did not turn often to poor Thagraine—they prayed for him and, in their minds and hearts, put him to rest—but among the grumbling crew, little was whispered that did not concern Taddy Sway, the youth who had tried for the island and who had not returned. Avelyn felt burning, accusing eyes on his back every time he walked the deck.

Whispers bred open talk in the heat and boredom of the passing days, and open talk bred accusing shouts. Avelyn, Pellimar, and most of all, Quintall, were not surprised then, one early morning, when Captain Adjonas came to them, warning of a mounting call for mutiny.

"They want the stones," Adjonas explained. "Or at least, some of the stones, in exchange for the life of Taddy Sway."

"They cannot even begin to understand the power of these gems," Quintall protested.

"But they understand the value of a ruby or an emerald," Adjonas pointed out, "even without the magic."

Avelyn bit his lip, remembering the hours on the beach, surrounded by so vast a wealth of useless gems.

"Your crew is being well paid for the voyage," Quintall reminded the captain.

"Extra compensation for the lost man," Adjonas remarked.

"They knew the risks."

"Did they?" the captain asked sincerely. "Did they suspect that the four men they carried might turn against them?"

Quintall stood up and walked to stand right before the captain, the monk seeming even more imposing because Adjonas had to stoop belowdecks, whereas Quintall could stand at his full height.

"I am only echoing their sentiments," Adjonas explained, not backing off an inch. "Words that Quintall should hear. We are three months yet from St.-Mere-Abelle."

Quintall glanced around the tiny cabin, eyes narrowed as he planned his next move. "We must end it this day," he decided, and he moved to Avelyn's cot and took one of the gemstones, an orange-brown stone marked by three black lines—a tiger's paw, it was called—from the tumbling box.

The stocky monk led the way to the deck, the other three close behind. Quintall's physical attitude as he came out alerted the crew that something important was about to happen, and they quickly gathered around the group, Bunkus Smealy at their lead.

"There will be no compensation for Taddy Sway," Quintall said bluntly. "The foolish youth forfeited his life when he swam to the island."

"Ye killed him!" one man cried.

"I was on the *Windrunner*," Quintall reminded.

"Yer monks, I mean!" the man insisted.

Quintall neither denied nor confirmed the execution. "The island was for two men alone, and even one of them, trained for years to survive Pim—the island, did not return."

Bunkus Smealy turned about and waved his hand forcefully, quieting the rising murmurs. "We're thinking that ye owe us," he said, turning back to Quintall. He tucked his hands into his rope belt, taking on an important attitude.

Quintall measured him carefully. He understood then that Smealy was the linchpin, the organizer, the would-be captain.

"Captain Adjonas does not agree," Quintall said evenly, coaxing the mutiny to the surface.

Smealy turned a wicked grin on the captain. "Might not be Captain Adjonas' decision," he said.

"The penalties for mutiny—" Adjonas began, but Smealy stopped him short.

"We're knowing the rules," Smealy assured him loudly. "And we're knowing, too, that a man has got to be caught to be hung. Behren's closer than Honce-the-Bear, and they're not for asking many questions in Behren."

There—he had played his hand, and now it was time for Quintall to take that hand and crush it. Smealy's eyes widened when he looked back at the stocky monk, when he heard the low growl coming from Quintall's throat, when he looked at the man's arm and saw not a human appendage but the paw and claws of a great tiger!

"What?" the old sea dog started to ask as Quintall, faster then Smealy could possibly react, raked the man chin to belly.

The horrified crew fell back.

"He killed me," Smealy whispered, and then, true to his words, with three great lines of bright blood erupting across his neck and chest, he fell limp to the deck.

Quintall's roar, truly the roar of a tiger, sent the crew scrambling. "Know this!" the transformed monk bellowed from a face that looked human but with a voice that sounded much greater. "Look upon dead Bunkus Smealy and see the fate of any other who speaks against Captain Adjonas or the brothers of St.-Mere-Abelle!"

Given the expressions on the crewmen, Avelyn thought it unlikely that any of them would utter another mutinous whisper all the way back to the coast and to St.-Mere-Abelle.

The three monks exchanged not a word as they went back to their cabin, nor for the rest of that day. Avelyn took care to keep his accusing gaze away from Quintall. His mind swirled in a hundred different directions. He had come to know Bunkus Smealy well over the last few months and, though he was not over fond of the weasely man, he could not help but feel some sense of loss.

And agitation. The cool and callous way Quintall had dispatched the man, had murdered a human being, shook gentle Avelyn to his very bones. This was not the way of the Abellican Church, at least not in Avelyn's mind, and yet the efficiency of the executions of Taddy Sway and now of Bunkus Smealy made Avelyn suspect that Quintall was acting as he had been instructed by the masters before they had left port. The mission was vital, true enough, the greatest moment in seven generations. Avelyn and the other monks would give their lives willingly to see the mission successful. But to kill without remorse?

He chanced a look at Quintall early the next day as the man went about his business. He remembered the emotional torture the execution had exacted on Thagraine, the restlessness. None of that was evident in the dark, stocky man. Quintall had killed Bunkus Smealy as he had drowned the powrie, without distinction of the fact that the victim this time was not an evil dwarf but a human being.

A shudder coursed down Avelyn's spine. Without remorse. And Avelyn knew when they returned to the abbey, when their tale was told in full, the masters, even Father Abbot Markwart, would only nod their agreement with Quintall's brutal actions.

Avelyn could appreciate their notion of the "greater good," for that would surely be the excuse given, but somehow all of this was out of line with justice, and justice was supposedly among the major tenets of the Abellican Church.

For Brother Avelyn, who had just been through the most sacred event, who had just realized the most religious experience by far of all his young life, something here seemed terribly out of place.

The month had turned to Parvespers, the last month of the autumn, when the *Windrunner* swept around the northeastern reach of the Mantis Arm, past Pireth Tulme and into the Gulf of Corona. Cold winds and stinging spray buffeted the crew. At night, they huddled together around oil lamps and candles, trying to ward off the chill. But their spirits were high, every man. All thoughts of Taddy Sway and Bunkus Smealy were behind them now, for their destination and their reward were at hand.

"Will ye stay in the abbey, then?" Dansally asked Avelyn one crisp morning. Land was out of sight again as the *Windrunner* cut a direct course across the gulf to All Saints Bay.

Avelyn considered the question with a most curious expression. "Of course," he finally answered.

Dansally's shrug was telling to the perceptive monk. He realized suddenly that she was asking him for companionship! "Do you mean to leave the ship?" he asked.

"Might," Dansally replied. "We'll be puttin' in three times between St.-Mere-Abelle and Palmaris, where Adjonas means to dock for winter."

"I have to . . ." Avelyn began. "I mean, there is no choice before me. Father Abbot Markwart will need a full accounting, and I will be at work for months with the stones I collected—"

She silenced him by putting a finger gently across his lips, her eyes soft and moist.

"Would that I could come and visit ye then," she said quietly. "Might that be allowed?"

Avelyn nodded, fairly stricken mute.

"Would ye be bothered?"

Avelyn shook his head rather vigorously. "Master Jojonah is a friend," he explained. "Perhaps he could find you work."

"On me back in an abbey?" the woman asked incredulously.

"Different work," Avelyn answered with a chuckle, hiding his discomfort at the notion. Those wicked stories of Bien deLouisa flitted through his memory. "But would Captain Adjonas let you off the ship?" he asked, to change the uncomfortable course down which his mind was flying.

"Me contract was for the isle and back," she replied. "We'll soon be back. Adjonas got nothing on me after Palmaris. I'll get me pay—and more for the favors I did for the rest of the crew—and be gone."

"Then will you come to the abbey?" Avelyn asked, showing more emotion, more hopefulness, than he had intended.

Dansally's smile was wide. "Might that I will," she answered. "But first, ye got to do something for me." As she finished talking, she leaned closer, putting her lips to his. Avelyn recoiled instinctively, out of shyness. When he thought about his hesitation, it only strengthened his resolve. His relationship with Dansally was special, was something different from the physical connection she had with other men. Surely his body wanted what she offered, but if he gave in now, then would he be lessening that special bond, reducing his relationship with Dansally to the level of all the others?

"Don't ye pull away," she pleaded, "not this time."

"I could bring Quintall to you," Avelyn said, a bitter edge to his voice.

Dansally fell back and slapped him across the face. He meant to respond with an insult, but by the time he recovered, he noted that she was kneeling on the bed, head down, shoulders moving with sobs.

"I—I did not mean ..." Avelyn stuttered, feeling horrible about wounding his precious Dansally.

"So ye think I'm a whore," she said. "And so I am."

"No," Avelyn replied, putting a hand on her shoulder.

"But I'm more a virgin than ye know!" the woman snapped, head coming up so that her gaze, her proud gaze, could lock with Avelyn's. "Me body does its work, 'tis true, but me heart's never been there. Not once! Not even with me worthless husband—might that be why he threw me out!"

The thought that Dansally had never loved caught Avelyn off his guard and settled him back for a bit. Though he was completely inexperienced in physical lovemaking, he understood what she was saying.

And he believed her!

He didn't answer, except to lean forward and offer a kiss.

Brother Avelyn learned much about love that day, learned the completeness of body and spirit in a way more profound than his morning exercise could ever approach.

So did Dansally.

The *Windrunner* was welcomed at St.-Mere-Abelle with understated efficiency, just a handful of monks, Masters Jojonah and Siherton among them, coming down to the docks to greet the returning brothers and their precious cargo, and to direct the lesser monks in carrying aboard ship a pair of heavy chests. A new wharf had been constructed, reaching far enough out into the bay so that the *Windrunner* could dock.

To mollify his crew, Adjonas had the chests opened as soon as they were brought on deck, and how the men gasped!

Avelyn did, too, noting the piles of coins and gems and jewelry, such a treasure as he had never before seen. Something beyond the rich materials caught his eyes, though, as the lids were being secured in place once more. He didn't quite understand it, nor could he make out the aura of magic surrounding Master Siherton. The man had one of his hands behind his back, and Avelyn noted that he was fingering a pair of stones, a diamond and a smoky quartz.

Suspicious, but wise enough to keep his mouth shut, Avelyn bid farewell to Adjonas and the others—though not a man aboard the *Windrunner* regretted the departure of the three monks—and went ashore. His thoughts were on Dansally, hoping she would indeed leave the *Windrunner* at next port and make her way to St.-Mere-Abelle. Logically, Avelyn knew that she would indeed, knew that they had shared something precious. But still his doubts lingered. Had their encounter really been special to Dansally? How had he measured up against all the men she had known? Perhaps he hadn't really done it right, or perhaps Adjonas had ordered her to bed Avelyn, or even had made a wager with her that she could not bed the man.

Avelyn fought hard to dismiss all those ridiculous notions and doubts. Whatever logic assured him, Avelyn knew that he would not relax until he saw the dark-haired woman's blue eyes again, eyes to which Avelyn had brought back a good measure of sparkle, at the gates of St.-Mere-Abelle.

The reception awaiting the three returned monks inside the abbey was more in tune with what they had been expecting. The chapel hall was lined with the finest baked goods from all the region—muffins and sweet rolls, cinnamon and raisin breads—all to be washed down with mead and even some of the rare and precious wine known as boggle. The choir was there, singing joyously. The Father Abbot watched from his high perch on the balcony, and all the monks of the order and all the servants of the abbey danced and sang, and laughed the whole night through.

How Avelyn wished that Dansally were there! That thought led him to wonder why she and the others of the *Windrunner* had not been invited. With the tides, the ship could not put out until after midnight, so why hadn't the thirty, or at least the captain, been included in the much-deserved festivities?

The last bite of a cinnamon roll turned over in Avelyn's stomach, a sinking feeling. A group of monks were walking toward him—he recognized Brother Pellimar among them—no doubt to pester him about the events on the island. Avelyn knew that he could say nothing about that time until he had reviewed his words with the Father Abbot.

And at that moment, the young monk had other things on his mind. He considered the stones Master Siherton had carried to the ship: a diamond and a smoky quartz. He knew the properties of diamonds, the creation of light, but had never used quartz. Avelyn closed his eyes, ignoring the call of his name by Pellimar, and reviewed his training.

Then it came to him in a sudden, horrifying rush. Diamonds not for light but sparkles! Quartz to create an image that was not real! The crew and captain of the *Windrunner* had been cheated! Now Avelyn knew why Adjonas was not at the gathering, and as he considered the implications, his gut churned violently.

Avelyn rushed past the approaching group, muttering something about speaking with them soon, then ran about the room, taking a mental count of those in attendance. He noted with mounting trepidation that not all of the monks were in attendance, that one group in particular, the older students, tenth-year immaculates, those men on the verge of becoming masters, were absent.

Neither could he find Master Siherton.

Avelyn ran from the chapel, skittering down the empty halls, his footsteps echoing noisily. He didn't know the hour but suspected that midnight was near or that it had come and gone.

He ran for the south side of the abbey, the seaward side, and turned into one long corridor, its left-hand wall dotted with small windows that overlooked the bay. Avelyn rushed to one and peered out desperately into the night.

Under the light of a half moon, he saw the outline of the *Windrunner* gliding out into the bay. "No," he breathed, noting the bustle on the deck, tiny silhouettes rushing past a small fire near the stern. He saw a second fire on the water.

"No!" Avelyn screamed.

Another ball of flaming pitch soared out from the monastery, skipping in along the starboard rail of the vessel, igniting the mainsail into one tremendous flame.

The barrage intensified, more pitch, great heavy stones, and giant ballista bolts battering the ill-fated craft. Soon the *Windrunner* was adrift, the strong currents of All Saints Bay taking her toward a dangerous reef. Avelyn winced, seeing men leaping from the deck, their doom at hand.

The screams of the crew drifted across the dark water; Avelyn knew that the other monks, at their celebration, would not hear. He watched helplessly, hopelessly, as the ship that had been his home for nearly eight months jolted and listed, then broke apart on the reef as still more missiles soared in. Tears ran freely down his cheeks; he mumbled the name "Dansally," over and over.

The bombardment went on for many minutes. Avelyn heard the people in the cold water, and hoped against hope that some of them, that his dear Dansally, might make it to shore.

But then came the worst thing of all—a hissing, sizzling noise. A bluish film covered the dark water, snapping and crackling off the stones and the sailors, off the remnants of the proud ship. A sheet of conjured lightning silenced the screams forever.

Except in Avelyn's mind.

More missiles went out, though their task was certainly finished. The strong ebb tide of All Saints Bay would collect the flotsam and jetsam and carry it out to the open sea. All the world, save Avelyn and the perpetrators, would think this a tragic accident.

"Dansally," Avelyn breathed. His shoulders slumped, the young man needing the stone wall for support. He rolled away from the window, putting his back to the wall, facing the corridor.

"You should not have come," Master Siherton said to him, the tall, hawkish man standing quietly.

Avelyn noted the considerable bag of stones at his belt and the grayish graphite he held in his hand. Graphite was the stone of lightning.

Avelyn slumped back against the wall even more, thinking Siherton would use the stone to destroy him then and there and, in many ways, hoping Siherton would do just that. The master only reached out and grabbed Avelyn by the arm and led him to a small, dark room in one far corner of the massive abbey.

The next morning, a crestfallen Brother Avelyn was in Father Abbot Markwart's private quarters, Masters Siherton and Jojonah flanking him. It stung Avelyn even more to realize that the actions taken against the *Windrunner* had not been a rogue decision by brutal Siherton but had been sanctioned by the Father Abbot, apparently with Master Jojonah's knowledge.

"There can be no witnesses to the location of Pimaninicuit," Father Abbot Markwart said evenly.

As there will be no witnesses to my death, Avelyn thought, for the corridors of St.-Mere-Abelle had been deserted that morning, the monks and servants sleeping off their evening of revelry.

"Do you realize the implications to the world?" Markwart said suddenly, excitedly. "If Pimaninicuit became common knowledge, the security of the

Ring Stones would be lost and petty merchants and kings would hold the secret to wealth and power beyond their comprehension!"

It made sense to Avelyn that, for the security of the world, the location of Pimaninicuit should remain secret, but that thought did little to erase his revulsion at the destruction of the hired ship and the murder of her crew.

And the murder of Dansally.

"There could be no other outcome," Markwart said flatly.

Avelyn glanced around nervously. "May I speak, Father Abbot?"

"Of course," Markwart replied, resting back in his chair. "Speak freely, Brother Avelyn. You are among friends."

Avelyn tried hard to keep his expression calm at that absurd notion. "All aboard the ship would have been long dead before the next occurrence of the stone showers," he argued.

"Sailors make maps," Master Siherton said dryly.

"But why would they?" Avelyn protested. "The map would be of no use to them, since seven generations—"

"You are forgetting the wealth strewn about Pimaninicuit," Father Abbot Markwart interrupted, "a treasure trove of jewels beyond imagination."

Avelyn hadn't thought of that. Still he shook his head. The journey was too treacherous, and if the crew had been well paid, as promised, they would have had no reason to dare the perils of the South Mirianic again.

"It was God's will," Markwart said with finality. "All of it. You are to speak nothing of what you have witnessed. Return now to the room that Master Siherton assigned to you. Your punishment will be determined and revealed later this same day."

Avelyn's thoughts whirled, too confusing a jumble for him to utter even a sound of protest. He staggered away as if he had been struck. Markwart verbally hit him again when he got to the door.

"Brother Pellimar succumbed this morning to his grievous wounds," the Father Abbot informed Avelyn.

Avelyn turned, stunned. Pellimar would carry scars forever, but surely he had mended. Then Avelyn understood. The previous night, at the party, Pellimar had been loose with his tongue. Too loose. Even to utter the name of the island without Father Abbot's permission was forbidden.

"A pity," Markwart went on. "That leaves only you and Quintall of the four who went to Pimaninicuit. You will have much work before you."

Avelyn stepped out of the room, into the stone corridor, and vomited all over the floor. He staggered away, half blind, half insane.

"He is being watched?" Markwart asked Siherton.

"Every step," the tall master replied. "All along, I feared this response from him."

Master Jojonah snorted. "Avelyn worked alone on Pimaninicuit, yet the horde he retrieved is inarguably the finest ever brought back from the island. How can you doubt his value?"

"I do not," Siherton replied. "I only wonder when those qualities that give Avelyn such value will become dangerous."

Jojonah looked at Markwart, who was nodding grimly. "He has much work to do," the Father Abbot told them both. "Committing his adventures to the page, cataloguing the stones, even seeking out their true strength and deepest secrets. The crystal amethyst most of all. Never have I seen such a magnificent stone, and Avelyn, as its Preparer, has the finest chance to discern its true measure."

"Perhaps I can persuade him to our way of thinking before he is finished his work," Jojonah offered.

"That would be most fine," replied Markwart.

Siherton gave his fellow master a dubious glance. He did not believe that Avelyn, so full of idealism and ridiculous faith, could be corralled.

Jojonah noted the look and could not disagree. He would try, though, for he was fond of young Brother Avelyn and he knew the alternative.

"The summer solstice," Father Abbot Markwart remarked. "At that time, we will discuss the future of Brother Avelyn Desbris."

"Or lack thereof," Master Siherton added, and from his tone, it wasn't hard for Jojonah to figure out which event would most please the hawkish, brutal man.

Avelyn found himself secluded from the rest of the monks over the next few weeks. His only contacts were with Siherton, Jojonah, and a couple of other masters, as well as the pair of guards—more tenth-year immaculates, who remained with him wherever he went—and Quintall, who was often at work beside him in the room of the Ring Stones.

Disturbing questions haunted the young monk every day. Why did they have to kill the men of the *Windrunner*? Couldn't Father Abbot Markwart have simply imprisoned them? Or, if this procedure was always the case, then why didn't the monastery simply man its own ship and send only trusted monks to Pimaninicuit?

Every logical argument ran smack into a wall, though, for Avelyn knew that he would not impress any change over his superiors and the way of the Abellican Order. And so he worked, as he was instructed, penning the tale of his adventures in great detail, studying and cataloguing the newest stones, their type, their magic, their strength. Whenever he was allowed to handle a magical stone, Master Siherton was at his side, a potent and lethal gem in hand.

Avelyn realized his place now, and truly he felt like one of the *Windrunner*'s crew. His only solace came in his many discussions with Master Jojonah, to whom he still felt a bond. But while Jojonah continually tried to explain the necessity for the actions taken upon the monks' return, Avelyn simply would not accept it.

There had to be a better way, he believed, and despite the potential for disaster, there could be no justification for murder.

The spring of 822 was late when his work neared completion, and Avelyn noted with some concern that Master Jojonah spoke with him less and less, noted with some concern the tender master's sympathetic expression whenever he looked upon Avelyn.

Avelyn grew uneasy, and then desperate. So much so that he chanced to pocket a gemstone, a hematite, one day. Fortune was with him, for a mistake by Quintall caused a minor explosion that afternoon, and though no one was hurt and nothing too badly damaged, it proved enough of a distraction for the theft to go unnoticed, at least for the moment.

Back in his cell, Avelyn fell into the powers of the stone. He didn't really know what he would do, other than spy on the masters and confirm his fears of his approaching fate.

His spirit walked free of his body, passed through the porous wood of the door and past the pair of oblivious guards. Avelyn felt that tug of the stone, wanting possession, but his will was strong and he resisted, floating invisibly down the corridor and finally to Father Abbot Markwart's door.

Inside, Avelyn glimpsed Siherton and Jojonah with the Father Abbot, the old man livid about the mishap in the stone room.

"Brother Quintall is a bumbler," Jojonah pointed out.

"But a loyal one," Siherton snapped back, an obvious comparison to Avelyn.

"Enough of this," demanded Markwart. "How goes the work?"

"The cataloguing is nearly complete," answered Siherton. "We are ready for the merchants."

"What of the giant crystal?"

"We have found no practical use for it," Siherton replied. "Avelyn— Brother Avelyn," he corrected with a derisive snort, "is convinced that it is thick with magic, but how to extract that magic and what purpose it might serve, we do not know."

"It would be folly to auction it," Jojonah put in.

"It would not bring a good price unless we could determine its powers," Father Abbot Markwart agreed.

"There are merchants who would purchase it simply for the mystery," Siherton argued.

Avelyn could hardly believe what he was hearing. They were talking about a private auction of the sacred stones! How much that notion diminished the sacrifice of Thagraine and Pellimar, of the *Windrunner*'s crew and of Dansally! The thought of unbelieving merchants plying the gift of the stones, to amuse guests, perhaps, or even for sinister purposes, wounded

Avelyn deeply. His spirit drifted out of the room, unable to bear any more of the sacrilegious talk.

He was heading back for his physical coil when he realized that time was against him. His spirit hovered there in the hall. The missing hematite would surely be discovered, and even disregarding that stone, Avelyn's future was far from secure.

What was he to do? And how could he tolerate any of this madness, this insult to God?

Master Siherton came out of Markwart's room alone, his boots clicking on the floor as he made his way in the direction of the stone room. To check on the damage from Quintall's misstep, no doubt, the spying Avelyn realized; to check on the lists of reorganized stones.

Tugged by a sense of urgency, Avelyn gave in to the hematite, his spirit floating fast for Siherton's back.

The pain as he entered the man's body was excruciating, beyond anything Avelyn had ever felt. His thoughts mingled with Siherton's; their spirits clashed and battled, shoving and pushing for possession. Avelyn had struck the man off guard, but even so, the struggle was nothing short of titanic. Avelyn realized then that an attempt at possession was akin to fighting an enemy on his home ground.

If any had been about to bear witness, they would have seen Siherton's body lurching back and forth across the corridor, slamming into walls, clawing at its own face.

Then Avelyn felt the weight of a corporeal form again. He knew instinctively that Siherton's spirit was nearby, locked in some dimensional pocket that Avelyn did not understand. And he had control of the body; it moved to the commands of his spirit!

Avelyn went off with all speed to the stone room, entering forcefully and snapping his glare over the two guards and Quintall before they could utter a word of protest.

"You remain," Avelyn commanded one of the guards. "You," he said to Quintall, "your punishment has not yet been determined."

"Punishment?" Quintall echoed breathlessly. He had been told that there would be no consequences from his mishap, and indeed, such minor problems had not been uncommon in the month in which he and Avelyn had been at work with the new stones. Just a week before, Avelyn had melted a leg of one table while examining a ruby sprinkled with carnallite!

"Brother Avelyn was not—" Quintall began to protest.

"To your room and prayers!" the voice of Siherton commanded.

"Yes, my master," said a cowed Quintall, and he moved off out of the room.

"Be gone!" Avelyn commanded the other guard, and the man ran out of the room, swiftly passing Quintall in the hall.

Then Avelyn and the remaining guard began selecting and collecting stones: the giant crystal amethyst, a rod of graphite, a small but potent ruby, and several others, including turquoise and amber, celestine and a tiger's paw, a chrysoberyl, or cat's eye, some gypsum and malachite, a sheet of chrysotile, and a piece of heavy magnetite. Avelyn placed them in a bag, and in it he placed, as well, a small pouch of tiny carnallites, the one stone whose magic could be brought forth only a single time. Avelyn then went to the other end of the room and pocketed a valuable emerald, not an enchanted one, but one used as an example of a particular cut, and then he bade the guard to follow him—and quickly, since the use of the hematite was draining the monk and Siherton's spirit was nearby, trying, Avelyn knew, to find some route back to its body.

They made their way to the secluded cell that held Avelyn's body, the master's voice quickly and forcefully dismissing the two men who stood guard in the hall.

The one remaining guard, the man from the stone room, opened the door on Siherton's order. There stood Avelyn's corporeal form, as he had left it, clutching the hematite. Avelyn in Siherton's body stepped past the guard and deftly took the hematite, then instructed the guard to shoulder the inanimate body and follow him.

"Brother Avelyn is to be punished for treason against the Order" was all the explanation he offered, and the guard, who had heard rumors to that effect for weeks now, did not question the news.

It was vespers, so few were about to observe the master and the guard, bearing his extraordinary burden, as they made their way to the abbey roof overlooking All Saints Bay. The guard, as instructed, placed the body at the base of the low wall and stepped back.

Avelyn waited for many moments, gathering his strength. He bent over the body, slipping the hematite and one other stone, into its hand, tying the gemstone sack to the body's rope belt.

"The stones will allow us to find the body," he explained to the guard, noting that the man was growing increasingly suspicious. "They will take from Brother Avelyn the last of his physical strength as he dies."

The guard's face screwed up with curiosity, but he did not dare to question the dangerous master.

Avelyn knew that he had to be quick—that he had to be perfect.

With great effort, Avelyn tore his spirit free of Siherton's corporeal form and reentered his own, coming to his physical senses even as Siherton's body shivered with the return of his own spirit.

Avelyn was up, quick as a cat, clutching the stones in one hand and grabbing Siherton by the front of his robe with the other. Before the guard could come to the master's aid, Avelyn hauled the stunned Siherton and himself over the rail.

They plummeted past the abbey walls, down the cliff face, into the gloom, Siherton screaming his protests.

Avelyn kicked and pushed the man away, then called upon the second stone he held, the malachite.

Then he was floating, Siherton continuing to plummet.

Avelyn continued to push out as he descended gently past the angled cliff. Near the bottom, he pulled the amber from his pouch. He touched down lightly on the water, as he had done in an exercise that seemed to him a million years ago. He was glad that Siherton's body was not in sight; he could not have borne that spectacle.

Using the amber, he walked across the cold water to a point where he could get ashore, then he moved off down the road.

He knew that he would never look upon St.-Mere-Abelle again.

He used the stones. With the malachite, he floated gently over cliffs that any pursuing monks would spend hours climbing down. With the amber, he crossed wide lakes that his pursuers would have to circumvent. Using a chrysoberyl, a cat's-eye, he could see clearly in the dark and move along at daylight pace without the telltale glow of a light. At the first town he entered, he happened upon a caravan of several merchant wagons, and there he sold the common emerald, giving him all the funds he would need for a long, long time.

He put miles and miles behind him, between him and that terrible place called St.-Mere-Abelle. But the young monk could not pull his mind far from the horrors he had witnessed, the encroaching evil that nibbled at the very heart of all that young Avelyn Desbris had held dear.

He learned the truth of it one cold night as he lay curled beneath a tree, under the stars, under the heavens. As if his thoughts were magically transported, or his prayers for guidance divinely answered, his eyes looked across the scores of miles to a land of great jagged mountains, to a smoking cone in its midst, and the black devastation behind a slowly creeping line of red lava.

Avelyn understood then—all of it—for it was not without precedent. This gloom that had come to Honce-the-Bear had come before in a definite shape and manner that was oft-told in the historical volumes at St.-Mere-Abelle. All of it: the cancer that had grown in his world, the unpreparedness, the ungodliness of St.-Mere-Abelle. The monks were the sentinels of God and yet even they had given in to complacency, to the cancer. And because of that lapse, the darkness had returned.

Half-crazed, his entire world shattered, Avelyn understood. The dactyl was awake. The brooding demon that forever haunted the race of man had come back to the world. He knew it to be true. In all his heart, young Avelyn Desbris recognized the darkness that had murdered Taddy Sway and Bunkus Smealy, the evil that had destroyed the *Windrunner* and left his dear Dansally cold in cold water, the wickedness that had forced Brother Pellimar to "succumb" to his wounds.

He awoke from his fitful sleep before the dawn.

The dactyl was awake!

The world did not understand the coming darkness.

The dactyl was awake!

The Order had failed; their weakness had facilitated this tragedy!

The dactyl was awake!

Avelyn ran off—one direction seemed as good as any other. He had to tell the world of the evil. He had to prepare the men and women of Honce-the-Bear, and all of Corona. He had to warn them of the demon, warn them of the Order! He had to somehow show them their own unpreparedness, their own weakness.

The dactyl was awake!

❖ 20 ❖

The Oracle

"How many lights do you see?" The words were spoken in the elvish tongue, one that Juraviel was using more and more with Elbryan. The young man knew all the words, all the common phrases, now, after five years in Andur'Blough Inninness, and only his inflections still needed perfecting.

Juraviel held a candle, as did Elbryan; and a couple of stars had appeared in the sky, the sun just gone behind the mountainous western horizon.

The young man spent a long moment studying Juraviel. Elbryan's lessons had turned more toward philosophy during the fall and winter of God's Year 821 to 822, and he had learned that even the simplest questions carried many layers of subtle meanings. Finally, convinced that this was but a prelude to his lesson, and nothing dramatic, the young man looked up and did a quick count of the stars, noting four.

"Six," he announced cautiously, adding the two candles.

"They are separate, then," Juraviel stated. "Your light and mine, and those of the stars."

Elbryan's brow furrowed. Slowly, hesitantly, as if he expected to be rebuked, he nodded his head.

"So if you pinched the light from your candle, you would stand in darkness," Juraviel reasoned.

"More than now," Elbryan was quick to reply. "But still I would have some of your light."

"Then my light is not contained within the flame," Juraviel went on, "but rather, it spreads far and wide. And what of the light of the stars?"

"If the light in the stars was contained within the stars, then we would not see the stars!" Elbryan growled in mounting frustration. There were times, such as this, when he hated simple elven logic. "And if the light in your candle was contained within the candle, then I would not see it."

"Exactly," replied the elf. "You may go now."

Elbryan stamped his foot as Juraviel turned away. The elf was always doing this to him, leaving him with questions that he could not answer. "What are you talking about?" the young man demanded.

Juraviel looked at him calmly, but made no move to respond.

Elbryan took the cue—it was his lesson, after all. "You are saying that the light, since it is not contained, is a shared thing?"

Juraviel didn't blink.

Elbryan paused for a long while, backtracking the conversation, considering the options. "One light," he said finally.

Juraviel smiled.

"That was the answer," said Elbryan, gaining confidence. "One light."

"I count a dozen stars, at least, now," replied the elf. Elbryan looked up. It was true enough; the night was fast deepening, the stars coming out in force.

"A dozen sources of the same light," Elbryan reasoned, "or of different lights that all join together. Because I see them, they blend. The lights become one."

"One and the same," agreed Juraviel.

"But must I see them for this to be true?" Elbryan asked eagerly, but his anticipation dissipated as he saw the frown immediately come over the elf.

Elbryan paused and closed his eyes, remembering his earliest lessons, the axioms the elves had put to him so that he might view the world in a completely different manner. In elven philosophy, the first truth, the basis of reality was that the entire material, physical world was no more than the collection of perceptions by the observer. Nothing existed except in the consciousness of the individual. It was a difficult concept for Elbryan, because he had been brought up with the idea of community, and within that concept, such elevation of self was considered the worst of sins: pride. The elves didn't see things that way; Juraviel had once asserted to Elbryan that everything in the world was no more than a play put on for Juraviel's benefit. "My consciousness creates the world around me," the elf had proclaimed.

"Then I could never defeat you in battle unless you willed it so," Elbryan had then reasoned.

"Except that your consciousness creates the world around you," the elf had replied, and then, typically, he had walked away.

That seeming contradiction had left Elbryan in a quandary. What he came to understand from that viewpoint was a sense of self he had never before felt free to explore.

"The stars and my candle are one because I can see both," the young man said conclusively. "I make the world around me."

Juraviel nodded. "You *interpret* the world around you," he corrected. "And as you heighten your senses to become aware of the slightest details, your interpretations will grow, your awareness will grow."

Juraviel then left him, sitting in a field, holding his candle and watching the birth of so many stars, heavenly fires to join with his own. That simple shift in perception, that all the lights were truly one, gave Elbryan a sense of oneness with the universe that he had never truly experienced before. Suddenly the heavens seemed closer to him, seemed within reach. Suddenly he felt a part of that vast velvet canopy.

All through the rest of that year, and through the months of God's Year 822, Elbryan learned to view the world as an elf, to find a paradox of individuality and community, an elevation of the self, yet a oneness with all about him. The tiny shifts in perception brought on so many new experiences, allowed him to see flowers where he never before would have looked, allowed him to feel the presence of an animal—even identify its approximate size—by subtle scents and vibrations in the living world about him. He felt like a great empty sponge being dunked into the waters of knowledge, and he absorbed so much, taking incredible pleasure in each lesson, in each word. His entire concepts of space and time altered. Sequence became segment, memory became time travel.

Even Elbryan's sleeping habits changed, shifting to a more controlled, meditative process than a lumped time of uncontrollable unconsciousness. "Fanciful musing," the elves called it, or "reverie." In this semidream state, Elbryan could tune out his sense of sight, yet keep his ears and nose keen for external stimuli. And he replaced much of his dreaming with time travel, moved his mind back to another place in his life that he could replay the events about him and view them from a different perspective, and thus, learn from them.

Olwan was alive to him on those nights, as was Jilseponie, dear Pony, and all the others of Dundalis. Somehow the perfect recollections gave Elbryan a sense of immortality, as if all those people really were alive, just locked away in a different place to which his memory was the key.

He took comfort in that. He found that much of elven philosophy gave him solace, except that he could not really change what had happened, could not alter the past.

The pain remained, the horrible screams, the desperate fights, the mounds of bodies. On Juraviel's instruction, Elbryan did not avoid the anguish, but went to that terrible place often, using the harsh reality of the death of Dundalis to strengthen his nerve, to harden him emotionally.

"Trials past prepare us for trials future," the elf often said.

Elbryan didn't argue, but he wondered, and almost feared, what future trials could possibly match the pain of that awful day.

He stood atop the treeless hillock and he waited, his eyes glued to the eastern horizon, to the tiny sliver of light heralding the approach of dawn.

He was naked, every hair, every nerve feeling the tickle of the chill breeze. He was naked and he was free, and as the horizon brightened a bit more, he lifted his sword, a large but well-balanced weapon, into the air before him, both hands clasping its long hilt, the muscles of his arms bulging.

Elbryan brought the sword across in a gentle sweep, his weight shifting gradually with the movement of the outstretched blade to keep his balance perfect. Up went the blade over his left shoulder. He stepped right foot forward, then brought the sword back, again slowly, perfectly balanced. His left foot came forward, then went out to the side, blade and right foot following, turning the young man as if he were now facing a second opponent. Strike, parry, strike, all in harmonic and slow motion, and then he dropped his right foot back, coming around in a fluid movement to stalk back to the left. Strike, parry, strike—the same routine.

Then he dropped his right foot back again and half pivoted, so that he was facing exactly opposite from where he had started. He came ahead in three strong strides—strike, strike, strike with the blade as he moved, then repeated the same motions he had used, left and right, from this new position.

"Bi'nelle dasada," it was called, the sword-dance. The young man continued for nearly an hour, his arms and weapon weaving ever more intricate patterns in the empty air. This was the bulk of his physical training now, not sparring but gaining a memory of the movements within his muscles. Every attack and parry angle became ingrained in him; what had been conscious battle strategy melded into a reactive response or an anticipatory strike.

From the trees at the base of the hillock, Juraviel and some others watched the sword-dance in sincere admiration. Truly the muscled young human was a thing of beauty and grace, a combination of pure strength and uncanny agility. His sword swished with ease, as did his long and wavy, wheat-colored hair. Never losing the slightest edge of balance, Elbryan's muscles worked in perfect harmony, perfect fluidity, none battling, flexing and complementing each move.

And his eyes! Even from this distance, the elves could see the olive-green orbs sparkling with intensity, truly seeing the imagined foes.

The young Elbryan's movements improved with every day, and so Juraviel gave him more of the sword-dance, the most intricate battle movements known to the elves, who collectively were the finest swordsmen in all the world. Elbryan mastered the intricate movements, every one, soaked them into the sponge he had become and held them fast in his heart, mind, and muscles. No longer did any, even Tuntun, question his prowess or his bloodline. Never again in Andur'Blough Inninness were the words "blood of Mather" spoken derisively where young Elbryan was concerned. For he had passed through the "wall of nonperception," as Juraviel called it, had shrugged off the human societal inhibitions of consciousness, had become one with the greater powers, the natural powers, about him.

On those occasions when he did spar, he not only understood how to defeat any attack, deflect, dodge, or block, but also knew which tactic would offer appropriate counterattacks or would keep his defensive posture strong against subsequent attacks from that foe, or even from others. Elbryan now won far more often than he lost, even held his own when battling two against one.

His routines became more varied, more deadly, resembling in many instances the motions of an animal predator. He could put a dagger in his hand and curl his arm in such a way that he might strike as the viper. Or he didn't even need the dagger but could stiffen his fingers that he might drive them right through any obstacle.

And every morning, before the mist veil blanketed Andur'Blough Inninness, Elbryan came to this spot and watched the dawn, weaving his sword-dance, building the memory.

The blood of Mather.

The gifts—a heavy blanket, a small chair shaped of bent sticks, and a wood-framed mirror—surprised and confused Elbryan. The mirror alone was very expensive, he knew, and the craftsmanship and incredibly light wood of the chair allowed it to be folded and easily carried, but the only one of the three presents that made any sense to him was the blanket, a most practical item.

Tuntun and Juraviel let the young man look the gifts over for a long while, let him test the chair and even study his own image in the silvery mirror.

"My deepest gratitude," Elbryan said sincerely, though his measure of confusion was clear in his voice.

"You do not even understand the significance," Tuntun replied distastefully. "You believe that you have been given three gifts, yet it is the fourth that is most precious by far!"

Elbryan looked at the elf maiden, studied her blue eyes for some hint.

"The mirror, the chair, and the blanket," Juraviel said solemnly. "The Oracle."

Elbryan had never heard the word before; again his confusion showed clearly on his face.

"Do you think that the dead are gone?" Tuntun asked cryptically, apparently enjoying this spectacle. "Do you think that all there is is all you see?"

"There are other levels of consciousness," Juraviel tried to clarify, casting a stern glance at his teasing partner.

"Dreaming," Elbryan offered hopefully.

"And the memories of fanciful musing," Juraviel added. "In Oracle, the musing combines with the consciousness to bring the memory to the present."

Elbryan's brow furrowed as he considered the words, as their implications began to unfold before him. "To speak with the dead?" he asked breathlessly.

"What is dead?" Tuntun laughed.

Even Juraviel couldn't suppress a chuckle at his elven companion's unending games. "Come," he bade Elbryan. "It would be better to show than to tell."

The three left Caer'alfar, moving purposefully into the deep woods. The day was not bright above them, even darker than usual with the misty blanket, and a light rain tickled the forest canopy. They walked for nearly an hour, no one talking except Tuntun, who offered an occasional verbal jab at Elbryan.

Finally Juraviel stopped at the base of a huge oak, its trunk so wide that Elbryan couldn't put his arms halfway around it. The two elves exchanged solemn looks.

"He'll not do it," Tuntun promised, her melodic voice rising singsong.

"Nor could he ever defeat you in battle," Juraviel was quick to respond, drawing an angry stamp of Tuntun's delicate foot.

Elbryan took a deep breath and straightened his shoulders. So, this was but another test, he thought. One of his will and mental prowess, no doubt, considering the three gifts he carried. He was determined not to disappoint Juraviel and not to let Tuntun be right about anything.

Around the back of the tree, Elbryan saw there was a narrow opening between the roots, a tunnel that seemed to widen as it descended at a steep angle.

"There is a pedestal of stone inside on which you must place the mirror," Juraviel explained, "and a place before it where you might set up your chair. Use the blanket to cover the entry, so that it becomes very dark within."

Elbryan waited, expecting more instructions. After a long moment, Tuntun nudged him roughly. "Are you afraid even to try?" she chided.

"Try what?" Elbryan demanded, but when he looked to Juraviel for support, he found the elf was pointing to the narrow opening, indicating that the young man should enter.

Elbryan had no idea what they expected, what he should do, beyond the simple instructions Juraviel had offered. With a shrug, he took up his items and moved to the opening. Getting in would be test enough, for the cave was far more suited to one of elven stature. He slipped the chair in first, easing it down as far as he could reach, then closing his eyes and letting go. From the sound of its descent, the floor of the cave was not more than eight feet below the opening, he figured. Next he lay the blanket along the bottom of the shaft, using it to cover uneven jags of roots, that he wouldn't hook his clothing, get stuck, and look completely stupid in Tuntun's always-judging eyes. With a final glance at Juraviel, hoping futilely that some further information would come his way, Elbryan closed his eyes and started in, going headfirst and protecting the mirror with his body. As soon as he crossed under the tree, he opened his eyes, now more sensitive to the darkness, and scouted. A bear or a porcupine or even a smelly skunk might have slipped in here, and it was with great relief that Elbryan found the cave apparently empty, and not so large. It was fairly circular, perhaps eight feet in diameter. As promised, a stone pedestal rested near the wall just to Elbryan's side, and hooking his arm around a root in the ceiling, he turned right side up and swung his feet to the pedestal, then stepped down easily to the cave floor. A bit of water had accumulated in one low spot, but nothing threatening or even inconvenient.

Elbryan quickly set the mirror on the pedestal, leaning it against the back wall of the cave, and opened his chair, placing it before the mirror, as instructed. Then he went about draping the blanket over the cave entrance, darkening the room so that he could barely make out his hand if he held it in front of his face. That done, the young man felt about, found his chair, and slipped into it.

Then he waited, wondering. His eyes gradually adjusted so that he could just barely make out the larger shapes in the room.

The minutes continued to pass him by; all was quiet and dark. Elbryan grew frustrated, wondering what test this might be, wondering what purpose could be found in sitting in the dark, facing a mirror he could hardly see. Was Tuntun right in asserting that this trip was a waste of time?

Finally Juraviel's melodic voice broke the tension. "This is the Cave of Souls, Elbryan Wyndon," the elf half spoke and half sang. "The Oracle, where an elf, or a human, might speak with the spirits of those who have passed before them. Seek your answers in the depths of the mirror."

Elbryan steadied himself with the breathing routine of *bi'nelle dasada* and focused his eyes on the mirror—or at least on the area where he knew the mirror to be, for it was hardly discernible.

He brought out a mental picture of the pedestal and mirror, recalled the image from the few moments before he had draped the blanket. Gradually, the square shape was visible, at least in his mental image, and so he sent his gaze within the frame of that square.

And he sat, as the minutes became an hour, as the sun behind the elven mist and the clouds made its way toward the western horizon. Boredom crept into his concentration, along with the frustration of realizing that Tuntun might be right. Still, no further calls came from beyond the cave, so the two elves, at least, were apparently being patient.

Elbryan dismissed all thought of the elves, and each time one of those distracting notions—or any other thoughts from outside this one room— came back to him, he fought it off.

He lost all sense of the passing of time; soon nothing invaded his focus. The room darkened even more as the sun moved westward, but Elbryan, his eyes long past the gloom, didn't notice.

There was something in the mirror, just beyond his vision!

He slipped deeper into his meditative state, let go of all the conscious images that cluttered his mind. Something was there, a reflection of a man, perhaps.

Was it his own reflection?

That notion stole away the image, but only for a moment.

Then Elbryan saw it more clearly: a man, older than he, with a face creased by the sun and wind, a light beard trimmed low to follow the line of his jaw. He looked like Elbryan, or at least as Elbryan might look in a score of years. He looked like Olwan, and yet it was not, the young man somehow knew. It was . . .

"Uncle Mather?"

The image nodded; Elbryan fought for a gulp of air.

"You are the ranger," Elbryan said quietly, barely finding his voice. "You are the ranger who went before me, who was trained by these very same elves."

The image made no move to reply.

"You are the standard to which I am held," Elbryan said. "I fear that you stand too tall!"

Something seemed to soften in the visage of the spirit, and Elbryan got the distinct feeling that, in Mather's eyes at least, his fear was misplaced.

"They speak of responsibility," the young man went on, "of duty, and the road that lies before me. Yet I fear I am not all that Belli'mar Juraviel believes me to be. I wonder why I was chosen in this—why was Elbryan saved that day in Dundalis? Why not Olwan, my father, your brother, so solid and strong, so knowing in the ways of battle and the world?"

Elbryan tried to pause and collect his thoughts, but he found the words kept coming out as if compelled by the spirit, by this place, and by his own state of mind. Even if this was his uncle Mather, he realized he was speaking to the spirit of a man he had never known! But that fear couldn't hold against the river of his own soul, pouring forth in great release.

"What height must I attain to satisfy the judgment of Tuntun and the many other elves of like mind? I fear that they ask of me the strength of a fomorian giant, the speed of a frightened deer, the wariness of a ground squirrel, and the calm and wisdom of a centuries-old elf. What man could measure such?

"Ah, but you did, Uncle Mather. By all that they say of you, even by the look in Tuntun's eyes—one of sincere admiration—I know that you were no disappointment to the fairy folk of Caer'alfar. How will they judge me twenty years hence, a mere day by an elf's measure? And what of this world I will soon know?"

Terrifying images, mostly of other humans, flitted across Elbryan's vision, as if they were flying across the face of the mirror.

"I am afraid, Uncle Mather," he admitted. "I do not know what it is that I fear, whether it is the judgment of the elves, the dangers of the wilderness, or the company of other people! More than a quarter of my life has passed since I have seen another who stands as a human, who sees the world as a human.

"But then," he continued, his voice dropping low, "I fear most that I no longer see the world as a human, nor can I truly view it as an elf might, but as something in between. I love Caer'alfar, and all of this valley, but here I do not belong. This I know in my heart, and I fear that out there, among my own kind, I will not be among my own kind.

"Kin and kind," Elbryan decided, "do not always go together. What is left of me, then? What creature am I that is neither elf nor human?"

Still the image did not answer, did not move at all. But Elbryan felt that soft feeling—that sympathy, that empathy—and he knew then that he was not alone. He knew then his answer.

"I am Elbryan the Ranger," he asserted, and all the implications of that title seemed to fall over him, their weight not bowing but bolstering his broad shoulders.

Elbryan realized that he was bathed in a cold sweat. Only then did he notice the room had darkened almost to the point of absolute blackness. "Uncle Mather?" he called in the direction of the mirror, but the image of the specter and even of the mirror itself was no more.

Juraviel was waiting for the young man when he crawled out of the hole. The elf looked as if he meant to ask some question, but he stared instead at Elbryan's face and apparently found his answer. They said nothing all the way back to Caer'alfar.

CHAPTER
❖ 21 ❖

Ever Vigilant,
Ever Watchful

Jill looked out past the towering rocks to the dark waters of the wide Mirianic, great swells rolling lazily, then breaking fast against the rocks two hundred feet below her. The rhythm continued, through the minutes, through the hours, through the days, the weeks, the years. Through all eternity, Jill supposed. If she were to return to this place in a thousand years, the waves would remain, rolling gently and then crashing against the base of this same rocky rise.

The young woman looked back over her shoulder at the small fortress that she called home, Pireth Tulme. In a thousand years, the scene would be the same, she decided, except that this structure, with its single low tower, would not remain, would be taken by time, by the wind and the storms that swept into Horseshoe Bay with disturbing regularity.

She had only been here for four months and she had witnessed a dozen such storms, including three in one week, that had left her and her forty companions, all members of the elite corps known as the Coastpoint Guards, soggy and sullen.

Yes, those were the words, Jill decided. "Soggy and sullen," she said aloud, and nodded, thinking that a fitting description of all her life.

She had been given her chance, the one opportunity that most people, particularly women in the patriarchal kingdom of Honce-the-Bear, never had. Jill closed her eyes and let the ocean sounds take her back to another shore, a gentler shore on the banks of the Masur Delaval, to the city of Palmaris, the only home she remembered. How fared Graevis and Pettibwa? she wondered. And what of Grady? Had her disaster with Connor Bildeborough destroyed the man's attempts at entry into the high society?

Jill laughed and hoped that it had. That would be the one good thing to come of the tragedy. Nearly two years had passed since her "wedding night," but the pain remained vivid indeed.

She looked around again, then up at the sky and noticed that many of the stars had disappeared. A moment later, a light rain began to fall. "Soggy," she said again, shaking her head. No matter how many times she witnessed it, Jill could hardly believe how quickly the rain came on in Pireth Tulme.

Like the rain that came into her life, first in that frontier village, when the goblins came, then in Palmaris. She could hardly remember that first incident, but she knew that her life had gradually grown wonderful. And then, in the snap of fingers, in the space of a single kiss, it was all gone, all taken away.

How much more could she have hoped for above the wedding in Palmaris? She had been married in St. Precious, considered by many to be the most beautiful chapel in all of Corona. And Dobrinion Calislas, Abbot of St. Precious and thus the third-ranking priest in the entire Abellican Church, had performed the ceremony himself! What young woman would not swoon at the mere thought of such a day? And then the night, spent in the mansion of Baron Bildeborough!

A shiver traced Jill's spine as she remembered—the grand room, the change that had come over Connor, and then the look on his face, first feral and then, with the side of his nose and one cheek burned and blistering, even worse. His expression had softened only a bit the next morning when he and Jill had gone again before Abbot Dobrinion. Of course, since it had not been consummated, the marriage had been annulled immediately.

A snap of old Dobrinion's fingers.

There was still the matter of Jill's crime, though. Her assault on a nobleman, one that might well have left the handsome young man permanently scarred, was no minor matter in Palmaris. By right, Connor could have demanded her execution. Short of that, there was the very real possibility that Abbot Dobrinion would bind Jill into indenture to Connor, perhaps for the remainder of her life.

But Connor had been merciful, and ever was Abbot Dobrinion long on forgiveness. "I have heard of the incident with three rogues on the back roof of Fellowship Way," the old priest had explained, a warm smile coming to his face. "One with your skills should not be wasted serving at tables. There is a place for a woman of your talent and ferocity, a place where such wild anger is assuaged, even applauded." Thus the old abbot had bound her over into the service of the King of Honce-the-Bear, as a foot soldier in the Kingsmen, the army. That moment remained very clear to Jill: Dobrinion's words spoken sympathetically, while she looked back over her shoulder at Pettibwa and Graevis. There was no anger showing on the faces of her adopted parents, no hint that Jill and her irrational actions of the previous night had cost them, too, so much—just a most profound sadness. Pettibwa had nearly burst apart at Abbot Dobrinion's decree, at the notion that her Jilly would be taken from her. There was little joy that night at the Way, where Jill said her good-byes.

Soon after, with Palmaris behind her, Jill had come to see the wisdom of the abbot's decision. Indeed she had thrived, initially, at least, in the military.

She started as a common foot soldier, "fodder walkers" they were called, but soon enough worked her way into the more elite cavalry group. There were no real enemies to battle: Honce-the-Bear had been at peace for longer than anyone could remember. But in the weekly sparring contests, Jill released enough enemies from her memories to carry her through with a ferocity that had astonished her superiors. One by one, her sparring partners had been dispatched, usually painfully, until not a man or woman in the unit desired to go against her. Her notoriety had made her more than a few real enemies, though, and so she had been moved about, from one fortress to another, serving a variety of functions, from castle guard to cavalry patrol.

All in all, it had been a boring year; castle guards were no more than showpieces, and the worst incident Jill had seen in four months with the cavalry patrol was a fight between two peasant brothers, when one had bitten the other's ear off. And so it was with great expectations and hopes that Jill had received the news of her appointment into the second most elite unit, behind only the Allheart Brigade, in all of Honce-the-Bear: the famed Coastpoint Guards. These were the legendary fighters who had in ages past turned away a powrie invasion, the fearsome warriors who had tamed the region known as the Broken Coast, thus widening the domain of Honce-the-Bear's King.

She didn't get what she expected when she arrived at the small fortress of Pireth Tulme, overlooking Horseshoe Bay and the wide Mirianic. Pireth Tulme was but one in a series of keeps dotting Honce-the-Bear's coastline. Like all of its sister fortresses, Pireth Tulme was secluded, far from any large settlements, but strategically located to watch the waters for invasion. Pireth Tulme guarded the southern passes of the Gulf of Corona, while Pireth Dancard held post on the five small islands centering the gulf, and Pireth Vanguard watched the northern way.

To Jill, their mission seemed paramount, a stoic existence protecting the welfare of all the kingdom. It didn't take her long to realize that she was alone in her convictions.

Pireth Tulme, and apparently all the other Coastpoint fortresses, were far from the stoic bastions of their reputation. The partying had hardly slowed in all the four months Jill had been there. Even now, later into the night as she walked her watch along the low walls, she could hear the revelry—the clink of glasses lifted high in one toast after another, the bawdy laughter, the squeals of women pursued or pursuing.

The guards were forty in number, with only seven of them female. Jill, whose only experience with a man had been so very disastrous, did not like the odds. She shook her head distastefully as she walked her watch this night, as she did every night.

A short while later one haggard-looking soldier—a man of forty years by the name of Gofflaw, who had spent more than half his wretched life in the Kingsmen, including a dozen years in the Coastpoint Guards shuffling from one lonely outpost to another—came staggering out to the wall, making his way toward Jill.

She gave a sigh, resigned to the reality about her. She wasn't particularly afraid; she didn't think the drunken slob would even get to her before he fell off the narrow walkway, dropping the eight feet to the fortress's small courtyard. Somehow, bouncing against the blocks of the outer wall with each step, he got near the woman.

"Ah, me Jilly," Gofflaw slurred. "Walkin' again in the rain."

Jill shook her head and looked away.

"Why don't ye go inside and warm yer bones then, girl?" the man asked. "Quite a row this night. Go on with ye. I'll take yer watch."

Jill knew better. If she accepted his outwardly gracious offer and went inside, Gofflaw would soon follow, leaving the walls empty. Even worse, for him to be out here fetching her, there was likely a conspiracy inside. The long, low main house of Pireth Tulme was not large, only three medium-sized common rooms, each surrounded by a dozen anterooms, each barely large enough for the pair of cots and two footlockers it held. Most of the structure was underground, the main house being three identical levels but appearing as only one story from the courtyard. If Jill ventured into that tight place, if this man was out here to lure her in, she would likely find herself in grabby quarters indeed.

"I will keep my own watch, thank you," she replied politely and started away.

"And just what're ye watching for?" the soldier demanded, his tone suddenly sharp.

Jill spun on him, her blue eyes narrow and glaring. She knew the routine and even agreed that it seemed very unlikely that any enemies, or anyone at all, would approach the fortress or sail past it on their way into the Gulf of Corona. But that wasn't the point, not in Jill's estimation. If one invasion came every five hundred years, the Coastpoint Guards, the elite of the elite, must be prepared for it!

"You go to your party," she said evenly, her jaw clenched. "I choose to walk to honor the uniform I wear."

Gofflaw snorted and wiped a greasy hand down the front of his own red jacket. "The better of it, ye'll learn," he said. "Just ye wait until the days become a year, and then two and three and four and—"

"I believe that she understands your reasoning, Gofflaw," came a solid, unwavering voice. Jill looked past the drunk, who turned as well, to see Warder Constantine Presso, the commander of Pireth Tulme, approaching along the wall. By all appearances, the man was impressive—tall and straight, mustache and goatee neatly trimmed, his red-trimmed blue overcoat tailored straight and proper, black leather baldric crossing right shoulder to left hip and sporting an impressive sword, a family heirloom.

He was in his late twenties and had earned his position by defeating three bandits who had slipped into the house of a nobleman one evening. When she had first arrived at Pireth Tulme and had met the warder, Jill's hopes had soared with a sense of greater responsibility.

She had soon learned, though, that the ready appearance of the fortress, on that day when the Kingsmen's regional commander had taken her out to the isolated outpost, had been no more than a temporary show, and that Warder Presso, for all of his regal appearance, had long ago fallen into the same trap as the rest of her companions.

Presso eyed Jill directly—he was often doing that. "And I believe that she declines," the warder said.

"I do," Jill agreed.

Gofflaw muttered something under his breath and started past Presso, but the man stuck out his arm, blocking the way.

"But it grows late," Presso said to Jill, "or should I say early? Your watch surely is ended."

"I take the night."

"What part of the night?"

"The night," Jill snapped. "No one else will come up here. They view the setting of the sun as the end of their duties, what little duties they do bother to perform during the day."

"Calm, lass," Presso said, patting his hand in the air. Perhaps he was trying to be the levelheaded commander, but to Jill, it came off as condescending.

"I am well read in our rules of conduct and operation," Jill continued. "Our watch does not end with the setting sun. 'Ever vigilant, ever watchful,' " she finished, the motto of the once-proud Coastpoint Guards.

"And for what are you watching?" Presso asked calmly.

Jill's face screwed up incredulously.

"Would you see a powrie ship, or even a raft full of goblins, if it glided past us into the gulf, barely a hundred yards from our shore?"

"I would hear them," Jill insisted.

Presso's snort fast became a full-blown chuckle. "Dawn is not so far away," he said. "Pray you go inside now and get the rain out of your bones."

Jill started to protest, but the warder cut her short. He set Gofflaw up as sentry, then took Jill by the arm and pulled her in front of him, pushing her gently toward the tower door.

They went in together, and in truth, Jill was glad to be out of the rain. At the bottom of the tower stairs, through the small hallway that led into the main house, the pair passed a partly opened door. From the sounds emanating from within, it was quite obvious what was going on in there.

Jill hurried down the hallway and entered the common room of the upper level. A dozen men were in there, along with two women, all nearly falling-down drunk. One man was up on the tables, dancing, or trying to, and removing his clothing to the jeers of his male friends and the hoots of the women.

Jill looked straight ahead as she made for the door to the stairwell that would get her down to her room. Warder Presso caught her just as she reached that door, grabbing her by the shoulder.

"Stay with us and enjoy the rest of the night," he said.

"Are you commanding me to do so?"

"Of course not," replied Presso, who was really a decent sort. "I am merely asking you to stay. Your watch is ended."

"Ever watchful," Jill replied through gritted teeth.

Presso gave a great sigh. "How many months of boredom can you tolerate?" he asked. "We are out here alone, all alone, with nothing but time ahead of us. This is our life, and each of us must choose whether it will be pleasant or wretched."

"Perhaps we have different views of what is pleasant," Jill said, subconsciously glancing back across the room to the hallway and the partly open door.

"I give you that," Presso replied.

"May I go?"

"I could not order you to stay, though I truly wish that you would so choose."

Jill's shoulders sagged. Presso's conciliation somehow seemed to take the strength from her more than any order he might have issued. "I was put in service to the Kingsmen by a magistrate, the abbot of Palmaris," she explained.

Presso nodded; he had heard as much.

"I did not choose to enter, but once in the ranks, I came to believe," she said. "I do not know what it was—a sense of purpose, a reason for continuing."

"Continuing?"

"To live," she answered sharply. "My duty is my litany—against what, I do not know. But this—" She held her hand out to the revelry, to the half-naked dancer who, as if on cue, tumbled from the table. "This is no part of my duty nor my desire."

Presso touched her arm gently, but still she recoiled as if she had been slapped. The warder immediately raised both his hands unthreateningly.

Jill understood his concern to be both defensive and compassionate. On the very first night after her arrival, one of the men had tried to get too familiar with the fiery woman. He had limped for a week, one foot swollen, one ankle and both his knees bruised, one eye closed and a lip too fat for him to drink anything without it dribbling down the front of his shirt. Even without the very prominent evidence that she could defend herself, Jill believed that Presso would not try anything. Despite his acceptance of the behavior within Pireth Tulme, Jill recognized that he was a man of some honor. He had his way with the other women, probably all six of them, but he would not infringe where he was not invited.

"I fear that Gofflaw's reasoning was sound," the warder warned. "The months will wear on you, day after boring, lonely day."

"Indeed," remarked Jill, gesturing with her chin across the way. Presso turned to see Gofflaw entering the room. The warder sighed audibly, then turned back to Jill and merely shrugged. He really didn't care that the walls were unmanned.

Jill swung about and left the room, but as soon as the door was closed behind her, she veered down a side corridor and back out into the rain. She moved to a ladder and climbed to the seacoast wall, then sat on its outer edge, dangling her legs over the long drop.

There she stayed for the rest of the night, watching the stars return as the storm cloud raced away into the gulf. As the day brightened, the pillarlike rocks in the wide bay came clearer, standing tall and straight like sentinels, ever vigilant, ever watchful.

❖ 22 ❖

The Nightbird

"The snows will be soon in coming this year," Lady Dasslerond remarked, staring out of her high tree house at the gray clouds that loomed on the horizon just north of the enchanted valley.

"A difficult winter would be consistent," Tuntun replied, her expression even more grave than usual.

Lady Dasslerond turned back to the pair and considered the words. The raid on Dundalis, the sightings of goblins and even giants, the evidence of many earthquakes to the north of Andur'Blough Inninness—all pointed to the resurgence of the dactyl. There were even reports of a smoke cloud rising lazily over the Barbacan, streaming from a solitary mountain known as Aida.

It made sense; the dactyl could—and indeed, likely would—awaken a long-dormant volcano, using the magma to strengthen its underworld magic.

"How long is he?" Lady Dasslerond asked as her gaze returned to the west and north.

"He has just passed his sixth year with us," Juraviel answered without hesitation. "He was rescued from the goblins in the harvest season of the year the humans call 816. Their reckoning shows the turn of 823 approaching."

Lady Dasslerond turned to Juraviel, her expression showing that his answer was not acceptable. "But how long is he?" she asked again.

Juraviel sighed and rested back against the wide trunk of the maple. Measuring such things was never easy for the elf, especially since he feared he viewed Elbryan with favorable eyes.

"He is ready," Tuntun unexpectedly put in. "The blood of Mather runs thick in his veins. In a half century, we will be telling our next would-be ranger that he is of the blood of Elbryan."

Juraviel couldn't suppress a small laugh, even given the gravity of this meeting. To hear Tuntun speaking so well of Elbryan seemed to him the ultimate irony. "Tuntun speaks the truth," he confirmed as soon as the shock wore off. "Elbryan has trained hard and well. He fights with grace and power, runs silent and wary, and has visited the Oracle many times, almost always with success."

"He found a kindred spirit?" asked Lady Dasslerond.

"Only that of Mather," Juraviel replied, beaming as the smile widened across his lady's fair face.

"But he is not yet ready," Juraviel added quickly. "There is more for him to learn of himself and of the woodland arts. He has a year remaining, and then, he will indeed walk as a ranger."

Lady Dasslerond was shaking her head before the elf even finished his proclamation. "The winter will be difficult," she said firmly. "And the humans have settled several communities along the edge of the Wilder- lands, have even resettled that place which was, and is again, known as Dundalis. If what we fear is true, then Elbryan will be needed before the next season of harvest."

"Even if our fears of the dactyl prove false," Tuntun added, "many of the humans are unprepared for the Wilderlands. The presence of a ranger would do them well."

"The turn of spring?" Juraviel asked.

"You will have the boy prepared for his walk," Lady Dasslerond agreed.

"And what of Joycenevial?" Juraviel asked.

"The bowyer is ready for him," Lady Dasslerond replied. "And the dark- fern is tall this season."

Juraviel nodded. He knew that Joycenevial, the finest bowyer in all of Caer'alfar, in all of the world, had been cultivating a special darkfern all these six years since Elbryan had been brought to Andur'Blough Inninness. This would be Joycenevial's first human task since Mather, and, since the bowyer was aged even by elven standards, most likely his last.

This one would be special.

Elbryan thought that he knew every trail and grove in the enchanted valley, and so he was indeed confused on that day when Juraviel led him down a particularly twisting path, often branching and crisscrossing a stream more than a dozen times. Their destination must be important indeed, Elbryan realized, for this trail was even more difficult to follow than the winding ways that hid Caer'alfar itself!

Finally, after hours of backtracking, the pair came to a short descent down a steep, sandy bank. At the bottom of the ravine, past a blocking wall of low evergreen bushes, they came to a bed of ferns, bluish green in color. Most were about waist high to Elbryan, shoulder high to Juraviel. Elbryan understood immediately that this was their destination, that there was something unusual about these plants; they were growing in neat rows, evenly spaced, and the ground around them was bare. He wouldn't have expected much undergrowth, for the ferns cast shade, but this area was too clean, as if caring hands regularly weeded it.

"These are the darkfern," Juraviel said, his tone full of reverence. He led Elbryan to the nearest plant and bent low, bidding the young man to inspect the fern's stem.

The plant was thick and smooth, and the stem didn't seem to narrow at all as it came up high and spread, three-pronged, to the leafy fronds. Elbryan peered closer, and his green eyes widened in surprise, then narrowed again quickly as he moved even closer to inspect the stem.

Silvery lines wove gracefully about the dark green stem; they seemed to Elbyran consistent with the fishing lines and the bowstrings the elves used.

"The darkfern is one with the metal," Juraviel explained as soon as he realized that Elbryan had found the key. "This ravine was chosen for the planting because we learned that it is rich in minerals, particularly silverel, which the plant prefers above all."

"The plant brings the metal lines up with it?" Elbryan asked. Many implications came to him then, as if the fog veiling one of the mysteries of elven life had suddenly lifted. The elves used many metal implements—shields and swords mostly—and Elbryan had sometimes wondered where they got the material, since, to his knowledge, there were no working mines in Andur'Blough Inninness. He had assumed that they traded for the metal, but then he had come to realize that elven metal was unlike anything he had seen outside the enchanted valley. He remembered his father's sword, bulky and dark, but that hardly compared to the fine elvish blades, shining bright and holding so keen an edge.

"They are as one," Juraviel confirmed. "The darkfern is the lone source of silverel."

Elbryan stared hard at the lines of gleaming metal. He felt as if he had seen this same pattern before, though where that might have been, he could not remember.

"Treated and cured properly, the stems are incredibly strong and resilient," Juraviel explained; "and pliable."

"Even after you take the metal from them?"

"We do not always take the silverel from the harvested stem," the elf replied.

Elbryan thought on that for a moment, particularly on Juraviel's last claim that the plants were pliable. Then it came to him where he had seen this same design. "Elvish bows," he breathed as the fog flew from yet another mystery. Now he knew how the elvish bows, so small and frail, could launch an arrow a hundred yards on a straight line.

He looked up from the plant to see Juraviel nodding.

"There is no composite, not bone and wood, even when blended with sinew, that is stronger," the elf said. He motioned to the man. "Come with me," he bade.

They walked carefully past the cultivated rows to the tallest fern of all, one whose broad fronds were above Elbryan's head. Unexpectedly, Juraviel handed Elbryan his sword, then motioned the young man back a few paces.

Elbryan watched, mesmerized, as the elf closed his eyes and began to chant in the elvish tongue, using many words so arcane that Elbryan didn't recognize them. The song came louder, faster, and Juraviel began to dance delicate, spinning circles wrapped in a larger circle that encompassed the plants. Elbryan concentrated, looking for the root sounds that made up the elf's song, but still he could not decipher many of the ancient words. He did understand that Juraviel was praising the plant and thanking it for the gift it would soon give. This did not surprise Elbryan; the elves always showed respect for other living creatures, always prayed and danced over the bodies of animals they had hunted, and sang countless songs to the fruits and berries of Andur'Blough Inninness.

The twirling elf tossed several puffs of powder upon the plant, then bent low and with some reddish gel painted a stripe around the base of the stem just an inch or two from the ground. He finished with a leaping flourish and landed pointing to the stripe. "One clean strike!" he commanded.

Elbryan rolled to one knee quickly and brought the sword flashing across, severing the plant at exactly the stripe. The darkfern landed upright and held for a moment, then slowly tumbled to the side into Juraviel's waiting hands.

"Follow quickly," the elf bade, and ran off.

Elbryan had to work hard to keep up. Juraviel ran all the way back to Caer'alfar, to the side of the glen, to a tall tree that housed only a single elf.

"Joycenevial is as old as the oldest tree in Andur'Blough Inninness," Juraviel explained as the aged elf came out of his home and slowly descended. Without saying a word, he dropped between the pair, took the cut fern from Juraviel, and held it up near Elbryan. He turned it over and nodded, apparently pleased by the fine and clean cut, then started back up his tree, fern in hand.

"No markings?" Juraviel asked.

Joycenevial only shook his head, not even bothering to look back at the pair.

Juraviel praised him once, then started away, Elbryan in tow. The young man had a million questions stirring around in his head. "The red gel?" he dared to ask, trying to start a conversation, trying to unravel this most extraordinary day.

"Without it, you would never have cut through the darkfern," Juraviel replied.

Elbryan noted the curtness of the answer, the elf's crisp, almost sharp tone, and he understood that further questioning would be unwelcome, that he would learn what he must when the elves decided to tell him.

Juraviel sent Elbryan off to his duties then, but interrupted the young man again that afternoon, two bows, including one that was fairly large by elvish standards, in hand.

"We haven't much time," Juraviel explained, handing the large bow to his student.

Elbryan took it and, ignoring the multitude of questions that again swirled in his thoughts, silently followed. He studied the bow as he walked, and concluded at once that this was not formed of the darkfern such as he had cut, but from a smaller plant.

The old elf took up a curious-looking knife, bent upward on both sides and with its cutting edge on one side of a slit running down its middle. He grasped it firmly in his left hand and cradled the fern stem—now stripped of its fronds—in his right. He tucked the long shaft of the plant under his right shoulder, then gently, very gently, scraped the blade along the stem.

A tiny strip peeled away, so thin as to be nearly translucent. Joycenevial nodded solemnly; he had treated the fern stem perfectly for the carving.

The old elf closed his eyes and began a chant. He pictured Elbryan at the moment when the young human held the stem, envisioned the size of his hand, the length of his arms. Other bowyers would have marked the stem appropriately, but Joycenevial was far beyond such crude necessities. His was an act of the purest creation and not a mere crafting; his art was bound by magic and by the sheer skill that seven hundred years had honed. And so it was with eyes closed that the old elf went to work on the stem, singing softly, using the music of his voice to pace his cuts in depth and intensity. He would spend the better part of half a year on this one, he knew, scraping and treating, notching and weaving spells of strength. Twice a week during the carving, he would coat the stem with special oils to add to its resilience. And when at last the bow had taken shape, he would hang it over an ever-smoking pit, a secret, enchanted place where the magic was strong indeed, so strong that it continually filtered up from the ground.

Half a year—not so long a time as measured by the elves of Caer'alfar, a mere moment in the long history of Belli'mar Joycenevial, father of Juraviel. He closed his eyes and considered the final ceremony, for the bow and the boy: the naming. He had no idea what title he would give the bow; that would come to him as the weapon took on its own personality, its own nuances.

The name would have to be correct, for this bow would be the epitome of his crafting, Joycenevial determined, the highest achievement in a career so often marked by perfection. Every elf in the valley carried a bow crafted by Joycenevial, as did every ranger that had gone out from Andur'Blough Inninness in the last half millennium. Not one of them would hold their weapon up against this bow, however, for Belli'mar Joycenevial, as old as the oldest tree in Andur'Blough Inninness, knew that it would be his last.

This one was special.

At least this time he had hit the tree that held the target! Elbryan looked at Juraviel hopefully, but the elf just stood, shaking his head. In one swift movement, Juraviel put up his bow and let fly an arrow, then another, then a third in rapid succession.

It had come so fluidly, so fast, that Elbryan was still staring at the elf when he heard the third arrow hit. He was almost afraid to look up at the mark and wasn't surprised to find all three embedded squarely in the target, one in the bull's-eye, the other two right beside it.

"I will never shoot as well as you," Elbryan lamented, in as close to a whine as Juraviel had heard from the young man in years. "Or as well as any elf in the valley."

"True enough," retorted the elf, and he smiled as Elbryan's green eyes widened. That apparently was not the response the young man wanted to hear.

With a growl, proud Elbryan put up his bow and let fly, missing everything this time.

"You are aiming at the target," Juraviel remarked.

Elbryan looked at him curiously; of course he was aiming at the target!

"At the *whole* target," the elf explained. "Yet the tip of your arrow is not nearly large enough to cover the whole."

Elbryan relaxed and tried to decipher the words. He considered them in relationship to the entire elven philosophy of life, the oneness. Suddenly it seemed possible to him that his arrow and the target were one and that his bow was merely a tool he used that he might join the arrow and target.

"Aim at a specific, very precise point on the target," Juraviel explained. "You must tighten your focus."

Elbryan understood. He had to find the exact spot where the arrow belonged, the specific point where the two, target and arrow, were to be joined. He lifted the bow—which was too small for him—again, drew back to the length of the bend, though his long arms would have allowed him to pull much farther, and let fly.

He missed, but the arrow notched into the tree barely two inches above the target—by far the closest the young man had come.

"Well done," Juraviel congratulated. "Now you understand." And the elf began to walk away.

"Where are you going?" Elbryan called to him. "We have only been out for minutes. My quiver holds ten arrows yet."

"Your lesson for this day is completed," Juraviel replied. "Contemplate it and spend as long as you desire perfecting it." The elf walked off, disappearing into the thick brush of the forest.

Elbryan nodded grimly, determined that by the time Juraviel brought him out here the next day, he would be able to hit that target with ease. He would stay out here all the rest of the day, and would return as soon as his duties with the milk-stones were completed the next morning, so he thought.

Every time his concentration wavered even a bit, his arrow flew wide of the mark, disappearing into the forest scrub. Elbryan had come out to this place with a full quiver, a score of arrows, but within half an hour, his quiver was empty and not a one could be found. Just as well, the young man thought, for the fingers of his right hand ached, as did the muscle in the middle of his chest, and the inside of his left forearm was badly chafed.

The next day, Juraviel gave Elbryan a black leather guard to put on that left arm and a new bow, this one not of darkfern but the largest the elf could find in all the valley—though it was also too small for the towering man. Juraviel also brought with him a light green triangular huntsmen's cap, which Elbryan accepted with a confused shrug. This time they went out with two full quivers, and Elbryan, improving minute by minute, spent nearly three hours at the range. At the end of the day, Juraviel revealed a new tool for him, the very cap he wore upon his head. The elf showed him how to bring the front tip of the triangular hat low above his eyes and to use that point as a reference in lining up his shots.

The very next day, Elbryan hit the target two out of every three shots.

All through the fall and winter, Juraviel trained Elbryan with the bow. The young man learned the practical aspects of the weapon, learned how to fashion arrows, heavy for greater damage and light for longer flight, and how to replace bowstrings—though the elven silverel string rarely broke. Most important of all, Elbryan came to know that archery was more a test of the mind than the body, a concentration and focus. All of the physical aspects—the draw, the aiming, the loosing of the arrow—soon became automatic repetition, but each individual shot remained a mental measure of distance and wind, of the length of the draw and the weight of the arrow. The fingers of the young man's right hand were soon laced with calluses, and the leather on the inside of his black arm guard had been worn down to half its original thickness. For Elbryan went at this training with all the hunger he had shown in his other endeavors, with a pride and determination that had many of the often scatterbrained elves shrugging their shoulders in disbelief. Every day, whatever the weather, Elbryan was at the target, working, training, drawing shot after shot, and inevitably sinking his arrows into the target, near if not in the bull's-eye. He learned to shoot fast—and from different angles: to roll on the ground and come around with an arrow flying; to hang upside down from the branch of a tree, arcing his shot skyward so it held the appropriate range; to let fly two arrows at once and put them near each other, usually both on the target.

Every morning he performed *bi'nelle dasada* and then his physical conditioning with the milk-stones. He spent his lunches talking philosophy with Juraviel, then went with the elf to the archery range for more practice.

His evenings, to his surprise, were most often spent with Tuntun, for the female had been the primary instructor, and friend, of Mather, a man about whom Elbryan desperately wanted to learn more. Tuntun recounted many stories of Mather, from his training days in Andur'Blough Inninness—he had made so many of the same mistakes as Elbryan!—to his exploits in the Wilderlands. How many thousands of goblins and giants had fallen to Mather's deadly blade! That sword, too, became a topic of many discussions, for Tempest, as the blade was named, was one of but six ranger swords ever crafted, the most powerful swords to ever go out from Andur'Blough Inninness. Of the six, only one was still accounted for, a huge broadsword named Icebreaker, wielded by a rarely seen ranger, Andacanavar, in the far northland of Alpinador.

"You are of a rare breed indeed," Tuntun remarked one starry evening. "It might be that you are the only ranger alive, though we have not felt the sorrow of Andacanavar's demise."

The reverence with which she spoke touched Elbryan and at the same time laid a great weight upon his strong shoulders. He had come to feel special, in many ways superior. Because of the elves, he had been given a rare and precious gift: another language—physical and verbal—another way of looking at the world about him, another way of perceiving the movements of his own body. He had come so far from that frightened waif stumbling out of burned Dundalis. He was the blood of Mather, Elbryan the Ranger.

Why, then, was he so terrified?

To find his answer, Elbryan often visited the Oracle. Each time, it became easier for him to conjure the spirit of Mather, and though the specter never offered any words in response, Elbryan's own soliloquies allowed the young man to keep things fairly sorted out, to keep his perspective and his nerve.

The winter, a difficult one even in the enchanted valley—as Lady Dasslerond had predicted—passed slowly, the snows coming early and deep and holding on stubbornly as the season shifted to spring.

For Elbryan, life went along at its usual frantic pace, learning and growing. He was truly an archer now, not as proficient as some of the elves, but certainly an expert by the measure of humans. His understanding of the natural world about him would never be complete—there was simply too much for any individual to know—but it continued to deepen with each passing day and each new experience. The entire way in which Elbryan now viewed the world around him was conducive to such learning; truly he was the sponge and all the world a liquid.

The shift came dramatically, unexpectedly, when Elbryan was roused from his bed one blustery Toumanay night by Juraviel and Tuntun. The elves prodded and pushed him, finally getting him out of his low tree house wearing only a cloak and a loincloth. They escorted him to a wide tree-lined field, where all two hundred elves of Caer'alfar had gathered.

Juraviel pulled away Elbryan's cloak, while Tuntun pushed him, shivering, to the middle of the field.

"Remove it," she said sternly, indicating the loincloth.

Modesty caused Elbryan to hesitate, but Tuntun wasn't in the mood for a debate. With a flick of her daggers, one in each hand, she cut away the meager covering, caught it before it dropped two inches, then skittered away, leaving the confused, naked man standing alone, with all the eyes of Andur'Blough Inninness upon him.

Holding hands, the elves formed a wide circle about him. Then they began to dance, the circle rotating to the left. They broke their line often, individual elves leaping into pirouettes or simply following steps of their own choosing, but in general the rotation continued about Elbryan.

The elven song filled his ears and all his body, gradually taking him from his place of modesty, relaxing him, intoxicating him. All the forest seemed to join in—the gusty breezes, the birdsong, the croaking of frogs.

Elbryan tilted back his head, considering the stars, the few rushing clouds. He found he was turning as the circle turned, as if compelled, as if the elven movement had summoned a whirlpool about him, spinning him with its currents. All seemed a dream, vague and somehow removed.

"What do you hear?" came a question near him. "At this, your moment of birth, what do you see?"

Elbryan didn't even consider the source—Lady Dasslerond standing right before him. "I hear the birds," he answered absently. "The night birds."

All the world around him went silent, the dream state shattered by the sudden change. Elbryan blinked a few times as he came to a halt, though, to his dizzy perspective, the stars above him continued on their merry rotating way.

"Tai'marawee!" Lady Dasslerond cried out, and Elbryan, hardly conscious that she was out in the middle of the field with him, jumped at the sound of her voice. He looked down at her as the two hundred elves echoed the cry of "Tai'marawee!"

Elbryan considered the words: tai for "bird" and marawee for "night."

"The Nightbird," Lady Dasslerond explained. "You have been named Nightbird on this, the evening of your birth."

Elbryan swallowed hard, not comprehending what this was all about. Juraviel and Tuntun certainly had not prepared him for such a ceremony.

Without explanation, Lady Dasslerond then threw a handful of glittering powder in Elbryan's face.

All the world seemed to stop, then to start again but more slowly. The elvish singing and all the harmony of the forest had renewed, and he was alone again in the middle of the field, turning as the circle turned. So gradually that Elbryan never noticed it, the elven voices faded away one by one. He realized he was alone long after all the elves had gone, and before he could decipher any meaning to it all, sleep overtook him, right there, naked in the middle of the field.

The night of his birth.

Belli'mar Joycenevial nodded his head as he considered the product of his love. They had named the ranger Nightbird, and so the elf's dream had not deceived him. This bow, Hawkwing by name, certainly fit all that Elbryan had become.

Joycenevial held the beautiful weapon up before him. It was taller than he, rubbed and stained to glassy smoothness—even in the dim light of the single candle, Hawkwing's dark green, silver-lined hue shone clearly—with a sculpted hand-grip and delicate, tapered ends. The removable high tip was set with three feathers, so perfectly aligned that they appeared as one when the bow was at rest.

Hawkwing and Nightbird—the old elf liked the connection. This would be the last bow he ever crafted, for he knew beyond doubt that if he made a thousand more, he would never near the perfection of this weapon.

Elbryan awoke as he had fallen asleep, alone and naked on the field, except that he found a red strip of cloth tied about his left arm, a green strip tied about his right, both crossing the middle of his huge biceps. He considered them for a moment, but didn't even think of removing them. Then he turned his attention to the awakening world about him. The dawn had long passed; Elbryan knew that he had missed his sword-dance, for the first time since it had been taught to him. Somehow, that morning, it didn't matter. The young man spotted his cloak and wrapped it about him, but then, instead of returning to his tree house, he went to the Oracle, where he had left his mirror, blanket, and chair.

"Uncle Mather?"

The spirit was waiting for him, serene in the depths of the mirror. A thousand questions came to Elbryan, but before he could utter even the first, his mind was clouded by images of a road, of a moor and a forest, of a valley of evergreen trees that seemed vaguely familiar.

Elbryan fought to steady his breathing; he was beginning to understand. Dark terror crept up all around him, threatening to swallow him where he sat, and he desperately wanted to ask Uncle Mather about it all, to relieve himself one more time of those doubts.

But this time, Elbryan was a receptacle and not the speaker. This time, he rested back, even closed his eyes, and let that unknown path find its place in his mind.

He came out of the cave even less relaxed than he had been when he had gone in, his face reflecting his fear and uncertainty, more questions raised than answered.

When he got back to Caer'alfar, he was surprised to see the place deserted. He moved quickly to his tree house and found it empty of all his possessions—his clothing, his baskets for collecting the milk-stones.

A new set of clothes, finely made, was laid out on the floor before him. They had to be for him, for they would obviously fit none other in Caer'alfar. Unless, Elbryan pondered, another would-be ranger had been brought in.

He shook that thought away, shrugged off his cloak, and began donning the clothing: deerskin boots, high and soft; supple breeches with a narrow belt made of rope lined with silverel for strength; a soft sleeveless shirt with a leather vest lined in silverel; and finally, a thick forest-green traveling cloak and a lighter-green triangular huntsmen's cap.

Elbryan looked around, wondering what he was expected to do next. He thought of the field again and made his way there, to find all the elves of Caer'alfar waiting for him, this time standing quietly in neatly ordered rows. In front of the gathering stood Lady Dasslerond and Belli'mar Juraviel. They motioned immediately for Elbryan to join them.

When he got there, Juraviel handed him a full pack, a fine knife strapped on one side, a balanced hand axe on the other.

A long moment passed before Elbryan realized that the elves were waiting for him to properly inspect the gift. He fumbled with the ties and opened the pack, then bent low and gingerly dumped it out onto the ground. Flint and steel, a slender cord of the same silverel-lined rope as his belt, a packet of the same red gel he had seen Juraviel use on the darkfern, the blanket and mirror needed for Oracle—which must have been retrieved soon after he had left the place—and most telling of all, a waterskin and a supply of food, carefully salted and packed.

Elbryan looked up to his elven friend, but found no answer there. Carefully, his hands trembling, he repacked the satchel, then stood tall before Juraviel and the Lady of Andur'Blough Inninness.

"The red band is soaked in permanent salves," Juraviel explained. "Both bandage and tourniquet. The green will filter air when placed over nose and mouth, will even allow you to pass under water for a short time."

"These are our gifts to you, Nightbird," Lady Dasslerond added. "These and this!" She snapped her fingers and Belli'mar Joycenevial stepped forth from the ranks of elves, cradling the beautiful bow.

"Hawkwing," the old elf explained, handing it over. "It will serve as a staff, as well." With a simple movement, he removed the feathered tip, taking the bowstring with it, then just as easily replaced it, bending the bow to restring it with hardly an effort. "Fear not, for though it seems delicate, you'll not break it. Not by striking, not by a bolt of lightning, not by the breath of a great dragon!"

His proclamation was met by a sudden burst of well-deserved cheering for the old elf.

"Draw it," Juraviel prompted.

Elbryan put down the pack and raised the bow. He was amazed by its balance, by the smoothness of its long and comfortable draw. As the bow bent, the three feathers on its top tip separated from one another, looking like the "fingers" on the end of the wing of a gliding hawk.

"Hawkwing," the old bowyer said again to Elbryan. "It will serve you as bow for all your days, and as staff until you have earned your sword, if ever you do."

Tears in his eyes, the old elf handed over a quiver full of long arrows, then slowly turned and moved back to his place in line.

"Our gifts to you," Lady Dasslerond said again. "Which do you consider the most precious?"

Elbryan paused for a long while, understanding that this was a critical moment for him, a subtle test that he could not fail. "All the supplies and clothes," he began, "are worthy of a king, even a king of elves. And this bow," he said with all reverence, looking at Joycenevial. "I am sure that it has no equal and know that I am truly blessed in carrying it.

"But the Oracle," Elbryan continued, turning back to Lady Dasslerond, his voice firm, "that is the gift I hold most precious."

The Lady didn't blink, but suddenly Elbryan knew that he spoke mistakenly. Perhaps it was the slightly crestfallen look of his friend Juraviel that tipped him to the truth of his own thoughts.

"No," he said quietly, "that is not the greatest of your gifts."

"What is?" the Lady prompted anxiously.

"Nightbird," Elbryan replied without hesitation. "All that I am; all that I have become. I am a ranger now, and no gift in all the world—not all the gold, not all the silverel, not all the kingdoms—could be greater. The greatest gift is the name you have given me, the name I have earned through your patience and your time, the name that marks me as elf-friend. There could be no higher honor, no higher responsibility."

"You are ready to face that responsibility," Juraviel dared to interject.

"It is time for you to go," Lady Dasslerond stated.

Elbryan's first instinct was to ask where, but he held the thought private, trusting that the elves would tell him if he needed to know. When they did not, when they did nothing but bow to him once, then filter out of the field, leaving him, once again completely alone, he had his answer.

The Oracle had shown him the way.

The land was relatively flat and brown, with sparse low shrubs poking here and there. But the gentle slopes were deceiving and the ranger, running smooth, could not usually see very far in any direction. These were the Moorlands—the Soupy Bogs, they had been affectionately called by the settlers on the edge of the Wilderlands. To the child Elbryan, this had been the place of wildly exaggerated fireside tales.

Except that now, he ran through the Moorlands, and recalling those tales of howling beasts and horrid guardians wasn't very comforting.

The mist was light this day, not closing in on the man as it had the previous day, when Elbryan felt as if watching eyes were with him every step. He came over a rise and saw a silvery stream winding below him, meandering this way and that across the brown clay. Instinctively, the ranger's hand went to his waterskin, and he found it less than half full. He trotted down to the stream, which was just a few feet across and less than a foot deep, and dipped his hand, nodding when he found that the water was quite clear. The ground here was simply too compacted to be swept up in the light flow. Rivulets of runoff had been crystalline all through the Moorlands, except in those low basins where the water collected and remained, where the ground and water seemed to blend, to melt together into a thick muddy stew.

Elbryan continued his inspection of the stream to make sure that nothing ominous was swimming along its course, then hooked his pack on the stiff branch of a prickly shrub and gingerly removed his boots. He had been running for five days, the last two in the Moorlands. The cool water and the soft bed beneath it felt good indeed on his sore feet; he briefly considered pulling off all his clothes and lying down in the flow.

But then he felt something, or heard something. One of his senses subtly called out a warning to him. The ranger froze where he stood, tuned his senses outward to his environment. The muscles in his feet relaxed, nerves on end, feeling for vibrations beneath him. He turned his head side to side slowly, eyes sharp.

He noted a splash, not so far in the distance upstream.

Elbryan considered his position. The stream flowed around one of the deceivingly high rises, turning out of sight just a couple dozen yards from where he stood.

He heard another splash, closer, and then a voice, though he could not make out the words. He looked around again, this time searching for a vantage point, a perch from which he might ambush any enemies. The terrain wasn't very promising; the best he could do would be backtrack up the rise and crouch just beyond the ridgeline. He would have to time his move perfectly, though, for various areas of that high ground would be visible from around the upstream bend.

Elbryan dismissed the notion altogether; he was on the eastern edge of the Moorlands by now, not so far from human settlements. Whoever or whatever was coming certainly wasn't kicking up a storm—it could not be giants. There was no reason for him to think that these would be enemies.

Even if they were, Nightbird had Hawkwing in hand.

He pulled his forest-green cloak tighter about his shoulders, lifted the hood up over his head and cap, then went about his business, crouching low to dip his waterskin in the stream.

The noise increased—by the volume and consistency of the splashing, Elbryan figured there must be about a half dozen bipedal creatures approaching. More important to him, though, was the continuing conversation, not the words, of which he could understand only a few, but the high, grating tone of the voices. Elbryan had heard such voices before.

The splashing and talking stopped suddenly; the creatures had rounded the bend. Elbryan remained crouching. He peeked out around the side of his hood to make sure that they carried no bows.

Goblins, six of them, stood and gawked from barely thirty feet away, one with a spear up on its shoulder, but not yet ready to throw. The others held clubs and crude swords, but thankfully, no bows.

Elbryan stayed low. With his posture and his cloak the creatures couldn't be sure of his race.

"Eeyan kos?" one of them called.

Elbryan smiled under his hood and did not look the goblins' way.

"Eeyan kos?" the same one asked again. *"Dokdok crus?"*

"Duck, duck, goose," Elbryan said under his breath, the name of a game he had played perhaps a decade before. He smiled again as he thought of that innocent time, but it was not a long-lasting sentiment, swept away in the wave of darker emotions as he considered what creatures such as these had done to his world.

The goblin called out again. It was time to answer, he knew, and since he had no idea what the goblin was saying, he merely stood up tall, too tall to be any goblin, and slowly dropped back the hood of his cloak.

Half of the goblin party shrieked; the spear wielder accompanied its yell by rushing three strides forward and hurling its weapon.

Elbryan waited until the last possible moment, then flashed Hawkwing across in front of him, deflecting the spear. He moved the bow around and out as it connected, diverting then defeating the spear's momentum, turning it harmlessly in midair and then catching it mid-shaft in his right hand as his left brought Hawkwing back to his side.

Suddenly he held the spear, aimed right back at its original wielder. That stopped the goblins cold before they could even begin to charge.

Emotions churned confusingly in the young man. He remembered the teachings of the elves, mostly of tolerance, though they held no love for goblinkind or for any of the fomorian races. However, Elbryan was not in any human settlement, not in any land claimed by his kind, and quite possibly was within the boundaries of goblin territory. If that was the case, would he be justified in waging battle with these six?

Yet, one had just attacked him, though it might have come more from fear than aggression. And Elbryan, whatever logical reasoning he summoned, could not possibly dismiss those memories of Dundalis.

He hesitated; were these goblins responsible for what their kin had done to Elbryan's home? The one the elves had named Nightbird had to give himself an honest answer; he owed that much, at least, to Belli'mar Juraviel.

A flick of his powerful wrist sent the spear flying back the way it had come, to land with a splash and stick up from the stream just a foot or so in front of the creature who had thrown it. Elbryan cast a warning glance the goblins' way, then turned sideways to them, focusing on the water, and bent down to finish filling his waterskin.

He had given them one chance; a large part of him, that boy who remembered Dundalis, hoped they would not take it.

He heard and felt the water stirring as the creatures came on slowly. He sensed that at least two had broken away, moving out of the stream to flank him front and back.

Elbryan measured their approach, kept wary for any hint that the spear was coming his way once more.

Everything seemed to stop, all movement, all splashing. The creatures were not more than ten feet away, he knew. Slowly he turned square with the main group of four, rising to stand straight, a foot and more higher than his tallest foe.

"Eenegash!" the closest and ugliest of the group demanded, holding forth its sword, a two-foot blade not unlike the one Olwan had given Elbryan for his patrols.

"I do not understand," he replied evenly.

The goblins muttered something among themselves; Elbryan realized that they could not understand his language either. Then the ugly one turned back to him.

"Eenegash!" it said again, more forcefully, and it pointed its sword at the staff, then at the riverbank.

"I hardly think so," Elbryan replied, smiling widely and shaking his head. In a barely noticeable movement, the ranger pulled the feathered tip from the bow, tucking it and the bowstring into his belt.

The goblin gave a threatening growl. Elbryan shook his head again.

The creature rushed to close half the distance and prodded with its sword, a movement more of intimidation than an actual attack. But it was the creature who was surprised.

Elbryan grabbed the staff, right hand over left, reversed his grip with his left as the pole started moving, and snapped it across so quickly in front of him that the goblin never had a chance to move. The staff connected simultaneously on the sword and the goblin's hand, knocking the weapon from the creature's grasp and launching it a dozen feet away. A subtle shift, still too quick for the creature to dodge, and Elbryan stabbed the tapered end out straight, striking the goblin on its sloping forehead right above and between the eyes, laying it out straight in the stream.

With a whoop of delight, the other goblins, predictably, came on.

Elbryan brought his staff back in, letting go with his left hand, flipping with his right to send the forward tip under. Never breaking the momentum, he extended his right arm out, catching the closing goblin, the one that had run out of the stream to flank the man, completely by surprise, Hawkwing's tip stabbing right under its chin.

Back in came the weapon, a full and defensive spin between the ranger and the three goblins coming along in the stream. Elbryan caught the staff firmly in his left hand and extended that arm out in similar fashion so that the other flanking goblin was poked away. Back in came the staff, half spun and caught again in the right hand, half spun, angled outward diagonally, and caught again in the left, and then the right hand catching it, too, as the trailing end came around and over, Elbryan shifting the weapon's angle and striding boldly ahead. The downward chop connected squarely on the head of the center goblin, the spearwielder, Hawkwing's incredible hardness splitting wide the creature's skull with a resounding *crack!*

Elbryan swept his staff out to the left, knocking aside a club strike, then back to the right, parrying a sword. Back left, back right, each time the angle shifting to defeat the intended attack. Then back left, then left again, knocking wide the creature's club arm. Elbryan stepped left as well and spun, avoiding an awkward cut of its sword. He came around hard and low, Hawkwing flying before him. The goblin, to its credit, recognized the circuitous attack and managed to get its club down, but Elbryan merely lifted Hawkwing's flying tip, cracking across the creature's skinny forearm, shattering bone. The club fell into the stream; the goblin shrieked and clutched at its arm.

Elbryan stepped forward, facing the creature squarely, staff coming horizontal in front of him, and punched out with his left, right, left, Hawkwing swishing about to smack the goblin hard on alternate sides of its head. The ranger dropped his right foot back after the last strike, retracting the staff, then turned sidelong to his current foe, expecting an attack from the sword wielder. Seeing that creature in full flight, Elbryan stabbed the staff back out hard to his left, hitting the dazed and battered goblin right in the face.

He didn't see but heard the movement as the goblin that had come in at his left struggled to its feet. Hawkwing went swinging again, turning a vertical circle under and then over Elbryan's right shoulder as he turned and leaped out to the left. Down raced the staff above the angle of the terrified goblin's pitiful attempt to parry, crashing hard against the base of the creature's neck. The goblin jolted perfectly still and then, as if the wave of energy had rolled right down to its feet and then come rushing back up, the creature went into a weird backward leap, landing on its feet for a long moment, then slowly falling over.

Elbryan turned and dropped into a defensive crouch, but no enemies presented themselves. The first one he had hit, the leader, was on its hands and knees in the middle of the stream, facing away, too dazed to even get back to its feet. The one he had hit to the right of the stream was still on the ground, squirming and gasping for air that would hardly come. This last one he had hit was surely dead, as was the spear wielder, and the one who had taken four blows to the head lay unmoving at the stream's edge, its face in the water. The last of the group, the one with the sword, faced Elbryan from twenty paces, hopping up and down, hurling curses that the ranger did not understand.

Casually, in no hurry, Elbryan replaced the feathered tip of his bow and in one fluid motion, bent the shaft around his leg and hooked the bowstring over the bottom edge.

The goblin caught on, howled, and fled.

Up came Hawkwing; three feathers separated. Clear and straight for thirty-five feet.

The arrow slammed the goblin square in the back, lifting it clear of the stream and sending it another five feet. Arms and legs flailing, it flopped heavily, facedown in the water.

Grim Elbryan retrieved the axe from the side of his pack and finished the task at hand.

Then he was on his way, running across the Moorlands.

PART THREE

▼

CONFLICT

Did you go home, Uncle Mather? When you walked away from Andur'Blough Inninness, from your elven home, did you return to the place you had known in your childhood?

I had thought it a vision that led me across the Moorlands then north to a sweeping vale of knee-deep caribou moss and stark pines. Now I wonder if it wasn't merely a memory returned, a backtracking of the same course the elves had taken on that day when they pulled me from Dundalis. Perhaps they then placed a veil over my memory, that I had no desire to escape Caer'alfar and run back to the place of my kinfolk. Perhaps that last Oracle in Andur'Blough Inninness was no more than a lifting of the veil.

I had not even considered this until my northern trek led me back to these lands familiar. I feared that I had erred in my course, that I had returned home by memory, not by vision.

Now I understand. This land is my land, my ranger haunt. It is under my protection, though the proud and hardy folk here would hardly believe they need it, and certainly would refuse it should I ask.

They are more numerous than when I lived here last. Weedy Meadow remains a village of four score—the goblins never attacked after the sacking of Dundalis—and a new village, nearly twice that in number, has been built some thirty miles to the west, even further into the Wilderlands. End-o'-the-World, they call it, and a fitting name it seems.

And, Uncle Mather, they have rebuilt Dundalis and have kept its name. I do not yet understand how I feel about this. Is the new Dundalis a tribute to the last or a mockery? It pained me when, walking along the wide cart path, I happened upon a signpost—a new signpost, for we never had such things—proclaiming the village limits, the edge of Dundalis. For a moment, I admit, I even held fast a fantasy that my memory of the destruction, of the carnage, was in error. Perhaps, I dared to think, the elves had tricked me into believing that Dundalis and all its folk had died, to keep me from fleeing their custody, or from wanting to flee.

Under the name on the signpost, someone had scrawled "Dundalis dan Dundalis," and under that, another prankster had added, "McDundalis," both indications that this place was "the son of Dundalis." I should have understood the implication.

It was with great anticipation that I walked that last mile to the village proper—to see a place that I knew not.

There is a tavern now, larger than the old common house and built on the foundation of my old home.

Built by strangers.

It was such an awkward moment, Uncle Mather, a feeling of absolute displacement. I had come home, and yet, this was not my home. The people were much the same—strong and firm, tough as the deepest winter night—and yet, they were not the same. No Brody Gentle, no Bunker Crawyer, no Shane McMichael, no Thomas Ault, no Mother and Father, no Pony.

No Dundalis.

I refused the invitation of the tavern's proprietor, a jolly-looking man, and, without a word—I suppose that was the moment the folk of the village began to suspect that I was a bit unusual—headed back the way I had come. I took my frustrations out on the signpost, I admit, tearing off the lowest board, the scribbled references to the original village.

Never had I felt so alone, not even that morning after the disaster. The world had moved on without me. I meant to come and speak with you then, Uncle Mather, and so I crossed by the town, up the slope on the northern edge. There are several small caves on the backside of that slope, overlooking the wide vale. In one of those, so I believed, I would find Oracle. I would find Uncle Mather. I would find peace.

I never made it over that ridge. It is a funny thing, memory. To the elves, it is a way to walk backward in time, to rediscover old scenes from the perspective of new enlightenments.

So it was that morning on the ridge north of Dundalis. I saw her, Uncle Mather, my Pony, as alive to me as ever she was, as wonderful and beautiful. I remembered her so very vividly that she was indeed beside me once again—for a few fleeting moments.

I have no new friends among the current residents of Dundalis, and in truth, I expect none. But I have found peace, Uncle Mather. I have come home.

—ELBRYAN WYNDON

The Black Bear

"It came roaring down that hill," the man was saying, waving his arm frantically in the direction of the forested slope north of Dundalis. "I got my family into the root cellar—damned glad I dug the thing!"

The speaker was about his own age, the ranger noticed as he approached the group of ten—eight men and two women—who were gathered outside the nearly destroyed cabin on the outskirts of Dundalis.

"Damn big bear," one of the other men said.

"Twelve footer," the first man, the victim of the attack, remarked, holding his arms as far apart as he could possibly stretch.

"Brown?" Elbryan asked, though the question was merely a formality, for a twelve-foot-tall bear would have to be brown.

The group turned as one to regard the stranger. They had seen Elbryan about town on several occasions over the last few months, mostly sitting quietly in the tavern, the Howling Sheila, but none, save Belster O'Comely, the innkeeper, had spoken a word to the suspicious man. Their reluctance was clearly etched on their faces as they regarded the outsider and his unusual dress: the forest green cloak and the triangular cap.

"Black," the victim corrected evenly, his eyes narrowed.

Elbryan nodded, accepting that as more likely the truth than the man's previous statement. He knew two things from the color: first, that the man was surely exaggerating the bear's size and second, that this attack was far from normal. A brown bear might come roaring down the hill, hurling itself upon the cabin as if the shelter were some elk, but black bears were shy creatures by nature, far from aggressive unless cornered, or defending their cubs.

"What business is it of yours?" another man asked, his tone making it seem to Elbryan as if he were being accused of the attack.

Ignoring the comment, the ranger walked past the group and knelt low, inspecting a set of tracks. As he suspected, the bear was nowhere near the size the excited farmer was claiming, probably closer to five or six feet in height, perhaps two to three hundred pounds. Elbryan didn't really begrudge the man his excitement, though. A six-foot bear could indeed appear twice that height when angered. And the amount of damage to the house was remarkable.

"We cannot tolerate a rogue," a large man, Tol Yuganick, insisted. Elbryan looked up to regard him. He was broad shouldered and strong, forceful in manner as he was in speech. His face was clean shaven, seeming almost babyish, but anyone looking at powerful Tol knew that to be a deceptive façade. Elbryan noticed the man's hands—for hands were often the most telling of all—were rough and thick with calluses. He was a worker, a true frontiersman.

"We'll get together a group and go out and kill the damned thing," he said, and he spat upon the ground.

Elbryan was surprised that the burly man hadn't decided to go out alone and hunt the bear.

"And what of you?" the man bellowed, looking at the ranger. "You were asked what business this might be of yours, but of yet I've heard no answer." Tol moved closer to the stooping ranger as he spoke.

Elbryan came up to his full height. He was as tall as the man and, while not as heavy, certainly more muscular.

"Do you think that you belong in Dundalis?" the man asked bluntly, again the words sounding like an accusation, or a threat.

Elbryan didn't blink. He wanted to scream out that he belonged in this place more than any of them, that he had been here when the foundation of their beloved tavern was that of his own home!

He held the words, though, and easily. His years with the elves had given him that control, that discipline. He was here, in Dundalis, in Weedy Meadow, in End-o'-the-World, to give the folk some measure of protection that they had never known. If an elven-trained ranger had been about those seven years before, then Dundalis would not have been sacked, Elbryan believed, and in the face of that responsibility, the surly man's demeanor seemed a minor thing.

"The bear will not return," was all the ranger said to them, and he calmly walked away.

He heard the grumbling behind him, heard the word "strange" several times—and not spoken with any affection. They were still planning to go out and hunt the bear, Elbryan realized, but he was determined to get there first. A black bear had attacked a farmhouse and that alone was enough of a mystery to force the ranger to investigate.

Elbryan was amazed at how easy it was for him to track the bear. The beast had run off from the farmhouse, creating a swath of devastation through the brush, even knocking over small trees, venting a rage that the ranger had never before witnessed in an animal. The tracks were surely those of a medium-sized bear, but Elbryan felt as if he were tracking a fomorian giant or some other evil, reasoning creature, some creature purposefully bent on destruction. He feared that the bear was in the grip of some disease, perhaps, or was wounded. Whatever the source, with every passed scene of utter destruction, the ranger's fear mounted that he would not be able to spare the creature. He had hoped simply to drive the bear far away into the deeper woodlands.

He moved up the side of one steep hill, peering intently into every shadow. Bears were not stupid creatures; they had been known to backtrack hunters, taking the men from behind. Elbryan crouched by the side of one small tree. He placed his hand on the ground, feeling for subtle vibrations, anything that might offer a hint.

He caught a slight movement of a bush out of the corner of his eye. The ranger didn't move except to shift his head to better view the shadow. He noted the wind, noted that he was upwind of the spot.

Out came the bear in full charge, roaring.

Elbryan shifted to one knee, fitted a heavy arrow, and, with a sigh of complete resignation, let fly. He scored a hit, the arrow skipping off the bear's face and burrowing into its chest, but the bear kept coming. The ranger was amazed at the sheer speed of the thing. He had seen bears in Andur'Blough Inninness, had even seen one run off when Juraviel had banged two stones together, but this creature's speed was outrageous, as fast as any horse might run.

A second arrow followed the first, diving deep into the bear's shoulder. It bellowed again and hardly slowed.

Elbryan knew that he would not get the third shot away. If it had been a brown bear, he would have taken to the trees, but a black could climb any tree faster than he could.

He waited, crouched, as the bear bore down on him, then, at the last instant, the ranger went into a sidelong roll, down the hill.

The bear skidded to a stop and turned to follow. When Elbryan rolled to his knees, facing up the hill to the bear, the creature went up onto its hind legs, standing tall and imposing.

But leaving some vital areas exposed.

Elbryan pulled the bowstring back with all his strength; Hawkwing's three feathers were as wide apart as they could go. The ranger hated this business as he sighted the hollow on the bear's breast.

And then it was over, suddenly, the creature rolling, dead. Elbryan went to the corpse. He waited a while to make sure that it would not stir, then moved to its muzzle, lifting its upper lip. He feared that he would find foamy saliva there, an indication of the most wicked disease. If that was the case, then Elbryan would have his work cut out from him indeed, hunting almost day and night for other infected animals, everything from raccoons and weasels to bats.

No foam; the ranger breathed a sigh of relief. It was short-lived, though, as Elbryan tried to figure what, then, had caused this normally docile animal to go so bad. He continued his inspection of the mouth and face, noted that the eyes were clear and not runny, then moved along the bear's torso.

He found his answer in the form of four barbed darts, stuck deep into the bear's rump. He worked one out—not an easy task—and inspected its tip. Elbryan recognized the black, sappy poison, a pain-inducing product of a rare black birch tree.

With a growl, the ranger threw the dart to the ground. This was no accident but a purposeful attack on the bear. The poor beast had been driven mad by pain, and someone—some human, most likely, given the type of the darts—had done it.

Elbryan gathered his wits and began his dance of praise to the spirit of the bear, thanking it for its gift of food and warmth. Then he methodically went about skinning and cleaning it. To waste the creature's useful body, to leave the bear to rot or even to bury it whole in the ground would, by elven standards—and by Elbryan's—be a complete insult to the bear, and thus to Nature.

His work was done late that afternoon, but the ranger did not rest, nor did he return to Dundalis to inform the townsfolk of the kill. Something, someone, had brought on this tragedy.

Nightbird went hunting again.

They were not much more difficult to find than the bear. Their hut, a mere shack of logs and old boards—Elbryan got the distinct impression that many of these had come from the ruins of Dundalis—was at the top of a hill. Branches had been tossed all about for camouflage, but many of these had already withered, their dry and brown leaves a telltale sign.

The ranger heard them long before he caught sight of them, laughing and singing terribly off-key, though the voices were surely human, as he had suspected.

Elbryan glided stealthily up the hill, tree to tree, shadow to shadow, though he doubted the men inside would have heard him had he been accompanied by a hundred villagers and a score of fomorian giants! He recognized the implements of the trapping trade hanging all about the shack, along with dozens of drying pelts. These men knew animals, Elbryan understood. In a vat not far from the back wall of the shack, the ranger found a thick concoction of black liquid, and quickly surmised it to be the same irritant poison that had been used on the bear.

The walls of the shack were in bad disrepair, with cracks between every board. Elbryan peeked in.

Three men lay about on piled skins, black bear mostly, drinking foamy beer from old mugs. Every so often, one would shift to the side and dip his mug into a barrel, first brushing away the many flies and bees drawn to the liquid.

Elbryan shook his head in disgust, but he reminded himself to keep a measure of respect. These were men of the Wilderlands, strong and heavily armed. One had many daggers within easy grasp, hanging on a bandolier that crisscrossed his chest. Another sported a heavy axe, while the last carried a slender sword. From his vantage point, the ranger noted, too, that a bar was in place across the one door.

He moved around to the front of the house and took the dagger from his pack. The door did not fit the opening well, leaving a wide crack on one side, wide enough to admit the dagger's blade. A flick of the wrist dislodged the bar and Elbryan kicked open the door, striding a single step into the shack.

The men scrambled, spilling beer, one shouting aloud as he rolled across his sword, the hilt catching hard on his hip. They were up soon enough, Elbryan standing impassively by the door, Hawkwing, its feathered tip and string removed, in his hand like some unthreatening walking stick.

"Whad'ye want?" asked one of the men, a barrel-chested brute whose face was more scar than beard. Except for that hardened face with its wild, untended beard, this man could have passed as a brother of Tol Yuganick, Elbryan noted distastefully. Surely their bodies were cut from the same, rather large, mold. The fellow had his huge axe out in front of him, and if Elbryan couldn't offer a reasonable answer, there was little doubt what he meant to do with it. The swordsman, tall and lean with not a hair anywhere on his head, shadowed the burly man, gaping at Elbryan from over his companion's shoulder; while the third, a skinny, nervous wretch, moved to the far corner, rubbing his fingers—which weren't so far from his many daggers.

"I have come to speak with you about a particular bear," Elbryan answered coolly.

"What bear?" the burly man replied. "We got skins."

"The bear you maddened with poisoned darts," Elbryan answered bluntly. "The bear that destroyed a farm in Dundalis and nearly killed a family."

"Go on now." The man spat.

"The same poison you have brewing out back," Elbryan went on, "a rare concoction, known to few."

"That don't prove nothing," the man retorted, snapping his dirty fingers in the air. "Now get on out of here, else ye'll soon feel the edge of me axe!"

"I think not," the ranger answered. "There is the matter of compensation—to the farmers and to me for my efforts in hunting the bear."

"C-compen—?" the tall, bald man stuttered.

"Payment," said Elbryan. He saw the movement even as he spoke, the man from the corner drawing and throwing a dagger with practiced ease.

Elbryan planted the ball of his left foot and spun clockwise, the dagger flying harmlessly past to stick deep in the wall. The ranger came round as if he would launch a horizontal swipe, but he recognized the move was anticipated: the burly man's axe was up to block. As soon as he started around, then, Elbryan turned his right foot out and went around counterclockwise, pulling in his hip to avoid a swipe of that axe.

Now he launched his attack, dropping down to one knee, slapping his staff across to catch the inside of the overbalanced man's leg. A shift of the angle sent his staff poking straight up, smacking the man's groin. Faster than a cat, Elbryan retracted the staff a foot, shifted its angle, and poked ahead three times in rapid succession, prodding the burly man in the hollow of his chest.

He fell away and Elbryan came up hard, bringing Hawkwing horizontal above his head in both hands to catch the downward chop of the second man's sword. Up came the ranger's knee, slamming the man's belly, and as he started to double over, Elbryan turned his staff, deflecting the sword to the side. He twisted his staff around the man's arm, hooking him under the armpit, stepped with his left foot across his body behind the man's entangled side, then heaved with all his strength, launching the wretch into the air to land heavily on his back and the back of his head.

Elbryan immediately swung about, realizing he was vulnerable. Predictably, another dagger was on its way, and the ranger just got Hawkwing up in time to block its flight. He loosened his grip on his staff as the dagger connected so that it wouldn't bounce far away. As fortune would have it, the dagger went straight up, and Elbryan seized it, catching it by the tip.

In the blink of an eye, the ranger stood, staff in one hand out before him, his other hand holding a dagger cocked behind his ear, ready to throw.

The skinny man, two daggers in hand, blanched and let his blades drop to the floor.

Elbryan fought hard to restrain the rage that called for him to put that dagger right into the foul man's chest, a rage that only intensified when the ranger thought of what these three had done to the bear and of the potentially devastating consequences of their foolhardy actions.

With a growl, he let fly, the dagger slamming hard into the wall right beside the man's head. Never taking his eyes from Elbryan, whimpering all the way, the skinny man slumped to a sitting position in the corner.

Elbryan looked about; the other two were staggering to their feet, neither holding a weapon.

"What are your names?" the ranger demanded.

The men looked curiously at one another.

"Your names!"

"Paulson," the burly man answered, "Cric, and Chipmunk," he finished, indicating first the tall man, then the dagger thrower.

"Chipmunk?" Elbryan inquired.

"Skittery type," Paulson explained.

The ranger shook his head. "Know this, Paulson, Cric, and Chipmunk: you share the forest with me, and I will be watching your every move. Another prank, another cruelty, as with the bear, will bring you more harm than this, I promise. And I will be watching your trap lines—no longer shall you use the jaw traps—"

Paulson started to complain, but Elbryan glared so fiercely at him that he seemed to melt.

"Nor any other traps that inflict suffering on your prey."

"We've to earn our money," Chipmunk remarked in a shaky voice.

"There are better ways," Elbryan answered evenly. "And in the hopes that you will find those ways, I'll demand no coins from you for compensation . . . this time." He looked at each of them, meeting their stares, his own showing clearly that he was not speaking empty threats.

"And who might ye be?" Paulson dared to ask.

Elbryan shifted back on his heels, considering the question. "I am Nightbird," he answered.

Cric snickered, but Paulson, locked with that intense gaze, held a hand up in his companion's face.

"A name you would do well to remember," Elbryan finished, and he headed for the door, boldly turning his back on the dangerous threesome.

They didn't begin to entertain any thoughts of attacking.

The ranger went around to the back and dumped out the cauldron of poison. As he left, he took a few of the jaw traps, nasty pieces of toothy iron hinged and set with heavy springs so that they would clamp hard on the leg of any passing animal.

His next stop was the tavern, the Howling Sheila, in Dundalis. A dozen men and women were in the common room, boisterous until the stranger entered. Elbryan went to the bar first, nodding to Belster O'Comely, the closest thing he had to a friend in the area.

"Just water," the ranger said, and Belster mouthed the predictable words right along with him, then pushed a glass out to him.

"Word of the bear?" the jolly innkeeper asked.

"The bear is dead," Elbryan replied grimly, and he walked to the far side of the room, taking a seat at the corner table, his back to the wall.

He noted that several other patrons shifted their seats, one woman even bluntly turning her back on him.

Elbryan brought the tip of his triangular cap down low and smiled. He understood that it would be like this. He was not much like these folk; no longer was he much like any human, except for those rare few who had ventured to the valley of the elves, who had spent years beside the likes of Bel-li'mar Juraviel and Tuntun. Elbryan missed those friends now—even Tuntun. It was true that he had been out of place in Caer'alfar, but in many ways the ranger felt even more out of place here among folk who looked so much like him but who saw the world through very different eyes.

Still, despite the prominent reminders of his position, Elbryan's smile was genuine. He had done well this day, though he regretted having to slay the bear. His solace came in duty, in his vow that this Dundalis and the two neighboring villages would not share the fate that had befallen his own village.

He remained in the Howling Sheila for nearly an hour, but not a person, save Belster on Elbryan's way out, offered him so much as a glance.

❖ 24 ❖

The Mad Friar

"Tinson," Warder Miklos Barmine said to Jill as she walked her watch along the sea wall of Pireth Tulme.

Jill regarded the short, stout man curiously. She recognized the name Tinson as that of the small hamlet some dozen miles inland from the fortress. The place was no more than a score of houses and a tavern, a place of rogues and whores servicing the soldiers of Pireth Tulme.

"The Waylaid Traveler," Barmine added in his typically curt manner.

"Another fight?" Jill asked.

"And something more," replied the warder, walking away. "Gather ten and go."

Jill watched the man depart. She didn't like Miklos Barmine, not at all. He had replaced Constantine Presso only three months before, the previous warder sent north to command Pireth Danard. At first, Jill thought the new warder more her style, a stickler for detail and duty. But he was a letch, a drooling, grabby slob, who took it personally when Jill refused his advances. Even his strict rules for duty had relaxed within the week, Pireth Tulme reverting to its typical partying ways. Also, it had surprised Jill how much she missed Constantine Presso, a decent man—by Pireth Tulme's standards, at least. She had served under Presso for more than a year, and he had always been a gentleman to her, always respected her decision not to partake in the unending festivities. Now, with Presso gone and the brooding Miklos Barmine in command, Jill feared that the pressure on her would only increase.

She shook that dark thought away, turning her attention to the task at hand. Barmine's punishment for her refusal to bed with him was always work—little did the fool understand that his punishment was more like a reward to Jill! There had been another fight, the fourth in less than two weeks, at the Waylaid Traveler, the apparently appropriately named tavern in Tinson. What this "something more," that Barmine had hinted at might be, Jill could not guess, though she suspected it to be nothing extraordinary. The woman shrugged; at least there was something to do now besides walking the wall.

She collected ten of Pireth Tulme's Coastpoint Guards, using their hangovers as a tool for rejecting more of the others, then set out, double-timing the march down the dirt path. They arrived in dirty Tinson late that afternoon. The town square was empty and quiet—it was always quiet, Jill noted, for on the three previous occasions she had visited the place, she hadn't seen a single child. The majority of Tinson's residents slept the day through, preferring the revelry of the night.

A shout from the Waylaid Traveler caught Jill's attention.

"We must prepare!" came a bellow, a tremendous voice, clear even out here at a distance and with a wall between the speaker and Jill. "Oh, evil, what a foothold you have found! What fools are we to sleep as darkness rises!"

The group of soldiers entered the tavern openly through the front door, doubling the number of patrons. The first thing Jill noticed was a huge, fat man standing atop a table, waving an empty mug, sometimes in a threatening manner to keep at bay the closer patrons, all obviously intent on knocking him from his perch. Jill ordered her troop to filter about, then went to see the man behind the serving bar.

"The mad friar," the barkeep explained. "He was in all the night, then came back just a short while ago. Has no shortage of money, I can assure you! They say he bartered jewels with merchants on the road, and though he didn't get a fair price—not even close—he left with pouches full of gold."

Jill regarded the fat friar curiously. He wore the thick brown robes of the Abellican Church, though they were old and threadbare in many places and weathered, as if he had been out on the open road for a long, long time. His black beard was thick and bushy, and he was tall, half a foot above six feet, and had to weigh near to three hundred pounds. His shoulders were wide, his bones thick and solid, but Jill got the feeling that the extra weight, most of which was centered about his belly, was something fairly recent.

What struck Jill most about him was his almost feverish intensity, his brown eyes showing a luster, a life, beyond anything she had seen in many years.

"Piety, dignity, poverty!" he yelled, and then he snorted derisively. "Ho, ho, what!"

Jill recognized the litany—piety, dignity, poverty—the same one Abbot Dobrinion Calislas had uttered on the fateful day of her wedding.

"Hah!" the huge man bellowed. "What piety is there in whoring? What dignity in foolhardiness? And what poverty? Gold leaf and jewels—ah, the jewels!"

"His song is not for changing," the barkeep said dryly. Then he yelled out to the guards, "Will you get him down?"

Jill wasn't sure that they should move in so straightforward a manner against the friar. The man's remark about whoring, in particular, had seemed to stir more than a few angry grumbles, and she feared that any overt action, a physical assault rather than trying to calm the man, would bring about a general row. She could do little to stop her soldiers, though, given the lax chain of command and the barkeep's permission.

She started across the room to try and keep things calm, stopping, though, when she heard the barkeep add, too low for any others to hear, "And take care, for he has a bit of magic about him."

"Damn," Jill muttered, turning back to see two of her soldiers, one of them Gofflaw, reach up to grab the monk.

"Hah, preparedness training!" the fat man howled joyfully, and he grabbed Gofflaw by the wrist and hoisted the surprised man into the air. Before the soldier could begin to react, the powerful friar lifted him above his head, spun him twice, then tossed him across the room.

A third soldier drew sword and swiped out one of the table legs, bringing the friar tumbling down atop the poor second man who had been reaching for him. The monk hit the ground in a roll, showing surprising agility for one his size, and came right back to his feet, shouting at the top of his lungs and barreling over the next two closest people, one a soldier, one a townsman.

The fight was on in full.

The sheer power of the friar astounded Jill. The man ran every which way, bowling over all who would stand before him, laughing maniacally all the while, even when one of those dodging his charge landed a solid punch about his face or neck. "Prepare!" he roared over and over, and he cried something about a dactyl and then about a demon.

Jill watched him for a few moments, honestly intrigued. The man was obviously out of his mind, or at least he appeared so, but to Jill, who had spent a year and a half in the Coastpoint Guards, a cry for preparedness and virtue did not seem like such a bad thing.

A group of soldiers encircled the friar, one man quickly putting his sword in line and calling for the monk to yield. There came a sudden, sharp flash of blue, and all the soldiers were flying, their hair standing on end. The friar laughed wildly.

And he charged on. He rushed to one terrified woman and picked her up by the shoulders. "Do not lay down for them!" he cried earnestly, and Jill had the feeling that the man had some personal stake in his plea. "I beg of you, do not, for you are part of the encroachment, do you not see? You are part of the dactyl's gain!"

A soldier jumped on the friar from behind, and he was forced to let go of the woman. He merely howled, though, and shrugged the man away, then charged on.

Jill cut in front of him; he recognized her as a woman and again slowed and softened his approach.

Jill dove at his legs, rolling and sweeping with her own legs, sending the burly friar tumbling headlong. Five men were atop him in an instant, grabbing and twisting. Somehow, the huge friar managed to get back up to his feet, but more soldiers and several of the townsfolk rushed in, finally subduing him. They ushered the man to the door and unceremoniously threw him out.

Jill noted that Gofflaw drew out his sword and moved to follow.

"Let him be!" she commanded.

Gofflaw growled at her, but under Jill's unyielding glare, he replaced his sword in its sheath.

"And if ye show yerself again," another of the soldiers yelled, "then know ye'll feel the bite of a sword!"

"Hear you the words of truth!" the mad friar yelled back at him. "Know me for what I am, and not for the insulting names you give to me. I am the hound of ill omen, the messenger of disaster!"

"Ye're a drunk," roared the soldier.

The fat man sputtered something unintelligible and turned away, waving his hand dismissively. "You will learn," he promised grimly. "You will learn."

Jill turned to the barkeep, the man merely shaking his head. "He's a dangerous one," the man said.

Jill nodded, but she wasn't sure she agreed. The fat friar had made no move to finish any of his attacks. He had tackled and punched, had thrown Gofflaw halfway across the room, but no one, not even the friar, had been badly injured. To frustrated Jill's thinking, Gofflaw could use a throw or two across a room. She moved to the door to see the friar shuffling down the muddy lane, weeping and crying out for the "sins of men" and the woeful state of preparation.

He swung about, some score of yards from the tavern entrance, and launched into a diatribe on the coming dark days, about a world unprepared to face the forces of evil, about a darkness being fed by the internal rot of the land.

"The man's crazy," one of the soldiers remarked.

"The mad friar," the barkeep replied.

Jill wasn't so sure of that. Not at all.

❖ 25 ❖

Brother Justice

Master Jojonah looked down from an inconspicuous balcony at the large chamber, bare of any furnishing but for a few practice riggings sitting against the far wall. In the center of the room stood the stocky young man, his face haggard from lack of sleep. He wore only a loincloth and stood defensively, shoulders hunched, arms crossed to cover his belly and loins. Even his head was bare, for his superiors had shaved it. He uttered a chant repeatedly, using it to bolster his failing strength, and De'Unnero, the new master who had taken Siherton's place, stalked about him, occasionally stinging him with a riding crop. Behind Quintall stood a tenth-year immaculate.

"You are weak and useless!" De'Unnero screamed, smacking Quintall across the shoulder blades. "And you were part of the conspiracy!"

Quintall's mouth moved to form the word "no," but no sound came forth, managing only a pitiful shake of his head.

"You were!" De'Unnero roared, and he whipped Quintall again.

Master Jojonah could hardly bear to watch. Quintall's "training" had been going on for more than a month now, ever since Father Abbot Markwart, looking old and tired indeed, had seen a vision of Avelyn alive.

Avelyn! The very thought of the young brother sent shivers along Jojonah's spine. Avelyn had killed Siherton—the body, or what remained of it, had been found only late that spring, almost a year to the day since the tragedy. And worse, if Markwart's vision was true, Avelyn had survived and had run off with a substantial supply of the sacred stones.

Jojonah closed his eyes and remembered all the times Siherton had warned him about Avelyn's almost inhuman dedication. Avelyn would be trouble, Siherton had promised, and the master's words had proven true. But why? Jojonah had to wonder. What had precipitated the trouble, a fault of Avelyn's or the man's lack of fault in an order grown perverse? Indeed, Brother Avelyn Desbris was trouble, a dark mirror that the masters of St.-Mere-Abelle could not bear to gaze into. Avelyn, by any measure that

243

Jojonah could discern, was what a monk was supposed to be, the truest of the true, and yet his manner could not agree with the increasingly secular ways of the monastery. That the Order should be threatened by the piety of a young monk was something Master Jojonah could not come to terms with.

And yet, the master was too tired, too wrapped up in a sense of loss, both for Siherton and Avelyn—and for himself—to try to make some peace within the monastery. Markwart had become almost feverish in his desire to see Avelyn and, more particularly, the sacred stones, brought back, and the Father Abbot's word was sacrosanct.

The crack of the crop brought Jojonah's attention back to the scene at hand. He had never held any love for brutish Quintall, but still he pitied the man. The conditioning ranged from sleep deprivation to long periods of hunger. Quintall's strength, both physical and mental, would be torn away piece by piece and then brought back under the guidance and control of the training masters. The man would be reduced to an instrument of destruction, Avelyn's destruction. Quintall's every thought would be focused on that singular purpose; Avelyn Desbris would become the source of all his ills, the most-hated threat to St.-Mere-Abelle.

Jojonah shuddered and walked away, trying hard not to picture the scene when Quintall finally caught up to Avelyn.

The cave seemed a gigantic caricature of a king's throne room. A huge dais, three steps up, centered the back wall, sporting a single obsidian throne that two large men could sit in together without touching each other. Twin rows of massive columns, each carved into the likeness of a giant warrior, lined the room. Like the throne, they were formed of obsidian, with graceful but somehow discordant lines swirling about them like the fibers of interlocking muscles. The floor and walls were clear of the black rock, showing the normal dullish gray of Aida's stone, and the single set of doors was made of bronze.

No torches burned within, the room's light coming from either side of the great dais where a continual flow of lava issued from the back corner of the wall and descended through holes in the floor, diving down into the tunnels of Aida, then reaching out along the mountain's black arms, engulfing more and more of the Barbacan.

Small indeed did Ubba Banrock and Ulg Tik'narn, powrie chieftains from the distant Julianthes, and Gothra, the goblin king, seem in that tremendous room. Even Maiyer Dek of the fomorian giants felt small and insignificant, eyeing the statue-columns as if they would come alive and surround him, dwarfing his sixteen-foot height. And Maiyer Dek, among the largest of his giant kind, was not accustomed to being dwarfed.

Still, even if all twenty of the columns, and a dozen more besides, surrounded the giant, it would not have been more imposing than the single creature reclining on the throne. All four of the dactyl's guests felt that imposing weight keenly. They were each among the most powerful of their respective races, leaders of armies that numbered in the hundreds for the giant, in the thousands for each of the powries, and in the tens of thousands for the goblin. They were the darkness of Corona, the bringers of misery, and yet, they seemed pitiful, groveling things before the great dactyl, mere shadows of this infinitely darker being.

Goblins and giants often aligned, but both races traditionally hated the powries almost as much as they hated the humans.

Except on those occasions when the dactyl was awake. Except at those times when the darker forces bound them together in singular purpose. There could be no struggles for power among the mortal leaders of the various races when the dactyl sat on its obsidian throne.

"We are not four armies," the dactyl roared at them suddenly, and Gothra nearly fell over from the sheer weight of the resonating voice. "Nor three, if the powries consider their respective forces to be allied. We are one army, one force, one purpose!" The demon leaped from its throne and tossed a small item, a fabric patch, gray in color and with the black image of the dactyl sewn in. "Go out and begin the work on these," the demon ordered.

Maiyer Dek was first to inspect the patch. "My warriors are not stitch women," the fomorian leader began, but as soon as the words left Maiyer Dek's mouth, the dactyl leaped down to stand before the giant, and seemed to grow. A feral growl escaped the demon's lips as its hand shot out, slapping the behemoth across the face with enough force to knock Maiyer Dek to the floor. Then the dactyl began a more insidious attack, a mental barrage of images of torture and agony, and Maiyer Dek, the proud and strong leader, the strongest mortal creature in all the Barbacan, whimpered pitifully and squirmed about on the floor, begging for mercy.

"Every soldier in my army shall wear such an emblem," the dactyl decreed. "In *my* army! And you," the beast said to Maiyer Dek, reaching down and easily lifting the massive giant to its feet. "Bring to me a score and four of your finest warriors to serve as my house guard."

And so the meetings went, through the days. The demon dactyl had been awake for several years, watching, feeling every slaughter of humans in the Wilderlands, tasting the blood of every corpse into which a powrie dipped its infamous cap, hearing the screams of sailors and passengers as each scuttled ship went under the swells of the merciless Mirianic. The darkness had grown; the humans had become ever weaker. Now the creature saw the time to organize its forces fully, to begin its unified attacks.

Terranen Dinoniel was dust in the earth; the dactyl meant to win this time.

To the twenty-four giants Maiyer Dek brought in, the dactyl presented suits of armor, demon-forged in the twin lava flows of the throne room, full plated, thick and strong. And the dactyl made even finer protection for its four chieftains, great magical bracers, studded with spikes, that would protect the wearer from the blows of any weapon. Among the three evil races, none had earned any reputation of loyalty or honor, but now, with the bracers, the dactyl could hold faith that its four chosen generals would survive the not-unexpected treachery of their underlings.

And those ranks were considerable indeed. Outside the cave, on the tree-covered slopes of Aida, thousands of goblins, powries, and giants milled about their respective camps, glancing up the southern face to the gaping hole that marked the main entrance to the demon's lair. All three camps were between the mountain's newest "arms," two black streaks of cooling lava, red-tipped as the stuff continued its slow roll from the bowels of the mountain, reaching out, southeast and southwest, as if they were extensions of the demon's own reach. There was no sign of tree or brush within those black lines; all life had been snuffed out beneath the darkness, burned away by the fires, and covered by the cooling lava. Even those creatures closest to the center of the area between the arms felt the residual heat, and on that shimmering air was brought the tingles of promised power, the itchy anxiety to go out and kill.

All for the dactyl.

"What is your name?"

"Quintall."

The man groaned as the whip struck him again, tearing a red line across his back.

"Your name?"

"Quintall!"

The whip cracked.

"You are not Quintall!" De'Unnero screamed in his face. "What is your name?"

"Quin—" He hadn't even gotten the word out before the whip, handled expertly by the tenth-year immaculate, ripped all sounds from his body.

Up on the balcony, unseen by the victim and his pair of torturers, Master Jojonah sighed and shook his head. This man was tough, admirably so, and Jojonah feared he would die from the beatings before he would relinquish his identity.

"Fear not," came a voice behind him, that of Father Abbot Markwart, "The treatises do not lie. The technique is proven."

Jojonah didn't really doubt that—he just wondered why in the name of God such a technique had ever been developed!

"Desperation breeds dark work," the Father Abbot remarked, coming to Jojonah's side just as the whip cracked again. "I find this as distasteful as do you, but what are we do to? Master Siherton's body confirms our fears. We know the tricks Avelyn used to escape, and his cache of magic stones is considerable. Are we to allow him to run free to the detriment, perhaps even the downfall, of our Order?"

"Of course not, Father Abbot," Master Jojonah replied.

"No living monk in St.-Mere-Abelle knows Avelyn Desbris better than Quintall," Father Abbot Markwart continued. "He is the perfect choice."

As executioner, Jojonah thought.

"As the retriever of what is rightfully ours," the Father Abbot said, reading Jojonah's thoughts so clearly that the master turned to regard him closely, Jojonah honestly wondering if Markwart was using some magic to peek into his mind.

"Quintall will serve as an extension of the church, an instrument of our justice," Father Abbot Markwart said grimly, more determination in his normally quivering old voice than Jojonah had ever heard before. The master understood the man's desperation, despite the fact that Avelyn's crimes and subsequent desertion were not without precedent. Nor did the stolen stones present any real danger to the Abellican Order; Jojonah knew that twice the number Avelyn had taken were sold at fairly regular auctions, that the powers of those stones possessed by merchants and noblemen far outweighed the cache Avelyn held. The only concern any in St.-Mere-Abelle's hierarchy held about the stolen stones was for the giant amethyst crystal, and that only because it was a stone whose magic they had not yet deciphered. So foolish Avelyn wasn't really any serious threat to the abbey or to the Order. But that wasn't the point, wasn't the source of the Father Abbot's desperation. Markwart would be dead soon, taken by that greatest enemy: time. And he did not desire to leave behind any legacy of failure—including the existence of the renegade Avelyn.

"We will put him on Avelyn's trail very soon," the Father Abbot remarked.

"Unless he continues to resist," Master Jojonah dared to say.

Markwart issued a coughing laugh. "The techniques are proven: the lack of sleep, of food, the rewards and punishments exerted by the eager young masters. Quintall's concepts of right and wrong, of duty and punishment, have been systematically replaced by the tenets given him at times of reward. He is a creature of singular purpose. Pity him, but pity Avelyn Desbris even more." With that, Markwart walked away.

Jojonah watched him go, shuddering at the sheer coldness of the man's aura. His attention was caught by yet another crack of the whip.

"What is your name?" De'Unnero demanded.

"Quin . . ."

The man hesitated; even from the balcony, Master Jojonah sensed they were near a breakthrough.

De'Unnero started to prompt the tortured man again, but he stopped, and Jojonah recognized that the young master had seen a change in Quintall's demeanor, a strange light in the man's eyes, perhaps. Jojonah leaned over the rail, listening to every inflection, every whisper.

"Brother Justice," the battered man replied.

Master Jojonah settled back on his heels. He still wasn't wholly convinced that he agreed with the technique—or the purpose—of Quintall's training, but he had to admit that it seemed effective.

❖ 26 ❖

Bradwarden

"Is it fear that inspires them? Is it jealousy? Or is it something more sublime, some inner voice telling them that they and I are not of similar ilk? They do not know, of course, of my days with the Touel'alfar, but certainly it is evident to them, as it is to me, that they and I do not share the same perspective."

Elbryan slumped back in the chair, musing over his own words. He put the tips of his fingers together and shifted his hands in front of his face, allowing his gaze to drift from the mirror.

When he looked back, the specter of Uncle Mather remained, passively and patiently standing in the mirror's depths.

"Belli'mar Juraviel warned me that it would be like this," Elbryan went on. "And, in truth, it seems perfectly logical. The folk of the Wilderlands frontier necessarily huddle together. Their fear isolates them, and they often cannot distinguish friend from foe.

"So it is concerning me whenever I venture into the Howling Sheila. They do not understand me—my ways and my knowledge, and most of all, my duty—and thus they fear me. Yes, Uncle Mather, it must be fear, for what have I that the folk of Dundalis should envy? By their measures, I am poorer by far."

The young man chuckled and ran his hand through his light brown hair. "Their measures," he muttered again, and he couldn't help but feel sorry for the folk of Dundalis, of Weedy Meadow and End-o'-the-World, huddled ever in their cabins. It was true enough that they enjoyed some amenities Elbryan did not: soft bedding, solid water basins, stored food. But the ranger had two things far more valuable, by his way of thinking, two things that he would not trade for all the treasures of all the kingdoms of Corona.

"Freedom and duty, Uncle Mather," he said firmly. "I draw no lines of property, because those lines serve as barriers both ways. And, in the end, it is a sense of accomplishment, of purpose, and not the wealth attained by such accomplishment, that equates to fulfillment and happiness.

"And so I walk my watch. And so I accept the barbs and open chiding. I take faith in what I am doing, in my sense of purpose, for I, above all others, understand the consequence of failure."

But I am alone, the young man thought privately, not yet ready to admit the truth aloud. He sat back again for a long moment, then braced his hands on the arms of his chair, preparing to leave.

He felt a soft and subtle vibration. Music?

He knew it was music, though it seemed too soft, too much in the background for him to actually hear it. Rather, Elbryan felt it in his bones, a gentle, delicate sound, sweet as an elvish harp, melodic as Lady Dasslerond's voice.

He looked at the mirror, at the distant image, and sensed a calm there.

Elbryan went outside his cave immediately, expecting the music to be louder. It wasn't; it hovered on the edge of his perceptions, whatever way he turned. But it was there. Something was there.

And Uncle Mather wanted him to find it.

He had planned to go to Weedy Meadow that day, then move on with the setting sun to the west, a circuit of End-o'-the-World. Now he could not go, for this subtle music, though Elbryan sensed it was not threatening, was surely intriguing. Had the elves come to visit? Then another thought nagged at the young man, a notion that he had heard this song before, though he could not place it.

The ranger spent the better part of the morning searching out the direction of the quiet notes. He used all his training, all his tools, focusing his senses one at a time in each direction, on every plant and every animal, seeking some hint of the source. Finally, he came upon a set of tracks.

A single large horse, he decided, unshod and walking at an easy pace. There were indeed wild horses in the area, some perhaps that had escaped the tragedy at Dundalis, others that had run off from caravans, and still others whose roots in the region were older than those of the human settlers. They were not numerous, and surely skittish, though Elbryan had entertained the notion of breaking one.

He soon came to believe that this would not be his chance, though, for as he followed the clear trail, he came to the conclusion that he was following, too, the source of the music. Thus, Elbryan believed, the horse was obviously ridden.

That thought didn't slow the ranger; it only intrigued him even more. Someone had come into his domain, someone not of the villages, for if it was one of the villagers, then this horse would likely have been shod.

Elbryan skipped down one tree-covered hillside, into a narrow vale and to the edge of a rushing river. He crossed with some difficulty, but had no trouble regaining the trail on the other side, for the rider was making no effort to conceal his tracks. Elbryan closed steadily. Soon he could make out the actual notes—of a wind instrument, he noted, and he searched his memory once again, for he was certain that he had heard that peculiar, haunting sound before. He remembered, then, the instrument, piped by a merchant on the occasion of Elbryan's tenth birthday, a curious thing, a leather bag and a series of pipes—a bagpipe, it was appropriately named.

The ranger moved swiftly and silently over a series of rolling hills. Then he stopped, suddenly, as the music stopped. Elbryan peered out around a tree. There, standing higher on the hill amidst a tangled grove of birch and low brush, stood a tall man, much taller than Elbryan, even considering the ranger's deceivingly low perspective. He had black, bushy hair and a tight beard. He was naked, at least from the belly up, with a powerful upper body, muscles clearly defined, and an arched back. He held the pipes under one arm, down low, his song finished.

"Well, ranger, are ye liking the way I fill me chanter and drones?" he asked, a wide, white smile across his face.

Elbryan crouched lower, though he was obviously seen. He could hardly believe that this man had noted his approach or that this man knew his title!

"And it took ye long enough to find me," the man bellowed. "Not that ye would have had I not piped for yer tracking!"

"And who are you?" the ranger called.

"Bradwarden the Piper," the man answered proudly. "Bradwarden the Woodsman. Bradwarden the Pine Father. Bradwarden the Horse Tender. Bradwarden the . . ."

He stopped as Elbryan came out from behind the tree, the ranger rightly sensing that this introduction could go on for some time. "I am called Nightbird," he said, though he figured that this man somehow already knew that.

The tall man nodded, smiling still. "Elbryan Wyndon," he added, and Elbryan nodded, then stared dumfoundedly when he considered the implications of that long-lost name. To everyone in Dundalis with the exception of Belster O'Comely, Elbryan was known only by the name the elves had given to him.

"Might be that the animals told me," Bradwarden remarked. "I'm smarter than I look, not to doubt, and older than ye'd guess. Might be the animals, might be the plants." Bradwarden stopped and offered an exaggerated wink that Elbryan, still a fair distance down the hill, saw clearly. "Might be yer uncle."

The ranger rocked back on his heels, unable to find even the words to ask the obvious questions. He was wary, though not afraid, and he continued up the hill, testing every step before he shifted his weight, as if he expected the place to be trapped.

"Ye should've killed the three," the piper went on.

Elbryan shrugged, not understanding.

"Paulson and his cronies," the tall man went on. "Nothing but trouble. I'd been thinking o' killing them meself, when I seen an animal chewing off its leg in one o' their wicked catchers."

Elbryan started to respond that he had eliminated the cruel traps, but the words were stuck in his throat. As he came around the low brush, he noted the hind quarters of a horse, noted that the man was mounted. As he came around another step, he saw that that was not the case, that the man, and no mount, had been the source of the tracks.

For Elbryan, Nightbird, who had battled fomorian giants and goblins, who had lived with the elves, the sight of a centaur was not completely unsettling. It brought many questions, though, too many for poor Elbryan to begin to sort out. And it brought, too, a memory of a piping song while he and Pony had stood quiet on the slope outside of Dundalis, and he recalled, too, the stories of the Forest Ghost, half man and half horse, that he had enjoyed as a child.

"They be nothing but trouble," Bradwarden remarked distastefully. "And I'll kill them if one more scream of me animal friends reaches me ears!"

Elbryan didn't doubt the claim for a minute. There was something too matter-of-fact about the centaur's tone, something dispassionate, removed from humanity. A shudder coursed the ranger's spine as he imagined what this powerful beast, easily eight hundred pounds and cunning enough to completely avoid the ranger for all these weeks, might do to Paulson, Cric, and Chipmunk.

"Well, Elbryan the Nightbird, have ye an instrument to join with me pipes?"

"How do you know of me?" the ranger demanded.

"Now if we're both for asking questions, then we're neither to be getting any answers," Bradwarden scolded.

"Then you answer mine," the ranger demanded.

"But I already did," Bradwarden insisted. "Might be—"

"Might be that you are avoiding an answer," Elbryan interrupted.

"Ah, me little human laddie," Bradwarden said with that disarming smile, though it surely seemed condescending coming from so far on high, "ye'd not be wanting me to give up me secrets, now would ye? What fun would ye have then?"

Elbryan relaxed and let down his guard. One of his friends had told Bradwarden of him, he figured, one of the elves, most likely Juraviel. Either that, Elbryan decided, or the centaur had eavesdropped when the young man was at Oracle, for Bradwarden knew of Uncle Mather, and of the "little cave." In any case, Elbryan felt in his heart that this was no enemy standing before him, and he thought it more than mere coincidence that this very day, for the first time since he had come to the region, he had hinted openly of his feelings of loneliness.

"I trampled me a deer this morning," the centaur said suddenly. "Come along for a meal then; I'll even let ye cook yer part!" With that, the centaur took up his pipes and started a rousing military march, thundering away on powerful legs. Elbryan ran full out, constantly seeking out shortcuts in the thick underbrush, just to keep pace.

They were not alike, very different in so many ways. True to his words, Bradwarden allowed Elbryan to start a fire and cook his venison, while the centaur ate his portion, nearly a quarter of the deer, raw.

"I do hate killing the damn things," the centaur said, ending his sentence with a resounding belch. "So cute they be, and appealing to one of me body in more ways than ye'd know. But fruits and berries are naught but ticklings. I'm needing meat to fill me belly." He rubbed a hand across his stomach, at the point where his human torso connected with the equine bottom half. "And I've considerable belly to fill!"

Elbryan shook his head and smiled—all the wider when Bradwarden belched again, a great, thunderous burp.

"You have been in the region all the while?" Elbryan asked. "And I never spotted you nor found any sign."

"Don't ye be too hard on yerself," the centaur replied. "I been in the region longer than yer father's father was alive. And what might ye spot? A hoofprint or me droppings? Ye'd think them both that of a horse, though if ye inspected the droppings a bit more, ye'd find that me diet's not quite the same as me horsie friends."

"And why would I look closer?" Elbryan asked, a sour expression on his face.

"Dirty business, that," Bradwarden agreed.

The ranger nodded, forgiving himself for missing the signs.

"Besides," Bradwarden went on, "I knew ye were coming, and ye didn't know I was here. Unfair advantage, I'd call it, so don't ye go chastising yerself."

"How did ye—you know?"

"A little birdie told me," the centaur replied. "Sweet little thing that says her name twice in a row."

Elbryan's face crinkled at the cryptic statement, but he just shook his head, thinking that it really wasn't that important. Even as he started to ask a question in a completely different direction, he remembered a certain friend who fit the description. "Tuntun," he stated more than asked.

"Aye, that's the one." Bradwarden laughed. "She warned me not to expect too much from ye."

"Indeed," the ranger said dryly.

"So I told her that I'd be watching over ye," the centaur went on. "Though I've come to know that ye don't need much watching."

"Then you are elf-friend," Elbryan said, hoping to find some common ground.

"Elf-acquaintance, I'd be calling it," the centaur replied. "They're a good sort for the wine, and they respect the animals and the trees, but they're too much for giggling and too long on manners!" To accentuate his point, he let fly the loudest belch Elbryan had ever heard. "Never heared an elf's belly-thunder!"

Bradwarden laughed riotously, then hoisted a huge skin and poured an amber-colored liquid—Elbryan recognized it as boggle—into his mouth, a considerable amount splashing over his bearded face.

"Ye should've killed them," the centaur said suddenly, spraying more than a little wine with each word.

Elbryan, thinking Bradwarden to be referring to the elves, crinkled his brow incredulously.

"The three men, I mean," the centaur clarified. "Paulson, Cric, and . . . what's the third, then? Weasel?"

"Chipmunk."

The centaur snorted. "Idiot," he muttered. "Ye should've killed them, all three. No respect, I say, and nothing but trouble."

"Then why has Bradwarden tolerated them?" Elbryan asked. "They have been in the area for some time, I would guess, considering their lodgings, and obviously you knew of them."

The centaur nodded at the simple logic. "I been thinking of it," he admitted. "But they didn't give me an excuse. And," he paused and offered a sly wink, "don't ye fear, for I'm not overly fond o' human flesh."

"You have tasted it then?" Elbryan reasoned, not taking the bait.

Bradwarden belched again, and then he launched into a long speech about the ills of humankind. Elbryan merely smiled and let the centaur ramble on and on, considering the creature's words carefully so that he could discover many hints about Bradwarden. Elbryan suspected, and would come to confirm over the next few weeks, that he and the centaur were not so different in purpose.

He was a ranger, a guardian of the frontier humans and also of the forest and its creatures. Bradwarden's mission, it seemed, was not so different, except that the centaur was more concerned with the animals, particularly the wild horses; he even hinted that he had given many of the wild horses their freedom, since their human masters treated them badly. He hardly cared for the humans. He had seen the raid on Dundalis years before, he confirmed for Elbryan, though the worst he would admit of the tragedy was that it was "a pity."

Theirs became a tentative friendship, an offered smile and exchange of news whenever the pair happened to be in the same area. For Elbryan, knowing Bradwarden was a wonderful thing indeed. He found that when he next ventured to Oracle, his previous feelings of loneliness did not follow him into the cave.

❖ 27 ❖

The Fat Prophet's Warning

News that she would soon be transferred to Pireth Vanguard, far to the north, did little to change Jill's sullen mood. By all reports, the weather was better on the northern side of the Gulf of Corona, more alive, with brisk winds and a greater change of the season. In Pireth Tulme, even the winter was one long gray sheet of clouds and cold rain, differing from the summer only in terms of temperature.

But Jill had settled into a routine here, akin to the continually gloomy season. Each day seemed as the last, an existence of perpetual watch and work. Seconds, minutes, and hours seemed to drag on endlessly, and yet, at the same time, once the weeks had passed, it seemed as if they had flown away.

The incident at the Waylaid Traveler had brought some measure of excitement, some break in the routine. Jill had taken the image of the mad friar back with her, could hear his words still, and found in them a kinship to that which lay in her own heart. There was no sense of duty or honor in Pireth Tulme, none in the Kingsmen or the Coastpoint Guards, none in all of Honce-the-Bear, she feared, or in all of wide Corona. And now this man, for speaking the truth with a level of enthusiasm that exceeded even the orgies in Pireth Tulme, this man, who would not be surprised by the tragedy that had touched young Jill's life, who would have expected it and called for preparation against it, this man, this holy prophet, was tagged "mad."

Jill sighed deeply every time she considered the man who had called himself the hound of ill omen. His words rang so true in her ears, echoing in the quiet lulls between the groans and shrieks that endlessly emanated from the rooms behind her. The mad friar foresaw disaster; Jill only wished that he had sung out his tune in a small frontier village several years ago.

Would the people of that village have heeded his warnings? Probably no more so than the soldiers of Pireth Tulme, their party resuming from the moment they returned from Tinson.

But despite her feelings, Jill kept her vigilant watch, day after day, often long into the night. And she kept her honor and virtue, refusing to give in to the temptations of the celebration, refusing to surrender to the hopelessness—and that precisely was the way Jill viewed the hedonism around her. The soldiers of Pireth Tulme engaged in the revelry, the pleasures of the flesh, to avoid noticing their empty souls. They had sacrificed their hearts, so to speak, for their loins.

So be it. Jill stoically suffered the barbs of her comrades, particularly from Warder Miklos Barmine, who seemed to covet her all the more since she would not give in.

Perhaps Pireth Vanguard would be better, she sometimes dared to hope; but inevitably, her wishes fell back on the dark reality that was life in Honce-the-Bear in God's Year 824.

It was a gray morning—no surprise there—with Jill on the wall, seated between crenelations, her legs dangling over the two-hundred-foot drop, her gaze on the dreamy mist that hung over Horseshoe Bay. Pireth Tulme was especially quiet after a night of tremendous drinking, a night which Jill had spent on the tower roof, quietly tucked under the beam of the fortress' lone catapult, her blanket tight about her.

She kept her senses tuned totally to the present, thinking of nothing but the rocky pillars standing like quiet sentinels in the foggy bay, the continual lap of the ebb tide waves against the rocks so far below, the occasional bleat of a sheep in the sloping field on the other side of the fortress.

And of the square sail that was drifting her way through the gray mist.

She scrambled to her feet and leaned out over the battlement, peering hard out to sea. It was indeed a sail, moving toward Pireth Tulme and neither in nor out of the Gulf of Corona. Jill's first instinct was to find some way to warn the obviously wayward craft. The fortress did have a signal barrel, a cask of volatile ingredients—though it hadn't been used in so many years that Jill feared it wouldn't even burn brightly—that was designed for signaling the larger fortress of Kingsmen some dozen miles inland, close beside the catapult. Jill realized that she wouldn't likely rouse enough help to get the barrel up in the air in time, and so she began waving her arms and calling out loudly, warning the ship's crew of the rocks and the impending disaster.

How Jill's mouth dropped open in shock when the vessel responded with the swish of its own catapult, a huge rock smashing against the cliff face some thirty feet or so below her!

It was exactly the situation for which the young soldier had trained all these years, just as Jill had imagined it might happen. And yet, for some reason, it seemed all too unreal for Jill. She stood there another long moment, perfectly stunned.

She noted then that the vessel was not alone, but was moving in accord with other craft, low to the water. One—at least one—had already gone by Pireth Tulme, making for the beach of Horseshoe Bay, and two flanked the sailing ship on the right, a third on its left.

A second ball soared in, this one soaring high over the fortress wall, and over the back wall as well, bouncing down the green field.

Jill cried out at the top of her lungs, then again a moment later, the ships moving ever closer, when she heard no response. She could see the activity on the deck of the sailing ship now, small forms darting this way and that, tacking hard to put the large caravel in between the bay's many sentry stones. She noted their red berets.

"Powries," she muttered under her breath. She had no time to wonder where they could have stolen or captured the ship; she cried out again, then turned to view the tower door.

There should have been a second sentry there, the relaying voice to the soldiers within. Jill shook her head, her short shock of blond hair bouncing about. Frustration boiled in the young woman, mingling with desperation. Another shot came thundering in, this one scoring a hit on Pireth Tulme's front wall, taking down some stones.

Jill ran along the wall, angling for the door. She noted the bay as she went, saw that the low craft was nearing the beach and that another was already there, its hatch open and dozens of red-capped dwarves pouring onto the shell-strewn sand!

Yet another shot came in as Jill grabbed the heavy door's latch and pulled it wide, this missile not of stone, nor pitch, but a jumble of dozens of wide-flying grapnels.

"Oh, damn," she sputtered, seeing many of the hooks gaining a firm hold on the walls. She screamed into the tower then, calling for all hands to the walls, warning of powries in the bay.

Then she ran, drawing her sword, cursing at every step. They had been caught unaware; she noted no allies had yet exited the tower even as she got back to the front wall. Likely, half the soldiers either didn't believe that call or were simply too drunk to heed it, and the other half probably couldn't even find their damned weapons!

The ropes were tight from the ship to the wall, with lines of dwarves on each, moving steadily with surprising strength, hanging under, hands and ankles locked about the cord. Jill first tried to dislodge the grapnel, but found that it was too tightly secured, with too much weight on the heavy line. Then she went at the line ferociously, hacking and chopping, chipping her sword from one ill-aimed blow, the blade ringing off the stone wall. The ropes were thick and strong, and Jill knew then that she could not cut them all down, could not cut more than one or two down before the evil powries began gaining the wall.

"Hurry!" she cried, glancing back to the open tower door.

Finally, Miklos Barmine wandered out, rubbing his eyes, blinking repeatedly as if the light, though the day was dim, stung him profoundly. He started to call out to Jill, to ask her what all the shouting was about, but he stopped, as he noted the woman at work on the heavy rope.

Another man came up behind the warder. "To the walls! To the walls!" Barmine cried desperately, and the man disappeared again into the blackness of the tower, crying out for his comrades.

A final hack from Jill sent the rope flying free, half a dozen powries splashing down hard into the cold waters. Jill ran to the next line but moved right past it, seeing that a dwarf was nearly to the wall some distance down. She got to the spot first, slashing the powrie hard as it tried to scramble to the stone. The creature grabbed on stubbornly, but Jill hit it again, right across the face, and it fell away, shrieking, to its doom.

Jill went to work on the rope. Soldiers were coming from the tower by this point, but powries were coming over the front wall. Jill wasn't halfway through the heavy cord when she had to stop and run to fight another of the dwarves as it pulled itself onto the parapet. The creature drew a small sword but too late to parry the woman's first savage attack, Jill's sword slashing across the dwarf's eyes, blinding it. The dwarf countered viciously, but Jill had already stepped beside it, then behind it, and when the powrie finished its wild swinging, coming back to full defensive posture, Jill locked one arm over its shoulder, her other under its crotch, and lifted and twisted, sending it plummeting from the wall. She didn't even have time to slice once at that particular rope, though, for another dwarf was already running her way, hooting and howling, whipping a cudgel about in the air before it.

Charging soldiers met the red-capped dwarves all along the wall, battling fiercely. Jill saw a pair of dwarves go flying over, saw a man slump to his knees, hands clutching a mortal chest wound.

Then she was fighting again, hopping back from the swing of that nasty cudgel—she saw more than a few spikes protruding from its wide end. On she came with a snarl, stabbing straight ahead with her sword, then, when that attack was neatly deflected, kicking her foot out beneath the sweep of the cudgel, connecting solidly with the dwarf's belly.

The powrie didn't even flinch, came right back to the offensive with one, two, and then a third swiping attack.

Jill was backing steadily, but realized that she would soon run out of room, for she sensed that another powrie was fast coming in at her back. She started ahead a step, then turned about abruptly, dropping to one knee and lunging ahead, her free hand catching the second dwarf's swinging sword arm, her own sword driving deep into its chest.

Jill came up in a short run, bowling the wounded powrie away, then she pivoted again and came in hard, moving too close for the cudgel to score a solid hit and accepting the weakened blow in exchange for her own attack, a stab into the dwarf's throat.

Breathing hard, the woman surveyed the scene.

They could not win. The Coastpoint Guards of Pireth Tulme were fighting well, but they were badly outnumbered and they had lost their one advantage: the walls. If they had been prepared, if they had been alert, then most of the powrie lines would have been cut before the dwarves ever gained the wall. If the soldiers had drilled for such an attack, then their defenses would have been coordinated, then the signal barrel would already be in the air, spinning high and far for reinforcements. Jill did see that a detachment of six soldiers was at the catapult, three working the levers, three desperately trying to hold a handful of powries at bay. She should get to them, she realized, but she understood, too, that there was no chance of that. Fighting was general all along the wall, more and more powries pouring in, and another group, those from the two barrelboats that had gone into Horseshoe Bay, screaming wildly and charging up the sloping field behind the fortress.

Pireth Tulme was lost.

Jill saw Warder Miklos Barmine shouting commands from the wall near the tower, powries swarming all about him. He took a vicious hit, then another, but responded with a slash of his own, knocking one powrie from the wall. One of Jill's female comrades came to the tower door then, but she was swept away by a host of bloody caps as they charged in.

Barmine continued to scream, though his words soon became but grunts and howls of agony. He was bloodied in a dozen place and took hit after hit, though he stubbornly continued to swing that sword.

Then Jill lost sight of him, finding herself facing another dwarf. This one came in hard and, thinking that it had the woman by surprise, launched a wild sidelong swing. Jill dodged easily, then kicked out behind the flying weapon, just nicking the powrie on the back but solidly enough so the overbalanced dwarf fell from the parapet eight feet to the ground below.

Another was quick to take its place, snapping off a series of thrusts with its short sword. Jill managed to glance back toward the tower, saw the host of powries flooding in, saw Barmine kneeling, his face, his arms, all his body covered in blood.

Spurred by the gruesome sight, she attacked fiercely. Up went her sword, cutting across left to right, then back again, then another strong backhand, each swing sounding with the ring of metal on metal. She shifted her right foot forward with the last stroke, then turned her blade and came straight ahead, driving the powrie back. But another dwarf was behind it to bolster the defense, and another behind that. Jill heard the dying scream of a soldier to her rear and fully expected that she would soon be overwhelmed.

She started forward, then leaped atop the wall, hopping from high point to high point, once over the surprised powrie's stabbing sword. She outdistanced all three with a few long strides, moving to the far corner of the front wall.

There was yet another rope secured at that point, the last dwarf on it barely five feet from the wall.

Jill glanced back at the carnage. Many powries were down, but more remained, and each of the still-standing soldiers was surrounded, battling desperately. Barmine was kneeling but offering no resistance, a powrie wiping its beret across his face.

Jill winced as the dwarf lifted its cap up high and in the same motion, slammed its spiked cudgel into the dying warder's face.

She had seen enough.

She could have taken out the dwarf on the rope, but doing so would have allowed the three pursuing her to catch her. Jill sheathed her sword instead, pulled her belt off, and leaped out from the wall, beyond the climbing dwarf. She caught the rope with one hand, barely, and hung on with all her strength, two hundred feet of empty air below her.

The powrie immediately reversed direction, deftly turning about on the rope with sure, strong grips. Its three companions, with typical powrie loyalty, went to work at once on the grapnel and rope, caring not at all if they dropped a comrade along with the dangerous woman.

Jill had no time for a fight. She kicked out to the side, trying to keep the dwarf at bay, but her main focus was on getting her belt, held fast in her other hand, up over the rope. She looped it up on one try, but lost her grip on the rope and started to tumble.

Her free hand somehow caught hold of the other end of the belt. She was holding both ends now, hanging lower, and then she was sliding away from her enemy, sliding fast into the mist, toward the ship, which was holding steady more than a hundred feet from shore.

The other end of the rope was fixed to the yard of the mainmast. There were many powries on that deck, though none had, as yet, spotted her. She figured she'd let go as she came over the prow, in the hope that she would land on deck clear enough for her to roll a few times to absorb the impact. If she could get across the deck to the stern catapult or more particularly, to the cauldrons of pitch and the firepit near the catapult, then she might be able to cause more than a little havoc.

Her plan was moot, as it turned out, for as Jill approached the front of the craft, the rope gave way, and suddenly her descent was much sharper than her forward momentum. She let out a scream, thinking that she would slam headlong into the ship's prow.

Luck was with her and she hit the cold sea short of the ship. She came up sputtering, her mouth full of water, her ears still filled with the sound of dying men ringing down from the fortress walls. Anger welled within her, directed at both the powries and her own comrades. Had they been prepared, this disaster would not have befallen them. Had they heeded their own code of conduct, the powries would have been repulsed.

She had lost her sword in the fall, but Jill didn't care. Feral growls escaped her lips as she started to swim around the vessel, moving all the faster for fear that her limbs would soon be too numb to propell her. She got around to the stern and found the anchor line, a heavy rope down from the port side. Her arms aching from cold and weariness, she grabbed hold and pulled herself up the ten feet to the rail. She peeked over even as the catapult fired again, a ball of flaming pitch soaring up over Pireth Tulme's wall. Jill noted that the missile was far more likely to burn a host of powries than any human, but the dwarves hardly seemed to care, howling with glee as they loaded the next ball.

Three of them had the ball, cradled in a heavy blanket, up above their heads near the basket when Jill hit them with a flying body block. They fell away toward the taffrail, but could not let go of their load. Over the rail the pitch ball went, taking the three powries with it.

A fourth was on Jill in a moment, grabbing for her throat. She couldn't believe the weight of the diminutive thing! Nor the strength! In an instant, the powrie had her on her back and was choking her hard.

She tried desperately to break its grip, locked her fingers about its thumbs and turned them outward.

She might as well have been pulling against iron shackles.

Jill changed tactics and began slugging the dwarf in the face instead, then poking for its eyes. It held on tight and even tried to bite her fingers.

Soon Jill's hands were flapping inconsequentially at the powrie's barrel-like torso, her strength fast deserting her. She would die as Pireth Tulme died, she realized, again silently cursing the unpreparedness, the slovenly men and women to whom she had been forced to entrust her life. She would die, not of any fault of her own, but because the Coastpoint Guards had grown weak.

Her hands flailed wildly; darkness crept into the edges of her vision. One hand banged against the powrie's solid waist, against a metal ball above the dwarf's belt.

The hilt of a dagger.

Jill had struck the dwarf four times before it realized that it was being stabbed. With a howl, it finally let go, scrambling about to evade the jabbing dagger.

Jill wounded it again, between its flailing arms and right in its chest, and then again, higher, in its throat. The dwarf rolled away, but Jill could hardly move to follow. She lay there for what seemed like minutes, then finally found the strength to come up to her elbows.

The powrie was near the rail, facedown.

Jill took in another blessed gulp of air and staggered to her feet. She turned to the catapult, its arm low and ready to fire, then looked at the vats of burning pitch, wondering what mischief she might cause.

The powrie slammed her hard from behind, driving her into the bent beam. Jill came about, dagger slashing, cutting a line across the dwarf's face, just inches above the garish cut she had put in its throat. The dwarf fell back a couple of steps, but came on again.

Jill dropped to her knees and lowered her shoulder, accepting the impact. She curled her legs under her and lifted the dwarf high, stepping fast and shoving with all her strength, putting the creature into the catapult basket. Jill rolled away immediately, falling to the side, grabbing at the release pin and pulling hard.

The powrie was almost out of the basket when the catapult fired, launching the dwarf in a wild, spinning flight straight up, arms and legs out wide.

Many other dwarves heard the scream, took note of the curious missile, and turned to the stern deck; Jill was out of time. She kicked over the pitch barrels, spilling one onto the capstan that held the anchor line and knocking another down the stairs to the lower main deck. Then she turned to the taffrail, thinking her only escape to be the cold water.

Again sheer luck saved her, for she found a boat hanging from the stern. She had it falling free in an instant, then, with powries scrambling up to the stern deck, with fires growing all about her on the capstan and on the catapult, she leaped out as far as she could, taking care to avoid the burning pitch that was floating in the water and the three dwarves, bobbing low, barely keeping their heads above the waves. They made for the boat as did Jill, the woman overtaking one and easily dispatching it with her borrowed dagger.

Powries weren't so tough in the water, she noted as she closed on the second. She swam right by that one, realizing if she delayed, the third would get to the boat before her. She caught that last floundering dwarf, stabbing it hard on the shoulder, then swimming right by it, grabbed desperately for the small craft.

A crossbow quarrel skimmed the water right beside her head.

Jill worked to get behind the boat, to use it as a barrier against the powrie archers on the deck. She knew that the angle was all wrong, though, that they were too high above her, the boat too close, and that they would get fairly clear shots no matter where she moved.

And she knew from the profound numbness that was creeping into her limbs that she had to get out of the water, and quickly.

The groan of wood alerted her to the powries' newest problem. She dared to peer over the small boat's rail, and saw that the ship's anchor line had burned through, and the ship, caught on a swell, had swung hard

about. Suddenly, the archers had more on their minds than the woman in
the water.

Jill started to climb into the boat, but had to stop and turn to strike again
at the struggling powrie. Finally she was in the boat, setting the oars, then
pulling away with all her strength, the third powrie frantically trying to
catch up.

It got near enough for Jill to slam it on the head with one of the oars.

❖ 28 ❖

Siblings

S he dragged herself onto the beach, battered, cold, and angry. She looked back at the small boat, even then being dashed against the rocks, tossed about by the powerful surf. She had drifted all through the rest of that fateful day, all through the night and the better part of the next morning as well. She had meant to go right from the battle to the nearest spot she could find to land the boat, to then run off and find some help, and lead the charge back to Pireth Tulme. The powrie ship was barely out of sight when her wounds overtook her, pains and aches she didn't even realize she had suffered. The heat of battle had left her body and unconsciousness had descended over her like some great hunting bird, wings out wide to block the light of day.

She had awakened that night, drifting somewhere in the gulf, praying that the currents had not pushed her out into the open Mirianic. Luck was with her, though, for the coastline remained in sight, towering black mountains marking the southern horizon. It had taken Jill hours to manage to row the craft near shore and then to find some place where she could put in. She had settled for a narrow inlet, but as soon as she entered, she found that many sharp rocks were in the water, lurking right below the surface. Jill worked the small boat hard, but understood the futility. So she shed her red Coastpoint jacket and her heavy boots and went over the side, fighting the undertow every inch of the way through the icy water.

The rocks took her boat.

She didn't recognize any landmarks but figured she must be somewhere west of Pireth Tulme on the north coast of the Mantis Arm. Her suspicions were confirmed when she moved inland, found a road, and then, an hour of walking later, a signpost pointing the way, three miles hence, to Macomber.

Jill found herself circumventing the town and approaching it from the west, not from the east the way any stragglers fleeing Pireth Tulme would. She tried to straighten her still-damp clothes, but realized that she would be conspicuous indeed to any, walking as she was without boots, and without the dirtied, calloused feet of a peasant woman. And though she was not wearing the telltale red jacket, a woman dressed in a simple white shirt, tan pants, and bare feet was not a common sight. Jill wished that she had a cloak, at least, to gather closely about her.

She got more than a few curious looks from the townsfolk as she passed the fairly sizable settlement of more than three score buildings, some two stories high. Some folk pointed, all whispered, more than a few turned their shoulders and scurried away, and it seemed to the young woman that they were on edge. Perhaps word of the disaster had preceded her.

These suspicions were bolstered by the snatches of conversation Jill caught, words of a contingent of Kingsmen riding hard to the east. She nodded to herself; she should go out and join the force, should go to Pireth Tulme to avenge—

The thought hit Jill like a cold slap. To avenge what? Her comrades? The letch Miklos Barmine? Gofflaw, whom she'd imagined killing several times herself?

She found a tavern, its sign too worn for her even to make out the name, though the image of a foaming mug was clear enough. Before she entered, a familiar voice, raised in dire warning, assaulted her.

"What demons do we invite into our midst?" the man inside cried, and Jill knew before she saw him that he was surely standing atop a table, one finger pointed high into the air.

She went in expecting a brewing row, but found instead that the mad friar, this time, had a fairly attentive audience.

And a large one; there had to be forty people inside, filling the tavern from wall to wall. Jill sifted through the crowd to get to the bar, started to order a mug of ale, but then realized she had no money. She turned instead, put her elbows on the bar, and watched the monk and, more particularly, the reactions of his audience.

She heard whispers of a fight, of goblins, some said, though others more accurately named the enemy powries. Estimates of the enemy force ranged from a thousand warriors to a thousand ships full of warriors.

Jill wanted to tell them that it was but one captured sailing vessel and no more than five barrelboats, but she kept quiet, fearing to reveal too much of herself and also thinking it would do these folk good to be afraid.

The mad friar apparently shared her feelings, for his speech became more dire, more frantic, as if he envisioned an army of monsters marching down the road, right to the border of Macomber.

The fever reached a critical point, and then, all of a sudden, it broke. The barkeep came around the bar with a heavy club, moving pointedly for the fat monk. "Enough from you," he warned, waving his weapon. "Whatever happened is the business of the Kingsmen, and not for the folk of Macomber!"

"All the world must prepare!" the fat man retorted, throwing his arms out wide, inviting the people to join.

But it was too late; he had pushed past the fear and into the realm of anger, and when the barkeep called for assistance, the man found no shortage of volunteers.

The mad friar put up a terrific fight, tossing men about, howling about his "preparedness training!" In the end, though, predictably, the monk was sailing out the door to land unceremoniously in the street.

Jill was beside him at once, on one knee as he sorted himself out. He reached into a pocket of his robe and produced a small flask, popping the top and sucking a huge swig. He did well to stifle his belch and looked at Jill as if embarrassed.

"Potion of courage," he explained dryly. "Ho, ho, what!"

Jill regarded him sourly, then rose and offered an arm. "You are consistent," she chided.

The friar looked at her more closely. He knew he had seen her before, but he could not place her. "Have we met?" he asked finally.

"Once," Jill said, "in a place not so far away."

"I would not forget so pretty a face," the friar insisted.

Jill was too bedraggled to blush or even to care. "Perhaps if I were still wearing my red jacket," she said, though she could hardly believe she had just admitted her position to this man.

He paused for a long moment, then his face brightened in recognition— and then it darkened immediately as he realized the implications. "Y-your home," he stuttered, as if not knowing which direction to go. "Pireth Tulme."

"Never would I call Pireth Tulme my home," Jill retorted. The mad friar started to speak again, but she stopped him with an upraised hand. "I was there," she said grimly. "I saw."

"The rumors?"

"Powries," she confirmed. "Pireth Tulme is no more."

The friar held out his flask, but Jill refused. He nodded and put it back under the folds of his weathered robes, his expression more serious. "Come with me," he bade her. "I have an ear for what you might need to say."

Jill considered the offer for a long moment, then moved away with the man to a room he had rented in a small inn on the outskirts of Macomber. He expected her to speak of desertion, but of course, her tale, spoken simply and truthfully, was far different. She saw respect mounting in the man's brown eyes and knew that he was a friend, knew that he would not turn her in to the military authorities, that he held as little respect for them as did she.

When she finished, when she explained that she was glad again to hear his voice and could now appreciate his dire warnings, the friar smiled comfortingly and put his hand over hers.

"I am Brother Avelyn Desbris, formerly of St.-Mere-Abelle," he confided, and Jill understood she was probably the first person he had told his true name in a long, long time. "It would seem that we are both dispossessed."

"Disappointed would be a better word," Jill replied.

A dark cloud passed over Avelyn's face. He nodded. "Disappointed indeed," he said softly.

"I have told you my tale," Jill prompted.

It came out in a burst of emotion Avelyn had not known since that night he had cried for his dead mother. He told Jill much—more than he would have ever believed he could confide—holding back only the specifics of the Ring Stones, the secret island, the method and fatal result of his escape, and the fact that he carried with him a stolen cache of powerful magic. Those things did not seem paramount to Avelyn, anyway, not when weighed against the tragedy of the *Windrunner*, the loss of his dear Dansally Comerwick.

"She told you her name," Jill put in quietly, and Avelyn's brown eyes misted at the realization that this woman could understand the significance of that.

"But you have not," Avelyn said to her.

"Jill," she answered after a short hesitation.

"Jill?"

"Just Jill," she assured him.

"Well, Just Jill," Brother Avelyn said with a widening smile, "it would seem we are two lost lambs."

"Yes, mad brother Avelyn Desbris," she replied in the same singsong voice, "two lost lambs in a forest of wolves."

"Pity the wolves, then!" Avelyn cried, "Ho, ho, what!"

They shared laughter, a relief of tension both of them so desperately needed—Jill for her recent trials and Avelyn because he had spoken openly at last of his dark past, had relit the candles about those desperate images and feelings that had driven him out on the road.

"Piety, dignity, poverty," the monk said distastefully when he had caught his breath.

"The credo of the Abellican Church," Jill replied.

"The lie," Avelyn retorted. "I saw little piety beyond simple rituals, found little dignity in murder, and poverty is not a thing the masters of St.-Mere-Abelle tolerate." He gave a snort, but Jill knew she had him beaten on this point.

"Ever vigilant, ever watchful," she recited dryly, and Avelyn recognized her words as the motto of the Coastpoint Guards. "Tell that to the powries!"

They laughed again, all the louder, using the very sound of mirth as a shield against tears.

Jill spent the night in Avelyn's room; the monk, of course, acting the part of a perfect gentlemen. He considered the tale he had told her, his life's story, and then looked to regard himself, the extra hundred pounds, the battered appearance.

"Ah, Jill," he lamented. "You should have seen me in my idealistic youth. What a different man I was then, before I saw the terrible truth of the world."

His thoughts hung on those words for a long, long while, and then it struck him that if he were to truly call this woman his friend, he would have to search hard for a part of himself that he had thought long lost. To be a friend to Jill, to be a proper companion to anyone, would mean recovering some of that idealism, some of that belief that the world was not so dark and terrible and that, with effort, it might get even better.

"Yes," the monk whispered over the sleeping woman, "we'll find our way together."

The next morning, they purchased some supplies, including a short sword, boots, and a warm cloak for Jill, and then they walked out of Macomber together, down the road to the west, ignoring the stares and whispers, feeling somehow as if they shared a secret and a wisdom the rest of the world, fools all, could never comprehend.

That bond alone held Jill together with Brother Avelyn over the first weeks of their journey; they were siblings, Avelyn insisted, two alone against the encroaching darkness. Jill accepted a large part of that argument, but hardly considered herself brother to the mad friar. The man drank almost constantly, and whatever town they entered, Avelyn found some way to get into a fight, often brutal. So it was in the town of Dusberry along the Masur Delaval halfway between Amvoy and Ursal. Avelyn was in the tavern, as usual, standing atop a table, spouting warnings and curses. Jill came in just as the fight broke out, two dozen men swinging at the closest body, not bothering to ask if it was enemy or ally. In these general rows, as opposed to the occasions when all in the bar teamed up against the monk, Avelyn more than held his ground. The huge bear of a man tossed his attackers with ease, punched and twisted deftly, hollering "Ho, ho, what!" every time he felled another.

Jill came in hard and fast, simply to defend herself as she made her way to her comrade. She, too, could handle the drunken townsfolk without much effort, turning easily as one man lunged for her, walking right past his lumbering reach, then kicking back hard on his instep, sending him down to the floor.

"Must you always?" she asked when she at last reached Avelyn's side.

The monk replied with a wide grin. Then he quickly brushed Jill aside with his right hand, straightening the man who was charging in at her back with a stiff left jab, then knocking him flying with a heavy right cross.

"Ho, ho, what!" Avelyn boomed. "The town will be the better for it!"

He started away, but Jill kicked him hard in the rump. He turned to her, wounded emotionally at least, but she would not back down, pointing resolutely at the door.

It wasn't until they had exited the tavern, the fight raging still, that Avelyn suddenly stopped and looked at his beautiful companion, a most curious expression on his face. Not even blinking, he reached under his robes, then quickly retracted his hand.

It was covered in blood.

"My dear Jill," Avelyn said, "I do believe I have been stabbed." His legs started to buckle under him, but Jill caught him and guided him off the main road to a porch in a nearby alley. She thought to leave him there, to run off and find Dusberry's healer—every small town had one—but Avelyn caught her by the arm and would not let her go.

Then she saw it. Brother Avelyn produced a grayish-black stone, its polish so deep that it seemed almost liquid, so smooth that Jill felt as if she could slip right into it. Her gaze lingered on the stone for a long while, the young woman sensing there was something extraordinary, something magical about it.

"I need to borrow some of your strength, my friend," Avelyn said, "else I shall soon perish."

Jill, on her knees before him, nodded, eager to help in any way.

Avelyn wasn't satisfied with that response, though, fearing that Jill did not understand the true measure of what he needed from her. "We shall become one," he said, his voice growing ever more breathless, "more intimate than anything you have ever known. Are you prepared for such a joining?"

"I hardly think you are in condition—"

"Not physically, oh no, not that!" Avelyn quickly corrected, wheezing out a laugh despite his obvious agony. "Spiritually."

Jill rocked back on her heels, regarding Avelyn curiously. A physical union she could not abide—not with this man, not with Connor! But this cryptic talk of a spiritual joining did not seem so imposing. "Do what you must," she begged.

Avelyn regarded her a while longer, then finally nodded. He closed his eyes and began chanting softly, falling into the magic of the powerful hematite. Jill likewise closed her eyes, listening to the inflections of the chant.

Soon she no longer heard them, but rather felt them as if they were emanating from within her own body. And then she felt the intrusion, the spirit of Avelyn making its way into her.

Just his body was there, she realized, as again his spirit sought entry. Jill tried to break down her defenses, knew logically that if she did not let Avelyn have his way, he would surely die. She knew, too, that she had come to trust this man. He was a friend, of like mind and, on most points, morals.

She focused all her strength, trying vainly to invite the man in, trying vainly to facilitate the joining.

Then she was screaming, not aloud—or perhaps aloud, she was too consumed to know. Avelyn came closer, so much closer. Too close. They seemed to be as one; Jill caught images of the brown and gray walls of a monastery, of an island covered with lush vegetation and trees with wide-fingered branches. Then she felt as if she was falling, looked into the face of a hawkish man who was falling beside her.

And then she felt the pain, of a stab wound, sharp and hot. It was not on her; she knew that. But it was right there beside her, pulling at her life force, sucking her into its depths. She resisted, tried to push Avelyn away, but it was too late now. They were joined and the monk fed as a vampire would feed.

Jill's eyes popped wide in horror and she jumped, startled, to find that the monk was still reclining in front of her.

The pain became another sensation, hot and private. Too private and yet shared. Jill instinctively recoiled, but she had nowhere to hide. She had let Avelyn in, and now she must suffer the experience.

For Avelyn, the union of spirits proved something wondrous. Even as he explored this unfamiliar use of hematite, he gave to Jill his understanding of the stones—and it was so easy! He felt her response immediately, Jill passing her energy through the hematite into Avelyn's wounded body as smoothly as any fifth-year student of St.-Mere-Abelle. It struck Avelyn profoundly then that the monks might be teaching the usage of the stones in a terribly wrong manner, that if the instruction came in the spiritual mode, through the use of hematite, the students might progress much faster. Jill, he knew, would come away from this with more than a casual understanding of how to use the magic stones, and she was strong! Avelyn felt that. With practice, and more joinings, she could quickly rival all but the most powerful stone users of St.-Mere-Abelle—and all because of this simple technique.

But dark images began to wash over Avelyn, scenes of men running amok with stone power. He dismissed the notion of training stone use through this method as quickly as he had entertained it, for he realized that the discipline involved in handling such power could not be taught in any easy way. Suddenly he felt guilty for what he had just given this woman he hardly knew, felt as if he had somehow betrayed God, giving a blessing without first asking for any guidance or sacrifice.

It was over in a few moments, with Avelyn back in his nearly healed body. Jill turned away, could not look upon the man.

"I am sorry," Avelyn said to her, his voice weary but all trace of physical pain gone. "You have saved my life."

Jill fought away the black wings of her past, the barrier that had for so long protected her against intimacy, the barrier that Avelyn had not crashed through but had somehow circumvented. With great effort, she managed to turn back and face him.

He was sitting upright now, smiling sheepishly, the cloud of pain and death gone from his plump features. "I am—" he started to apologize again, but Jill put a finger over his lips to silence him. She stood up and offered her hand, helping the portly monk to his feet.

Then Jill started down the road, like all the other roads that led them out of all the other towns. She offered not a word as they walked long into the night, replaying those terrible moments of their joining over and over in her mind, constantly telling herself that it had been necessary, and trying to fathom the images that Avelyn had given her, images, no doubt, from the monk's past. There was something else, though, some gift that Avelyn had left behind. Jill had never even heard of the magic stones before, let alone used one, but now she felt as if she could handle them fairly well, as if their secrets had been unlocked to her in the blink of an eye. On this point, as well, she kept quiet, not knowing yet whether Avelyn had given her a gift or a curse.

Avelyn, too, did nothing to break the silence. He, too, had much to contemplate: the feelings he had viewed within the tortured woman and the scenes that the joining had shown him—images of a slaughter in a small town, probably somewhere in or near the Wilderlands. And Avelyn had a name for the place, a name the woman could not remember. He inquired privately about it in the next town the pair ventured through, and then, as the monk gained more and more knowledge, he began to steer Jill generally north.

It was with mixed feelings that Jill followed Brother Avelyn into Palmaris. The woman desperately wanted to seek out Graevis and Pettibwa, to tell them she was all right, to hug them and fall comfortably onto Pettibwa's soft bosom. All of that was, of course, tempered by her realization that she was, in effect, a deserter. A meeting with Connor could prove disastrous, and if Grady happened to spot her or learn of her visit, the greedy man would likely set the Kingsmen on her trail, if for no other reason than to ensure his inheritance.

Jill did go out one night, while Avelyn went down into the common room of the inn they had chosen, spouting his diatribes. She made her way silently across town, taking up a spot in the alleyway across from Fellowship Way. She sat there as the minutes became an hour, taking some comfort in the fact that many patrons came and went; apparently her little disaster hadn't ruined the Chilichunk name. Sometime later, Pettibwa came out of the inn, rubbing her hands on her apron, wiping the sweat from her brow, smiling, always smiling, as she went about the business of her life.

Jill's heart tugged at her to go out and embrace the woman, to run to Pettibwa as she would have run to her natural mother.

Something within, fear for Pettibwa, perhaps, stopped her though.

And then, quickly, the plump woman was gone, back into the bustle of the Way.

Jill left the alley hurriedly, thinking to go back to her room across town. Somehow she wound up on the back roof of the Way, in her private spot, basking one final time in those familiar feelings. Up here, she was, in effect, in Pettibwa's arms. Up here, Jill was Cat-the-Stray again, a younger girl in a world less complicated, with feelings less confusing.

She spent all night watching the stars, the gentle drift of Sheila, the occasional lazy cloud.

She returned to her room as dawn was breaking over Palmaris, to find Avelyn snoring loudly, his breath smelling of ale and more potent drinks, one eye blackened.

They remained in Palmaris, a city large enough to suffer the likes of the mad friar, for several more days, but Jill never ventured near Fellowship Way again.

❖ 29 ❖

Of Singular Purpose

They gave him but two stones: a smooth yellow-hued sunstone and a cabochon garnet, a carbuncle, the deepest shade of red. The former, among the most valued stones at St.-Mere-Abelle, could protect the man from almost any stone magic, could kill all magic in an entire area and render all spells useless within it, and the latter, the seeking stone, could show him the way to magic. Thus was Brother Justice equipped to find and destroy Avelyn.

He set out from the abbey one dark and dreary morning, riding an ash-gray mare, not swift of hoof but long in heart. The horse could go for many hours, and Brother Justice, so focused on the completion of his vital task, pushed her to her limits.

He traveled first to Youmaneff, the village where Avelyn Desbris had been born, some three hundred miles from St.-Mere-Abelle. He went to the small cemetery on the hill outside the place first, found the stone raised in memory of Annalisa Desbris, and noted with some satisfaction that the name of Jayson Desbris had not been added.

"You have come to tell me of my son Avelyn?" the old man asked as soon as Brother Justice, his brown robes marking him as an Abellican monk, knocked at his door.

The simple question, asked so very sincerely, put the monk on edge.

"Is he dead?" Jayson asked fearfully.

"Should he be?" Brother Justice retorted.

The old man blinked many times, then shook his head. "Forgive my lack of manners," he bade the visitor, moving to the side of the door and sweeping his hand, an invitation for the monk to enter. Brother Justice did so, his head bowed to hide his cruel smile.

"I had only assumed that a visit from a man of St.-Mere-Abelle would be to give tidings of Avelyn," Jayson explained. "And since the visit was not from Avelyn—"

"Where is Avelyn?" The monk's tone was flat and cold, a snapping question that sent Jayson back on his heels and had the hair on his neck standing on end.

"You would know better than I," the old man replied quietly. "Is he not at the monastery?"

"You know of his long journey?" the monk asked sharply.

Jayson shook his head, and Brother Justice sensed that he was truly confused.

"I last saw my son in the fall of God's Year 816," Jayson explained, "when I handed him into the care of St.-Mere-Abelle, into the arms of God."

Brother Justice found he believed every word, and that fact only made him all the more angry. He had hoped for information from Jayson Desbris, a direction to take that he might end this foul business quickly and efficiently. But Avelyn had apparently not come home, or at least, had not made contact with his father. Now the monk was torn, not knowing whether he should kill the old man, erasing any trace of his pursuit of Avelyn should he come home, or simply brush away any sense of misgivings Jayson might hold, putting the visit in a more congenial light.

That would not work, Brother Justice realized, for if Avelyn did come home and learn of a visit from a monk, then he would know that this had been no social call. Still, to slay the old man might make things even more complicated, for then he would be marked by the local officials and perhaps even hunted.

There was one other way.

"I fear to tell you that your son is dead," he said with as much conviction as he could muster—and that was not considerable.

Jayson leaned heavily on a table, and seemed suddenly very much older indeed.

"He fell from the abbey walls," Brother Justice went on, "into All Saints Bay. We have not recovered his body."

"Then why did you come here with questions as to his whereabouts?" came a sharp question from the side of the room. A large man, perhaps ten years older than Brother Justice, stormed into the room, his dark brown eyes filled with outrage.

Brother Justice hardly paid the man any heed—at least outwardly. He kept his focus on Jayson and tried to cover his previous questions. "Avelyn has taken his long journey," the monk said quietly, and that reference, put in terms of a spiritual flight, slowed the mounting anger in Avelyn's brother Tenegrid.

"He is with God now," Brother Justice finished.

Tenegrid came right up to the monk, glaring down at the shorter man. "But you never found his body," he reasoned.

"The fall is too great," Brother Justice said quietly. He had his hands in front of him, buried within his voluminous sleeves. They were not clasped, rather, his right hand was cupped, fingers set tight, forearm muscles twitching from the strain.

"Be gone from this house!" Tenegrid commanded. "Foul messenger who comes and taunts with questions before speaking the truth!" It was an obviously misplaced anger, an expression of pain and with no real resentment aimed at Brother Justice. Tenegrid was wounded as much by the sight of his grief-stricken father as by the news of his brother's death. Brother Justice understood this, though he hardly sympathized.

Still, the vicious monk would have let it go, but then Tenegrid made a dangerous mistake.

"Be gone!" he repeated, and he put his hand on the stocky man's strong shoulder and started to push him toward the door. Faster than his eyes could follow, Brother Justice's cupped hand snapped up and out to the right, striking Tenegrid squarely across the throat. The man fell away a couple of staggering steps, grabbed the back of a chair for support, and then fell over anyway, the chair tumbling down about him.

It took considerable willpower for Brother Justice, his blood so hot for the kill, to turn away for the door. He wanted to vent his rage on this brother of foul Avelyn, wanted to rip the man's head right off before his father's eyes and then slowly murder the father as well. But that would not be prudent, would likely make his course to Avelyn, the grandest prize of all, much more difficult.

"We of St.-Mere-Abelle are sorry for your loss," he said to Jayson Desbris.

The old man incredulously looked up from his son, who was still lying on the floor holding his wounded throat and gasping for breath, to see the monk depart.

The one obvious lead fruitless, Brother Justice had to turn to his magic, to the carbuncle, a stone also called Dragon Sight for its ability to detect things magical. He rode out of Youmaneff shortly thereafter, finding no magical emanations in or about the pitiful village. This was worse than a cold trail, Brother Justice realized, for this was no trail at all.

The world seemed wide indeed.

His first contact with magic came a few days later on the open road when he happened by a merchant caravan. One of the merchants had a stone—and admitted as much when Brother Justice cornered him alone inside his covered carriage. It was merely a diamond chip, useful for saving the candles and oil on long journeys.

The monk was soon again back on the road, riding steadily and making a general course to the north. The largest city in Honce-the-Bear was Ursal, so that, he figured, might be a good place to start. Brother Justice knew the pitfalls, though. Many merchants in Ursal likely possessed stones; the monastery was not averse to selling them. His garnet would lead him down a hundred different avenues, to one dead end after another. But still, considering the limited range of the Dragon Sight stone—it could not locate magic more than a few hundred feet away—Brother Justice would have more of a chance in a confined city than in the vast open spaces of central and northern Honce-the-Bear.

He wasn't a third of the way to Ursal, though, when his course took a different direction, when the trail suddenly heated up.

It happened purely by chance in a hamlet too small even to have a name, a place a certain "mad friar" had passed through only a few weeks before on his way to Dusberry on the Masur Delaval. The reaction of the inhabitants to Brother Justice's brown robes tipped the monk off to the fact that he was not the first Abellican monk to come through this place recently. People sighed when he walked in, seemed fearful at first, and then, as if recognizing that he was a different man than they had originally feared, they sighed again, this time in obvious relief.

When questioned, they were all too ready to give an account of the "mad friar" who had visited their village, offering portents of doom and starting a wild fight in the tavern. One man showed Brother Justice a broken arm, still far from healed.

"Not good business for the church, I'm thinking," the man offered, "to have one o' yer own wandering about hurting folks!"

"More than a few folk have turned away from St. Gwendolyn of the Sea since the fight," the bartender of the tavern added.

"This monk was of St. Gwendolyn?" Brother Justice asked, recognizing the name of the monastery, a secluded fortress nestled high on a rocky bluff, perhaps two days' ride to the east.

The man with the broken arm shrugged noncommittally, then turned to the bartender, who likewise had no answers.

"He wore robes akin to yer own," the bartender remarked.

Brother Justice wanted desperately to inquire if the man carried any magical stones, if there was any magic about him at all, but he realized that these two would not likely have held back such information if they had it, and he didn't want to tip his hand too much to anyone, fearing that Avelyn would be all the more difficult to find if he realized he was being hunted.

So the monk got a description, and though it was not an exact image of the Avelyn Desbris he had known, it was enough to hold his curiosity. So, suddenly, he had a description, a title—"the mad friar"—and a direction, the folk of the hamlet uniformly insisting the monk had gone down the western road with his companion, a beautiful young woman of about twenty years, close beside him.

The trail was warm, and it led Brother Justice from town to town, across the countryside to Dusberry on the Masur Delaval. He picked up even more clues as he went, for in one skirmish in a bar this mad friar had apparently sent a pair of men flying with a blue shock.

Graphite.

Less than a month after he had set out from the tiny hamlet, confident that he was steadily gaining on this rogue monk, Brother Justice walked through the fortified gates of Palmaris.

Only two short days later, Brother Justice used his Dragon Sight stone to detect the use of strong magic, coming from the northeastern quarter of the city, the high ground of rich houses overlooking the Masur Delaval. Convinced that his prey was in reach, a lion staring down the face of an old and weary zebra, the monk rushed through the streets, through the crowded marketplace, knocking over more than one surprised person. He was a bit apprehensive when he got to the gates of the indicated house, a huge structure of imported materials: smooth white marble from the south, dark wooden beams from the Timberlands, and an assortment of garden artwork that could only have come from the galleries of the finest sculptors in Ursal. Brother Justice's first thought was that Avelyn had hired on with this obviously wealthy merchant, perhaps to perform some necessary feat with the stones, perhaps merely as a court jester. The fierce monk tried to hold hard to that hope, for, logically, he could not dismiss his doubts. Would Avelyn, who held the stones as most sacred, rent out their powers? Only in emergency, Brother Justice realized, and since Avelyn could not have been in Palmaris for more than a couple of weeks, this was not likely a familiar house to him.

That left another possibility, one the monk did not wish to entertain. He went over the gate easily, lighting down in the front yard without a whisper of sound. There were many hedges and high bushes; he could get to the door without drawing notice from within or from the wide street behind him.

He understood his error before he had gone a dozen paces when he heard the growl of a sentry dog.

Brother Justice spat a curse and saw the animal, a massive, muscled beast, black and brown with a huge bony skull and wide jaw full of gleaming white teeth. The dog hesitated only a moment, taking full measure of the man, then came on in a dead run, lips curled back to show Brother Justice those awful teeth with every stride.

The monk crouched low, bent his legs, and tightened his muscles, measuring the dog's swift approach. The beast came in fast and hard, but just as it was about to leap for the man's throat, Brother Justice confused it by jumping high into the air, curling his legs under him.

The dog skidded to a stop, its momentum too great for it to effectively change its angle of attack, and then Brother Justice came down hard on its back, kicking both his legs straight down as he descended.

The dog's legs splayed wide; it gave one yelp, then lay still, its back broken, its lungs collapsing.

The monk, convinced that the animal could not cry out any further warnings, walked on toward the house. He decided to take a straightforward approach and went right to the front door, knocking hard with the large brass knocker, another imported and sculpted item, he knew, this one in the shape of a leering, stretched face.

As soon as he saw the handle begin to turn, the monk lifted one foot and went into a spin, timing it perfectly so that his foot connected with the door just as it began to open. The man on the other side, a servant, flew to the floor as the door swung wide and Brother Justice entered.

"Your master?" the monk asked flatly.

The stunned man stammered, taking too long for the impatient monk's comfort.

"Your master?" Brother Justice demanded again, grabbing the man by the collar and lifting him to his feet.

"He is indisposed," the man replied, at which Brother Justice slapped him hard across the face, then clutched him on the neck, a grip that left no doubt in the man's mind that this intruder could rip out his throat with hardly an effort. The man pointed toward a door across the foyer.

Brother Justice dragged him along. He let go before he reached the door, though, tossing the poor servant to the floor as he felt the first waves of intrusion, magical intrusion, an attack aimed his way and coming from within the room.

The monk quickly took out his yellow sunstone, falling immediately into its defensive magic. The attack was fairly strong—though he would have expected more from powerful Brother Avelyn—but the sunstone was among the most potent of all the stones of St.-Mere-Abelle, its defenses even more complete than the chrysoberyl more commonly used, and its power was more tightly focused than any other, a simple shield against magic. In an instant, a yellowish glow surrounded the monk, and the waves of intrusion were halted.

The monk snarled in defiance and kicked at the heavy door. It jolted but did not open. He kicked again and again, repeatedly slamming the lock, until finally, the wood of the jamb gave way, the door flying wide to reveal a portly man, richly dressed, standing behind a large oaken desk, a loaded crossbow in hand.

"You have one shot," Brother Justice said evenly, striding directly into the room, his eyes locked on those of the merchant. "One shot, and if it does not kill me, I will torture you to a slow death."

The man's hands trembled; Brother Justice knew that without even looking at them. He saw the merchant flinch as a line of sweat rolled from his brow into one eye, saw the man chewing his lip.

"Not another step!" the merchant said with all the courage he could muster.

Brother Justice stopped and smiled wickedly. "Can you kill me?" he asked. "Is this the end you desire?"

"I desire only to defend what is mine," the merchant replied.

"I am no enemy."

The merchant stared at him incredulously.

"I had thought you to be another," Brother Justice said calmly, turning his back on the merchant to close the door as tightly as the shattered jamb would allow. He sneered at the curious servants gathering in the hall to keep them at bay. "I am hunting a dangerous fugitive, one who employs the magic of the stones," he explained, turning back to the merchant, a disarming look on his face. "I had not thought that any but he would be so powerful with the magic." Brother Justice did well to hide his wicked grin as the crossbow slipped down.

"I am always ready to lend aid to those of St. Precious," the merchant declared.

Brother Justice shook his head. "St.-Mere-Abelle," he corrected. "I have traveled the breadth of Honce-the-Bear in my most vital quest. I had thought it to be at its end. Forgive my entrance; my Father Abbot will reimburse you for all the cost."

The merchant waved his hand, his face brightening at the mention of the man. "How fares old Markwart?" he asked, his tone one of familiarity.

Again the monk restrained his feeling of outrage that this man—this simple, pitiful, wretched merchant—could speak of Father Abbot Markwart as if he were the man's equal. Obviously he had dealt with Markwart—where else would he have garnered so powerful a stone?—but Brother Justice understood the relationship between the merchants and the abbey far more clearly than did the merchants. Father Abbot Markwart was always willing to take their money, but never in exchange for honest respect.

"Perhaps, then, I can help you with your quest," the merchant offered. "Ah, but where are my manners? I am Folo Dosindien, Dosey to my friends, to your Father Abbot! You must be hungry or perhaps in need of a drink." He lifted his hand and started to call out, but Brother Justice cut him short.

"I require nothing," he assured the merchant.

"Nothing but help in your search, perhaps," the man said teasingly.

The monk tilted his head, somewhat intrigued. The man had at least one powerful stone—he knew that and suspected it to be hematite. Many things could be accomplished with such a stone.

"I seek a fellow monk," Brother Justice explained. "He is known as the mad friar."

The merchant shrugged; the name obviously meant nothing to him. "He is in Palmaris?"

"He came through, at least," the monk explained, "not more than two weeks previous."

The merchant sat down behind his desk, his features tightening with concentration. "If he travels, if he is an outlaw, then likely he would have sought out the lowlier regions of the southern docks," he reasoned. He looked up at the monk, his expression resigned. "Palmaris is a large place."

Brother Justice did not blink.

"I have offered my name," the man prompted.

"I have no name to offer," replied Brother Justice, and the tension grew once more, instantly emanating from the monk's cold stare.

Dosey cleared his throat. "Yes," he said. "I wish that I had more answers to give to one of Markwart's underlings."

Brother Justice narrowed his eyes, not appreciating the sentiment, the way the foolish merchant tried to dominate him by referring to his superior in such familiar terms.

"But there is a place," the merchant whispered, coming forward suddenly in his chair, "where one might get answers. Answers to any question in all the world."

Brother Justice had no idea where this conversation was going, had no idea what to make of the man's sudden, almost maniacal expression.

"But not until we have dined," Dosey said, falling back in his chair. "Come, then, I will set for you a table unrivaled in Palmaris, that you might return to St.-Mere-Abelle with kind words for Markwart's dear old merchant friend."

Brother Justice played along, and, indeed, the merchant Dosey was not exaggerating. His servants—the man Brother Justice had dropped to the foyer floor and three women, one undeniably beautiful—brought in course after course of the finest cuts of meat and the sweetest fruits. Juicy lamb and thick cuts of venison buried in brown sauces and mushrooms, oranges that exploded in a shower of juice as soon as the integrity of their peels was breached, and large, round, yellow melons that the monk had never before seen but that were sweeter than anything he had ever tasted.

He ate and he drank, neither to excess, and when the meal was over, some two hours later, he again sat quietly and let the merchant guide the conversation.

The man rambled on and on, telling mostly stories of his dealings with the various monasteries of Honce-the-Bear, even with St. Brugalnard in far-away Alpinador. Brother Justice knew that he was supposed to be impressed, and he worked hard to pretend that he was as the minutes dragged on into yet another hour. Dosey interrupted his tales only for an occasional belch; so lost was he in his own sense of importance that he hardly bothered to gauge the monk's reaction. Brother Justice figured that the man was accustomed to dealing with people in need of or with great desire for his wealth, and, thus, he could ramble on and on to an attentive, though captive, audience. Such were the trappings of power that Dosey did not realize what an ultimate bore and ridiculous buffoon he truly was.

But Brother Justice needed the merchant, as well, or at least it seemed plausible that the man might aid the monk in his all-important quest. That alone held the monk at the table long after the sun had set.

Finally, so suddenly that the surprise shook the monk from his almost dreamlike state of boredom, Dosey announced that it was time to get some answers and that these things were better done in the dark.

The mysterious tone of his voice set the monk on his guard, though, in truth, Brother Justice really didn't expect much from the merchant. Perhaps the fool Dosey would use his hematite to invade the bodies of several innkeepers from the lowlier sections of the city, using their forms to inquire about the mad friar.

The pair went back to Dosey's study, to the great oaken desk. Dosey had his manservant retrieve a second chair, placing it at the desk's side, and then he bade the monk to sit and relax.

"I could go," the merchant offered, and then he shook his head, as if not liking that notion, almost as if he were afraid of that thought.

Brother Justice made no move at all to reply, no verbal or body language to let the man know that he was even the least bit intrigued.

"But perhaps you should see for yourself," the merchant went on, a wry smile on his face as he spoke. "Would you like to go?" he asked.

"Go?"

"For your answers."

"I know not of this place of which you speak," Brother Justice admitted. "You have a stone, that much I know."

"Oh, much more than a simple stone," Dosey teased. He reached under the lapel of his fine gray jacket and produced a pin, a large broach, and held it out for Brother Justice to see. Now the monk could not fully hide his interest. The central stone of the broach was a hematite, as he had suspected, an oval of liquid gray, deep and smooth. Encircling it, set in the yellow gold, were a series of small, clear, round crystals. Brother Justice did not immediately recognize them, for they might have been several different types, but he sensed that they were indeed magical, in some way tied to the powers of the hematite.

"My own design," Dosey bragged. "The fun of the stones is in combining their powers, is it not?"

The fun, Brother Justice silently echoed, hating this man and the irreverence with which he spoke of something so sacred. "This broach presents a combination not known to me," the monk admitted.

"Simple clear-crystal quartz," Dosey explained, running his finger about the large broach's edge. "For distant sight."

A stone of divining, Brother Justice then realized, and he was beginning to catch on. With the clear quartz, a man could send his vision across the miles; perhaps combining that with the spirit-walking of the hematite . . .

"With this, you can go to a place to find your answers," Dosey promised, "a place that only I know of. The home of a friend, a powerful friend indeed, one that would impress your Markwart, to be sure!"

Brother Justice hardly noted the familiar reference to the Father Abbot this time, so caught up was he in the implications. His intrigue was fast shifting to trepidation now, as he got the distinct feeling that he had stumbled on to something potentially dangerous. He recalled Dosey's fearful expression when he hinted that he would make the journey, a mixture, it seemed, of the sheerest horror and the highest titillation. What manner of being could so inspire such a reaction? What, then, lay at the end of this spirit-journey?

A shudder coursed up the monk's spine. Perhaps the monastery should reconsider its practice of selling stones to fools like Dosey.

The thought flew away in an instant, for this monk, this Brother Justice, had been trained to be unable to hold long to any ill feelings, any questions at all, concerning the decisions of his superiors.

"Go," Dosey bade him, handing over the broach. "Let the stone guide you. It knows the way."

"Am I to possess the body of another?"

"The stone knows the way." It was spoken simply, calmly, and, somehow wickedly. That part of Brother Justice, that small flicker of memory that recalled his life as Quintall, recognized Dosey's expression as that of an older boy pressing a youngster to mischief.

He took the broach, felt its power in his hand, eyeing Dosey cautiously all the while. His physical body would be vulnerable while spirit-walking, he knew, but he doubted that Dosey would strike against one of Markwart's emissaries. Even if he did attack, Brother Justice, already using the hematite, figured that he would have little trouble possessing the merchant's body. And Dosey likely knew the same thing, and that understanding, the monk decided, would give him the insurance he needed.

So Brother Justice sat back in the chair, closed his eyes, and let the magic of the broach engulf him. He visualized the hematite as a dark liquid pool and he waded in slowly, letting the physical world dissipate into gray nothingness. Then his body and spirit were apart, two separate entities. The monk looked about the room from this new perspective, but his eyes could not remain fixed on anything but the clear stones surrounding that hematite. They pulled at him as forcefully as anything he had ever felt, a compulsion too great to ignore. Doubts about the wisdom of his choice, about the wisdom of selling such powerful stones to fools, flapped up about him, flashes of dark wings that beat at the will of the powerful monk.

He was sinking, ever sinking, into that crystal glare, away from the room, away from his corporeal body and the fool Dosey.

And then he was flying, faster than thought, across the miles. Time and distance warped. It seemed as if an hour went by, but then as if only a second had passed; what appeared as an infinite plain was crossed by a single step. On and on Brother Justice flew, north to the Timberlands, to

the Wilderlands, across great lakes and deep forests, and then to mountains, towering peaks.

So many times he thought he would collide with jags of stone only to
watch them rush under him at the last possible second. He had never imagined such an attunement of stone magic, that these crystals could be so
focused in their divination. It was something dangerous and beyond his
understanding—and he knew as much about the stones as any man alive,
with, as far as he knew, the exceptions of only Father Abbot Markwart and
Avelyn Desbris!

He crossed the range into a huge, high valley, a great plateau ringed by
the towering mountains. Below him, massed like ants, were the campsites of
armies. He wanted to go lower, to distinguish the individual forms, to see
what force had gathered in such unbelievable numbers, but the compelling
crystals would not let him out of their grasp. He flew on above the plateau
to a singular, smoking mountain, its southern face tree covered, but with
two black arms reaching down, reaching out to encompass the gathered
armies.

Brother Justice nearly swooned, his senses overwhelmed by the sheer
speed at which his spirit entered a series of connecting narrow tunnels.
Every breakneck turn jolted him, though his physical form was hundreds of
miles away. Every dip and sudden rise blurred his vision, scrambled his
thoughts.

He came up fast on a pair of great bronze doors, inlaid with a myriad of
designs and symbols. They opened but a crack, and through that tiny space
flew his disembodied spirit into a huge chamber lined by stone columns
that resembled gigantic sculpted warriors. He soared through their twin
lines, his attention stolen as he approached the far end of the chamber, a
raised dais, and a creature whose strength was beyond anything Brother
Justice had ever known, whose emanations of power and of evil mocked life
itself.

The flight stopped, leaving Brother Justice standing right before the dais.
He considered his own form, for normally spirit-walkers were invisible. Not
in here, though. The monk could see himself, as he appeared within his corporeal trappings, except that he was a singular shade of gray and translucent, so that he could look right through his form to see the gray stone
beneath his feet.

But that spectacle couldn't hold Brother Justice's attention for any length
of time, not with this huge monstrosity leering at him from on high. What
monster was this? the monk wondered as he studied the reddish skin and
black eyes, the bat wings, horns, and claws. What manifestation of hell had
come to walk the material world? What demon?

The questions spiraled into a singular line of thought, a singular fear that
threatened to break the monk's very mind. He knew! From his lessons,

years of religious training, years of his masters imparting the fears of that which opposed their God.

He knew!

You have destroyed the fool Dosey, then, the creature telepathically imparted to the monk, and have stolen his treasure. The instant that last thought ended, Brother Justice felt an intrusion that he could not deny, a sudden scouring of his brain, of his identity, his intentions. Sheer revulsion saved him, catapulted his spirit out of that terrible place like a slingshot snapping back through the tunnels, across the plateau, above the swarming soldiers that he knew then were an army of evil, across the mountains and then the forests, the lakes, careening all the way back to Palmaris, to the merchant's study, and back into his body so suddenly that the physical form nearly toppled over.

"Do you know now?" Dosey asked him even as his eyes blinked open.

Brother Justice looked into that maniacal expression and saw the result of contact with such a creature clearly etched on Dosey's face. He wanted to shake the man and ask him what he had done, what he had awakened—but it was far beyond that, Brother Justice realized before he ever uttered a word. The man had passed the point of redemption and had perhaps awakened a dangerous curiosity in the demon.

Up came the monk's hands, locking fast on Dosey's throat. Dosey grabbed at the monk's wrists, tugging futilely, trying to cry for help, scream, anything. The muscles on Brother Justice's arms stood taut and too strong to fight. The monk drove the feeble merchant to his knees and held fast long after the struggling stopped, long after the merchant's arms fell slack at his sides.

His mind whirling with outrage and fear, Brother Justice stalked about the house, finding the servants and the merchant's family.

He left long after midnight, battling his confusion with a wall of sheer anger. The broach was in his pocket, the house of Folo Dosindien was dead.

❖ 30 ❖

Symphony

"I am at peace, a greater sense of belonging than I have ever known," the ranger said at length after more than half an hour sitting in his wooden chair in the darkness, staring at the barely perceptible mirror. He gave a chuckle at the irony of his own words. "And yet, Uncle Mather, I count my current friends as but two, and one of them is no more than a shadowy image, a specter that cannot speak!"

Elbryan laughed again as he considered the preposterous illogic of it all. "I belong here," he declared. "This area, these towns—Dundalis, Weedy Meadow, and End-o'-the-World—are my towns, these folk, my folk, though they hardly tolerate the sight of me. What is it then that gives me acceptance in this place, a greater sense of peace and belonging than I knew among the Touel'alfar, who became my friends, who cared for me much more deeply than any of the folk of the three villages, than any but you and Bradwarden?"

He stared hard at the image at the edge of the dark mirror for a long while, considering his words, seeking his answers.

"It is duty," Elbryan said finally. "It is the belief that here I am doing something to better the world—or at least my corner of the wide world. With the elves, I felt a sense of personal growth, learning and training, perfecting my skills, always moving toward something better. Here, I use those skills to better the world, to protect those who need protection—whether or not they believe they need protection.

"So here I belong. Here I fit into a necessary niche and know that my daily toils, my watchful eye, my rapport with the forest—creatures and plants—is surely valuable, if not appreciated."

Elbryan closed his eyes and kept them shut for a long moment, his mind filling with the thoughts of the many duties left to him this day. He soon realized that Uncle Mather would not be in the mirror when he again opened his eyes, for the trance was broken. That was the way it always happened, the needs of the day dispatching the spirit soon before the dawn, turning Elbryan's thoughts from philosophical to pragmatic. He used the Oracle regularly now, sometimes two or even three times in a week, and he never failed to bring up the image of his relative, the ranger who had gone before him. He wondered often if he might also find the image of Olwan in that mirror or of his mother or Pony, perhaps.

Yes, Elbryan would like to converse with Pony, to see her again, to remember that innocent time when patrolling was play and nightmares were not real.

He left the small cave, crawling out past the large tree roots, with a sincere smile on his face, rejuvenated and ready for the day's work, as always. He was hoping to find Bradwarden, for the centaur, after weeks of Elbryan's teasing, had at last promised him an archery contest. Perhaps Elbryan would make his prize, should he win—and he had no reason to believe that he would not—an indenture of the centaur, forcing Bradwarden to accompany him on his coming visit to the forest about the western village of End-o'-the-World.

First things first, the ranger told himself. He took up Hawkwing, removed its feathered tip and its string, and went to a place he had claimed as his own, a nearly treeless hillock much like the one he had frequented in Andur'Blough Inninness, one that lifted him up into the heavens on starry nights and brought him the first rays of dawn and the last rays of the sunset.

The ranger quickly removed his clothes, the grass feeling scratchy but not unpleasant to his feet. He greeted the dawn with his dance, weaving the staff about as he would wield a sword, stepping slowly, perfectly balanced, the moves coming with hardly a thought, since the movement memories were ingrained deep within his muscles. The sword-dance was perfected now, and there were no steps to be added, no more difficult maneuvers, no increase in speed. These movements alone would continue to heighten Elbryan's balance, his sense of control over his body. In the half hour that it now took Elbryan to perform the dance, he would put his body through every movement needed in battle, he would reinforce in his muscles the memory of which action properly followed which.

Truly the ranger was a thing of beauty, moving with animal-like grace but with human control. A combination of strength and agility, a balanced, thinking warrior. The greatest gift of the Touel'alfar was his name, Nightbird, and all the training that had come with it. The greatest gift of the elves was this harmony the man had achieved, this joining of two philosophies, of two ways of looking at the world, of two ways to do battle.

Sweat glistened in the morning light, beading and rolling about the man's hard, sculpted form. For though he was not moving quickly, the energy required to maintain the balance of the sword-dance was tremendous, often a working of muscle against muscle or an isolation of a muscle group so completely that it was worked to its limits.

When he was done, Elbryan gathered up his clothing and ran to a nearby pond, diving into the chilly water without hesitation. A quick swim refreshed him, and he dressed and went at once to his morning meal, then set off to find the centaur.

To Elbryan's relief, Bradwarden was in the appointed area, though not exactly in the spot where he had told Elbryan their contest would be held. To make things even easier for the tracking ranger, the centaur was playing his pipes this morning, a haunting melody that seemed akin to the dawn, gentle and rising, rising, until the notes burst forth as the rays of the sun, cresting the long hill and spreading wide. Following that music, compelled by its notes, Elbryan soon came upon the half-equine beast, standing amid a tumble of boulders.

The centaur stopped his playing when he spotted his friend, his white smile growing wide within his bushy black beard. "I feared ye would not have the courage to show yer face!" Bradwarden roared.

"My face and my bow," the ranger replied, holding Hawkwing up before him.

"Aye, that elven stick," the centaur remarked. Bradwarden held aloft his own bow then, the first time Elbryan had seen it, and he was truly astonished. Mounted sidelong on a platform, the thing would have passed for a fair-sized ballista!

"You throw arrows with a tree?" the ranger scoffed.

Bradwarden's smile didn't lessen a bit. "Call 'em arrows," he said evenly, placing his pipes on the ground and hoisting a quiver that would have passed for a sleeping bag for Elbryan, with arrows each as long as the man was tall. "Call 'em spears. But if ye get hit by one, know that ye'll call 'em death!"

Elbryan didn't doubt that for a minute.

Bradwarden led the way out of the area to an open meadow upon which he had placed a series of six targets, each a different distance from the appointed line.

"We'll be starting close and working our way to the back," the centaur explained. "First one to miss a target is the loser."

Elbryan considered the rules, so befitting the centaur's blunt style. Normally in a test of archery, each contestant would be granted a specified number of shots, with the best total score serving as the measure. With Bradwarden, though, it was a simple challenge of hit or miss.

Elbryan stepped up and let fly first, confident that the first target, no more than thirty paces, would pose no difficulty. His arrow slapped into the target near the bull's-eye, a straight, level shot.

Without a word of congratulations, Bradwarden lifted his monstrous bow and drew back. "Ye only stung the giant," the centaur remarked, then let fly. His great bolt thudded into the target near Elbryan's arrow and overturned the whole three-legged thing. "Now," the centaur declared, "the beast is properly killed."

"Perhaps I should shoot first at each target," Elbryan said dryly.

The mighty centaur laughed heartily. "If ye don't," he agreed, "then ye'll be aiming high for the clouds and hoping yer bolt drops straight down on the mark, don't ye doubt!"

Before the centaur had even finished, Elbryan's second arrow thudded dead center into the next target, ten paces farther away than the first.

Bradwarden hit it as well, and again the target fell over.

They were up to the fifth target in no time, the first three having been knocked flat, and the fourth still standing, for Bradwarden's great arrow, though true in aim, had not pushed it all the way over. This fifth target, some hundred yards away, was the first for which Elbryan had to elevate his shot. Not much, though; so strong was Hawkwing that the arrow's flight was barely arched, cutting a sure line through the gentle wind to strike perfectly.

The centaur, for the very first time, seemed honestly impressed. "Good bow," he muttered, and then he took aim and let fly.

Elbryan clenched a fist, thinking himself victorious as he marked the flight. Bradwarden's arrow did hit the target, though, barely catching hold in its outer edge, as far to the left of center as it could go.

Elbryan turned a wry gaze on the centaur. "A bit of luck," he remarked.

Bradwarden pawed hard at the ground. "Not so," he insisted in all seriousness. "I aimed for the beast's weapon hand."

"Ah, but if it was left-handed . . ." the ranger replied without hesitation.

Bradwarden's smile was gone. "Last shot," he said evenly. "Then we'll be picking out farther trees to substitute for targets."

"Or leaves," Elbryan replied, and lifted his bow.

"A bit too much," the centaur said suddenly, and the ranger eased the tension on his bowstring, having almost lost his concentration and the shot.

"Too much?"

"Too much faith in yerself," the centaur clarified. "Next, ye'll be wanting to wager."

Elbryan paused and thought hard on that line, then looked back to consider the centaur's last shot, so near a miss. Or had it been planned that way? he had to wonder. Was Bradwarden setting him up? Certainly the centaur was a fine archer, but was he even better than Elbryan had recognized?

"Me pipes'll be needing a new bag," Bradwarden mused. "Not a difficult chore, but a dirty one—taking a hide."

"And if I win?" Elbryan asked. His eyes betrayed his idea, roaming to the centaur's strong back.

Bradwarden started to laugh, as if the notion that Elbryan might win was absurd. The centaur stopped abruptly, though, and glared hard at his human companion. "I know ye're thinking ye might be riding me, but if ever ye try, I'll be giving human flesh another taste."

"Just to End-o'-the-World," Elbryan clarified. "I wish to be there and back in a hurry."

"Never!" the centaur declared. "Only a maiden I'd let ride, and then she'd be letting me," he finished with a lewd wink.

Elbryan didn't even want to conjure the image.

"What, then?" he asked. "I'll wager against you, but the prize must be named."

"I could make ye a real bow," the centaur chided.

"And I could put an arrow up your arse from a hundred paces," Elbryan retorted.

"Big target," the huge centaur admitted. "But what might ye be needing, me friend, not that ye've a chance at winning."

"I already told you," Elbryan replied. "I enjoy my walks, but I fear that I need a faster method to cover the ground about the three towns."

"Ye'll never climb on me back."

"Do you lead the wild horses?" Elbryan asked, surprising the centaur.

"Not I," Bradwarden replied. "That's the work of another." A strange smile came over the centaur, a strange expression as if he had found the solution to some puzzle. "Aye," he said at length, "that'll be yer prize. If lightning hits me arrow—for that's the only way ye'll beat me—I'll take ye to the one who leads the wild herd. I'll take ye, mind ye, but then ye'll make yer own deals."

Elbryan realized that he was being duped, that this prize, in Bradwarden's estimation, was more a punishment. The ranger felt the hairs on the back of his neck standing up, felt a tingling of trepidation. Who might this leader of the herd be to inspire such uncharacteristic respect from cocky Bradwarden? Along with the realization came an undeniable sense of intrigue, however, and so the ranger agreed.

Up came Hawkwing and off flew the arrow, striking hard on the far-distant target.

Bradwarden gave a grunt of respect, then let fly, his arrow, too, hitting the mark.

"Three," said Elbryan, and he put up his bow three times in rapid succession, each bolt flying unerringly.

Bradwarden followed and scored three hits.

"Fourth, fifth, sixth!" Elbryan cried, letting three more shots fly, the first hitting the fourth target squarely, the second striking the fifth—splitting Elbryan's previous shot on that target—and the last zipping into the final target, dead center.

The centaur sighed, beginning to understand that he had, for the first time, possibly met his match in a human. He got the fourth target easily enough, and then the fifth, but his shot at the last in line skipped off the top of the target and flew away into the brush beyond the far edge of the meadow.

Elbryan smiled widely and clenched a fist. He looked up at Bradwarden and found the centaur eyeing him with an expression he had not really seen from the creature before: respect.

"Ye've got yerself one dragon-killer of a bow, me friend," Bradwarden offered. "And be sure that I've not seen a steadier hand."

"I had the best bowyer," Elbryan replied, "and the best tutors. None in all the world can match the archery of the Touel'alfar."

Bradwarden snorted. "That's because the skinny little folks don't dare to get close to an enemy!" he replied. "Come on then, let us go and get our arrows, and then I'll show ye something fine."

They gathered together their arrows and their belongings and set off at once, the centaur leading Elbryan deep into the forest, past the pine and the caribou moss, down a deep valley, then up its other side. They walked for several hours, speaking little, but with the centaur often lifting his pipes to play. At last, the sun moving low in the western sky, they came to a secluded grove of pines, neatly tended into roughly a diamond shape. It sat on the gentle slope of a wide hill, surrounded on all sides by a meadow of tall grass and wildflowers. Elbryan could hardly believe that he hadn't found this grove before, that his ranger instincts hadn't guided him to a place so naturally perfect, so in tune with the harmony of the forest. This grove—every flower, every bush, every tree and stone, and the trickling brook that crossed it—was something more than the ordinary forests of the region. It was something sacred, something befitting Andur'Blough Innin-ness, and not of the tainted world of men.

There was some magic here; Elbryan felt that as clearly as he had felt the magic of the elven valley. Reverently, almost as if in a trance, the ranger approached, Bradwarden at his side. They crossed the outer line of thick evergreens into the heart of the grove and found bare paths weaving through the dense undergrowth. Elbryan walked along without speaking a word, as if fearing to disturb the stillness, for not a hint of a breeze came in through that wall of pines.

The path meandered, joining another, then forking three ways. The grove was not large, perhaps two hundred yards across and half again that measure in length, but Elbryan was certain that the paths, if straightened and laid end to end, would cover several miles. He looked back often to Bradwarden for guidance, but the centaur paid him no heed, just followed silently.

They came to a dark, shady spot where the path forked left and right around a great jut of rock covered with a thick patch of short yellow flowers. Elbryan glanced both ways, then, figuring that the paths converged just the other side of the boulder, went right. He soon came to the expected joining, and, looking ahead, he almost continued on.

"Not so perceptive for one trained by elves," the centaur remarked, Bradwarden's deep voice shattering the stillness. Elbryan spun around, meaning to hush him, but all thoughts of that, all thoughts of Bradwarden at all, left him as he glanced past the centaur, to the back side of the boulder that had split the path. Elbryan glided back, moving beside the centaur, staring hard at the pile of rocks, eight feet by six and roughly diamond shaped. The ranger glanced all about. They were in the very center of the grove, he realized, and he realized, too, that this cairn was the source of the magic, that the tree-lined borders of the grove seemed to be a reflection of this place.

He went down to one knee, studying the stones, marveling at the care with which they had been placed. He touched one and felt a gentle tingling there, the emanation of magic.

"Who is buried here?" the ranger whispered.

Bradwarden snorted and smiled. "Not for me to tell," he replied, and Elbryan couldn't discern if the centaur meant that he did not know, or that it was not his place to reveal the person's identity.

"Put in the ground by the elves," the centaur said, "when I was no bigger than yerself."

Elbryan looked at him curiously. "And how long ago might that be," he asked Bradwarden, "in the measure of human years?"

The centaur shrugged and pawed the ground uneasily. "Half a man's life," he replied, as exact an answer as Elbryan was going to get.

The ranger let it go. He didn't need to know who was buried here. Obviously the man, or elf or whatever it might be, was important to the Touel'alfar; obviously they had graced this place, this cairn and the grove that had grown about it, with more than a small measure of their magic. He could be satisfied with that; Bradwarden had promised to show him something fine, and indeed the centaur had fulfilled that pledge.

There remained, however, the matter of Elbryan's prize for winning the archery contest. He looked up at the centaur.

"Ye just keep coming here," Bradwarden remarked, as if reading Elbryan's thoughts, "and ye'll find the one who leads the horses."

The notion filled the ranger with both excitement and fear. They left the grove soon after, to find an evening meal. Elbryan returned later that night, and then again the next day, but it wasn't until his fourth journey, some two weeks later, after he had returned from his rounds to End-o'-the-World, that he found Bradwarden's payment.

It was a brisk autumn day, the wind whipping—though inside the grove, the air remained still—leaves and clouds alike, the puffy white mountains drifting swiftly overhead across the rich blue sky. Elbryan went right to the heart of the grove, paying homage to whoever was buried there, then came back to the edge, wanting to feel the breeze in his face.

Then he heard the music.

At first he thought it was Bradwarden at work with his pipes, but then he realized that it was too sweet, a subtle vibration in the ground and air, a natural song. It didn't increase in volume or intensity, just played on, and Elbryan soon realized it to be a heralding call, the run of hooves and the wind. He turned and ran along to the southern tip of the grove, though he had no idea of what might be guiding him.

Across the wide meadow, past the flowers and the grass, he saw perfection of form, a huge stallion, milling about the shadows of the distant trees.

Elbryan held his breath as the great horse, shining black except for white on the bottoms of its forelegs and a white diamond above its eyes, came out onto the open field. It was taking his measure, Elbryan knew, though he was not downwind and too far for most horses even to notice him.

The stallion pawed the ground, then reared and whinnied. It came forward in a short burst, a show of strength, then turned and thundered away into the forest.

Elbryan breathed again. He knew the magnificent steed would not return that day, and so he walked away, not in the direction in which the horse had run but back toward Dundalis. He found Bradwarden, at work crafting some devilish arrows, and the centaur's face immediately brightened.

"Welcome back," Bradwarden offered with a chuckle. "I see ye've already been to the grove."

Elbryan blushed to think that his emotions were so clearly displayed on his face.

"I told ye," the centaur gloated. "So fine a creature is—" He stopped and laughed again.

"The stallion has a name?"

"Different to all," Bradwarden remarked. "But ye must be knowing it if ye want to get close to him."

"And how might I learn it?"

"Silly boy," said Bradwarden. "Ye do not learn it, ye just know it."

The centaur walked off then, leaving Elbryan with his thoughts.

The ranger was back at the grove the next day, and the next after that, and every day, until finally, more than a week later, he heard, or rather, felt the music once more, this time from the west.

"Smart," he quietly congratulated when the horse came into view on the edge of the shadows, for the stallion's approach was downwind this time, that it might get a scent of this intruder to the grove without offering its own scent in return.

After a few minutes, the horse came out onto the open field, and again Elbryan's breath was stolen away by the sheer beauty of the thing, by its muscled flanks and wide chest, by the intelligence of its features, those knowing black eyes.

A word came to the ranger then, but he shook his head, not understanding. He took a step forward and the horse ran off, breaking the spell and ending the encounter.

Their third meeting came only a day later, the same way as the previous, the stallion approaching tentatively from the west, eyeing Elbryan and pawing the ground.

That word was in his head again, a word that perfectly described the appearance of the great horse.

"Symphony!" the ranger called out, stepping boldly from the grove. To Elbryan's surprise, to his delight and his horror, the horse reared and neighed loudly, then fell back to all fours and pawed hard at the ground.

"Symphony," Elbryan repeated over and over as he cautiously approached. What other name could so fit such a horse? What other word could describe the beauty and harmony, the working of muscle with muscle, the songlike vibrations, as if all of nature heralded the run of the great stallion.

Before the ranger even realized it, he was within five strides of the great horse.

"Symphony," he said quietly.

The horse nickered and threw back his head.

Elbryan moved closer, his hands out wide to show that he was not a threat. Respectfully, he put his hand on the stallion's neck, stroking firmly and evenly. Slowly, slowly, the horse's ears came up.

Then the great stallion leaped away, thundering back into the shadows, into the brush.

The pair met day after day, each time growing more comfortable. Elbryan soon realized that this horse was meant for him, as surely as if the elves had put him here as companion for the ranger—and that thought, too, did not seem so ridiculous.

"Did they?" he asked his uncle Mather at Oracle one night. "Is Symphony, for I know that to be the stallion's proper title, a gift to me from the elves, from Juraviel, perhaps?"

There came no reply, of course, but hearing his own words, Elbryan discovered one distinct flaw in his reasoning.

"Not a gift, then," he said, "for no such animal could ever be given. But surely the elves have played some role, for this was no chance meeting and the response from the horse was not as would be expected from a creature running fully wild all its life.

"The cairn," Elbryan whispered a moment later, discovering his answer. It seemed so perfectly clear to him then; the magic of the cairn had somehow brought Symphony to him—no, it had brought the two of them together, ranger and stallion. Now more than ever, Elbryan wanted to know who was buried there, what great man—or elf or centaur, perhaps— had been placed so reverently in the ground by the Touel'alfar, with magic strong enough to tend that perfect grove, strong enough to call Symphony and to give the horse such intelligence. For surely it was the magic of the cairn that had done all of this; Elbryan knew that without doubt.

The next day, he rode Symphony for the first time, bareback, clutching tight to the horse's thick mane. The wind rushed past his ears, the landscape flying along beneath, such a thrill of the run, such a smoothness of stride, that Elbryan would have sworn he was flying across a cushion of air.

As soon as he dismounted, back in the meadow by the grove, Symphony turned and ran off, and Elbryan made no move to stop the stallion, for he knew that this was not the normal rider-horse relationship, not a relationship of master to beast but a friendship of mutual respect and trust.

Symphony would come back to him, he knew, would let him ride again, but on the stallion's own terms.

Elbryan gave a salute to that place on the forest's edge where the stallion had disappeared, a motion of respect and understanding that he and Symphony had their own separate lives but were joined now.

❖ 31 ❖

Home Again, Home Again

Over the next couple of weeks, as they marched along the trails, Avelyn showed Jill just how much he had come to trust her, for he began formally tutoring her in the ways of the stones. At first, the monk used the conventional methods, the same lessons that had been given to him in St.-Mere-Abelle. He saw at once, though, that Jill was far beyond an average beginning student, was nearly as strong as he had been when Master Jojonah had played the out-of-body game with him that first time. Avelyn understood the source. Jill was naturally strong, but surely not as strong as he had been. But she was no beginner. That joining by means of the hematite when he had been sorely wounded had given her an understanding of accessing the powers on a level that other monks spent months, even years, trying to attain. As their friendship deepened, their trust becoming so strong, Avelyn again dared to use the hematite to instruct Jill. Not only was her gain exponential, but so was the monk's understanding of this secretive woman—and of her dark past.

"Dundalis." The word fell from Jill's lips like the peal of a church bell, a chime that could be of celebration, of hope and the future promise of eternal life, or one that could signify death. The young woman ran a hand through her hair, which had grown thick to her shoulders again, and looked at Avelyn suspiciously. "You knew," she accused.

Avelyn shrugged, having no practical response.

"Somehow you discovered my history," the woman went on, using excitement, a sense of betrayal, to block away the more urgent feelings that were welling up inside her as she considered that long-lost name, the name of the village that had been her home and apparently the name of a new village, built on the same spot. "In Palmaris," Jill reasoned, "you spoke with Graevis!"

"Pettibwa, actually," Avelyn admitted dryly.

"You dared?"

"I had no choice," Avelyn retorted. "I am your friend."

Jill stuttered incoherently for a moment, trying to sort it all out. Avelyn had led her north of the city, along the Masur Delaval to its delta, then turning inland, heading for the wilderness. It had happened in a round-about manner; Jill feared that she might be wandering into once-familiar territory, but really nothing had sparked recognition within her, not until the pair had ventured into a town called End-o'-the-World and had heard that name "Dundalis" spoken aloud. She wanted to lash out at Avelyn at that moment, but she could not deny his last words. Indeed the monk was her friend, among the best of friends Jill had ever known. She need only look at the gift he was giving to her with the stones to confirm that he loved her.

"You run from ghosts, my friend, my dearest Jill," Avelyn explained. "I see your pain and feel it as though it were my own. It is evident in every stride you take, in every smile you feign—yea, feign, I say, for have you really smiled, Jill? In all of your life?"

Tears welled in the young woman's shining blue eyes and she looked away.

"You have, I say!" Avelyn insisted. "Of course you have! But that was before the disaster, before the ghosts began to walk in your footsteps."

"Why did you bring me here?"

"Because here those ghosts have nothing to hide behind," Avelyn remarked firmly. "Here, in this new village that was once your home, you will confront those ghosts and banish them to the peace they deserve, and the peace you deserve."

It was spoken with such resolve, such strength, that Jill could no longer be angry with him. Brother Avelyn was indeed her friend, she knew, and he wanted only what was best for her, would fight and die for her sake. But still she feared that his decision was folly, based on his underestimating the pain within her. Avelyn could not truly appreciate that grief; nor could Jill, but she feared it lurked right below the surface and, if loosed, would surely consume her.

She nodded mutely, having no answers, having only fears. She walked in the back door of the tavern, then to the private room she and Avelyn had rented. She didn't know what memories the familiar name might conjure, but she wanted to be alone when she faced them.

He had been angered beyond words, had spat and kicked down the door of his room, had even broken the jaw of one woman of the night who had offered her wares. For Palmaris had deceived him as much as his encounter with the merchant Dosey had unnerved him. Brother Justice had not gained on his intended prey—had, in fact, lost ground, wandering aimlessly about the large city. Only chance had brought him in contact with a man named Bildeborough and a rake named Grady Chilichunk, drunkards both.

Brother Justice found their stories, sputtered for the price of a few cheap ales, quite interesting. Especially Grady's, when the man mentioned that he had seen yet another Abellican monk only a month before, talking with his mother, Pettibwa, in Fellowship Way. "How uncommon that two of you should come out together," Grady remarked, not politely. "Normally your kind are so reclusive; and what do you do to entertain yourselves within those abbey walls?"

The implications were clear, considering the man's lewd manner, and Grady and Connor shared a laugh.

Brother Justice used a fantasy of twisting the fool's head off to force a smile. The monk remained polite long enough to learn that this other Abellican monk, whom he suspected to be Brother Avelyn, had gone out to the north to the Wilderlands and the Timberlands, to a place called Weedy Meadow.

There were no merchant caravans going north from Palmaris at that time, with autumn settling thick over the land and the promise of a deep winter, but that hardly deterred the resourceful Brother Justice. He set out alone, moving swiftly, running more than walking, determined to make up the ground and be done with this business.

She remembered that long-ago morning on the tree-covered slope, looking at the sky, at the shining Halo, with its rainbow of colors, its heavenly allure. She remembered the music filling all the air. She had not been alone that morning, Jill now realized, for she had called out her discovery.

"A boy," she whispered to the empty corners of her small room. The name "Elbryan" nipped at the edges of her mind, but with it came an overwhelming sense of grief and loss: that black wall of pain that caused her to shrink away, that had made her put the glowing ember in Connor Bildeborough's face.

Jill took a deep breath and forced all the memories away. She did not sleep at all that night, but still, she was packed for the road early the next morning, leading a groggy—and hung-over—Avelyn by the hand out of the inn, tugging him down the eastern road, toward the village known as Dundalis.

They arrived late that afternoon, the sun settling on the western horizon, the long, slanted shadows rolling out from the buildings of the new village. Jill didn't recognize the place, not at all, and she was surprised by this fact. She had held her breath along the last expanse of road before Dundalis came into sight, expecting to be overwhelmed by sudden memories. It simply didn't happen like that. This was Dundalis, built on the remains of the former Dundalis, but it resembled Weedy Meadow, End-o'-the-World, or any other frontier village as much as it resembled its namesake—at least at first glance.

Avelyn let Jill lead him through the village, down the one main road, heading north. There was an old, broken-down fence on the northern edge of town, formerly a corral, Jill realized, and beyond it was the slope.

The slope.

"I saw the Halo from there," she remarked.

Avelyn smiled, but only briefly, remembering his most vivid encounters with the Halo, so far, far away on board a swift sailing ship on his most important and sacred mission.

"It was real," Jill whispered, more to herself than to Avelyn. She took some satisfaction in that, in knowing that the small fragment of her past life that was clear to her was indeed something real and not imagined. Looking up from the northern edge of Dundalis to the slope that separated the town from the valley of evergreens and caribou moss, to the slope that had been so important to her in her youth, Jill knew beyond any doubt that her memory of sighting the majestic Halo was indeed real. She felt it again, that tingling sensation, that removal of mortal bonds to soar into the infinite universe.

"The boy," she remarked.

"You were with someone?" Avelyn asked, trying to coax her on.

Jill nodded. "Someone dear," she replied.

The moment passed; Jill turned back toward the town. She paused before she got all the way around, though, staring hard at the old corral fence. "I used to play on that fence," she announced. "We would climb up to the top rail and bet on how long we could walk it."

"We?"

"My friends," Jill said, without really thinking about her answer.

Avelyn had hoped that his latest prompt would get her to name some of those lost friends, but he wasn't too disappointed with its failure. The trip north had been a wise thing, the monk believed, for now, only a few minutes after entering Dundalis, Jill had recaptured more of her past than she had known in many years.

"Bunker Crawyer," she said suddenly, her expression turning curious.

"A friend?"

"No," Jill replied, pointing to the old fence. "It was his corral. Bunker Crawyer's corral."

Avelyn smiled widely, but hid it when Jill turned to regard him, her frustration evident. It was coming back, but painfully slowly, for now she was growing quite impatient.

"Let us go and get lodging for the night," the monk offered. "We passed an inn on our way to this place."

Avelyn knew that another memory had come over Jill, this one more powerful, as they approached the front door of the place called the Howling Sheila, a large tavern near the center of Dundalis. The woman looked not at the building, but at the ground beneath it, her expression shifting from curiosity to fear to outright horror.

She turned away, trembling, and Avelyn caught her even as she started to run. If he let her go, the monk suspected that she would run all the way back to Weedy Meadow, all the way back to End-o'-the-World, all the way back to Palmaris!

"You know this place," Avelyn said, holding her fast.

Jill's breath came in gasps; she smelled smoke, thick and black. Though she was outside, she felt as if she were suffocating, closed within a space that was too tight.

"You know!" Avelyn declared forcefully, giving her a shake.

Jill's deep breath resonated like a growl and she turned, pulling free of the monk, staring hard at the tavern, at its stone foundation. "I hid in there," she said, working hard so that her voice would not break apart. "While all the town burned down around me. While all the screams . . ."

Her words faded to a choking sniffle, her straightened shoulders slumped suddenly, and she would have fallen to the ground had not Avelyn held her tight.

There was no other inn in Dundalis, and besides, Avelyn had not come all this way simply to allow Jill to run again from her terrible past. He paid for a single room, for there was but one vacancy, pointedly explaining to the jolly Belster O'Comely that there was nothing romantic or lewd between him and the girl, that they were merely good friends and traveling companions. That was the first time he had ever bothered to offer such an explanation, Avelyn mused as he led Jill up the stairs from the common room to their sleeping quarters. The monk believed that they might remain in this town for some time, and since the community was so small and so closed, he felt the need to protect Jill's reputation. She would face enough trials in Dundalis, Avelyn knew, without hearing the nasty whispers of gossiping townsfolk.

Jill went right to sleep, overcome by the sheer power of the memory. Avelyn remained with her for a long while, fearing that disturbing dreams would visit her.

She slept soundly, perhaps too drained for dreams. Finally Avelyn could not ignore the commotion from the common room below any longer. Most of the village was gathered there, the monk knew, and for all of his love for Jill—and he did indeed love the girl, as a father might love a daughter—the battered monk had needs of his own.

He was downstairs soon enough, drinking and talking amid a huge crowd, for many of the area trappers had come in to lay in provisions in preparation of the coming winter. They were a tough bunch indeed, reclusive and opinionated, men and a few women who lived by their weapons and their cunning, and Avelyn was soon enough arguing with one rake that a town whose history was as dark as that of Dundalis should be better prepared to face the danger.

When the trapper scoffed that the most dangerous thing in the area was the occasional hungry raccoon, Brother Avelyn promptly put his fist in the man's face.

The monk was alone with Belster O'Comely in the common room when he woke up, a slab of steak positioned over one eye. "Ho, ho, what?" he asked the innkeeper. "Best training the folk around here have seen in years!"

Belster gave a laugh. The folk of Dundalis were a hardy bunch, not shying from the occasional fight. In a weird way, Avelyn—who had fought well, though he hardly remembered it—had earned a bit of respect that night, though most of the men and women who had been in the common room thought him mad.

Belster presented him with a piece of paper, a bill. "They decided that you would pay for the last round of drinks," the innkeeper remarked.

"Ho, ho, what!" Avelyn howled, and he was smiling wide as he turned over the pieces of silver.

That jolly smile turned to one of warmth as the monk entered his rented room to find Jill curled up about her pillow, seeming like such a little lost girl. Avelyn knelt by her bed and stroked her thick golden hair, then kissed her on the cheek.

❖ 32 ❖

Darkness Rising

E lkenbrook was a village not unlike Dundalis or Weedy Meadow, except that, being on the western border of Alpinador, it was a colder place, with more hardy evergreens and fewer deciduous trees. Winter in Elkenbrook began in the eighth month of the year, Octenbrough, usually within a few weeks of the autumnal equinox, and lingered on until the month of Toumanay had passed, giving way to a short spring and shorter summer. The folk of Elkenbrook were light skinned and light of eye and hair, as was true of most of their Alpinadoran brethren. And, again as befitted the race, they were undeniably hardy, tall and square shouldered, accustomed to hardship. Even the children of the Alpinadoran frontier—and most of the still-wild kingdom was considered frontier!—could wield a weapon, for goblins and fomorian giants were much more common up north than in the more civilized southern kingdoms. The settlement, in attitude and posture, reflected this, for Elkenbrook, unlike the villages of northern Honce-the-Bear, was walled by an eight-foot fence of spiked logs.

Thus, when the scouts of Elkenbrook reported goblin sign, the hardy folk were not too concerned. Even when giant footsteps were noted mingled in with those of the wretched smaller humanoids, the village leaders only shrugged stoically and began sharpening their long broadswords and heavy axes.

It wasn't until the very moment before the attack, eight hours after the dawn, the pale sun already touching the western horizon, that Elkenbrook truly appreciated its enemy and understood its doom. Normally the goblins would have come in as a mob, a rushing horde, barreling past the trees and scrub, throwing themselves wildly against the pickets and barricades. This time, though, the wretches ringed the village, completely encircling it with ranks ten deep! And the goblin line was bolstered every twenty paces by a fomorian giant wrapped in layers and layers of thick furs.

The folk of Elkenbrook had never known such a huge gathering of goblins, could not conceive of the notion that the hateful, selfish creatures could ever band together in such numbers. Yet here they were, countless spearheads glistening in the last slanted rays of day, countless shields, emblazoned with the standards of many different tribes, standing side by side.

As one, the village folk held their breath, too overwhelmed to speak, to offer any new directives or strategies. Often marauding goblins would send in a messenger before the attack to ask for surrender, to barter for a bribe, warning that battle would otherwise be joined. The usual answer to such a request came in the form of the messenger's head staked before the village wall.

This time, though, more than a few of the village folk were considering their options should an emissary approach.

The goblins held their line for several minutes, then, on command, their ranks parted, doubled in depth as each warrior stepped left or right, a single, brisk movement.

Out from the gaps in the line came the next surprise, a goblin cavalry, the diminutive creatures astride shaggy ponies. Goblin riders were not unknown but were considered a rarity—never had any of the folk of Elkenbrook imagined that so many could be together.

"Four hundred," one man estimated, and that guess put the goblin cavalry alone at twice the number of Elkenbrook's entire population.

Just as stunning to the hardy folk was the manner in which the goblin lines had parted. "Trained army," another man muttered.

"Disciplined," yet another agreed, his expression incredulous—and desperate, for it was no secret among the Alpinadorans that the only thing that had kept the fierce and prolific goblins from overrunning the entire northland was their inability to band together. Goblins fought goblins more often than they fought humans—or any other race, for that matter.

Directly before Elkenbrook's main gate, four creatures emerged from the ranks: a huge fomorian, nearly three times a tall man's height, wrapped in furs and the skin of a white bear and carrying the largest club any of the villagers had ever seen; an incredibly ugly goblin, its face scarred and disfigured, one arm chopped away just below the elbow; and two curious creatures, goblin sized but not goblin shaped, with barrel-like stout bodies and spindly arms and legs that seemed too skinny to support them. Most striking of all about these last two creatures were their berets, shining bright red in the fast-dimming light.

"Bloody Caps," one man offered, and there were nods of agreement, though none of Elkenbrook's folk had ever before actually seen one of the infamous powries.

Again, the enemy line held its formidable posture as the seconds slipped by. Then one of the powries motioned to the giant, and the fomorian, grinning wickedly, lifted the dwarf high into the air. His eyes locked firmly on Elkenbrook, the dwarf removed his beret and waved it about in the air, high above his head.

The folk recognized the dramatic movement as a signal and braced for the charge, determined to take their toll, whatever the final outcome. What they heard, though, was not the thunder of hooves or the howls of charging goblins but the creaking swish of powrie war engines. Great stones, twelve-foot spears, and balls of burning pitch soared through the air, turning the tensed, frozen town into a frenzy of screams and cries, splintering logs, and hissing flames.

Few folk remained on the wall when the second volley roared in, for they were engaged in tending wounded, in battling flames, and shoring up defensive barricades. Most did not see the charge then, a splendid thing indeed; but they heard it, the very ground shaking under their feet.

The third volley, more than two hundred spears hurled by the rushing infantry, flew in just before the cavalry arrived, and thus as the riders poured through the many openings in the walls, they found more dead villagers than remaining defenders. Those folk who had survived the bombardment soon envied their dead companions.

Elkenbrook was flattened before the sun dipped below the horizon. Maiyer Dek of the fomorians, Gothra of the goblins, and Ubba Banrock and Ulg Tik'narn of the powries stood at the center of the massacre, hands and eyes uplifted, crying out to their leader, their god-figure.

Far away, on its obsidian throne in Aida, the dactyl heard them and savored the kill, the first organized attack by its trained minions. The demon could smell the blood and taste the fury as surely as if it had been on the scene with its chieftains.

And this was but the first, the appetizer, the dactyl knew, for its army continued to grow, black masses swarming into the embrace of Aida's dark arms, and Alpinador's lonely villages were merely a testing ground. The real challenge lay in the south, in the most prosperous and populous kingdom, in Honce-the-Bear.

They would be ready as winter began to relinquish its grip on the land, when the snows receded enough to free up the higher passes.

They would be ready.

Jill meandered this way and that on the forested slope north of Dundalis. The first snows had fallen, a light and gentle blanket, and the air was chill, the sky above showing the richest blue hue. That air alone brought to the young woman familiarity, a crispness that she had not known in the city of Palmaris nor in Pireth Tulme, where the dull and damp fog seemed eternal. Jill had known this air, so crisp and so clean, in her youth, in this place; and images of that past life flitted past the edges of her consciousness now, brief glimpses of what had once been.

She knew that her life had been happy, her youth full of freedom and wild games. She knew that she had had many friends, coconspirators in one grand and mischievous scheme after another. Life had been somehow simpler and cleaner, hard work and hard play, good food fairly earned, and laughter that came from the belly, not from any sense of good manners.

Still, the details of that past existence escaped her, as did the actual names, though many of the faces returned. Such was her frustration that bright morning as she walked about the forested slope to the tip of the ridge, to a pair of twin pines overlooking the wide vale of ever-white mossy ground and squat trees, their dark branches dusted by the recent snow.

More images came rushing to her as soon as she sat in the nook of those pines. She pictured a line of hunters weaving in and out of the trees in the mossy vale. She envisioned shoulder poles, and recalled her excitement that the hunt had apparently been successful.

Then the images began to crowd back, of herself running to the group, losing sight of them as she entered the low vale, weaving in and out of the barrier pines and spruce, running with a friend. She remembered rushing through that last obstacle, the feel of the prickly pine branches on her arms, and coming face-to-face with the returning hunters—yes, she could see their faces, and among them was her father!

She remembered! And their poles were laden with the deer they would need, and with . . . something else.

Jill's eyes opened wide, the memory suddenly too vivid, the recollection of that ugly, misshapen dead thing assaulting her, telling her mind to run away.

She held the image fast, though her breath would hardly come to her. She remembered that morning, that bright morning, so much like this one. She had seen the Halo, and then the hunters, including her father, had returned with the winter provisions—and with the goblin.

"The goblin," Jill whispered aloud, the very name assuring her that this past event had been the foretelling of doom for Dundalis, for her home, her family, and her friends.

She fought hard to steady her breathing, to keep her hands from trembling.

"Are you well, my lady?"

She nearly jumped out of her boots, spinning fast to face the questioner: a monk of the Abellican Church, wearing the same style brown robe as Brother Avelyn, its hood pulled back to reveal a shaven head. He was much shorter than Avelyn, but with wide shoulders, obviously strong.

"Are you well?"

He asked the question softly, gently, but Jill sensed a hard edge to his voice and that his concern was merely for show. He studied her intently, she noted, staring long at her hair, at her eyes and lips, as if he was taking a measure of her.

Indeed he was. Brother Justice had heard many descriptions of the woman traveling beside the mad friar, and as he looked upon this woman now, upon her lips, so thick and full, her stunning blue eyes, and that thick mane of golden hair, he knew.

"You should not be up here all alone," he mentioned.

Jill scoffed and brushed her fingers across the hilt of her short sword, not to threaten but merely to display that she was not unarmed. "I served in the army of the King," she assured the monk, "in the Coastpoint Guards." The way the man's eyes narrowed in recognition suddenly caught Jill off guard and made her think that perhaps she had not been wise in mentioning that fact.

"What is your name?" he asked.

"What is your own?" Jill snapped back, growing ever more defensive. It struck her as curious that a brother of the Abellican Church should be this far to the north and should be out alone away from the village. She considered Avelyn's story then, his abandonment of the order. Might there be consequences for such an action? Might the mad friar's increasing reputation have brought unwanted recognition from the strict order?

"My name has never been important," the monk replied evenly, "except to one. To a man once of my order but who deserted the way and who stole from my abbey. Yes," he said, viewing clearly Jill's growing look of apprehension, "to Brother Avelyn Desbris, I am Brother Justice. To your companion, my girl, I am doom incarnate, sent from the church to retrieve what he stole."

Jill was up on her feet, backing steadily, sword drawn.

"You would attack a lawful emissary of the church?" the monk demanded. "One whose title as Brother Justice is fair and true, and who carries the punishment rightfully earned by the outlaw monk you name as your companion?"

"I will defend Avelyn," Jill assured the man. "He is no outlaw."

The monk scoffed, standing easily. Then suddenly, brutally, he leaped ahead, fell low in a spinning crouch, and kicked up hard at Jill's extended sword.

A deft twist by the woman turned the sword out of harm's way, allowing Brother Justice merely a glancing hit that forced Jill back a step.

Brother Justice squared himself, ready to spring again, his respect for the woman growing. She was no novice to battle, this one, with finely honed reflexes.

"It is rumored that you, too, are an outlaw," he teased, edging closer, "a deserter from Pireth Tulme."

Jill didn't flinch, didn't blink.

"Perhaps the Coastpoint Guards will offer a bounty," the monk said, and he came on fiercely, spinning another kick, then turning straight and kicking out three time in rapid succession, his foot snapping hard at Jill from various heights. She dodged each, sidestepping, then came in hard with a thrust of her own.

Her conscience held her, forced her to realize that she was about to kill a human being.

She needn't have worried, for her sword would never have gotten close to striking the deadly monk. Brother Justice let it come in at him, turning subtly at the very last moment, his left arm rolling under, then up and out, against the flat of the blade. He stepped ahead as he parried, launching a heavy right cross.

Jill retreated immediately, but got stung on the ribs, her breath blasted away. She staggered backward, setting her feet as she went, ready to fend off the expected attack.

As her thoughts cleared, she saw that the monk was not pursuing, was not capitalizing on the advantage he had earned. He stood calmly, a dozen feet away, one hand in a pocket of his robe. To Jill's amazement, his eyes closed.

The woman's questions were lost suddenly in a dizzying rush, for though the monk had not physically moved, he came at her again, at her very spirit, and suddenly the woman was fighting, through sheer willpower, to retain control of her body!

Intense pain shot through Jill's body and soul, and through the monk's, as well, she knew—though that thought gave her little comfort. She felt his obscene intrusion as a shadowy wall, pushing into her, pushing her away from her own body. At first, she felt overwhelmed, felt as if she could not possibly resist. But soon she came to understand that in this body—in this, her home battleground—she could indeed withstand the monk's wicked intrusion. The shadowy wall edged back as Jill pushed hard with all her considerable willpower. She envisioned herself as a light source, a blazing sun, rightful owner of this mortal coil, and she fought back.

Then the shadow was gone, and Jill staggered a step and opened her eyes.

He was right in her face, leering at her. She understood then that his mental attack had been but a ruse, a distraction from which he could recover much faster than she.

She knew that, in the split second of consciousness she had remaining. She knew all of it and yet that knowledge brought only despair, for he was too close, too ready, and she could not hope to defend.

Brother Justice knifed his hand into her throat, dropping her back to the snow and dirt. A single clean blow, but a punch pulled, for the monk did not want the woman dead. Her knowledge would be valuable in locating treacherous Avelyn, he presumed, and her presence as his prisoner would certainly aid in bringing the outlaw monk to him.

He did not want the woman dead, not yet, but the monk knew that when his business with Avelyn was finished, this woman, Jill, too, would have to die.

Brother Justice cared not at all.

❖ 33 ❖

The Telling Blow

Elbryan sat far in the back of the Howling Sheila, pushing his chair right into the corner that he might have the security of walls on both his rear flanks. The ranger wasn't expecting trouble—the people of Dundalis might not like him, but they had never been openly hostile—it was simply his training at work, always reminding him to place himself in the most defensible position.

The crowd was loud this night, the tavern packed full, for a light snow was falling outside and the people feared that it might intensify. A blizzard could effectively shut the folk in their homes for a week straight.

The drinks were flowing, the conversation rowdy and mostly about the weather, except in one corner of the bar where a fat, brown-robed man and several townsfolk were arguing about the potential of a goblin raid.

"Happened before," Brother Avelyn declared dryly. "Whole town flattened and only one—or perhaps none—survived." The monk snorted and hoped his slip would not be noticed. Jill's secret was his to keep, and hers—and hers alone—to reveal.

"But only after Dundalis' hunters killed a goblin in the woods," protested a man named Tol Yuganick, a bear of a man, though he did not seem so large next to three-hundred-pound Avelyn. "And that was nearly a decade ago. The goblins would not come back. No reason."

"And not with Dusty on the prowl," another man laughed, turning to glance across the room to the ranger, alone at his table in the back corner. The other three townsfolk joined in the laughter, more than willing to do so at Elbryan's expense.

"And who is this man?" Avelyn wanted to know.

"An attentive ear for your tales of doom," remarked Tol, quaffing his entire mug of beer, so that his lips and chin were covered in foam.

"And was it not Elbryan who took care of that marauding black bear?" asked Belster O'Comely, moving down to that end of the bar, wiping it rather enthusiastically to force two of the men away. "The same bear that sacked your own home, Burgis Gosen!"

The smaller man, Burgis, shied away at the declaration.

"Bah!" Tol snorted, a cloud of anger crossing his brutish features. The huge man had never appreciated Belster's relationship with the strange Nightbird and had said so often and loudly.

Belster held his ground behind the bar. For a long time, the innkeeper had kept his friendship with Elbryan quiet and low-key, knowing that his own reputation might be at stake. Lately, though, Belster had begun changing that. He had recently commissioned a specially designed saddle from the local leatherworker, and had made no secret that it was for Nightbird, payment for some work the ranger had done for him.

"The bear was sick and dying anyway," Tol Yuganick blustered on. "Doubt that Elbryan there, our lord protector, ever saw the damned thing."

Several grunts and nods of agreement followed. Belster, understanding that he would get nowhere with this surly crowd, just shook his head and moved along with his work. He knew that any reminder of the bear incident bothered Tol, for the hunter had sworn to get the bear himself—and would have been paid a fairly substantial reward if he had!

Brother Avelyn, too, ignored Tol Yuganick's cheering gallery. He studied the man in the distant corner, the one Tol had referred to sarcastically as "our lord protector," with new interest. Perhaps this one understood the truth of the world, he mused.

"I should think you would all be grateful," the monk remarked absently, more thinking out loud than any directed comment.

A moment later, Avelyn, still focused on the man across the room, felt a hard poke against his chest.

"We need no protecting!" Tol Yuganick declared, moving his contorted, though still childish, face right before the monk's.

Avelyn looked long and hard at the man, at the cherubic features so twisted by an almost maniacal rage. Then the monk glanced back over his shoulder, to see Belster shaking his head resignedly; the barkeep knew what was coming.

Avelyn stepped back and produced a small flask from under his cloak. "Potion of courage," he whispered to Burgis Gosen, giving a wink, and then he took a deep draw. He finished with a satisfied "Aaah!" then rubbed his free hand briskly over his face while replacing the flask in his thick robes.

Then Avelyn eyed Tol squarely, matching the man's ominous expression with one of pure excitement. Tol growled and came forward, but Avelyn was ready for him.

"Ho, ho, what!" the monk bellowed as Tol moved to poke him in the chest again. With a single sweeping left hook, Avelyn laid the big man low.

Two of Tol's companions jumped the monk immediately, but they were shrugged away and the fight was on.

Behind the bar, Belster shook his head and sighed deeply, wondering how many would be left standing to help him clean up the mess.

Brother Justice smiled wickedly as he approached the Howling Sheila, as he heard the commotion of a fight, confirmation that Brother Avelyn was within. The monk had shed his telltale brown robe in favor of the more normal dress of a villager. He wondered if his old friend Avelyn would recognize him without the Abellican trappings, and that thought prompted the man to pull low the hood of his traveling cloak.

Better for the surprise.

Avelyn was outnumbered five to one—and those odds were only due to the fact that three other men were fighting on his side, or at least, against the mob that was moving against the monk.

Elbryan, on his feet and ready, watched it all curiously, not quite knowing what to make of the wild monk, as Avelyn, fighting wonderfully, kept bellowing out for "preparedness," and calling the brawl a "readiness exercise." The ranger was not unhappy at seeing Tol Yuganick and his friends getting a beating, as long as things didn't get too out of hand.

Elbryan allowed himself a smile when brutish Tol pulled himself up from the floor and charged the monk with a roar, only to have the huge man sidestep at the last possible second, tripping Tol over a trailing leg, then helping him along with a stiff forearm to the back of the flying man's head.

"Ho, ho, what!" Avelyn howled in glee.

So Elbryan stood back from it all, figuring it to be one of those dangers for the villagers to work out on their own. He kept Hawkwing, unstrung, ready at his side, though, already deciding that no deadly revenge would be taken once the monk was put down.

If the monk was put down, Elbryan soon corrected his thinking, for the fat man moved with the grace and precision of a trained warrior. He dodged and punched, took a hit and laughed it away, then buried his latest attacker with a heavy punch or a well-placed knee. He flipped two men at once over his huge shoulders, laughing all the while. A chair shattered against his back, but while Belster O'Comely groaned at the hit, the monk only laughed all the louder, giving his habitual cry, "Ho, ho, what!"

Elbryan leaned on his staff, thinking this quite a show. As soon as his posture eased, he was challenged almost immediately as an enthusiastic villager used the opportunity of a general fight to take a punch at the disliked ranger.

Elbryan casually put Hawkwing out vertically in front of him, picking off the punch with the hard wood. The attacker moaned and clutched his hand, and Elbryan pulled hard down and toward himself with his upper hand so that the staff's lower end shot up and out, right between the groaning man's legs.

Elbryan retracted the weapon and poked it straight out, setting it firmly against the man's chest and pushing him away to fall, clutching hand and groin, to the floor. Then the ranger went back to watching, thinking that the mad monk would soon tire. If the man made but a single mistake, the mob of villagers would overwhelm him.

Then Elbryan would step in.

The ranger smiled once more as Tol Yuganick attacked again, only to be hammered away. Elbryan's grin faded fast, though, his expression turning to one of curiosity, as a newcomer slipped in the tavern doors, moving easily through the battling crowd. When one man turned to punch at him, the newcomer leveled him with a series of three sharp, perfectly placed blows, launched with such rapidity that the man hadn't even moved to respond to the first when the third dropped him.

Even without the fighting display, Elbryan knew that this was no ordinary villager. The man walked with the balanced gait of a warrior and sifted through the crowd with the focus of an assassin—and like an assassin, his face was half-covered, a scarf pulled up high and tightly tied.

It wasn't difficult for the ranger to discern the man's target.

What enemies had this wild monk made? Elbryan wondered, as he, too, worked through the tangled crowd, angling to intercept the newcomer.

The deadly punch was headed for Avelyn's throat, though the fat monk, already engaged with two others, never saw it coming. Elbryan's staff picked it off in midair, deflecting the blow up high. The newcomer, his balance and timing perfect, hardly noticed, but followed with his second strike, his other hand coming across hard.

Elbryan snapped his staff down low, quite hard, stinging the man on the forearm.

Now Brother Justice did turn his sights on Elbryan, spinning to face him with the sudden knowledge that this, too, was no ordinary villager who had come to Avelyn's aid. A man tried to jump on the monk's back then, but Brother Justice elbowed him hard in the chest, then the neck, then the face in rapid succession, sending him tumbling away. None of those nearby who had seen the defense wanted any part of the stranger, and none in the tavern—except perhaps for Tol, who was still on the floor—wanted a fight with Elbryan. That left the two, Elbryan and Brother Justice, standing face-to-face, an island of calm in a raging sea, weirdly isolated from the rest of the thrashing mob.

The monk leaped ahead, feigning a punch and kicking straight out for Elbryan's knee. Elbryan put his staff up high to block the expected punch, but even though he seemed to fall for the ruse, the ranger was not caught. He spun a reverse circuit off his back foot even as Brother Justice kicked, moving his leg out of range.

Brother Justice came ahead hard, trying to beat the turn, to catch his foe on the back before Elbryan could get all the way around.

Elbryan halted in mid-spin, reversed his energy, and sent the staff straight out and back. He turned right under the weapon and launched it again in a straight poke, driving his opponent backward. Then the ranger went into a flurry: poking, swishing the staff side to side, then pulling it straight across, and alternating a series of heavy blows, left hand leading, right hand leading.

Brother Justice picked every attack off, his arms waving in a blur, hardened forearms smacking against the polished wood. He tried to find some hole in the ranger's press, some opening through which he might go on the attack once more. But Elbryan's form was perfect, each strike following the previous too closely for any countering move.

Still, the ranger did not get through the defenses of the skilled monk, and soon enough, didn't even have Brother Justice backing any longer.

The attack flurry played itself out, Elbryan coming to a crouched stance, Hawkwing horizontal in front of him. Now the monk did come on fiercely, chopping at the staff as if he meant to snap it in half.

Elbryan was ready, had anticipated the move perfectly. He brought the staff in close to his chest, Brother Justice's downward swipe falling short, then rolled Hawkwing over the descending arm and snapped it down hard. In the same motion, Elbryan came ahead a step and thrust both his hands, and thus the staff, straight out horizontally, driving it under the monk's chin.

Brother Justice fell away as the wicked strike came in. He rolled his free arm up, taking some of the momentum from the blow, then knifed his hand out straight, scoring a hit of his own.

The two staggered apart, Elbryan gasping for breath, Brother Justice trying to shake away the dizziness. Immediately the mob rolled in around them, for all the Howling Sheila was flying fists and breaking chairs.

"Ho, ho, what!" came the exuberant bellow above the din, and it was obvious to Elbryan that the fat monk was enjoying this row.

Elbryan heard the movement behind him, recognizing it as an attack. He spun, Hawkwing extended, to pick off a lumbering hook, then brought the high tip of his staff down hard diagonally, drawing blood on the face of Tol Yuganick. Seeing the huge man dazed, Elbryan let go his weapon with one hand and snapped his palm into Tol's chin, dropping him heavily to the floor. Then the ranger began his scan again, seeking the newcomer, this skilled fighter, this assassin. The ranger elbowed through the brawl, blocking punches whenever necessary, felling with three shortened blows yet another villager who tried to pounce upon him.

Brother Justice moved in a wide circuit of the dangerous ranger. He took a small pin from the rope belt of his robe and held it in tight, against his sunstone. Sunstones were used as wards, primarily against magic but also against various poisons. The stone's magic could be twisted, though—could be inverted.

Soon the monk spotted the ranger, predictably walking a guard near fighting Avelyn. Slowly Brother Justice closed, using bodies as camouflage.

Elbryan noted the man's approach and was ready when the deadly monk came in. He started for Elbryan but shifted suddenly and darted fast for Avelyn, who was standing with his arms high above his head, spinning Burgis Gosen in circles.

Elbryan had to move fast, had to throw his weight to the side frantically to intercept. He noted the tiny flicker of silver in the newcomer's hand, noted that the man held some weapon.

He caught the newcomer by the wrist, accepted a punch from the man's other hand in exchange for his own strike with Hawkwing. Brother Justice had the better balance at that time, though, and Elbryan took the worst of it. He staggered to one knee, trying to find a defensive posture, expecting to be pummeled.

The attack never came. Elbryan saw a shadow cross before him—Burgis Gosen in Avelyn-launched flight—and when the tangle sorted out, the newcomer was not to be seen.

Only then did Elbryan realize that the wrist of the arm with which he had grabbed the assassin was bleeding, a thin line of red. Not a serious wound, surely, but one that seemed to burn with an anger of its own. The ranger shrugged it away and hustled to the side of the fat monk.

Avelyn was ready for the charge, his hands moving in swift defense. Elbryan had no time for that, though. "I am no enemy!" he declared, but when Avelyn, howling his usual "Ho, ho, what!" punched out anyway, Elbryan skittered down to one knee, hooked his staff behind the fat man's legs, and uprooted him. The monk fell hard to the floor.

Elbryan was over him in an instant, more to protect him from the angry crowd than in any fear of retaliation. "I am no enemy!" he yelled again, and he caught the fat man by the wrist and yanked him to his feet, then rushed him out of the tavern.

The fight continued without them; Avelyn had merely given the villagers and the visiting trappers an excuse for a wild party.

Brother Avelyn was full of questions, full of protests, but the ranger would hear none of them. He ushered the monk away, his own eyes darting from shadow to shadow, expecting the deadly stranger to be about. Finally they got behind the back wall of the northernmost house in the village, just beneath the forested slope.

"Preparedness training," Avelyn explained, and the look on his face showed that he meant to carry on the fight out here, with just this one "trainee."

One good look at Elbryan changed Avelyn's mind, though. Lines of sweat streaked the ranger's face and his breath came in short gasps. Elbryan held up his wrist, staring at the wound, presenting it as explanation to the now-curious monk.

Avelyn caught the arm and held it up in the moonlight. It was not a serious wound, a tiny slice, too small to have been caused by a dagger, even. That alone told the monk that this man was in serious trouble. For a wound so minuscule to cause such pain could only mean . . .

Avelyn fumbled to find his hematite. He suspected poison and understood that the longer it took him to go after the insidious substance, the more deeply he would have to join his spirit with his patient's and the more agony it would cause both of them.

As soon as he started, however, Brother Avelyn found a frightening twist. This man had been poisoned, no doubt about it, but the poison was not based in any *substance*, in any herb or plant or any animal venom. It was magically based; the monk could feel that keenly. As such, it was quite easy for Avelyn to counter the effects with his powerful hematite, and soon Elbryan was breathing steadily again, soon the burning pain was no more.

"No enemy?" Avelyn asked when he saw that Elbryan was fine and steady.

"No enemy," the ranger replied. "But know that you will make enemies, my friend, with such talk and such—"

"Preparedness training," Avelyn finished with a wink.

"Indeed," the ranger said dryly. "And they will surely prepare the ground for your interment if you continue to battle with some of the scoundrels about Dundalis."

Avelyn nodded and shrugged helplessly. "Your wound will heal," he assured the ranger, and then he started away, into the dark night, heading back toward the Howling Sheila, where the fighting was gradually diminishing.

Elbryan watched him go, taking some comfort in the fact that the man swerved for the inn's side door and was apparently going to his room, not back to the common room. The fat monk was in real trouble, the ranger realized, for that man he had fought, that man with the poisoned needle, was much more than an overzealous ruffian. Elbryan didn't know exactly where he might fit in to such a private affair, but he expected that he and the fat monk—and likely the deadly stranger, as well—had not seen the last of one another.

❖ 34 ❖

Justice

Brother Avelyn was not overly concerned when he returned to his room to find that Jill was not about. The woman had mentioned her plans to walk to the valley beyond the north slope, and the monk was confident that Jill could take care of herself. In their weeks together, it seemed to Avelyn that Jill looked after him more than he protected her.

So the monk, exhausted from fighting and then curing the stranger's magical poisoning, his mind heavy with drink, plopped down on his bed and was soon snoring loudly. His dreams were not content, though, not with the prospects of a magic-wielding assassin nearby. Likely, the man was in no way connected to Avelyn, but still the fugitive monk remained concerned.

He awoke late the next morning, to find himself alone in the room. Again, he was not concerned, figuring that Jill had come in after he had fallen asleep, and was long up and about, probably down in the common room having her breakfast.

"Or lunch," the monk remarked aloud with a self-deprecating chuckle. "Ho, ho, what!"

When he got downstairs, though, Avelyn saw no sign of Jill; indeed, Belster O'Comely informed him that he had not seen the woman all night. "Perhaps she found better company to keep," the innkeeper said snidely, leaning on the broom he was using to sweep up the remnants of the previous night's activities.

"Indeed would Jill be better off away from one as mad as I," Avelyn replied, wincing with every word, for his head was pounding. The monk had long ago noted, with complete frustration, that the hematite, powerful as it was, could do little to relieve a hangover.

Avelyn ate a light meal, then shuffled outside and promptly regurgitated it. He felt better after. The day was cool and gray, the sky spitting light snow every so often. "Oh, where are you, girl?" Avelyn asked loudly, more frustrated than afraid. The question would have to wait, though, for the monk made his weary way back to his room and went back to bed.

He didn't wake up again until the next morning, to discover, once more, that Jill was nowhere to be found. Now Avelyn was indeed growing fearful; it wasn't like Jill to disappear for so long without forewarning him or without finding some way to contact him. That, combined with the presence of this magic-wielding assassin, surely concerned the monk. Perhaps the incident in the common room was no accident. Perhaps the monastery was on his trail. Had they caught him at last, up here in the most remote corner of Honce-the-Bear? And had Jill paid dearly for Avelyn's crimes?

He went to speak with Belster again, and, after hearing from the innkeeper that Jill still had not been seen, Avelyn begged the innkeeper to tell him how he might locate the stranger who had shuffled him out of the fight.

"The ranger?" Belster asked incredulously, and from his tone, it was obvious to Avelyn that few inquired as to this man's whereabouts.

"If that is what he calls himself," Avelyn replied.

"He calls himself Elbryan," Belster explained, "to me, at least, though to others he carries another title. And he's one of the rangers, do not doubt." He saw that the term held no meaning for Avelyn. "Some say they're elf trained, others that they're merely misfits who find some comfort in thinking themselves better than anyone else, walking their vigilant patrols, protecting all the land—not that there's any need for protection, of course."

"Of course," Avelyn politely echoed. He found that he was beginning to like this man called Elbryan more and more with every word. "Where might I find this ranger, then?" the monk pressed.

Belster's shrug was surely sincere. "Here and there," he replied. "Walks the woods from here to End-o'-the-World, from what I'm told."

Avelyn's expression soured and he looked down at the bar. "What of the other stranger?" he asked. "The small mysterious man who fought so well?"

Belster's face screwed up. "There are many strangers in Dundalis this season," he answered. "And all of them fight well, else the forest would have taken them by now!"

"The small and agile man," Avelyn tried to clarify, "the one who battled Elbryan so fiercely."

Belster nodded his recognition. "He was in here again last night," the innkeeper explained. "No fighting this time."

Avelyn took a deep breath and cursed himself for sleeping the afternoon and all the night through while a potential clue to Jill's whereabouts was right below him.

"Direct me, then," the monk said at last. "Point me in the most likely direction where I might find Elbryan."

Again Belster shrugged, then he considered the fact that every time he had seen Elbryan enter Dundalis, it was down the north road. He pointed to the north. "That way," he declared, "up and over the slope, through the vale, and turn west."

Avelyn automatically looked that way, though of course, all he could see was the north wall of the Howling Sheila. He nodded as he considered the words, glad for them. Traveling north, he might find Elbryan, it would seem, and he would also be able to search for signs of his dear Jill.

He set off after a quick meal, huffing and puffing up the forested slope, then, after a long pause spent staring down at the stark pines and white ground, he started down the back side of the ridge, into the valley, angling northwest.

There were no signs to be found—Brother Justice had made certain of that—and oblivious Avelyn passed by within thirty feet of the concealed entrance to the cave that now served as Jill's prison.

She had not been treated badly . . . until Brother Justice had returned, the night before last, in a foul mood and visibly bruised, to find that she had nearly escaped her tight bonds. Then the monk had beaten her severely and had subsequently tied her up so tightly that her hands and feet were now completely numb.

When she wouldn't—couldn't—tell him anything about the staff-wielding stranger who had intervened in the inn, the ferocious monk had beaten her again, and now one of her eyes was swollen closed.

Brother Justice had spent all that next day with her, talking mostly to himself about how he might get word to the fat monk that he held her captive. Then the assassin had gone out; Jill knew that his plan still was not fully clear and that he was simply searching for more information. Now, with a gray morning fast turning to midday outside, Brother Justice had not returned.

Jill hoped that Avelyn had killed him; Jill, who could not possibly get out of the bindings and gag that the monk had put on her this time, hoped that Avelyn had first forced the man to disclose her whereabouts!

To Avelyn, who had lived all of his life in the more populous and defined central region of Honce-the-Bear, and who had lately traveled the breadth of the land along well-defined roads, with clear landmarks and signposts, the prospects of finding the ranger had not initially seemed dismal. It wasn't until Avelyn got deep into the wide forest, where the view varied little from direction to direction, where the landmarks were so much more subtle, that he understood the true scope of his hunt. The distance from Youmaneff to St.-Mere-Abelle was over two hundred miles, the distance from Dundalis to End-o'-the-World but two score, yet, given the winding trails and the areas where there were no trails at all, Avelyn soon realized that he would have had a better chance of finding the ranger had he been pursuing the man in the miles from his home to the abbey.

He wandered in circles, taking care to note the direction of the sun as it slipped behind the gray canopy, looking for some sign. Of course Elbryan, trained by the elves, left little or no trail at all, and Avelyn's frustration steadily mounted. He wasn't even sure, after all, that Elbryan had left Dundalis in this direction.

Thus, by midday, the monk was ready to give up the hunt. He would return to Dundalis—and perhaps Jill would be there waiting for him—and then take the more conventional road through Weedy Meadow to End-o'-the-World. There was simply no possibility, he now understood, that he would find the ranger in this forest.

But Avelyn was no ranger, and this was not his domain, and while he had no chance of locating Elbryan, the ranger had little trouble finding him.

The monk was huffing and puffing along a flat trail, arching around the base of a hillock, when he first heard the hooves. He scrambled for some brush, thinking to hide, and then, when that seemed futile, he fumbled about his magical stones, trying to sort out some defensive measures.

A moment later, Avelyn relaxed as a powerful black stallion thundered by.

"No rider," the monk said aloud, mocking his own worries. "Ho, ho, what!"

"But a beautiful horse nonetheless," came a remark from right behind and above him. "Would you not agree?"

Avelyn froze in place, a lump rising in his throat. He turned slowly to see the ranger crouched in the brush along the side of the hillock, just a few feet back. "H-how did you—" the monk stammered. "I mean, you were there all along?"

Elbryan shook his head and smiled.

"But how . . ."

"You were busy listening to the horse," the ranger explained.

Avelyn glanced back the other way to see the stallion standing tall and pawing the ground, looking at him and Elbryan with eyes that seemed too intelligent for such a creature.

"His name is Symphony," Elbryan explained.

"I am not well acquainted with horses," Avelyn admitted, "but he seems a wonder."

Elbryan uttered a soft clicking sound, and Symphony responded by lifting his ears and nickering. The stallion pawed the ground once more, then thundered away back along the trail.

"You will have a hard time catching that one again!" Avelyn blurted, trying to ease his own tension. He looked back at Elbryan. "Ho, ho, what!"

Elbryan didn't blink and the ranger's lack of interest stole the bubbly grin from Avelyn's face.

"Well, yes," the monk began uncomfortably. "Why am I here, then, you would like to know. Of course, of course."

Elbryan squatted perfectly still, arms across his bent legs, fingers locked together, his gaze fixed upon the man.

"Well . . . to find you, yes, yes," Avelyn finally explained, finding his wits against that uncompromising stare. "Of course, yes, I came into the forest looking for the one they call the ranger."

Elbryan gave a slight nod, prompting Avelyn to continue.

"Well, it is about the fight, of course," he said. "About the man, actually, the one who tried for me but poisoned you."

Elbryan nodded; this visit wasn't totally unexpected, since the stealthy fighter from the Howling Sheila was still in the region, as was this monk whom Elbryan believed the assassin's target. Elbryan suspected that the mad friar would need help, and suspected, too, that he would find little among the folk of Dundalis.

"He attacked you again?" the ranger asked.

"No—no," Avelyn stammered. "Well, yes, actually, or he might have. I cannot be sure."

Elbryan sighed wearily.

"It is my companion, of course," the nervous monk went on. "Beautiful young woman, and a fighter, too. But she is gone, nowhere to be found, and I am afraid—"

"You should be afraid," Elbryan replied. "That was no ordinary brawler in the common room the other night."

"The magical poison," Avelyn reasoned.

"The way he moved," Elbryan corrected. "He was a warrior, a true warrior, long trained in the art of battle."

Avelyn nodded enthusiastically, but the ranger's words only heightened his fear that this was indeed no coincidental attack, that the fighting monks of the Abellican Church were after him.

"You must tell me of this man," Elbryan said, "everything you know."

"I do not *know* anything," Avelyn replied in exasperation.

"Then tell me everything that you suspect," the ranger demanded. "If he has your friend, then you need my help—help I willingly give, but only if you remain forthright with me."

Avelyn nodded again, glad for the words. Elbryan rose and moved down to the trail, Avelyn following close behind.

"I do not even know your name," the monk remarked, though he remembered the name that Belster had given to this man.

"I am El—" the ranger began reflexively, but he caught himself and looked hard at the monk, the first man who had actively sought out his help since he had left Andur'Blough Inninness, the first man who would admit that he needed the ranger's assistance. "I am Nightbird," Elbryan said evenly.

Avelyn cocked an eyebrow at that curious title, not the response he had expected. Whatever the man's reasons for offering a different title were not important, Avelyn decided, and so he accepted the name without further question. The pair walked back toward Dundalis then, Avelyn telling Elbryan his suspicions about the pursuit from the church. Of course, the conversation grew uncomfortable for Avelyn when the ranger asked why St.-Mere-Abelle might be after the monk, and Avelyn had not the time nor the inclination to explain all the events that had led to his fateful decision. How does one justify murder and theft, after all? Elbryan didn't press the point, however; at that time, all that truly seemed relevant was that Avelyn's companion was missing, possibly kidnapped by a man the ranger knew to be dangerous.

And Avelyn's description of his companion, added to the fact that the monk hinted that they had come to Dundalis for her benefit, gave the ranger much to think about.

The hunt began soon after, Elbryan searching hard to find some trail leading out of Dundalis, while Avelyn inquired of Belster and some other patrons in the Howling Sheila whether the stranger had returned to the inn today.

Their answers came near dusk, when Avelyn returned to his room to find a note pinned to his bedding. It was short and to the point, confirming the monk's worst fears. If Avelyn wanted to save his companion, he was to travel to the slope overlooking the pine valley, alone, and wait at an appointed spot.

He showed the note to Elbryan down in the Howling Sheila's common room, the pair ignoring the many derisive remarks aimed at them by the early customers there.

"Go, then," the ranger bade the monk.

"And you will be there?"

Elbryan nodded.

"But it says that I have to go alone," the monk protested.

"To our enemy, you will seem alone," Elbryan assured him, and, after considering this man beside him, after recalling the fact that this one called Nightbird had moved to within five feet of him without his ever knowing it, Avelyn nodded his agreement, took back the note, and started out of town.

All the way, the monk fumbled with his pack of gemstones, then, on sudden intuition, he stored all but three—graphite, hematite, and protective malachite—in the nook of a tree. If his suspicions were correct, this man had come for him, but even more for the stones. If Avelyn carried them with him, and the dangerous warrior managed to wrest them away, then the monk would have no bargaining power with which to save himself and even more important, to save his dear Jill.

At the appointed place, a bare spot on the side of an otherwise full-branched pine tree some twenty feet below the ridge, Avelyn did not have to wait for long.

"I see that you decided to follow my instructions, Brother Avelyn," came an all-too-familiar voice. "Very good."

Quintall! It was Quintall, Avelyn knew at once, and the monk felt as if the very ground were about to rush up and swallow him—and he almost hoped that it would. The monastery, the Order, was after him, and there would be no corner of the world far enough away, no shadows dark enough to hide him.

"I had little faith that a thief and murderer would be so honorable as to come to the aid of a friend," the voice went on.

Avelyn glanced all about nervously, wondering where Nightbird might be, wondering if the ranger was close enough to hear those words, and if he was, how he might now feel about this man he had chosen to help.

"I have her," the voice teased. "Come to me."

The reminder of Jill's predicament bolstered the monk's failing courage. Perhaps his Abellican brothers would get him, Avelyn decided, but they would not harm Jill. Slipping the graphite all about the fingers of one anxious hand, the monk followed the direction of the voice, soon discerning the dark rim of a cave opening and the shadowy form of a man inside. He went in as the form retreated, to find a fairly substantial cave, this one chamber—and it seemed plausible to Avelyn that the place had more than one chamber—larger than his room at the Howling Sheila.

Quintall stood at the back of the dimly lit cave, leaning easily against the wall, flicking flint against steel until a light caught on the torch he had propped there.

When the light flickered to life, when it fully illuminated the face of the man Avelyn had known all those years, the man who had traveled to Pimaninicuit beside Avelyn and knew the truth of the stones, Avelyn was nearly overcome with grief. All that he had lost—his home, his companions, and most important, his faith—assaulted Avelyn; all the memories of the good times at St.-Mere-Abelle, his instruction with Master Jojonah, the revelations about the sacred stones, the studying of the charts, the revealed mysteries of the magic, came rushing back to him.

And then they were buried beneath the subsequent memories: the death of Thagraine, of the boy who had foolishly gone onto Pimaninicuit, of all the crew of the *Windrunner*, of Dansally, of Siherton.

"Quintall," Avelyn muttered.

"No more," the other monk replied.

"Why have you come?" Avelyn asked, hoping against reason that this man, too, had deserted the Order and was as much a renegade as he.

Quintall's cackle rocked him. "I am Brother Justice," the man replied harshly, "sent to retrieve what was stolen." Quintall snorted. "I hardly recognized you, fat Avelyn. You have lost all, so it seems, and have more than doubled your size. Always you took your physical training lightly!"

Avelyn steeled himself against the insults. It was true, he had taken on more than a few bad habits, drinking too much and eating too much, and the only exercise or martial training he now performed was in the fights he inspired.

"Did you not believe that we would discover your treachery?" Brother Justice went on. "Did you think that you could murder a master of St.-Mere-Abelle and steal such a treasure, and then walk free for the rest of your days?"

"There is more—"

"There is no more!" Quintall shouted. "You fell, my former brother. All that remains for you is the pit of hell. I shall have the stones!"

"And my life," Avelyn reasoned, making no move.

"And your life," cold Brother Justice confirmed. "You forfeited that when Master Siherton went over the wall."

"I forfeited that when I refused to accept the perversion of the Order!" Avelyn shot back, drawing some courage with words of conviction. "As Brother Pellimar—"

"Silence!" Brother Justice ordered. "Your life is forfeit, I assure you, and no explanation is worth the time to utter. I will have the stones, as well, but if you hand them to me without battle and accept the fate you deserve, then I will let the woman go free. On my word."

Avelyn snorted at that. "Is your word as solid a thing as the word of the masters you serve?" he asked. "Is your gold but an illusion, meant to coax a ship into waters where it might be destroyed?"

Quintall's expression showed that he neither understood nor cared about what Avelyn was saying, showed Avelyn beyond any doubts that the man was single-minded and would not be swayed. That left the fat monk two choices: to surrender the stones and his life and hope that Quintall was speaking truthfully, or to fight.

He didn't trust the man, not at all. Quintall would kill him after he got the stones, without doubt; then he would kill Jill, that there would be no witnesses. Avelyn believed that in his heart. He took his hand, and the graphite, out of his pocket, pointing it in Quintall's direction.

"You would forfeit the life of a friend?" Brother Justice asked and then he laughed again.

"I would spare your own life," Avelyn replied, "in exchange for the woman."

The man's laughter continued, and it gave Avelyn pause. Quintall above all others understood Avelyn's proficiency with the magic stones. Quintall should have understood that Avelyn could loose a bolt of lightning with that piece of graphite that would fry the man where he stood. And yet

Quintall, this man who called himself Brother Justice, this extension of St.-Mere-Abelle's vicious order, was not afraid.

Avelyn turned his thoughts away from the man, to the chamber Quintall had chosen for this encounter. He felt the emanations, the subtle pulse of magic, and when he looked then into the stone he held, when he realized that the powers of the graphite seemed far, far away, he understood.

"Sunstone," Quintall confirmed, seeing the expression. "There will be little magic used in this cave, foolish Brother Avelyn."

Avelyn chewed his lip, looking for an out. Back in St.-Mere-Abelle, he had seen Master Siherton create a magical dead zone while he and several others had tried to discern the powers of the giant amethyst crystal. Only the most powerful magics could function within such an area, and even then, their powers were greatly diminished.

Avelyn might be able to effect a lightning stroke within this chamber, but he doubted that it would do much more than anger Quintall even more.

Quintall held out his hand. "The stones," he said calmly, "for the woman's life."

"The woman is no part of this," Elbryan declared, slipping into the cave to stand beside Avelyn. "I know not of Brother Avelyn's crimes, but you have offered no charge against the woman."

Quintall's expression grew suddenly grave at the sight of the imposing ranger. "Treachery again!" he growled at Avelyn. "I should have expected as much from the likes of Avelyn Desbris."

"No treachery," Elbryan insisted, "but justice."

"What do you know of it?" Brother Justice insisted. "What do you know of this stranger, this mad friar, who has come into your midst, begging aid? Did he tell you that he was a murderer?"

"And is the woman a murderer?" Elbryan asked calmly.

"No," Avelyn answered when the other monk hesitated.

"A thief?" asked Elbryan.

"No!" Avelyn said determinedly. "She has committed no crimes. As for my own, I will speak of them, openly and honestly; and when all the account is told, let someone other than a monk of St.-Mere-Abelle serve as judge."

Brother Justice narrowed his eyes and glared at the monk. Of course, he had no intention of allowing any court. He was judge, jury, and executioner, assigned by the Father Abbot. "You were a fool to follow Avelyn to this place," he said to Elbryan, "for now your life is forfeit, as is Avelyn's, as is the woman's."

"More justice?" Elbryan started to ask, but his question was lost as Brother Justice spun about, pulling aside some hanging vines that blocked the entrance to another chamber. A flick of the monk's wrist sent a silver item flying and from within the deeper chamber came a gurgled groan.

"Go to her!" Elbryan cried to Avelyn, and the ranger leaped forward to meet the monk, Hawkwing spinning to a ready position.

"Not by surprise this time," Brother Justice sneered, setting himself in a crouch. He tried to keep near the door, to prevent Avelyn from getting to the woman, but Elbryan's attack was too fierce, too straightforward. The ranger came rushing in, accepting a punishing blow to the chest but managing to duck his shoulder low against the monk and drive the man back a step. Brother Justice dug in, locking himself in place—until Avelyn came roaring in at Elbryan's back, the monk's three-hundred-pound frame blasting the two combatants away.

Elbryan took three quick punches—two to the chest and then one to the face that nearly sent him down—before he managed to break the clench and get away from the dangerous monk.

Facing the man squarely, the ranger wasn't quite sure what to make of him. Brother Justice turned sidelong and lifted his leading foot, drawing it slowly up his balanced leg, arms lifting as well, as certain snakes might rise before the strike.

It was a dagger, small but nasty, and thrown perfectly to hit the gagged and bound woman right in the throat, just under her jawbone. Her main artery severed, blood was pumping wildly from the wound, already forming a puddle around her slumped form.

"Jill, Jill! Oh, my Jill!" Avelyn wailed, rushing to her. He pulled the dagger free, his hands going to the wound, trying futilely to stem the flow. She had little time left, he knew. Her skin felt cold.

Avelyn pulled out his hematite, then remembered the antimagic shield that Quintall had constructed. He thought to carry Jill from this place, but realized immediately that she would be dead before he ever got her outside.

He clutched his hematite in both hands, putting them to the wound, putting his lips against his hands, praying with all his will, with all his heart. If there was a God above, if these stones were indeed sacred, then the hematite must work!

The monk's fighting prowess was indeed remarkable, his movements quick and fluid, his frame always in perfect balance. He was too fast for most humans, dizzying them with winding, sweeping feints before the lightning strike killed them.

But Quintall, for all his training, was no faster than Tuntun or Belli'mar Juraviel, or any of the elves that had trained Elbryan, and when he snapped a strike from that snakelike pose, thinking to tear out Elbryan's throat and move on to finish his business with Avelyn, the monk's expression showed he was surprised to find his extended fingers hit only air, while Elbryan's staff gave him a wicked smack on the elbow. With incredible flexibility, both physical and mental, the monk adjusted, rolling his pained arm down across the staff to open a hole in Elbryan's defenses, then snapping off a quick blow with his other hand, followed by a kick that caught the ranger inside the knee and nearly buckled his leg. Elbryan countered by letting go of his staff with his top hand, rolling it under the blocking arm, then grabbing it and sweeping low for the monk's supporting leg.

Brother Justice hopped over the swing, but was forced back.

The monk circled, a confident expression mounting.

Two running steps launched Brother Justice into a double kick. Elbryan jammed one end of Hawkwing into the dirt and swept the staff powerfully across in front of him, left to right, deflecting the blow. He stepped ahead with his left foot then, continuing to turn as Brother Justice landed on his feet and pivoted the other way. Elbryan dragged Hawkwing up and around, slapping a backhand with the staff that connected squarely on the monk's lower back at the same time Brother Justice let fly an elbow to the back of Elbryan's head.

The ranger reacted well, diving forward as the elbow connected, leaping and tumbling over his staff as if it were a tree branch. He came back to his feet and turned as Brother Justice spun around, the two men circling once more.

"I give you one more chance to leave," the monk offered, drawing a smile from his adversary. That smug look by the ranger spurred the proud Quintall into a charge. He skidded to a stop right before Elbryan, throwing a vicious overhead chop.

Up came Hawkwing in a solid horizontal block. Anticipating the following moves, Elbryan snapped his left hand down, taking the power from a right cross, then stepped in closer, putting his right leg inside the monk's left, defeating an attempted kick. Brother Justice wriggled his left arm about the staff, reaching for Elbryan's face, but the ranger pulled the staff and the arm out wide, moving even closer to the monk, then drove his forehead hard into the monk's face.

Brother Justice grabbed hard onto the staff with both hands, as much to support himself as to prevent any attacks. Elbryan let go with his left hand at that same moment and snapped off a series of short, heavy jabs into Brother Justice's face.

The monk was dazed; Elbryan seized the moment. He grabbed the staff again, hard, and tugged it in close, pushed it away to the end of his reach, then pulled it in again. Brother Justice should have let go, but he was fighting to clear his thoughts. Following the tug, he came rushing in close to Elbryan, and his face met the ranger's forehead again.

Still dazed, still hanging on, the monk felt the change in his adversary's angle as Elbryan fell back to the floor, pulling hard, taking the monk right over him. Both his feet planted squarely in Brother Justice's belly, the ranger heaved him right over, sent him flying, to land heavily at the base of the chamber's hard wall.

Pure rage drove the monk on, forced the pain away. He rolled and came up fast—but not fast enough. His defenses were not in place when Elbryan grabbed his staff down low with both hands and swept it across mightily, smashing in the side of Brother Justice's face. The monk went with the blow, turning to a dead run that launched him out the cave's outer opening, into the daylight.

Elbryan was quick to follow, but by the time he got out, the monk was many strides ahead, in a full run. Hardly thinking of the motion, knowing only that he could not lose this advantage against so deadly an adversary, Elbryan popped the feathered tip onto his weapon and bent it low, quickly setting the bowstring. He ran ahead a dozen strides, seeking an angle to best view the top of the ridge, where the monk was fleeing.

Brother Justice came into view for only a split second, darting between two trees. Elbryan's arrow caught him in the calf, right below the knee, and with a howl of pain the monk tumbled sidelong, gaining momentum as he rolled along the steep slope.

Elbryan scrambled to get to the spot, saw the monk land heavily atop one rocky outcropping and then tumble right over it, a fifteen-foot plummet to hard stone.

Elbryan groaned sympathetically, running to get in view of the man once more. He spotted the monk from a distance, lying among the boulders, one leg bent back up under him, one arm across his chest, the other out straight, then turned back under, obviously broken. The man, gasping for breath, reached inside the folds of his clothing and produced something that Elbryan could not discern from this distance.

The ranger halted as the monk suddenly glowed, limned in blackish flames. Elbryan's mouth dropped open as the monk's features twisted, twisted, as his face blurred and seemed to double, and as that second face stretched grotesquely and pulled free of the man's corporeal form, his visible spirit ripping out of that flesh and blood coil, down to the object he clutched in his hand.

There came a bright flash and then the monk lay still, low flames licking his lifeless body.

"Nightbird!" came a cry from the cave, and Elbryan, thoroughly shaken, scampered back within.

He was careening, flying fast above the forest, across the lakes, over the lands where the snow had already settled deep—too fast for his senses, too fast for the man to understand. The pain was gone, that much he knew. Then he came upon the mountains, whipping through passes, over peaks, to a plateau he had seen before above a vast encampment between the black arms of a smoking mountain. Then came the dizzying ride through tight tunnels, cutting left, right, down and down again to a stone wall creased by a single crack, through that crack, the stone rushing past him so close that his mind screamed out in terror.

Then he was in the room between the columns before the obsidian throne.

Quintall stood on semitransparent legs, caught halfway between the mortal and spirit worlds. He stood on the legs of a wraith facing the dactyl demon.

It was the end, the end of hope, of any pretense of godliness. It was the truth, the dark-shining truth, the reality of what he had become, the only honest end of the road upon which his Abellican masters had set him. It was the dactyl demon, Bestesbulzibar—he knew its name!—in all its horrible beauty, in all its magnificence.

Quintall, Brother Justice, fell to his wraith knees before the dactyl, bowed his head, and spoke.

"Master."

Elbryan took the torch with him as he pushed aside the vines and entered the inner chamber. Avelyn squatted on the floor, cradling the woman. Her wound was closed and she was very much alive, though thoroughly exhausted, as was Avelyn, who had gone into the hematite, who had, by sheer willpower and faith, fought past the sunstone barrier, fought his way into the healing magic.

The monk asked about Quintall, but Elbryan didn't hear him. Avelyn shifted on the floor and tried to rise, nearly toppling for the effort, but Elbryan didn't notice. All that the ranger saw was the woman, all that he heard was her breathing. His eyes roamed over her—the thick mop of blond hair, the blue eyes, shining in the dim light, despite her weary condition, and her lips, those thick and wonderful lips, those so soft lips.

He could hardly breathe, could hardly keep the strength to stand, all his thoughts, all his energy, tied up in a single word, a name he had not spoken for so very long.

"Pony."

CHAPTER

❖ 35 ❖

Escape?

P *ony.*
The name hit the young woman like a thunderbolt, spoken with
such familiar inflection. She watched, mesmerized, as the strong
young man eased toward her, his green eyes growing misty.

"Pony," Elbryan said again, and he was stating the name, not asking.
"My Pony, I thought . . ."

He slipped down to his knees before her, closed his eyes, and tried hard
to steady his breathing. When, after a long while, he opened his eyes and
looked again on this image from his past, he found that her expression was
more confusion than anything else.

"Do you not remember me?" Elbryan asked, and the question alone, the
need to ask it, seemed to pain him greatly.

The woman didn't know how to respond. She did remember the man—
he was there, prodding somewhere in the back of her mind, screaming
at her to let him out. The way he said the name, her name—her nickname,
she suddenly knew, for her name was not Pony, nor Jill, but Jilseponie!—
was so familiar; surely she had heard this man call her *Pony* before in just
that way.

"Give her time, I beg, Elbryan," Brother Avelyn remarked.

That was it. Elbryan. The name hit Pony as hard as Brother Justice
ever could, jarred her, sent her thoughts spinning back across the span of
years.

"When you ran from me on the slope, running into burning Dundalis, I
thought you lost to me forever," the ranger went on, spurred by the sudden
sparkle of recognition that came to the woman's blue eyes. "My Pony. How
I searched! I found your mother and father, my own, our friends. Carley
dan Aubrey died in my own arms. And I would have died, too, trapped by a
fomorian giant and a band of goblins, had it not been for—" He stopped,
realizing that he was going too fast for the poor young woman, realizing
that he had overwhelmed her.

329

But it was indeed his Pony; Elbryan knew that beyond any doubt. He moved closer to her then, put his face barely inches from hers.

"Elbryan," she said softly, lifting a weary arm to stroke the ranger's face. All those scattered images in her head spun and dropped together, like a vast puzzle, all the pieces magically falling together. She *remembered* him as if she had never forgotten him, remembered their talks and walks, remembered their friendship, and more than that. In her mind, she saw him moving closer to her, to kiss her.

But then he was Connor, poor Connor, and Pony was suffocating, reaching for the hearth, grabbing a glowing ember.

When she shook the image away, she found that Elbryan had backed away from her and was looking to Brother Avelyn for answers.

"We have much to discuss," the monk said.

Elbryan nodded and looked back at her, as beautiful now—more beautiful!—than he remembered her.

"Brother Quintall?" Avelyn asked.

Elbryan looked at him curiously.

"Brother Justice?" Avelyn clarified. "The hunter from my own Order, sent to kill me and to kill my friends, do not doubt."

"He is dead," Elbryan replied evenly.

"Take me to him."

Elbryan nodded to Avelyn. "Why did he come after you?" the ranger asked, the question that Avelyn knew he would be forced to answer truthfully. He looked from Elbryan to Pony, then back to the ranger.

"Not all of his claims were untrue, I fear," the monk admitted. "I will explain all when we are far from this place, and then I will accept your judgment," Avelyn offered, squaring his shoulders. "Judgment from both of you. You decide if Brother Quintall's mission was truly one that deserved the name of Justice, if Brother Avelyn, the mad friar, is truly an outlaw."

"I am no judge," the ranger remarked.

"Then I am a doomed thing," Avelyn replied. "For the only ones who presume to judge me have made their decision, and it is based on greed and fear and in no way on justice."

Elbryan stared long and hard at Avelyn. Finally he nodded, and he helped both Avelyn and Pony to their feet, then led them out of the cave and to the spot where Brother Justice had fallen.

The monk's body was hardly recognizable, a charred, smoldering thing.

"How did this happen?" Elbryan asked, inspecting the corpse but finding no indication of what had caused it to burst into flame.

"Here is your answer," Avelyn explained, indicating the side of the corpse, where one hand was nearly burned to ashes. On the ground beside the body lay the ruined broach, its hematite core melted and misshapen, an elongated black egg. Scattered around it were the small quartz crystals, blackened, some stuck in the remains of the golden setting.

Avelyn scrutinized the broach carefully. "Its power is no more," he announced after a few moments. "Somehow the magic of the hematite and the crystals erupted when Quintall fell." Avelyn paused and considered his own words. Had there been some contingency placed on the magic? he wondered. Avelyn could feel the magical reverberations in the area and knew that some strong energy had been released. Perhaps the stones served as a warning device to the masters back in St.-Mere-Abelle, a signal that Quintall was dead, that Quintall had failed. Or was the magic even stronger than that? Given the powers of hematite, might this have been some transport for Quintall's soul?

Avelyn, who had spirit-walked, who had once possessed the body of another, shuddered at the possibilities.

Elbryan continued to prod at the corpse, searching for clues. What he found instead were two stones intact: a sunstone—which did not surprise Avelyn in the least—and a carbuncle.

"That is how he trailed me across the country," Avelyn remarked, noting the carbuncle. "It is a stone used to detect magic."

"And you have magic about you," Elbryan reasoned.

"A great cache," Avelyn admitted. "Perhaps the greatest individual cache in all the world."

"Stolen from St.-Mere-Abelle," said the ranger.

"Taken from those who did not deserve it, who abused it and brought only misery from the God-given stones," Avelyn said firmly. "Find us a camp, my friend. I will tell you my tale, in all detail, in all truth. You decide which of us, myself or Quintall, deserves the title he carried."

When they arrived at Elbryan's camp, when the ranger and Pony settled beside a fire, Avelyn did as promised. He told his tale, all of it, from the journey to Pimaninicuit to the sinking of the *Windrunner* and the murder of Dansally, to his escape from St.-Mere-Abelle and the death of Master Siherton. It was the first time Avelyn had told his story, though he had hinted at many parts of it to Jill over the course of their travels. It was the first time the monk was able to purge his soul openly, to admit his crimes, if they were crimes. When he finished, he seemed a miserable wretch indeed; his huge form had wilted upon the hard ground, his eyes teary.

Pony went to him, loving him all the more, feeling a true kinship with the man, feeling a great deal of pity, as well. She was sorry that Avelyn had been forced to act as thief and killer, sorry that this gentle man—and despite the barroom brawls, Pony knew Avelyn to be a gentle man—had been put into such an uncompromising position.

Both of them looked at Elbryan after some time, fearing the ranger's judgment. They saw only sympathy on his handsome face.

"I do not envy that which you were forced to do," the ranger said firmly. "Nor do I consider your actions criminal. You acted in self-defense, always justifiable. You stole the stones because you rightly judged that they were being abused."

Avelyn nodded, so glad to hear those words. "Then I must be on my way," he announced unexpectedly. "Jill—Pony, has found her way home, it would seem." He put a hand to the woman's face, and his own brightened suddenly. "Ho, ho, what!

"She needs me no more," Avelyn finished.

"But does Brother Avelyn need her?" Elbryan asked.

The monk shrugged. "St.-Mere-Abelle will not give up the search, thus I must keep on the move. I would not bring danger to my friends, now that I know of it."

Elbryan looked hard into Pony's eyes, then the both of them burst into a fit of laughter, as if the whole notion was perfectly ridiculous.

"You stay," Elbryan remarked, demanded. "Pony is home, 'tis true, and her home is Avelyn's, unless I miss my guess."

"Her home is Avelyn's," she said firmly.

A light snow had begun to fall all across the forest, but it seemed to shy from the ranger's camp, from the heat of the ranger's fire, from the warmth of Brother Avelyn's newfound home.

PART FOUR

▼

THE

RANGER

How I desire to go to her, to be with her, that we might know again the peace that was in our lives before that terrible day. How I want to hold Pony, to kiss her, to tell her all my feelings, all my secrets, my pain, my hopes. To see Pony now is to see what was and to wonder what might have been had the goblins not come to Dundalis. To see Pony now is to ponder what other road might have been before me— might I have farmed the land and hunted, as Olwan my father did? Would Pony and I be wed, perhaps with children?

How would the world look to Elbryan had he not spent those years in Andur'Blough Inninness?

But that is the problem, Uncle Mather. I cannot know, can only guess, and I fear that any guess I make will be tainted by the observations of my current life. Perhaps my life would have been better if God had presented me a different path, one more like Olwan's. I wish all those folk of Dundalis—my mother and father, Pony's parents, and all the others—had been spared their grim fate. I wish with all my heart that the goblins had not come to Dundalis!

But where would that leave me? At peace, I suppose, and probably with Pony, and that is a fate about which no man could complain.

Yet I refuse to dismiss or diminish my years with the Touel'alfar; those elven friends helped to shape the man Elbryan. Those elven friends created Nightbird, this ranger, hopefully for the betterment of the world and surely for the betterment of me. Looking through the perspective of their shining eyes, I have gained a newer and brighter appreciation of the world about me, one I would never have known had the goblins not come to Dundalis, had the elves not rescued me and taken me to their secret valley. Through that tragedy, I, Elbryan, have come to know and love life all the more. Through that tragedy,

I have become the man I am, the man who can see the world through the vision of an elf as well as the vision of a human.

That is my guilt, Uncle Mather, for why should I have been chosen, and not another of Dundalis—not Olwan or Shane McMichael, not Pony or Carley dan Aubrey. That is my guilt, and seeing Pony alive, so beautiful, so wonderful, only heightens my pain, reminds me of those who died, tempts me to ask what might have been, and makes me wonder if I would indeed prefer that lost course.

It is only worse for poor Pony. The sight of me, of Dundalis, has brought back to her memories long buried. I have seen her little in the few days since Brother Avelyn and I rescued her from Quintall. She is avoiding me, I know, and I do not begrudge her that. She needs the time; she has seen again so much of her lost past in so short a time.

Everyone in Dundalis died except the two of us. And we have continued from that moment of tragedy, have grown strong and true, have found lives pleasing, and, now that we are together again, the potential seems all the greater. Yet, in our pleasures . . .

That is the guilt, Uncle Mather, our guilt. I cannot rescue Pony from the pain of her memories, as she cannot rescue me from mine. I only hope that she comes to accept our fate and that she desires to forge ahead in the best manner that we may.

I knew it from the moment I saw her in that cave. I love her, Uncle Mather, as I loved her that fateful day on the ridge above our home. I love her, and all the world will be sweeter indeed if I may hold her in my arms and feel her soft breath against my neck.

—ELBRYAN WYNDON

❖ 36 ❖

Confrontation

"They think me madder still!" Brother Avelyn roared happily. "Ho, ho, what!"

Elbryan looked at Bradwarden, and the centaur only shrugged, not about to disagree with the volatile friar's estimation of himself.

"Cavorting with the likes of you, after all," Avelyn went on. "And, oh, would they talk if they knew that I was dining with a centaur!"

"They would talk respectfully if they knew Bradwarden as I know him," Elbryan put in, "else, I fear the centaur would trample them."

Bradwarden swallowed a huge chunk of mutton and gave a great belch.

"Ho, ho, what!" Avelyn howled, charmed by it all. The monk was feeling better now, feeling more at home than he had since his earliest days in St.-Mere-Abelle, since that innocent time before he had learned the truth of the Abellican Order. In Elbryan, Avelyn had found a man he could honestly respect, a stoic individual, wary of the very real dangers of the world, ready to fight against evil and injustice. He had told his tale in full to the ranger, and the ranger had judged him not according to the penned laws but by the true ideal of justice.

Now Avelyn spent his nights in Dundalis or in Weedy Meadow or End-o'-the-World, and his days in the forest with Elbryan and Pony—and sometimes with the ranger's more unusual friends, such as Bradwarden and that magnificent horse Symphony. There was something right about it all to Avelyn, some sense of godliness here that he had not felt in many years. His only lament was that Pony seemed truly shaken by her return to this area. She spent little time with any of them, preferring to walk alone, mostly near Dundalis. She was confronting her past, the monk knew, and he was glad of that, though he wished he could be of more help to the young woman.

Bradwarden took up his pipes then, following the meal with a mournful, soulful tune that conjured in Avelyn images of the rolling hills, the wheatfields, and grapevines of Youmaneff. He thought of his mother and father, hoped that his father was still well. Of course, Jayson Desbris would not know it, but he could rest well when thinking of his youngest son now.

On a hillock not so far away, Pony, too, heard the centaur's haunting music. Her thoughts rolled back to the carefree days of her childhood, of her times with Elbryan—Elbryan! All those terrible images of that fateful day in Dundalis remained with her, but somehow they were easier to deal with. She could look at the tragedy rationally, and now, with Elbryan beside her, she was beginning to come to terms with her fate.

Pony came to know that it was not simple terror and grief that had forced her to bury those awful images, but guilt. She had lived, but everyone else, so she thought, had perished. Why her?

Seeing another from her village, seeing dear Elbryan again, had allowed Pony to remove some of that guilt. She knew the truth now, all of it, and she was strong enough to accept that truth—and on those occasions when she found she was not strong enough, she knew Elbryan would be there for her, as she would be there for him. For the first time in many years, Pony was not alone.

"You are not going into town this night?" Elbryan asked Avelyn, the monk tarrying near to the fire.

"Jill—Pony went into Dundalis," Avelyn clarified, "but I believe I will spend this night in the forest."

"Cold wind and a hard ground," Elbryan warned, and indeed, winter was fast approaching.

"Ho, ho, what!" Avelyn laughed. "You would not guess the hardships I have endured, my friend. This round body does not tell of them."

Elbryan smiled and considered the monk, understanding there was indeed a hardened frame beneath the soft exterior.

"No, I will stay this night," Avelyn went on. "I feel it is time for me to begin repaying you the debt I owe."

"Debt?" Elbryan asked incredulously.

"I owe you my life, as does Pony."

"I followed the only course open to me," Elbryan replied.

"And glad I am that you did!" Avelyn snorted. "Ho, ho, what!"

Elbryan gave a smile and shook his head, entertained, as usual by the complex man. "So you shall repay me with your company," the ranger reasoned.

"Oh, more than that," the monk replied. "And I fear that if I offer too much of my company, then I shall owe you all the more!"

Again came the laughter, but it died away quickly, Avelyn's face growing suddenly serious. "Tell me of your horse," he bade the ranger.

"I have no horse."

"Symphony?"

"Symphony is not mine," Elbryan explained. "Symphony is free and belongs to no man."

"All the better then!" said Avelyn. He fumbled about his robes, then with his pouch.

Elbryan caught a glimpse within that pouch as Avelyn searched for a certain stone, the ranger's jaw dropping low at the myriad sparkles, shimmering brightly, magnificently, even in the light of the low fire. No wonder, then, that the Abellican Church had come after Brother Avelyn!

Finally the monk found the stone he was looking for and held it up before him: a turquoise.

"Is Symphony about?" the monk asked.

Elbryan nodded slowly, cautiously. "What magic do you intend for Symphony?" he wanted to know.

Avelyn snorted. "Nothing the horse will not desire," he assured the ranger.

They went off together into the night, finding Symphony in a moonlit field, grazing calmly. Avelyn bade Elbryan to wait at field's edge, then the monk walked slowly toward the horse, holding forth the stone and chanting quietly.

Elbryan held his breath, not certain what the powerful Symphony might do. The stallion had accepted the ranger, but Elbryan knew that to be an unusual thing for proud and wild Symphony. If the stallion now bolted forward suddenly, trampling the monk into the earth, Elbryan would not be surprised.

But Symphony did no such thing. The horse nickered quietly as Avelyn came right up to him. The monk continued to chant—it seemed to Elbryan as if he were conversing with the horse—and whatever he was saying, Symphony was listening! After a long while, Avelyn motioned for the ranger to join him.

The monk was still whispering softly when Elbryan moved up beside him. Symphony had gone perfectly still, his head raised high, his magnificent, muscled chest presented openly to the two men.

Avelyn handed the turquoise to Elbryan. "Finish," he instructed.

Elbryan took the stone, having no idea what he should do with it. Before he could begin to question the monk, he felt an urge, a calling. The ranger looked up into Symphony's dark eyes, understanding suddenly that it was the stallion calling to him! Elbryan blinked in disbelief, then looked back at the turquoise and realized that its glow was not reflected moonlight but its own inner light, a radiating magic; only then did Elbryan realize how warm the stone had grown.

"Touch it to the horse's breast," the monk instructed.

Elbryan moved his hand slowly toward the stallion. Symphony closed his eyes, seeming as if in a deep trance. The ranger put the stone right against the horse's breast, right in the "V" where the muscles of the powerful shoulders came together. He held it there for a long time, while Avelyn took up a louder, more insistent chant that sounded as a song.

Elbryan was hardly conscious of the stone's action, and Symphony seemed perfectly at ease, as the turquoise burrowed into the horse's flesh, as the stone set itself perfectly upon Symphony's breast.

The ranger retracted his hand suddenly, his expression horrified as he regarded the stone, which seemed now a natural part of the horse. Avelyn stopped his chanting and put a comforting hand on Elbryan's shoulder; Symphony opened his dark eyes and seemed perfectly calm, pained not at all.

"What have I done?" Elbryan asked. "What have you done?"

Avelyn shrugged. "Not exactly sure," he admitted. "But the stone's magic was for animals, of that I am certain."

"To heal?" Elbryan asked. "To strengthen?"

"Perhaps both," the monk replied. Avelyn's face crinkled as he tried to sort out a feasible explanation. "You see, I do not always know what magic the stones will provide," he began. "They call to me; they tell me what to do."

"Then you have no way of knowing what we just did to Symphony," Elbryan reasoned, his tone showing clearly that he was not pleased. Symphony was no toy for experiments, after all! "Beneficial or baneful?"

"Beneficial," Avelyn said with all confidence and without hesitation. "Ho, ho, what! I told you that I meant to repay a debt."

"But you do not even know what you did!" Elbryan protested.

"But I know the nature of what the stone did," Avelyn explained. "Turquoise is the stone of animals, a true blessing of beasts. I suspect that your bond with Symphony has been heightened, that you and the stallion are more deeply and profoundly joined now."

"Master and beast?" Elbryan demanded, clearly not happy with the prospect.

"Friend and friend," Avelyn corrected. "Symphony cannot be owned, so you said, and I would not presume to break this most wonderful stallion's spirit! Ho, ho, what! Never that! Trust, my friend, hold faith in the stones, in the gifts of God. You will soon learn the truth of this magic that Symphony now holds, and you will be pleased, as will Symphony, do not doubt."

As if in answer, Symphony reared suddenly and whinnied, then came back down and thundered about the pair in a tight circle, hooves rending the turf. The stallion showed no sign of pain or even agitation other than a sudden elation.

Elbryan felt that emotion very clearly. It was as if he could read Symphony's mind, and not just by the visible movements of the stallion's body.

He read the stallion's thoughts!

Elbryan looked at Avelyn, the monk smiling widely. "Do you 'hear' them?" the ranger asked, for lack of a better word. "Do you know what the stallion is feeling?"

"I was but the mediator," Avelyn explained, "the facilitator, ho, ho, what! I brought forth the stone's magic, but you are the one who used it, my friend. You and Symphony, and now you two are joined more closely. But I do indeed know the stallion's thoughts," the monk finished with a mischievous smile. "I see them clearly on your face!"

Symphony stopped abruptly and reared again, calling into the night. Then the horse thundered away out of the field, out of sight.

But Elbryan knew where the horse was; if he concentrated, the ranger could visualize the very ground before Symphony's pounding hooves. He did so then, and saw and felt the rush of the wind and the night as the horse raced through the darkened forest. And it went deeper than that; the ranger came to perceive the world about Symphony through the eyes of the magnificent horse. Only then did Elbryan truly appreciate the intelligence of the animal, filtered through a different perspective, perhaps, but no less intense than his own. The horse knew things simply, without the interference of reason that was the domain of men, elves, and the higher races. What was, in the horse's eyes, simply *was* with no interpretation, an efficient and perfect way of perception that sorted through emotion, that lived in the present without concern for the future or interference from the past.

Perfect, simple, beautiful.

After a long while, Elbryan opened his eyes and looked at Avelyn. He nodded his appreciation, for he understood already that this gift Avelyn had given to him and to Symphony was as profound and precious as the bow Joycenevial had crafted for him.

Elbryan put his hand on Avelyn's shoulder and nodded again, for he could find no words to properly thank the man.

Avelyn went into Dundalis the next morning, passing Pony on the trail as she made her way back to the ranger's camp. The monk started to ask the woman if she wanted him to accompany her, but, in studying the expression on Pony's face, Avelyn thought the better of it and continued on his way. Soon after, he was whistling gaily, for upon some closer examination, Avelyn had indeed come to understand the expression on the young woman's face.

Pony found Elbryan burying the embers of his fire. She came into the camp quietly and moved right across the way from him without a word.

Elbryan stood tall, looking at her. They were alone, completely alone, for the first time, and so many questions came to each of them that they remained silent, just started circling each other, as combatants might, as a stalking panther might when confronted with another of its own kind.

Pony's eyes reflected an intensity Elbryan had never before encountered, a hunger, perhaps, or a rage—some inner passion that kept her from blinking, that kept her chewing on the corner of her bottom lip as she paced about him, her gaze locked on his.

The ranger soon fell into a similar trance, his focus becoming squarely, singularly, Pony. There was only her and nothing else, only those burning blue eyes, those tender lips.

Circling, they moved slightly, but ever closer with each rotation.

A harsh noise from somewhere in the forest startled the pair and stole the moment. Neither recognized it, and neither wanted to search it out.

"Come," Elbryan bade Pony, taking her hand and leading her down a snow-covered path. They moved out from under the canopy of the forest onto a clearing, and Elbryan smiled wide, for there, across the field, stood Symphony. The ranger had known that the stallion would be there, had even telepathically called out to Symphony to wait for him.

Spotting him, the great stallion reared and snorted, its breath coming out as a great cone of steam.

"Come," Elbryan said again, leading Pony quickly across the field. Now that Symphony was with them, the ranger knew his destination, knew the only place that would suit this first private meeting with Pony. He became tentative when he neared the magnificent horse. Would Symphony accept two riders?

"Easy, friend," the ranger said softly, stroking the horse's muzzle and muscled neck. He looked hard at the horse, sharing his thoughts, hearing the answer, then looked at Pony and nodded.

"He is beautiful," she said. She thought her words lame, somehow hollow in the face of such magnificence as Symphony, but she had no other words to offer to the stallion. Elbryan took her hand and helped her up tentatively onto the powerful animal's back.

Symphony snorted again and jostled about, but gradually came to accept the woman. Then came the real test as Elbryan went up on the stallion in front of Pony.

The horse settled easily, ready to run.

And run Symphony did! Fast as the wind, flying along the trails, weaving through the trees in a dizzying blur that had Pony screaming with terror and delight, and holding so tightly to Elbryan's waist that every time the horse came down hard the ranger's breath was blasted from his body.

Soon they came to the diamond-shaped grove, the spruce and pines blanketed by snow but the ground about the grove blown bare by the wind. Symphony pulled to a stop and the pair slid down.

Pony went right up to the horse's face and stared hard into one dark eye. Her breathing would not steady; there was something too primordial, too untamed and uncontrollable, about this beast, something fearfully strong. And yet she had come through the ride unscathed, breathless with joy and excitement.

She had come through the ride!

She turned to Elbryan, who was walking to the glade, and followed him. He disappeared through the thick branches; Pony paused when she got to that spot, considering the implications, considering her own feelings.

The young woman shook her head defiantly, then looked back at the stallion, who reared and whinnied, as if to prod her on. Untamed, uncontrollable, fearfully strong, he embodied the feelings that bubbled at the edges of Pony's thoughts, threatening to overwhelm her.

She pushed through the thick branches into a small clearing, where Elbryan crouched, the first flickers of a fire already starting before him. Pony watched him as he worked, blowing softly, turning sticks.

Untamed, uncontrollable, fearfully strong. The thoughts stayed with her, repeated in her head like a warning, like a temptation. She clenched her fists at her sides, chewed the corner of her bottom lip again, and stared hard at this man, no more the boy she had known and yet so much that boy with whom she had shared her youth.

She feared those few memories she had not yet uncovered, and yet, looking at Elbryan, she knew that she would soon face them.

She walked over to him and he rose, the fire burning. Face-to-face they stood for many seconds, for minutes, staring in silence at each other.

Then he moved for her, his lips drawn to hers, and she gave a slight gasp, expecting black wings to rise up all around her, expecting a scream to reverberate within her mind. But then he was there, against her, his lips brushing gently over hers, softly, softly, and all she felt was him, and all she heard was his soft breathing and his slight moan.

The kiss became more urgent, and gradually Pony's fears melted away, swept up in the sudden torrent of passion that overcame her. He kissed her hard, and she kissed him back, tongues entwined, lips pressing hard.

And then they were apart, Elbryan staring at her, locking her deep in his gaze. His hand came up and unlaced her cloak, and she let the garment drop without protest, cool air on her skin. Then he reached for the buttons of her shirt, and on and on until the last layer of her clothing fell away. And she was not ashamed, not embarrassed, and no black wings of horrors past swept up about her.

Elbryan pulled off his own cloak and shirt and stood bare to the waist before her. They moved closer, the hairs of his chest just brushing her breasts, little tingles shared. With his prompting, she lifted her arms high above her head and he locked his fingers about hers.

Then he broke the hold and began to run his hands down her arms, slowly and, oh, so gently, the tips of his fingernails just grazing her soft skin. Down came his hands, past her elbows, across her arms, and then around to the back, to her shoulder blades and to the base of her neck, so softly and gently, fingertips just lightly brushing.

She felt the electric pull of those fingers, the tingle that made her want to pull them in closer—and yet, she knew that if they were pulled in closer, their teasing tingle would be no more. Her head went back, mouth opened as she basked in his stroke, as his hands went down her back, so gently, to the top of her buttocks and then brushing about, to her hips and past her hips. Again with his prompting, Pony turned and melted back into his strong embrace. He lifted one hand to push her hair aside, and gently kissed the nape of her neck, the soft kiss turning slowly more urgent, a harder kiss, a gentle bite, and when she cooed quietly, a harder bite still.

"Do you feel me?" he whispered into her ear.

"Yes."

"Are you alive?"

"So alive."

"Do you want me to make love to you?"

Pony paused, searching for the threat of terrible memories. She recalled her wedding night, glanced down at the glowing fire as if it were some enemy or some forewarning. But this was different, the young woman knew, different from Connor. Stronger.

Untamed, uncontrollable, fearfully strong, her mind recited. And right, she silently added. So very right.

"Yes," she answered quietly.

They sank down to the ground together, onto the still-warm cloak, and there they were, caught in the present and encircled by their past. For Elbryan, it was the culmination of his youth, where every waking thought had led him to this point with this woman, his soulmate, his Pony. This moment, so many years in the waiting, was the marker of the end of that relationship with the girl, the beginning of the new and deeper relationship with the woman. Now he was a man, and Pony a woman, and all the love that had brought them to this moment came crashing together with their bodies. He was happy to the point of giddiness, and yet he was vulnerable suddenly, so vulnerable, for if anything happened to Pony, if he lost her now as he had thought he had lost her before, then a rift would be torn in his heart that would never mend, then his life ever after would be without meaning.

For Pony, that moment in the grove was the denial of blackness, a dark barrier torn down and thrown away, the harsh memories overwhelmed by the gentleness, the love, and the warm memories of her youth with Elbryan: the time when he had pulled her hair and she had laid him out flat; the times when his friends had teased him, but he'd stood up to them, not denying his feelings for the girl; their long talks and walks on the northern slope; that moment on the slope when they shared in the vision of the Halo; that moment on the ridge when they first kissed—yes, that moment of the kiss!—and this time, it did not end in blackness and screams, but went on and on, kissing and touching, feeling each other wholly. They had shared lives and were bonded by common memories, by love lost and love found, and though they hadn't been together in years, they each knew everything about the other, the truth of the moment.

They lay together for a long time afterward, nestled in their cloaks, saying nothing, staring at the fire. Elbryan got up once to add wood to the fire, and Pony laughed at him as he hopped about, naked, his bare feet stumbling on the cold ground. She pulled the blanket tight about her when he returned, not letting him in.

But her smile gave away her true feelings, the warmth of it egging Elbryan on until he tackled her and fought with her, and then he was under the blanket again, their bodies pressed together, and for Pony, all the world was spinning once more.

Untamed, uncontrollable, fearfully strong.

Later, he was above her, looking down at her in the light of the low fire.

"My Pony," he whispered. "How empty was my life, so empty that I had not the heart even to recognize the hole in it. Only now, when you have returned to me, do I understand how empty it had been, how meaningless."

"Never that."

He nodded, denying her words. "My Pony," he said again. "The colors of the world are returned to me."

Then he closed his eyes and kissed her.

The night deepened about them, the wind moaned through the trees and those few birds that braved the northern winter whistled. Somewhere in the distance a wolf howled, and another took up the song, and for Elbryan, the music was sweeter now than ever before, than even in those years he had spent in the enchanted elven forest.

He fell into a most contented sleep, but Pony did not. She lay awake all the night, Elbryan close to her, Elbryan one with her. She thought of Connor and her wedding night, of the black memories that had swallowed her. Unconsciously, she rubbed the palm of her hand, burned once so long ago by glowing embers.

Now, for the first time, Pony saw those memories clearly, heard the screams of Dundalis, saw the fires and the carnage, saw Olwan die in the grasp of a giant, and in her mind, she crawled again under the burning house, into the darkness.

Only this time, they were just memories and not threatening black demons. This time, with Elbryan beside her, with Elbryan a part of her strength, she could face them and accept them.

Tears streamed down her cheeks, but they were honest tears for the loss of Dundalis; when they were gone, when the moment of grief at long last was past, Pony hugged sleeping Elbryan close and smiled, truly free for the first time since that moment on the ridge, since the moment of her first kiss.

❖ 37 ❖

Catch of the Day

"**D**amn me," the skinny, nervous man whimpered, skittering away from the noose trap and from the ugly humanoid creature hanging from it. "Damn me, oh, damn me! Cric! Cric!"

He realized soon enough that his screaming would only bring in more of these creatures, if any were about, so he slapped a hand over his own mouth and tumbled down to the field, his free hand moving to one of the many daggers on his broad shoulder belts. He found little cover, however, for though the grass was tall, it was sparse, with only a few blades sticking up through the blanket of light snow.

A few moments later, Chipmunk breathed a little easier as a bald, lean man rushed into view, his sword at the ready. "Chipmunk?" Cric called softly. "Chipmunk, are ye here?"

Chipmunk scrambled to his feet and ran for his friend, tripping and falling several times on the slippery ground.

"What do ye know?" Cric asked him repeatedly as he stumbled to approach. Finally, Chipmunk caught up to his friend, but he was too excited to explain in words. He hopped up and down, pointing back across the field to a small copse of trees.

"Our trap?" the bald man asked calmly.

Chipmunk nodded so rapidly that he bit his tongue.

"What'd we catch something?"

Again the wild nod.

"Something unusual?"

Chipmunk was in no mood for any further questions. He grabbed Cric by the arm and shoved him ahead in the direction of the copse. Cric straightened and, seeing that Chipmunk would not be following, just shook his head and went alone to the trap.

A minute later, there came a howl from the trees and Cric ran from the spot nearly as quickly as had Chipmunk.

"It's a g-goblin!" the tall man sputtered. "A damned goblin!"

"We got to get Paulson," reasoned Chipmunk, to which Cric only nodded and ran off, the skinny man in close pursuit.

They found barrel-chested Paulson, their leader, sitting, relaxing against the sunny side of a wide elm, his ragged boots standing off to the side, his dirty toes wriggling near a small fire. The pair slowed as they approached, knowing that to disturb Paulson usually meant a slap on the head.

Cric motioned for Chipmunk to approach the man, but Chipmunk only motioned back.

"State yer business," Paulson demanded under half-closed eyelids. "And yer business better be worth stating!"

"We caught something," Cric remarked.

Paulson opened his eyes and rubbed a hand across a face that was more scar than beard. "Good pelt?" he asked.

"No pelt," said Chipmunk.

"No fur," added Cric. "Just skin."

"What?" Paulson sat up straight and reached for his boots. "Don't ye tell me ye hanged a man now!"

"Not a man," said Chipmunk.

"It's a damned goblin!" spouted Cric.

Paulson's face went suddenly grave. "A goblin?" he echoed quietly.

Both men nodded eagerly.

"Just one?"

Again the nods.

"Ye damned fools," scolded Paulson. "Don't ye know there's no such thing as 'just one' goblin?"

"We should go home," said Chipmunk.

Paulson looked all around, then shook his head. Cric and Chipmunk were fairly new to the area, having come north a little more than three years before, but Paulson had lived on the border of the Wilderlands for most of his life, had been living just outside Weedy Meadow when the goblin raid had flattened Dundalis. "We got to find out how many," he replied, "and find out where they're heading."

"Aw, who's to care for the folk o' Dundalis?" asked a frightened Cric. "They never cared any for us."

"Yeah," added Chipmunk.

"It's more than for them," said Paulson. "For ourselves. If goblins're coming hard, then we'd be wise to go south for a bit."

"Can't we just go south then, anyway?" asked Cric.

"Shut yer mouth and keep yer sword ready," Paulson ordered. "Goblins ain't so tough—it's their numbers ye got to fear. And their friends," he added grimly, "for goblins and giants get on well."

The other two were trembling.

"But all we got to do is see them afore they see us," the burly man went on. "Might be that there's a bounty on goblin ears."

That seemed to catch the pair's attention.

The three went back to the trap first, Paulson unceremoniously cutting the goblin down, then slicing off its ears and putting them in a pouch, pausing only to note that the creature was surprisingly well armed for one of its kind and that it wore an insignia on its leather jerkin, a black emblem of a batlike creature on a light gray background. Paulson didn't think too much of it, figuring that the jerkin was stolen anyway.

"Not been here more than a few hours," Paulson announced, after a quick inspection of the body. "If this one traveled with friends, then they're likely still about." The creature's tracks through the copse were not hard to follow, but any marks it had made on the open field beyond had been erased by the wind. Still, just by the direction from which it had entered the copse, the trackers could make a reasonable guess about where it had come from, and so they set off quickly across the field and into the forest.

Chipmunk found the first goblin sign—three sets of tracks with one branching back the way the three men had come, the other two moving off down a different fork in the trail.

"Well, now we're outnumbering them," Paulson said wickedly, the big man never fearful of a fight.

Less than a mile on, they spotted the goblin pair, resting amid a tumble of rocks on a forested hillside. Paulson drew out his large sword and motioned for Cric to go in at his side, while Chipmunk was to go to the higher ground around to the right, getting an angle for his dagger throws.

"Hard and fast?" Cric whispered.

Paulson considered the words, then shook his head. He held Cric back, hiding behind some scrub, while agile Chipmunk worked his way into position. Then Paulson started out, slowly, pacing evenly and calmly toward the goblin pair. He and Cric were within a dozen strides before the goblins spotted them, and then how the creatures howled!

They jumped to their feet, one producing a long, iron-tipped spear, the other a well-fashioned short sword. Paulson was surprised that these two, like their dead comrade, were so well armed and also that their jerkins so closely resembled the one on the dead goblin, even down to the emblem. The large man's knowledge of goblins simply didn't reconcile with this sight before him.

Nor did the goblins act in any manner that Paulson would have expected. He and Cric came on fast, but only one goblin, the spear wielder, jumped out to meet them, blocking the way, covering its companion's sudden retreat.

Both swordsmen came in fast; the goblin swished the spear back and forth, the weapon's sharp tip scratching Cric's arm and holding him at bay. Paulson stepped inside the range and caught the spear by the shaft and rushed up its length, quickly and efficiently embedding his sword deep in the creature's chest.

"Two more ears!" Cric laughed, but Paulson wasn't thinking along those lines just then.

"Get him, Chipmunk!" he called.

The fleeing goblin angled up the hill, and Chipmunk moved to intercept, sliding to his knees and sending a pair of daggers spinning at the goblin. The creature managed to dodge one, but the other caught it on the hip and hung there.

The goblin squealed but hardly slowed, even when Chipmunk's next blade stuck deep into its shoulder.

Then the goblin was out of throwing range, and Chipmunk fell in with Paulson and Cric, taking up the chase. Tall Cric was by far the fastest of the three and he forged ahead, gaining steadily on the goblin as it scrambled down the back side of the hill, then over the wooded floor of the next valley. The creature went up over a rise, Cric in close pursuit, and Paulson howled out for his companion to "take the damned thing down!"

Cric went up to the top of the hill, eager, sword ready, and then, to the surprise of his two friends, he skidded to a stop.

When Paulson and Chipmunk caught up to him, they understood his hesitance, for there, in a wide valley below the ridge, loomed the largest army that any of the three had ever seen—and both Cric and Paulson had spent a few years in the Kingsmen. All the valley was filled with tents and campfires; a thousand, thousand forms milled about down below, most seeming about goblin sized, some even smaller, but with a fair number of fomorian giants among them. Even more surprising to the three men were the war engines, a dozen at least, great catapults and spear-throwing ballistae, and huge corkscrew devices, obviously for burrowing through fortified walls.

"How far south were you planning to move?" Cric asked Paulson.

To the barrel-chested man at that moment, Behren seemed a distinct possibility.

"I'm knowing that ye're up to something no good!" the centaur roared. "An assumption I'm sure to make every time I glance upon yer ugly faces!" Bradwarden had heard the stirring in the small ramshackle hut and, upon investigation, had found the three trappers packing their gear, stripping everything from the shack walls.

The three men glanced nervously at one another. Even huge Paulson seemed a small thing indeed when standing before the eight-hundred-pound centaur—and the creature's demeanor at that moment made him even more imposing.

"Well?" boomed Bradwarden. "Have ye an explanation?"

"We're leaving, that's all," said Chipmunk.

"Leaving?"

"Going south," Cric added, ready to concoct an appropriate lie, but when Paulson glared at him, the tall, bald man went silent.

"What did ye do, then?" demanded Bradwarden. "I know ye—ye'd not be leaving if ye hadn't angered someone." The centaur backed off a bit, then smiled, thinking he had it figured out. "Ye got Nightbird on yer trail," he reasoned.

"We ain't seen the ranger in weeks," Paulson protested.

"But ye've seen his friends," said Bradwarden. "Might be that ye've killed one o' his friends."

"No such thing!" growled Paulson.

"Goblins ain't no friend o' the Nightbird!" added Chipmunk before he could properly think his words through. Cric pushed the skinny man hard, and Paulson's glare promised Chipmunk that he meant to do him even more harm for his slip.

Bradwarden backed off a step, eyeing the three curiously. "Goblins?"

"Did I say goblins?" Chipmunk asked innocently, trying to backtrack.

"Ye did!" Bradwarden roared, ending any forthcoming lies from the man and his two companions. "Ye said goblins, and if there be goblins about, and ye know o' them, then tell yer tale in full, or be sure that I'll trample ye down to the dirt!"

"Goblins," Paulson said grimly. "Thousands of goblins. We seen them, and want no part o' them." He went on to recount the tale in full, and ended by dropping four goblin ears to the ground before Bradwarden.

Paulson then asked the centaur to be gone so that he and his friends might finish their packing and be on their way, but Bradwarden wouldn't let them get away that easily. They would go with him, the centaur decided, to find Elbryan and Pony and tell their tale once again. The three trappers weren't keen on the idea of wasting a single moment, but neither were they ready to battle the fierce centaur.

They found the pair and Brother Avelyn at Elbryan's camp just north of Dundalis, nestled within the shelter of a grove of closely growing spruce trees.

Bradwarden called out long before his group approached—Elbryan could set a trap as well as any elf, and the ranger was always on his guard. The ranger invited the centaur in, of course, but was surprised indeed to find his half-horse friend in the company of such rogues.

"I believe that Mr. Paulson there has a tale ye'll be wanting to hear," Bradwarden explained.

Paulson laid it out simply and to the point, and his words hit especially hard on Pony and on Elbryan. For Pony, the possibility of an approaching goblin army sent her mind careening back to the day of the tragedy, threatening to overwhelm her with feelings she had only recently reconciled.

For Elbryan, though, the trapper's tale was more complicated. While he, too, carried those terrible memories within him, he also had his sense of duty. How many times had the ranger told himself that he would not allow such a tragedy to befall Dundalis again? And here, before him, loomed the threat, the same threat. For Pony, it took great strength to master her fears, to keep her wits about her; for Elbryan, it was simply a matter of duty and pride.

The ranger took a stick from the edge of the low fire and drew a rough map of the area on the ground. "Show me the exact location," he ordered Paulson, and the man readily complied, understanding that if Elbryan wasn't satisfied, the ranger would probably force him to go along, the better to investigate.

Elbryan paced about the campfire, looking down often at the map.

"They must be told," Pony said.

Elbryan nodded.

"On the word of these three?" Bradwarden asked incredulously.

The ranger looked from Paulson to the centaur, then nodded again. "It is never too soon to issue a warning," he said.

Paulson appeared vindicated, but Elbryan wasn't ready to concede that the man's words were true. "I will go north," the ranger said, "to this place described."

"I'll not go with ye," Paulson protested.

Elbryan shook his head. "I will fly fast, too fast for you." He looked at Bradwarden, and the centaur nodded, understanding the plea and more than ready to go along with his ranger friend.

"You," Elbryan said to Paulson, "and your friends will go to End-o'-the-World, bearing word of warning."

Paulson held out his hand to quiet Cric and Chipmunk, their protests and fears bubbling up in the form of unintelligible whimpers. "And then?" Paulson wanted to know.

"Where your heart takes you," Elbryan replied. "You owe me nothing, I say, beyond this one favor."

"We're owing ye even that?" Paulson asked skeptically.

Elbryan's grim nod was all the reply that the man was going to get, a poignant reminder of that day in the trappers' shack when the ranger had shown mercy.

"End-o'-the-World," Paulson agreed angrily. "And we'll tell the fools, but I'm not thinking that they'll be listening."

Elbryan nodded and looked at Pony. "Weedy Meadow," he instructed. "You and Avelyn."

"And what of Dundalis?" the woman asked.

"Bradwarden and I will return to Dundalis with word of the goblins," the ranger explained. "But first, we will return here." The ranger pointed down at the map with his stick, to a spot on the map northwest of Dundalis, a point nearly equidistant from Dundalis and Weedy Meadow, and not much further from End-o'-the-World.

"The grove?" Pony asked.

Elbryan nodded. "A diamond-shaped grove of fir trees," he explained to the trappers.

"I'm knowing the spot," said Paulson, "and not much caring for it."

Elbryan wasn't surprised by that response—likely the same elven magic that drew the ranger to the grove made a rogue like Paulson feel uncomfortable around it. "One week, then," the ranger explained. He looked to Paulson. "If you go straight to the south from End-o'-the-World, be certain that the folk of the town know where I can be found."

Paulson waved him away, the man seeming quite displeased by it all.

Elbryan motioned to Bradwarden. "Symphony is about," the ranger said confidently.

Before the next dawn, the ranger and the centaur were racing to the north, Bradwarden working hard to keep up with magnificent Symphony.

Avelyn and Pony, walking side by side, set a more gradual pace, for they figured that they could arrive in Weedy Meadow before the nightfall.

The road was a bit longer for Paulson, Cric, and Chipmunk, but though the latter two pressed Paulson hard for desertion, telling him every step of the way that they should abandon End-o'-the-World and go straight on to the south—all the way to Palmaris, perhaps—the big man, duty-bound for the first time in years, would hear nothing of it. He had given his word to the ranger that he would go and warn the folk of End-o'-the-World, and so he would.

Pony and Avelyn had underestimated the distance and camped outside Weedy Meadow that night, the monk reasoning that it would be better for them to go into town with such grim warnings during the brightness of day. They rested easily in the quiet forest, having learned much of camp building from Elbryan over the last few days, and Pony was soon asleep.

She awakened to the screams of Avelyn, the fat man in the throes of a nightmare, rolling about on the ground. Finally Pony managed to stir him from his slumber, and the look upon his face as he stared at her was one of madness, one that sent chills up and down Pony's spine.

Avelyn lifted his hand and opened it, revealing several small stones, the burned smoky quartz that he had taken from the corpse of Brother Quintall.

"I felt that they had magic left in them," the fat monk explained. "Distance sight is their trademark."

"You looked for the goblins," Pony reasoned.

"And I saw them, my girl," said Avelyn, "a vast host. Paulson did not exaggerate!"

Pony breathed hard and nodded.

"But that was not all!" Avelyn said to her, grabbing and shaking her. "I was compelled beyond the army. *Compelled,* I say, pulled by the magic of the stones, by a distant power that long ago attuned itself to these special stones."

Pony looked at him curiously, not really understanding.

"Something terrible is awake in Corona, my girl!" Avelyn spouted. "The dactyl walks Corona!"

The words were nothing new to Pony; Avelyn had been making such claims for a very long time. Indeed, he had spouted similar words in the common room in Tinson on the night Pony had first met him. This time, though, there was something more to the claim, something personal. Always Avelyn had been firm in his belief, but now his expression showed him to be far beyond simple belief. At that moment, in the light of a dying fire, Pony had no doubt that Avelyn's knowledge of the awakened dactyl was now something more than the suspicions aroused by ancient texts. It was something entirely personal.

"So there ye have it," Bradwarden said quietly, ominously, he and Elbryan looking out over a vast field of dark tents. "Them three wasn't lying."

"Or even exaggerating," Elbryan added in subdued tones. When first he had crested this ridge, looking down upon the massive army setting its camp, the ranger's heart had dropped. How could the folk of Dundalis, Weedy Meadow, and End-o'-the-World resist such an army, even if all of them stood together behind fortified walls?

They could not, of course.

And it was quite obvious that this force was moving southward. The army was many miles below the spot where Paulson, Cric, and Chipmunk had indicated they had seen it, and the swath the goblins and giants had cut in the forest on the northern side of the encampment was visible even from this southern ridge.

"We'll find us a hole to hide in," Bradwarden said calmly. "Goblins been through afore, and'll be through again. I've waited them out afore, and I'll wait them out again!"

"We need to know more of their intentions," Elbryan said suddenly, drawing a curious stare from the centaur.

"Not so hard to figure out what a goblin means to do," Bradwarden replied dryly.

Elbryan was shaking his head before the centaur ever finished. "This is different," he explained. "Goblins and giants should not be together in so large a group. And working in concert," he added, sweeping his arm across the panorama of the encampment, indicating the disciplined manner in which the creatures were organizing their camp. "And what of those?" he went on, pointing to a dozen huge war engines circled on the far end of the camp.

"They're a bit hungrier this time, is all," replied Bradwarden. "So they'll kill a few more than usual, maybe sack two towns instead of one. It's an old tale, me friend, repeated again and again, though always do ye human folk seem surprised when it falls on yer heads."

Elbryan didn't believe it, not this time, not in looking at that military camp. He glanced to the west, taking note that the sun was touching the horizon. "I have to go in," he remarked.

"Do ye now?" the centaur asked sarcastically.

Elbryan slipped down from Symphony and handed his reins to Bradwarden. "Scout the area," he said. "See if any branches of the army have moved past our location. I will return at the setting of Sheila to this spot or to the back of the next ridge if the goblins have claimed this area as their own."

Bradwarden knew that it was futile to argue with the stubborn ranger.

Elbryan made his way from tree to tree, to bush and to the back of hills, moving ever closer to the great army. Soon, goblin scouts were about him, walking through the trees, talking in their whining voices, complaining about this or that, about the fit of their uniforms or some particularly nasty commander who talked more with his whip than his voice. Elbryan couldn't make out every word; the goblins were using the language spoken by the common folk of Corona, but the creatures' accents were so thick, their slang so heavy, that the ranger could only get a general impression of their conversation.

That impression did little to calm Elbryan's fears. The goblins were speaking of being a part of an army, that much was certain.

Elbryan got his next surprise an hour later. The ranger was up in a tree, lying low across a thick branch barely ten feet from the ground when a group of soldiers walked into the clearing below the tree. Three were goblins, but the fourth, holding the torch, was a creature the ranger had never before seen, a dwarf, barrel-chested but spindly limbed, wearing a red cap.

A cap red with blood, Elbryan knew, for though he had never seen a powrie before, he remembered well the childhood tales of the wicked dwarves.

The four decided to rest right at the base of the wide-spreading tree. Fortunately for Elbryan, none of the creatures bothered to look up into the tangle of branches.

The ranger wasn't sure how to proceed. He felt that he should steal that bloody cap, as further proof for the townsfolk that danger was sweeping their way. Reports of goblins would do little more than stir up some interest and maybe incite a few patrols, Elbryan knew, a response he remembered from his own days as a villager. But a bloody cap tossed in their midst, proof that powries were in the region, might scare more than a few folk from their homes, might send them running down the road to the south.

How to get the cap, though?

Stealthy thievery seemed the order of the day. The four were down and resting; perhaps they would drift off to sleep. One of the goblins brought out a bulging waterskin, and as soon as the creature poured some of the foaming liquid into a mug, Elbryan knew that it held some potent drink indeed.

Elbryan's blood began to boil with rage as the goblins talked of flattening the towns and killing all the men, as they described in detail the pleasures that might be had before they killed the women.

The young man found his breath hard to draw; the brutish talk brought him back to that awful day in his youth, made him see again the carnage in Dundalis, made him hear again the screams of his family and his friends.

All thoughts of stealthy thievery flew from the fierce ranger's mind.

A few minutes later, one of the goblins went off a short distance into the brush to relieve itself. Elbryan could still see the creature, a darker spot in the brush, its back to him, swaying back and forth as it watered a bush.

The ranger shifted slowly to a sitting position. He lifted an arrow to Hawkwing's string and gently pulled back. He glanced down at the other three, growing louder and more boisterous as they drank deeply. The dwarf was telling some rowdy story, the two goblins laughing riotously at every grotesque detail.

Elbryan measured the words, waiting a moment longer, sensing that the dwarf was at some high point.

Hawkwing's bowstring hummed, the arrow flying true, diving into the back of the peeing goblin's head. The creature gave a slight moan and tumbled headlong into the brush.

The dwarf stopped abruptly and hopped to its feet, staring out into the night.

The goblins were still laughing, though, one of them making some crude remark that its companion probably passed out on top of its own urine.

The dwarf wasn't so sure and waved the pair to silence, then motioned for them to move out a bit.

Up on the branch, the ranger fitted two arrows to his bow, one above the other and drew back the string. The two goblins paced out in front of the dwarf, side by side, calling softly to their missing companion, though neither seemed overconcerned.

Elbryan shifted his bow to horizontal, took careful aim, and let fly. The arrows whipped out, not quite parallel, their angle separating them as they flew. They were two feet apart as each burrowed into its respective goblin, dropping the creatures where they stood. One made not a sound, the other, hit below a lung, let out an agonized howl.

Elbryan leaped from the branch, letting fly another arrow in midair, this one silencing the wounded goblin forever. The ranger hit the ground in a roll, flicked the feathered tip and string from Hawkwing, and came to his feet, staff at the ready.

The dwarf was ready, too, a two-headed flail spinning in its hands. It came on in a wild rush, showing no sign of fear.

Elbryan leaped back, easily avoiding the short reach of the flail, then stepped ahead and poked hard with the tip of his staff, smacking the dwarf right in the face.

The stout creature hardly slowed, rushing ahead, whipping its flail back and forth.

Elbryan dodged and darted out to the side and, when the dwarf turned to chase, swinging its weapon with extended arms, Elbryan presented his staff vertically, both balls of the flail wrapping about it.

The ranger pulled hard, expecting to take the weapon from the dwarf's hand, but the powrie was stronger than Elbryan believed, and only pulled back even harder. Always ready to improvise, Elbryan eased his muscles and ran straight ahead into the dwarf, turning his staff to smash its tip into the dwarf's face once more.

Elbryan tugged again and the chained balls slipped off the staff's end, freeing both weapons. The ranger had the advantage, though, and he batted Hawkwing back and forth, clubbing the dwarf twice on either side of its hard head.

The powrie retreated a step and shook its head fiercely, then, to Elbryan's disbelief, came charging right back in. Its swing was awkward, the flail coming in from a wide angle, and Elbryan thrust his staff out that way in one hand, enwrapping the balls once more. The ranger stepped straight ahead, cupped his fingers, flattened his palm, and slammed the powrie with a series of short heavy blows, each one snapping the dwarf's head back.

His attacks showing little effect, the ranger spun to the side, grabbed up his staff in both hands, and tugged hard, pulling the flail free of the powrie's grasp and launching it across the clearing. Sensing that the furious dwarf would be charging again, Elbryan came all the way around and jabbed Hawkwing hard into the creature's throat, stopping it in its tracks.

The ranger spun again and smashed the staff down diagonally across the powrie's jaw, cracking bone, but the dwarf only growled and pursued. Elbryan simply could not believe the punishment this creature had accepted!

The powrie dipped its broad shoulder, trying to tackle the ranger. Elbryan set his feet and launched a vicious uppercut jab with the staff, using the powrie's momentum against it.

But still the dwarf came on, locking its thin arms about Elbryan's waist and squeezing him tight, driving him back toward the trunk of the huge tree.

The ranger dropped Hawkwing, reached behind him to his pack, and tore free his hatchet. With a growl, he chopped it down hard on the back of the powrie's neck.

Still the dwarf drove him backward.

Elbryan hit the creature again and again, then nearly lost his weapon when he collided with the tree, the powrie's legs driving on, as if the dwarf meant to push him right through the bark.

And given the unearthly strength of the dwarf, Elbryan wondered if the creature might actually do so!

Now the ranger's arm pumped frantically, and finally after perhaps the tenth blow, the powrie's grasp at last loosened.

Elbryan timed his maneuver, hit the dwarf once more, then spun out to the side, and the overbalanced, semiconscious powrie ran headlong into the tree, hugging it now, holding on to it dearly, for if the dwarf let go, it knew it would fall to the ground.

Elbryan walked up behind the creature and bashed his hatchet with all his strength into the back of the dwarf's neck, splintering bone. The powrie whimpered, but held on.

Elbryan, horrified, hit it again, and the dwarf slumped to its knees, finally dead, but still hugging the tree.

Elbryan looked at his weapons, so ineffective against the sturdy powrie. "I need a sword," the ranger lamented. He took the dwarf's cap and gathered up Hawkwing, quickly replacing the feathered tip and stringing the weapon. As he started out of the clearing, he heard a gasp, and turned and fitted an arrow so fluidly and quickly that the newest goblin that had stumbled upon the scene hardly moved before an arrow took it through the throat, sending it stumbling backward into another tree.

Elbryan's next shot pierced its heart and drove deep into the tree behind it, and the goblin slumped, quite dead, but standing, pegged to the tree.

The ranger ran off, arriving at the appointed spot as the moon settled behind the western horizon. Bradwarden and Symphony were waiting for him, the centaur bearing ill news. A section of the army had indeed broken off from this main group, so the tracks had shown, heading south and west.

"End-o'-the-World," Elbryan reasoned.

"They're near to the place already," said Bradwarden, "if not sleeping in the village itself."

Elbryan hopped up on Symphony. There would be no sleep for him this night, he knew, nor the next.

❖ 38 ❖

Mercy Repaid

"Remain here," Elbryan bade Bradwarden when the pair reached the diamond-shaped grove, "or in the region, at least. See what the news is from Weedy Meadow and prepare the folk of Dundalis for the decision that will soon be before them."

"The humans aren't much for talking to the likes of a centaur," Bradwarden reminded the ranger. "But I'll see what I can see and set me animal friends about to the north and west, looking for goblin sign. Ye're for End-o'-the-World, then?"

Elbryan nodded. "I pray that I arrive in time, or that the three trappers got word to the folk."

"Pray for the second, for hoping for the first, I fear, will be a waste o' yer time," Bradwarden replied. "And for the trappers, pray instead that the folk're smart enough to heed their words."

Elbryan nodded grimly and tugged his reins, swinging Symphony about. The stallion was already lathered from the long run south, but Symphony had more heart than any other horse and understood his rider's urgency. Off the stallion pounded through the predawn forest, running on all through the next day. From one high hillock, Elbryan noted hopefully that no smoke appeared in the west, that End-o'-the-World apparently was not burning.

Elbryan first noticed the ghostly figures moving through the mist as twilight descended. The ranger still had a dozen miles before him to get to End-o'-the-World, and so shapes moving through the forest, moving eastward, did not bode well. He brought Symphony up behind a thick tangle of white birch and strung Hawkwing, ready to fight all the way to the westernmost village if need be.

Somewhere not far ahead and to the side, a small shadow glided through the trees, a slender form not much higher than Elbryan's waist. The ranger put up his bow and drew back, finding the mark. He saw the form stumble out of some brush and stagger along the trail. It was the right size for a

goblin—a small one—but the way it moved did not seem right to the perceptive ranger. This was not a lead soldier in an army's march, but one
exhausted, in desperate flight. The ranger waited a few moments longer as
the figure neared, as it came out into a clearing under the moonlight.

A young boy, no more than ten years.

Elbryan prodded Symphony into a short gallop, too quickly for the
frightened youngster to scramble away. The ranger bent low to the side and
caught the fleeing boy under the arm, easily hoisting him up into the saddle,
trying to quiet his cries.

A movement from the other side caught the ranger's attention. He
pushed down hard to secure the squirming youngster and swung about,
Hawkwing in his free hand, ready to fend off an attack.

The would-be attacker skidded to an abrupt stop, recognizing the man.

"Paulson," Elbryan breathed.

"And to yerself, Nightbird," the large man replied. "Be easy on the boy.
He's been through the fighting."

Elbryan looked down to his diminutive captive. "End-o'-the-World?" he
asked.

Paulson nodded grimly.

Other people walked into the small clearing then, dirty, many with
wounds, and all with that hollow, shocked expression showing that they
had just come through hell.

"Goblins and giants hit the place two days after we arrived," Paulson
explained.

"And dwarves," added Cric, coming into the clearing beside Chipmunk.
"Nasty folk!"

"Powries," remarked Elbryan, holding up the cap he had procured.

"We got some o' the folk on the road south before the fight," Paulson
went on, "some smart enough to hear our words o' doom. But most stayed.
Stubborn."

Elbryan nodded, thinking of his own village. Few in Dundalis would
have left even if they knew a goblin force was coming to avenge the goblin
that had been killed by the hunting party. They would have stayed and
fought and died, because Dundalis was their home and, in truth, they had
nowhere else to go.

"They came in hard, Nightbird," Paulson went on, shaking his head,
"and in numbers I'd not've believed possible had I not seen the army in the
north for meself. We got out, me and Cric and Chipmunk, and we took
about a score of folk with us, running blind through the woods these few
days, thinking that we've got goblins on our heels all the way."

Elbryan closed his eyes, sympathetic to the tale, understanding completely the plight of these people, the horrible emptiness that some of them
now felt, the complete hopelessness.

"There is a sheltered meadow two hundred yards from this spot,"

Elbryan told Paulson, the ranger pointing back the way he had come. "Take your band there and huddle together to fend off the cold. I will scout out the lands west and return quickly, that we might make our choice."

Paulson gave a quick nod. "We could be using some rest," he admitted.

Elbryan let the boy down to Paulson's waiting grasp, and the ranger was touched by how gently the bearish man handled the youngster. He sat for a while atop Symphony, regarding the refugees, wondering what he might do for these people.

Then he set off, riding hard through the moonlit woods. He was out an hour and more before he decided that there were no goblins in the area, no dwarves, and certainly no giants. Elbryan thought that a curious thing; why hadn't the wretched humanoids pursued the fleeing humans? And why, he wondered, had the western sky been clear of smoke? Surely the goblins would have burned End-o'-the-World, as they had burned Dundalis years before.

Back at the sheltered meadow, Elbryan gave his permission for the refugees to start a couple of low fires. It was risky setting a light in the dark forest, but these folk sorely needed the warmth.

Elbryan slipped down from Symphony at the side of the meadow, bade the horse to stay in the area and listen close for his call, then he went into the small encampment and found a place about the fire with the three trappers.

"I would have thought that you three would take the south road with those who were wise enough to flee," Elbryan remarked after a short, uncomfortable silence. The ranger noted then the way Cric looked hard at Paulson, the way Paulson kept his own gaze low to the fire.

"Wasn't time," the big man replied unconvincingly.

Elbryan paused for a long while, studying Paulson, trying to find some clue to this uncharacteristically chivalrous action. Finally, Paulson looked up, locking stares with the ranger.

"So we're with ye, then," the big man growled. "But don't ye think for a moment that we three give a beaver's damn for Honce-the-Bear or any town between here and Ursal!"

"Then why?" Elbryan asked simply.

Paulson looked down at the fire. He stood up and kicked a stick that had fallen from the flames, then walked off.

Elbryan looked at the man's companions. Cric motioned across the way to the boy Elbryan had captured.

"Paulson had a boy once," Cric explained, "about the same years as that one. Fell from a tree and breaked his neck."

"That one there lost his folk, by me own guess," Chipmunk added.

"You could have gotten away," said Elbryan, "to the south."

Cric started to respond, eagerly and angrily, it seemed to Elbryan, but the tall man went silent as Paulson stormed back over to the fire.

"And I'm not liking smelly goblins!" the large man snarled. "I mean to get me enough goblin ears so that a single gold piece bounty'll put me in a big house with a dozen serving wenches on a hundred acres o' land!"

Elbryan nodded and smiled, trying to calm the brute, but Paulson only kicked the dirt again and stormed away. It was more than any bounty, the ranger knew. And, given the fact that Cric and Chipmunk had remained, it was more than the tale of a child lost. These three, for all their faults and all their vocal protests, carried some degree of humanity within them. Whatever complaints Cric and Chipmunk might offer, they had remained in the area because of the refugees, out of simple compassion.

In the end, Elbryan hardly cared what reason Paulson or the others gave for staying. Given the increasingly desperate situation about him, Elbryan was only glad to have these trappers, fierce fighters who knew the area as well as—or even better than—he, on his side.

The next day, Elbryan set the refugees on their way—for Dundalis, if possible, though he gave Paulson several alternate choices, caves and sheltered vales. Then the ranger set off, riding hard for End-o'-the-World, looking for answers or hints of what might yet come, and hoping to find more refugees.

The forest was perfectly quiet as he neared the town. Still, he saw no smoke blackening the sky. He left Symphony in the forest and moved tree to tree, crossing past goblin sentries undetected, at last finding a good vantage point on the edge of the village.

Goblins, dwarves, and giants swarmed in the place, moving as if this was their home. Elbryan saw the bodies, dozens of dead, human and humanoid, thrown in a ditch on the western edge of town, but this was not as the sack of Dundalis had been. The buildings showed very little damage; none had been burned. Did the humanoid army mean to settle here? Or, as the ranger thought much more likely, did they mean to use End-o'-the-World as a base camp, a supply depot?

Elbryan didn't like the prospects. From End-o'-the-World, this force could swing south and then east, cutting off the roads for any people fleeing Weedy Meadow or Dundalis, the next obvious targets. And if the humanoids didn't sack the town, that indicated they meant to continue on.

Elbryan recalled the image of the vast encampment. The humanoids could indeed advance, and the ranger had to wonder if all the men of Honce-the-Bear could even slow them.

He could do nothing here, so he thought, and he turned to leave, picking the course that would get him back through the forest to Symphony.

Then the ranger heard the cry, a child's cry, from a house nearby.

Elbryan squatted low and considered his options. He could hardly leave such a desperate wail, but if he was caught here, then the information he possessed might never reach Weedy Meadow or Dundalis. There was more at stake here than his own life.

But the cry sounded again, seconded by another whimper, that of a woman.

Elbryan dashed across the clearing between two houses, held still long enough to survey the area, then ran on to the house in question.

"A meal for a dog!" he heard inside, a harsh voice, like that of the powrie he had killed. "You get me some proper food or I'll eat the arm from your ugly son!"

The woman cried out again, followed closely by the sound of a sharp slap, then of a body falling hard to the floor. Elbryan moved along the side of the house, finally spotting a small window.

The powrie advanced on the sobbing woman, its hand raised to deliver another heavy blow. It stopped, though, a couple of feet from its intended victim, looking down at the woman curiously.

And she looked at the dwarf, not understanding—until the powrie toppled forward, an arrow deep in its back. The woman looked past it, her eyes wide, to the window, where stood the ranger, motioning to her and to her son to be quick.

The three got from house to house, then across the short clearing to the woods. As they entered the shelter of the trees, they heard a scream from the town.

Elbryan looked back upon End-o'-the-World to see another powrie come running out of the house, shouting that there was an archer about.

"Run!" Elbryan whispered urgently to his companions. They scrambled through the woods desperately, hearing horns from the town. Elbryan realized that the goblin sentries would soon be all about them, swarming about the forest.

He saw the shapes of two such goblins paralleling the movements of his group. Up came Hawkwing, and two shots later, the immediate threat was ended.

But there were more, many more, and the pursuit from the town was organized and systematic, calls from sentries gradually narrowing the possible area.

The three came upon Symphony, the big stallion pawing the ground and snorting warnings. Elbryan hoisted the woman onto Symphony's back, into the saddle, then placed the boy behind her.

"Tell the centaur what you have seen in End-o'-the-World," he instructed the woman, who only shook her head as if she didn't understand. "Tell Bradwarden—remember that name!—and all the others that the goblins will likely move south and east to cut off their escape." The ranger's tone was adamant, so forceful that the woman finally nodded her consent. "I will join you as soon as I can."

"Run," the ranger instructed the horse, "all the way to the grove to Bradwarden!"

"What of you?" the woman asked, grabbing the ranger's hand. "How will you get away from this place?" Elbryan had no time for answers. He pulled his hand free, and Symphony leaped away, thundering down the trails, slamming down two goblins that foolishly jumped in his path to intercept.

Elbryan watched for a moment, confident that the woman and boy would be safe enough with Symphony carrying them. Then the ranger turned his attention to his own predicament, looked about at the many shapes moving among the shadows of the trees, and listened to the many calls of goblins and dwarves and the fearsome bellows of giants.

CHAPTER

❖ 39 ❖

The Difference

T hey were readying to attack Weedy Meadow. Elbryan knew that, could hear it in the shriek of every bird, in the movements of squirrels, agitated by the presence of such numbers, by the thunder of a giant's step or the rolling war machines, by the croaks of powrie generals, the eager whines of bloodthirsty goblins.

They were readying to attack Weedy Meadow, and Avelyn and Pony had not been able to convince the townsfolk to leave—not many, anyway, though now with the storm cloud that was the goblin army hovering about the village, many of the folk began to recognize their folly.

From a high vantage point some two miles south of the village, Elbryan saw the villagers shoring up walls, scrambling about in preparation. None of it would make any difference, the ranger knew. The only hope for Weedy Meadow's four score people was to get out of the village and far away. And with the goblins moving in from all sides, the only possibility of that was with the help of the ranger and his friends.

But Elbryan had so few to work with. Besides Pony and Avelyn, who were somewhere down amid that scrambling group, Elbryan had only the three trappers and Bradwarden. The refugees from End-o'-the-World were nowhere near ready for another fight; half of them hadn't even uttered a word yet. The one advantage on the ranger's side was his knowledge of the region surrounding Weedy Meadow. The village was nestled in a land of steep hillsides and narrow valleys, where a hundred sneaking people might pass unnoticed only a few dozen yards away. This was a place of natural noises: running streams, cackling birds, and chattering animals. A living forest, with enough pine and spruce to offer cover even now, with winter fast holding the land.

"What're ye thinking?" Bradwarden asked, moving up quietly beside the ranger.

"We have to get them out."

"Not so easy a task, I'd be betting," replied the centaur, "else Avelyn and

Pony'd have them far away already." Bradwarden paused, watching Elbryan's pained features as the man continued to stare to the north. The centaur understood what the man was feeling, the sense of his own loss those years before and the helplessness now in the face of a repeat of that disaster. Bradwarden had watched Elbryan closely these last two days, since he had evaded the monsters about End-o'-the-World and had crawled out of the forest. Always had the ranger seemed stoic and often stern, but never as grim as now.

"We'll get Pony and Avelyn, at least," the centaur offered, "and some others, I'm not doubting. Most won't go. Ye know that. They'll be staying with their homes until they see the enemy, then they'll know their doom. Then, it'll be too late for them."

Elbryan cocked an eyebrow. "Will it?" he asked simply.

Bradwarden didn't quite understand. Even if Elbryan and the trappers, all the refugees from End-o'-the-World, and all the folk of Dundalis went in to bolster the defenses of Weedy Meadow, the village would be flattened within an hour. Elbryan knew that as surely as did the centaur, and yet, the sudden gleam of determination on Elbryan's face left the centaur believing that the man had some plan.

"There," Elbryan said, pointing to a position just east of the village, to a pair of two-thousand-foot-tall mountains, their steep sides white with snow, crossed by the dark lines of many leafless trees.

"The valley between those hills is full of boulders and pine groves," the ranger explained. "Cover enough, if we move the folk quickly." Elbryan looked down and patted Symphony's muscled neck, knowing full well that the horse not only understood the plan but would help facilitate it.

"Ye'd choose the low ground for yer escape?" the centaur asked incredulously.

"Too many trees," Elbryan answered without hesitation as the puzzle sorted out before him. "They will get no clear shots or spear throws from above."

"They'll come down like a mass o' swooping hawks," Bradwarden protested.

Elbryan smiled wickedly as he considered those steep hillsides, all of varied angles and deep with virgin snow. He thought of Avelyn and the magic stones and some of the properties the monk had explained to him. He thought of Paulson, Cric, and Chipmunk, and their undeniable skills. "Will they?" he said calmly, his tone so even and assured that the centaur sucked in his breath and argued no more.

"How did you get in here?" Pony asked breathlessly, grabbing Elbryan in a hug as soon as she spotted him entering the common room at Weedy Meadow. "We know the goblins are all about."

"Thicker than you believe," Elbryan agreed, returning the hug tenfold. It felt so good to him, so warm and fulfilling, that a very large part of the stoic ranger wanted to whisk Pony away into the night, to run far away from this place and its troubles and just live peacefully and lovingly.

He could not do that, could not forsake his duty and the destiny that he had been shown by the Touel'alfar. For every thought of running away with Pony, the ranger held five memories of the tragedy that had befallen his own family and community.

Avelyn bounded over to the pair a moment later, the boisterous monk seeming not so animated now. "Ah, but they wouldn't go," he wailed at Elbryan. "They would not listen to our words, and even now, with darkness looming in the forest, many insist that they will stay and fight."

"Any who choose to stay and fight will surely die," Elbryan said, loud enough for several nearby townsfolk to hear. A pair of grizzly men at a table near the common room entrance stood up, one kicking the table away as he rose. They glared at Elbryan for a long moment, but finally walked away, moving to the other side of the large hall.

Undaunted, Elbryan moved to the long table that served as the bar, and hopped atop it. "I tell you this only one time," the ranger proclaimed, and the score of men and half that number of women in the room looked his way, most disdainfully but some too fearful to show any outrage. "I have just crawled through the ranks of our enemy, deep lines of goblins and giants and powrie dwarves."

"Powries?" one woman echoed.

"Bah, a tale o' lies," someone answered from one corner.

"Your only chance will be to get far from this place," Elbryan said bluntly, tossing the bloodred beret to the floor. "And even now, escape will not be easy. I will take those that I can with me tonight, soon after the moon has set." The ranger paused and glanced around, locking stares with each of the patrons, letting them see the intensity of his green eyes, the determination on his face. "As for the rest of you, your window through the monstrous force will be small and any hesitation will cost you dearly."

"Who are you to come in here and give orders?" one man demanded. Agreeing protests rang from every corner of the room.

True to his word, the ranger did not repeat his message. He hopped down from the table, gathered Pony and Avelyn in his wake, and bade them follow him outside, where they might talk in private.

Elbryan didn't flinch nor did he look back threateningly when a mug shattered against the wall beside the exit, a missile obviously aimed at the back of his head.

Elbryan conferred with Avelyn first, to confirm the potential of the magical stones. Then he talked more to Pony, who better understood the terrain of this region, with its hilly forests and many streams.

"They, too, will come in through that valley," Pony reasoned as Elbryan laid out the plan before her. "If they are as organized as your description of the assault on End-o'-the-World indicates, they will not leave so open a route behind them. They will come in through that valley, and will take the tops of both hills."

"Not many will make it through," the ranger promised. "The goblin line will be thin, and speed and surprise will be our allies. As for those on the hills, three friends are already preparing for them."

Pony nodded, not doubting the ranger's words, but still, another part of the plan troubled her deeply. "How can we place so much hope on animals?" she asked.

Elbryan looked to Avelyn. "The turquoise," he explained. "It has given me insight into Symphony's thoughts. I can talk to the horse with my mind, and he understands. Of that I am sure."

Avelyn nodded, not doubting the power of the turquoise. The stone, as if it were something sentient, had called to the monk on that day when he had presented it to Elbryan and Symphony, and Avelyn, who had floated down the face of a cliff, who had walked on water and unleashed tremendous fireballs, who had held the power of a thunderstorm in his puny, mortal hands, would not discount any possibilities of its God-given power.

"We have few options," Pony admitted.

"No other," Elbryan replied.

Avelyn saw the look that passed between them and he walked away, at first aimlessly but then turning toward the cabin of the one family—a widow and her three small children—that the three friends had agreed should leave with the ranger this night.

Pony and Elbryan spent a long and quiet moment together, ending it wordlessly with a kiss that passed as a promise from Elbryan to the woman that she would not be abandoned, and as a promise from Pony that she and those who would leave would be ready when the moment of opportunity was upon them.

The ranger left Weedy Meadow that night, moving through the winding valley east of the village with the fleeing family. The forest was quiet, but, as Elbryan had suspected, it was not empty.

"Goblins," he mouthed silently to the woman, and he held up his open hand to indicate their number at five. The ranger had an arrow ready on Hawkwing, but he didn't want to kill any monsters this night, not in this pass, where any bodies might alert the army to a possible hole in its raiding lines.

So they sat tight and waited, the woman working hard to keep her youngest child, a mere infant, from crying.

The goblins moved close, so close that the five could hear their whining voices, so close that the crack of a stick underfoot sounded loud to the ranger and the family.

Elbryan kept them down, tried to reassure them all by patting the other two children softly, by showing them his weapons and that he was ready should they be discovered.

The ranger, lying up front, said nothing when a goblin boot stepped firmly on the cold ground barely three feet from his head. Elbryan held his breath and clutched his hand axe, playing out in his mind the quickest and surest attack should the goblin make any sudden move to indicate that it had spotted the group.

But then the moment had passed, the goblins wandering on along their patrol route in the valley, oblivious of the man and his refugees. The goblins' ignorance saved the creatures' lives that night, for death was barely an arm's length away; more important, the goblins' ignorance also saved Elbryan's plan.

The sky brightened to a dull gray shortly before the dawn, another lazy snowstorm dropping scattered flakes that floated to and fro during their descent. Elbryan and Bradwarden, on that same hill far to the south of Weedy Meadow, watched for the start of it all, for the first signs of the attack they knew would come this day.

"Ye left her there," the centaur said unexpectedly.

Elbryan cocked a curious eyebrow.

"The girl," the centaur explained. "Yer lover."

"More than a lover," Elbryan replied.

"And ye left her there," the centaur went on, "with ten thousand monsters moving her way."

Elbryan continued to stare curiously at his half-equine friend, not sure whether Bradwarden was congratulating him or criticizing him.

"Ye left the woman ye love in harm's way."

The words hit Elbryan strangely, showed him a perspective that he had hardly considered. "It was Pony's choice to stay, her duty—"

"She could die this day."

"Do you enjoy torturing me with your words?"

Bradwarden looked the ranger squarely in the face and laughed heartily. "Torturing?" he asked. "I'm admiring ye, boy! Ye love the girl, but ye left her in a town that's about to be sacked!"

"I trust her," Elbryan protested, too defensive to understand the centaur's sincerity, "and trust in her."

"So I'm seeing," said Bradwarden. He put hand on Elbryan's shoulder and gave the man a sincere, admiring look. "And that's yer strength. Too many of yer folk would've forced the girl by their side, to protect her. Ye're smart enough to see that Pony needs little protecting."

Elbryan looked back to the north, to Weedy Meadow.

"She could die this day," Bradwarden said evenly.

"So could we," Elbryan countered.

"So could ten thousand goblins." The centaur laughed.

Elbryan joined in, but the mirth was ended when a streaking line of fire cut across the sky, a ball of flaming pitch, soaring for Weedy Meadow.

"Powrie catapult," Bradwarden said dryly.

"Time to go," replied Elbryan. He gave one last look at the distant village, at the small fire that had come up. Pony was in there, in harm's way.

Elbryan grimaced and let it go. He looked at the centaur, moving steadily ahead of him, and at first he was angry with Bradwarden for bringing up the grim possibilities. Until this time, Elbryan hadn't even considered the danger to Pony on a personal level, so great was his trust in her. She would lead the people out of Weedy Meadow, he had supposed, and though some of them might be killed, Pony would not.

Bradwarden had made him face the truth of this day, and gradually the ranger's anger became gratitude. He didn't trust Pony any less; he could control his desires to rush to her side and protect her. Bradwarden had shown him the truth of his relationship, the true depth of his love and trust for this woman who had come back into his life. Elbryan nodded and smiled as he regarded the centaur, sincerely grateful.

"Ho, ho, what!" the monk bellowed, running to the newest fire, clutching the sheet of serpentine in his plump hand. Using the magical protection, Avelyn walked right into the midst of the blaze, standing with flames licking to his shoulders but smiling widely, to the amazement of those villagers witnessing the sight.

The monk fell deeper into the magic of the stone, calling forth its shielding powers, expanding its area of influence until this particular fire was smothered.

Avelyn came out of his trance, only to find that another blaze was burning, not so far away. "Ho, ho, what!" he bellowed again, pushing aside the would-be village firefighters so that he could use his much more effective method.

Despite the efforts of the mad friar, the rain of powrie fireballs increased, coupled with bouncing boulders that smashed more than one home to kindling. One fireball hit against the village's east wall, splattering the two men standing nearby with burning pitch. Pony was quick to one, wrapping him in a heavy blanket, and Avelyn got to the other, using the serpentine effectively.

"The gray stone!" Pony cried to the monk, indicating the hematite and the badly burned man on the ground beside her. Avelyn went to him at once and eased his pain, but the monk's expression turned more grim.

He was beginning to admit that he could not keep up with the barrage, and he knew that even this was but a prelude to worse.

Pony left the man in Avelyn's caring hands and ran about the frantic villagers, berating them for their folly in staying and reminding them that a
way out might soon be open.

She was not surprised that now, with fireballs lighting structures by the
minute and boulders crashing down about them, she found more people
willing to listen to Elbryan's plan. Still, despite the flaming evidence, many
of the proud and stubborn folk refused to admit that this was more than a
simple goblin raid.

"We'll push them back," one man argued to her, "chase them into the
woods so far, they'll never find their stinking way out!"

Pony shook her head, trying to argue, but the man had too much support
from the five fellows standing shoulder-to-shoulder with him along the wall.

"Goblins!" the man insisted, and he spat at Pony's feet.

The others started grumbling but went strangely silent an instant later,
and Pony looked up at them, then followed their gaze across the short field
that stood between the village and the edge of the trees.

A pair of fomorian giants, fifteen feet tall and ten times the weight of a
heavy man, paced back and forth in the shadows, eager to rush the wall.

"Damn big goblins," Pony replied sarcastically. She looked down at the
weapons the group carried—shovels and pitchforks mostly, with only a
single, rusty old sword among them. Pony had given her own sword to the
mother who had left with Elbryan, and now she carried only a slender club
and a small axe, weapons that looked puny indeed against the sheer bulk of
those two giants.

She left the stubborn group with one final reminder. "The east wall," she
said grimly.

She found Avelyn near that wall, and paused as she approached, seeing a
slight bluish glow among the timbers of the one east gate. She looked at the
monk curiously.

Avelyn shrugged. "I did not know that the serpentine could enact a
lasting barrier," he said, "nor do I know how long I might maintain it. But
be assured that any fires brushing that gate will find no hold."

Pony put a hand to the monk's broad shoulder, glad indeed to have
Brother Avelyn on her side.

The pair turned abruptly a moment later when a shout from the north
wall told them that the attack was on.

Elbryan was running hard to keep up with Bradwarden; Symphony had
taken to the woods, disappearing as a shadow might when the sun goes
behind dark clouds.

"I cannot slow!" the centaur called, and then he grunted as the ranger
grabbed fast to his tail, the man half running, half flying behind the swift
creature.

They came to their base camp, where Paulson, Cric, and Chipmunk waited.

"They're filling the valley," Paulson explained, "a long line, goblins mostly, and not so deep."

"Powries on the hills," Cric piped in.

"But the traps are set?" Elbryan asked.

All three nodded eagerly.

Elbryan closed his eyes and sent his thoughts out to Symphony, and heard the horse's response clearly. Satisfied, he looked again at his immediate companions. "We must pick our targets carefully," the ranger explained. "We must thin their line wherever we may, and take out any giants or those monsters that can get out of harm's way." The ranger looked back to the east. "Let Symphony do the rest," he explained.

The group started off quietly, Paulson, Cric, and Chipmunk going along the base of the north hill, Elbryan and Bradwarden making their way to the south.

Agile Pony got to the roof quickly and fell flat to her belly, crawling low as spears arched over her, as the monstrous horde came on toward the north gate. She peeked over the edge of the roof, back into the village, and saw that only three of the five at the wall remained alive, and they were fleeing fast.

The two giants banged against the fortified wall for a moment, then simply stepped over it.

Pony held her breath at that dangerous moment, but fortunately the two giants were too concerned with the townsfolk to notice her. They strode past into the village, men and women fleeing before them, screaming, finally admitting their folly in staying.

"Ho, ho, what!" came a familiar cry, and Pony looked past the giants to see Brother Avelyn standing steady before them.

A spear nearly got the distracted woman. She spun about as a goblin's head appeared above the edge of the roof. Pony's club sent the monster tumbling away, but she noted that a hundred more were climbing all about the wall, eager for human blood. With a growl, the woman threw her club into the face of the closest one, and it, too, fell back. Then she gave a quick glance to the east, which was still quiet.

"Damn," the woman muttered and she put her legs under her and ran for the southwestern corner of the roof, leaping far into the air and grabbing the closest giant by the hair. Her momentum brought her right in front of the monster, their faces inches apart, and Pony wasted no time in planting her axe into that gruesome visage.

The giant howled, the woman fell away, landing in a roll, and the second giant turned to her, ready to squash her flat.

"Ho, ho, what!" Avelyn bellowed his signature cry, one he used now to release the mounting energies of the graphite he held.

A forked blast of blue-white lightning erupted from the monk's hand, one finger of the bolt striking each giant. The one Pony had hit in the face, its hands up to cover the wound, went flying backward, hitting the wall waist high and flipping right over it, crushing a goblin in the process. The other giant, its foot high to stamp Pony, jolted straight and stood trembling, too stunned to react as its intended victim ran off.

Pony rushed to Avelyn. She looked all about desperately. Goblins were crawling over the walls like ants, hundreds and hundreds, their sheer numbers burying any townsfolk who stood to challenge them.

"Fighting in the east!" one man yelled, running to Pony and Avelyn. "Where is your plan?" he added sarcastically, hopelessly.

Pony ran with him back toward the eastern gate, while Avelyn held the rear guard, loosing another lighting bolt that launched a dozen goblins from the rooftop Pony had just abandoned.

A powrie crawled atop the eastern wall directly in front of Pony and the villager, not so far from the gate.

"Where is your plan?" the man demanded again of Pony, his desperate question echoing off the anxious faces of all the villagers gathered near the wall.

The powrie stood tall on the eastern wall, but then kept moving forward, curiously, falling headlong over the structure and landing in the dirt, very still.

A long arrow protruded from its back, an arrow with fletchings familiar to the woman.

"There is my plan," she replied confidently.

A moment later came the thunder of hoofbeats to the east, many hoofbeats accompanied by the screams of those unfortunate goblins caught in front of the wild horse stampede.

"Avelyn!" Pony yelled.

"Ho, ho, what!" the monk replied, loosing yet another lightning bolt, this time into the ground at the feet of a horde of goblins that were charging straight for him. The jolt sent the entire group of monsters two feet off the ground.

Pony grabbed a pitchfork from one of the men nearby and ran to the eastern gate, bravely throwing it open.

There stood a pair of goblins, stunned that the gate had opened before them. Pony took one in the throat with the pitchfork. The other turned to flee, but was cut down almost immediately, an arrow striking it right between the eyes. Pony looked back and spotted Elbryan sitting on a low branch of a tree on the northern side of the ravine. Below the ranger, Bradwarden ran back and forth, trampling goblins and powries or bashing them down with his heavy cudgel. The centaur tapped one powrie on the head, then scooped up the dazed dwarf and dropped it into a sack.

Pony didn't have time to consider the move, for the thunder approached, led by powerful Symphony. Goblins and powries scattered or were crushed beneath the charge, a hundred wild horses stampeding along the ravine.

"Avelyn!" Pony cried, and the monk rushed past her; she noted that he was glowing slightly, that same bluish hue as the eastern gate.

Pony held the townsfolk back as Avelyn ran out among the goblins. Most were too confused and frightened to attack, but some did charge.

Avelyn held forth his hand—Pony caught sight of a red sparkle from within his grasp.

A huge ball of fire encircled the monk and consumed all the nearby monsters. A hot wind brushed Pony's face and blew into the stunned villagers standing beside her.

When the flames dissipated an instant later, Avelyn stood alone and the way was open.

Almost open; a powrie came rushing out from behind a stone, its hair burned away, its face blackened, its club no more than a withered and charred stick. But the dwarf was very much alive, and very angry. It howled and whooped and charged Avelyn, ready to throttle the monk with its bare hands.

In his other hand, Avelyn clutched a third stone, brown and striped with black—tiger's paw, it was called. Now the monk fell into this stone's magic, letting go the fire shield of the serpentine. A moment later, Avelyn was screaming in agony, not from the powrie—that enemy hadn't caught up to him yet—but from the work of his own transforming magic that was bending and breaking the bones in Avelyn's left arm. Fingers crunched and shortened, fingernails narrowed and slipped back under the knuckles, and then came a great itching as orange and black fur erupted all along the length of the arm.

The powrie got to the monk, but Avelyn had recovered now. He was whole again—except that his left arm was no longer the arm of Brother Avelyn but that of a powerful tiger.

With a mere thought, Avelyn extended his claws and raked them across, taking the face off of the stunned powrie.

Now the way was clear.

From further down the valley, Symphony charged in, followed by his equine minions. The stampede came to a skidding halt, the wild horses accepting riders, villagers. Pony climbed atop Symphony, and Avelyn, standing with Elbryan as the ranger ran in, waited behind to cover the retreat.

Both Pony and Elbryan sucked in their breath at the sight of Avelyn's arm, but neither spoke of it at that desperate moment.

Then away thundered Symphony and the hundred horses, fifty of Weedy Meadow's eighty inhabitants holding fast to manes, terrified, and scores of goblins and powries scrambling to the hills, trying to get out of the way.

Down those hills came the powries, outraged by the apparent escape, but Paulson, Cric, and Chipmunk had done their work well. Deadfalls, pit traps, and jaw traps stopped many; in one place a dropping pile of logs triggered a small avalanche of loose snow and rock.

Those monsters that did make it down found Bradwarden and his cudgel waiting for them, the centaur kicking and smashing with abandon. Avelyn's graphite shot out again, back toward Weedy Meadow's eastern gate, scattering those goblins coming in close pursuit and opening the way for Elbryan, who insisted that he go back for any stragglers.

The ranger found a giant coming hard his way, stomping across the village, outraged and already hurt by one of the monk's lightning blasts.

Hawkwing's bowstring hummed repeatedly, an arrow thudding into the giant's chest, followed by one to its belly, another to its chest, and then a third nicking off huge ribs, and then a second in the belly.

Each hit slowed the behemoth a bit more, allowed Elbryan yet another devastating shot. Finally, the stubborn monster slumped down.

Several frightened men ran right over its back as it tumbled, a horde of shrieking goblins close on their heels.

Elbryan knelt by the gate, taking careful aim and picking off the closest monsters one by one.

"Avelyn, I need you!" the ranger cried. The situation was even more desperate than Elbryan initially believed, as he discovered when he looked up to see a goblin standing atop the wall, some five feet to the side of the gate, ready to pounce upon him.

But Avelyn couldn't immediately help, the monk preoccupied with a group of powries coming hard down the south hill, having dodged the trappers' pitfalls.

Elbryan turned to meet the pounce, but even as the goblin came on, silver flickers caught the ranger's eye. The monster landed right beside the ranger, but it was dead before it hit the ground, three daggers sticking from the side of its neck and chest. Elbryan glanced back to a smiling Chipmunk, the man running off to engage another confused powrie.

"Avelyn!" Elbryan called again, more insistently. The ranger put up his bow and cut down one more goblin as the group of men ran out the gate and scrambled past him.

Elbryan fell back in a roll; goblins filled the gate and poured out.

Avelyn's lightning blast laid them low.

Then they were off and running, all of them, Elbryan and the three trappers, Bradwarden and Avelyn, and all the latest refugees of Weedy Meadow, following the tentative trail opened to them by the horse stampede.

They ran all the morning, fighting often, but only quick skirmishes. They followed the obvious trail and were guided along even more cunning ways by Elbryan, the ranger following Symphony's call.

One stubborn group of thirty powries stayed with them all the way, hooting and hollering, throwing daggers and axes whenever they got close enough, and only crying out with more fervor whenever Elbryan or Bradwarden paused and let fly an arrow, inevitably taking one of the dwarves down.

Avelyn, huffing and puffing, and too weary to attempt another stone use, moaned and complained that the others should leave his fat body behind. Elbryan would hear none of that, of course, and neither would Bradwarden. The powerful centaur was still carrying the sack with the kicking powrie, and somehow managing to put his great bow to use every so often, but he still had enough strength to allow the fat monk up on his back.

The horse trail continued to the east, but Elbryan called for a turn to the south, leading his group, more sliding than running, down a thickly wooded hillside that ended in a half-frozen stream and a field covered with snow beyond that. They splashed across and ran on, the powries coming in furious pursuit now that their prey was in the open.

"Why'd we go this way?" one villager cried out in desperation, seeing the stubborn, untiring dwarves gaining steadily.

The man got his answer as grim-faced Pony, sitting tall atop Symphony, came out of the trees across the way, flanked on each side by a score of angry villagers and their spirited mounts.

Elbryan's group ran on; the powries skidded to an abrupt halt and tried to turn.

Pony led the thunderous charge and not a dwarf got off that field alive—except for the unfortunate one kicking futilely in Bradwarden's sack.

The encampment that night, closer to Dundalis than to Weedy Meadow, was filled with a bittersweet atmosphere. More than sixty of the village's eighty folk had escaped, but that meant that nearly a score had died, and all their homes were lost.

"You sent him away?" Pony asked Elbryan as the ranger approached the campfire she and Avelyn shared.

"I could not tolerate that in the camp," Elbryan explained.

"How could you tolerate it at all?" Avelyn asked.

"How could I stop it?" Elbryan was quick to reply.

"Good point," the monk conceded. "Ho, ho, what!"

Elbryan looked at Pony, and each shuddered, thinking of brutal Bradwarden and his planned meal. Elbryan had interrogated the captured powrie, getting no information of any value, and then the centaur had claimed the dwarf as his catch—and as his dinner.

He had promised Elbryan that he would kill the wretched creature quickly, at least.

The ranger had to be satisfied with that; he and the refugees were in no position to take on a prisoner, especially one as fierce and stupidly bold as that powrie.

"We did well," Avelyn remarked, handing a bowl to Elbryan and motioning to a cauldron not so far away.

The ranger held up his hand, having little appetite this night.

Avelyn only shrugged and went back to his meal.

"You did well," Elbryan remarked to the man. "Your fireball opened the way for Symphony—and even the help of the horses would not have been possible without the magic of the turquoise. And your lightning bolts saved many lives, my own included."

"And mine," Pony added, rubbing the fat monk's back.

Avelyn looked at her, then at Elbryan, his expression truly content. He even forgot his food for a moment, just sat back and considered the events and the role he and his God-given stones had played.

"For years I have wondered if I chose correctly in taking the stones," Avelyn explained a moment later. "Always have I been followed by doubts, by fears that my actions were not truly in the spirit of God but only in my own misguided interpretation of that spirit."

"Today proves you right, then," Elbryan said quietly.

Avelyn nodded, feeling truly vindicated. A moment later, he caught the look that passed between Elbryan and Pony, and politely excused himself. There were many wounded in the encampment that night, including some who might need further help from Avelyn and his hematite.

"I could not save Weedy Meadow," Elbryan said to the woman when they were alone.

Pony looked all around, leading Elbryan's gaze to the men and women, to the children who would have surely died this day had not the ranger and his friends ushered them away.

"I am satisfied," Elbryan admitted. "The town could not be saved, but so different this is from the day of our own tragedy."

"We did not have a ranger to look over us," Pony replied with a grin.

That smile could not hold, though, lost in the bittersweet blend of tragedy present and tragedy past. The two moved closer together, huddled in each other's arms before the fire, and said not another word, each lost in their memories of their own loss but with the satisfaction that this day, they had been the difference.

❖ 40 ❖

Nightbird the Leader

"They are not burning the town," Elbryan remarked as he, Pony, Bradwarden, and Avelyn looked toward Dundalis.

"Why would they?" the centaur asked. "The place was empty before they ever got there."

"True enough," Elbryan replied, for the folk of Dundalis, with sixty-three witnesses from Weedy Meadow and a score from End-o'-the-World telling tales of utter disaster, had not been hard to convince. All of Dundalis' folk had followed Elbryan into the woods to the camps the ranger and his friends had constructed, hidden deep and far from the trails.

"But neither did they burn Weedy Meadow," Pony observed, "nor End-o'-the-World before that."

Elbryan looked grimly at Bradwarden.

"Supply towns," the centaur said, his tone grave.

"That means they are continuing south," Avelyn remarked, his voice cracking on the words. "How far?"

"Few villages south of here," Bradwarden said. "Nothing much all the way to the great river."

"Palmaris," Avelyn muttered helplessly.

A long, silent moment passed as the gravity of the situation settled more deeply over the four friends.

"We can do little to stop such an army," Elbryan declared. "But our duty is threefold: to hurt the monsters in any way that we can, to send word ahead so that the villages and even the great city are not caught unaware, and to care for those who have fallen under our protection."

"A hundred and sixty," Bradwarden said. "And I haven't yet counted them all. Worse, no more than a third o' them're able to fight against the likes of a single goblin."

"We must work with them, then," Elbryan declared, "usher those who cannot fight to safety and use those who can and will do battle to our best advantage."

"A huge task, ranger," Bradwarden remarked.

Elbryan stared at him long and hard.

"I'm with ye," the centaur grumbled a moment later, "though not for the taste o' powrie, I tell ye. Tough little bugs!"

"Ho, ho, what!" Avelyn howled.

They went to the task that very day, sorting the refugees into those who would stay and fight with Elbryan, and those who would be sent to safer havens, into caves that Bradwarden knew of some distance to the east of Dundalis or even into the more human-controlled southlands, if a route could be found. When they finished the initial round, Elbryan found that he had more than seven score who would need to be relocated, leaving him just over twenty able-bodied warriors. And they were indeed a ragtag band; the best among them, other than Pony, Bradwarden, and Avelyn, was probably unreliable Paulson or the always-irritating, disagreeable Tol Yuganick.

Pony pointed out that very fact to Elbryan when they sat together that evening. "You should send him south with the refugees," she noted, indicating the grumbling Tol, who was walking about the encampment, bullying any who crossed his path.

"He is strong and good with a spear," Elbryan countered.

"And he'll fight you all the way," Pony said. "Tol will demand control, and his continuing rage will certainly put him, and any who follow him, into a position from which there will be no escape."

Elbryan couldn't really disagree. At least with Paulson, the ranger had some idea that the man was willing to follow directions; Paulson and his two companions, after all, had laid traps on the hillsides east of Weedy Meadow exactly as Elbryan had bade them.

"Send him off with the unfit," Pony said again, more forcefully. "Let Belster O'Comely deal with the brute, else I fear that you and Tol will cross swords, and it would not do for you to be killing one of our own in front of the others."

Elbryan thought she was perhaps being a bit overdramatic, but he had to admit that he and Tol had come close to blows several times over the previous few months—and then in situations not nearly as tense as the one that surely lay before them.

"When will you send the band south?" Pony asked, wisely giving Elbryan some breathing room before he was forced into such a difficult decision.

"Paulson, Cric, and Chipmunk are off scouting the area even now," the ranger replied, "swinging west to confirm the occupation of Weedy Meadow and End-o'-the-World and then south to see what roads lie open. When they return in a few days, we might decide what to do with the refugees."

Pony nodded, considering the plan. "If they will soon return, then they will not go far to the south, not to the next villages in line, Caer Tinella and Landsdown, and certainly not to Palmaris," she reasoned. "You must send an emissary soon if the southland is to be properly warned."

Elbryan sighed deeply, agreeing fully with her observation. He knew the proper course before him, knew the perfect choice, a person possessed of both tact and skills, battle and horsemanship, but it was a decree the ranger did not wish to utter.

Pony did it for him. "Symphony will bear me?" she asked, drawing the ranger's gaze to her own.

Elbryan paused and looked long and hard at the woman, at his love. They had been reunited for so short a time, how could he bear to part with her again? Despite that turmoil, Elbryan found himself nodding. Symphony would indeed carry Pony; the great stallion had already indicated as much to Elbryan.

"Then I will be away before the dawn," Pony said firmly.

Elbryan sighed again, and Pony took his face in her hands, turned him to her, and pulled him close, kissing him gently.

"I will go all the way to Palmaris, if I must," she promised, "and then I will return to your side. Symphony will see me there and back again. No goblin, no powrie, no giant will catch me."

Elbryan, who had felt the wind, the rush of Symphony's run, didn't doubt that for a minute. "And you must return to me," he whispered, "to fight beside me and to lie beside me in the quiet night, when all the troubles of the day must be put to peace."

Pony kissed him again, longer and harder this time. All around them, the camp was settling down, save the occasional grumble from ugly Tol, and the pair slipped away sometime later into the forest to a private place.

True to her word, Pony was riding hard to the south as the sun crested the eastern horizon. She had not gone without two meetings, though, one a very private discussion with Elbryan and the other, unexpectedly, with Brother Avelyn, who was waiting for her when she walked out of the camp.

"Symphony is not far," the monk explained. "I saw him on that ridge just a few minutes ago. Waiting for you, I should guess."

Pony gave a crooked smile, her wonderment at the continuing intelligence shown by the animal—now seeming to be so much more than an ordinary horse—clearly displayed on her features.

"As I was waiting for you," Avelyn huffed.

"Symphony would not carry us both," Pony said dryly.

"What?" asked Avelyn. "Ho, ho, good laugh, that!"

The man's mirth disappeared almost immediately, and the suddenly grim set of his heavy jowls made Pony believe he was concerned for her safety.

"I will return," she promised.

Avelyn nodded. "And all the faster," he explained, holding forth a silver circlet, "with this."

Pony took the band tentatively, knowing as soon as she saw the gemstone set in the silver in front that this was much more than something ornamental. The gem was unlike anything she had seen before, yellowish-green with a black streak down its middle.

"Cat's eye," Avelyn explained. He took the circlet back from her and set it about her forehead.

"With it, you will see clearly in the dark of night," the monk explained.

Indeed, the mounting light of dawn still a while away seemed suddenly brighter to Pony. Not brighter, exactly, but every object became much more distinct. Pony looked at Avelyn, suddenly very appreciative of the training he had given her with the magical stones but somewhat surprised that she could call forth the magic of this cat's eye so readily.

"How is it that the stone will work so easily for me?" she asked. "And am I now ready to unleash fireballs and bolts of lightning as you did in the battle in Weedy Meadow?" Pony's expression grew sly. "Is the power, then, wholly of the stones?" she asked. "And if that is so, then why is Avelyn so blessed?"

"Ho, but that hurt!" the good-natured monk bellowed. "Ho, ho, what! Blessed indeed, say some, but cursed, say I, with such a supportive friend as this!"

"Ho, but that hurt!" Pony echoed, imitating Avelyn's voice, and they shared a much-needed laugh.

"The power comes from both stone and user," Avelyn explained in all seriousness, a lesson he had explained to her many times during their weeks on the road. "Some stones, though, such as the turquoise I gave to Elbryan and he to Symphony, can be altered to perform their magic continually, whoever their holder might be. Stones become magical items, so to speak, useful to the layman. I have seen such minor charms, and so have you, I would guess, among the farmers or the minor seers of the lands."

"And you prepared this one," Pony reasoned, tapping the cat's eye.

"For you," replied Avelyn, "or for myself or perhaps for Elbryan. Ho, ho, what! Wherever it is most needed, I say, and now, that will be with you. Take it and use it to guide Symphony well through the night when our enemies will not be aware."

A snort from the side caught their attention and they turned to see the magnificent stallion standing again atop the nearby ridge, eager to run, as if he had been eavesdropping on their conversation.

"I doubt Symphony will need much guidance," Pony said, "day or night."

"Use it to keep your head from smacking into low branches, then." Avelyn laughed, drawing a short-lived smile from Pony.

Short-lived, because it was time for the woman to go.

Avelyn turned her around suddenly as soon as she had started away. The monk held his hand out to her, and when she took it, he gave her another stone, a piece of graphite, the stone used to create lightning.

"Perhaps you are ready," Avelyn said with respect.

Pony clenched the graphite tightly, nodded once, and walked away.

The day was clear and crisp but bitterly cold, the north wind blowing steadily, and Elbryan had to wonder if winter would ever give up its grip upon the land.

Later that morning, the ranger gathered together the men and a few women who would remain with him as his fighting force. "We cannot defeat the enemy that has come to our homes," he told them bluntly. "They are too great in number."

That brought a few grumbles, including a sarcastic, "Inspirational," from Tol Yuganick.

"But we can hurt them," Elbryan went on. "And perhaps our efforts here will make the war—"

"War?" Tol demanded.

"You still think this no more than a raiding party?" Elbryan scolded. "Ten thousand goblins have passed through Weedy Meadow since its fall, passed through and continued south."

Tol snorted and waved his hand dismissively.

"Our efforts here will make the war easier on those in the south," Elbryan said loudly, to quench the rising dissent, "to help Caer Tinella and Landsdown, and even Palmaris, where we believe this army to be headed."

"Bah!" Tol snorted. "The words of a fool, I say! The goblin scum have taken Dundalis, so to Dundalis we must go, to drive them far."

"To die," Elbryan put in before the big man could gain any momentum. "Only to die." Elbryan walked over to stand right before Tol, the tension mounting with each step. They were about the same height, but Tol, with his barrel-like torso and ample belly, was heavier.

The man puffed out his chest and glared hard at the ranger.

"I'll not stop any who wish to follow Tol Yuganick into Dundalis," the ranger said after a long and tense moment, "or into Weedy Meadow or End-o'-the-World or wherever else you choose as your graveyard. These woods have many places I can camp so you'll not be able to betray me when the goblins pull off your fingernails or hold you down and smash your privates with hammers."

Even Tol blanched a bit at that notion.

"No, you'll not betray me or my cause, but neither will I cry for your pain, neither will I risk those who wisely choose my way, to rescue those who willingly went to such a death."

It was enough for one day, Elbryan decided, for the first day of putting his soldiers in line, so the ranger slowly walked away from Tol, then off the field to the edge of the forest, where stood an amused Bradwarden.

"Oh, nice touch with the hammer story," the centaur greeted him.

Elbryan gave a wry smile, but it couldn't last. He was too concerned with Pony's opinion of Tol as a troublemaker and with the fact that Pony was probably already many miles away.

"We've—ye've a long way to go to get them in line," the centaur remarked.

Elbryan was all too aware of that grim fact.

"But I gave ye little credit when ye didn't kill the three rogues," Bradwarden offered.

"You said I should have killed them," the ranger reminded, drawing an embarrassed snort from the centaur.

"So I did! So I did!" Bradwarden replied. "And the three've proven themselves worthy o' yer mercy ten times over!"

"They are valuable allies," Elbryan added.

"Ye'll have a tougher time with that one," Bradwarden remarked, lifting his bearded chin toward Tol Yuganick, who was still standing in the small field, looking none too happy. "He's not for respecting ye, ranger. Might that ye should take him into the woods and beat him about."

Elbryan only smiled, but Bradwarden's suggestion did not seem like such a bad idea.

The mood of all the encampment brightened considerably that night when a dozen stragglers—more refugees from End-o'-the-World and mostly under the age of fifteen—wandered in, seeming dazed and sorely hungry; several had minor wounds, but otherwise all were physically sound. They told their remarkable tale to the group, and then their two leaders, a middle-aged couple, repeated the story in depth to Elbryan and Avelyn.

They had fled the town with the others as the goblin horde descended upon it, heading for the forest. But they had not gotten away cleanly and were forced to separate from the main group. Later that night, they had found themselves cornered in a rocky ravine by powries and a pair of giants, but, as the woman explained it, "The air came alive, like the buzzing of a million bees," and when the confusion ended, all their would-be murderers lay dead, the victims of many small puncture wounds.

It sounded all too familiar to Elbryan Wyndon.

"Then we were guided," the man added, "through the woods by night, camping in the day."

"By whom?" the ranger asked eagerly. "Who was it that led you to this place?"

The man shrugged and pointed to one young boy, sleeping near the fire, a lad of no more than six years. "Shawno said he talked to them," the man explained. " 'Tools,' he called them."

"Tools?" echoed Avelyn, mystified.

"Not 'Tools,' " Elbryan explained. "Touel." The ranger looked hard at the boy. He would have to speak with that one in the morning, after the child had rested and eaten.

❖ 41 ❖

Tempest

"Uncle Mather?"

Elbryan waited for a long while in the dimly lit cave, the day outside gray and hinting again of snow. He was not physically uncomfortable, for this place he had been using as Oracle, a hole beneath a wide pine, remained surprisingly dry; and, sheltered from the bite of the north wind, the air was not so cold.

The ranger was anxious, and he wanted to converse with the spirit this late afternoon, to tell his uncle Mather of the responsibilities that had befallen him, of the abrupt change that had come into his life, into the lives of all the folk on the borders of the Wilderlands. He realized then that Pony had been his sounding board, his confidant, and that since she had returned to him, he had not often been to Oracle.

But now Pony was gone, on the road with Symphony.

The ranger prayed that his uncle Mather would respond openly this time, would offer him some solid answers, as Pony had done, but that had never before been the way of the Oracle. This time, Elbryan feared, the answers and the strength were not within him, waiting for him to discover them.

He called again, softly, then again nearly half an hour later, when the cave had grown so dark that the keen-eyed ranger could hardly make out the edges of the mirror, let alone any spirit image within the glass.

Elbryan closed his eyes and recounted the events in his mind. The boy from End-o'-the-World, Shawno, had been of little help, but Elbryan remained convinced that it was indeed the Touel'alfar who had rescued that fleeing group from the monstrous hordes.

But where were the elves, then? Surely Belli'mar Juraviel, if he was in the area, would have made some contact with Elbryan. Surely Tuntun would have to come to him, if for no other reason than to tell him how miserably he had failed in protecting the three towns!

The ranger was startled when he opened his eyes to see the reflection of a small light, a candle, burning softly in the depths of the mirror, its sharp glow dulled by a whitish haze whose source Elbryan could not discern.

No, it was not a reflection, the ranger suddenly realized, but a light within the glass!

A moment later, Elbryan sucked in his breath, for there, at the corner of the glass stood the quiet apparition of, he knew in his heart, his father's brother.

"Uncle Mather," he said softly, "glad I am that you heeded my call this troubled day."

The image stood silently, unblinking.

Where to begin? Elbryan wondered. "The towns have fallen, all three," he blurted, "but many of the folk escaped, including nearly all those from Weedy Meadow and all of Dundalis."

The image hardly moved, but Elbryan sensed the spirit was pleased— with Elbryan, if not with the situation.

"And so we are hiding," the ranger went on, "and it is difficult, for winter remains. Now I must get those who cannot fight to safety in the south; that I know and am already seeking to arrange. And the southland will be warned by Pony, my beloved, returned to me and flying fast across the miles upon Symphony. But as for the rest, Uncle Mather, for those who would remain and fight, my course is unclear."

The ranger paused and waited, hoping for some response.

"I would choose to use them against the invaders," Elbryan said at length, when no answer was forthcoming. "I can form them into something devilish, a swift and secret band that strikes our enemy in the night and flies away before the goblins and powries can retaliate."

Again, the ranger had the feeling that the specter was pleased.

"So much stronger shall we be if my suspicions are correct," Elbryan went on, "if the Touel'alfar are in the area, ready to lend their silverel bows to our cause. Do you know? Are they somewhere close . . ."

Elbryan's voice trailed off as the image in the mirror shifted, as though the lens that was the mirror was drawing back from that single shielded candle, widening to include many others, little burning huts of snow, they seemed, set in a familiar field.

"Uncle Mather?" Elbryan asked, but the image of the specter was no more, just the field of candles, flickering under the dulling whiteness, dying, gradually dying, until the mirror, until all the small cave, went absolutely dark.

Elbryan sat there for a long while, considering the course before him. The moon had set when he at last crawled out of the hole, and there, waiting for him, fiddling with some stones, was Brother Avelyn. The monk had set a torch in the nook of a low branch of a nearby tree, its orange light casting twisted shadows across the ground.

"Cold night," the monk remarked dryly. "A true friend would have come out much earlier."

"I knew not that you were here waiting," Elbryan replied, and then he paused and looked hard at the man. "I did not know that you even knew of this place."

"Shown to me by the stones," the monk replied, and he held up one of the stones, a coin-sized quartz.

"You sought me out, then."

"We have much work before us, my friend," said Avelyn.

Elbryan didn't disagree.

"This is no simple raid, not even a simple invasion," said Avelyn.

"A simple invasion?" echoed Elbryan, for surely the words sounded curious when put together. "Can an invasion be simple?"

"If it is without greater purpose," replied the monk. "Powries have oft come to Honce-the-Bear's coastline, striking hard and charging inland until their thirst for blood and pillage is sated. Then their ranks break apart from their constant infighting, they go away, and the land heals. It has been that way for all of time, I believe."

"But this time is different," reasoned the ranger.

"That is my fear," said Avelyn.

"Yet it would seem as if this monstrous force of creatures so hateful and so different from one another would be more likely to turn on itself," Elbryan said.

"So they would," muttered Avelyn. "So they would, were it not for a guiding hand of the greatest strength."

Elbryan leaned back against the wide tree, having nothing to offer on that point. He remembered the murmuring of the elves soon before his departure, the whispers of a dactyl demon awakened in the north. "And if you are right?" he asked finally.

Avelyn's face turned grave. "Then I see my destiny," the monk remarked. "Then I understand what prophetic, divine being guided my hand when I filled my pouch with the stones of St.-Mere-Abelle. Even the choice of which stones to take was made for me, then, by something above—"

"I envy you your faith," said the ranger. "For myself, I feel that our destiny is our own to choose, our mistakes our own to make, our choices wrought of freedom."

Avelyn thought for a moment, then nodded. "A different way of looking at the same thing," he decided. "My choice that day was based on all that had transpired previously in my life, was the culmination of a course that had begun long before I entered the Abellican Order. I feel that I am right with my God, ranger, and if my suspicions as to the nature of the beast are true, then I see my course before me. That is all. I thought I should let it be known to you."

"Because you are leaving."

"Not yet," Avelyn replied quickly, "and know that I am with you, at your command. I will use the stones and all my talents and all my body in whatever course you set. For now."

Elbryan nodded, satisfied that the monk would be of great help—as he had already been. The ranger didn't underestimate Avelyn in the least; without the man and his magic, many more would have fallen at Weedy Meadow. And by Elbryan's measure, Avelyn's bravery in all that he had done—in taking the stones and fleeing St.-Mere-Abelle, in facing Brother Justice, and in aiding against the monsters—was above question.

"Do you believe in visions?" the ranger asked suddenly. "In prophecy?"

Avelyn looked at him hard. "Did I not just say as much?" he returned.

"And how is one to know if a vision is true or a deception?" the ranger asked.

"Ho, ho, what!" Avelyn boomed. "You've seen something this night in your hole!"

Elbryan smiled. "But how am I to know its source and its outcome?"

Avelyn laughed all the harder. "The responsibility weighs on you heavily," the monk replied. "You consider the vision more closely because so many people depend upon you now, because any course you take will draw many others in your wake. Ho, ho, what! Relieve your mind of the burden, then decide, my friend. What would be your course had you seen this vision without the responsibilities that have been placed on your strong shoulders?"

Elbryan paused for a long while, studying this man, thinking Avelyn as wise as any of the elves who had been so instrumental in the making of Elbryan the Nightbird.

Then he knew what he must do. And with only a few hours of darkness left before him, and without Symphony to take him swiftly, he knew that he must make haste.

"Your pardon, my friend," he said.

"A vision calls?"

Elbryan nodded.

"Would you need my company, then?" Avelyn asked.

Elbryan looked at him again and was glad of the man's offer. He felt that he might indeed need help this night, but he understood, too, that the vision, whatever it foretold, was for him alone. He walked to Avelyn and patted the huge man on the shoulder. "I need you to help Bradwarden," he explained, "to keep the people on the right course."

Avelyn didn't look over his shoulder to watch the ranger disappear into the night.

The diamond-shaped grove was eerily quiet, with no rustle of wind nor the call of any animal, of any night bird, to stir the still air. Elbryan wished that he had gotten here before moonset, when he could better see the rolling fields of snow surrounding the dark grove. He considered the sack he had retrieved before coming out to this place, bulging with candles, and he wondered if he should first light the area.

It didn't matter, the ranger decided boldly, and went to work. He moved slowly and carefully about the field, building domes of snow the size of his two cupped hands. Then he carefully hollowed each out and placed a single candle within. When he was finished with his task, when he had but one candle remaining, the ranger put flint to steel and lit it, then went steadily about the field, lighting each candle in turn, until all the area was glowing softly from two score muffled lights, points in the darkness.

Elbryan knew not how long the candles would last, how long it would take their heat to melt the snow domes above them, the droplets falling to extinguish the flames. He stood for a long time and the domes burned—too long, it seemed to him, and he suspected then that something beyond the ordinary was happening here, that some other force was at work in keeping those candles burning.

He heard his name called softly. Turning to the dark row of stately pines, the ranger instinctively understood the source. He moved inside the grove, across the covering of snow to the secret cairn.

Something was terribly wrong, Elbryan realized, terribly out of sorts, as if the very harmony of this place had somehow been stolen away. Suddenly this holy place, this place he had presumed prepared by the Touel'alfar themselves, seemed to him no sanctuary at all.

Elbryan leaned heavily on Hawkwing, staring at the cairn, and it took him some time to realize that he could see the stones far too distinctly, that there was simply too much light here.

Its source was the cairn itself, glowing green!

Elbryan could hardly draw breath as he noticed one of the top stones shift. He wanted to turn and flee; every survival instinct within the ranger told him to run away.

But he could not flee, held in place by something he did not understand, by something beyond the power of his own will.

The cairn blew outward, weirdly, slowly and not violently, all the rocks rolling up atop one another to form walls on either side of the grave; the light intensified so that Elbryan could see clearly the remains within, rotted and withered, a hollow shell of the man they had once been.

His staff was up in front of him now, defensively, as if ready for whatever would come next, but the alert ranger nearly swooned when that corpse opened its eyes, showing two red dots of light—when it sat up suddenly, its back too stiff and straight, that posture alone showing that it was far from natural.

"Be gone, demon," the ranger whispered ineffectively.

As if some wire were attached to its back, the zombie stood suddenly, moving straight up without use of its hands, without bending its legs.

Elbryan fell back a step—again came that urge to flee, his mind telling him that this monster was too great for him—but he planted Hawkwing firmly and used it to support his position, holding steady before the undead thing.

"Who are you?" Elbryan demanded. "What manner of creature? Of what weal, good or evil?"

That last question echoed in Elbryan's mind, sounding ridiculous, for what manner of goodly force could so torture a body at rest? Still, the ranger did not dismiss his knowledge that this was a blessed place, that this body, and the soul that had inhabited it in life, had been elf-friend, at least.

The creature's arms came up, reaching straight out toward the ranger, in a posture that might be threatening or pleading.

But then the undead thing was there, right before him, propelled by something other than its legs—was there, barely a foot away, its bony fingers clasped about the ranger's throat!

Elbryan grabbed at the arm and tried futilely to break the impossibly strong hold. He tried to yell out in protest, but had no breath. How he wished that Avelyn were there! That the monk would step in and blast this wicked thing with the magical stones!

But no, the ranger remembered. The vision was for him alone; this fight was for him alone. Clearing his panic, Elbryan brought Hawkwing up between the zombie's arms, grabbed the staff at both ends and twisted it, using its leverage to break the hold.

For a moment, he thought the twist would break his own neck instead, but finally, he wriggled free, jumped back a step, and smashed his staff hard against the side of the creature's head.

He might have hit it with a blow of his breath, he realized, as the monster didn't flinch in the least, just came on steadily, those straight arms reaching again for his throat.

Elbryan went into a sidelong dive, meaning to put some distance between himself and the monster, thinking that he should string his bow and let fly some stinging arrows.

But when he came up from the roll, the zombie was there, suddenly, magically. The ranger got his staff and his arm up to block, but the creature's backhand sweep was too heavy, sending Elbryan tumbling back the other way.

He came up in a run and ducked low to avoid another blow—for again, the zombie had somehow beaten him to the spot—and scrambled through the thick pine branches, cutting this way and that, trying to keep away from any predictable course.

Twice he turned corners to see the monster waiting for him. One time he ducked the attack, skidding to his knees but coming right back up agilely to run on. The second time, the ranger got grabbed painfully by the shoulder but somehow squirmed free before the monster could crush him in a hug.

Soon Elbryan was at the edge of the grove, standing before the candled field.

The monster was across the way, off to the side.

Elbryan's jaw slackened at the familiar sight, at the exact image he had last seen in the mirror, except that the zombie now stood where the specter of his uncle Mather had stood before. All was too quiet, too serene.

"Uncle Mather?" he asked the thing.

Then it was before him, so suddenly, clubbing him with those rock-stiff arms, sending him tumbling back into the pines.

Elbryan felt warm blood rolling from one ear and had to shake his head repeatedly to force the dizziness away. The creature, whatever it was, could hit like a giant!

He turned a corner within a triangle of tight pines, expecting correctly that the zombie would be there. Up came Hawkwing in a blurring defensive circle, Elbryan working brilliantly to parry and dodge the deceptively quick strikes of the stiff-limbed monster, then even countering once, twice, thrice with a deft stab, a sudden club to the side of the monster's head, and a third stab, this one nailing the zombie right between the eyes.

The vicious blows seemed not to affect the creature at all.

Across came its clubbing arm, and Elbryan, confused, dove away from the blow, taking the hit but not hard as he fell. He rolled through several branches, coming to his feet again in full flight, wondering what he might do against the likes of this monster, fearing that the dactyl itself had come against him, had lured him to this spot that he might be destroyed once and for all.

He crashed through a tangle of branches to find the zombie standing before him. Not surprised, the ranger continued on, bringing his staff down hard, right into the creature's face.

It didn't flinch, except to smack Elbryan across the shoulder with one arm, stealing his forward momentum and launching him sideways instead.

"I have to get a sword," the ranger lamented, glad that the branches had softened his tumbling fall. Then he was up and running, hoping to put some distance between himself and the creature, that he might devise some strategy. He wondered if he should flee the area, into the deeper forest where he was more at home.

Elbryan dismissed that thought; however futile his efforts seemed, he had played a part in bringing this creature to the world, and he must see to its destruction.

He ran on instead through the winding ways of the grove, cutting down every side path, trying to keep his movements unpredictable so that the monster could not appear before him. All the while, he was circling in toward the heart of the grove, moving determinedly toward the ruined cairn.

He came through the last line of trees into the green light. The opened grave loomed before him, and the zombie monster appeared right behind him! The creature pounded him hard between the shoulder blades, launching him into a forward roll that ended abruptly when he crashed against some of the cairn rocks.

Dazed, bleeding, Elbryan pulled himself up to his elbows, looking over the edge of the cairn. He knew that he must get up and run, knew that the monster was stalking in from behind.

The ranger froze in place, staring wide-eyed into the open pit. There, positioned as if it were the very heart of the grave, lay a sword—and not just any common sword but a work of art, a beautiful, gleaming treasure. If the tip of its blade was set upon the ground, the end of its balled hilt would not have reached Elbryan's waist, and the width of the blade was no more than the distance between the knuckle and first joint of Elbryan's smallest finger, but there was an unmistakable solidity and strength to the weapon, an aura of power.

The ranger reached in to the limit of his arm, to find that the sword was just out of range.

He heard the zombie right behind him.

Then, somehow, the sword was in his hand, and Elbryan spun and swept the weapon in a furious arc. Bluish-white light trailed the length of its path, stealing the green hue, and the zombie fell back and growled.

Elbryan scrambled to his feet, trying to inspect the blade without losing sight of his dangerous opponent. The sword was incredibly light; a blood trough ran down the center of the blade—and that blade was forged of sil-verel, the ranger suddenly recognized! The crosspiece, which curved back toward the tip of the blade, was similarly forged of the precious elven metal and tipped in gold; the hilt was wrapped in blue leather, tied tight by unmistakable silverel strands. Most wondrous of all, though, was the ball anchoring the hilt, a balance to the blade, for it, too, was of silverel, but was hollowed and set with such a gemstone as Elbryan had never seen—blue and with patches of gray and white like storm clouds crossing an autumn sky. And there was a power in that gem, the ranger knew, magic such as the magic of Avelyn's stones.

Elbryan let Hawkwing fall to the ground—he wondered if he would ever again need to use the bow as a staff—and brought the sword out before him, weaving it slowly, feeling its balance.

He tossed it easily from hand to hand, moving it in the sword-dance, then thrusting the sword out to keep the zombie at bay, swinging it wide to entice the monster in.

But the zombie showed the man new respect and stayed back, growling, the red dots of light that were its eyes glowing furiously.

"Come on, then," Elbryan said quietly. "You would have me dead, so come along and play."

The zombie fell back into the branch tangle; Elbryan rushed to follow.

But the creature was gone, out of sight, and the ranger realized that he, too, had to keep moving, that the fight had become even more a game of cat and mouse, for this time, both he and the zombie were the cats.

He stayed on the narrow trails mostly, using his speed, hoping to spot the monster before it was right beside him. He decided to angle his way back to the candlelit field and was not surprised when he arrived there to find the zombie waiting for him. The ranger understood then that this was how it was supposed to be, that this challenge on this field had been predetermined. He stalked toward the monster, and it came to him slowly at first, then in a furious rush, its arms flailing wildly.

Elbryan parried and struck, fell back on his heels, tumbled sidelong in a roll, and came right back in a ferocious charge, that magnificent sword leading. Now his hit did indeed sting the zombie, the sword tearing a deep gash in the rotted flesh, smacking hard against a rib.

The zombie came across with a sweeping backhand that caught ducking Elbryan hard across the shoulder. But the ranger stubbornly held his position and stood straight, stabbing at the ribs again and then sweeping the blade in an arc for the monster's neck.

Up came a zombie arm to block; the sword's gemstone flared with sudden power and the blade crackled with energy, as if it had caught a bolt of white lightning and held it fast.

The sword severed that blocking arm cleanly, right above the elbow and slashed across the face of the ducking monster.

Blinded, the zombie fell back and howled in agony, but Elbryan was upon it in an instant, the mighty sword diving through the monster's chest in a quick thrust, then coming out and sweeping down diagonally, shearing through the collarbone, down and across, deep into the rotted chest.

The zombie went hard to the ground and burst apart with a bright green flash that sent Elbryan stumbling backward, that sent all the world spinning in the ranger's eyes.

Elbryan awakened sometime later, the eastern sky just brightening with dawn, his head cradled in his arms atop the bottom stones of the intact cairn.

"Whole again?" he asked skeptically, or perhaps, he realized, it had been whole all along.

The ranger started to rise but found that every bone in his body ached, and only then did he realize how cold he was. He put his head back down, wondering if he would die out here, alone and cold, wondering what had brought such a nightmare.

Then a curious thought hit him, and he looked up, truly puzzled, staring hard at the cairn.

"Uncle Mather?" he asked breathlessly, and he knew that it was true, that this was the grave of his uncle Mather, the ranger.

But, he wondered, had it all been a dream, then? The monster? The sword?

Too intrigued to feel his pain, the ranger struggled to his feet, and as he came up above the stones, he saw, on the ground at the head of the cairn, a familiar, beautiful sword.

Elbryan stiffly reached out his hand and started around to retrieve the weapon, but the sword came to him, floating to his grasp!

He held it up before his admiring gaze, studying the craftsmanship, the gleaming silverel, the magnificent gemstone pommel, the blue, the storm clouds.

"Tempest," he whispered, suddenly realizing the significance of that unique gemstone. This was Tempest, Mather's sword, one of the six ranger swords forged by the elves in a time long past.

"Indeed," came a melodic voice from behind and above. Elbryan spun to see Belli'mar Juraviel sitting calmly on a low branch, smiling at him.

"Mather's sword," Elbryan said.

"No more," replied Juraviel. "Elbryan's sword, earned in the dark of night."

The ranger could hardly draw breath.

"My old friend," Elbryan said at length, "all the world has gone mad, I fear."

Juraviel only nodded, unable to disagree.

CHAPTER

❖ 42 ❖

Reputation

Winter's icy grip weakened at last, more than three weeks after the vernal equinox. Snow still fell, but often it turned in mid-storm to a cold rain, and ground that had been deep with white powder was now slick with gray slush. The change came as a mixed blessing to Elbryan and his forest band. While their lives certainly became more comfortable, their nights no longer spent so closely huddled to a fire that their eyebrows singed, winter's relaxed grip offered the invading monsters even more mobility. Now goblin, powrie, and fomorian giant patrols struck deep into the forest, and though these scouts were often discovered and destroyed by Elbryan's people, the danger to the group increased daily.

Pony still had not returned from the south. After three weeks, though, Paulson and his two trapper companions had come back with a fairly thorough description of the monstrous army's movements. It was as they had feared—the monsters using the occupied towns as base and supply camps while they sent their dark tendrils further south, first in probes, but soon, so Paulson believed, in great numbers.

"They'll strike Landsdown within a week, unless we get hit with another storm," Paulson explained grimly.

"The season's past," Avelyn remarked. "There will be no more storms severe enough to slow our enemies."

Elbryan agreed; Belli'mar and the other elves—who remained far in the shadows about the human camps, hidden from all save the ranger and the centaur—had told him as much.

"Then Landsdown's to fall," said Paulson.

"We must get word to them," Avelyn offered, looking at the ranger, who in turn looked at Paulson.

"We already told some farmers," Paulson explained, "and yer girl's been through with the same news."

Elbryan perked his ears up considerably at that bit of news.

"But will they listen?" Avelyn wanted to know.

"Who's to make them?" asked Paulson.

Elbryan closed his eyes and considered that. Indeed, the men and women of the frontier towns north of Palmaris could be a stubborn lot! The ranger decided then that it was time to put Belli'mar's troop to good use. The mobile elves could get to Landsdown ahead of the monsters, and if the sight of an elf didn't shake some sense into thick heads, then let the folk of Landsdown get what they deserved!

"I will see to Landsdown," the ranger promised, and he moved on to other matters. "What of our own folk?"

"We've got a hundred not taking well to the life," said Bradwarden. "Tough enough folk, but we've asked too much o' them."

"Is there any place we might take them?" the ranger asked.

The three trappers were at a loss; Brother Avelyn could think of no sanctuary closer than St. Precious in Palmaris, but how they could ever get a hundred people that far south without alerting the monsters was beyond the monk. Bradwarden's expression told the ranger that the centaur was thinking along the same lines as he, that the elves and the sanctuary of their hidden home might prove valuable here. But Elbryan, who had lived long in Andur'Blough Inninness, didn't think it likely that so many humans, however desperate their situation might be, would be invited in. Belli'mar Juraviel, easily the friendliest of the elven band, and the one most acquainted with humans, had even refused to be seen among the encampments, explaining that his presence would probably only frighten those too foolish to know friend from foe.

"Then we must make a place for them," the ranger decided, "and keep them away from our enemies until such time as we may usher them far to the south, behind the militia lines of Honce-the-Bear's Kingsmen." He looked at Paulson, Cric, and Chipmunk. "See to it," he bade them, and they nodded.

Good soliders, Elbryan mused.

The next week moved along uneventfully. Elbryan, Bradwarden, and Avelyn came upon a group of a dozen goblins chopping firewood, and summarily destroyed them. When a fomorian came rushing to the goblins' rescue, Bradwarden tripped the giant, and the first thing it saw when it looked up—and the last thing it ever saw—was the fierce ranger glaring down at it, powerful Tempest sweeping down.

Elbryan had little contact with the elves that week. He had met with Juraviel soon after his fireside discussion with his more conventional commanders, and the elf had reluctantly agreed to send a handful of his fellows south to warn Landsdown.

"I fear that we are being dragged into the middle of a fight that is meant for humans," Juraviel had groaned, to which Elbryan only lightly responded, "Of your own accord."

At the end of the week, Juraviel and Tuntun came to the ranger with welcome news indeed. "The folk of Landsdown are on the road south ahead of the advancing monsters," Juraviel explained. "Every one."

"And they are being met and ushered more swiftly by soldiers of your king," added Tuntun.

"My thanks to you and yours," the ranger said solemnly with a low bow.

"Not to us"—Tuntun laughed—"for the folk were on the road before we ever arrived."

Elbryan's expression turned quizzical.

"Your thanks to her," explained Juraviel, and on cue, Pony stepped out of the shadows of a thick spruce.

Elbryan rushed to her, embracing her in a huge hug. It took him some time to realize that the elves had announced her, and thus, that the elves had met her! He looked from Pony back to Juraviel and Tuntun.

"You had already told her of us," Juraviel said dryly.

"But I believe our appearance shocked her anyway," added Tuntun, again, in better spirits than was normal for the surly elf.

"I was still in Landsdown, the last one there, when they came upon me," Pony explained.

Elbryan looked her over carefully, satisfied that she was not injured, only muddy and weary from so long a ride.

"All the way to Palmaris," she answered his unspoken question. "No horse will ever match the run of Symphony! He took me all the way to Palmaris without complaint, and all the way back at equal speed. The kingdom is alerted now, the soldiers are on the road, and our enemies will win no more victories by surprise."

Elbryan lifted his hand to brush back a stray lock of the woman's thick, dirty hair. He turned his fingers gently to flick a speck of mud from her cheek, though his gaze never left her shining blue eyes. How much he loved her, admired her, respected her! He wanted to crush her to him, to make love to her forever, and to protect her—and that was his dilemma, for if he tried to protect this marvelous woman, Jilseponie Ault, then he would surely be stealing the very essence of her, the will and the strength that he so loved.

"All the world should thank you," he whispered. He turned to make a remark to the elves, but the pair, so wise in the ways of all the world, were long gone, granting the lovers their privacy.

"They knew we were out here, in great numbers, and now they wonder why the signs have lessened," Elbryan explained to Avelyn, the ranger astride his horse, beside the standing man just inside the cover of thick trees lining a bowl-shaped field. A blanket of slushy snow still covered the field, shining blue-white in the pale light of a bright half moon. Diagonally, across the field to the northwest, moving through the stark lines of thinner trees, came three forms, obviously goblin scouts.

"Perhaps they will believe that we have all departed," Avelyn offered hopefully. Indeed, more than two thirds of the human group had gone further to the east, leaving less than forty warriors at Elbryan's disposal, not counting the secretive elves, whose number even the ranger didn't know.

"That would be their mistake," the ranger answered grimly.

The tone of his voice made Avelyn glance his way, and the monk was glad to see that Tempest was still sheathed at the side of the saddle Belster O'Comely had commissioned for Elbryan before the coming of the monsters, and that Hawkwing was likewise in place, on a holder that looped the bow about a quiver of arrows.

But then, to Avelyn's surprise, Elbryan stepped Symphony out of the shadows onto the mild southern slope of the bowl-shaped vale, out of cover.

Across the way, perhaps a hundred yards, the goblins stopped and stared, then scrambled among the trees, fitting arrows to bowstrings.

"Elbryan!" Avelyn whispered harshly. "Come back!"

The ranger sat quietly, cutting a regal figure, his bow and sword at rest.

Three arrows went up into the night sky, errant shots that landed far short or far wide of the ranger.

"They do not even believe that we can see them," Elbryan said quietly, obviously amused.

Avelyn scrambled out to Elbryan's side, putting Symphony between him and the goblins. "Better that we had not seen them," the monk huffed, "or better still that they had not seen us!"

"Calm, my friend," the ranger replied as another arrow thudded into the snowy ground, barely twenty feet away. Brave Symphony held perfectly steady; Elbryan wished that his human friend had as much faith.

Avelyn peeked under Symphony's head, to see that the goblins had gone to the bottom of the field's slope, still under the respectable cover of the stark deciduous trees.

"Three shots at a time, and they're likely to get lucky," Avelyn remarked. The monk looked up to see Elbryan slowly bringing Hawkwing to bear, then, with hardly a movement, letting fly an arrow.

Avelyn looked back in time to see a goblin catch it in his chest. He couldn't see the arrow, of course, just the sudden jerk of the dark silhouette, followed by a backward drop to the ground. The other two scrambled in sudden retreat, slipping as they tried to get back up the slope.

Elbryan held his pose, his bowstring fully drawn and perfectly steady.

"Get them quick," Avelyn prodded.

"It must be sure," Elbryan answered. "There can be no miss." He waited as the goblin pair weaved, then at last found his opening and let fly, the arrow cutting a straight, swift line to take a second goblin in the side of the head. The one remaining howled and scrambled, fell to its belly, and slid halfway back to the bottom.

"Oh, get him!" cheered Avelyn. "Ho, ho, what!"

But Elbryan had put up his bow, sitting calmly on Symphony, his head tilted back, his eyes closed, as if he were simply enjoying the breeze of the moonlit night.

"What?" Avelyn asked, the monk watching the goblin running off once again to the top of the ridge and then beyond, lost from view. "Ho, ho, what?"

Elbryan slowly opened his eyes and looked down at the man. "It is all about reputation," the ranger explained, and he turned Symphony and started walking back to the trees.

"Reputation?" Avelyn echoed. "You let the last one get away! It will surely report that we have not left, that we, that you, at least, remain . . ." The monk's voice trailed off and a smile spread across his round face. Of course, the terrified goblin would return, blabbering its report. Of course, the goblin would tell them that the mysterious ranger on his mighty stallion remained, would tell them that death waited for them in the forest.

"Ho, ho, what!" Avelyn bellowed in sincere admiration. "Let them know of Elbryan, then!"

"No," the ranger corrected. "Let them know of Nightbird. Let them know and let them be afraid."

Avelyn nodded as he watched the ranger and his mount melt away into the forest night. Indeed, he thought, and well they should be afraid!

Elbryan did his sword-dance, as he had done so many times in Andur'Blough Inninness. Tempest weaved its wondrous lines about him slowly—turning, stooping, and rising in perfect balance. One foot followed the other and then took up the lead: step, step, thrust, and retreat.

All flowed slowly, beautifully. He was the embodiment of the warrior, this muscular naked man, the height of harmony, one with his weapon.

From the trees behind Elbryan, Pony and Avelyn watched awestruck. They had come upon the scene quite accidentally, and the monk, seeing Elbryan first and seeing that he was quite naked, had tried to turn Pony down a different path. But she, too, had spotted the man, and no amount of coercing from Avelyn would deflect her.

In watching Elbryan, his graceful moves, his trancelike intensity, Pony came to know so much more of him, to see him as clearly as if she were lying in his arms, sharing his heights of passion and joy.

This was different but no less intense, she realized. Like their coupling, this was a joining of body and spirit, a physical meditation somehow above the norm of human experience, somehow sacred.

Avelyn had seen this type of practice before—it was not so different from the physical training the monks received at St.-Mere-Abelle—but he had never seen a dance as graceful as Elbryan's, as perfectly harmonious.

And Tempest, seeming no more than an extension of the ranger, only added to that beauty, the light sword swishing about, leaving a glowing trail of bluish-white.

"We should be away," the monk whispered to Pony as Elbryan came to one long pause in his routine.

Pony didn't disagree; perhaps they were indeed peeping at something which was Elbryan's alone. But as the ranger started his movements again, as Tempest came up and about, perfectly level and parallel with his broad shoulders, she found that she could not turn away.

Nor could Avelyn.

Elbryan finished soon after and slumped to the grass; Pony and Avelyn stole away.

When Pony met Elbryan more than an hour later, she had to work hard to hide her feelings of guilt, her feelings that she had somehow violated him. Finally, it was too much.

"I saw you this morning," she admitted.

Elbryan raised an eyebrow.

"At your exercise," Pony admitted. "I—I did not mean . . ." She stopped, stammering, and lowered her gaze.

"And were you alone?" said Elbryan.

Something in his tone brought Pony's gaze up to meet his, and in the hint of a smile at the corner of his mouth, the woman found the truth revealed.

"You already knew!" she accused.

Elbryan brought a hand to his chest, as if wounded.

"You knew!" Pony said again, and she slapped her hand against his shoulder.

"But I did not know if you would tell me," the ranger said evenly, and Pony backed away.

"We came upon you by accident," the woman explained.

"We?"

Pony glared at him.

"Yes, you and Avelyn," Elbryan revealed.

After a long pause, Pony asked bluntly, "Are you angry?"

Elbryan smiled warmly. "There is nothing I wish to hold secret from you."

"But I remained," she went on, "I watched you until the end of your dance."

"I would have been disappointed if the sight of me so could not hold you in place," Elbryan said playfully, and all tension was abruptly gone.

Pony wrapped the man in a hug then, and gave him a deep kiss. "Will you teach it to me?" she asked. "The dance, I mean."

Elbryan looked hard into her face. "It was a gift to me from the Touel'alfar," he explained. "A gift that I will, in turn, offer to you, but only with the blessings of the elves."

Pony was honored, and she moved to kiss Elbryan again, but a rustle at the side caught her attention.

Paulson moved out of the brush. "The caravan must've traveled half the night," he said, referring to a goblin supply train they had been watching, coming from the north. "We hit it today, or it makes Weedy Meadow."

"Are they still along the river?" asked Elbryan.

The big man nodded.

Elbryan looked at Pony, who understood her role, and without further bidding, she ran off to find Avelyn and gather together those warriors who had been put under her charge.

Elbryan closed his eyes and sent his thoughts into the forest, to Symphony—the stallion grazing, as always these days, not so far away.

"Let us be off," the ranger then said to Paulson, "to prepare the battlefield as best suits us."

There was no high ground in the path of the caravan, except those hills surrounding Weedy Meadow, and that locale would be too close to the occupied village. Elbryan and his forces had to go out further to the north, had to intercept and destroy the caravan before any aid could come from the monsters already encamped in the area.

But there was no high ground, just thick woodlands, giving way to the brown and gray stones that lined the riverbank. At least the river would form a barrier to their enemies, the ranger thought, preventing an easy escape.

"Two groups coming," Bradwarden explained, catching up to Elbryan and the others as they determined their attack routes. "Small one in front, goblins mostly, but with a giant helping, cutting the trees and clearing the way."

"For wagons?" Elbryan asked, and he hoped that he was right.

"War engines," the centaur explained. "Two big contraptions, catapults, all set on wheels and pulled by three giants each."

"Too many," muttered Paulson, standing at Elbryan's side.

The ranger looked at the man, no coward certainly, and wasn't sure that he could disagree. Seven giants—at least—and a host of powries and goblins might indeed be more than the ranger and his band could handle.

"Well, we can hit at them anyway," Paulson offered a moment later. "But we best be ready to run off if the tide turns against us."

Elbryan looked at Bradwarden. "What of scouts?" he asked.

"Oh, they've plenty o' goblin rats running about the trees," the centaur replied, smiling widely as he lifted a twig to pick his teeth. "Two less, now," he said mischievously.

The ranger made a subtle movement, one that only Bradwarden caught, putting his finger up beside his ear, indicating a pointy ear, thus an elf.

The centaur nodded; the elves were in the area, and Elbryan was confident that he and his band would not have to worry much about any goblin scouts.

Pony came riding in then on a roan mare, one of several wild horses that would allow themselves to be ridden. Brother Avelyn came huffing and puffing behind her, the monk trotting along without complaint.

"The most important task before us is the destruction of the war engines," Elbryan decided. "For surely they will be put to deadly use against the towns to the south, even against the high walls of Palmaris."

The ranger paused for a while and considered all that he had heard. "How many in the front group?" he asked the centaur.

"Ah, a motley bunch," Bradwarden replied sourly, as if even speaking of the creatures left a foul taste in his mouth. "A dozen, I'd say, hacking at the trees, tearing at them, while the giant clears what's fallen. Ugly wretches. I'll kill the lot of them, if ye want."

Elbryan almost believed that the centaur would do just that. "Can you handle a giant?" he asked.

Bradwarden snorted as if the very question was insulting.

The ranger turned to Pony. "Take ten and the centaur," he explained. "You must destroy that front group and quickly. The rest will come in with me to cut off the main caravan, right in between the groups."

"Facing six giants?" Paulson asked skeptically.

"Drawing their attention," the ranger explained, "long enough for Avelyn to burn the powrie catapults. After that, we can scatter as we must, but my hope is that many monsters will be dead in the wreckage."

"But they have scouts," Paulson argued. "They might be knowing we're about afore e'er we get near them."

"The scouts are all dead," Elbryan said firmly. Paulson, and many others, looked at him hard.

"Yer elfin friends?" the big man asked. "I'm not sure I'm liking that."

"Tell me that after the battle," Elbryan replied wryly, then to Pony he shouted, "Be off!"

Paulson sighed, accepting the ranger's word for it. He was surprised when Pony tapped him on the shoulder, indicating that she wanted him and Cric and Chipmunk to work with her group up front.

"We will come straight in at them along the riverbank," Pony explained to Elbryan as she and the others moved away.

"And we hit from the side, through the trees," the ranger replied. He nodded at his beloved. He could feel that tingling excitement, prebattle, and he knew Pony felt it, too. Indeed, there was danger for him and for Pony, but this was their life, this was their destiny, and for all the horror and all the fear, it was exciting.

Elbryan had to grit his teeth and let the front group of monsters move past his position, though with every hack of a goblin axe against one of the beautiful trees, the ranger wanted to rush out and cut the creature down.

The goblins and their giant escort moved along slowly but steadily, and soon after, Elbryan and his companions heard the rumble of the war engines, the grunts of the towing giants.

"Hold until they are right upon us," the ranger instructed, "then let fly your arrows and loose your spears. Aim for the giants only," the ranger quickly added. "They are the most dangerous. If we can bring a couple of them down with the first volley, our enemies will be at a sore disadvantage."

"And if we don't?" surly Tol Yuganick grumbled. "Are we to run in front of six giants to be squashed?"

"We hit at them as hard as we safely can," the ranger replied evenly, trying to keep his continuing frustration with the disagreeable man out of his voice, "and then, when we must, we flee. A single caravan is not worth risking many casualties."

"Easy for you," Tol snapped back, "up on that fast horse of yours. The rest of us are running, and I'm not thinking that many can outrun the likes of a giant!"

Elbryan glared at the man, wishing that Pony had taken him with her group, or even that Tol had been sent off to the east with the other refugees. Tol was a fierce fighter, but the amount of discord he caused made him a detraction, not an asset.

"Wait until they close," the ranger said again, addressing the whole group. "They think that they have scouts in place, and will be caught unawares. Concentrate your missiles on the giants pulling the front catapult. Let us see what remains after the first volley."

He turned to Avelyn then. "How many will you need with you?"

The monk shook his head. "None," he replied. "Just keep their attention ahead of them, and I will get in behind! Stay back from the catapults, I warn you. I am feeling quite powerful this day!"

With that, the monk scrambled off into the brush, and Elbryan nearly laughed aloud watching him go, watching the light step that had come over Brother Avelyn Desbris. The monk had found peace within himself, ironically, in the midst of a war, a battle that Avelyn knew justified the actions that had weighed so heavily on him these last years.

Elbryan turned his attention back to the scene before him, ten yards of trees, followed by a few yards of cleared brush, a dozen feet of river stones, and then the river itself, waters rushing fast with the beginning of the spring melt. He heard the rumble of the war engines above that watery voice and discerned, by the alternating sounds, both sharp and muffled, that the caravan was moving right along the edge of the riverbank.

The ranger motioned to his companions, who started slinking from tree to tree, setting up their shots. Elbryan held his place, behind the tangled branches of two close hemlocks. He glanced about for the elves, and hoped that they were nearby. None in all the world could better concentrate their shots, and even a giant, the ranger knew from personal experience, could be brought down by the small arrows.

Up in front, one of the women signaled that the caravan was nearly upon them.

Elbryan fitted an arrow to Hawkwing and eyed his course. He contacted Symphony telepathically, and the horse nickered softly.

The first of the giants came into sight, bending low, pulling hard, a heavy harness strapped across its torso. Two others were close behind, in similar posture.

Elbryan felt the anxious gazes of his companions upon him, waiting for him to start it all. He was somewhat concerned that no sounds of battle came to him from further south, from the lead group, but he and his companions were committed, he knew, and would have to trust that Pony would not let the goblins and giant get behind them, cutting off any quick retreat.

The ranger let fly his first arrow even as he kicked his heels against Symphony's ribs and the horse leaped forward.

The lead giant grunted, more in surprise than in pain, when the bolt dove into his shoulder, and then all the air about the monster and its two companions erupted as a dozen arrows and nearly that many spears came slicing in.

Elbryan fired again and again, scoring a hit each time as Symphony guided him to the open ground before the caravan. By the time he got there, the lead giant was down and dead, the other two were scrambling to get out of their encumbering harnesses, while a score of powries and twice that number of goblins were hooting and rushing about, grabbing for weapons or diving for cover.

Out came several of Elbryan's companions, right behind him, and all of them, and the ranger too, breathed a sigh of relief to finally hear the sound of battle behind them.

One of the powries stood tall on the first catapult, barking out commands. The ranger's next shot laid the dwarf low.

Pony charged in hard, running her horse right across the lead line of goblins, her sword slashing hard across the face of one, then darting out to stick a second in the throat. This was the easy part, she knew, for she and her companions had caught the monsters by surprise, and diminutive goblins couldn't take a solid hit. Before the woman had even swung her sword, half the small creatures lay dead or squirming in agony on the ground.

But then there was the not so little matter of a fomorian giant.

Pony tugged hard on her mare's mane, turning the horse when she saw the behemoth moving to intercept. Out of the corner of her eye, she saw the galloping charge of Bradwarden, the centaur singing at the top of his considerable voice, waving a huge cudgel as easily as if it were a tiny baton.

The giant braced as the centaur came in, but Bradwarden skidded short and leaped about, putting his tail closest to the monster. Thinking that the centaur had changed his mind and was trying to flee, the giant lunged for that tail, but Bradwarden's haunches came up high, the centaur kicking out with both his hind legs, hard hooves perfectly aligned with the stooping monster's ugly face.

The giant staggered backward, its legs buckling under it.

Singing wildly, the centaur charged in, bashing the monster about the head with his heavy club.

Then Pony rushed by, her sword slashing a line across the side of the giant's neck.

"Hey, but ye're stealing me fun!" the centaur protested, leaping about again and snapping off a second mighty double kick, this one connecting on the giant's massive chest and throwing the monster flat to the ground.

Bradwarden smiled, seeing Pony run down another goblin, seeing all the wretched creatures falling fast before the deadly group. And seeing, most of all, the giant, dazed and helpless, up on its elbows, its head lolling about.

Perfect height for an underhand swing.

The second giant went down before it ever got out of the harness. The third did get out, but Elbryan put an arrow into its eye, and half a dozen other arrows hit it in the neck and face.

It, too, slumped to the ground.

Of more concern, though, were the powries, taking up their weapons, and the giants from the second catapult, out of their harnesses and with hardly a scratch on them.

"Hurry, Avelyn," Elbryan muttered under his breath. "Do not delay."

"Here comes Jilly! Flying fast!" one man cried, and Elbryan was truly glad for the timing and for the much-needed boost to his group's tentative morale. The monstrous troop in the south had been overrun, so it seemed.

"Concentrate your shots on the giants!" the ranger bellowed, and then under his voice, he repeated, "Hurry, Avelyn."

Bradwarden galloped off to catch the woman and her fast-flying roan, but the centaur skidded to a stop, seeing Chipmunk tearing free a pair of daggers from a dead goblin, but with tears streaming down his face.

"It's Cric!" the man wailed. "Oh, my Cric!"

Bradwarden followed his gaze to a tumble of a pair of goblins and, unmistakably, a bald-headed human lying among them.

"He's dead!" the small nervous man declared.

"Where is yer third?" the centaur asked. "The big one?"

"Paulson's running up ahead," Chipmunk explained. "Says he'll kill every goblin, every powrie, every giant."

"Get on me back, man, and hurry!" the centaur ordered, and Chipmunk did just that. On they charged, Bradwarden singing a rousing song and Chipmunk forcing away his tears, locking them behind a wall of sheer anger.

Avelyn crouched behind a tree, barely ten feet from the side of the trailing catapult. The monk's frustration mounted, for though two of the giants had run off toward the fighting up front, the third had remained defensively in place, with a host of powries staying up on the catapult, some of them with crossbows.

Avelyn would have to get closer, he knew, for his fireball to have any real effect, but if he went out in the open, he figured that he would be grabbed or shot down before he ever loosed the magical blast.

The monk understood the situation up front, understood that Elbryan could not buy him very much more time without endangering many lives. He called up his serpentine shield and, purely on instinct, he rushed out of the brush and dove to the ground, rolling right under the catapult.

He heard the powries crying out, knew that he hadn't much time, and tried to focus on the ruby, on its mounting energy.

Then the giant was kneeling beside the catapult, its face down to the ground, its long arm reaching under for poor Avelyn.

He had to roll away, but then stopped suddenly as a small crossbow bolt skipped off the ground right beside him. He glanced back to see a pair of powries crawling under the war engine, coming for him with prodding spears.

Avelyn closed his eyes and prayed with all his heart. He felt the tingling power of the ruby, as if it were begging for release; he imagined the sudden stabbing pain when the powries drew near.

Avelyn's eyes popped open, the man staring into the ugly face of the giant.

"Ho, ho, what!" the monk howled in glee, and *boom!* a ball of flame engulfed the catapult, incinerated the powries crawling in behind the monk, and blinded the giant in front of him. The great wooden structure went up like a huge candle; those unsuspecting powries standing atop it cried out and dove for the ground, rolling to extinguish the flames. One unfortunate dwarf dove right in the path of the howling giant. The fire on that particular dwarf was indeed extinguished as a huge booted foot crushed the diminutive creature flat. The burning giant continued on with hardly a thought for the dwarf, running blindly, swatting futilely at the flames. It slammed into a young tree, snapping branches and stumbling, but held its balance—stupidly, for the ground offered its only chance of smothering the flames—and ran on.

Avelyn clutched the serpentine tightly as burning chips of wood sizzled down around him. The gem wouldn't protect him from smoke, he knew, and so he realized he had to get out from under the burning war engine. He started to work himself to one side, but then a wheel succumbed to the flames and the gigantic catapult creaked and rocked to the side, pinning the monk.

"Oh, help me," Avelyn breathed, trying to squeeze back the other way. "Ho, ho, what?"

Avelyn's blast did much to even the odds, leaving only two giants and a score of powries against Elbryan's thirty. The ranger could not accept such an even fight, though, for if he lost a fifth of his force, it would be too many for the gains of this one encounter. He started to call for a retreat, holding Pony back as she galloped up beside him on her strong roan, but then Bradwarden came by, singing again, a rowdy tune, with a growling Chipmunk on his back, daggers in hand.

"Halt!" Elbryan called to the centaur, but even as he spoke there came a sudden humming sound, a noise the ranger recognized as the thrumming of many delicate but deadly elvish bows.

Several powries tumbled from the lead catapult.

Bradwarden bore down on the closest giant, Chipmunk leading the way with a hurled dagger, then a second, third, and fourth in rapid succession, all aimed perfectly for the behemoth's face, all hitting the mark and digging in deeply with the strength of the man's rage driving them.

The giant howled in agony and clutched at its torn face with both hands, and Bradwarden hit it in full stride, bowling it to the ground.

Elbryan could not halt the flow of his furious forces then, certainly not wild-eyed Paulson, who dodged the thrust of a powrie spear, lifted the dwarf into the air, and tossed it a dozen feet, to crack its head against a tree trunk.

The remaining giant ran away into the woods; those powries out of the immediate rush scattered, wanting no more of this wild band.

"Take apart the second catapult!" Elbryan commanded his forces. "Feed its logs to Avelyn's fire."

"Where is Avelyn?" Pony asked as her roan trotted past Symphony.

"In the forest with the elves, likely," said Elbryan. "Perhaps in pursuit of the giant."

As if on cue, the burning catapult creaked again and slanted over farther. Elbryan stared at it, sensed something amiss.

"No," the ranger murmured, slipping down from his horse. He started walking toward the burning thing, then began running, scrambling to the ground as close as he could get to the catapult's highest edge. Elbryan peered through the thick smoke. There were two bodies near him, and he was relieved to recognize them as powries.

"But what were the powries doing *under* the catapult?" the ranger asked with sudden horror.

"Bring a beam!" he shouted, standing tall and hopping excitedly. "A lever! And quickly!"

"Avelyn," Pony breathed, catching on to the source of her lover's distress.

Most of the fighting was finished—several men and the centaur had already begun taking apart the intact catapult. Bradwarden, working at the catapult's long arm and great counterweight, heard the ranger's desperate call.

Chipmunk popped out the last fastening peg, and, with the strength of a giant, the centaur lifted free the huge beam. Men scrambled to help him, but even with all of the hands, the best they could do was drag the beam to Elbryan and the burning catapult.

"Ropes to the other side," Elbryan commanded, as he and several others began setting one end of the long pole under the highest side of the burning catapult. "It must be pulled right over, and swiftly!"

They tugged, they lifted with all their strength. Pony got Symphony and her roan around the back, ropes looped about the war engine and tied to the tugging horses. Finally, with one great heave, the group uprighted the catapult, which fell over with a tremendous groan of protest and a huge shower of orange-yellow sparks.

There lay Avelyn, motionless and soot covered.

Elbryan rushed to him, as did all the others, Pony pushing her way through to be beside this man she had come to love as a brother.

"He does not breathe!" Elbryan cried, pushing hard on the man's chest, trying to force the air into him.

Pony took a different tack, going for the monk's pouch, fumbling with the stones until she at last brought forth the hematite. She had no idea how to proceed—Avelyn had not formally trained her with this most dangerous of stones—but she knew that she must try. She sent her thoughts into the stone, remembered that Avelyn had done as much for her, and indeed, for Elbryan.

She prayed to God, she begged for help, and then, though she did not believe that she had accessed the stone's power in the least, she felt a soothing hand above her own, and looked down to see the monk staring up at her, smiling faintly.

"Hot one," Avelyn said between coughs that brought forth black spittle. "Ho, ho, what!"

*   *   *

"The design was impressive," Elbryan admitted to Belli'mar Juraviel and Tuntun, the elves sitting with the ranger at Avelyn's bedside much later that night.

Avelyn opened a sleepy eye to regard his newest companions. He had known the elves were about, of course—everyone in the camp did—but he had never actually seen one of the Touel'alfar before. He stayed quiet and closed his eyes once more, not wanting to scare the sprites away.

Too late; Elbryan had noticed the movement.

"I fear that your prophecies of doom hold much truth," the ranger said, shaking Avelyn a bit to show that he was speaking to him.

Avelyn opened one eye, locked stares not with Elbryan but with the elven pair.

"I give you Belli'mar Juraviel and Tuntun," the ranger said politely, "two of my tutors, two of my dearest friends."

Avelyn opened wide his eyes. "Well met, what," he said boisterously, though he wound up coughing again, not yet ready for such exertion.

"And to you, good friar," said Juraviel. "Your power with the stones is encouraging."

"And great will that power need to be," added Tuntun. "For a darkness has come to the world."

Avelyn knew that all too well, had known it since the days immediately after his departure from St.-Mere-Abelle—had known it, in retrospect, since his journey to Pimaninicuit. He closed his eyes again and lay still, too weary to speak of such things.

"We know beyond doubt that these monsters are not simple raiders but a cohesive and organized force," Elbryan stated.

"They are guided," Tuntun agreed, "and held together."

"We need to speak of this another time," said Juraviel, indicating the monk, who seemed as if he had drifted off to sleep once more. "For now, we have the immediate battles before us."

Both elves nodded and slipped quietly out of the tent, past the sleeping soldiers and the alert guards without a whisper, seeming to all about as no more than windblown leaves or the shadow of a bird.

Elbryan sat with Avelyn for the rest of the night, but the monk did not stir. He was deep in thought, in sleep at times, recalling all that he had heard of the darkness that was on the land, of the demon dactyl and the blackness within men's hearts.

"Our master will not be pleased," Gothra the goblin whined, the one-handed creature hopping frantically about the small room.

Ulg Tik'narn regarded his fellow general sourly. The powrie had little love of goblins and found Gothra a pitiful whining creature. The powrie could not deny Gothra's statement, though, and gave the goblin more credit than he gave Maiyer Dek, for the giant was perfectly oblivious of their increasingly desperate situation. The villages had been captured, that was true, but too few humans had been killed, and this mysterious Nightbird and his friends were wreaking havoc on every supply group that came down from the north, something the merciless dactyl had certainly noticed—the arrival of the spirit who called himself Brother Justice confirmed that fact.

And Ulg Tik'narn knew that he, most of all, would be blamed for the interfering humans. But the powrie was not without allies of its own, and was not without a plan.

CHAPTER

❖ 43 ❖

A Place of Particular Interest

"Tearing and scarring!" the centaur wailed, stomping about, splashing in the mud and puddles and smashing his heavy club against the ground. A drenching rain fell all about the region, turning the last of the snow to slush and softening the ground.

"They are cutting the evergreens in the vale north of Dundalis," Elbryan explained grimly to Pony. "All of them."

"Then the day is all the grayer," she replied, looking in the general direction of what had once been her home. Of all the places in the area, only Elbryan's private grove was more beautiful than the pine vale and the caribou moss, and none elicited more wistful memories from the young woman.

"We can stop them," the ranger said suddenly, seeing the profound pain on Pony's fair features. He sighed as he finished, though, for he and Bradwarden had just concluded a similar conversation in which the centaur had called for an attack, but Elbryan had reasoned that the clear-cutting might be no more than a trap set for their band. They had become a large thorn in the side of the invading army, and no doubt the monstrous leaders in Dundalis and the other villages wanted to get the secretive band out in the open and deal with them once and for all. Goblins were stupid things, but powries were not, Elbryan knew, and he understood that these dwarvish generals would recognize the importance of beauty to the humans.

"Too close to Dundalis," Pony lamented. "They would have reinforcements upon us before we could do any real harm to their clear-cutters."

"But if we sting them and send them running," Bradwarden argued again, "might that they'll be thinking twice before going back in that valley!"

Pony looked at Elbryan, the Nightbird. This was his game, his force to command. "I would like to hit at them," she said quietly, "if for no other reason than to show my respect for the land they despoil."

Elbryan nodded grimly. "What of Avelyn?"

"He is in no state to entertain thoughts of battle," Pony replied with a shake of her head, the movement spraying little droplets of water from her thick, soaked hair. "And he is busy with his gemstones, looking far, so he said."

Elbryan had to be satisfied with that; any work Avelyn was doing was likely vital, for the monk was at least as dedicated as Elbryan himself, or any of the others out here. "Symphony can bring us only a handful of horses," the ranger stated, improvising, thinking out loud. "We'll take only as many as can ride, and only volunteers."

"My roan will bear me," said Pony.

"I ride when I'm walking." The centaur laughed.

Elbryan replied with a smile, then fell within his thoughts, calling out through the rain and the trees to Symphony, the black stallion not so far away. Within the hour, seven riders, Paulson and Chipmunk among them—both still fuming over the loss of Cric—and Bradwarden beside them, set out through the forest, making their winding way toward the evergreen valley. The elves were with them, as well, Elbryan knew, shadowing their every move, serving as silent scouts.

They arrived at the northern slope of the valley without incident, to look down upon a score of powries, a like number of goblins, and a pair of giants, clearing away the trees. This was one of the few times of the year when the ground in the vale was brown, for the caribou moss wasn't in season and the snow was all but gone. Still, the sight of the low, neat evergreens was impressive, a reminder to the ranger and Pony of the beauty of this place, this valley that they had so treasured in their youth.

"We stay close, we hit fast, and we get away," Elbryan explained, addressing them all but eyeing Paulson directly. The big man, so pained by the loss of his friend, was likely to ride right out the other end of the valley, the ranger realized, and charge into Dundalis, killing everything in his path. "Our mission here is not to kill them all—we've not the numbers for such a task—but to scare them and sting them, to chase them away in the hope that they will fear to leave the shelter of the village."

Pony, Paulson, and Chipmunk went with Elbryan, moving down to the left, while the other three followed Bradwarden down to the right. The rain intensified then, as did the wind, sheets of water blowing past, making them and their mounts all thoroughly miserable. But Elbryan welcomed the deluge. The monsters were as miserable as they, he knew, and the noise of the storm would cover their approach, perhaps even their first attacks. The one drawback was that the elves, even then moving into position lower on the slope, would have a difficult time with their bows.

No matter, the ranger mused as he picked his way among the low pines, wide of the area where the monsters hacked away. Today was a day for swords, then, and Elbryan felt comfortable indeed drawing Tempest and laying the magnificent sword across his lap.

The blade came up swiftly as the ranger passed around one bushy spruce, to see the branches jostled by something within.

Belli'mar Juraviel popped his head out in plain view; Elbryan heard Paulson and Chipmunk suck in their breath behind him, their first real sight of the ever-elusive elves.

"They are behind the ridge in great numbers," Juraviel said to the ranger. "Many giants among them, and those with stones for throwing! Be gone from this place, oh, be gone!"

Before Elbryan could begin to respond, the elf disappeared within the thick boughs, and then a rustle across the way told Elbryan that Juraviel had exited the back side of the tree and was probably long gone already.

"Trap," the ranger whispered harshly to his three companions, and he kicked Symphony into a run. The four widened their line, weaving about the trees, coming suddenly upon a group of powries and goblins, the monsters too startled to react.

Elbryan leaned low in the saddle and slashed one across the face, then drove Tempest into the chest of another as Symphony thundered past. Chipmunk took one in the eye with a dagger and cut the ear off another as it tried to dive aside, while Pony scattered a trio of goblins, the whining creatures more than willing to run away.

Paulson's maneuvers were more direct, the bearish man running down one powrie, trampling it under his mount, then splitting the skull of another with his heavy axe. Roaring and charging, looking for another target, the big man guided his horse out to the side of the others, cut a close circuit of one tree, and ran smack into a fomorian giant, the horse and rider bouncing more than the behemoth.

Paulson fell from his mount into the mud and looked up to see the giant, a bit dazed but far from defeated, shove his horse aside, then take up its monstrous, spiked club.

He knew that he would soon be with poor Cric.

He was weak and sore, but he could wait no longer. Brother Avelyn understood that he and his friends, that all the world, needed answers, needed to know the exact cause of this invasion. And so he fell into the enchantment of his powerful hematite, let his spirit walk free of his battered body, and then let it fly upon the winds.

He looked to the south, to Dundalis and the fight in the vale. He saw the monsters readied on the hill, beginning their charge, organized as an army and not a simple collection of marauding tribes.

Avelyn could do nothing except pray that Elbryan and his riders were swift enough and lucky enough to get away.

The monk's thoughts turned him back to the north, and there he went with all speed. Soon he was far beyond the sounds of battle, the forest rushing past beneath his floating spirit. How free he felt, as he had on that long-ago day—that day a million years ago in another life, it seemed—when Master Jojonah had first let him walk outside of his corporeal form, when he had floated above St.-Mere-Abelle to see the carvings on the monastery roof.

Yet another caravan of monsters, laden with engines of war and moving inexorably south, washed those peaceful thoughts from Avelyn's mind.

He came past the storm, out of the rain, but though the sky was brighter, the scene before the monk, the towering outline of the Barbacan, was not. Avelyn felt the evil, feared the evil, and knew suddenly that if he went in that dark place now, he would not get out.

Still, his spirit moved toward the Barbacan, drawn by the monk's need to know. He floated up past the towering spires of natural stone, over the southern lip of the barrier mountains, and looked down upon a blackness more complete than any moonless night.

If ten thousand monsters had marched south, five times that number were gathered here, their dark forms filling the valley from this southern mountain wall all the way to the plain between the black arms of a singular, smoking mountain some miles to the north.

A smoking mountain! It was alive with the magic of molten stone, the magic of demon dactyls.

Avelyn didn't need to go any closer, and yet he felt compelled to do so, driven by curiosity, perhaps.

No, it wasn't curiosity, the monk realized suddenly, nor was it any false hope that he might do battle with the creature then and there. Yet he could not deny the tug of that lone, smoking mountain, calling to him, compelling him . . .

He had been noticed; there could be no other answer! The demon dactyl had sensed his spirit presence and was trying to draw him in, to destroy him. That realization bolstered Avelyn's strength, and he turned away, the southlands wide before him.

"You have come to join with us," came a soft call, more a telepathic message than an actual voice, though Avelyn recognized the tone of the speaker. His spirit swung about again, and there, coming over a rocky bluff, was the ghost of the man who had trained beside him all those years in St.-Mere-Abelle, the man who had gone to Pimaninicuit to share in the glory of their God, and who, so it now seemed, had fallen so very far.

"To join with us," Quintall had said. To join with *us.*

"You court demons," Avelyn's spirit cried out.

"I have learned the truth," Quintall countered. "The light within the shadows, revealing the lies—"

"You are a damned thing!"

Avelyn sensed the spirit's amusement. "I am with the victor," Quintall assured him.

"We will fight you, every mile, every inch!"

Again, the amusement. "A minor inconvenience and no more," Quintall replied. "Even as we speak, your mighty champion and your precious companion are dying. You cannot win, you cannot hide."

The spirit stopped abruptly as Avelyn, boiling with outrage, attacked, his spirit flying fast against the nearly translucent outline of the evil ghost, locking with the creature, their battle as much one of wills as of physical strength.

They wrestled about, their power borne of faith, Avelyn's for his God, and Quintall's for the demon dactyl. They twisted and gouged, floating about and through the bare windblown rocks of the Barbacan. Quintall's grasp was the darkness of the demon—cold, drawing the very life force from his opponent. Avelyn's grasp was the sharpness of light, burning his foe.

They locked in agony, neither gaining an advantage, rolling and floating, and finally, they were apart, facing each other, circling, loathing.

Avelyn knew he could not win, not here, not with the demon dactyl so close, and the notion that the ghost knew something about Elbryan and Pony that he did not bothered Avelyn more than a little. Even worse, their fight would draw unwanted attention from the smoking mountain, the monk feared; and if the dactyl came upon him as he battled this evil spirit, he would surely be destroyed.

Avelyn was strangely unafraid of that possibility, would go willingly to his God's side if his death came in a battle with this purest of evil. But the monk had to put his own desires aside, for the others back in the forest would need to know what he had learned, would need to know of the smoking mountain and the Barbacan, the confirmation of their dark suspicions.

Avelyn would get his fight, he decided, but not until the world was properly warned.

"You are a damned thing, Quintall," he said to his dark foe, but the ghost only laughed and came on.

Avelyn resisted the urge to meet that charge and his spirit flew away, soaring fast for the south. He heard the taunts of Quintall, the ghost wrongly thinking the monk had fled in fear, and he ignored those barbs as meaningless.

Avelyn hoped that he and Quintall would meet again.

Pony and Chipmunk continued their wild ride, weaving about the pines, cutting sharp corners, Pony's sword flashing, Chipmunk's seemingly endless stream of daggers spinning out. Or, when either of them was too close for such weapons, they merely spurred their powerful steeds on, running down the helpless powries or goblins that ventured into their path.

Even those monsters not in panic, even those trying to get some angle on the riders, could do little against the sheer power and speed of the rushing horses.

"To me! To me!" Pony heard Bradwarden call, and she led the way to the centaur and his three companions, who were enjoying similar success.

Elbryan, though, did not follow. He was not surprised by the disappearance of Paulson; the man was too consumed by grief and rage, and in truth, the ranger feared that he should not have brought Paulson out here, not now, not so soon after Cric's demise.

The ranger was surprised, however, when he saw the big man's delay was not by choice, when he saw Paulson scrambling in the mud, trying desperately to stay out of reach of a giant's smashing club. Elbryan kicked Symphony into a straight charge. He wished that he had Hawkwing readied, that he could lead the way with a stinging arrow. He let the horse serve as missile instead, rushing in right beside the engaged giant, slamming against the creature as it stooped low in its attempt to get at Paulson.

The giant slipped down into the mud; Symphony staggered and slid but held his balance.

"Run!" Elbryan cried to the man, and terrified Paulson didn't have to be told twice. He scrambled about the pines, blinded by the rain and by sheer terror. He fell in the mud, but was scrambling up even as he hit the ground, his legs pumping desperately.

Elbryan tried to keep a rear guard, thought to go and scoop Paulson into the saddle behind him, but then realized that such a maneuver would cost them both too much time, would allow the stubborn giant to fall over them. And Elbryan had no time to spend in battling such a foe, not here, not now, for all the southern slope of the valley was thick with monsters, including many giants, most carrying sacks of heavy stones. Rocks began bouncing all about the valley floor, skipping in the mud, more likely to squash powrie or goblin than any of the eight attackers, though that possibility did little to dissuade the monstrous reinforcements.

Elbryan noted to his relief that Pony, Bradwarden, and the others were making a clean escape, running fast in a line up the north slope, back for the cover of the deeper forest. The ranger noted, too, that Paulson's riderless mount was close behind them, and while he was glad that the horse had escaped, he was not pleased by the sight.

Now Paulson would have to run all the way out of the valley, and he would never make it unless Elbryan and Symphony could cause enough confusion behind him. On the ranger went, now taking and deftly stringing Hawkwing, weaving a zigzag course about the pines, and letting fly an arrow whenever a monster showed its ugly face.

He kept up the dodging, the quick bursts to break free of any flanking movements, for several minutes, but time was soon working against him as more and more monsters poured onto the valley floor, as his options for flight lessened. A glance back showed the ranger Paulson's lumbering form—at least he thought the dark speck scrambling up the southeastern slope was Paulson—but showed him also the huge form of the stubborn giant, in close pursuit.

His game was ended, the ranger knew, and he spun Symphony in a tight circle about the next tree—poked a powrie hiding amid the thick boughs in the eye with Hawkwing for good measure—then cut a straight line in pursuit of Paulson and the giant.

Huge stones splattered in the mud all about him, stripping the branches from the sides of nearby trees, and the shouts of a hundred monsters followed Elbryan out of that valley.

But those shouts were fast receding, Symphony's great strides outdistancing the pursuit, and sheer luck saw the ranger through the shower of giant-thrown stones. He got over the lip of the valley, spotted the distant form of the lumbering giant, and plunged fast among the skeletal forms of the leafless trees.

Paulson was caught; he tripped over an exposed root and went facedown into the mud and slush. He heard the giant's victorious laughter, imagined the spiked club coming up high, and covered his head with his hands, though he realized that meager defense would do him little good.

The giant was indeed closing for the kill, lifting its deadly weapon, when an arrow thudded hard into its back, turning its evil laughter into a sudden wheeze. Outraged, the behemoth spun.

Elbryan stood right up on Symphony's back, the horse in full gallop. He drew out Tempest and put his bow to the saddle. The giant was near a wide-branching elm with thick, solid limbs.

"Be quick and be sure," the ranger said to Symphony, who understood his plan perfectly.

The horse angled near a second elm, its branches intertwined with the one near the giant, and Elbryan leaped away, running, surefooted, along one rain-slicked limb.

The giant turned and stared curiously as the suddenly riderless horse continued to bear down upon it, but the monster, after a moment's thought, seemed satisfied with that and lifted its club to meet Symphony's charge.

At the last second, the horse veered sharply to the side, and the giant lunged, and only then did the stupid fomorian notice the second form, running along the branches, running right by its bending form.

Tempest flashed like blue-white lightning, tearing a long line across the monster's throat. The giant came up with a roar and swung hard, but Elbryan had already dropped off the back of the limb, and that sturdy branch stopped the club far short of the mark. Under the limb came Elbryan, Tempest stabbing, then slashing upward into the monster's loins as it tried futilely to extract its spiked club from the stubborn branch.

And even worse for the giant than the stabbing, searing pain down low was the wound across its throat, the wound that spurted blood wildly and refused to allow the monster to draw breath. Its rage played out, as the terrible wound and the flying blood took away the monster's strength. The giant let go of the club, then, and staggered backward, grasping at its torn throat. It looked down through blurred eyes to see the wicked man back atop his stallion, the other man, the easy prey, climbing up behind him.

The giant reached for Elbryan and Paulson, but its senses were playing tricks now and the men were fully twenty feet away. Reaching, reaching, the giant overbalanced and fell to the ground.

The behemoth heard the hooves receding into the forest, heard the distant voice of a human female, and then the darkness closed in.

❖ 44 ❖

The Revelations
of Spirits

"I t was a trap, set for you, who lived once in Dundalis," Juraviel said. The elf sat with Pony and Elbryan near Mather's grave in the diamond-shaped grove. Tuntun was nearby, along with the other elves who had come to the area, and who, Juraviel had informed Elbryan, would soon be returning to Andur'Blough Inninness.

"How would they know that?" Elbryan asked, not yet willing to believe that the cutting in the evergreen vale had been done specifically for them.

"They knew that many of the folk battling them had fled Dundalis," Juraviel answered. "The village was deserted before they arrived. It would follow that they understood the valley north of the town to be an important place, perhaps even a sacred place."

"No," Pony argued. "They would not believe it to be more important than was the village itself, and that we deserted."

"And I doubt that powries, and certainly not goblins and giants, hold any appreciation for beauty," Elbryan added.

Juraviel fell silent, digesting the logical arguments. Still, it bothered the elf that the monsters had gone into that particular valley.

It bothered Elbryan, too, for the scarring of the evergreens made no sense. The monsters' take of lumber would not have been useful; the spruce and pines were too short for catapults, too wet and sappy for wood fires, and too pliable for any construction. With deeper forests all about them, filled with taller trees of harder wood, why would the powries go into the evergreen valley? Only to lure their enemies, Elbryan had to reason, particularly Jilseponie and him, the two to whom the valley was indeed sacred.

But it made no sense to the ranger, for the plan was too subtle. How might the monsters have garnered such information about the leaders of their enemies?

"They knew," Elbryan said flatly. "They had to know."

"How?" Juraviel demanded.

A whistle from the trees—from Tuntun, they realized—alerted them of a visitor, and a moment later, Brother Avelyn ambled in to join them. He looked much better, seeming his old bouncy self, except for a slight limp.

"Ho, ho, what?" Pony said to him playfully, drawing a smile from the monk.

"They knew," Avelyn remarked as he sat down hard on the ground. "They knew, and they know much of us. Too much."

"How have you discerned this?" Juraviel asked.

"A ghost told me," Avelyn replied. Elbryan perked up his ears, wondering if the monk had been in contact with Uncle Mather.

"While you fought in the valley, I went far to the north," the monk explained. "I tell you now that this force which has come upon us is but a predecessor, a testing probe, and that our enemy, the demon dactyl, has many times this number of soldiers to send down upon us."

"Then we are doomed," Pony whispered.

"Our enemy has another ally, as well," Avelyn went on, looking directly at Elbryan. "The ghost of a man you killed, in my defense."

"Brother Justice," the ranger reasoned.

Avelyn nodded. "His name is Quintall," he said, for the other title seemed perfectly ridiculous now. "I spoke with this ghost briefly, before we battled, and I tell you, he knew of us, of you and of Pony."

"He and I once did battle," the ranger reminded.

Avelyn was shaking his head before Elbryan even finished the predictable sentence. "He knew that you were in trouble, in the valley. He predicted that both of you would be slain."

"Then it was a trap," Juraviel said.

"Indeed," remarked Avelyn. "They knew how best to draw us—you, two, at least," he said to Elbryan and Pony.

"How could they?" Pony wanted to know. "Brother—Quintall did not know us well, certainly did not know our affinity with the pine vale."

"Perhaps the ghost has been about us," came a voice from a nearby tree. The group glanced over to see Tuntun sitting calmly on a branch.

That seemed plausible enough, but Avelyn suspected that he would have sensed Quintall's presence had the spirit indeed been about. "Perhaps," the monk admitted, "or might it be that Quintall is not the only one who has fallen to the darkness of the dactyl?"

To the small group whose very lives depended on absolute secrecy, there could have been no more unsettling possibility than that of a traitor in their midst. A thousand questions filtered through Elbryan's and everyone else's thoughts as he considered each person of the band. When he came to privately question the loyalty of Bradwarden, the ranger realized that this exercise was truly folly.

"We know no such thing," Elbryan said firmly after a lengthy pause in the conversation. "Likely it was the ghost, a spy for our enemies. Or perhaps the powries are more cunning than we first believed. Perhaps they have prisoners hidden away and have tortured information from them."

"None from Dundalis, surely," argued Pony. "None who might know of our fondness for the valley."

"It is all speculation," the ranger insisted. "Dangerous thoughts. How will we function if there remains no trust among us? No," he decided, his stern tone showing that he would brook no compromise on this point, "we will not cast suspicion on any in our group. We will not speak of this outside our immediate circle, and not speak of it at all unless some more substantial evidence can be found."

"We must be careful then," Avelyn offered.

"Will this grove be next?" Pony asked, a question that unnerved Elbryan.

"All the world will be next," Tuntun said, shifting the focus, "if Avelyn's words are true."

"They are," the monk insisted. "I saw the monstrous gathering in such numbers as I would never have imagined."

"In greater numbers than their nature would allow," agreed Juraviel, "were they not guided."

Pony, who hadn't been involved in the previous discussion at Avelyn's bedside, seemed not to understand.

"Powries and goblins would not ally for long if there was not a greater power, a greater evil, holding them together," Juraviel explained.

Pony looked at Avelyn, thinking of his prophecies of doom all those weeks together on the road, thinking of the weakness of the world the monk constantly berated and of the name he gave to it. "The dactyl?" she asked. "You are certain?"

"The dactyl is awake," Avelyn said without hesitation.

"As we feared in Caer'alfar," Juraviel added.

"But I thought that the dactyl was the weakness in men's hearts," Pony reasoned, "not a physical being."

"It is both," Avelyn explained, recalling the training he had received at St.-Mere-Abelle and thinking it ironic now that those same men who had taught him of the demon dactyl had, through their own weakness and impiety, helped to facilitate the return of the monster. "It is the weakness of man that allows the demon to come forth, but when it does, it is a physical monster indeed, a being of great power who can command the wills of those with evil in their hearts, who can dominate the monstrous hordes and tempt men such as Quintall, men who have fallen from the ways of God, to its side."

"There are more beliefs than those of your church," Tuntun put in dryly.

"And all our gods are one God," Avelyn replied quickly, not wanting to offend the elf. "A God of differing names perhaps, but of similar tenets. And when those tenets are misinterpreted," the monk went on, his voice turning grave, "when they are used for personal gain or as a means of exacting punishment or forcing submission upon others, then let all of Corona beware, for the demon dactyl will rouse from its slumbers."

"It is a dark time," Juraviel agreed.

Elbryan bowed his head but in thought and not in despair. Such philosophical discussions did not elude the ranger, but Elbryan understood that his role here was to consider their position in terms of their day-to-day existence, that he might properly guide those folk, closer to two hundred than to one, who had come under his care. At that moment, the ranger had more immediate problems than some mythical monster hundreds of miles away, for if there was indeed a traitor in their midst, then the threat would increase.

"They knew, Uncle Mather," Elbryan whispered when at last the image came to him at Oracle. "They knew that scourging the valley would wound me, would, perhaps, even bring me out of hiding. Yet, how can they know of me, more than the name of Nightbird, which I have not hidden, and of my exploits against them? How could they know of my loves, of a place that is special only within my heart?"

The ranger sat back, leaning on the back wall of the small cave. He continued to stare silently, not expecting an answer but hoping that, as was often the case, the image of his uncle Mather would guide him through the jumble of his own thoughts, to reason through his dilemma.

He saw another image in the mirror—or was it merely in his mind?—one of a man he had selected to go along on the raid to the evergreen vale, but who had refused, claiming sickness. Elbryan knew well that the man had not been ill, and he considered the sudden cowardice truly out of character. But with no time for such petty problems, the ranger had dismissed the incident.

Elbryan envisioned again the return of the battered group to the main encampment: Paulson dropping down wearily from Symphony's back, Pony leaning against Bradwarden as if, were it not for the centaur's solid frame, she would have simply tumbled over to the ground. He saw reflected in the mirror those images that had been peripheral to him at that time: a supposedly ill man standing at the side of the camp and, more important, the expression on that man's face, hardly noticed at the time, but clear now to Elbryan.

The man was surprised, truly surprised, that they had returned.

Using all the stealth he had learned in his years with the Touel'alfar, Elbryan followed Tol Yuganick out of the encampment late one dark night, several days after the abandoned raid on the evergreen valley.

The big man, supposedly in search of firewood, looked back over his broad shoulders often, Elbryan noted, obviously trying to ensure that he was not being followed. His precaution did little against the stealthy skill of the ranger, though, and so Tol was oblivious of Elbryan's presence, obviously so, when he met with a bandy-limbed powrie less than two miles from the band's present hideout.

"I did as you demanded," Elbryan heard the big man complain. "I delivered them, right where I said I would."

"Yach! Ye said the ranger," the powrie grumbled back, "and his woman friend. Ye made no talk of other warriors or of that wretched centaur!"

"Did you think Nightbird would be so foolish as to go so near Dundalis alone?"

"Silence!" the powrie snapped at him. "Take care yer attitude, Tol Yuganick; Bestesbulzibar is not far, I promise, and he hungers for human flesh."

Elbryan silently mouthed the unfamiliar name and noted how Tol's ruddy face blanched at the mere mention. The ranger didn't know what this creature, Bestesbulzibar, might be, but his respect for it as an enemy was already considerable.

"We must defeat Nightbird," the powrie insisted, "and soon. My master has noticed the problems here, though we are many leagues behind the battle lines, and my master is not pleased."

"That is your problem, Ulg Tik'narn, and not my own!" Tol growled. "You have used me, powrie, and left a foul taste in my mouth that no river could wash out were I to swallow the whole of it!"

Elbryan nodded, glad that the man felt some remorse for his traitorous actions.

"And I'm done with you and with Bestesbulzibar the winged devil!" He turned indignantly on his heel and started to stride away.

"Yach, and with the ghost that finds yer dreams," the powrie asked slyly, "the ghost who beckons to Bestesbulzibar's every call?"

Tol Yuganick hesitated and turned back.

"And what might Nightbird do if he discovers your treachery?" Ulg Tik'-narn asked.

"We had a deal," Tol protested.

"We *have* a deal," Ulg Tik'narn corrected. "Ye'll do as I say, fool human, or me master will destroy ye most unpleasantly."

Tol bowed his head, his face contorting as he struggled, pragmatism against conscience.

"Ye're are already a fallen thing," the powrie went on, chuckling. "Yer course cannot be reversed, yer errors cannot be corrected. Ye delivered Nightbird to us once, and now ye must do so again, for unless he's taken, there'll be no rest for ugly Tol Yuganick, no sleep that will evade the intrusions of the ghost Quintall, no path that will get you far enough from the flight of Bestesbulzibar, who is all-powerful."

Elbryan could hardly draw breath at the realization that he and his little band had made such an impact on the very heart of this monstrous army. He recognized the name of the turncoat spirit, of course, and considering that the powrie referred to Quintall as but a pawn of Bestesbulzibar, the ranger suspected the identity of that creature.

"There is a grove," Tol began reluctantly, "diamond-shaped."

The words stirred Elbryan; he put an arrow to Hawkwing before he even realized and had the bow leveled, its mark the space between treacherous Tol's eyes.

"It is even more special to the ranger, a place that he will not allow to be defiled, whatever the odds," Tol went on.

Elbryan didn't want to kill the man; whatever Tol's weakness, the ranger didn't want to shoot him dead without explanation, without hearing the threats that had been laid upon the man to turn him so.

But Elbryan held no such sympathy for powries, and so he shifted the angle of the bow just a bit, gritted his teeth, and let fly, the arrow whipping across the twenty feet, unerringly, so he thought. At the last moment, the arrow turned in mid-flight, thudding hard into a tree. Ulg Tik'narn was away in the blink of an eye, running fast into the forest night, but before Tol could move, the ranger leaped before him, Tempest in hand. A glance at the fleeing powrie told Elbryan that the creature posed no immediate threat.

Tol, on the other hand, had his huge sword in hand, eyeing Elbryan nervously.

"I heard," the ranger said, "everything."

Tol didn't reply, just glanced around, looking for an escape.

"You cannot outrun me in the woods at night," Elbryan said evenly.

"Then you outrun me," the big man retorted. "I've wanted your head since the first day we met, smelly ranger, and be gone now or be sure that I'll get it!"

Elbryan recognized the true fear behind that bluff. Tol had no desire to fight him, had no desire to face the mighty cut of Tempest.

"Throw your weapon to the ground," Elbryan said calmly. "I'll not play judge to you, Tol Yuganick, not out here. You come with me back to the camp and speak your crimes plainly, and let us see what the people choose for you."

Tol scoffed at the notion. "Drop my weapon that you might more easily wrap a noose about my neck?" he said.

"Unlikely," the ranger replied. "The folk are merciful."

Tol spat at him. "I give you one last chance to run," he said.

"Do not do this," Elbryan warned, but Tol came upon him in a wild rush, his heavy sword slashing.

Tempest flashed left, parried up, went out left again and then right, Elbryan easily fending off the clumsy attacks. The ranger poked the smaller blade ahead, bringing its tip near the hilt of Tol's jabbing sword as he deftly sidestepped the large man's forward thrust. A twist of Elbryan's wrist brought Tempest's blade hard against the big man's hand, and a further twist turned Tol's hand right over awkwardly.

Elbryan shoved wide his sword arm, and Tol's weapon went flying harmlessly to the side, splashing down into a muddy puddle.

The big man gasped in desperation, unarmed and eyeing the deadly ranger.

"Do not," Elbryan began, but Tol turned and stumbled away.

Elbryan flipped Tempest up above his head, lining the blade for a throw. He held back, though, as Tol passed the nearest tree, as a pair of muscled equine legs flashed out, connecting solidly on the side of the man's head, launching him head over heels to crash hard at the base of a wide ash tree.

Bradwarden stepped into the small clearing.

"I followed him out here," Elbryan explained.

"And I followed yerself," the centaur replied. "And I was carrying Avelyn on me back. Ye should be more to looking past yer arse, though yer target's past yer nose."

Elbryan glanced all about. "And where is the monk?"

"Chasing a powrie," Bradwarden explained. "Said not to worry about that little one."

Elbryan looked over at Tol, the man's head lolling about on his shoulders. He was in a sitting position, wedged in tightly against the hard trunk.

"I'll not presume to judge him," the ranger said.

"Always for mercy, as ye were with the three rogue trappers."

"And that choice was the best," Elbryan reminded.

"Aye, but this one is not," the centaur insisted. "This one's a fallen thing, with no redeeming. His crime cannot be tolerated, so I say, for he'd have given us all to the beast to save his skin." Bradwarden eyed the dazed man contemptuously. "He knows it, too. Suren that ye're showing him less mercy by letting him live with the terrible thing he's done."

"I'll not play judge."

"But I will," Bradwarden said firmly. "Ye might want to be going now, me friend. Avelyn might be needing ye, and ye might want to not be watching this."

Elbryan eyed the brutal centaur squarely, but understood that he had little power to sway Bradwarden's determination. And whatever his feelings of mercy, Elbryan would not battle Bradwarden for the sake of Tol Yuganick, who had indeed fallen too far. He looked back at Tol, the man oblivious and probably already mortally wounded by the powerful kick.

"Be merciful," the ranger said to Bradwarden. "He laments his choice."

"He made the choice willingly."

"Even if that is true, mercy is friend to the just," Elbryan insisted.

Bradwarden nodded somberly, and Elbryan scooped up Hawkwing and ran off into the night, behind the departing powrie, though the ranger held faith that Avelyn would know how to deal with the dwarf. Less than ten steps into the woods, he heard a single thump, a centaur's kick against a head propped by a tree trunk, and he knew that it was finished.

He felt sick to his stomach, but he could not disagree, not out here with so many lives at stake. Tol had chosen, and Tol had paid for his choice.

Around a bend far down the dark trail, the ranger happened upon a band of powries lying on the ground, most dead but some still twitching in the last moments of their lives. A lightning bolt had hit them, the ranger realized, and he knew that he was close.

He paused and tuned his senses to the night, and he heard speaking, not so far away. Running fast, but silently, Elbryan soon spotted Avelyn, making fast work of yet another powrie, the burly monk holding the dwarf under his arm, repeatedly slamming the creature's head into a tree trunk.

Elbryan meant to stop there, but a movement farther to the south along the trail caught his attention. He came in sight of the last powrie—the one, Ulg Tik'narn, who had been speaking with Tol Yuganick. Sliding down to one knee, Elbryan had Hawkwing up and leveled. Again his shot was true, but again, the arrow swerved at the last possible moment and flew off harmlessly into the night.

Frustrated, the ranger abandoned his bow and ran on, sword in hand.

The powrie, apparently realizing that it could not possibly outdistance the long-legged human, skidded to a stop and turned about, a gleaming, serrated sword in hand.

"Nightbird," the dwarf breathed. "Yach, ye die!"

Elbryan said nothing, just came in hard and fast, batting Tempest twice against the powrie's blade, then thrusting the sword through the opened defenses, straight for the unarmored dwarf's heart.

The blade turned aside, compelled by some force Elbryan did not understand, and the startled ranger was overbalanced suddenly, falling forward. He slapped his free hand across desperately, accepting the hit on his open palm from the smiling powrie's sword.

"What?" the ranger asked, skidding aside and turning to squarely face this deceptive foe.

Laughing, Ulg Tik'narn advanced.

From a short distance away, Brother Avelyn watched the scene curiously, saw Elbryan perform another apparently successful attack, only to have Tempest fly wide at the last instant. The ranger was not caught unaware this time, though, and he held his balance and reverted to defensive posture quickly enough to prevent any stinging counters.

Avelyn put away the stone he was holding, graphite, for the lightning had been of little effect on this one when he had last used it. There was something very unusual about this powrie, the monk realized, some defensive magic that Avelyn did not understand.

He took out the carbuncle he had taken from dead Quintall, fell into its magic even as Elbryan slashed his weapon—to no avail—twice at the laughing powrie's head.

Then Avelyn saw the reason, saw clearly the powrie's studded bracers, glowing fiercely with enchantment.

"Good enough, then," the monk growled. "Ho, ho, what!" Avelyn took out the other stone he had retrieved from dead Quintall, the powerful sunstone, and he sent its focused energies out.

"Yach, ye can not kill me, foolish Nightbird," Ulg Tik'narn was saying, holding wide his short arms and steadily advancing on the confused Elbryan. "Me master protects me. Bestes—"

The word ended with a gurgle as the waves of magic-suppression rolled over the dactyl-forged bracers, as Tempest pierced through the dwarf's chest.

"I do not know the name," Juraviel admitted, looking across the campfire at Elbryan.

"But I do," Avelyn put in, resting his bulk against a fallen log. "Bestesbulzibar, Aztemephostophe, Pelucine, Decambrinezarre—"

"All names of the dactyl demons," Juraviel said, for two of the strange titles rang familiar to the elf.

"Then we know, if the powrie can be believed, that there is indeed a beast, a physical beast, guiding our enemy," said Pony.

"Then we know," Avelyn said with certainty, and he threw down the enchanted bracers, evil items that the monk would not allow to be worn. "I have known for some time of this beast and of its home."

"The Barbacan," said Elbryan.

"The smoking mountain," Avelyn added.

A long moment of silence ensued, all five—the three humans, Juraviel, and Tuntun—feeling the weight of confirmation and feeling suddenly vulnerable. There was indeed a very real dactyl, and it controlled Quintall's ghost, and—whether through Quintall or reports from its monstrous forces—it knew of their raiding band, knew of Nightbird.

Avelyn stood up and started away; Pony rushed to catch up to him.

"I know my destiny," he said to her quietly, though Elbryan, who had moved to follow, and the two elves, with their keen ears, heard him clearly. "I know now why I was compelled by the spirit of God to steal the stones and run from St.-Mere-Abelle."

"You mean to go to the Barbacan," Pony reasoned.

"I have seen the army that has gathered there," Avelyn replied. "I have seen the darkness that will soon sweep down upon us, upon all the kingdom: St.-Mere-Abelle and Palmaris, Ursal, and even to Entel on the Belt-and-Buckle. Perhaps far Behren is not safe."

The monk turned back to look Pony directly in the eye, then past her, to Elbryan. "We cannot defeat the dactyl and its minions," Avelyn insisted.

"Our people have grown weak, and the elves have become too isolated and too few. The only way in which the darkness might be averted is if our enemy is decapitated, if the binding force that holds powrie beside hated goblin, if the sheer evil willpower that focuses the wild giants is destroyed."

"You mean to travel hundreds of miles to do battle with a creature of such power?" Elbryan asked skeptically.

"No army gathered by all the human kingdoms could get near the dactyl," Avelyn replied, "but I might."

"A small group might," Pony added, looking at Elbryan.

The ranger considered that notion for a moment, then nodded grimly.

Pony looked back at Avelyn, stared deeply into the eyes of this man who had become to her as a brother. She saw the pain there, the fear that was not present when the monk had proclaimed that he alone would go. Avelyn was afraid for her, and not for himself.

"You say it is your destiny," Pony remarked, "and so, since fate has put me beside you, is it mine."

Avelyn was shaking his head, but Pony pressed on.

"Do not even think to try to stop me," she insisted. "Where am I to be safe, in any case? Here, when the powries lay traps meant for us? In the southland, perhaps, running ahead of the advancing hordes?"

"Or even in the elven home?" Juraviel added grimly, unexpectedly lending support to Pony's argument.

"Where indeed?" asked the woman. "I would rather confront the monster face-to-face, to stand by Avelyn's side as he meets his destiny, as all the world holds its breath."

Avelyn looked at Elbryan as if he expected the ranger to protest. How could Elbryan, so obviously in love with Pony, allow her to go?

But Avelyn didn't fully understand the nature of that love.

"And I will stand by Pony's side," the ranger said firmly. "And by Avelyn's."

The monk's expression was one of sheer incredulity.

"Was not Terranen Dinoniel an elf-trained ranger?" Elbryan asked, looking about and finally settling his gaze on Juraviel and Tuntun.

"He was half-elf, as well," Tuntun put in, as if that fact put the legendary hero somewhat above Elbryan's station.

"Then I will have to go along to make up the other half," Juraviel said somberly. He met Tuntun's wide-eyed stare without surprise. "With Lady Dasslerond's blessings, of course," he said.

"Ho, ho, what!" Avelyn burst out suddenly, surprised and obviously pleased by the unexpected support. But the boisterous moment could not last, not with so grim a prospect as a journey to the Barbacan before them. The monk looked in turn at each of them and nodded, then walked off to be alone with his conscience and his courage.

When Elbryan and Pony left the elves, they were surprised to find an eavesdropping friend, standing only a dozen or so paces into the forest, unseen and unheard despite his great bulk.

"Ah, but I knew it'd come to this," Bradwarden said. "Humans"—the centaur spat derisively—"always thinking o' ways to be remembered." He shook his head. "Get yer saddlebags for me, then, ye'll need one to carry supplies, and better if that one knows how to get away from trouble."

"You intend to accompany us?" Elbryan asked.

"A long road," the centaur replied. "Ye'll be needing me pipes to soothe yer nerves, don't ye doubt!"

PART FIVE

▼

THE
BEAST

It is settled, Uncle Mather, a new stasis, a level of play. Our enemies know of us, and there is certainly concern among their ranks, but they have a bigger goal before them and that diversion gives us some hope, gives us the ability to proclaim with confidence that they will not catch us.

But neither will we deliver any significant blows. A pair of catapults fell before our fires, but what are they compared to the hundreds of war engines in a line rolling down from the Barbacan? We have killed nearly a dozen giants in the last two weeks, but how significant are they when a thousand more march against Honce-the-Bear? And now that we are known, our enemies take precautions, moving about in larger, better-prepared bands. Each kill comes harder.

So we will survive for the time, I believe, but we will do nothing decisive, not here, halfway between the fighting front and the source of the invasion. Yet, if Brother Avelyn is correct, if his destiny lies in the north and we can deliver him there, if he can battle and defeat the demon dactyl, then our enemies will be without their binding force. Who will quell the ancient and deep hatred between powrie and goblin when Bestesbulzibar is gone? It is likely that all the invasion will disintegrate into separate groups, fighting one another as much as the folk of the kingdom. It is likely that most of the giants, normally reclusive beasts, will turn back for their mountain homes, far from the villages of humans.

I do laugh when I consider how simple it all sounds, for I know that the path ahead is the darkest that ever I will tread, and that the end of that path is darker still.

Dark, too, is the journey for those men and women I leave behind, who will continue the fight while ushering their more helpless kin to a safer place—if one can ever be found. I hold no comforting illusions; that group is in danger as great as my own. Eventually, if they cannot find a haven, they will be killed, one at a time, perhaps, as was poor Cric, or perhaps the goblins will discover their camp in the night and slaughter them all.

What clouds are these that so cover our heads, blacker than the blackest storm?

It is the life that fate has chosen for us, Uncle Mather. It is the life that fate has thrust upon us, and I am proud indeed that few, so very few, have shrunk before their sudden, unasked-for responsibilities. For every Tol Yuganick, there are a hundred, I say, who will not give in to any threat, to any torture, who share loyalty and courage and who willingly take up the fight, even if that means their death, that their kin might win out.

I am a ranger, trained to accept duty, however harsh, and to accept whatever fate holds for me during the execution of that duty. That is my debt and my honor. I will fight, with all the skills the elves gave me, with all the weapons at my disposal, for those tenets I hold dear—for the protection of innocents and for the higher principles of justice above all else. And in that course, in these times, I have by reason of necessity become leader of the folk of the three villages. But they, these innocents placed in the path of war, and not I, are the true heroes of the day, for each of them—the trappers who could have been far from harm's way; Bradwarden, whose fight this is not; Belster O'Comely and Shawno of End-o'-the-World—each of them willingly fights on, though they are not bound by debt. Every man, every woman, every child willingly takes up arms because of their common heritage, because they understand the value of unity, because they care for the fate of those in the towns to the south.

I understand now what it means to be a ranger, Uncle Mather. To be a ranger is to accept the frailties of humanity with the knowledge that the good outweighs the bad, to serve as an example, often an unappreciated one, that when darkness descends upon those about you—even many of those who, perhaps, persecuted you—they will recognize your value and follow that lead. To be a ranger is to show by example those about you what they might be when the need arises, to reflect openly the better aspects of what is in every human character.

The men and women I leave behind will serve as I have served, will lift up the spirits and the will, the courage and the conviction, of all those they subsequently meet.

And for myself, I pledge now that I will deliver Brother Avelyn to the Barbacan, to the fiendish head of our enemy. And if I perish in the journey, then so be it. If all of us, my beloved Pony included, perish and fail, then let another take up my sword and my cry.

The blackness will not fall complete until the last free human spirit has succumbed.

—ELBRYAN THE NIGHTBIRD

❖ 45 ❖

Parting

I t took Elbryan and the other leaders of the rebel force several days to get everything organized with the twenty-five warriors and eight score refugees they would leave behind. The remaining band would cease its hit-and-hide warfare and concentrate on getting all the folk to safer points in the south, trying to parallel the advancing army without engaging it.

For those few heading north to the Barbacan, it was a difficult parting, but especially so for Elbryan, who had come to feel as a father to these people, as their trusted protector. If they were found and destroyed, the ranger knew he would never forgive himself.

But the other argument was more compelling; if the dactyl could not be defeated, then there would be no safe havens, then all the world as the humans knew it would be destroyed. Pony reminded the ranger often that he had trained those warriors who would escort the refugees, that they went with not only his blessing but also his woodland skills. And, like a father who has watched his children grow beyond his protection, Elbryan had to let them go.

His course, a darker road by far, lay the other way.

They set out at an easy pace, with Elbryan riding Symphony—but only for a short distance—that he might hasten out to run a perimeter guard, and with Pony and Avelyn walking beside Bradwarden, who had pipes in hand, but wouldn't start playing until they had put the monstrous enclaves of Dundalis, Weedy Meadow, and End-o'-the-World far behind them.

Just out of sight of the encampment, the small group came upon a party of elves—there might have been five or there might have been twenty, so fleeting were their glimpses of the ever-elusive sprites—dancing amid the budding branches of several trees.

"What says Lady Dasslerond?" Elbryan inquired of Belli'mar Juraviel.

"Fare well, says she," replied the elf. "Fare well to Elbryan the Night-bird, to Jilseponie, to good Brother Avelyn, to mighty Bradwarden, and," he finished with a flurry, beating his tiny wings furiously to set himself gently down on the ground, "to Belli'mar Juraviel, who will represent Caer'alfar on this most important quest!" The elf dipped a low bow.

Elbryan looked up at Tuntun, who was sitting on the branch and smiling—a grin that did not seem so sincere to the perceptive ranger. "See to him, Nightbird," the elven female said threateningly. "I will hold you personally responsible for my brother's safety."

"Ho, and a mighty responsibility that is, when facing the likes of a demon dactyl!" howled Bradwarden.

"If I had my say, Belli'mar Juraviel would remain with his own," Elbryan replied. "Of course, if I had my way, then Pony—Jilseponie—would remain with the folk of the three sacked villages, as would Avelyn, and Bradwarden's pipes would greet the dawn each day in this forest, his home."

"Ho, ho, what!" bellowed Avelyn. "Brave Nightbird would fight the beast alone!"

"Aye, and cut a killing swath through the army ye seen 'tween the arms o' the dactyl's mountain!" added Bradwarden.

Elbryan could only laugh at their jibes. He kicked Symphony into a short gallop, rushing down the path.

"Fare well to you, Nightbird!" he heard Tuntun call, and then he was alone, riding the perimeter, glad for this newest addition to the party, despite his comments to the contrary.

He sensed a movement not far away and asked Symphony to walk slowly. He relaxed when Paulson and Chipmunk came onto the path, some distance ahead and apparently oblivious of him.

"If we missed them, I'll beat ye silly," the large man huffed at Chipmunk, who wisely shifted to the side, out of arm's reach. Elbryan did not miss the fact that they were dressed for the road, though the others would not be going to join with the refugees until the next morning. The ranger moved his mount into the cover of a pair of pines and let the two approach, hoping to discern their intent, thinking that they might have had enough of it all and were striking out on their own.

Aside from Paulson's typical grumbling, he caught no direction to their conversation.

"My greetings," he said suddenly as they neared, startling the pair.

"And to yerself," said Paulson. "Glad I am that we did not miss yer departure."

"Have you plans of your own?"

Paulson eyed him directly. "What's for us with Elbryan gone?" he wanted to know.

The ranger looked hard at the man, then shrugged. "We will need to get the refugees to the south. There can be no further delays."

"Ye've got more than a score of fighters for that task," Paulson answered.

"A score that will need Paulson and Chipmunk to lead them," Elbryan reasoned.

"They'll more listen to Belster O'Comely," Paulson argued. "And the able man's already taken charge, by all accounts from the big camp. Our job here is done."

"Then you are free of responsibility," Elbryan replied, "to go as you will, where you will. And to go with my thanks and the gratitude of all who survived the invasion."

Paulson looked at Chipmunk, and the small man nodded nervously.

"With you," Paulson said suddenly. "The way we're seeing it, the goblin that killed Cric was sent by this Bestesbulzi—thing, so we're holding it responsible."

Elbryan's expression was skeptical.

"Are ye knowing anyone better for the woods?" Paulson argued.

"Ye just said that we were free to choose," Chipmunk added sheepishly, ducking behind Paulson's bulk as he spoke.

The others caught up to the ranger then, Bradwarden—with Juraviel nestled comfortably on his back, the elf tucked between the heavy packs— moving up right beside Elbryan.

"Our friends Paulson and Chipmunk would like to join us," the ranger explained.

"We decided that a small group'd get through all the better," Bradwarden complained.

"The two of us take up less room than yerself alone, centaur," Paulson argued.

Elbryan smiled wryly at Bradwarden before the fearsome centaur could take offense. "True enough," the ranger agreed.

"And we're knowing the ways of the woods," Paulson went on, "and the ways of our enemies. Ye get in a fight and ye'll be glad that me and Chipmunk are with ye."

Elbryan looked at Bradwarden again, since he and the centaur had been unofficially accepted as the leaders of the expedition. Bradwarden's hardened visage fast softened under the ranger's plaintive look. "Come along then," he said to the two men. "But one bad word for me piping and I'll be eating more than the meat that's on me back!"

So they set out then, seven strong. Seven against the tens of thousands, and—in odds that seemed even less favorable—seven mortals against one demon dactyl. At the edge of the forest surrounding Dundalis, Elbryan slipped down from his mount.

"Run free, my friend," he said to the horse. "Perhaps I shall return to you." The horse did not immediately run off, but stood stamping the ground, as if in protest.

The ranger sensed that the stallion did not want to remain behind, and for a moment, Elbryan entertained the thought of riding all the way. But how could he do that in all good conscience, when he knew that Symphony might not be able to cross the mountainous Barbacan, and certainly would not be able to go into Aida's tunnels with him.

"Run on!" he commanded, and Symphony bolted out of the immediate area, but stood quiet in the shadows of some trees not far away.

So it was Elbryan, and not the horse, who walked away, when the others caught up to him. It was not an easy thing for the ranger to do.

They struck out west more than north, wanting to cut a wide circuit around the long caravan that Avelyn had magically observed. Even from several miles to the north and west of End-o'-the-World, from atop a hillock, they could see a long line of dust rising into the air, moving south, descending upon Dundalis and the other towns.

"All the way to the Belt-and-Buckle," Avelyn remarked grimly, and from that vantage point, it seemed impossible that the monk might be wrong.

There were no roads out here once the group got beyond the logging areas of End-o'-the-World. The forest was old, with tall, dark trees and sparse undergrowth, and there were rivers to follow, some whose waters had come all the way down from the high peaks of the Barbacan. Occasionally, the group came upon a lone house or a few clustered together, the real frontier families, living beyond even the meager civilization of the three small villages. It was not a comforting thing for the seven to find that every house they chanced upon, including one whose occupants had been friends of Paulson's band, was deserted.

They found the reason the tenth day out, when Elbryan noted a line of tracks preceding them in the muddy riverbank.

"Goblins," the ranger informed his companions, "and a few humans."

"Could be a rogue band," Bradwarden offered, "and nothing to do with our enemy in the north."

"Goblins been in this region for a thousand years," Paulson added. "Me friends've fought with them often, so they told me."

"But do goblins normally take prisoners?" the ranger wanted to know, and that admittedly unusual circumstance tipped them off that this was no chance incident, no rogue band.

The demon will draw all the goblins from all the holes, Avelyn had warned.

How Elbryan wished he still had Symphony with him, that he could ride fast to catch up to the band!

"We slip back into the woods to avoid them," Bradwarden said. "No problem with that."

"Except that they have prisoners," Pony was fast to interject.

"We're not knowing that," Bradwarden replied.

"Human tracks with the goblins," Avelyn argued.

"Might be that they *had* prisoners," Bradwarden answered bluntly.

Elbryan was about to argue the point with the centaur, to point out that, whatever their mission, they first had to see if there were people in need of their assistance, when he got some unexpected help from Paulson.

"They're running an army," the big man reasoned, "so they're needing slaves. If this raiding group is in league with the dactyl, then they're knowing better than to kill those who might be worked to death."

Bradwarden threw up his arms in defeat, and motioned for Elbryan to run on and see what he might see. The ranger did just that, circling west of the riverbank as he made his way to the north. He came upon them at last at a bend in the river, where the goblins—many goblins!—had stopped to drink, but were keeping a score of humans, three quarters of them women and children, back from the badly desired water.

The ranger bowed his head as he considered the options. Thankfully, there were no giants or even powries to be seen, but there were at least fifty goblins down there, with several, Elbryan noted, wearing the black-and-gray insignia of the dactyl's army. Even if he and his powerful band attacked the group, how might they stop the goblins from killing the prisoners?

Elbryan went back to report to his companions, expecting that a furious argument would ensue. Was their mission the overriding factor here, for if they attacked and were beaten back, killed, or captured, then who would go on to the smoking mountain to stand against the demon dactyl?

"Only fifty?" Bradwarden huffed. "And only goblins? I'll warm me bow on the first score, trample the second score, and give me club a taste on the last ten!"

"How do we hit them without endangering the prisoners?" the ever-pragmatic Pony asked. The question was not meant to dissuade any attack, Elbryan knew in looking at his determined companion, but to logically guide the group in the best possible direction.

"We separate them," Elbryan answered. "If even one or more ventures away into the woods, lags behind, or gets too far in front . . ."

Six grim nods came back at the ranger. Within the hour, they were shadowing the caravan, learning their enemies' movement, discerning the pecking order among the goblin ranks. At one point, when the riverbank grew more narrow and impassible, the goblins sent a group of six out to find a new route.

They died quickly, quietly, cut down by bows and daggers, by flashing sword and crushing cudgel. So fast and complete was the massacre that Avelyn never used his magic. The monk did get in close enough to one wounded goblin to finish it with a flurry of deadly punches, but he kept his magical energy in reserve.

When it became apparent that the first six would not return, the goblins sent out a couple more to find them. Elbryan, Juraviel, and Bradwarden shot them down as soon as they were out of sight of the caravan.

"They are onto us," Pony reasoned when the band of seven moved back to view the main group, goblins rushing about nervously, tightening the ropes on the prisoners, herding the miserable humans together. The worst of it for the onlookers came whenever a goblin beat a human, particularly when one slapped a small child to the ground. Gritting his teeth, holding discipline supreme to emotion, Elbryan held his companions at bay. The goblins were wary, he reminded them all; this was not the time to strike.

"We hide the bodies," Elbryan plotted, "and let any more scouts they send out go unhindered. Let them find the paths. When they are on the move again, the forest thick about them, we hit them hard."

"Aye," the centaur agreed. "Give them a couple of hours to think that their miserable kin just ran away. Let them drop their guard again, and then we'll take the lot of them and pay them back for every slap."

Elbryan looked to Avelyn. "You must play an important role," the ranger said. "We will cut the goblins to pieces, I do not doubt, but only your magic can protect the prisoners long enough."

The monk nodded grimly, then looked at Pony. Elbryan did as well, sensing that the pair, Avelyn and Pony, shared a secret. The ranger's expression grew even more incredulous when he noticed Avelyn hand a piece of graphite to her, and green malachite after that.

The goblins did indeed send out another pair of scouts, and these two moved unhindered through the woods, then went back to the main group reporting no sign of their missing eight companions. Since desertions among goblin ranks were surely not an uncommon thing, the goblin leaders seemed to relax almost immediately, and with new trails found, they soon started the caravan along its plodding way once more.

And again, they were shadowed, every step, and even led, though they did not know it, by the ranger as he scouted out the perfect spot for the ambush. Elbryan had found just what he was looking for, a narrow pass between a steep, high ridge and a muddy pond, and was returning to lay out the plans when he found that his hand was being forced.

Pony's expression was the first indication that something was wrong, and as soon as he gained a vantage point on the monsters, the ranger figured it out. A dispute had arisen between one or more of the prisoners and their goblin captors, and now the humans were being punished once more. Elbryan winced with every blow, feeling the pain as acutely as if the goblin's club had been aimed at him; but again, he tried to hold back, tried to keep perspective and hold the greater goal above his emotions.

But then one prisoner, a young man of about the same age Elbryan had been when Dundalis was first overrun, was pulled from the line. The goblins' intentions for this one soon became obvious; they meant to make him an example. The young man was forced to his knees, his head pulled low, exposing the back of his neck.

"No, no, no," Elbryan whispered, and truly he was torn. All the plan and all the prisoners had a better chance if the ambush was carefully plotted and choreographed, and yet how could the ranger stand idly by and watch this unfortunate young man be sacrificed?

Elbryan could *not* watch idly, of course, and as soon as Hawkwing came up, the others realized that the time for action was upon them.

The goblin's sword went up high, but fell harmlessly to the ground as Elbryan's arrow slammed into the creature's chest. Elbryan came charging through the trees, screaming wildly, readying another arrow.

Goblins scrambled, one calling out commands—until its words became a gurgle, its mouth filled with its own blood, Elbryan's second arrow deep in its throat.

"Oh, hurry!" Avelyn cried to Pony, for the two had laid plans of how they might get to the prisoners.

Pony was trying to hurry, concentrating with all her will on the malachite. She had done this before, in practice with Avelyn, but now the pressure was intense, the price of failure too great.

"Ho, ho, what!" Avelyn howled at her. "You know that you can do it, and do it well, my girl!"

The encouragement pushed her over the edge, into the depths of the stone's magic. She felt her weight lessening, felt as light as a feather.

Avelyn lifted her easily from the ground and threw her in the direction of the monstrous caravan. Pony floated up as she went, grabbing the branches of trees and propelling herself along. She crossed over Elbryan, the ranger engaged with sword now, battling a line of goblins and, amazingly, driving them back.

She crossed over the goblins, scrambling high and keeping quiet, until she was, at last, directly above the huddled group of prisoners. Pony held her breath, noting the movements of the goblins, thinking by their actions and by the snatches of screamed commands she caught that they were indeed planning to harm the human prisoners.

The woman looked worriedly at the other stone Avelyn had given her, then at her own sword, wondering which she would be better to trust. Either way, her situation was about to become desperate.

Elbryan's rage did not relent. Two goblins rushed to intercept him, but he batted their weapons aside with a furious two-handed swipe of Hawkwing. He dropped the bow as it moved past the creatures, and in the same lightning-fast movement, drew out Tempest, thrusting it into the belly of the closest creature. The ranger punched out with his free hand, connecting solidly on the other goblin's chin, and he charged on, tearing free his sword.

The stunned goblin rubbed its chin and tried to rise to follow, but Bradwarden was right on the ranger's heels and was quick to trample the wretched thing into the dust.

Then the centaur was beside Elbryan, singing at the top of his voice, running goblins down and clubbing goblins down. Their momentum carried them deep into the goblin ranks, but began to ebb as the creatures finally organized a defense about them.

The goblins came at them in a semicircular formation, but the integrity of the monstrous line was compromised quickly, for Belli'mar Juraviel, perched on a branch some distance away, plucked at them with his tiny but deadly bow.

At the same time, Paulson and Chipmunk caught up to their fighting companions, the small man leading his way in with a line of hurled daggers.

"On me back!" the centaur roared to Elbryan. "We'll get to the prisoners!"

But not in time, Elbryan thought, looking past the goblin ranks to the pitiful group. He prayed that Pony and Avelyn would do their part well, and wondered if his rage had betrayed them all.

Avelyn could hardly see the goblin ranks and knew not at all which creature was in charge. As soon as Pony was away, the monk searched for some hiding spot for his bulky frame, but realized that he had little time to spare. He settled for a clump of birch trees, throwing his body into their midst as he threw his mind into the hematite he tightly clutched. He was into his spirit-walking, already rushing fast away, before his great bulk ever settled amid the tangled branches.

The monk's spirit flew past Juraviel, the sensitive elf taking note, though the ghostly form was surely invisible. He swept past Paulson and Chipmunk, past Bradwarden and Elbryan, past the front ranks of goblins, until he came to the miserable prisoners and the monstrous guards about them. One in particular was calling out commands, and Avelyn's spirit made a straight line to that body, pushed into the physical form, and battled for control.

Possession was never easily accomplished, a difficult and dangerous practice, but no one in all the world could summon the powers of the stones as thoroughly as Avelyn Desbris, and the monk was desperate now, for the safety of others and not for himself.

He ejected the goblin's spirit almost immediately and continued barking out commands, but these did not concern the prisoners at all. "Flee!" he yelled to his charges. "Run to the trees, into the forest. Run away! Run away!"

Many goblins did just that, more than eager to be gone since the furious ranger and the powerful centaur were crushing through their ranks.

Others, though, meant to get their taste of human blood before they left.

Pony saw them, two of them, running from the area of the fight but angling their course and their weapons to pound the prisoners as they passed. The woman's concentration was taxed to its limit as she tried to fall into her other stone while maintaining the weightlessness of the malachite, all the while, keeping her eyes on the monsters, measuring their progress.

She was out of time. Her mind let go of the malachite and she dropped the ten feet to the ground, landing right between the surprised goblins.

They screamed, Pony screamed, and they spun about, bringing their weapons to bear, as the woman grabbed their shoulders.

Pony was quicker, falling into the stone, the graphite.

There came a sharp crack, a sudden black flash, and the two goblins fell to the ground, twitching violently as they died.

"Forget the woman!" Avelyn the goblin chief cried to another monster that was swinging about to bear down on Pony, and the monk rushed to intercept. He tried something new then, connecting his mind back to his physical body and bringing in new magic from a second stone that his own form clutched, as he went.

"Kill humans!" the goblin howled in Avelyn's face, but the monk reached up with an arm that more resembled that of a tiger than of a human or a goblin. He took away the creature's protest as he took away its face.

"Ho, ho, what!" the monk-turned-goblin roared, eyeing the transformed arm. "It worked!"

Indeed it had; Avelyn had reached out across the distance, had connected with his own physical being while holding control of the goblin's form. But the strain had been great, too great, and the monk felt himself losing control immediately, his spirit soaring back past the fighting, back to the birch trees. In his last effort of will, right before he lost consciousness, the monk reached back out to the goblin's body, and as the creature became aware of its physical form once more, it found its own arm—or at least an arm that was connected to its body—moving up to claw viciously at its own face.

The surprised, confused creature stumbled backward, its other, normal appendage grabbing at its torn face. Surprise turned to horror, to agony, as it stumbled near Pony, and the woman drove her sword into its back, its tip poking right through the goblin's chest.

Pony then turned her attention to the prisoners, bidding them to run off, out of harm's way. Most of the men and a few women would not go, however. Wearing masks of grief, no doubt for loved ones this monstrous band had slain, they charged the other way, into those monsters battling Elbryan and the others, fighting with weapons they snatched from goblin dead, with sticks or rocks found on the ground, or with their bare hands.

It was over in a matter of minutes, with more than a score of goblins lying dead, the rest running, scattering into the forest. Several humans had been injured, as had Bradwarden—though the tough centaur thought little of his cuts and bruises—and Avelyn returned to them shortly, on unsteady legs, carrying the worst headache the monk had ever known. Still, without complaint, the good monk used his hematite once more, this time to lessen the wounds of the injured.

Elbryan gathered up Paulson and Chipmunk and called to Juraviel, the four moving out from the gathering to ensure the goblins were not rallying for any counterattack.

In more than an hour of searching, the foursome found only a pair of goblins hiding in one spot, and another running stupidly in circles.

So the ambush had worked, near to perfection, and the prisoners were free, but that left the ranger with a new dilemma and a new and unasked-for responsibility.

"Belster is no doubt many miles to the south by now," Avelyn reasoned, "out of our reach. Even if I use the stones to contact him, we'll not easily get to him and hand off our new friends."

"They are a tough lot," Pony added hopefully, "but inexperienced with goblins and the like."

Paulson gave her a sidelong, incredulous glance.

"With these goblins, at least," the woman corrected. "They've not battled the army of the dactyl before."

Paulson conceded that point.

"It would take us weeks to prepare them correctly, that they might have a chance of escaping on their own," the woman finished.

Elbryan absorbed all their words, sifted through their suggestions. After a moment, his gaze settled on Paulson and Chipmunk.

The big man understood that gaze well; Elbryan had never asked him and Chipmunk to come along, had, in fact absolved them of all responsibilities. But the ranger was about to place a new responsibility on the pair, Paulson realized. He wanted Paulson and Chipmunk to shoulder the burden of the new refugees and find a way to take them south. Paulson, full of anger at the loss of his dear friend, did not want to abandon this quest and neither did Chipmunk, but they would for the sake of the refugees. That realization struck the big man profoundly; for the first time in many years, he felt like a part of something larger than himself, a cohesive circle of comrades, of friends.

"There is another choice before us," Belli'mar Juraviel said from the low branches of a nearby tree. The elf had been keeping a low profile, not wanting to frighten the skittish refugees. The sight of Bradwarden had unnerved the folk almost as much as had the sight of the goblins, and the elf thought it better to hit them with one surprise at a time.

The group looked up to the elf, resting easily, his legs crossed at the ankles, feet dangling a few yards above their heads.

"There is a place where they might know shelter, not so far from here," the elf remarked.

Hopeful nods came from every head, except for Elbryan. Juraviel's tone intimated something more profound to the ranger, that not only was there a mere place for shelter, but a very special place indeed. Elbryan remembered the run that had brought him to Dundalis, Nightbird's first journey.

He had crossed the Moorlands, coming from the west. Now he and his troop were once again west of the Moorlands, though miles farther north.

"We can get them there, then, and continue on our way," Pony reasoned.

"Not we," Juraviel replied, "but I alone. This place is not so far, but not so close, a week's march, perhaps."

"In a week, we could bring them almost all the way back to Dundalis," Bradwarden reasoned.

"To what end?" asked the elf. "No one remains to help them there, and all that area is full of monsters. The place I speak of holds many allies, and there are no monsters, of that I am sure."

"You speak of Andur'Blough Inninness," Elbryan reasoned, and when the elf didn't immediately deny it, the ranger knew that his guess was correct. "But will your Lady accept so many humans into the elven home? The place is secret, its borders closed and well hidden."

"The times are not normal," Juraviel replied. "Lady Dasslerond gave a score of us leave to join in your struggles, to go out and take stock of the happenings in the wider world. She will not refuse entry to the humans, not now, with darkness all about them." The elf gave a smile. "Oh, do not doubt that we shall put enchantments over them, a bit of boggle in their meals, perhaps, to keep them disoriented that our paths remain hidden when they are turned out into the wider world once more."

"We should all go," reasoned Pony, who desperately wanted to view the elven home, who could sit for hours and hours to listen to Elbryan's tales of the magical place.

Elbryan, too, was tempted, would have loved to see Andur'Blough Inninness again, especially now, to bolster his resolve before he completed this all-important, perilous journey. The ranger knew better, though. "Every day we spend moving to the south, and every day it takes us to get back even to this spot, our enemies strike deeper into our homeland and more people die," he said calmly.

"I shall take them alone," Juraviel announced. "As you recognized your destiny, Brother Avelyn, so I recognize my own. You will introduce me to the folk in the morning and I will lead them away to safety."

Elbryan looked long and hard at his winged friend. He wanted Juraviel along on this journey, needed the elf's wisdom and courage to bolster his own. But Juraviel was right; he alone could take the refugees to safety, and though the quest to the Barbacan was paramount, the needs of so many innocents could not be ignored.

In the morning came the second painful parting.

"So there you are at long last!" Tuntun cried to Symphony when she spotted the stallion trotting across a field north of Weedy Meadow. Most of the elves were long gone, some shadowing the human band that had gone to the south, but most on the road back to Andur'Blough Inninness.

Tuntun and a couple of others had remained in the area, though, to continue their survey of the invading army.

This wasn't the place where Tuntun wanted to be.

The elf had been searching for Symphony, her desires formulating into a definite plan.

She approached the horse tentatively, but soon found that she could indeed connect with the stallion. The turquoise was tuned to Elbryan, but Tuntun, with her elvish blood, could make some sense of it, could fathom the horse's greatest desires, at least, if not his actual thoughts.

Symphony was apparently in complete agreement with her.

Tuntun had little trouble getting the great stallion to accept her, and Symphony leaped away as soon as the elf climbed atop him, running fast for the north and west.

❖ 46 ❖

The Fiend's Fiend

H e couldn't feel the stone beneath his feet, and he hated that fact of his existence more than anything else in all the world, more even than he hated this monster, this demon, his savior. For all the benefits of this wraithlike existence, Quintall missed the tangible sensations of his mortal form, the feel of grass or stone on his bare feet, the smell of dinner cooking, of brine when he looked out over All Saints Bay, the taste of shellfish or of the exotic herbs the *Windrunner* had taken on at Jacintha.

He stood now, or rather floated, in the dactyl's great columned hall at Aida before the obsidian throne and the monstrosity that was his god.

"We will be in Palmaris by midsummer," Bestesbulzibar explained, coming forward in his seat, the rough folds of its red hide shining in the orange glow of the lava rivers, pouring down through the walls and onto the floor at either side of the wide dais. "And Ursal shall be besieged when the season turns to autumn. Then the winter snows will not work against us as we roll on to the south, to Entel and the mountain range that separates the kingdoms."

"And will we stop there?" the spirit asked.

"Stop?" scoffed the dactyl. "We will entreaty with Behren's many chieftains, then find ways to use them against one another, and finally, when they do not expect war, we will sweep south. And all the world will be mine. Let humanity know its age of darkness."

Quintall couldn't disagree with the dactyl's reasoning. There were minor points untouched, to be sure. Alpinador, despite the brutal border raids and the subsequent, determined march to the coast, remained intact, but the northern kingdom was not an organized place and was not populous enough to pose any real threat.

"It is an age well earned," Bestesbulzibar said. "Your kin have only themselves to blame for the coming storm; their own weakness opened the way." The demon waved its wings and a rush of hot air passed through

Quintall, a sensation the spirit somehow felt. And with that blow, Quintall remembered.

He remembered in incredible detail: all that he had been, all the promises of his mortal life. He remembered St.-Mere-Abelle, the journey to Pimaninicuit. He remembered Avelyn, damned Avelyn, and the rivalry. He heard again Avelyn's voice, his screams of protest when the *Windrunner* had been sunk, a voice touched, Quintall now knew, by God. He remembered chasing the rogue monk, the tales in town after town of the mad friar and his words of warning, words that rang all too true now.

Quintall looked at his demon master; he knew the dactyl had shown him his mortal memories only to torment him. Since he had come to Aida, since the moment of his mortal death when the hematite broach had somehow transported his spirit to Bestesbulzibar, Quintall had remembered only that last encounter and not the path that had led him to Avelyn and the monk's powerful friends.

But now—now he remembered. Everything. And he knew that he was a doomed thing, knew the dactyl's claims were true, that Avelyn's warnings were true. The weakness of mankind, the impiety of the Abellican Church, the murders of the *Windrunner*'s crew, his own jealousy of Brother Avelyn—all these things had fed the demon dactyl, had awakened the darkness that now encroached upon the world.

Quintall loathed Bestesbulzibar but realized he was powerless against the fiend, realized he had fallen to the dactyl and that he could not escape.

Bestesbulzibar extended its hand palm down and telepathically demanded that Quintall pay homage.

The doomed spirit took the hand and kissed it.

There could be no redemption.

And Quintall knew the demon read his every thought, that his hopelessness only made the creature something more.

"You are useful to me," Bestesbulzibar said suddenly, "as you visit the dreams of men such as the fool Yuganick, as you walk unnoticed among our enemies. But I can do all that, Quintall."

The dactyl paused, and Quintall, in light of the last statement, expected that his time was at its end, that he would be blasted out of existence or thrown into a bottomless pit of eternal torment.

"I need more from you," the dactyl decided. Bestesbulzibar looked from Quintall to one of the lava rivers. "Yes," the creature muttered, talking more to itself than to the ghost. It moved across the dais, dipped one arm into the molten flow, then looked back at Quintall.

"Yes," the dactyl said again. "Do you not long to feel the sensations of the corporeal world once more?"

Quintall did indeed.

"I can do that, my stooge. I can give you life, real life, once more."

Quintall felt his spirit drifting toward the creature, though it was surely an unconscious movement.

"I can make you something greater," the demon whispered, and again the great black wings beat softly and a gust of hot wind passed through the spirit. After the gust, the heat remained.

The heat remained, and Quintall understood he was feeling the warmth of the lava!

Bestesbulzibar began a long, slow chant in a language the spirit did not understand, a guttural, cracking language of clicks and sounds that could only be equated with an old man clearing his phlegm-filled throat. Bestesbulzibar then spat upon Quintall, and the goo did not pass through the spirit, but struck him and stuck to him. Bestesbulzibar repeated the action over and over until Quintall was thoroughly slimed, then the fiend grabbed the spirit and, as Quintall screamed out in instinctive protest, plunged Quintall into the lava.

All the world was blackness, was searing heat and unbearable agony, and Quintall knew no more.

He awoke later, much later, though he was unaware of the passage of time. He was in the throne room still, standing, not floating, upon the solid floor.

He was a creature of lava, shaped like a man, shaped roughly as he had once been with arms and legs, rock hard torso and head, and joints somehow fluid, molten and glowing bright orange but not dripping away. He felt awkward, but he felt! He looked on in amazement as he opened and closed his black, orange-striped hand, understood the unearthly strength in that grip, and knew he could crush a stone—or the head of an enemy.

The head of Avelyn.

Bestesbulzibar's wicked laughter drew Quintall from his contemplations.

"Are you pleased?" the demon asked.

Quintall did not know how to answer. He began to speak, but the sound of his own voice, of a voice that resonated like a rock slide, frightened him.

"You will grow accustomed to your new body, my stooge, my general," the dactyl teased, "my assassin. No giant could stand before you, and no man. When Palmaris falls, you will lead my army into the city, and you will take the seat of Honce-the-Bear's deposed King when Ursal is mine."

His power, sheer strength, was dizzying, overwhelming. Images of conquest flooded Quintall's every thought. He felt he could destroy Palmaris all by himself, that no weapon, that no man, could possibly stand before him.

"Train your new body," Bestesbulzibar instructed. "Feel its powers and limitations and apply all that you once learned of the martial arts to this form. You are my general now, and my assassin. Let all men, let all creatures of Corona, tremble before you."

The fiend ended with yet another hideous laugh, but this time, Quintall heard his own grating voice joining in.

"The war goes well, my pet," the dactyl went on. "While you were asleep, your spirit binding to this gift I gave you, I viewed the southland, the unstoppable progress. Palmaris falls before midsummer, I say, and another powrie force sails to join us, makes fast for the Broken Coast. One army will march south, the other west, inland, until they join at the very gates of Ursal! Who will stand before them? The feeble King of Honce-the-Bear?"

"I know nothing of kings," Quintall replied.

"But you do!" the dactyl teased. "You know of your Father Abbot, the doddering old fool, and even he is a more worthy foe than the jester who sits on the throne of Honce-the-Bear. Who will stand before the beast then?"

The answer seemed obvious to fallen Quintall. No one would stand before the beast, before his master, before his god. Suddenly, the man-turned-spirit-turned-lava monster wanted desperately to smash through the gates of Ursal, to take his place on the throne of Honce-the-Bear.

Even more than that, Quintall wanted to visit St.-Mere-Abelle, to face Father Abbot Markwart and Master Jojonah, to make them grovel at his stony feet and then step upon them and squash them, grind them to death. They had used him, he understood now, all too clearly. They had used him in sending him to Pimaninicuit, and then again when they turned him into something less than human, when they turned him into Brother Justice, the instrument of their anger. So now Bestesbulzibar had done the same thing, but in Quintall's estimation, the demon dactyl was by far the worthier master.

"You will watch over Aida and serve in my absence," Bestesbulzibar announced.

Quintall knew better than to question the beast at all.

That very night, the demon swept out of its mountain home, flying fast to the south to its minions. In mere hours, Bestesbulzibar covered the hundreds of miles to the base at Dundalis, where it found a rattled Gothra of the goblins and Maiyer Dek of the fomorian giants arguing fiercely.

How their words caught in their throats, how all the camp about them fell to stunned silence, when the dactyl dropped between them, when the absolute darkness fell from the night sky.

"Tell me!" the dactyl demanded, and both started talking at once, and both were silenced by a mere threatening glare. Bestesbulzibar looked at Maiyer Dek squarely.

"Our camps swell to bursting," the giant chieftain explained, even its thunderous voice seeming meek before the demon. "More should be sent south to face the armies of our enemy!"

The demon's eyes flared with fire. Its head snapped about, an accusing glare falling over the trembling goblin.

"Ulg Tik'narn cannot be found," Gothra stated. "Likely he is dead."

"So?" The demon snorted, for there seemed no shortage of potential replacements.

"The region is not secured," the goblin went on. "Nightbird owns the forest."

"He is a thorn!" Maiyer Dek roared. "And a charging giant does not stop to pluck a thorn!"

"A thorn that interrupts supply—" Gothra began, but he was cut short by the bloodcurdling shriek of the demon dactyl.

"Enough!" the beast thundered. "You mean to stall our thousands for the sake of this one man, this Nightbird?"

"Each area must be secured in t-turn," the goblin stuttered, realizing that this discussion was not going very well. Goblins by nature were conservative in their warfare tactics, securing territories one by one, then methodically moving along, rarely attacking unless complete victory could be assured.

Bestesbulzibar had little patience with that.

"I demand Palmaris, yet you hold back thousands to retain this pitiful village?" the dactyl roared.

"No," Gothra protested. The goblin general wanted to explain its reasoning, wanted to make its master see that supply lines might be interrupted, equipment and needed reinforcements destroyed or delayed, and that the result in the south, at Palmaris's very gate, perhaps, could be disastrous.

Gothra, no fool—at least by goblin standards—wanted to argue his point in logical, rational terms, but all that came from the goblin's mouth was an agonized scream as Bestesbulzibar reached out with one hand, clamping the goblin's head and pulling Gothra in. Smiling wickedly, Bestesbulzibar lifted its other hand so that all could see, then extended one finger, and with a thought, lengthened the fingernail into a terrible claw. A sudden, impossibly long swipe brought a shriek from Gothra, and the demon shoved the goblin back.

Gothra stared down at the line of blood running from forehead to crotch, then looked back at the demon.

Bestesbulzibar's hand reached out and clenched the air, and the demon's magic grabbed at Gothra—or at least at the goblin's skin, pulling it from the goblin's body as completely as if the demon were helping Gothra out of clothing. The fleshless thing fell quivering, dying, to the ground.

Not a sound came from about the beast as, clothing and all, the dactyl devoured the torn skin of Gothra.

"Who was Ulg Tik'narn's second?" Bestesbulzibar asked.

There came no immediate reply, but then one trembling powrie was pushed forward from the ranks to stand before the master.

"Your name?"

"Kos—" the dwarf's voice trailed off, lost in the terrified gasps.

"He is Kos-kosio Begulne," Maiyer Dek offered.

"And where did Kos-kosio Begulne stand on this issue?" the dactyl asked.

Maiyer Dek smiled confidently. "He wished to move south," the giant lied, for Maiyer Dek liked the thought of Kos-kosio, not a strong personality, in command of the powrie forces. "Or at least to strike hard and quickly at the petty human raiders, that the issue be settled and the greater road be open."

The demon nodded, seeming pleased, and Kos-kosio stood a bit straighter.

"You are the powrie commander now, Kos-kosio Begulne," Bestesbulzibar announced. "And you and Maiyer Dek shall share the leadership of the goblins until a suitable replacement for Gothra can be found." Bestesbulzibar shared his glowering visage with all gathered near. "You two I charge with delivering Palmaris on the Masur Delaval by midsummer's eve. I will see you at the gates of Palmaris, my generals, and if I find need to see you before those gates are mine, then look upon Gothra's fate as your own!"

With a flourish, a thunderous beating of wings, and a bit of magic to make the flames of the main fire in the camp leap high into the night, the demon dactyl took wing, flying fast for the west to view the other occupied villages, to see its massing might spread out beneath it. Satisfied as End-o'-the-World was left behind, the beast turned northward, thinking to swoop low over the newest caravan plodding south, to encourage its minions and to strike fear in their hearts all at once.

But something else caught the beast's attention, some sensation, some presence the dactyl had not felt in many centuries. Lower went the demon, and slower, turning tight circles, sharp eyes scouring the terrain, keen ears tuning to every sound.

There was an elf about, Bestesbulzibar knew. One of the Touel'alfar, the dactyl demon's most ancient and hated of enemies.

❖ 47 ❖

One Harmony

The night was still, and undeniably beautiful. Every so often a cloud would rush overhead, pushed by southwestern breezes, but for the most part the stars shone crisp and clear, and the smell of spring was everywhere, the smell of new life.

It was a lie, Elbryan knew, all of it. The smell of new life would fast give way to the smell of goblins, powries, and giants, and the stench of death. All this serenity would be shattered under the thunderous march of the black horde, the crack of powrie whip, the rolling war engines.

It was a cruel lie: the quiet, the serenity, the spring breeze.

A movement to the side caught the wary ranger's attention, but he did not go for his weapon, recognizing the light, graceful step and the smell—like a field of distant flowers, the gentle fragrance carried on soft breezes—of the woman so dear to him. Pony came through the brush lightly, wearing only a soft silken nightshirt that didn't reach her knees. Her hair was down now, loose and wild, and it framed her fair face in a sensual manner, brushing her cheeks, one thick lock wrapped down and about her chin, that sent Elbryan's heart pumping.

She looked at the man and smiled, then crossed her arms to ward the breeze and turned, staring up at the night canopy.

"How could I have brought you out here?" the ranger said to her, moving up behind her and touching her gently on the shoulder.

Pony bent her head atop that hand and shifted backward, leaning against Elbryan. "How might you have stopped me?" she asked.

The ranger chuckled softly and kissed the woman's hair, wrapping his strong arms about her. How indeed? he wondered, marveling, as always, at Pony's free spirit. He could not truly love Pony, he knew, could not love who she was, if he meant to control her, for surely any attempt to harness Pony would defeat the very free spirit that Elbryan so adored. She was his in heart, but her own in will, and the ranger could not have stopped her from coming along, short of knocking her unconscious and tying her in a cave!

The woman turned within Elbryan's grasp, her soft face just below his, looking up at him.

Elbryan stared at her for a long, silent moment. An image of her lying dead at the end of a goblin spear came to him and he looked away suddenly, looked up at the stars, and wondered how he would live, what point there would be in going on with his life, if anything happened to Pony.

He felt her hand brushing against his cheek, and then the touch grew more firm as Pony turned his face back to look into her own. "We are each of us in danger," she reminded him. "And I might die, as Elbryan might die."

"Do not even utter such horrors."

"Possibilities," Pony corrected, "chances that we each took of our own volition, chances borne in duty. I would not want to live in the world that will be if the dactyl is not destroyed; rather that I had died fighting the fiend in the faraway Barbacan . . ." Her voice trailed off and she rose to her tiptoes, her lips brushing Elbryan's in a gentle kiss. "Rather that I died beside my friend, my love."

He started to look away again, unable to come to terms with that distinct possibility, but Pony's hand caught his chin firmly, forcefully, and turned him back to face her, all gentleness suddenly gone from her fair features.

"I am a warrior," the woman declared. "I have fought all of my life, since the day I wandered the road from destroyed Dundalis. I see my duty as no less than your own."

"Of course not," Elbryan quickly agreed.

"And if I am to die, then let it be in battle," Pony said through gritted teeth. "Let it be against the demon dactyl, delivering Avelyn, that the foul beast might be destroyed. I am a warrior, my love. Do not begrudge me a fitting end!"

"I would rather that your end and my own be together a hundred years hence," Elbryan replied, a helpless smile finding its way across his face.

Pony reached up to touch that smile and felt the sharp stubble of the ranger's beard, several days grown. "Ah, but my love," she said quietly, "put that fine elvish blade of yours to use on that beard, else I fear my face will glow from your scraping."

"More than your face, my love," Elbryan teased, and he lifted Pony up before him, biting her softly just under the chin, then turning his face so that his beard rubbed against her neck.

She slid back down, keeping tight to him, until their eyes met, and suddenly the play was gone from their smiles, all teasing lost in sudden intensity, in the knowledge that their time together might be nearing a very brutal end. Pony kissed him then, hard and passionately, her hands moving to grab tightly at his thick hair, to pull him even closer, though there was already no space between them.

Elbryan wrapped her even more tightly, squeezing her in his powerful grasp. One arm slipped down to the back of her bare leg, then up under the nightshirt, over the smooth skin of her buttocks, gently up her back, bracing her as Elbryan slowly shifted her down to the ground.

"Potion," Avelyn argued.

Bradwarden snorted. "Potion o' dizziness, then. What fool brewed such a magic as that? A drink to set ye on the ground, when a club might do a better job!"

"Potion of courage!" Avelyn protested, taking a deep swig, then wiping his forearm across his face.

"Potion o' hiding," Bradwarden said seriously, changing the tone.

Avelyn stared hard at the centaur.

"Oh, I been known to have me drinks," the centaur said. " 'Tis boggle I'm favoring, and not a potion in all the world'll kick ye harder than that. But I'm drinking at times for celebrating, me friend, at the solstice and the equinox, and not for hiding."

The accusation hit the monk hard, especially considering the source. Avelyn had grown quite close to Bradwarden over the first weeks of their journey, a bond more of respect than friendship. Now there was no mistaking the somber, accusing tone of the normally jovial centaur; Bradwarden did not approve of the monk's little flask.

"Perhaps you simply do not have as much to hide from," the monk said quietly, defiantly lifting the flask to his lips.

He didn't drink, though, not then, held back by an unrelenting stare.

"The more ye hide, the more ye need to hide," Bradwarden replied. "Ye look at me, Brother Avelyn. Ye look into me eyes to know that no lie comes from me lips."

Avelyn lowered the flask and stared hard at Bradwarden.

"Ye did no wrong in taking the stones," the centaur said.

"What foolishness is that?" the monk protested.

"Ah, but ye cannot hide from me, Avelyn Desbris," Bradwarden said without hesitation, his confidence only bolstered by the monk's too-loud protestation. "Ye're not afraid of yer kinfolk, not the monks, not any other Brother Justice that might come hunting ye. No, me friend, ye're afraid o' Avelyn, of what ye did and of yer eternal soul. Did ye stain it, then?"

"You know nothing."

"Ho, ho, what!" the centaur boomed in a fair imitation of Avelyn. "I know the ways o' men, the ways o' Avelyn. I know that yer drinking yer 'potions o' courage' is no more than yer hiding from yer own past, from decisions ye made—and good ones at that! Hear me now, because I would not lie to ye, I'd have no reason to lie to ye: ye did right in running, in taking the stones, even in killing the man who meant to kill yerself. Ye did what ye had to do, me friend, and so let go yer guilt, I say, and see better the road ahead. Ye said ye knew yer destiny, and I'm believing in that destiny, else I'd not have come. Ye're meant to face the dactyl, I say, to destroy the beast, and so ye will, but only if yer mind's clear, and only if yer heart's clear."

The words, coming from so mysterious, so wise, and aged a creature, hit Avelyn profoundly. He looked back at his flask and saw it for the first time as an enemy, a sign of weakness.

"Ye're not for needing yer potion," Bradwarden said. "Aye, but when ye beat the dactyl, then I'll take ye out for a bit o' boggle, and ye'll know what it means to see the world turn!" He reached out and grabbed Avelyn's wrist, pulling the flask further from the man, and locking gazes. "Avelyn needs not to hide from Avelyn," he said in all seriousness, and the monk, after a pause, nodded slowly.

"From the dactyl, now!" Bradwarden said suddenly, satisfied that he had gotten his point through. "Now, ye're wanting to hide from the dactyl until the time's right, but ye'll find yer flask a bit small for that!"

Avelyn said nothing, just nodded again. He was amazed that Bradwarden had so seen through him, had looked so clearly into his heart and soul, and had recognized the taint of guilt there. This drink that he always kept handy was no potion of courage but an admission of cowardice, a means for hiding from his own past.

Avelyn continued to stare at Bradwarden, and smiled as the centaur smiled, as the monk tossed the flask into the brush.

Now, finally, Avelyn could face his destiny with no regrets for the path that had led him to this place.

The centaur took up his pipes then and softly played, for such was the magic of Bradwarden's song that no goblin, no monster, no human, no animal even, could possibly discern its source in the forest night. His tune, mournful and hopeful all at once, calmed Avelyn and bolstered his resolve. It floated through the trees to caress the lovers, and further out to where Paulson and Chipmunk kept a watchful eye on the forest night.

And thus the group was bound by Bradwarden's song, one band, one purpose, one harmony.

The quiet night brought no such rest for Tuntun and Symphony. The elf watched the stallion closely to see if he was tiring, but the great horse ran on and on, slipping through the leafy shadows like the passage of Sheila herself, running to the horizon and beyond.

They had a quest, these two, every bit as vital to them as the hunt for the dactyl was to the seven who had left before them. For Tuntun, the sting of being left out of that all-important journey had not diminished, and no logical arguments could change the way the elf felt about it. Tuntun's stake in destroying the dactyl was no less than Juraviel's or that of any other elf or human. But it was more than that, the elf knew, and she had to admit it to herself, for it was her heart and not her mind that had forced her out here. Tuntun had to rush along, had to chase the group, in part because Belli'mar Juraviel—her closest friend despite their constant squabbling—was among them, but also in part because Nightbird led that troop. The elf could no longer deny her feelings for the ranger. She had played an important role in getting Elbryan to this point and, as a mother clings to her child, Tuntun could not bear to let him go off without her.

Yes, it was Nightbird more than anything else that had the sprite riding hard through the forest night. It was the man she had trained, the man she had grown to love. She trusted in the ranger—never had she seen Elbryan's better—but even so, she would stand beside him in this, his darkest of hours, in this, his pinnacle of glory.

The elf bent her head low over Symphony's flying mane and bade the horse to run on, and Symphony, as connected to the ranger as she, needed no encouragement and no outward guidance.

❖ 48 ❖

Enemies Ancient

"You and your friends saved us all, I do not dispute," Jingo Gregor said, his voice cracking from the strain of the last few weeks, the overwhelming surprises and horrors. "Yet are we to walk willingly to a place of enchantment?" He looked pleadingly at the boughs, at the rarely seen guide who had led him and his companions through a trackless region, heading south and with towering mountains now in sight.

"Better that than to face the goblin hordes," Belli'mar Juraviel answered. "I offer refuge, a haven as safe as any place in all the world. And the offer is not given lightly, I assure you, Master Jingo Gregor. You are as strange to the Touel'alfar as are we to you, and the valley that is home to my people is not open to humans. Yet I take you there, for if I do not, then surely you and all your companions will perish."

"I am not ungrateful, good Juraviel," Jingo Gregor replied.

"Just wary," Juraviel finished for him, moving down the tree so that the man could see him clearly, one of the few views the elf had allowed to any of the humans. "And well you should be, given the tragedies that have come to you and your clan. But I am not your enemy."

"That much has been proven," Jingo agreed.

"Then rest easy, for Andur'Blough Inninness is not so far," Juraviel said to him. "Consider yourself blessed to look upon the elven valley of mists." There was an unconscious edge to that last statement, reflecting Juraviel's own doubts about this decision to take humans to the secret valley. True, Elbryan had been taken in and trained; true, Lady Dasslerond had allowed Juraviel, Tuntun, and the others to go out to find the ranger and help him with his fight. But to take humans to Andur'Blough Inninness without the express permission of Lady Dasslerond was indeed a stretch of the Lady's compassion, and Juraviel was not certain that the troop wouldn't simply be turned away; perhaps the paths into the misty valley would be altered and hidden even from Juraviel. Lady Dasslerond was merciful, the elf knew, but she was, above that, pragmatic and protective of her realm. The welfare of the Touel'alfar she placed above all else, perhaps even above the lives of a score of unfortunate human refugees.

Despite the hints of doubt in Juraviel's tone, Jingo Gregor seemed satisfied with the words—a speech Juraviel had offered to the man several times over the last few days. Juraviel held nothing but sympathy for this ragged group, many of whom had lost loved ones in the goblin raids upon their homes, and most of whom had been tortured and violated by the wretched creatures. The elf would offer those comforting words to any and all, as often as they needed to hear them, reassuring the poor folk even though he himself wasn't so certain of the outcome.

Jingo Gregor moved off then, back to the warmth of the campfire and his eighteen companions. Juraviel, too, moved back toward the campfire, tightening his perimeter watch, though the humans had no idea of the elf's movements, so silent was he as he crossed the higher boughs of the budding trees.

The fire burned low—it had never been truly high, for Juraviel opted for caution, though he was fairly certain there were no monsters in the area, no organized groups anyway. Now the fire was no more than embers, their orange glow casting faint illumination over the resting forms of the humans, the light seeming appropriate for the rhythmic breathing of the sleeping folk.

Juraviel, too, was near to sleep, the elf comfortably nestled in the V of a high branch. He should have been watching the ground, he knew, but in accord with the wistful nature of his kind, his eyes kept lifting skyward to the stars and the mysteries.

And then to something else, something darker and more sinister, moving swiftly across the sky, heading for the camp, for Juraviel. The elf sensed the presence of the demon dactyl as surely as the dactyl sensed him, felt the awfulness, the sheerest of evil, the coldest of deathly chill.

With great effort, Juraviel pulled his thoughts from the night sky and the approach of doom and slipped quickly down, branch to branch, finally dropping right in the middle of the camp. He ran about, kicking at feet, whispering harshly, until all the humans were roused.

"Be gone!" the elf commanded. "Flee to the forest in groups of five and four, each in a direction of your own!"

Questions came at him, and at the stupefied leaders of the group, but Juraviel did not relent. "Tarry not!" the elf warned. "For death comes on wing! Be gone to the forest!"

The dactyl was close, so close! The humans scrambled, trying to gather some things, trying to put on boots, at least, as they stumbled and were pulled to the darkness of the forest night.

Juraviel remained at the glowing fire pit until all had gone, his eyes ever skyward, looking for the blackest of forms.

He felt it, he saw it, the dactyl swooping down from on high, rushing past the tangle of branches with hardly a care, spinning at the last moment, halting its descent to land lightly on the ground opposite the diminutive elf.

Juraviel drew out his slender sword but wondered what use it might be against the horrific demon. He prayed that all the folk would rush back in at the monster and join in his fight, but it was a wish that the elf had to dismiss, knowing that if the folk did come to his aid, they would all perish with him.

"Touel'alfar," the demon dactyl remarked in its mighty voice. "Not many are your kind. Not so strong, not so strong."

"Be gone from this place, demon," Juraviel responded in as firm a voice as he could muster. "You have no hold over me, no claim to my heart or my soul. I am the master here, and I reject you and your lies!"

The dactyl laughed at him, mocking his words and his courage, making him feel like an insignificant thing. "Why do you believe that I want claim to such worthless things as your heart and soul, elf?" the demon growled. "Your heart, perhaps," Bestesbulzibar teased, "that I might feast upon it, savoring the sweet blood of a Touel'alfar."

As he spoke, Bestesbulzibar slowly began to circle the fire, and Juraviel moved as well, keeping the embers between him and the demon—though when he thought about it, the elf realized that the flames, were they blazing high, would prove no barrier at all to the creature of the fiery pits of the underworld.

"Why are you out, Touel'alfar?" Bestesbulzibar asked. "Why are you away from your valley—yes, I know of your valley. I have seen many things since I have awakened, foolish elf, and I know that your kind is diminished greatly, that your world is smaller now, a mere canyon in a world that is grown too wide and too human. So why are you away, elf? What is it that brings you so far from home?"

"The darkness of the demon dactyl," Juraviel answered firmly. "Your shadow has roused the Touel'alfar, foul beast, for you are not unknown to us."

"But what shall you do about Bestesbulzibar?" the dactyl roared suddenly, and sudden, too, was the monster's rush, a quick burst right across the fire, scattering embers in a blinding shower. Juraviel struck fast and hard with his small sword, scoring a solid hit, but that hardly slowed the great beast whose armored hide held even the elvish blade at bay, whose clawed hand slapped the sword from Juraviel's hand while the demon's other hand grabbed the elf by the throat, lifting him easily up into the air.

"Oh," Bestesbulzibar moaned, as if in ecstasy. "I could tear it out, elf," the demon teased, running the claws of his free hand over Juraviel's tiny chest, "and hold it up before your eyes, biting into its red flesh even as you watched it beat its last."

"I do not fear you," Juraviel gasped with what little breath remained to him.

"Then you are a fool," Bestesbulzibar replied. "Do you know what comes after life, elf? Do you know what awaits you?" The demon laughed wickedly, bellowing thunderously into the still night.

"No torment . . ." Juraviel gasped.

"For you are true of heart," Bestesbulzibar mimicked evilly, and then the beast laughed again all the louder. "No torment," the fiend agreed. "Nothing! Do you hear? *Nothing*, elf. There is no afterlife for a miserable wretch such as thee! Only unknowing blackness. Savor your precious seconds, foolish elf. Beg me to let you see one more dawn."

Juraviel said nothing. He tried hard to hold to his faith, whose precepts insisted that a good life would indeed be rewarded in the afterlife. He considered Garshan Inodiel, who was God to the elves, a god of justice and promise, not unlike the god of the humans. But in the face of the darkness that was Bestesbulzibar, Belli'mar Juraviel knew despair.

"But why are you out?" the demon asked again, giving a sidelong, scrutinizing glance at the elf. "And what do you know?"

Juraviel closed his eyes and said nothing. He expected to be tortured, to have his limbs torn from his body, perhaps, until he confessed all he knew, until he betrayed his friends who had gone to the Barbacan. No, I must not think of that! the elf told himself firmly, and he turned his thoughts once more to Garshan Inodiel, trying to blanket everything else under the serenity of his God.

But then, in perhaps the worst torture of all to the valiant Touel'alfar, Juraviel felt the encroachment, felt the dark and cold presence of Bestesbulzibar creeping into his thoughts, scouring his mind. He opened his eyes in horror to see the demon's contorted features, flaming eyes closed as Bestesbulzibar concentrated, using his magic to scour the elf's brain.

Juraviel fought valiantly, but he was overmatched. The more he tried not to think of Elbryan and the others, the more they were revealed to Bestesbulzibar. The demon would get what it wanted, he feared, would devour him, and then would be off to devour his friends!

"Avelyn," Bestesbulzibar whispered.

"No!" Juraviel cried, and he kicked out with all his strength, his foot slamming the demon right in the eye. The wriggling elf broke free and tumbled to the ground. He tried to scamper away, but Bestesbulzibar towered over him, looking down, laughing, teasing.

"You do not belong here," came a sudden, melodious voice, one that caught and held the demon's attention. Both Bestesbulzibar and Juraviel turned to see Lady Dasslerond come out of the brush, flanked by a dozen other elves, bows and swords in hand.

"You live still!" the demon howled at the sight of the Lady of Caer'alfar, an elf he had known centuries before.

"And you walk Corona again," the Lady replied, "and surely all of the world weeps at the sight."

"Surely all of the world should!" Bestesbulzibar retorted. "Where is your Terranen Dinoniel now, Dasslerond? Who will stand before me this time?" As he spoke the last, he turned his ominous gaze upon Juraviel, and the poor elf shook with the fear that he had given his friends away.

"Who, Dasslerond?" the demon insisted. "You or this pitiful elf that cowers before me?" Bestesbulzibar looked all around at the encircling sprites, and laughed more loudly than ever. "All of you together, then? Well done, I say, and let us commence. Better for me that the nuisance of the Touel'alfar be done with here and now!"

"I'll not fight you," Lady Dasslerond replied coolly. "Not here." That said, she held aloft a huge green gemstone, shining with power, its illumination turning everything in the area a shade of green—everything except Bestesbulzibar, for the shadow of the demon could not be overcome by any light.

"What trick is this?" the fiend protested. "What foolish—" The words were lost in the demon's throat as all the world began to shift and change, features blending together in a greenish mist and then growing clear again, crystalline under the stars, bright and beautiful.

They were in Andur'Blough Inninness, all of them. Lady Dasslerond and Juraviel, all the elves and the refugees, and Bestesbulzibar.

"What trick?" the fiend roared, suddenly angry, suddenly recognizing that he should not be in this place, the very heart of elvish power.

"I invite you to my home, creature of shadow," Lady Dasslerond answered, her voice edged with weariness from the tremendous exertion of power it had taken to transport the group—or, in effect, to change the very ground beneath their feet. "You cannot defeat me here, not now."

The demon growled and considered the words, felt the strength of the Lady and her fellows in this, their domain. "But soon," Bestesbulzibar promised.

The Lady held aloft the green gemstone, the heart of Andur'Blough Inninness, now shining fiercely.

Bestesbulzibar's unearthly roar, one of pain and outrage, stole her breath. "So you saved the pitiful elf and the humans he escorted," the fiend sneered. "What good will it prove when all the world is mine?" Out came the black wings and the demon dactyl lifted away to the hum of elvish bows, the melodious tumult of elvish insults.

Any true joy felt by the Touel'alfar at the demon dactyl's retreat was short-lived, though. By necessity, Lady Dasslerond had allowed Bestesbulzibar to tread upon this, their most sacred and secret of places, and though the fiend was correct, Bestesbulzibar could not yet face them all in Andur'Blough Inninness, they had done nothing to diminish the demon.

Juraviel joined Lady Dasslerond as she stood over the spot from where

Bestesbulzibar had departed. The ground that had been under the fiend's clawed feet was blackened and torn.

"A wound that will not heal," the Lady said despondently.

Juraviel knelt to better inspect the ground. He could smell the rot there: the earth itself was tainted from the fiend's presence.

"A festering wound that will slowly spread," the Lady admitted. "We must tend the ground about this spot vigilantly, for if ever we fail to counter with our magic and our song the rot that is Bestesbulzibar, it will grow within our valley."

Juraviel sighed and looked hopelessly at his Lady, his guilt obvious upon his fair face.

"The dactyl grows strong," she said, not accusingly.

"I have failed."

Lady Dasslerond looked at him incredulously.

"The demon knows," Juraviel admitted. "The demon knows of Elbryan, of Avelyn, and the plan."

"Then pity Elbryan," the Lady replied. "Or hold faith in Nightbird and in Brother Avelyn, whose heart is true. They went north to do battle with Bestesbulzibar, and so they shall."

Juraviel continued to look down upon the black scar that the demon had left upon the ground of his precious home. Indeed, Bestesbulzibar had grown strong to so taint the very land of Andur'Blough Inninness. Juraviel's Lady had bid him to hold faith, and so he would, but the fear was obvious on his face as he looked from the scar to the north.

"And now we have duties," Lady Dasslerond went on, speaking more loudly, directing her words at all the elves. "All of us. We have unexpected guests who must be comforted and then taken from our homeland to a place of their own kind, a place of safety—if any place in the world remains safe." She looked back down at the black scar upon her beautiful valley. "We have much work to do," she said softly.

❖ 49 ❖

Hunted

"The terrain grows more wild, Uncle Mather, more fitting to the nature of our enemies. The trees are older, never harvested by humans, and darker. The animals do not fear us, do not respect our weapons or our cunning."

Elbryan rested back against the diagonal tree root in this impromptu room of Oracle, digesting his own words. They were true enough; in this region so far to the north of any known human settlements, all the world seemed somehow larger and more imposing. The towering mountains that formed the dread Barbacan loomed less than a day's march away, dominating the northern horizon, making the travelers feel smaller still.

"It brings me mixed feelings," the ranger went on. "I fear for our safety—will I be able to protect my friends, not necessarily from the threats of our enemy but from the simple truths of survival in this region? And yet, out here, I am somewhat more free than ever, more true to the training the elves have given me. There is no room for error in the far north, no margin of safety, and that keeps me ever vigilant, on my guard, tingling with wariness. I am afraid, and thus, I am alive."

Again, Elbryan sat back, smiling at the irony of it all. I am afraid, and thus, I am alive.

"If given the opportunity, most people would choose a life of quiet luxury," he said softly, "would choose to surround themselves with servants, with concubines, even. That is their mistake, for out here, danger ever present, I am ten times more alive than ever they could be. And with the challenge that is Pony—and with the challenge I hope that I pose for her—I am many times more satisfied. It is, I believe, the difference between physical satisfaction and true lovemaking, the difference between release and passion. I may die soon following this course before me, but out here, at one with my spirit and my nature, on the edges of catastrophe, I have lived many times more than most will ever know.

"So I do not regret this journey that fate has laid before me, Uncle

Mather, nor do I regret that the others—Bradwarden and Avelyn, Paulson and Chipmunk, and most of all, Pony—have been swept along this course. I pity Belli'mar Juraviel, that he could not see it through, that duty turned his path."

Elbryan put his chin in his palm, resting, thinking, and staring always at the faint image at the corner of the mirror. It was true, all of it; he hated the death and the suffering, of course, but he could not deny his excitement, and the sense of righteousness, the belief that he was indeed making a difference in the world.

He looked closely at Mather's image, seeking a smile of approval or a frown that would indicate his feelings were not true but merely a contrived defense against despair. He looked closely, and he saw a shadow beginning to creep in across the glassy surface within the depths of the mirror. The ranger sighed, thinking this a sign of disapproval, thinking that he might have fallen into a trap of justifications, but gradually he came to understand that it was not a cloud emanating from Mather or from his own true feelings. Elbryan began to understand that it was something else, something darker by far.

Elbryan sat bolt upright, unblinking. "Uncle Mather?" he asked breathlessly, a coldness creeping into his very body.

A coldness, a blackness, a living death.

The ranger's mind was whirling, trying to make sense of the undeniable event. Only one creature could bring such darkness, he realized, and then, suddenly, he understood. Whether Mather had facilitated the warning from the other side of life, or whether it was simply a connection wrought of the magic of Oracle, Elbryan neither knew nor cared. What he did know was that the demon dactyl was searching for him, for them, sending its otherworldly vision out far and wide.

Fear gripped Elbryan as he realized that his own use of Oracle might be helping his enemy locate him and his friends. He leaped up, slamming his head against the roots and ground that formed the cave's ceiling, and rushed to the mirror, turning it down, breaking all connection. He scrambled for the exit then, pulling down the blanket and wrapping it about the mirror, then crawled out into the waning daylight, calling for Avelyn.

From the flow of molten lava, the demon dactyl pulled its latest creation—a glowing spike, a tapering spear—and held it aloft.

"Fools all." The beast laughed, eyeing its masterpiece, a weapon that would find and destroy the pitiful humans seeking Aida. Into the spike, the beast sent its vision, the telltale tracings of human-woven magic. Into the spike, the demon sent its power, the strength of the underworld, the strength to burn.

Then the beast called to its elite guards, the armored giants, and to their leader, Togul Dek.

When the brute was before the dark master, Bestesbulzibar held forth the glowing spear.

Togul Dek hesitated, feeling the heat, the intense magical strength.

Bestesbulzibar thrust the nine-foot spike forward and growled a final warning, and Togul Dek, more fearful of the demon than of the fiery implement, grasped it without further hesitation, though the giant winced as his flesh touched the diabolical weapon.

Togul Dek's expression became one of surprise, for the spike felt cool to the touch.

"Take ten with you," Bestesbulzibar commanded. "Humans approach my throne. The spear will lead you."

"Does Bestesbulzibar who is King want any living?" the giant asked, barking each word.

The dactyl scoffed as if the notion were absurd, revealing that he did not think these pitiful few worthy of his time and energy. "Bring me their heads," he instructed. "You may eat the rest."

The giant stamped one boot and spun away, collecting its ten closest allies among the elite guard and sweeping out of the throne room.

The dactyl dismissed the remaining guards and moved back to one of the glowing lava rivers, dipping his clawed fingers into the fiery stone, feeling the power of the magic that was his alone to command, musing again about the darkness of his complete rule.

"How could I have been such a fool?" Avelyn lamented, dropping his round head into his plump hands.

"How so?" Pony demanded, realizing they had no time for doubts and blame. Each challenge had to be met without regret for past decisions.

"I should have known that the dactyl would search us out, should have anticipated his magical vision," Avelyn replied.

"We do not know that the dactyl has searched us out," Elbryan interjected. "Perhaps the shadow at Oracle was but a warning. We have met with few enemies since our departure, only one organized group that we even know was part of the demon's army. Why should Bestesbulzibar—"

"Speak not that name aloud so close to the dactyl's home!" Avelyn warned. "Do not even think it, if you can so discipline your thoughts!"

Elbryan nodded an apology to Avelyn and to all the fearful others. "We do not know that it is too late," the ranger said softly.

"Ye put up the guard, then?" Bradwarden asked.

Avelyn nodded. Using the sunstone he had taken from Quintall, he had enacted a shield against divining magic. It was not a difficult enchantment, actually, and one that powerful Avelyn could maintain with the focused sunstone for a very long time without severely taxing his energies for other magics.

It was one that Avelyn should have enacted, he now realized, even as they set out from the region of Dundalis.

"Stupid!" Paulson grumbled, eyeing the monk dangerously, and then he stormed away.

Elbryan was quick to follow, catching up to the man, grabbing him by the elbow, and leading him farther from the camp behind a shielding wall of evergreens where they could speak in private.

"You did not mention that we should enact such a protective shield," the ranger pointed out.

"I ain't no wizard," Paulson argued. "I didn't even know about such a thing."

"Then it is good that we have Avelyn with us, who can block the demon's sight."

"If the damned demon ain't upon us even now," Paulson retorted, and he glanced about nervously as he spoke the grim words.

"I'll not tolerate any placement of blame on this journey," Elbryan said sternly.

Paulson stared at him long and hard, finally relenting under the ranger's unblinking stare. Instead of growing defensive, as was his nature, the big man tried hard to see things from Elbryan's perspective. Finally, he nodded. "It's good that Avelyn is with us," he said sincerely.

"We'll get there," Elbryan promised, and started away.

"Hey, ranger," Paulson called after Elbryan had gone a few steps. Elbryan turned to regard the man, noting his grin.

"We'll get there, eh?" Paulson cracked. "Ye sure that's a good thing?"

"I am sure it is not," Elbryan replied, matching the big man's grin.

From the edge of a high, rocky bluff, crouched defensively behind the stone, the companions watched the latest caravan wind its way out of the Barbacan. Goblins comprised the bulk of the line, trudging with heads down, looking thoroughly miserable, especially those chained to the various powrie war engines—catapults, ballistae, and great corkscrew boring machines meant to drive huge holes in castle walls.

The caravan went on and on, exiting a pass in the dark mountain wall and forming a line that went out of the companions' sight to the east.

"Alpinador, too, is under siege," Elbryan reasoned.

"The dactyl will use the summer months to drive right to the coast, no doubt where more powries await his armies," Avelyn added, and then, considering his own words, he snorted loudly. "Unless of course the demon's soldiers have already driven to the coast. Ho, ho, what!"

"Then no time for wasting," remarked Bradwarden, a few feet away, behind the others on a lower point. The centaur obviously could not climb up the stone and crouch, and so he had spent the last half hour waiting rather impatiently, listening to descriptions of the exotic powrie war machines and to Paulson's unending giant count.

"We have to wait for Pony," Elbryan reminded the anxious centaur.

"Then wait no more," came a voice from ahead, and the group turned as one to see the woman moving lightly down the trail.

"There are several passes that will get us through," she explained. "This trail branches a quarter mile from here; the left road winds back down and out of the range, but the right climbs higher and into the mountains, which are not so deep."

"Is there cover?" Elbryan asked.

Pony shrugged. "As much as we can hope for," she replied. "Boulders line the trail on both sides, but if our enemy has guards posted in proper position, they will likely spot us."

"Then we must spot them first," Elbryan said determinedly, taking up Hawkwing. He sent Chipmunk off and running, flanking them to the left, bade Pony guard the right, and he, himself, moved in front of Avelyn, Paulson, and Bradwarden, taking a long lead.

Within an hour's time, they had climbed high across the southern face of the dark mountain, to the edge of the tree line, where the wind blew chill. Elbryan, far in the lead and out of sight of the others, left markers showing his course, but even with this, the ranger was fearful that they would all get separated and lost. The Barbacan was a wild place, as untamed as any land the ranger had ever seen; a place of huge, rocky outcroppings, jagged stones, and thick copses of dark trees. It was a place where a trail ended abruptly in a hundred-foot drop, or a boulder might come suddenly down upon an unwary traveler's head. A place of the most primal danger, it was a place where the ranger felt most alive.

A slight noise to his right put Elbryan into a crouch, his hand going from his bow to his sword. He slipped to shelter behind a stone, then dropped flat on his belly, peeking out around the edge at a small ravine, a cut in the mountain filled with trees and brush.

The noise came again, soft footsteps, and Elbryan followed it to its source, just a shadow moving gracefully through the tangle. He took up Hawkwing again, his eyes never leaving the target.

And then he relaxed as the shadow moved through a clear area.

"Pony," he called softly, catching her attention. He noted the stealthy manner in which she approached, and that kept him on his guard.

"Goblin," she whispered from a short distance, not daring to cross the last clearing to come beside Elbryan, "high and to the left beyond the twin pines and behind the jutting stone."

Elbryan scanned in that direction, but had to move out from his rock even to spot the jutting stone. He nodded as the place, though not the goblin, came into view.

"How many?"

"I saw but one," Pony answered. "There could be more, further to the left and down."

Elbryan glanced back along the trail. He had moved from shadow to shadow, and it was unlikely that the goblin had spotted him from that distance, but Avelyn, and particularly Bradwarden, would have trouble being inconspicuous. By the ranger's calculations, the trailing trio would soon be well within the goblin's view.

He noted a movement up above, a dark shape coming atop the jutting rock. Torn and uncertain, the ranger fitted an arrow to Hawkwing. "If there are more, they'll soon know of us," he whispered.

"Perhaps I can get behind the spot," Pony replied.

Elbryan started to ponder that possibility, then noted the goblin's attention was occupied—by something back along Elbryan's path.

"It knows of us," the ranger explained, and up came his bow. The shot was fully a hundred yards, and he had no more of a target than the goblin's head and shoulders, and in the crosswinds of a mountain face. His arrow hit the mark right down the middle, and the dark form fell away.

There came a cry and a second shape darted out from behind the boulder, scrambling away.

"We are known!" the ranger called to Pony and the pair jumped up and started in pursuit, though they had little hope of catching a creature in this wild tangle. Just a few steps away, though, they skidded to a sudden stop, seeing the goblin coming back, staggering out of a copse and across an expanse of bare rock.

They watched curiously as the monster jerked suddenly, then fell over, and a moment later, Chipmunk appeared from the brush behind the creature, scampering up to retrieve his daggers.

"Well done," Elbryan said, though the man was far from earshot.

"And a good thing it is," Pony added.

"All three of us," the ranger instructed, "and get Paulson as well. We must search the area to make sure that no other sentinels were nearby to witness the kills."

The four did just that, circling the area and spying out the spot from every conceivable angle, looking for goblins or any signs that goblins had been about. When they were at last convinced that the kills had been unnoticed, Elbryan hustled them along, coming to a bowl-shaped depression as night descended across the wild mountains. The ranger would have liked to go farther, but they could not travel the difficult and dangerous terrain in the dark, and they certainly could light no torches.

They set their camp with confidence that their progress had gone undetected; they could not know that a giant carried a weapon which had sensed the kills and had led its wielder right to the spot of the disposed goblin carcasses, a spot not so far from their encampment.

The night was cool and quiet, save the moan of the wind across mountain stones. Elbryan and Pony sat close, huddled under a blanket. To the side loomed the huge shape of Bradwarden, the centaur using its bulk to shield Avelyn from the wind. Paulson and Chipmunk were out and about, guarding the perimeter.

"Tomorrow we climb more sheer faces," Elbryan said with some concern.

"Oh, don't ye worry," Bradwarden assured him. "I'll find me way."

"I am more concerned with Avelyn," the ranger remarked. As if on cue, the snoozing monk rolled over and snored loudly. "He is in no shape for this."

"He will make it," Pony said with determination. "I have traveled with Avelyn for many months and have never known him to complain. He sees this as his destiny; he will not be denied by any mountain obstacles."

Elbryan studied Avelyn for a long while, considering his own experiences with the man, and conceded the point.

"Besides," noted the centaur, "he's getting the best of sleep."

Again as if on cue, the monk shifted and snored.

"Chipmunk?" Paulson whispered, his voice quickly buried under the moaning wind. "Is that yerself?" The big man crouched lower, peering intently at a group of trees, the source of the unmistakable sound of a footstep.

Only then did Paulson realize that there seemed to be one extra tree in the group. "Damnation," he whispered, turning to run.

A spinning sliver, flickering in the quiet light, spun right past his head, causing him to cry out and fall away. He hit the ground, looking back toward the giant, noting its surprised, jerky movement as Chipmunk's dagger hit it squarely in the chest with a metallic ring.

"Come on, then!" the big man cried, scrambling to his feet, gaining confidence in the knowledge that his trusted comrade was nearby. The ringing sound of that last impact played in his mind, though; giants were tough enough adversaries without metal armor!

And this one was indeed armored, Paulson realized as the monster closed on him. Again came the spinning slivers, two in rapid succession, this time angled higher to hit the monster about the head. Both did, and both were repelled by a metal helm.

"Don't stay to fight!" Paulson called and he turned to flee, noticing then an orange glow emanating at the giant's side. Mesmerized, the big man hesitated, then he screamed out, realizing that the glow was a spearlike weapon carried by a second giant! He got his weapon up to block, but the demon-forged spike blasted right through it, right through Paulson's raised forearm, and deep into the man's belly.

Waves of searing agony ripped through Paulson. He had never imagined the possibility of such pain. Hardly conscious, he felt himself lifted high into the air and then, with a flick of the giant's huge arms, he was flying free, launched into the night, into death.

Chipmunk ran screaming for his life, tears of fear and horror and the loss of yet another friend streaking his cheeks. Giants were all about him. He could feel the heat of the orange glow following his path. He had to get back to the camp, and yet, he realized that to do so would put them all in jeopardy, would likely bring about the end of the quest!

Chipmunk found a hole instead, burying himself quickly under piled leaves at the base of a thick tree. His confidence mounted as a pair of giants stomped past, oblivious of him. A third came rushing by, and then came the one carrying the glowing spike.

That giant, too, started past, but skidded to a stop just beyond the hole, compelled by the demonic weapon.

Chipmunk tried to cry out as his covering was pushed aside, as he looked up at the towering, fifteen-foot-tall monster, up at the huge, awful spike. He tried to cry out, but no sound would come forth, only a breathless gurgle, that ended abruptly as the monstrous spike fast descended.

The cries of the doomed pair had alerted Elbryan and the others to the danger, so they were not unprepared when the first of the giants crashed through the brush and charged over the rim of the bowl-shaped encampment. The leading brute, apparently thinking the centaur a mere horse, tramped right by Bradwarden, who stood with head and torso bowed.

As the giant passed, Bradwarden turned, lifting his heavy bow and letting fly. The arrow hit solidly, denting the armor plate and driving through, but not so deep as to cause any serious wound. Three quick strides later, the centaur was upon the giant, ramming hard into the behemoth's back. Bradwarden's heavy bow, swung as a club, rang off the plated armor, splintering as it hit. The giant stumbled and went down, the centaur in fast pursuit, cursing his foolishness in using the bow and reaching for his cudgel. But two more giants were close behind, following their friend in, now bearing down on Bradwarden.

"What does it do?" Pony asked Avelyn as the monk held aloft a stone the woman had not seen before, a clump of black octahedral crystals.

"It is lodestone," Avelyn explained. "Magnetite." He went silent then, sending his thoughts into the stone, using his magical energies to ignite those powers within the stone. The giants were bearing down on Bradwarden in a straight line; Elbryan had gone off to the side and was now calling out the presence of more of the huge fomorians.

Pony left Avelyn's side then, rushing to join with Elbryan.

The orange glow outlined them, three more behemoths closing in. Hawkwing went to work at once, arrow after arrow rushing down to bang hard against metal armor, into the breastplate, then repeatedly into the visor, several tips slipping through to sting the giant face, to make the monster howl in agony.

One of the three fell back from the charge, clutching at its face, blinded by the sting.

Elbryan dropped his bow and drew out Tempest as Pony scrambled by. He ordered her to the left, toward the giant without the glowing spike, for he sensed that the spike held some diabolical power.

Pony readily complied, thinking that the remaining giant, smaller than the spike wielder, would be a quicker kill—not that any giant was an easy kill! She rushed right for it, feigning a dodge to the side as it lifted its huge sword. By far the quicker, agile Pony went one step left, then back to the right, then straight ahead, under the awkward cut of the giant's weapon, falling into a headlong roll that brought her right between the monster's widespread legs.

The giant reacted quickly, snapping straight and tall, closing its legs to entrap the foolish human.

Pony's graphite defeated that maneuver, though, sent a crackling bolt of energy along the monster's inner thighs that left it swaying, legs wide-spread, as the woman worked her way out the back. Now Pony went to more conventional weaponry, drawing her sword and turning right back in on the monster, slamming the weapon hard against the giant's lower back, seeking an opening between the protective plates.

She found none, but stayed behind the staggering brute, belting away as the giant tried to turn and grab her.

Elbryan didn't know what to make of this armored foe, and especially of its glowing spike. Why weren't the monster's hands burning? the ranger wondered, for surely that spike was brutally hot.

The giant stabbed straight ahead, and Elbryan left those thoughts behind, suddenly more concerned with keeping his body from sporting very large holes. He went around to the side with a flourish, snapping Tempest against the pursuing spike, each hit sending a shower of orange sparks into the air.

Elbryan knew that he had to get up higher, within striking distance of the giant's head. He knew the terrain, had marked it clearly in his thoughts before the night had fallen. He ran hard to the side, then leaped up atop a rounded boulder, gaining a foothold and turning back in a quick charge to meet the rushing monster.

Tempest snapped in, level with the giant's eyes. Up came the spike to block, but too late, and Tempest slashed hard against the visor, twisting the giant's head from the force of the blow.

Out came a straight thrust of the spike; Elbryan turned his hips and skittered back. The ranger leaped ahead and launched a vicious sidelong swipe as the heavy, awkward spike retracted. He connected solidly on the side of the giant's head, knocking the helm away, the behemoth staggering a long stride to the side.

"The next will not be so blocked!" the ranger promised.

The giant was not without a trick of its own, though. It came at Elbryan, but shifted as Tempest came up to parry, as Elbryan's feet turned defensively sideways, allowing the ranger to retreat back or to either side. The giant plunged the spear down low instead, right into the boulder, and Elbryan was too surprised to seize the momentary opening and charge ahead.

He had to leap away instead, far out to the side, crashing through twigs and saplings, for the boulder superheated, turned red, and then melted away right below him!

The ranger was dazed but knew that he had to keep moving as this pile of molten stone rolled down, igniting small, smokey fires among the twigs.

In the sudden glow, Elbryan saw more forms moving about the perimeter, giant forms, and between the reinforcements and that terrible glowing spike, the ranger knew that he and his friends were overmatched.

Avelyn fell deeper into the stone, felt its energy building to a critical mass. Lodestone was highly magnetic; its enchantment would send it fast to a metal surface. Impossibly fast, faster than a crossbow bolt.

The monk fell back, nearly toppling, as the stone suddenly zipped away, flying unerringly for the armored chest of the giant closest behind Bradwarden. It hit with a tremendous thump, jerking the behemoth from the ground, and then, to Avelyn's amazement, for he had never really used magnetite before, the second giant in line shuddered violently as well.

Bradwarden had forced the helm off the fallen giant by then, his cudgel turning the monster's head to mush before it could rise up. The centaur heard the commotion close behind and turned to see both giants slumping to the ground, the closest showing a neatly blasted hole right through its breastplate, right through its chest, right through its back.

"Oh, good shot!" Bradwarden congratulated Avelyn.

The monk was already running toward Bradwarden, toward the fallen giants, thinking to retrieve the stone. But then there were other giants, all about, huge shadowy forms blurring the otherwise straight line of the perimeter.

"On me back!" the centaur cried.

"My stone!"

"No time!"

"Everyone out!" came a call, Elbryan's voice. "Avelyn with Bradwarden! Myself with Pony! Paulson with Chipmunk!" If the two are still with us! he added silently. "Out and away, to a direction of your own choosing!"

Pony could hardly believe what she was hearing, what she was seeing. They had come so far together, and now they were being forced into an impromptu, hardly organized retreat. She waited for her turning giant to align itself properly, then scrambled back between its legs once more.

Again there came that nasty crackle of energy, and this time, the giant's muscles betrayed it, tensing with the current, and the brute tumbled down.

Pony had no time to stop and take advantage of the situation, though, as she scrambled for the center of the encampment, for Avelyn and Bradwarden, hoping against hope that they might all link together once more.

She saw the monk lying across the centaur's back, Bradwarden's powerful legs pounding away up the north face of the bowl, the same direction from which the first giants had come. They made the lip and went over, and almost immediately after, all the sky lit up with the bright flames of a tremendous fireball.

Pony fell back, all the battle stopped for a moment, and when she caught her breath, the woman was satisfied to hear the receding hoofbeats. Avelyn and Bradwarden, at least, had gotten away.

But how might she and Elbryan? Pony had to wonder as she skittered down the rocky slope, a pair of giants in fast pursuit. Purely on instinct, the woman dove ahead, over the giant Bradwarden had killed. She felt a rush of wind and heard a crash behind her, a giant club smashing against armor.

Still she scrambled, expecting to be buried at any moment, expecting her life to end with a sudden, burning explosion.

Over the next giant she went, trying to regain her footing. But she tripped and stumbled, falling atop the third dead behemoth, her hand tearing against a jagged edge in the monster's breastplate, then slipping into the gore of its torn guts.

There was fighting right behind her! She turned and saw Elbryan darting about the giant pair, Tempest working furiously. But he could not win! Even if he beat these two, others were coming fast, including the one with the glowing spike!

Pony's hand instinctively clutched onto something hard and she retracted it to find the stone Avelyn had used. She stared at it curiously for just a moment, trying to discern its energy.

"Run!" came Elbryan's cry.

Pony looked to the fight as she rose, saw Elbryan, Hawkwing in one hand, Tempest in the other, jump out of the path of a fast-descending club, then leap back suddenly as a sword swished across. Pony cried out, thinking her love cut in half, but Elbryan had been quick enough to dodge out of harm's way.

He planted his feet as he landed and rushed straight ahead, screaming wildly, his sword now glowing a furious bluish-white, snapping to and fro, darting straight ahead, sparking as it banged against unyielding armor.

But the ranger's tactic worked, the sudden rush forcing the giants into a short retreat, forcing them off balance. One went down over a fallen body, reaching out as it fell to grab its companion. Another short hop and attack by Elbryan had that one tumbling, too, both landing in a tangled heap.

The ranger had no intention of jumping atop them, not with other giants bearing in. He turned and ran as Pony ran, catching up to Pony as they scrambled together up the north slope, following the trail of their friends. Over the lip, they saw the effects of Avelyn's fireball, small fires here and there, the largest being the one still burning atop the curled and blackened corpse of yet another giant. Down the pair ran through the heat and the smoke, stumbling, but using each other for support. They heard the roars behind them, knew that to stop was to die.

Into the night, the four survivors went, stumbling blindly, separated, two and two, with a third of their party dead.

CHAPTER

❖ 50 ❖

Flight

Avelyn lay across the centaur's back, staring more behind than ahead, praying for his companions.

Bradwarden, though, would not turn back and would not slow. Determined, purposeful, the centaur pounded along the mountain trails, hooves digging firm holds and propelling him and his all-important passenger mightily. Soon after they had left the encampment, Avelyn had looped the cat's eye about Bradwarden's head, and so the centaur could see in the dark and was not slowed as were the pursuing giants—as were their own companions.

"We must find a defensible spot!" the monk kept shouting.

"We'll not be stopping!" the centaur finally answered and, as if to accentuate that point, Bradwarden lowered his human torso forward and gained speed.

"A defensible spot!" Avelyn insisted. "To await Elbryan and Jilseponie, to bring them in to our side and together ward off the giants!"

"No giant'll be catching us," the centaur assured him. "Nor will Elbryan and Pony, though I lament their loss."

"They are not dead!" the monk insisted.

"No," agreed Bradwarden. "Resourceful, the both o' them. Not dead, but not for catching us, and when ye kill the dactyl, we'll come back out and find them both, I'm not doubting!"

Avelyn, dumbfounded, had no answers. He could hardly believe that Bradwarden would so leave their friends behind, deserting the pair in so perilous a situation. Avelyn came to understand then just how determined the centaur was, just how determined all his companions were, that he was the hope, that he alone might do battle with the dactyl and win. Avelyn believed, and had spoken it openly and often, that it was his destiny to meet with the hellish creature; and so his friends meant to get him there, and if all of them perished in the process then by their thinking, at least—so be it.

A great weight fell over the monk as he came to that realization, a responsibility beyond anything Avelyn Desbris had ever known: greater even than his eight-year dedication that had gotten him into St.-Mere-Abelle, to the fulfillment of his dearest mother's lifelong desire; greater even than the task assigned him by the Church, and by God, to go to Pimaninicuit and prepare this latest generation of gemstones. Avelyn had been ready to argue with Bradwarden, to insist, even if it meant dropping from the centaur's back, or using some magic against Bradwarden, that they stop and wait for their friends. But now the sobered monk remained silent and uncomplaining. Bradwarden meant to deliver him, and so Avelyn must be delivered.

Or all the deaths would be for naught.

They came through the pass of the great Barbacan with night still thick about them, having put many miles behind them in a furious rush. Bradwarden, clearly exhausted, would not think of stopping, though he was glad when Avelyn announced that he would walk and not ride for a time.

Overlooking the valley within the mountain ring, the pair were overwhelmed—particularly Bradwarden, who had not viewed the great encampment before. Thousands of campfires dotted the dark plain below them, thousands and thousands.

And beyond the masses loomed a single dark silhouette, a conical mountain tipped by a steady stream of dark smoke.

Aida.

"The dactyl's home," Avelyn whispered to the centaur, and Bradwarden needed no clarification, for both of them were staring squarely at the ominous mountain.

"We can get down and about the camp," Bradwarden said a few moments later, after pausing to inspect the layout. The centaur pointed to the left, to one of the great black arms running down from the lone mountain, nearly to the base of the mountains Bradwarden and Avelyn had just come through. "Though we're looking at a full day o' walking," the centaur finished.

"Out in the daylight near that swarm?" Avelyn asked doubtfully.

"Not a choice," Bradwarden replied. "We'll get behind the mountain arm and hope our enemy has not an army on the other side of it."

Avelyn nodded and silently followed the indomitable centaur, denying his obvious exhaustion.

They were scrambling in the right direction, Elbryan knew, following their friends, though they certainly were not gaining any ground. Every so often, the pair crossed a low spot, a muddy puddle, and Elbryan spotted the deep tracks of Bradwarden. Widespread tracks, he noted hopefully; the centaur was in full run.

That was what Elbryan and Pony wanted. Duty told them that they must follow, but their higher purpose reminded them that all that mattered was the delivery of Avelyn. "Run on, Bradwarden," Elbryan muttered more than once, and always Pony nodded her agreement.

Elbryan was surprised at how easy the mountain trails were to navigate, even in the dark. The Barbacan was an imposing range of tall rocky mountains, capped in snow year-round with many sheer cliffs, some with drops of two or even three thousand feet. But in this particular region, with the trail cutting between two such peaks and thus bringing the climbers nowhere near the top, the going remained steady and fairly easy. The ranger believed that they might see the other side, the slope down to the valley beyond, before the dawn. Avelyn had described the general layout to them all, had told of the valley and of the lone mountain that maps named Aida. In that description, the monk had noted often and hopefully that the barrier mountain range, though tall and ominous, was not wide.

So it was with some hope that Elbryan and Pony ran on, and though they could not possibly match the pace of the galloping centaur, they found many occasions when they could cross over a blocking outcropping of stone that Bradwarden would have had to circumvent. Perhaps with the dawn, they would sight their friends again and would be able to link up.

Even the pursuit seemed left behind, the fumbling giants not keeping pace. Elbryan's one fear, though, was that the behemoths knew the region and thus knew a quicker way.

That fear came to fruition when Elbryan and Pony entered one long narrow pass, a jumble of boulders and scraggly trees sheltered from the strong winds, but, the pair both silently noted, without any obvious escape routes. Halfway along the trail through the gully, an ominous and familiar orange glow appeared—*ahead* of the pair.

Out stepped the giant, Togul Dek, still wearing no helm, its huge features twisted with rage. Roaring at the two humans—and all the louder when Elbryan banged an arrow off its tremendous breastplate—the behemoth jabbed its glowing spike first into the tree at its left, then in the one at its right, sending both up instantly as towering candles. Between the trees stepped the brute, outlined by fire, not bothered by fire, and Elbryan and Pony noted the dark silhouettes of another pair of giants behind it.

"Take him head-on," the ranger instructed, and he dove to the muddy ground, wrapping his cloak tightly about him. He came up in a dash, to the side and not straight ahead, and Pony, trusting him, charged out from his wake, waving her sword menacingly, drawing the spike wielder's attention.

The giant set its huge feet wide apart and slapped the demon-created spear across its open palm. It paid no heed to the ranger, for it knew he had nowhere to flee, and concentrated instead on the woman, brave and foolish, walking steadily to her doom.

Each step came more difficult to Pony. She heard a commotion far behind and understood that the other giants—probably three or four more, if her count at the previous fight was accurate—had sealed off that end of the gully. Where had Elbryan gone, she wondered, and why? Why hadn't he just put Hawkwing to use, shooting arrow after arrow at the spike wielder's unarmored head until the thing fell over dead? Then they could fight two against two, and try to break out into the night.

Pony shook the confusing possibilities from her thoughts. This was Elbryan, she reminded herself: the Nightbird, the ranger, elven trained.

Even as her resolve began to mount once more, she saw him, running right through the fires, along a low branch on the tree to the giant's right. Flames licked at him, at his soggy muddy cloak, but he scampered along, buried by the blaze, bearing down on his unsuspecting enemy.

Pony howled and charged, drawing the monster's full attention. She skidded up quickly and loosed a forked bolt of crackling lightning, striking hard the leader and both of the giants behind it.

Then, before Togul Dek had recovered from the lightning, Elbryan was upon the brute, the ranger running full out to the end of the branch, leaping high and hard, sword extended, throwing his arms wide to thrust the smoldering cape behind him. Tempest dove right into the giant's face, while Elbryan's booted feet were planted hard against the behemoth's massive chest.

He had only one quick strike; he had to be perfect. And so he was, mighty Tempest blasting through bone and flesh, diving into the giant's brain.

Togul Dek tried to respond, tried to lift the spike and bring it to bear, but the weapon flew from the suddenly weak hands, drawing a bright line in the dark air. It landed far to the side, upon a stone it fast reduced to flowing, molten lava, rolling down the side of the mountain, taking the spike with it, and that, in turn, melting all subsequent stone, the fiery avalanche gaining momentum.

Elbryan viciously wrenched his blade free, but held his footing as the giant fell backward, the ranger riding the behemoth like some felled tree. The two giants behind their leader did not know what to make of the scene, had not even noticed Elbryan until Togul Dek began that backward fall. And then, it was too late.

Elbryan hit the ground in a graceful forward roll, rushing up and stabbing hard, finding the crease between one giant's huge breastplate and its pelvic armor. Throwing his momentum firmly behind the sword, the ranger drove it in to its hilt, then scrambled past, right between the brutes, drawing Tempest back out as he went. He cut a sudden, sharp turn, diving into yet another roll, this one aimed at the second giant as it swung its club. The weapon swished high of the mark, harmlessly—for Elbryan, at least. The wounded giant, clutching its torn guts, bent right into the weapon's path and got clipped across the forehead. It went down hard, groaning, trying to shake the dizziness, growling against the searing pain.

Elbryan got in a fast strike on the still-standing brute, then darted out into the night. He didn't think himself quick enough, though, thought the giant would get in one hit, but then the monster inexplicably dropped its club and howled, grasping at its visor.

Pony ran by, stabbing the standing giant hard in the back of the leg, then rushing out to join Elbryan.

"What did you do to its eyes?" the ranger asked, but Pony had no answer, only shrugged and kept on running.

Pursuit was close and fast, forcing the tired companions to stay at full speed. They came to a wall of stone, climbable, but Elbryan feared the giants would have an easier time than he and Pony, that the brutes would close in and simply pluck them off the wall before they got over.

No other options, the ranger decided, and so he scrambled ahead, hoping to get a firm handhold, that he might propel Pony over him, over the stone, out to freedom in the dark night. He neared the top when he heard Pony, just a few feet below him, cry out in surprise.

Elbryan turned and screamed, seeing a giant reaching for his lover. Pony had no weapon in hand—no weapon that Elbryan saw, at least—though she had her arm extended out toward the giant.

She yelled again, and something flew out from her grasp, rocketed into the giant's visor with a resounding ring, and though the missile did not penetrate the helm, but rather bounced off, it hit with tremendous force, bending and creasing the metal into the giant's face, and the brute fell away. Pony was quick to retrieve the stone, not willing to abandon such a powerful weapon.

Elbryan grabbed Pony by the shoulder and hauled her up, pulling her right past him, then pushing hard until she went over the lip of the ridge. The ranger dug in and scrambled for all his life, and got over the rim just ahead of reaching fingers, a second giant coming in for him.

Pony was fast to those fingers, her sword slashing hard, taking a couple from the hand, and then the pair were running again; and this time no pursuit was close behind.

"What did you do to the first at the base of the wall?" the ranger asked her.

"Lodestone," Pony replied. "The gem rushes to targeted metal. I wish I had a hundred more like it!"

Elbryan looked back in the direction of the ridge and shuddered at the sheer power of the stone. He had thought his sword impressive, had thought himself a marvelous warrior, and so he was, but how did that measure against the power of the stones?

Elbryan was glad that Pony was on his side and that Avelyn, much more powerful than the woman, was on his side. That thought gave him hope that his monk friend would indeed defeat the demon that had come to Corona.

Though she didn't understand its source, Tuntun watched the growing spectacle of the fiery avalanche with satisfaction. The elf had played only a minor role in the battle, fired only a single arrow. But such a shot! Tuntun had put her arrow right against a giant's visor, right through the slit! In her mind, she replayed again its howl and saw again the sight of Elbryan and Jilseponie running out to the safety of the dark night.

Convinced that they were safe for the time being, the elf had then circled back, down below the scene of the fight, to rejoin her precious companion.

"I'll take you no farther," she said to Symphony, patting the muzzle of this animal that had served her so well. Even though the trails seemed easy for at least a short distance, Tuntun decided that it would be better for her to use stealth. Alone, the elf could run full out without any fear of detection.

"I know that you are smart enough to get away," Tuntun whispered, and the great horse snorted as if he understood. The elf took her pack and her weapons—bow and a long dagger—and with a final look Symphony's way, a final nod of appreciation, she ran off into the night.

❖ 51 ❖

Aida

Elbryan and Pony were coming down the northwestern face of the mountainous barrier when dawn broke over the Barbacan. Only then was the size of the dactyl's gathered army revealed, a swarming black mass that filled the whole valley between the long arms of a lone, smoking mountain, some ten miles or so to the north.

"How many?" Pony breathed.

"Too many," the ranger said helplessly, having no better answer.

"And how are we to get to the mountain?" Pony asked. "How many thousands must we defeat even to reach its black rocky base?"

Elbryan shook his head determinedly, somehow sure his companion's assessment was not correct. "A few sentries perhaps," he replied. "Nothing more."

Pony eyed him skeptically.

"The demon is confident," Elbryan explained, "inviting us in. The dactyl fears no mortal man and no monster, and it has no reason to believe that we would ever dare to move against it in such small numbers, small enough to enter the Barbacan unnoticed."

"That has been our hope since the beginning," Pony agreed.

"And that is our only hope now," Elbryan said, "a hope to which we must hold fast. If the demon sets its army to block us, then so we shall be blocked, and not my sword, nor Avelyn's magic, not Bradwarden's strength, nor your own assortment of weapons, will possibly get us through so many swarming monsters.

"But it will not come to that," the ranger went on. "Even if the demon dactyl thinks that some enemies have come to its home, as the armored giants and that terrible spear might indicate, it remains supremely confident that none in all the world can stand against it."

"How do you know this?"

The simple question seemed to catch Elbryan off his guard. Indeed, how did he know so much about this enemy that he had never seen and had never battled before? In the end, the ranger realized that he did not know, that he was guessing, and hoping. He answered Pony only with a shrug, and that seemed enough. They had come too far to worry about things they couldn't control, and so they started along once more, quickly picking a path down the side of the mountain. They were both weary after the long night of running, but neither entertained any thoughts of stopping to rest, not with so many monsters before them—and perhaps more than a few chasing them.

An hour later, moving across an open expanse of bare rock—the two friends feeling very exposed indeed!—Elbryan stopped suddenly and dropped to a crouch. Thinking danger at hand, Pony crouched as well, and reached her hand into a pocket, fingering her few stones.

"There!" the ranger said excitedly, pointing down across the valley to his left, toward the western arm of Aida. Beyond that black line of stone, a black dot, a solitary figure, moved steadily across the green carpet, making fast for a thick copse of trees.

No, Pony realized, not one figure, but two, a man atop a horse . . . a man atop a centaur!

"Avelyn and Bradwarden!" she whispered.

"Running hard for Aida," Elbryan agreed. He looked back at Pony, his smile wide. "And with none chasing them, and none standing before them."

Pony nodded grimly. Perhaps her love was right, perhaps the dactyl was indeed inviting them in. She had to wonder, though she said nothing aloud, was that a good thing?

The pair were off the mountain within the hour, making their way along its base, weaving in and out of boulders and patches of trees. They easily avoided the few bored goblin sentries that were about, and every so often came upon tracks that told them they were following the exact route Avelyn and Bradwarden had taken.

Finally they crossed over the mountain's long arm and were surprised to find the ground very warm under their feet. Only then did the pair realize that this line of stone was not a solid ridge, but rather, like a living thing, was growing and changing. Most of the ridge was hard, but every so often, the pair caught a sudden glimpse of fiery orange, the lava flow bubbling up to the surface, then meandering across the hardened black stone like a crawling orange slug. Within a few minutes, each of these movements would cease, the lava gradually rolling over itself or gathering in a depression, and then quickly cooling, its glow fading to blackness.

"Like a living thing," Pony remarked, taking more care where she subsequently stepped.

"Like the dactyl," Elbryan replied. "Flowing out from Aida, encompassing all the world under its blackness."

It was not a pleasant thought.

They were several hours behind their friends, Elbryan and Pony realized when they at last came upon the same expanse they had seen their friends traversing. There was no apparent resistance; behind this arm of Aida, this blocking ridge of black stone some twenty to thirty feet high, no monsters moved about and no sentries were visible.

They went into a copse of trees, such a stark contrast of teeming life next to the black wall of stone, and found again the centaur's tracks. Soon a second set—the tracks of a heavy human, of Brother Avelyn—were visible beside those of Bradwarden, and it was not hard for the pair to surmise that the centaur might be getting tired.

But Bradwarden continued on, and so did Avelyn; and so did Pony and Elbryan, increasing their pace in the hope that they might catch up to their friends before they entered the caverns of the mountain. Perhaps, Elbryan pondered, if Avelyn and Bradwarden were scrambling about, looking for some way into the mountain . . .

It didn't happen that way. The ranger and Pony exited the copse of trees, then crossed through a second and then a third, climbing to the lower reaches of Aida. As soon as they cleared that last copse, they saw an entrance, a great gaping hole, defying the slanting rays of the westering sun. If the appearance proved true, if this was indeed a way into the heart of Aida, then Avelyn and Bradwarden had long ago gone into the mountain and might even now be standing before the demon dactyl as Elbryan and Pony stood staring at the entrance. The anxious couple went back into the last copse and cut sticks, wrapping them with cloth to make torches.

Then, fearful that they would be too late, the pair split, left and right, and moved quickly and stealthily right up to the edge of the cavern entrance. Elbryan peeked around the stone and into the gloom; Pony did likewise from across the way; and they were somewhat relieved to find that this was indeed a deep cavern and that it was apparently empty.

Just inside, Elbryan noted the hooflike depression of the centaur's track.

Keeping near the side wall, not daring to light a torch, the pair moved in tentatively, allowing their eyes to adjust to the rapidly diminishing light. All too soon, they were faced with a dilemma: light the torch or walk on in near-complete darkness.

Elbryan winced as the fire flared to life, as if expecting all the minions of the dactyl to descend upon him. After a few tense but uneventful moments, he motioned to Pony, and the pair crept along, coming to a place where the tunnel forked: one branch going right and level, the other left and down. Looking down the right-hand side, Pony noted that the tunnel forked again just a short way in, and the tunnel continuing to the right beyond that second fork showed yet another side passage.

"A veritable maze," Elbryan moaned. He fell to his knees and moved the torch low, searching for some sign of his friends' passing, but the ground was bare, unmarked stone.

"Straight ahead," Pony declared a moment later, seeing her companion's frustration. "Deeper into the mountain, and then down and to the left at the next fork."

She spoke with determination, though it was only a guess—a guess that seemed as good to Elbryan as any he might make. They moved in deeper, then began a descent along a smooth and angled passageway. Elbryan gave up any thoughts of continuing his scan for tracks, knowing that to do so would only slow their progress. Avelyn and Bradwarden were wandering in here, probably as lost as were Elbryan and Pony. Sooner or later, one of the pairs, or perhaps both, would stumble upon the dactyl or some of its deadly minions.

It was a desperate situation, and both Elbryan and Pony had to remind themselves often that they had known it would be like this from the moment they had set out from Dundalis.

Bestesbulzibar was outraged, and yet the demon was somewhat amused as well as it stood with Quintall and a pair of very nervous giants, looking down the ruined slope of a mountain. How powerful indeed was the demon-forged spike! To cause such devastation as this, simply because it left the hand of its dying wielder and fell across the stone!

One of the giants continued to stammer on about bad luck and other such nonsense, trying hard to concoct some excuse that might keep its skin attached to its body. Bestesbulzibar wasn't listening.

"Have they made the mountain?" the dactyl asked Quintall, indicating Aida.

The rockman scrutinized the terrain ahead and considered the distance. He put a hand to his chin, an oddly human gesture. And indeed, Quintall now seemed physically human. The rough edges of his rocky body had smoothed and rounded, shaping more and more to the exact human form the spirit had left behind. The rockman was recognizable again as Quintall; the features, the size, and the body dimensions were all the same, as if the man's spirit were somehow determining the shape of this new stone coil. Of course, his "skin" was now obsidian in consistency as well as hue, and red lines of molten stone still striped his joints; his eyes, too, were red pits of liquid stone. But he looked like Quintall, and the rockman could hardly wait until the moment that Brother Avelyn saw his new and superior body.

"Have they?" Bestesbulzibar prompted.

Quintall nodded. "If they ran on through the night," he answered, "and if no others rose up against them."

"Perhaps they will be seated upon my throne when I return to it." The dactyl sneered, eyeing the pair of giants wickedly.

"B-bad luck," one of the behemoths stammered.

"We will—" the other began to promise, but the dactyl cut it short.

"You will go and take your places with the army," Bestesbulzibar instructed. The demon badly wanted to rip the hide from these two, and from any others of the hunting party who had survived their encounter with the intruders and who were now hiding nearby, fearing the demon's wrath. Or perhaps Bestesbulzibar could take them back to Aida and throw them in the path of the deadly Nightbird. Or, the demon mused, perhaps it would give the job of punishment to Quintall, that Bestesbulzibar might witness the power of its newest weapon. But the dactyl was not a stupid creature and could control its impulses, even those bent upon destruction, which the demon loved above all else. Bestesbulzibar had lost too many of its elite giant guardsmen already, considering the effort he had taken to outfit the giants with armor, but, in truth, the demon figured that it had lost little by the failure of the giants. So Brother Avelyn and the one called Nightbird may have entered Aida; that only meant that Bestesbulzibar might enjoy a bit of the fun of killing them.

"Come along," the dactyl instructed Quintall. The rockman moved closer and Bestesbulzibar lifted from the ground, hooking its powerful legs about Quintall, and then speeding the instrument of its wrath across the valley, above the heads of the cowering minions, and back to Aida.

Quintall, possessed of heightened senses, whose glowing eyes could light the way along dark tunnels, was sent to find the trail.

"We are too low," Avelyn complained, leaning against a wall of the stuffy, tight cavern. He kept the light of his enchanted diamond low, hoping that it would be less conspicuous and not attract any more guards like the two powries Avelyn and Bradwarden had just overwhelmed. That thought in mind, Avelyn kicked aside the bloody leg of one of the dwarves and shifted himself so that he was looking back the way they had come.

"Now wouldn't the demon thing be at the heart?" Bradwarden asked casually, tearing at the second powrie as he spoke. "And wouldn't a mountain's heart be below?"

Avelyn shook his head immediately; he just didn't feel right about the path. They had gone down and to the left at the first fork, too soon perhaps, to be heading into the lower chambers of this tunnel-crossed mountain. "Our enemy might be higher," he said, "near the smoking cone, where the winged demon might quickly fly out among its minions."

He looked back at Bradwarden as he finished his argument, and he was sorry that he did.

"Bah, 'tis a guess and nothing more," the centaur replied, taking a huge bite out of a powrie leg.

Avelyn closed his eyes.

"We go along, I say," the centaur continued, talking through its full mouth, "choosing trails as we find them. It's all a guess, yer knowing as well as I'm knowing."

The monk sighed and didn't disagree. Whatever course they chose, Avelyn would second-guess. Too much was at stake here; the monk was too much on the edge of his nerves.

"Now why're ye here?" Bradwarden asked simply. "Ye've come to face yer destiny, so ye said, and so ye shall. We'll get there, me friend, and if that's what's scaring ye, then I'm not for blaming ye. But turning back won't put us any closer to anything, and every lost step gives more of our enemies the chance to stumble upon us." He spat at that last thought and tossed the tough powrie leg to the ground. "And the damned things aren't even good eating!"

Avelyn managed a smile and walked by the centaur, taking great care to avoid stepping on the discarded meal. They started off again, side by side, their bulky forms filling the narrow passageway.

"I am not pleased by the sight," Elbryan whispered, looking down the long, narrow descent, a ledge bordered on the left by an uneven wall and on the right by a long drop of more than two hundred feet from where the ledge began and only gradually diminishing as the trail moved lower. Height hardly seemed to matter when considering the danger, though, for the drop ended in a pool of red fire, a swirling lake of molten stone. Even from this great height, Elbryan and Pony could feel the intense heat, and the sulfuric stench was nearly overwhelming.

"And I am not pleased at the prospect of backtracking all the way," Pony replied. "Down we decided to go, and down this goes!"

"The fumes . . ." the ranger protested, and his fears were not lost on the woman. Pony fumbled in her pack and took out a strip of cloth, an intended bandage. She tore it in half and wetted both strips thoroughly from her waterskin, then tied one about her face after she handed the other to Elbryan.

The ranger, though, had a better idea. He took the green armband from his right arm, the one the elves said would defeat any poison, and tore it in two, handing one strip to Pony. With a trusting nod, the woman donned the mask, as did Elbryan, the ranger eyeing Pony all the while, admiring her gumption. The brave woman was not easily deterred.

They needed no torch in this place, because of the glow of the lava, and so their hands were free as they started down, at first hugging the wall tightly—the ledge was not narrow, but the prospects of slipping over were far too grim. Gradually, they eased out from the wall, their pace increasing, and soon they had put a couple hundred feet behind them, nearing the halfway point of the descent.

Pony, holding the lead, grew hopeful when she spotted a dark shadow along the wall far below, a side passage, running into the mountain and away from this place. So intent was she that she never noticed the crack running right across the ledge in front of her.

She stepped over it, and as she brought her weight down, the stone beneath her foot gave way.

Pony screamed; Elbryan grabbed her and pulled her back to safety, the pair falling to the ledge in a jumble. The ranger scrambled to the very lip and watched the eight-foot stone slab falling. It bounced off a jag in the wall, then spun over and out, tumbling into the magma, where it was swallowed, disappearing with hardly a splash.

Pony, horrified and breathing deeply, had to slow herself down consciously. She managed it, but the deep breaths had taken their toll, the sulfuric fumes overwhelming her, for in the fall, she had dislodged the elven mask. She rolled to the lip of the ledge, pulled her mask further down, and vomited.

"We must go back," Elbryan said, putting a hand on the woman's shoulder, trying to comfort her.

"Shorter down than up," Pony said stubbornly, and she retched again. Then she sat up quickly, determinedly, pulled out her waterskin and washed her face briskly, replacing the mask and standing firm.

"A long jump," Elbryan remarked, eyeing the break in the trail.

"An easy leap," Pony corrected, and to prove her point, the woman took a single running stride and sprang across the gap, landing easily and skidding down defensively, on the lower level.

Elbryan stared at her long and hard, admiring again that stubborn determination but honestly wondering if she wasn't being foolhardy just to prove a point. They had no idea if that passage down below led anywhere, after all, and the eight-foot leap would be decidedly more difficult coming *up* the angled walkway.

"Easy leap," Pony said again. The ranger managed a smile; they were going to face a demon, after all, so how could he berate the woman for what he considered recklessness?

Pony's eyes widened, and Elbryan realized that she was about to scream.

The ranger spun, drawing Tempest as he went, but the danger was not behind him, but to the side, coming out of the solid wall. Stones burst outward; Elbryan skipped back up the slope a few scrambling steps and dove to the ground. He turned about, confused, and when he saw the source, he was even more confused.

Quintall walked out onto the ledge.

Elbryan was up in a defensive crouch, Tempest defensively before him, though he knew not what to make of this moving rockman, this obsidian image of Brother Justice.

Quintall's intentions were easy enough to discern. The rockman looked at Pony, then turned back fully upon Elbryan, red-striped fingers clenching the air menacingly. "Do you think you can win this time, Nightbird?" the demon's lackey asked, his voice grating like stone rubbing stone.

"What are you?" Elbryan asked breathlessly. "What manner of being, what tormented soul?"

"Tormented?" Quintall scoffed. "I am free, mortal fool, and shall live forever, while your life is forfeit!" On came the rockman, stalking straight in.

Elbryan slashed his sword across, scoring a scraping hit that didn't even slow Quintall. The ranger jumped back a step, then lunged forward, Tempest squealing as it deflected off Quintall's face. This hit was more substantial, Elbryan was glad to realize, for the fine elven-forged sword cracked through the rockman's hard skin, drawing a slight orange line.

But the line cooled to black almost immediately, and if Quintall was hurt, he did not show it. He came on furiously then, and launched a roundhouse left hook.

Elbryan ducked the blow, just barely, and scampered back as Quintall's hand thundered against the wall. The ranger glanced at that impact spot and his respect for this enemy heightened, for where Quintall's hand had struck, the stone was cracked and smoking.

"Will you run away, then, and leave the woman to me?" the rockman taunted. "I can get to her, do not doubt."

The words made Elbryan glance down at Pony, and he saw, to his horror, that she was readying for a jump back across the gap. "Stay down!" the ranger yelled to her. "I will come to you!"

"You will never get past me," Quintall remarked, accentuating his point by slamming the stone wall again, even harder.

That movement left an opening that the ranger could not resist. He came forward in a rush, Tempest driving in hard and straight, striking hard, cracking through the black shell and diving into the monster's magma interior.

Quintall howled and launched a series of blows, but Elbryan was the quicker, already retracting his glowing sword—and the ranger was glad to know that the fine weapon had survived the immersion in the obviously hot interior of this wicked foe—and snapping Tempest up left, up right, up left, in three quick parries, then straight ahead to poke the rockman in the face once again.

But even the great wound in the monster's belly fast closed, while Quintall's movements became more cautious, more dangerous.

From down below, Pony was shouting out, but Elbryan hardly took the time to consider her words. He had to find some way to hurt this thing, and though his sword might inflict some sting, it seemed that the wound could only be so deep.

The answer seemed obvious, and so the ranger spent no time considering the problems with such a course, plotting out the appropriate attack. He darted ahead again, stabbing hard, then turned as if to run by the monster on its left, on the outside of the ledge.

Pure instinct dropped Elbryan to one knee, Quintall's heavy arm swishing above his head—a blow that would have launched the ranger over the edge! Then Elbryan came up in a reverse spin, turning in front of the rockman, going hard against the wall, and angling to get in between Quintall and the stone.

The monster's other arm shot out hard, slamming the wall in front of Elbryan, preventing him from running past. He had no intention of such a course, anyway, for he stopped short of the barrier, braced himself against the wall, and shoved back with all his great strength.

He hardly moved; Quintall, so solid, so strong, laughed at him.

Then Elbryan felt the press and the heat, intense and burning from those points on the rockman that were not hardened stone. Elbryan punched and twisted, but the press grew ever tighter. He heard Pony scream out, but her voice seemed to come from far away.

Then came a sudden rush of air above the slumping ranger, and the rockman cried out, and the grip was lessened.

Elbryan stumbled back up the slope, wriggling away, and turned to see Quintall clutching at his molten eyes, drops of hot magma glowing on his cheek. A second puzzle faced the ranger when he noticed a cord, thin but strong, strung to his left, along the wall, going past him and past Quintall. A quick tug showed Elbryan that it was tied off a short distance up the ledge.

The ranger had no time to stop and figure it out, for Quintall's eyes, like his other wounds, quickly healed. On came the Nightbird, having no answers but to attack fiercely and hope his sword would find a weakness. He slashed left, back right, straight ahead, back to the right again, the sword ringing loudly and throwing sparks with each impact upon the rockman.

Despite the fact that Tempest offered no real threat, Quintall instinctively reacted, using his solid arms to parry, using the same martial routines he had learned long ago at St.-Mere-Abelle.

Elbryan pressed on, Tempest hitting so often that the ringing song never paused. He drew crack after crack in the rock man, and entertained the fleeting hope that Quintall would simply split apart.

"Tie it off, there!" Tuntun instructed, tossing the strong elvish cord to a stunned Pony and pointing to a large, loose boulder, a dozen feet further down the slope. "And be quick!" the elf demanded.

Pony was already running, not really knowing what Tuntun had in mind, but not daring to waste the moment in questioning. Any plan, however desperate, was better than nothing, and nothing was exactly what Pony could figure to do. As the woman began looping the rope, she felt the tension from the other end and, considering that it was on the inside of the rock-man, she began to figure things out.

Tuntun flew away, back up toward the combatants, her slender daggers in hand, both dripping magma from Quintall's eyes.

Elbryan was still on the offensive when the elf buzzed in, the ranger's heavy blows whacking repeatedly against the rockman's blocking arms or every so often slipping through to smack the monster about the torso or even across the head. He didn't know how long he could keep it up, though, and understood that if he did no real damage soon, his momentum would be lost, and then it would be Quintall's turn.

But then, suddenly, the rockman howled again, as Tuntun's arms came about his head, tiny daggers finding their way to glowing eyes. Quintall threw his arms up mightily, connecting a glancing blow that sent the elf fluttering way up high, one dagger flying free, spinning down to disappear in the magma.

Elbryan grabbed up Tempest in both hands and surged ahead, swinging an over-the-shoulder chop with every ounce of strength he could muster. Quintall's arm got down to block, and Tempest blasted right through it, severing the limb halfway between wrist and elbow.

The rockman howled again, hot magma pouring from the wound, though it, too, like all the others, hardened fast and cooled to black, leaving a stump below the monster's red-striped elbow joint.

Quintall continued to roar, coming on with sheer outrage. Up above, Tuntun was screaming at the top of her melodic voice, "Now! Now!"

Elbryan had no idea of what the elf could mean, but Pony did. The woman put her back to the roped boulder, squeezed in between it and the wall and braced her feet, then pushed out with all her strength. The strong muscles in Pony's legs corded taut; she groaned with the great effort, and the boulder slid only a fraction of an inch.

Pony heard the renewed fighting, the ringing blade, the roaring monster. Strength alone would not dislodge this heavy stone; she had to be smart. She turned her shoulders, shifting the angle a bit upward, and pushed out again. She felt the closest edge of the stone lift from the ledge, knew that she only had to go a bit more to get over that back edge.

Tuntun dove for the combatants, but veered at the last second as Quintall spun, not surprised this time. The turn cost the rockman another sting as Elbryan seized the moment and thrust ahead, Tempest cutting hard.

"Over the cord!" Tuntun yelled to the ranger. "Over the cord."

The meaning came clear to Elbryan even as Pony overturned the boulder, the heavy rock rolling off the ledge. The ranger started to leap over the suddenly taut, suddenly moving, cord, but only made it halfway. He dropped Tempest to the ledge and grabbed on for all his life as the boulder plummeted, its fall pulling the elven cord from the wall, swinging it, and Quintall and Elbryan, over the ledge.

Down they went, screaming. They came to a sudden, jarring stop as the rope played out to its length, the boulder jolting free of Pony's knot and spinning down, down, to plop into the magma, where it was swallowed.

Elbryan held on, and some five feet below him, so did Quintall, the rockman clenching his one impossibly strong hand about the rope so powerfully that his hold was more solid than that of the two-handed man above him.

"Climb!" Pony cried to her love, and so Elbryan did, driving on with all speed and all strength.

Faster still was Quintall, the rockman, heaving mightily, launching himself up a foot or more, then grabbing tight again. Heaving and grabbing, he was closing fast on Elbryan, who had at least twenty feet of scrambling still ahead of him.

Pony continued to call out encouragement. She ran up and leaped the eight-foot gap, slamming her shin hard against the higher lip, but driving on, running to her love.

Hand over hand went the ranger; Pony thought he might make it. He threw one arm and shoulder over the ledge and the woman dove to him, tugging hard. But then, Quintall gave a great heave and caught the rope again, barely inches below Elbryan's feet. One more leap and the ranger would be caught.

In swooped Tuntun. Elbryan saw the desperate move and cried out for the elf to go back. He let go with one hand, trusting in Pony to brace him, and even tried to catch the elf as she swept below him.

Elven cord was fine and strong, but Tuntun's dagger, too, was of elvish make, and a quick flick of her wrist snapped the stretched rope right below Elbryan's feet.

Elbryan caught the elf's forearm; Quintall caught her by the foot.

Then they hung, twisting and turning, Pony looping the rope about her as a firmer brace and tugging Elbryan's tunic desperately. The ranger's hand tightened on poor Tuntun's forearm, his muscles bulging from the strain, but down below, heavy Quintall's grip was even stronger.

"Pull!" Elbryan begged Pony, for though they were working with all their might, the ranger was slipping back over the lip.

Tuntun, stretched, fearing that she would simply be ripped in half, recognized the dilemma, understanding that her friends could not hoist her and the heavy rockman. Her free hand, holding the dagger, moved upward, and she looked into Elbryan's shining eyes.

"No," the man pleaded, his voice barely a whisper for the lump in his throat. He shook his head.

Tuntun stabbed him hard in the wrist, and then she and Quintall, were falling fast. The stubborn rockman did not let go, would not let the elf, this wretched creature who had doomed him, use those wings to save herself! Tuntun tried to turn, tried to use her dagger . . .

Elbryan and Pony looked away, could not watch the final drop into the molten pool, could not witness the end of Tuntun.

They lay in a heap on the ledge for a long while, until the continuing fumes began to overwhelm them.

"We have to press on," the ranger said.

"For Tuntun," Pony agreed.

They leaped the gap and hurried along, relieved indeed to find that the side passage at the bottom was no dead end, but long and fairly straight.

They relit the torch and rushed ahead, glad to put the sickening fumes and the terrible sight behind them. Soon after, however, they came to a quick stop, spotting a distant glow far ahead in the tunnel. Elbryan looked helplessly to the torch in his hand; if he could see the glow . . .

Suddenly, the light far ahead intensified, and then narrowed, shooting down the corridor, falling over Elbryan and Pony, who had to throw up their arms to shield their eyes.

Images of demonic monsters filled their thoughts, images fast shattered by a cry of "Ho, ho, what!" from the other end of the beacon.

Through the Maze

Avelyn and Bradwarden were thrilled to see their companions again, but their smiles could not hold against the tears running down Pony's cheeks and the unmistakable mist in Elbryan's eyes.

"Tuntun," Elbryan explained, rubbing at one eye. "She came to our aid and saved my life, but the cost was her own."

"Perhaps she is not quite dead," Avelyn replied, fumbling with his stone sack. "Perhaps the hematite—"

"Into the magma," the ranger explained grimly, putting a hand on the monk and shaking his head.

"A brave lass to the end," Bradwarden noted. "Such is the way of the Touel'alfar—finer folk I've never known." The centaur paused, letting the eulogy hang in the air for a moment. "And what of Paulson and the little one?" he asked.

"I do not know that they escaped the giant fight," the ranger said.

"And why did ye not go back and look for them?" the centaur went on, and all three glanced Bradwarden's way with stunned expressions. How dare he accuse Elbryan and Pony, if that was indeed what he was doing.

"Our goal was Aida, our mission to deliver Avelyn, to destroy the dactyl," Elbryan said firmly, and even as he spoke the words, he understood Bradwarden's cunning verbal maneuver. In so pointedly reminding Elbryan and the others of the higher goal, the centaur helped them to put Tuntun's demise in proper perspective. She was gone, but because of her, they might move on and their higher purpose might be achieved.

That thought driving them, the four companions pushed hard along the corridors, looking for some sign as to which direction would get them to the demon. The passages forked many times, and they had to choose, without any guidance other than their own perceptions of where they might be and where the demon's lair was likely situated.

But then, at one such fork, Avelyn stopped suddenly, and held his arm out to prevent Elbryan from moving down to the left.

"Right," the monk insisted.

Elbryan looked at him carefully. "What do you know?" the ranger asked, surmising from the monk's firm tone that this was no blind guess.

Avelyn had no practical answer for his friends; it was a feeling, nothing more, but a definite feeling, as if he were sensing the magical radiations of the otherworldly monster. Whatever the source, Avelyn knew in his heart that he was correct, and so he started down the right-hand corridor.

The others followed without delay, and their hopes mounted when they came to a heavy grate, bars set floor to ceiling, blocking the passage.

All went well in the south, the dactyl knew. Its armies, led by Maiyer Dek and Kos-kosio Begulne, were pressing fast for Palmaris, while Ubba Banrock's northern force had crossed the breadth of Alpinador, right to the coast, cutting the northern kingdom in half. Banrock's powries had linked up right on schedule with the great powrie fleet that sailed from the Julianthes, and now that fleet had put out once more, sailing south for the Gulf of Corona.

Despite the promising events, the demon now paced about its obsidian throne anxiously. It felt the intrusion, the powerful magic; it knew that Quintall had been destroyed.

The dactyl would no longer underestimate these foes that had come to Aida. If any of them got through the final defenses . . .

The demon creature narrowed its eyes and grinned wickedly at the thought, at the pleasures it would take in personally killing these intruders. For all the misery its army caused, for all the death and agony, Bestesbulzibar had not truly participated, other than the murders of a few upstarts or incompetents within its own ranks.

The dactyl, anxious as it was, hoped that some of these intruders, at least, would survive to get to the throne room.

"Stand far from it," Avelyn instructed, fumbling with his pouch, but Elbryan had another idea.

"No," the ranger said. "Your magic will be too loud, I fear. There is another way." Elbryan pulled off his pack and sorted through it, finally producing the red gel the elves had given him, the same substance Belli'mar Juraviel had put upon the darkfern those years ago in Andur'Blough Inninness, allowing Elbryan to fell the sturdy plant with ease. Elbryan knew how strong and resilient his bow was, and so he figured that if the softening gel would work on darkfern, it might even defeat the metal.

He striped the center bar, near the corridor's low ceiling. Then he took out Tempest and called Bradwarden to him, climbing up on the centaur that his cut would be flat across. Hoping his instincts were true, hoping that he would not damage his marvelous sword, Elbryan drew back and swung mightily for the spot, both his hands clenched tightly on the hilt.

Tempest sliced right through the metal bar, then banged with a ring off the next in line. Elbryan hopped down from the centaur and pulled the sword blade near his face, sighing with relief when he noted it was not damaged, not even nicked.

Mighty Bradwarden reached to the cut bar and pulled it far to the side, enough so that the others, at least, could easily slip through.

"Well done," Pony congratulated.

"Aye," Bradwarden agreed, "but I'll not be getting me bulky body through that narrow hole."

Elbryan gave the centaur a wink. "I've more gel," he assured them, and soon the next bar in line was free on the top end, as well.

So they went on, even more urgently, accepting the grate as a sure sign that they were in an important area, probably the dactyl's own.

The passage went on and on, widening at times so that all four could move abreast, and then narrowing so that only Elbryan and Pony could remain in front, Avelyn behind them, the bulky centaur at the rear of the line. They passed several side tunnels, but this one they were traveling seemed the finest, the smoothest, and certainly the widest, and so they continued along their chosen course. Avelyn took care to modulate the diamond light; he cupped the gem so that the beam would shoot out more toward the front, while he, with the cat's eye chrysoberyl, continually glanced into the gloom behind them.

And so it was Avelyn who first noticed the large shadowy forms slipping into the main corridor from a side passage far behind.

"Company," the monk whispered, and even as he spoke, the telltale flickers of a torch bounced across the wall from around a bend in the tunnel some three dozen paces ahead of Elbryan.

The ranger quickly surveyed the area, then moved the group to a narrow point—if they were to be attacked both front and back, better that they fight in an area too narrow to allow more than one or two enemies to come at them from either end of the line.

The light came around the bend, another flared behind them, showing their foes to be fomorian giants, four in front, four in back, and all armored, as had been the ones chasing them at the mountainous entrance to the Barbacan.

Elbryan was glad indeed that they were not in an open field, for then they would each have been fighting two at a time—and would have had little chance indeed. In these tight quarters, the giants had to come in, front and back, in two ranks of two.

"Pony and I have the front," the ranger called.

"And I've the back!" Bradwarden responded, clumsily turning his bulky frame about in the narrow tunnel.

"Not alone," Avelyn assured him, the monk moving as far up beside the centaur as his own bulky frame would allow. Avelyn reached into a smaller pouch and took out a handful of small prismatic celestite crystals, pale blue in color, and began calling forth their enchantment.

"We cannot give them the offensive edge," the ranger said to Pony. Then, suddenly, the pair charged ahead, temporarily confusing the giants, who were certainly not used to little people rushing at them!

Elbryan started furiously, slapping his sword many times against the blade of the giant's sword, finally pushing the weapon out wide enough for the ranger to get in a solid, screeching slice that dented the monster's breastplate.

Pony went in with equal ferocity, though her attacks were not quite as effective and she scored only a minor hit.

It was Elbryan, though, and not Pony, who first lost momentum, the ranger involuntarily glancing at the side, looking at his love nearly as often as he studied his opponent. Soon, he was dodging frantically, barely parrying a swipe of a giant sword that would have easily lopped off his puny head.

"I wish ye might get up here," the centaur grumbled, eyeing the leading giants. The huge brutes couldn't quite stand side by side in the narrow corridor, but they really didn't have to, for one of them, the trailing giant, carried a long spear. "Oh, they'll get me two to one," the centaur groaned, swinging his cudgel back and forth, loosening up his joints.

"We shall see," Brother Avelyn promised sneakily, continuing his magical summoning.

In came the giants at full charge; Bradwarden braced and set his hind legs firmly. And then Avelyn threw, and the corridor before the centaur erupted in a shower of popping, stinging explosions, snapping bursts, a dozen or more, that stopped the charge fully and had the giants scrambling, crying out in pain.

Bradwarden recovered his wits and seized the moment, charging straight ahead, ramming the lead giant and knocking it back and to the floor, then turning out the spear with his free hand, launching a heavy swing with his cudgel that connected on the side of the second giant's helmet, knocking the protective armor clear off the brute's head and knocking the giant against the passage wall.

Bradwarden's second swing was even harder, all the centaur's great strength behind it connecting solidly with the giant's vulnerable head, which was still braced against the stone. The massive skull cracked with a tremendous sound and the giant slumped to the floor.

But the other fomorians were back and ready, though one seemed to be partially blinded from the celestite explosions, and Bradwarden's momentum came to a swift halt.

Pony saw what was happening here, and she was not pleased. She knew Elbryan trusted her—how could he not after all their fights together?—and yet, fighting in such proximity had him on the defensive for her sake.

That the young woman could not tolerate, more for the practical reason that they could not hope to win with such a posture than for any reason of pride. Pony had to hit fast and hard, to remind her love of her prowess. She slipped the graphite rod into her sword hand, clutching it tightly against the weapon's hilt, and wondered if her plan would work.

Elbryan ducked another swing, a clear opening to score a wicked hit, but he went to the side instead, picking off a sword strike aimed for Pony—and one she could easily have avoided on her own.

The ranger's move did leave an opening, though, the surprised giant glancing to regard Elbryan, and Pony rushed ahead, jabbing hard into the brute's belly. Her sword found a bit of a crease in the armor but couldn't sink in far enough to score a decisive hit.

No need for that, the giant—and Elbryan—discovered a moment later, when Pony released the stone's magical energy. A crackling black arc raced up the weapon and leaped from its tip, right into the fomorian's belly. The giant jolted violently, again and again, and then, when the electrical barrage finally ended, fell back off the sword to the floor, stunned, if not dead.

The lesson was not lost on Elbryan, who marveled at the powerful combination of sword and stone, even as he berated himself for thinking that Pony might need his help. Not to be outdone—and with another giant ready to take the fallen one's place—the ranger leaped ahead and launched a series of furious attacks, right and left and straight ahead, Tempest moving too quickly for the fomorian's heavy sword to keep up. The mighty elvish weapon scored hit after hit, sparks flying as it banged hard against metal armor. Finally, Elbryan found that crease between breastplate and girdle, mentally marking the spot.

The ranger let up for an instant, and as he expected, the giant roared and cut mightily. Elbryan was down in a low squat before the blade ever got close to hitting him, and he skittered under as it swooshed past. The ranger came up hard, his aim perfect for that slight crease.

In slipped Tempest, past the armor, tearing guts and diving deep. Elbryan moved ahead again, wanting to be well within the arc of that monstrous sword, pushing his blade in to the hilt. The giant reached across his back with its free hand, but there was little strength in that grip. Elbryan jerked fiercely, once and then again, the tearing jolts straightening the agonized fomorian. Then, seeing his work with this one finished, the ranger tore free the blade and let the brute fall.

The last in line was quick to join in, swinging its huge torch as a weapon.

Pony, thick into it with the third giant, took out a stone for yet another trick. But then she heard more clearly the situation at the back of the line, Bradwarden grunting, taking hits.

"Avelyn!" the woman called, and she tossed the stone, one she knew that the monk could put to much more deadly effect than she, over her shoulder.

It bounced off the monk's back, catching his attention, for he was falling into the magic of yet another gem. He noted the gift Pony had offered, though, and halted his spell, quickly retrieving the fallen stone, the lodestone.

"Ho, ho, what!" the monk bellowed happily, bringing the deadly gem in line. "This is going to hurt!"

"Well, be quick about it!" Bradwarden pleaded and then grunted, accepting a heavy club hit on his left flank, for he was too busy keeping his other opponent's sword at bay. The centaur had already taken a hit from that sword, and had a huge gash on the side of his human torso to prove it.

Avelyn called forth the energy of the stone and let it fly, swifter than any crossbow quarrel, more powerful than any ballista bolt. It hit the sword-wielding giant towering right in front of Bradwarden square in the chest, blasting a huge hole, lifting the brute clear of its feet and hurling it backward, crashing past the club wielder to slam heavily into the last in line, the pair going down in a heap.

Bradwarden used the moment of distraction to spin completely about, and as the club wielder regained its balance, the centaur launched a mighty double kick against its breastplate, knocking it back into the jumble.

"Forward!" Avelyn cried to the group.

Elbryan agreed wholeheartedly, and he leaped back to get beyond the swishing torch, then rushed ahead, angling to dive between the two remaining giants at the front, thrusting Tempest at Pony's foe as he went. The one battling Pony had to turn to meet the attack, and took a hit from the woman even as it parried the ranger's blade. Then, even worse for the fomorian, it got a swishing torch across the face as its partner tried to catch up to the scrambling ranger.

Pony rushed ahead and struck hard, sinking in her sword, calling forth the jolting energy of the graphite once again. Though her lightning was much weaker this time, her magical energies taxed, the giant slumped back, stunned.

Then came a series of popping explosions in the air ahead of Pony, another celestite barrage from Avelyn, singeing and confusing the fomorian pair.

Pony stared curiously at the behemoth that had been battling Elbryan, at its suddenly too-straight posture, hips forward, shoulders back. She understood as the torch dropped away, as the brute toppled forward, sliding off the blood-dripping Tempest.

Avelyn flattened himself against the wall and instructed Bradwarden to run by, for only one of the four giants that had come in at the back had any fight left in it. Bradwarden, wounded more seriously than he had at first believed, didn't argue, but slipped past the bulky monk, moving beside Pony, stubbornly bearing down on the last giant in front.

The last in the pile at the rear finally extracted itself and, seeing Avelyn standing alone, no weapon visible, it came on wildly.

Avelyn waited until the last possible second, then loosed the magic of his latest stone, the malachite, into the corridor.

Suddenly, the giant was off balance, feet barely scraping the stone. Every movement forced a countermovement from the weightless behemoth, and so, when the stupid thing brought its club high overhead for a mighty chop, the energy lifted the giant from the ground and turned it right over in midair, a slow-motion somersault. The giant tried desperately to get at the trickster monk, but each twist and turn only made its predicament even worse, and soon it was tumbling, floating helplessly back down the corridor. As soon as it cleared its fallen companions, Avelyn was upon them, reaching into the chest of one to retrieve his deadly magnetite. He looked up to see that last giant upside down, flailing wildly, futilely, floating even farther away.

Avelyn snorted at the sight and turned to watch his three friends finishing the last of that group. Then, with an almost apologetic shrug, when he noted that the giant was far enough from his friends, the monk ran toward it, enacting a serpentine shield and then pulling forth his powerful ruby.

Elbryan winced as he noted the centaur's wicked wound, a bleeding gash that was fast draining the life from poor Bradwarden.

"We need the hematite," Pony remarked, looking back toward Avelyn.

"Try this instead," Elbryan offered, taking off his other armband, the red one, the one the elves had soaked in permanent healing salves.

Pony took it and went to work, while Elbryan ran ahead, both pausing, nearly tumbling, when they heard the tremendous blast of Avelyn's fireball.

Avelyn trotted back down the corridor, the charred giant, still floating headdown, far behind him.

The tunnel continued straight for a dozen paces, then turned sharply to the right, where Elbryan had run.

"Move along," Avelyn instructed his weary friends, and they nodded, understanding that their task was far from finished. Pony looked at Bradwarden, but the centaur was smiling widely, the healing salves already at work under the red bandage.

So on they went, Avelyn in the lead. All three stopped suddenly as Elbryan came rushing back around the corner. The ranger hit the wall hard, using it to turn himself so he could dive back down the corridor, and when he came up out of the roll, the others looked past him curiously to see glowing stones fast hardening on the floor.

"A great red man!" the ranger explained, "with the black wings of a bat—"

"No man," Avelyn interrupted, knowing the truth of this newest foe, knowing that they had at last met with the demon dactyl.

❖ 53 ❖

Destiny

A wave of molten stone splashed around the corner, driving the group back, the heat nearly overwhelming them. A second wave, and then more—a river of the magma—coursed around the bend, and three of the group turned in full flight. Avelyn stood his ground, though, and went quickly to work, calling upon his stone magic to enact a shield, constructing a magical wall, floor to ceiling across the corridor.

The demon fires rolled on, bearing down on the praying monk. Pony skidded to a halt, realizing that Avelyn was not with her. She turned and screamed out to him, even took a running step back toward the monk, but Elbryan held her fast.

Avelyn's faith was put to the test as the magma flow approached, as the heat intensified. He had used this gem, serpentine, to survive in the midst of a fireball, but he had no real knowledge of how it would work against the demon magma. It might defeat the heat, he supposed, but what of the sheer weight of the flowing stone?

Avelyn had no room for such doubts. He fell deeper into his prayers, into the depths of the stone magic. The magma was only a couple of feet away, rolling, bubbling.

The monk felt no heat, then, felt no hot wash from the molten stone. As the leading edge passed through the serpentine barrier, it cooled suddenly, turning black and solid, and the magma behind it began to flow over it, until it, too, cooled and hardened.

Now Avelyn saw a new problem brewing: if the lava continued to pile up, it would rise too high and block the corridor, the only way they knew to get at the demon dactyl. Boldly the monk strode forward, stepped up on the leading wall of obsidian, and forward, too, went his magical shield, stealing the demon's heat.

Seeing the spectacle, realizing that their friend had beaten the dactyl's attack, the other three were quick to join him, Elbryan, Hawkwing in hand, moving right to the side of the praying monk. They went around the bend, Avelyn stopping the magma river fully, the demon dactyl coming in sight.

Elbryan lifted his bow and let fly, and the dactyl, so obviously surprised to see its enemies, took the hit squarely in the chest between its humanlike arms.

Bestesbulzibar's eyes flared, and the demon opened wide its mouth, vomiting a stream of magma at the group, and while the serpentine shield blocked the heat, the sheer force of the missilelike spew knocked Avelyn and Elbryan back against the wall. The ranger recovered quickly, growling and sending a second arrow after the first, again with perfect aim.

The dactyl howled, more in rage than pain, for Elbryan's arrows were but a minor inconvenience to the mighty creature.

Avelyn, though . . . that one presented a more troubling power.

The demon's arms shot forward, fingers extended, and black tendrils of crackling electricity spouted from them, biting against the wall and running the length of the straight passage, nipping and snapping at Elbryan and Avelyn, at Pony and Bradwarden as they followed their friends around the bend. Avelyn had no counter ready and the demon's magic caught him and Elbryan, holding them fast in its sparking grasp for a long painful moment, and then hurled them both backward to crash hard against the wall. Smoke wafting from various parts of their clothing, the pair darted in a quick retreat around the bend, pushing Pony and Bradwarden back the way they had come.

Avelyn desperately searched his magical repertoire, but it was Pony who struck next, thrusting forth the graphite rod and letting loose a bolt of streaking lightning, bouncing it off the wall, angled perfectly to skip around the bend and bear down on the demon. Her aim was true, it seemed from the howl that came back at them, but that howl was followed closely by a second crackling black bolt, this one hitting with a thunderclap that launched Pony and Avelyn—and would have sent Elbryan, as well, except that he was holding to the sturdy centaur—flying to the floor.

"Time for running!" Bradwarden cried.

"Take it!" Pony called to the monk, tossing him the graphite, knowing that he could put it to more powerful use.

"Forward, I say!" Avelyn corrected the centaur, catching the stone and pulling Pony to her feet. He paused for just a moment, considering the fact that his hands were full of a confusing jumble of gems, and none of them were the particular stone he now desired. He quickly handed two stones, the malachite and the lighted diamond, back to Pony, then he scrambled on, taking the lead toward the bend once more. "Now the darkness is before us, so forward, I say!" Avelyn reached into his pouch and retrieved yet another gem, a stone he had used to defeat dactyl-inspired magic before, in a fight with a powrie general.

Avelyn focused the energy of the sunstone, building a wall before him, shaping it and thrusting it forward, taking some comfort in the fact that Pony, who was behind him, kept the diamond glowing brightly.

The dactyl loosed another tremendous bolt as Avelyn rounded the bend, but the crackling magic fell away to nothingness as it entered the disenchanted zone.

"Ho, ho, what!" Avelyn roared, and all the friends came on in full charge.

Bestesbulzibar was confused, had not seen such a display of antimagic in all its millennia of life. It narrowed its gaze upon Avelyn, upon the gemstone the monk held tightly in his extended hand, and, ignoring the charge, thinking nothing of the next stinging arrow that soared its way, the dactyl gathered all its magical energy.

They were barely thirty feet away.

Twenty—another arrow zipped in, deflecting off the dactyl's bone-hard forehead.

Ten feet away, Avelyn roaring wildly, the ranger hooking his bow over his shoulder and drawing forth his sword—an elvish sword!

The dactyl's shriek echoed all through the tunnel maze of Aida, deafened the four friends, and made them reach for their ears. The demon, recognizing the power of Elbryan's silverel blade and wanting nothing to do with an elven-forged weapon—Dinoniel had wielded such a weapon!—loosed a stream of its purest magical force, a green line of sizzling, tingling energy aimed directly at Avelyn, at the monk's extended hand.

The beam stopped right before the monk, wavered there, holding Avelyn in his place, crackling sparks flying wide, forcing Elbryan to slow and shield his eyes.

Avelyn screamed, and the dactyl shrieked again, throwing all its magical strength, every ounce, behind the beam.

On came the green line, engulfing Avelyn's hand, the sunstone glowing fiercely. They held for a long moment, the monk's will against the demon's hellish strength.

The sunstone absorbed the dactyl energy, stole the line from the demon's hand. But Avelyn's expression of joy, of victory, was short-lived, for the stone could not contain such energy, and it threw it out, dispersed as green smoke into the air, the sheer force of the expulsion throwing Elbryan and Avelyn backward into Pony and Bradwarden, the resulting smoke filling the corridor.

None of the group was hurt, but the momentary distraction gave the drained dactyl the time to retreat.

"Ho, ho, what!" Avelyn bellowed when he saw the creature half running, half flying down the corridor, and the roaring monk was the first in pursuit.

Elbryan scrambled to untangle himself from Pony, and charged off behind the monk, the woman coming next, and bulky Bradwarden bringing up the rear.

They sped past several side passages, around turns in the corridor, Avelyn leading boldly, trying to keep the demon in sight, ready but without fear in case the creature was waiting for him around each bend.

They raced up some stairs, pounded fast down a long, narrow descending slope, and came at last into a long, straight corridor, the demon visible before them. Elbryan tried hard to get past his monk friend, then, to take up the lead and close the distance to the monster. But Avelyn was too focused even to notice the ranger's attempt, even to consider letting the faster Elbryan squeeze by him.

The monk was trying furiously to bring up the magic of the sun-stone again, but even if he couldn't manage it, Avelyn meant to get to the dactyl, to tackle the damned thing and beat it with his bare hands if he had to!

Up ahead, the corridor widened, like the top half of an hourglass, and then ended in a wall, broken only by a large archway, through which the demon dactyl scrambled. Beyond this portal, Avelyn saw a huge room, braced by columns and lit by the orange flow of molten stone.

This was the throne room, he knew, the very heart of the demon's power. That notion only spurred the furious monk on even more, Avelyn lowering his head and running full out, with his telltale cry of "Ho, ho, what!" He charged through the archway with no consideration that it might be trapped, and Elbryan, though he slowed a bit for caution, was but two running strides behind.

The dactyl, back on its obsidian throne, was ready for them. As Avelyn passed into the room, he was hit full force with more demonic magic: a great gust of wind that held the monk in his tracks, that sent the huge bronze doors to the side of Avelyn swinging mightily.

Elbryan, too, felt the wind and saw the doors. He screamed out and tried to buck the force and dive ahead, arm extended, Tempest leading.

The doors swung closed, brushing Avelyn, spinning him about, and then slamming together on Elbryan's forearm, smashing his bones, tearing his flesh. Tempest fell to the floor; the doors pushed on, threatening to rip the ranger's arm off.

Bradwarden threw Pony aside and barreled into the doors full force, but even the centaur's great weight and strength could only move them slightly, just enough for Elbryan to extract his arm and fall back, semiconscious, into the corridor. Bradwarden caught him and scrambled back with him, and the bronze doors slammed closed, leaving Avelyn alone in the throne room with Bestesbulzibar.

Or so the monk thought. Bestesbulzibar kept his concentration on the door, using his magic to hold it closed against the repeated slams of stubborn Bradwarden. But then the demon's second trick became apparent as a grinding sound filled the room and the massive stone columns began to twist and shift.

Avelyn, grasping at the opening, was quick to retrieve Tempest, but he was no swordsman. He felt the power of the weapon's gemstone, but it was a magic to strengthen and enhance the blade, he believed, and nothing that the monk could access beyond that.

The closest two columns stretched out their stony arms, broke through the inanimate stone holding fast their legs, and started the monk's way. With a yelp, Avelyn skipped to the side, bringing the puny sword up defensively. These two behemoths weren't going for him, however, but for the bronze doors.

Avelyn held his breath, thinking that the pair would throw wide the doors and fall over his friends. To his relief, they did not, but rather they fell against the metal, using their bulk to seal off any chance of entry. The fact that the maneuver put those two obsidian giants out of the fighting did little to bolster Avelyn, for eighteen of the gigantic black animations remained, all stepping forth now, and with the doors thus barricaded, the dactyl was free to deal with this one intruder.

The demon leered down at the monk from its obsidian throne. "Destroy him," Bestesbulzibar commanded, and all the stone monsters started Avelyn's way, except for the two holding the doors.

Avelyn took a careful measure of their approach; they were not fast-moving things, and the monk believed that he could keep his distance, for a while at least. He meant to do just that, and loose whatever magic he could muster against Bestesbulzibar, but to his surprise, the demon did not remain, leaping up from the throne, moving to the side of the dais, and diving headlong into the lava flow, disappearing through the floor.

Avelyn growled in frustration and entertained the thought of using his serpentine shield and chasing after Bestesbulzibar. He found that he had more immediate problems, though, as two of the massive columns bore down on him. He thought to use the sunstone, to counter the magic and disenchant the obsidian, but he feared that the stone itself had not yet recovered from the strain in the corridor. Up came the graphite instead, and Avelyn let loose a tremendous blast of lightning, a thundering forked bolt that slammed both the columns and knocked them back a step, sending cracks running up and down their length.

Avelyn ran between the pair, easily avoiding their lumbering attempts to grab him. The monk lashed out with Tempest as he passed, for good measure, and the sword took a slice of stone from the back of a giant leg. Avelyn hardly took comfort in that successful strike, though, realizing by the extent of the damage that he would have to hit the thing a hundred times, at least, to destroy it, and probably a score of times on the same spot on the leg to topple it!

So it became a game of cat and mouse, and Avelyn was the mouse. He ran all about the great hall, igniting a fireball, and then, when that proved ineffective, resorting to the graphite, falling into its magic again and again, stinging giant, cracking the black stone.

After a few minutes, the monk amazingly had three of the behemoths down, no more than great piles of broken rubble, but Avelyn couldn't possibly maintain the pace, he realized, for he was huffing and puffing and his magical energies were fast depleting.

He took a different tack then, rushing to the dais and scrambling up the steps. How simple the evasion proved, for the giants could not maneuver their great bodies to follow!

Now Avelyn focused his energy on the pair holding the door, thinking to clear the path for his friends.

He didn't know it, but his friends were long gone.

Elbryan was hardly conscious, with Pony holding him up and holding his smashed arm out from his body, trying to keep it steady. Waves of pain assaulted the ranger with every slight shift, turned his stomach and dulled his vision. He did see Bradwarden, slamming repeatedly, stubbornly, at the doors, not budging them in the least.

How helpless the ranger felt then! He had come all this way, and now was denied. Was denied!

Summoning every ounce of his remaining strength, Elbryan managed to pull away from Pony, taking two unsteady steps toward Bradwarden, meaning to help with the door.

"Hit it with a bolt o' yer lightning!" the centaur bade Pony.

"I gave that stone to Avelyn," she replied, holding up her hands, showing only the glowing diamond and the green-ringed malachite.

That news seemed to take the resolve from the centaur. "Then it's Avelyn and the demon," Bradwarden said, "as the monk knew it should be."

Elbryan swooned and tumbled to the floor. His friends were beside him in an instant, Pony propping up his head.

"Might that ye give him this," the centaur offered, indicating the red bandage.

Pony considered it for just a moment, but when she pulled the bandage down a bit, she realized that Bradwarden's garish wound wasn't nearly healed, and that if she took the bandage away, it would only open once more. Elbryan's arm was agonizing, but not life threatening, and Pony knew her love well enough to realize that he would be angry indeed if she risked the centaur's life to alleviate his pain.

The woman shook her head and looked back at Elbryan.

"Side passages," the ranger mumbled.

Pony turned to Bradwarden, who glanced back helplessly at the great bronze doors. "Got nothing better," the centaur agreed, and so the three were off, Pony supporting Elbryan and Bradwarden leading the way back down the tunnels, up the slope and down the stairs, searching for a side passage that would get them into the throne room from a different entrance.

Their hopes were bolstered shortly thereafter when they heard a voice— Avelyn's voice—cursing the demon, then crying out in pain. On they ran with all speed; Elbryan was so strengthened by the indication that his friend might be in trouble that he pulled away from Pony and made his own unsteady way, stumbling often, but using Hawkwing as a crutch and moving faster than the woman could have ushered him.

They went down the next side passage, a narrow, winding affair, and the talking continued, spurring them on.

Around a bend, they saw their folly, for it was not the throne room that loomed before them, not Avelyn at all, but the demon dactyl, standing tall across a wider expanse of the corridor, leering at them.

"Welcome," the beast said in a voice that sounded like Avelyn's.

Pony looked helplessly at her diamond, then wondered if she could make the light shine so brightly that this creature of darkness could not withstand it. Bradwarden's method was more straightforward, however, the centaur charging straight ahead, singing at the top of his lungs. Elbryan moved to follow, but could not hope to keep up.

The dactyl's laughter mocked them. The beast lifted its arms, summoning its hellish magic. Pony cried out, thinking they would all be destroyed.

Bestesbulzibar did not aim the strike at them but rather at the floor beneath their feet, a blast of explosive energy that shattered the stone, dropping the corridor's floor out from beneath them.

The demon cackled and turned away, its work finished.

And so it seemed to be, as the stones and the three friends fell far away— a hundred feet, at least, two hundred—toward a floor of jagged stalagmites.

It came up fast through the hole in the floor at the side of the dais, rushed past the flowing lava quickly, spewing the red stone all about. Up the demon soared, and then it dropped, landing heavily on its muscular legs.

The monk refused to be distracted, though this demon dactyl, the darkness of all the world, was but a few strides away. Avelyn growled and fell deeper into the stone, grabbed up all the power the graphite would give him, and hurled it in three rapid blasts at the pair of stone giants guarding the door.

They blew apart into rubble; the way was clear for Avelyn's friends, except that Avelyn's friends were nowhere near the door.

"Well done!" Bestesbulzibar congratulated, clapping his human hands together. "But all for what end?"

"Nightbird!" Avelyn cried. The monk thought to run for the doors, but there remained too many animated columns, crowding around the dais, waiting for him to come down.

Avelyn called out again, but the dactyl's laughter stole his voice. "They cannot hear you, fool," Bestesbulzibar explained. "They are already dead!"

The words nearly knocked Avelyn from his feet, assaulted his mind and tore at his heart. His lips moved in denial, but he suspected Bestesbulzibar would not lie to him; given the demon's awful power, he suspected the demon wouldn't have to lie to him!

So that left Avelyn against the fiend, just them, facing off from five paces. Avelyn was past grief suddenly, and without fear. He had come here to Aida, into this very room, to battle Bestesbulzibar, to pit his God against the hellish power of the demon. And now he was here, the best scenario he could rationally have hoped to find. If he won now, then his friends, all of them, would not have died in vain.

That thought sobered the monk and calmed his nerves. He considered his repertoire, wondered what stone magic would prove most effective against the beast, then went with what he had in hand, his graphite.

"Wretched beast!" Avelyn boomed, his voice resonating throughout the room. "I deny you!"

He thrust out his arm and loosed a tremendous bolt of sizzling blue lightning, a sharp, crackling flash that slammed Bestesbulzibar right in the chest and drove the demon back a couple of steps.

"You are strong, Avelyn Desbris," the fiend growled, all its body quivering from the continuing grasp of the electricity. The demon spread wide its black wings and reached back with one humanlike arm, claws extended toward the flowing lava, grabbing the power and channeling it.

Then the demon's arms clutched tight at its chest, right where Avelyn's bolt was holding fast, and red crackles shot forth from Bestesbulzibar's clawed hands, red to meet Avelyn's blue bolt, joining together end to end in a showering display.

Avelyn growled low and called to God, begging for more energy, channeling it, as pure a conduit of godly might as ever had stood upon Corona. And that power staggered Bestesbulzibar, nearly threw the demon to the floor.

Nearly—for Bestesbulzibar was no conduit of power, but a source of power, and the red bolts fought back terrifically, grabbing the ends of Avelyn's lightning and pushing the bolt back toward the monk. Red extended to cover half the distance between the pair, and continued to close. Avelyn shut his eyes and growled louder, throwing every bit of himself behind the energy, and the blue bolt gained again, drove on toward the demon.

But then the red bolt strengthened and pushed the blue back, pushed the sizzling point of joining inexorably back, toward Avelyn. The monk opened wide his eyes, straining, straining, but it would not be enough, he knew then.

The demonic red lighting inched closer.

She shouldn't have been able to do it; none of Avelyn's training nor her own experiences with the stones should have allowed Pony to bring forth such energy. But sheer terror, sheer instinct, and an unselfishness that bordered on foolhardiness, allowed for nothing less.

Pony took up the malachite and reached out with it, somehow lending its magic not only to Elbryan, who was within her reach, but to Bradwarden, who was far ahead of the pair, and all three, tumbling with the broken corridor floor, were suddenly floating more gently, drifting down as a feather might, and it took little effort for each of them to step aside from the stalagmite teeth as they lighted on the lower level.

"I'm not for knowing how ye did it, girl," a thoroughly shaken Bradwarden congratulated, "but suren I'm glad that ye did it!"

But for all their joy, for all the centaur's gratitude toward Pony, the three found themselves in a precarious position. Pony knew that she might fall into the malachite once more and become nearly weightless, but the prospects of getting anyone back up to the broken ledge seemed remote indeed, for they had no rope to hang from such a height.

"One way's as good as another," the centaur was quick to point out, motioning toward a tunnel that led out of the stalagmite-filled chamber and wound its way along the deeper tunnels of Aida.

So on they went, with Pony holding the diamond light steady and holding poor Elbryan steady; and Bradwarden, cudgel in hand, taking up the lead. To their dismay, this tunnel complex proved no less a maze than the higher passageways, and most of these corridors seemed to be leading further down and not up.

"One way's as good as another," Bradwarden kept repeating, but it seemed to the others that the centaur was trying to convince himself more than them.

Avelyn could not hold it at bay. The demon's red lightning hit him with the force of a giant's punch, launching the monk to the very edge of the raised dais. One of the stone behemoths was at the spot almost immediately, leaning over the helpless man, its huge hand chopping down to squash Avelyn flat.

Avelyn cried out, thinking himself doomed, thinking that he had failed and that all the quest was ended.

But the stone behemoth creaked and twisted, arm moving back against its massive chest, legs shifting together. In a few seconds, it was no more than a column again, leaning over, and then falling.

Avelyn rolled out of the way; the inanimate stone crashed down and rolled from the dais.

"He is mine!" the dactyl shrieked at the impertinent behemoth, at the giant-turned-column that had almost stolen the fiend's most savored kill.

All the other columns retreated then, going back near the door, dispelling any of Avelyn's thoughts of escape.

The monk stubbornly pulled himself up to his knees, then struggled to stand tall before the monster. The dactyl, eyes narrowed, showing respect for Avelyn but no fear of the monk, stalked in.

Perhaps this would not be a battle of magic, the monk thought suddenly. He had Elbryan's sword after all, that most powerful of weapons. Perhaps this was to be a test of his body against the dactyl's, a contest of physical strength.

In one fluid movement, Avelyn lifted Tempest high and darted ahead at his foe, slashing wildly.

He missed, the cunning dactyl easily sidestepping and then countering with a beat of its leathery wing, slamming the rushing Avelyn on the shoulder and launching him head over heels to the other edge of the dais.

"You are no swordsman," the fiend remarked, and Avelyn could hardly disagree. Still the monk stubbornly climbed back to his feet and stalked toward the monster more cautiously this time, prodding Tempest with shortened, measured thrusts.

Bestesbulzibar began to slowly circle to Avelyn's right.

Avelyn's free hand came up, launching a handful of celestite crystals that popped in minor explosions all about Bestesbulzibar's face. Thinking that he had his opening, the monk charged ahead.

Bestesbulzibar was gone in a puff of smoke, in the blink of a surprised monk's eye. Avelyn skidded to a stop, then understood his sudden dilemma and swung about hard.

The demon, standing right behind him, battered him with its wing again, knocking him to the ground before the swinging sword ever got close.

Avelyn struggled to his feet once more, stumbling toward the rear of the raised platform.

Bestesbulzibar, cackling with laughter, walked around him, putting Avelyn squarely between itself and the solid wall, cutting off the one route of escape.

Avelyn had no ideas, no plan at all. He came forward a step and began waving Tempest, again in shortened strikes, more to buy time, to keep the fiend at bay, than with any hope of winning.

But the demon's patience was at its end, and Bestesbulzibar came forward in a sudden, terrifying rush.

Out went Tempest, a quicker thrust, aimed for the dactyl's heart, but Avelyn, for all his training in those years at St.-Mere-Abelle, was no Terranen Dinoniel, and the dactyl accepted a minor hit and swept aside the awkward attack with one forearm, then quick-stepped into the opening.

Always ready to improvise, Avelyn launched a heavy punch with his free hand and connected solidly with the powerful beast's chest.

Before the monk could begin to congratulate himself, he found Bestesbulzibar's free hand around his throat, lifting him from the ground. Avelyn tried to whack with Tempest, but the demon understood the power of the ranger sword and would not allow the monk to bring it to bear.

"Fool," Bestesbulzibar thundered, squeezing harder—and Avelyn feared his head would simply pop off! "Did you think that you could even hurt me? Hurt me, Bestesbulzibar, who has lived for centuries, for millennia? Every day I destroy creatures ten times your worth!"

"I deny you!" Avelyn gasped.

"Deny?" Bestesbulzibar echoed. "Tell me that I am beautiful."

Avelyn stared incredulously at the demon's angular face, at the fiery eyes, the white, pointed canines. Something about Bestesbulzibar, the sheen of the demon's skin, the strong angles of its features, struck Avelyn profoundly as beautiful indeed. The monk felt an overwhelming urge then to do as the demon had asked, to admit Bestesbulzibar's beauty.

But Avelyn saw the lie, the temptation, for what it was. He stared Bestesbulzibar right in the eye. "I deny you," he said evenly.

The dactyl heaved Avelyn across the dais, to slam hard into the back wall.

Avelyn slumped low, his vision blurred, sharp explosions going off in the back of his head. He tried to stand but slumped again, and the room at the edges of his vision began to grow dark.

The monk tried to get to his sunstone, thought to kill the magic in this area as he had done in the hallway. But to what end? his reeling thoughts screamed back, for Bestesbulzibar needed no magic to destroy him.

The dactyl paced in, towered over him.

Avelyn swooned; his thoughts went flying back to the glories of his life, back to Pimaninicuit, the closest he had ever felt to his God. He saw again the island at the start of the blessed showers, saw Brother Thagraine, poor Thagraine, running desperately, reaching out toward the cave, toward Avelyn.

Then falling dead, and Avelyn remembered rushing to him, remembered his horror, fast turned to curiosity . . .

Avelyn reached into his second pouch and pulled forth the giant amethyst crystal, the mysterious stone humming with magical energy.

The dactyl hesitated at the sight, at the stone aglow with teeming magic.

"What have you?" it demanded.

In all truth, Avelyn didn't know the answer to that question. Growling with every inch, all pain vanished, Avelyn Desbris forced his legs under him and slid back up the wall to stand before the hellish fiend.

The dactyl growled and came on.

Following instincts that he could only hope were from God, Avelyn tossed the stone into the air, and then he and the dactyl both hesitated, surprised, for the heavy crystal did not fall but hovered in place.

Again, with no logical basis for the movement, Avelyn exploded into action, grabbing Tempest in both hands and swinging mightily even as Bestesbulzibar reached for the tantalizing stone.

Mighty Tempest sheared right through the crystal, and the whole of it blew into dust, shattered a thousand times.

The demon stared dumbfoundedly at the dusty cloud, at Avelyn, as if to ask what the man had done, and again, Avelyn had no answers.

From within that dust cloud came a low humming noise, a growling almost, and, like a ripple in a pond, a purplish ring emanated, rolling through Avelyn and the dactyl, rolling out to the edges of the room, deflecting off the stone again and again, crossing back in on itself.

More rings, rolling, humming, mounting.

"What have you done?" Bestesbulzibar demanded.

Avelyn, his head throbbing once more, clutched desperately at his sunstone, though he thought the thing a pitiful counter to the mounting strength.

The ominous growling increased tenfold, a hundredfold, deafening Avelyn, blocking the sounds of the dactyl's shrieks. The creature watched in amazement as its stone columns crumbled to dust, as if the very vibrations had shattered the obsidian.

Bestesbulzibar turned on Avelyn, murder in its flaming eyes.

The dais lurched; a great crack opened in the floor and a gout of steam hissed through.

"Fool!" the dactyl shrieked wildly. "Fool! What have you done?"

"Not I," Avelyn answered under his breath, though he knew that the demon could not possibly hear him. "Not I." The monk understood then, knew his fate and willingly accepted it.

He hooked the bag of stones, all but the sunstone which he still clutched tightly, over Tempest's blade. He noticed then the stone in Tempest's pommel, and recognized it for the first time as some sort of sunstone, an accessible gem. It was too late for him, though, and so he grabbed the sword at mid-blade, and thrust it straight up above his head.

The left-hand wall of the throne room crumbled; the twin lava flows intensified, spurting molten stone across the room.

The dactyl shrieked and loosed a bolt of black lightning at Avelyn, but the monk was fully into the sunstone shield then, and the magic was stolen before it ever got to him.

Bestesbulzibar leaped away, flew all about the room, looking for an escape. Then, with none evident, the fiend came straight for Avelyn, thinking to punish, to tear and to kill.

But then the demon was tumbling, the resounding, deafening roar overcoming it in mid-flight, stealing its concentration, stealing its strength. Bestesbulzibar crawled across the dais, away from Avelyn—who was standing tall, shining, praying—and toward one of the lava flows.

The hundreds of purplish rings converged in the middle of the room.

Aida, the very mountain itself, exploded.

Far below the jolt sent all three of the friends, even sturdy Bradwarden, flying wildly about the tunnel. Elbryan slammed hard into the wall of the narrow passageway with his already broken arm. Waves of agony assaulted him, and despite all the courage and determination he could possibly muster, he found himself slumping down into blackness.

Pony, too, was dazed but not so much that she couldn't hold fast to her diamond and keep the precious light glowing, though in the sudden burst of dust, it seemed a meager beacon indeed. She struggled back to her feet as the rumbling continued, as the walls and the floor beneath her feet shifted and bounced. She somehow got to Elbryan and propped him up, hugged him tightly, thinking it fitting that they die in each others' arms.

But then, after what seemed like an hour but was in fact no more than a few minutes, the rumbling stopped, and the ceiling did not fall in on them.

Pony's relief lasted only until she managed to locate Bradwarden through the dust; the centaur was by far the worst off. He stood braced against the corridor's right-hand wall, wedged in tight, his human torso bent far back, arms widespread with muscles bulging, to hold back the largest slab of stone imaginable, to hold up the very mountain itself!

Pony gently eased Elbryan down, then ran for the centaur, crying out his name. She pulled out the malachite as she went, thinking to levitate the block that the centaur might escape.

She couldn't begin to move it; Avelyn himself, with a piece of malachite ten times this one's strength, would not have budged so huge a slab. To Pony's surprise, Elbryan came up then, groggily, barely conscious, Hawkwing in hand. With great effort, the battered man wedged the bow in tight against the wall, trying to use it as a lever to relieve some of the pressure on the centaur.

"Ah, me boy, ye'll not be moving this one," the doomed centaur groaned. "She's got me stuck, and got me dead, don't be doubting!"

Elbryan fell back against the wall, dizzy, defeated, with no answers.

"Bradwarden," Pony breathed helplessly. "Oh, my friend, all the mountain would have fallen on us but for your great strength."

"And all the mountain'll be falling soon enough," the centaur replied. "Run to the outside and yer freedom."

Pony's horrified expression was all the reply Bradwarden was going to get.

"Go on!" the centaur yelled, and the exertion cost him an inch, the huge slab sliding ever lower, bending him backward. "Go on," he said again, more calmly. "Ye cannot move the damned mountain! Don't ye make me death a meaningless thing, me friends. I beg ye, get out!"

Pony looked at Elbryan for guidance, but the man was past reasoning, slumping once again into blackness. She stared hard at the centaur then, thinking this to be the cruelest play of all. How could she leave so gallant a friend? How could that be expected of her?

And yet Pony realized the sincerity of the centaur, saw it clearly in his calm features. She imagined herself in his position and knew what she would expect of her friends.

Pony moved up very close to Bradwarden, bent over to him, and kissed him on the cheek. "My friend," she said.

"Always," the centaur replied, and then his visage and his voice hardened. "Now run. Ye owe me that!"

Pony nodded. It was the most difficult thing she'd ever had to do, and yet she did not hesitate. She pulled Elbryan up to his feet, hooked her arm under his shoulder, and started off without looking back. The pair had barely left the corridor when they heard the rock shift once again, heard the resigned groan of the breaking centaur.

Pony wandered for hours in the twisting darkness, with only the diamond light to guide her, and that growing ever dimmer as exhaustion sapped her energy. She found tunnels blocked by flowing lava, others by thick concentrations of sulfurous fumes, and still others that simply ended in a solid wall or in a deep chasm that she could not cross.

Elbryan tried hard to keep up with her, to be less of a burden, but his legs were too wobbly, the pain too intense. Several times, he whispered for Pony to leave him behind, but that, of course, she could not do. Another idea came to her, then, and she took out the malachite, lending some of its levitational magic to Elbryan's body, greatly lessening her load.

And then finally, as hope began to fade to empty despair, as her magical energies at last began to fade to nothingness, the woman felt a breeze, and it was cool and soft, not like the hot wash of flowing lava.

Pony concentrated hard. The diamond was all but out, a pinprick of light that showed her nothing in the heavy air. The malachite's power was no more, Elbryan leaning heavily against her. She stumbled on, following the current, backtracking the gentle breeze. She stumbled and fell, crawled back to her knees and tugged Elbryan along, and then she stumbled again. It wasn't until, exhausted beyond her limits, she rolled onto her back, that she realized that she was out of the mountain, under a sky darkened by smoke.

Just before Pony drifted off to sleep, one patch of that sky cleared, showing a single, shining star, then a second, then a third.

"Avelyn, Bradwarden, and Tuntun," the woman whispered, and merciful sleep took her.

Epilogue

It was Elbryan and not Pony who was the first to wake, the sky still dark before the dawn and still heavy with billowing smoke. The ranger tried hard to remember what had happened, then he did, and he sat, head bowed, fighting away despair.

Worst of all, Elbryan did not know Avelyn's fate, though he suspected the monk was dead. What of the dactyl? Had the creature been consumed, or had it merely flown away before the blast?

Elbryan lifted his eyes at that unsettling notion, looked at the sky as if he expected the dactyl demon to be swooping upon him even then.

What he saw was a glow, coming from higher up on what remained of the mountain, a soft white light atop the blasted peak.

Pony awakened shortly thereafter, the dulled dawn just beginning, but still the glow from atop the mountain was faintly visible. Without saying a word, the battered pair gathered up their things and started off, up the mountain trails, supporting each other through every step. Only when the dawn broke fully—dimmed by the huge smoke cloud—could they appreciate the absolute devastation that had come to the mountain and to the valley before it.

Nothing lived down there, they both knew. Nothing could possibly have survived. All the trees that had been on Aida's slopes were laid out flat, leafless, most of their branches blown away. Empty logs, gray with ash, stretched away in the gloom. Nothing moved across that gray sea, save the occasional flutter of ash, caught by a swirl of wind. No birds flew above it, no sounds at all broke the eerie stillness of the devastated morning.

Neither did Elbryan or Pony speak out, too overwhelmed by the sight. They continued on their way, struggling past broken stones and through patches of warm ash hip deep, hoping for some answer.

They came over the edge of the now flat-topped mountain, in sight of a huge plateau of empty grayness—except for one tiny spot of light. Toward it they went, trudging on, plowing through the heavy ash. They could not discern the source until they were very close, within a dozen strides, and then they hesitated.

An arm, Avelyn's arm, protruded from the ash, holding fast Tempest at mid-blade and with a bag hanging below that.

Elbryan rushed ahead, thinking to dig his friend from the ground, thinking that Avelyn had somehow survived, had enacted a magical shield to protect himself even from this level of destruction.

When he reached the spot, he found his folly, found that the ground around Avelyn's arm was solid and only lightly covered in ash, and the monk was surely dead, his arm and hand withered, dried out, as if the great heat of the explosion had taken all the fluid from his body.

"The dactyl is destroyed," Pony said firmly when she arrived beside Elbryan. "Avelyn killed it."

Elbryan looked at her.

"Else his gift to us would have been stolen away by the demon," the woman reasoned, and she reached over and worked the sword and bag free of the withered hand. The glow went away instantly, but the arm remained, extended.

Pony handed Tempest to the ranger, and she was not surprised when she opened the bag to find all of Avelyn's stones, except the amethyst and the sunstone, within.

"It is a message," she said with confidence. "He gave this to us as a message that the dactyl is defeated."

"A message and a responsibility," Elbryan replied, looking from Pony's eyes to the bag of gemstones. "Avelyn saved us, saved us all, but the friar is demanding repayment."

The woman nodded and looked, too, at the precious bag, at Avelyn's choice, at her responsibility. "There may already be another Brother Justice on our trail," Pony remarked.

Elbryan lifted Tempest with his healthy arm. "Then I must mend my arm," he replied. "Or learn to fight left-handed."

Thus, Elbryan and Pony walked away from Avelyn's chosen grave, from Tuntun's last breath, from Bradwarden's tomb. They crossed the ash-filled valley with great difficulty, having to stop often from weariness, and that only making things worse since they had no food or water.

Finally, they made the mountains bordering the Barbacan, and just over the ridges, they found life again and water to drink. They spent more than a day at rest, and when she felt strong again, Pony used the hematite to relieve much of Elbryan's pain and to set his bones fast on the mend.

And so it was with strides much stronger that the pair continued on their way down the southern slopes of the Barbacan. Near the bottom, wary for any goblins or other monsters that might be about, they found another friend.

Elbryan sensed Symphony's approach long before the horse came in sight. The ranger didn't know how the stallion had gotten out there, but then he thought of a certain elf, a stubborn and mischievous elf that had never learned to accept an order.

"Tuntun," Pony remarked, figuring the riddle.

Elbryan managed a smile. He slid Tempest into its sheath, looped Hawk-wing over his back, then climbed up, offering his hand to Pony.

They rode easily that day, picking their careful way, wary of enemies. That night, they camped on a high plateau, which they agreed to be the most defensible position in the area. No monsters presented themselves, no threat at all, but the choice of the high plateau proved a good one, for in the southern sky, reaching about the horizon like the arms of God, shone the blessed Halo.

Pony and Elbryan rode fast with the break of dawn, south along the wild trails, the weary and grieving victors, the new protectors of the holy stones.

ABOUT THE AUTHOR

R. A. SALVATORE was born in Massachusetts in 1959. His first published novel was *The Crystal Shard*. He has since published more than a dozen novels, including the *New York Times* bestsellers *The Halfling's Gem*, *Sojourn*, *The Legacy*, and *Starless Night*. He makes his home in Massachusetts with his wife, Diane, and their three children.

Enter THE REALM
The Official R. A. Salvatore Fan Club

Benefits include:

- THE REALM Membership Card
  — signed by the author!
- A subscription to *The Realm Herald*
  — the club's quarterly newsletter
- Advance notification of new releases!
- Advance notification of author appearances!
- Exclusive interviews!

And more!

To join for one (1) year, send $20.00 ($25.00 if outside USA), check or money-order, along with:

Your Name
Street Address
City, State, Country (if not USA),
ZIP code
and Date of Birth

To:
THE REALM
P. O. Box 535
South Windsor, CT 06074

THE REALM is not for profit.
All proceeds not needed in the administration of the club will be donated annually to Reading Is Fundamental.

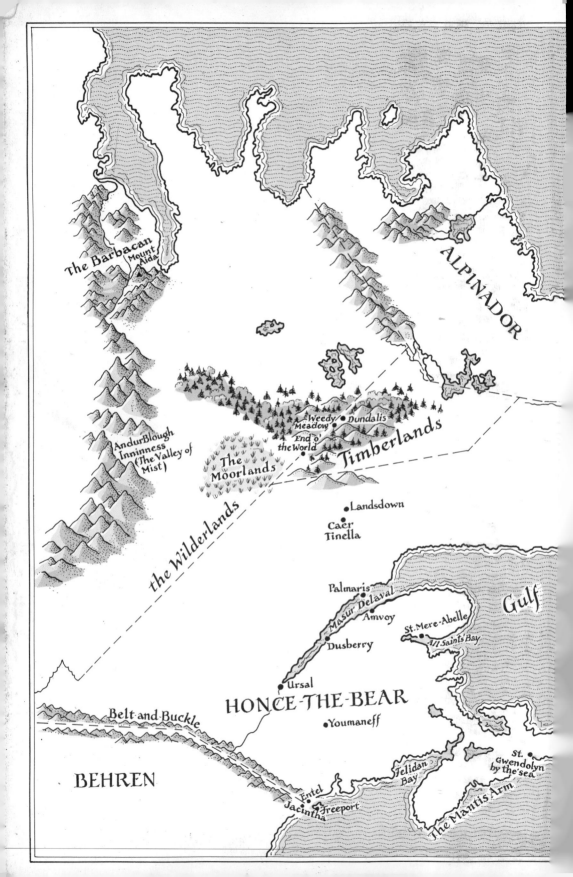